III
FRENCH

III

FRENCH

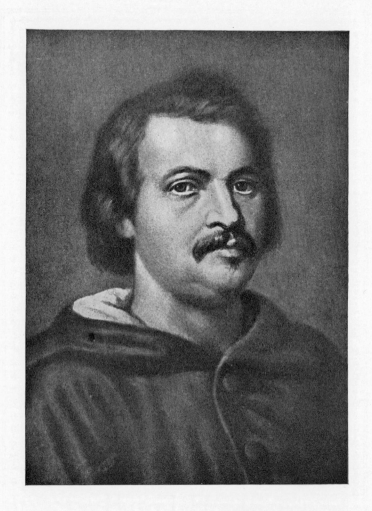

(Honoré de Balzac)

THE
Masterpiece Library of Short Stories

The Thousand Best Complete Tales of all Times and all Countries

Selected by

AN INTERNATIONAL BOARD
OF EMINENT CRITICS

Sir William Robertson Nicoll, LL.D.

Sir Arthur Quiller-Couch   Sir Frederick Wedmore
Clement Shorter   Sir Edmund Gosse, C.B., LL.D.
George Saintsbury, LL.D.   W. P. Trent, LL.D.
Richard le Gallienne   Carl Van Doren
Brander Matthews, Litt.D.   Thomas Seccombe

Edited by

Sir J. A. Hammerton

III. FRENCH

LONDON
THE EDUCATIONAL BOOK COMPANY LIMITED

Editorial Board

Editorial Note

A SHORT story may be a mere anecdote of three hundred words or a work of ten or fifteen thousand. In content it may be anything from a glimpse of character, an incident, to a highly finished picture of life. But it should be a complete work of imagination, its effect achieved with a minimum of personages and events.

TO select the best thousand examples was a task that could be achieved only on arbitrary lines. As to length, three thousand words was the ideal average, but this excluded some of the finest stories, so exceptions had to be allowed. National characteristics also had consideration. Another test was the value of a story as illustrating the development of the art.

PROBLEMS of arrangement were not entirely solved by classification according to the country of each writer's origin. This puts Richard Steele into the Irish volume and separates those ideal literary partners Agnes and Egerton Castle. But it is the best possible arrangement for the work, and the index makes reference easy. The inclusion of a series of stories of the War became possible when the War itself ruled out all modern German work.

A WORD as to the method of selection. The General Editor prepared a trial list of titles which were submitted to all the members of the Editorial Board, who rejected and added according to their individual tastes and knowledge. These individual lists were then collated and the final list evolved. The thousand stories selected are therefore representative of the combined opinion of the whole group of editors. A very few modifications of the final list were made necessary by difficulties of copyright and considerations of Anglo-Saxon taste in certain translations from foreign literatures.

MOST of the foreign stories have been specially translated, and all copyrights, in both stories and translations, the use of which authors and publishers have courteously permitted, are duly credited at the end of each volume.　　　　　　　　J. A. H.

Contents of Volume III

THE FRENCH STORY-TELLERS

From La Sale to Dumas

THE modern short story is French ; all the rest are merely anecdotes. That is somewhat exaggerated, but, taken generally, it is passable. Other nations have produced a few men with a fine genius for this form of literature ; but the French are as supreme in the modern art of the short story as the Italians were in the art of the little novel in the age of Boccaccio and Bandello. There seems to be something special in the turn of mind of the French that makes them fitted to excel in this form of prose fiction. In matter of fact, they were some centuries ahead of the earliest Italians in the production of the short story. They were the originators of this literary form in northern Europe. Their wandering minstrels and jugglers of the eleventh and twelfth centuries took up the simple anecdote and transformed it into a work of art, in the shape of a *fabliau*—which was a short, entertaining tale in rhyme.

If the Board of Selectors had not decided to confine their choice of THE THOUSAND BEST SHORT STORIES to works of prose fiction, the early French short-story writers would have been far more abundantly represented in our first volume. It would have been seen from their verses that Boccaccio and his successors had in many cases merely adapted in prose ideas to which the French minstrels had first given a brilliant poetic shape. When, in the seventeenth century, La Fontaine turned some of Boccaccio's stories into verse, he was often only withdrawing from Italy, what Italy had taken from France. Some of the gayest of the Canterbury Tales of Chaucer are also based on the old French *fabliaux* ; and it is probable that a good many of the more amusing satirical folk-tales of Europe were first minted by the French mind.

ANTOINE DE LA SALE

The French lost their position in the arts during the Hundred Years' War with England—from the battle of Crécy to the marvellous appearance of Joan of Arc. Our bowmen shattered the old civilisation of France and left it in ruins ; and it was not until our civil Wars of the Roses gave the French breathing space that they were able to turn again to literature. It is from the court of our ally in the conquest of France—Philip the Good, Duke of Burgundy—that there comes the first modern collection of French short stories. These are the somewhat too well-known *Cent Nouvelles Nouvelles*, or Hundred New Tales. At the Duke's court in Brabant there was a brilliant novelist, Antoine de la Sale, a Provençal by birth, who had studied in Italy, and had then entered the service of the Duke of Burgundy. La Sale was a writer of high genius, with some of the qualities of Sir Walter Scott and more of the qualities of Cervantes. The extraordinary merit of his long novel, *Le Petit Jehan de Saintré*, has only lately been fully recognised. It is a mixture of a romance of chivalry and a fierce satire on the knightly manners of the age.

But La Sale's short stories are still more striking evidence of the utter corruption of the noble society of his time. They are supposed to have been related by Philip the Good and his courtiers, and some authorities think that King Louis XI. of France was also one of the composers. In no thieves' kitchen at the present day could such filth be heard as these kings and noblemen poured out by way of courtly entertainment in the middle of the fifteenth century. La Sale professes to be only the transcriber of most of the tales, and among the few contributions under his own name is the honest, amusing satire of "The Cynic Testament," in which the avarice of the French bishops of the age of decadence is satirised. Then in "A Tune on the Bagpipe" we have a vivid dramatic picture of an adventure between the Burgundians and the French about the time of the battle of Agincourt.

PHILIP THE GOOD

Philip the Good recovers somewhat of the fine feeling of chivalry in his touching story of "The Honest Woman with Two Husbands," remarkable alike for its sincere piety and its high respect for women. Practically all the other tales in the collection, however, are gross and degrading in both language and idea. They show what depth the French mind touched in the overthrow of its old culture.

MARGUERITE DE NAVARRE

The moral atmosphere of the French Court was not improved about a hundred years later when King François' sister, Marguerite of Navarre, went to the Pyrenees to bathe in the waters at Cauterets. She came to the spring with her poets, her musicians, her men of learning ; and she was poet and theologian herself, infinitely curious, reading Greek, learning Hebrew and studying the doctrines of Calvin. There she wrote her *Heptameron*, a collection of tales that rivals in indecency the *Cent Nouvelles Nouvelles*. Towards the end of her life Queen Marguerite wrote *The Mirror of the Sinful Soul*, so possibly she repented of the scandalous work of her early days. Probably her stories about the vices of monks, such as "The Crime of the Cordelier," did not shock her pious friend Jean Calvin ; for the early Protestant reformers were not averse from spreading scandals about Catholic monks, priests and nuns. Most of the tales, however, would shock any decent man, and though there are seventy-two stories in the collection, it has been most difficult to find two suitable for publication.

"The Unhappy Lover," however, is an admirable example of the talent of the learned religious Queen in an unusual mood of decency.

BONAVENTURE DES PERIERS

It is thought that Marguerite of Navarre may have been helped in the composition of her stories by Bonaventure des Periers, who was one of her valets de chambre. Des Periers was the most sceptical and daring writer of the sixteenth century. While the disputes between the Catholics and Protestants were raging, he dumbfounded both parties by an infidel work that started the free-thinking movement in France. Probably it was his early death in 1544 that enabled Marguerite to think for herself about matters of religion, and repent of the loose thoughts of her younger days. Des Periers was a man of the stamp of Montaigne and Voltaire—witty, indelicate, and full of worldly wisdom. His philosophy of life is charmingly expressed in his tale of "The Cobbler Blondeau," who threw away his money when he found he could not sing as light-heartedly as he did in the days of his poverty. It is one of the household tales of France.

NOEL DU FAIL

Another master of the French story unknown outside his own country is Noel du Fail. He was a Breton gentleman and Councillor of the Parliament of Rennes in 1571. A man of law, with a wise deep view of life, he is one of the first writers of the realistic school. Unlike most of his contemporaries, he is not interested entirely in affairs of gallantry ; with the trained penetration of vision of a man of business, he surveys the whole field of human life. There is something about him that reminds an Englishman of Defoe ; he keeps remarkably close to facts, and traces the workings of a motive with the skill of a criminal lawyer. As a study of avaricious old age and youthful adventuresomeness, his story of "The Miserly Father " is a little masterpiece of humour.

VERBOQUET LE GENEREUX

It is impossible to say anything about the last of our French story-tellers of the sixteenth century—Verboquet Le Genereux. For he is one of those strange creatures who never existed. He is merely a name under which some unknown writer—probably a Norman living in Paris—published a little book of amusing tales. "If any one asks who I am," he says, "tell him I am a man who does not waste his time in sadness or boredom." His tale of "The Three Drunkards" shows that he was not wanting in wit, originality and gaiety. And that is all we can say of him.

PAUL SCARRON

His successor, Paul Scarron, on the other hand, is one of the most famous of French men of letters. He was a poor, helpless, witty cripple who took a handsome young girl to wife, in order to get a good nurse cheaply. He left her a widow when she was twenty-five years of age, and after one of the most extraordinary careers in history, she married at the age of fifty the greatest monarch of the time— Louis XIV. ! Scarron's entertaining studies of stage life, in his *Roman comique*, naturally have a reflected lustre from the career of his amazing widow. We read his works to see what the first husband of Madame de Maintenon was like ; then we find him well worth reading for his own sake. The tale of "The Two Jealous Ladies " is told by one of the characters in his *Roman comique* ; it is a curious study of feminine snobbishness.

BISHOP FÉNELON

The fairest side of French life in the days of Louis the Great is seen in the stories by Bishop Fénelon—one of the finest of prose writers. This noble prelate was appointed preceptor of the grandson of the King, and his tales, " The Story of Alibea " and " The Isle of Pleasures," were written with a view to forming the mind of the young prince. Exquisite is the art with which they are composed, and "The Isle of Pleasures," especially, is one of the pearls of fiction. It is as satirical as Swift's work, yet it breathes tenderness, humanity and charm. If the generality of French ecclesiastics had possessed some of the qualities of heart of Fénelon, the history of France might have been altered.

LE SAGE

As it was, the free-thinking wits prevailed ; and among them Alain-René Le Sage is very eminent. He is in prose fiction what Molière is in play-writing—a prince of comedy with all human life for his dominion. His work is deeply coloured with Spanish ideas ; he borrowed his plots freely ; but he improved everything he took, and the general effect of his great novel, *Gil Blas*, is his own. He was not a robber, but a conqueror. By force of genius he annexed the Spanish novel of low life, and made out of it one of the finest monuments in French literature. His brilliant tale of gallantry and injured honour is one of many short stories that occur in *Gil Blas*.

ABBÉ GRÉCOURT

The French short story of the eighteenth century is one of the most remarkable things in European literature. It is mainly the work of men of irreligious character and religious profession—the *abbés*. An *abbé* of course is an abbot—the head of an abbey of monks. But the typical French *abbé* was the younger son of a noble family, who took his vows in an offhand manner, and remained in Paris without an abbey, playing the part of a young gallant about town, and amusing the great ladies in the hope of winning, through them, some Church appointment that would increase his income. Gay, witty, licentious, and entertaining, these young gentlemen had only one virtue—that of being able to write in a light and graceful way. The first of them, Abbé Grécourt, is the best and worst of his school. His satire on the curiosity of woman, " The Linnet of the Pope," is scarcely characteristic of his talent. For Grécourt seldom deviates into decency ; but he is a witty rogue, and this story is worthy of a place in our great collection.

COMTE DE CAYLUS

Many of the *abbés* met in some kind of club, held usually in a tavern or in the house of an actress. A good many of them collected round the lovely Mademoiselle Quinault Dufresne, in a society over which a very learned man of science, the Comte de Caylus, presided. The club was called "The End-Bench Society," and it devoted a large part of its time to the composition of short tales. Some ten volumes of the works of the club were published under the name of the president, and it is probable that the lively and humorous tale of "The Chaudron Girls" belongs to him. For in spite of his learning, the Comte de Caylus had a keen sense of life. His favourite recreation was to walk about the slums of Paris and listen to the talk of the street women. He has done some extremely vivid sketches of slum life, but the best of them are somewhat too coarse for our purpose. The tale of "The Letter" is probably by some other member of the club—perhaps the younger Crébillon, perhaps Voisenon, perhaps Duclos—perhaps some one now unknown. But it is a remarkably fine piece of work.

VOLTAIRE

It was in literary clubs of this kind that Voltaire, the Paris lawyer's boy, trained his mind. If Voltaire was not the actual son of the French *abbé* who introduced him into the aristocratic bohemian life of Paris, he was at least the spiritual child of his earliest patron. Had he not been exiled to England owing to a quarrel with a French noble-man, he would never have made the mark he did. It was Englishmen who taught him to think, and from English literature he obtained many of his ideas, and a good many of his short stories. His best short story, "What Women Want," is taken almost word for word from Chaucer ; but being, like its original, in verse, it cannot be included in our collection. So we must fall back on the charming story of "Jeannot and Colin," and the brilliant "Bababec and the Fakirs," for the inimitable "Candide" is too long.

BOURDELOT

After Voltaire come three brilliant *abbés*. Abbé Bourdelot was probably one of the precursors of Voltaire. His entertaining history of the troubles of "Monsieur Oufle" was intended to ridicule the super-stitions of the peasantry. Out of the belief in bears that assume human shape the *abbé* wove this gay, high-spirited farce, that is now one of the rarest pieces of French literature. Our version, made by the Rev. S. Baring-Gould in 1865 for *Once a Week*, is rather an adaptation than a translation, as it takes considerable liberty with the original, which is many times longer, and not really a short story.

BLANCHET—DE VOISENON

When a Frenchman had something very stinging to say about the great men of his country, he usually placed the scene of his tale in Spain, as Abbé Blanchet did in his "Dean of Badajoz." It saved the writer from the trouble of going to the Bastille, which was not a healthy place to live in. At the same time it enabled his readers to amuse themselves by discovering in Paris the man whose portrait had been placed in a Spanish frame. Blanchet's study of the greed and ingratitude of the princes of his Church is a fine piece of literature, that derives additional weight from the character of the man who wrote it. By reason of his greatness of mind he was much sought after by the leaders of society, but he spent most of his time in the service of the poor. The Abbé De Voisenon was a more worldly creature, and his sketch of Mondor in "He Was Wrong" throws a surprising light on his own character. He was one of the most successful men about town of his day, dazzlingly witty, the favourite of everybody and a friend of the King. He had a Court position as well as a Church appointment, but he spent a good deal of money in secret in helping the poor and the unfortunate. Very few French writers of his age cared to do good without claiming immediate applause ; in fact, Voisenon almost stands alone. There was much of his own Mondor in him, despite appearances.

DIDEROT

The more famous Denis Diderot, who treated his own wife and children like a beast, has written exquisitely about the sufferings of the poor in his "Two Friends of Bourbonne." This is one of the first, and still one of the best, sympathetic studies of the French labouring classes. It is part of a large propaganda of a revolutionary kind into which Diderot threw himself. He was a very active agent in arousing the French mind to that effort of social reform which began with the French Revolution, and which has not yet ended. His *Encyclopaedia* was the chief engine of the great movement of French thought ; but Diderot could write gaily and lightly, as is shown by his tales of "The Plaster of Desglands" and "Friar Côme and the Corpse."

CHARLES NODIER

Diderot, like Voltaire, stood for rationalism ; but the rationalists did not in their scheme of things allow sufficient scope for the kindly play of human feelings. So under the influence of Rousseau, a man of most vehement emotions, many of the writers of the younger generation rebelled against the too narrow and arid rationalism, and formed themselves into the romantic school in French literature. The magnificent Breton prose writer, Chateaubriand, was the leader of the new school ; but all his novels are too long for our purpose. To get an early example of the French short story of the romantic school, we must turn to the obscure but charming figure of Charles Nodier, the author of the first *Trilby*. His Trilby is very different from Du Maurier's. She is a Scottish fairy who falls in love with Jeanie, a crofter's pretty wife. The tale, however, is long and somewhat thin ; so we have chosen as an example of Nodier's delightful but uncertain talent "The Legend of Sister Beatrice," which has recently attracted the attention of hundreds of thousands of persons who are ignorant of the name of Nodier. It will be seen that the wordless play, "The Miracle," is really an adaptation of Nodier's picturesque version of the ancient legend of an erring nun whose place in the convent was taken by the Holy Virgin.

STENDHAL

Then, by way of contrast with the romantic work of Nodier, we have two stories, "The Philtre" and "The Jew," by one of the masters of realistic fiction—Stendhal. Stendhal, whose real name was Marie-Henri Beyle, fought under Napoleon in Italy, and took part in the terrible Russian campaign of 1812. Settling down to literature in middle age, he exerted on the art of fiction almost as much influence as Napoleon exerted on the art of war. For Stendhal can count among his disciples the four princes of modern French prose—Balzac, Mérimée, Taine, and Renan. He also inspired the Russian novelist, Dostoievski, and the German philosopher, Nietzsche. What other modern writer has such a following ? Stendhal was an embittered sentimentalist, but in his struggles to regain a healthy balance of mind, he penetrated further into the recesses of the heart than any other novelist. Within his narrow limits, he goes deeper than Shakespeare. He is the supreme psychologist, interested in the wildly passionate moments of life.

SCRIBE

Compare his two tales, in which life is seen in lightning flashes, with the little dramatic idyll " The Price of a Life " by Scribe. Scribe was a master of theatrical effects ; he dominated the theatres of Europe until the arrival of Ibsen ; and Sardou, and other well-known playwrights, lived mainly on his stock of dramatic tricks and methods. His remarkable skill is well displayed in " The Price of a Life " ; the tale is a lesson in construction, but in vital qualities, how meagre it is beside the work of Stendhal !

DE VIGNY

Chronological arrangement brings men into as strange company as life does ; for next to Scribe, the fashionable, superficial playwright, stands the sombre, handsome figure of the Comte de Vigny—one of the loneliest souls in the universe. He was a brilliant army officer, who married a lovely Englishwoman, and won immediate fame both as a poet and as a novelist. But he was discontented with life, mainly through a lack of religious faith, and in his latter years he gave strong and majestic expression to his pessimistic view of the universe. His story of " Napoleon and Pope Pius VII." is an admirable example of his art. It has the picturesqueness of his early romantic style, and somewhat of the deep thought of his last period. In its combination of romance and philosophy it resembled the short stories of Honoré de Balzac—the supreme master of modern prose fiction.

BALZAC

There are men who excel Balzac in some particular—such as Dickens, Tolstoi, Stendhal, and Sir Walter Scott—but in general range and power Balzac is the greatest of all novelists. Most of his short stories were written before his long novels, and written in a different style. They are romantic in conception ; that is to say, they deal with strange, bizarre and even fanciful incidents of life. In one of the earliest, " An Episode of the Reign of Terror," the feelings of the executioner of the French King are strangely depicted. In " A Passion in the Desert " a panther conceives a doglike affection for a fugitive soldier. In " The Conscript," Balzac, who was always deeply interested in the spiritual forces of human existence, gives a memorable study of the phenomena known as telepathy. But the " Grande Bretèche " is

probably the best of his short stories. It is a striking example of the
workings of the romantic imagination. It gives in the form of fiction
the impression that the writer received when looking at a grim,
picturesque and mouldering castle. As R. L. Stevenson made a
remarkable story out of a door that impressed him, so Balzac turns
the sinister aspect of an old fortress into a little prose drama.

In "The Atheist's Mass " he plays with the odd contradictions that
beset a materialist with warm feelings, than in "The Christ in Flanders,"
outrivals Nodier in handling an old legend, and introduces a deeper
meaning into it. His other three short stories, "El Verdugo," "A
Sea Shore Drama " and "Facino Cane," have the picturesqueness,
the savagery and the strangeness of pure romance of the modern sort.
Similar to them in character is the tale of "The Unknown Masterpiece " ;
this, however, is a short novel rather than a short story, and by reason
of its length has been omitted from our selection.

VICTOR HUGO

Victor Hugo resembles Balzac in his superb imaginative power,
but he had less sense of the realities of life. He is the greatest of
romantic prose writers, as well as one of the greatest of lyrical poets.
As his two fine short stories, "Claude Gueux " and "Jenny," show,
he had a keen sympathy for the poor and the unfortunate. The
first of these tales is especially famous ; it is a powerful plea for the
redemption of men who have been driven into crime by poverty.

MÉRIMÉE—DUMAS

Great as Balzac and Hugo are in general literature, they have not
so high a position in the special art of the short story as Prosper
Mérimée has. Mérimée is the creator of the modern *conte*. He was
a very versatile man—government official, historian, traveller and
archaeologist ; but his permanent achievement is to have moulded
the form that Maupassant, Kipling and Chekof have developed into
the principal literary art of our period. In his hands the modern
short story has become as important a branch of literature as the lyric.
His "Taking of the Redoubt " is one of the most brilliant pieces of
picturesque writing. "Mateo Falcone " is a strange tragedy of
Corsican life, and "Tamango " is one of the first, and one of the finest
studies in the wild romance of the tropics. In the "Blue Room "
that Mérimée wrote for the amusement of the Empress Eugénie, we
have an admirable example of the humorous short story, in which a
joke is played on the reader. Then in "The Game of Backgammon "
and in the "Etruscan Vase," Mérimée displays his remarkable powers
of tragic irony and keen observation. Compared with his work,
the short stories of Alexandre Dumas are somewhat old-fashioned.
Dumas, with his negro gaiety and French exuberance, required a larger
canvas for the full display of his genius. In "Zodomirsky's Duel,"
"Marceau's Prisoner " and "A Bal Masqué," we have a fresco painter
trying his hand at the art of the miniature. Of the three tales the
last is the best. It is a vivid little picture of a good woman's jealousy.

E. W.

ANTOINE DE LA SALE
1398–1470

THE CYNIC TESTAMENT

Now listen, if you please, to a thing that happened the other day to a simple village priest, who by his simplicity was amerced by his bishop in the sum of fifty good golden crowns. The good priest had a dog he had brought up from puppyhood, and that surpassed all the dogs of the parish in fetching sticks thrown in the water, or bringing back the hat his master forgot or purposely left behind him in any place. In short, all that a good and wise dog ought to know and do he was a champion at ; and for this reason his master loved him so much that he was quite besotted about his dog.

But it happened, I know not by what mischance, whether he got too hot or too cold, or ate something that hurt him, that the dog became very ill and died, and went straight from this world to the paradise that good dogs go to. But what did the good priest do ? Just below his presbytery was the parish graveyard ; and when he saw his dog had passed away from this world, he thought that such a good and wise beast had a right to a proper burial. So he dug a grave just outside his door, and there he buried him like a Christian.

I do not know if he erected a marble stone above the grave and engraved an epitaph on it, so I will keep silent about this part of the affair. But it was not long before the death of the worthy dog was known to the village of the neighbouring parishes and spread from there to the ears of the bishop, together with the rumour about the Christian burial that his master had given him. So the bishop summoned the priest to appear before him.

" Alas ! " said the priest to the lawyer who brought the summons, " what have I done that I should be brought before the bishop's court ? I am amazed at the summons, and cannot guess what I have done wrong."

" As for myself," said the bishop's man, " I cannot tell what they want you for, unless it is that you have buried your dog in holy ground in which the bodies of Christians are placed."

" Ha ! " thought the priest, "so that is it ! "

And for the first time it came into his head that he might have
gone a little too far, and he thought to himself he would have to
prepare for the worst. For his bishop was the most covetous in
the kingdom, and the people around the bishop knew how to bring
grist to the mill by ways God only could discern. And the priest
knew that if he were condemned to prison he would be very heavily
fined.

" Since I must lose my money," he said, " it is best to get
it over."

So he answered the summons, and went straight to the bishop,
who preached him a long sermon about the burial of the good dog.
And it seemed, to hear him, that the priest would have committed
a lighter sin if he had denied God. And when the sermon was
ended, he ordered the criminal to be thrown into prison.

When the priest saw they wanted to shut him up in the stone
box he was more terrified than a duckling, and begged his lordship,
the bishop, first to hear what he had to say. And his request was
granted. And you must know that at this trial there was a swarm
of folks of many sorts, such as the official, the promoters, the scribe,
notaries, barristers, procurers, and several others—and all of them
together rejoiced over the case of the good priest who had buried
his dog in holy ground. By way of defence the priest spoke but
a few words.

" Truly, my lord Bishop, if you had known as much as I do of
my good dog, you would not be amazed at the burial I gave him.
For his equal was never found and never will be."

Then he began to praise his dog. " And just as he was most
wise in his lifetime so was he more so in his death. For he made
and executed an excellent testament, and knowing your necessity
and your poverty, he bequeathed to you fifty gold crowns, which
I now bring you."

And drawing the money from his purse, he counted it out to the
bishop. His lordship gladly received the legacy, and then praised
and approved the good sense of the worthy dog, and the testament
he had made, and the burial that had been given to him.

A TUNE ON THE BAGPIPE

Antoine de la Sale

DURING the war between the Burgundians and the Armagnacs, there occurred at Troyes in Champagne a delightful adventure that is well worth relating. The people of Troyes had first been on the side of Burgundy and had then turned Armagnacs ; and among them was a half-witted fellow who kept with us. He had not quite lost his reason, but he inclined more to the side of madness than to that of sanity : yet at the same time he carried out by hand and mouth several tasks that wiser men than he would not have known how to manage.

This fellow was doing garrison work with the Burgundians at Sainte Menehoulde, and while talking one day with his companions he said that if they would trust him and help him, he would give them a good plan for capturing a great host of the rascals of Troyes. For he hated these townfolk mortally, and they did not exactly love him, but always threatened to hang him if he fell into their hands.

" I will go towards Troyes," he said, " and approach the outskirts of the city, and pretend to spy on the town and measure the moat with my lance. I shall be taken prisoner, and I am sure that the good bailiff will condemn me to be hanged, and none of the townsmen will object to it. For they hate me, all of them. So I shall be quickly led to the gibbet, and you will lie in ambush in the copse close by. And as soon as you hear me coming out of the gate into the field with my large following, you must spring out on the townspeople and make them prisoners and deliver me from their hands."

All the troops of the garrison agreed to help him if he were daring enough to undertake the adventure. So the game, gallant, half-witted fellow went to Troyes, and, as he wished, was taken prisoner, and the news of his capture quickly spread through the town. And there was not a man who did not wish to hang him. The bailiff, as soon as he saw him, swore by all his saints he would hang him up by the neck.

" Alas, my lord," said the adventurer, " I pray you have mercy on me. I have never done you wrong."

" You lie, scoundrel ! " said the bailiff. " You have guided the

Burgundians in their marches, and have harmed the good burghers and merchants of this town. But you shall have your reward and be hanged at the gibbet ! "

" For God's sake," said our good fellow, " since I must die, let it be in the early morning and outside the town. For I cannot bear to receive too public a punishment in this town, where I once had so many friends and acquaintances."

" Very well," said the bailiff, " we will think about it."

At dawn the next day the executioner with his cart arrived at the prison, and scarcely had he arrived than the bailiff came on horseback with his officers and a large number of people to accompany him. Our man was taken and trussed and bound on the cart, and, holding his bagpipe, on which he played continually, he was carried to the place of execution. Though it was so early, a larger crowd gathered to see him die than was usual at these scenes, so much was he hated in the town.

Now you must know that the Burgundian troops had not forgotten to lie in ambush in the wood close to the place of execution. They had come there at midnight, partly to save their man, though he was not the wisest of creatures, and partly to get prisoners and any spoil within reach. They disposed themselves ready for action, and sent a man up a tree to watch and tell them when the townsmen of Troyes were at the field of execution.

The watchman was placed so that he could do good duty. And the people of Troyes came to the gibbet, and the bailiff ordered that our poor fool should be despatched. He wondered where his companions were, and why they did not attack the scoundrelly Armagnacs. Ill at ease, he looked backwards and forwards, and chiefly at the wood. But he heard and saw nothing. He lengthened out his confession as much as he could, but he was taken from the priest and pushed on the scaffold. There, God knows, he was pretty well dazed, and he continued to stare at the wood. But all his trouble went for nothing. For the watchman, who had been ordered to start the rescue party, had fallen asleep on the tree.

So our poor fellow did not know what to do, and thought his last day had come. The executioner made his preparations to fix the rope round his neck to finish him. When our friend saw this, he thought of a trick that might turn to his advantage.

" My lord," he said to the bailiff, " for God's sake, let me play one tune on my bagpipe before your men lay hands on me. I ask nothing more, and shall be content to die and forgive you and everybody for killing me ! "

His request was granted, and his bagpipe lifted up to him. And holding it as easily as he could, he began to blow, and played a song that he companions in ambush knew very well. It was, " You stay too long, Robin, you stay too long ! " And at the skirl of the bagpipe the watchman awoke, and in his fear he let himself fall from the top to the bottom of the tree, and cried :

"They are hanging our man! On! on! Quick as you can!"

The troops were all ready, and at the sound of the trumpet, they sallied from the wood and fell upon the bailiff and all the folk round the gibbet. And in the tumult the executioner lost his wits, and instead of hanging his man told him to save his life. This our friend would willingly have done but it was not in his power. He did something better. Standing on the scaffold, he cried to his companions :

"Take that man! Capture this man! This one is wealthy, that one is worth nothing."

In short, the Burgundians killed a great heap of the men of Troyes, and took a large number captive, and saved their own man, who, never all the days of his life, was in such a state of terror as in that hour.

PHILIP THE GOOD, DUKE OF BURGUNDY 1396–1467

THE HONEST WOMAN WITH TWO HUSBANDS

IT is known not only in the town of Ghent, where the affair I am about to describe happened a few years ago, but by most folk of Flanders, that at the battle between the King of Hungary and Duke John, whom God absolve ! on the one part, and the Grand Turk in his land of Turkey on the other part, several knights and squires of France, Flanders, Germany, and Picardy were taken prisoners. Some were put to death by the Turk ; some were cast for life into prison ; others were condemned to the state and labour of slaves.

Among these last was a gentle knight of the land of Flanders named Messire Clayz Utenhoven. For several years he worked as a slave, and his labour was not light to him, but an intolerable martyrdom, seeing to what pleasure he had been bred and to what rank he belonged. For you must know that he had married at Ghent a very beautiful and good lady who loved him with all her heart. Daily she prayed to God that she might see him again, if he were still living, and that if he were dead he might be pardoned of his sins and placed amongst the glorious martyrs who, for the repulsion of the infidels and the exaltation of the holy Catholic faith, voluntarily abandoned themselves to temporal death.

This good lady, who was very rich, was continually urged by her friends to marry again. They assured her that her husband was dead. If he were alive, they said, he would have returned with the others ; if he had been taken prisoner, there would have been news of him in connection with his ransom. But no matter what they said, the good lady would not think of a second marriage, and did all she could to escape from it. Her efforts, however, went for little or nothing. For she was so constrained by her relatives and her friends that she had to obey them.

But, God knows it was with great regret, and after being widowed of her good and loyal husband for nine years and thinking him dead, as every one else did, that she married again.

But God, who guards and preserves his servants and champions, had not allowed Messire Clayz Utenhoven to die. He was still working miserably as a slave when his good lady married another knight. And about six months after this event some Christian gentlemen and merchants set him free, and took him aboard their galley and brought him back. And in the countries he passed on his return he met with several acquaintances, who were very joyful over his delivery. For in truth he was a very valiant man of virtuous character and high reputation. And the glad news of his deliverance spread into France and Artois and Picardy, where his virtues were not less known than in Flanders. It was not long before the rumour reached Flanders, and came to the ears of the good and lovely wife of the freed man. Greatly was she stricken by it, and so wrung with grief that she did not know her own face.

" Ha ! " she said, when she was able to talk, " my heart never consented to do that which my parents and friends forced me to do. Alas ! what will he think of it, my loyal lord and husband ! I have not kept faith as I should, but like a frail, light, timid woman I have given up to another that of which he should have been the sole lord and master. I am not worthy to await his coming, and I dare not do it. I am not worthy that he should look on me, or have me in his company ! "

And saying these words with great tears, her honest, virtuous, and loyal heart fainted away. She was carried on a bed, and her heart revived ; but it was not in the power of man or woman to get her to eat or sleep. So she lived for three days, continually weeping, in the greatest sorrow of heart that ever woman knew. After some time she made her confession and ordered her end like a good Christian, praying mercy from every one, and especially from her husband. And soon after that she died, and great was the sorrow over her. I cannot describe the grief of her husband when he heard the news ; and by reason of his sorrow he was in great danger of dying as his wife has done. But God, who had saved him from other great perils, preserved him also from this.

MARGUERITE DE NAVARRE
1492–1549

THE CRIME OF THE CORDELIER

THERE was in the dominions of the Emperor Maximilian of Austria a monastery of Cordeliers, held in high esteem, near which was the house of a gentleman. He was so infatuated with these Cordeliers that there was nothing he did not give them in order to have part in the benefit of their fastings and prayers. Among others, there was in this monastery a tall, handsome young Cordelier, whom the gentleman had taken for his confessor, and who was as absolute in the house as the master himself.

The Cordelier, struck by the exceeding beauty and propriety of the gentleman's wife, became so enamoured of her that he could neither eat nor drink, and lost all natural reason. Resolved to execute his design, he went all alone one day to the gentleman's house. Finding no one at home, the monk asked the lady whither her husband was gone? She replied that he was gone to one of his estates, where he was to remain two or three days; but that if he wanted him she would send an express to bring him back. The Cordelier told her that was not necessary, and began to go to and fro about the house, as if he had some affair of consequence in his head.

As soon as the monk had left the lady's room, she said to one of her woman (there were but two of them), "Run after the father, and learn what he wants, for I know by his looks that he is not pleased."

The girl, finding him in the courtyard, asked him if he wanted anything? He said he did, and, drawing her into a corner, he plunged into her bosom a poniard he carried in his sleeve. He had hardly done the deed when one of the gentleman's men, who had gone to receive the rent of a farm, entered the yard on horseback. As soon as he had dismounted he saluted the Cordelier, who embraced him and buried the poniard in his back, after which he closed the gates of the château.

The lady, seeing that her servant did not return, and surprised at her remaining so long with the Cordelier, said to the other woman:

24

"Go, see why your companion does not come back." The servant went, and no sooner came in sight of the Cordelier than he called her aside, and served her as he had done the other. Knowing that he was then alone in the house, he went to the lady, and told her that he had long loved her, and that it was time she should obey him. She, who could never have suspected him of anything of the kind, replied :

"I believe, father, that if I were so unhappily inclined, you would be the first to condemn me and cast a stone at me."

"Come out into the yard," said the monk, "and you will see what I have done."

The poor woman did so, and, seeing her two women and her man lying dead on the ground, was so horrified that she remained motionless and speechless as a statue. The villain, who did not want to possess her for an hour only, did not think fit to offer her violence then, and said to her :

"Have no fear, mademoiselle ; you are in the hands of that man in all the world who loves you most."

So saying, he took off his habit, beneath which he had a smaller one, which he presented to the demoiselle, threatening, if she did not put it on, that he would treat her as he had done the others.

The demoiselle, more dead than alive, made a show of obeying him, as well to save her life as to gain time, in hope that her husband would return. She took off her head-dress, by the Cordelier's order, as slowly as she could ; and when she had done so, the monk, without regard to the beauty of her hair, cut it off in haste, made her strip to her shift and put on the small habit ; and then, resuming his own, he set off with all the speed he could, with the little Cordelier, whom he had so long coveted, at his side.

But God, who has pity on the wronged innocent, was touched by the tears of this poor lady, and so ordered things that her husband, having despatched his business sooner than he expected, took that very road to return home by which the Cordelier was carrying off his wife. The monk, descrying the husband from a distance, said to the lady :

"Here comes your husband. I know that if you look at him he will try to get you out of my hands ; so walk before me, and do not turn your head in his direction, for if you make him the least sign I shall have plunged my poniard in your breast sooner than he will have delivered you."

Presently the gentleman came up and asked him whence he came.

"From your house, monsieur," replied the Cordelier. "I left mademoiselle quite well, and she is expecting you."

The gentleman rode on without perceiving his wife ; but the valet who accompanied him, and who had always been in the habit of conversing with the Cordelier's companion, named Friar John, called to his mistress, thinking that she was that person.

The poor woman, who durst not turn her head towards her husband, made no reply to the valet ; and the latter crossed the road that he might see the face of this pretended Brother John. The poor lady, without saying anything, made a sign to him with her eyes, which were full of tears. The valet then rode up to his master and said :

" In conscience, monsieur, Friar John is very like mademoiselle your wife. I had a look at him as I crossed the road. It is certainly not the usual Friar John ; at least, I can tell you that if it is, he weeps abundantly, and that he gave me a very sorrowful glance of his eye."

The gentleman told him he was dreaming, and made light of what he said.

The valet, however, still persisted in it that there was something wrong, asked leave to ride back and see to it, and begged his master to wait for him. The gentleman let him go, and waited to see what would be the upshot. But the Cordelier, hearing the valet coming after him with shouts to Friar John, and making no doubt that the lady had been recognised, turned upon the valet with a great iron-bound staff, gave him such a blow on the side that he knocked him off his horse, and springing instantly upon him with a poniard, speedily despatched him.

The gentleman, who from a distance had seen his valet fall, and supposed that this had happened by some accident, spurred towards him at once to help him. As soon as he was within reach, the Cordelier struck him a blow of the same staff with which he had struck the valet, unhorsed and fell upon him ; but the gentleman, being very strong, threw his arms round the Cordelier, and hugged him so roughly that he not only prevented his doing him any more mischief, but made him drop the poniard. The wife caught it up at once and gave it to her husband. At the same time she seized him by his hood and held him with all her might, whilst her husband stabbed him several times with the poniard.

The Cordelier, being unable to do anything else, begged for quarter, and confessed the crime he had committed. The gentleman granted him his life, and begged his wife to go for his people, and a cart to carry the prisoner away, which she did, throwing off her Cordelier's habit, and hurrying home in her shift and her cropped hair. The gentleman's retainers all hastened to help him to bring home the wolf he had captured ; and the culprit was afterwards sent by the gentleman to Flanders to be tried by the Emperor's officers.

He not only confessed the crime for which he was tried, but also avowed a fact, which was afterwards verified on the spot by special commissioners sent for that purpose, which was, that several other ladies had been taken to that convent in the same manner as this Cordelier had attempted to carry off the lady of whom we are speaking ; and if he did not succeed, this was owing to nothing else than the goodness of God, who always takes upon Him the defence of those who trust in Him.

The girls, and the other stolen spoil found in the monastery, were removed, and then the monks were burned with the monastery, in perpetual memorial of a crime so horrible.

We see from this fact there is nothing more cruel than love when its principle is vice, as there is nothing more human or more laudable when it dwells in a virtuous heart.

THE UNHAPPY LOVER

MARGUERITE DE NAVARRE

ON the confines of Dauphiné and Provence there lived a gentleman who was much better endowed with the gifts of nature and education than with those of fortune. He was passionately enamoured of a demoiselle whose name I will not mention, on account of her relations, who are of good and great houses ; but you may rely on the reality of the fact.

Not being of as good family as she was, he durst not declare his passion ; but though his inferior birth made his despair of ever being able to marry her, nevertheless the love he bore her was so pure and respectful that he would have died rather than ask of her anything which could compromise her honour. He loved her, then, only because he thought her perfectly lovable, and he loved her so long that at last she had some inkling of the fact. Seeing, then, that his love for her was founded on virtue only, she deemed herself fortunate in being loved by so upright a man ; and she treated him with such affability that he, who aspired to nothing better than this, was transported with delight.

But envy, the enemy of all quiet, could not suffer so innocent and so sweet an intercourse to continue. Some one told the girl's mother he was surprised the gentleman went so often to her house that people saw it was her daughter's beauty that attracted him, and that they had often been seen together.

The mother, who was thoroughly assured of the gentleman's probity, was greatly annoyed at finding that a bad interpretation was put upon his visits ; but in the end, dreading scandal and

malicious gossip, she begged he would for some time cease to frequent her house. The gentleman was the more mortified at this,
as the proper and respectful manner in which he had always
behaved towards the daughter had deserved very different treatment. However, to put an end to the gossip about him, he
withdrew, and did not renew his visits until it had ceased.

Absence, meanwhile, by no means diminished his love ; but one
day, when he was paying a visit to his mistress, he heard talk of
her being married to a gentleman not richer than himself, and
whom consequently he thought no better entitled to have her.
He began to take heart, and employed his friends to speak on his
part, in the hope that if the lady was allowed to choose, she would
prefer him to his rival ; but as the latter was really the wealthier
man, the young lady's mother and relations gave him the preference.

The gentleman, who knew that his mistress was a loser as well
as himself, was so grieved at being rejected, that, without any
other malady, he began by degrees to waste away, and became so
changed that one would have said he had covered his handsome
face with the mask of death, to which from hour to hour he was
gaily hastening. Still he could not refrain from going as often
as he could to see her whom he loved so well ; but at last, his
strength being worn out, he was compelled to keep his bed, but
would never let his mistress know of it for fear of distressing her.
So entirely did he give himself up to despair, that he neither ate,
drank, slept, nor rested ; and became so lean and wan that he
was no longer to be recognised.

Some one made his state known to the mother of the demoiselle,
who was very kind-hearted, and had besides so much esteem for
the gentleman, that if the relations had been of the same mind as
herself and her daughter, the personal merit of the invalid would
have been preferred to the alleged wealth of the other suitor ;
but the paternal relations would not hear of it.

However, she went with her daughter to see the poor gentleman,
whom she found more dead than alive. As he knew that his end
was near, he had confessed and communicated, and never expected
to see any more visitors ; but on beholding again her who was his
life and his resurrection, his strength returned, so that he at once
sat up in bed, and said :

" What brings you hither, madam ? How come you to visit a
man who has already one foot in the grave, and of whose death
you are the cause ? "

" What ! " exclaimed the lady. " Is it possible we should cause
the death of a person we love so much ? Tell me, I entreat, why you
speak in this manner ? "

" Madam, I concealed my love for your daughter as long as I
could ; my relations, however, who have asked her of you in

marriage, have gone further than I wished, since I have thereby
had the misfortune to lose hope. I say misfortune, not with
reference to my individual satisfaction, but because I know that
no one will ever treat her so well or love her so much as I would
have done. Her loss of the best and most faithful friend and
servant she has in the world touches me more sensibly than the
loss of my life, which I wished to preserve for her alone. Nevertheless, since henceforth it can be of no use to her, I gain much
in losing it."

The mother and daughter tried to comfort him. " Cheer up, my
friend," said the mother ; " I promise you, that if God restores
you to health, my daughter shall never have any other husband
than you. She is present, and I command her to make you the
same promise."

The daughter, weeping sorely, assured him of what her mother
said ; but he, knowing that although God were to restore him to
health he should not have his mistress, and that it was only to
cheer him that these hopes were held out, replied :

" Had you spoken in this manner three months ago, I should have
been the healthiest and happiest gentleman in France ; but this
succour comes so late that I can neither believe it nor rest any hope
upon it."

Then, as they strove to overcome his incredulity, he continued
" Since you promise me a blessing which can never be mine even
if you grant it, I will ask you to confer on me one much less, which
I have never ventured to demand of you."

They both vowed that they would grant his request, and that he
might declare it boldly.

" I implore you," said he, " to put into my arms her whom you
promise me for a wife, and to bid her embrace and kiss me."

The daughter, who was not accustomed to such caresses, was on
the point of making objections ; but her mother expressly commanded her to comply, seeing that there was no longer in him either
the feeling or the power of a living man. After such a command,
the daughter no longer hesitated, but going up to the bedside :

" Cheer up, my friend," she said, " cheer up, I conjure you."

The poor dying creature, notwithstanding his extreme weakness,
stretched out his emaciated arms, embraced with all his might her
who was the cause of his death, and, laying his cold pale lip to hers,
clung there as long as he could.

" I have loved you," he said at last " with a love so intense and
so pure that, marriage excepted, I have never desired any other
favour of you than that which I now receive. But as God has
not been pleased to unite us in marriage, I gladly surrender up my
soul to Him who is love and perfect charity, and who knows how
much I have loved you, and how pure my desires have been,

beseeching Him, that since I hold the dear object of my desires within my arms, He will receive my soul in His."

So saying, he clasped her again in his embrace with such vehemence, that his enfeebled heart, being unable to sustain the effort, was abandoned by all his spirits; for joy so dilated them, that the seat of the soul gave way and fled to its Creator.

Though it was already some time since the poor gentleman had expired, and could not retain his hold, the love she had felt for him, and which she had always concealed, broke forth at this moment in such wise that the mother and the servants had much difficulty in detaching the almost dead survivor from the corpse.

The poor gentleman was honourably interred; but the greatest triumph in his obsequies were the tears and cries of that poor demoiselle, who as openly displayed her feelings after his death as she had concealed them during his life, as if she would make amends for the wrong she had done him. And I have been told that for all they gave her a husband to console her, she never afterwards knew real joy.

BONAVENTURE DES PERIERS
D. 1544

THE COBBLER BLONDEAU

THERE was a cobbler of Paris who was called Blondeau. He lived near the Croix du Tiroir, and there he mended shoes, taking life joyfully and loving good wine above everything. And he was ready to share it with all who came : for if the whole parish had come to him, he would have given them a glass and they would have wanted more of it. For it was good. All day long he sang and delighted his neighbours. He was never mournful but twice in his life.

On the first occasion, he found in an old wall an iron pot containing a large quantity of antique pieces of money, some of silver and some of gold. He did not know what they were worth, and he began to grow moody. His songs ceased, and he thought only of his iron pot.

" If the money is not current," he thought to himself, " I shall not be able to buy either bread or wine with it. If I take it to the goldsmiths, they will either betray me, and I shall lose the treasure-trove, or they will stick me for a large share of the find, and I shall not get half of what it is worth."

Then he became afraid that he had not hidden the pot properly and that some one would steal it from him. He was continually leaving his tent to go and see if it was safe. He was in the greatest trouble in the world, but at last he pulled himself together.

" What ! " he said, " I do nothing but think of my pot ! Every one who knows my ways must see that something has happened to me. Bah ! the devil take the thing ! It only brings me bad luck ! "

So he took the treasure up gaily, and threw it in the Seine, and thus drowned his melancholy with his pot.

On another occasion he was much upset by a gentleman who dwelt opposite to his shelter. This gentleman had a monkey that played a thousand tricks on poor Blondeau. For the animal watched him from a high window when he was cutting his leather, and noticed how he did it. And as soon as Blondeau went to dinner or left on some other business, the monkey came down and darted into Blondeau's tent, took his knife, and cut the leather about in imitation of the cobbler. And this went on every time that Blondeau went away.

The poor man at last dared not go out to eat or drink or leave his business without locking up all his leather. And if sometimes he forgot to shut it away, the monkey never forgot to cut it up in shreds for him. The thing angered him greatly, but he was not able to hurt the monkey for fear of his master. But, being greatly annoyed, he resolved to find a means of avenging himself.

He clearly saw in what way the monkey acted : this was to imitate everything he saw the cobbler do. If Blondeau sharpened his shoe-knife, the monkey sharpened it after him ; if he waxed his thread, the monkey also did it. If he soled some old boots, the monkey came and took a boot between his knees and tried to do the same. Having studied the matter in this way, Blondeau sharpened his shoe-knife till it cut like a razor. Then, when the monkey came out to watch him, he took up the shoe-knife and drew it backwards and forwards over his throat. And when he had done this long enough to attract the notice of the monkey, he left his booth and went to dinner.

The monkey came down in desperate haste. For it wished to try this new game that it has just been studying. It took the shoe-knife and put it against its throat, drawing it backwards and forwards as Blondeau had done. The animal, however, brought the knife too close, and cut its throat so badly that it died within an hour.

Thus was Blondeau avenged on his enemy without danger to himself, and he returned to his early habit of singing and taking life joyfully, and in this way he continued till the day of his death. And in remembrance of the glad life he had led, this epitaph was made for him :

> Underneath this stone is laid
> Blondeau, who plied a cobbler's trade.
> Hoarded wealth he held in scorn,
> And died as poor as he was born ;
> Yet now for him his neighbours pine—
> He taught them all to know good wine !

NOEL DU FAIL
D. 1585

THE MISERLY FATHER

THE ancients thought so highly of neediness that they made a
goddess out of it ; thereby signifying that in the pressure of need
our spirit awakes and becomes brusque and lively, instead of being
heavy and torpid, as often happens when a man's desires are fulfilled
and he is profoundly happy and wrapped in comfort. If a man
has little money, or if his affairs are confused and worrying, he
will learn better how to make his way in the world than those who
are born booted and dressed ; as was said of King Louis XI., the
first prince who made his successors their own masters, and who
best knew what his neighbours were doing.

Being in the bad graces of his father—oh, what a sweet thing it
is to reign in absolute power !—he retired to his cousin, the Duke of
Burgundy, and there learnt to eat small bread and make the most
of a penny. This rendered him so admirable in the management
of his affairs that he had few peers among all princes, and he was
able to verify the prophecy of his father, King Charles VII., who
told the Duke of Burgundy that he was feeding a fox that would
eat all his chickens. For in the end King Louis carved up and
parcelled out the estates of his host so well that he got most of
the best pieces, which, he held, had been torn from his own property.

And with regard to fathers who are too rigorous with their
children, there was seen but a little while ago in my country a
man so grasping and peevish that he gave his son little or nothing
for his keep. The boy, for his part, borrowed here and there all
that he could, until he was riddled with writs by merchants, money-
lenders, and other folk of seizure and interest. Very often he
tricked them, and let his conscience sleep over the rest. All his
defence was a reference to the avarice of his father ; and he would
often say to his companions, who were running the same way of
life for the same reason, that he wished to God his father would
break his neck and take it with him to paradise ; with other
imprecations and maledictions of the same import.

The father, whom it cost more than I know to spy on the actions
of his son, was well informed of these things ; but he turned his deaf

26   33

ear to them, taking pleasure, which he esteemed profit, in keeping
the young man in privations and calamities. Sometimes he
threatened to marry again, or to give his property into such hands
that he could not get a look at it. In this extreme necessity, the son
thought of a good trick to play against his stingy father and restore
the honour of his ancestors and his race, by getting enough money
to take part in the King's wars, and thus strengthen his position that
all brave and gallant men would side with him.

He went to a merchant and bought much black cloth on credit.
You who do not pay your money down, judge of the loyalty of the
vendor, and the acclamations and beating of the breast he made in
connection with the price and the measuring! The young man had
his mourning clothes made, packed them in his trunk, and whipped
away towards Poitou, where his father had a fine, rich estate of
great value. The farmer of it, a wealthy peasant, had in hand a
year's revenue, ready to take it to his master. But he was saved this
trouble. For the young gentleman, dressed in his mourning attire,
and with a lackey sad and grim of face, alighted at the house of his
father and told the farmer of the death of the old man.

"In his last words," he said, "he recommended you to me. He
begged me, under pain of disobedience, not to make any change on
the estate, because he had always found you a straight man and a
good servant of our house. My father was a little hard and strict,
but, farmer, my good friend, you can well understand that the
niggardly way he managed things now means more money and
profit to me."

"Oh, sir!" said the Poitou farmer, all honey to keep the lease of
the farm, "we must all pass through the door or through the
window. Still it is a great solace that he has left an heir, who, unless
I am much deceived, loves me, and from whom I can be sure of
continuing to hold the farms that the rich man gave me in this
district. I beg you to excuse me," bending, as he said it, first one
knee and then the other, "if sometimes I have refused to give you
money. For, on my conscience, I had a prohibition from the
deceased—and I think I have it still in my pocket. No. It is in
the place I keep my letters—just as if he suspected you. And you
understand right well," bristling up and laughing like a bagpipe
drone, "that since the boots of us fathers can serve our children,
we are like cats, and do not want to see our offspring more than
once a year, to hear of their fortunes. For we have put into their
hands the tools and means to get a livelihood."

"There is one other thing," said the mourning son, "and then I
have finished. You have heard of the wars in which the King is
greatly worried. How reprehensible it would be of me, and what
dishonour would come of it, if I failed to give my services to His
Majesty! For no matter how poor I have been, I have done my

duty to him. And now that war has broken out, and I have done my part as a son to my dead father, whom God absolve ! I must in all haste go and find the regiment that is marching to the place where I must serve. Some of my men have already gone ahead. It would be a very great pleasure to me and pretty profitable to you to remain on my estate on the same conditions and charges as you held the farm from my father. And how much shall I have in addition if I renew the agreement ?

" Ho ! Pierre," added the young man to his lackey, " how much did that fat man offer me at dinner for the farm ? "

" Ah, sir," replied the pretended servant, " you don't know a man till you've buried him ! Never change your old servants. Your father, God keep his soul ! always had that saying in his mouth, but at each renewal of the farm he wanted a hundred crowns bonus and a year in advance. I do not know what you will require."

The farmer, who was full of fear that such a bargain should escape him, at once accepted the terms. Then the notaries got to work and a hundred crowns were given to the master and ten to Pierre who held he had well earned them. Then there were revenues for a year in advance, besides those due for the past year. Each thought he had got the best of the other. The farmer, reckoning on his fingers, thought he had gained a hundred per cent. The heir knew he might have obtained more by waiting, but he was well pleased with the plum that he was able to put in his pocket and he rode off with it.

He had been gone half a day when the trouble began, and the battle opened with a wild conflict of evidence. One of the father's men, an old notary, mounted on a mule and booted with straw, arrived with receipts ready to receive the money that had fallen due, and to make a new lease for the future. He showed the farmer his documents, his general and special power of attorney, properly drawn up and signed. The farmer, in turn, brought out his documents to prove that the new young lord had granted him a fresh lease. He said that the heir was in mourning, and that everything had gone well, and that the notary was a manifest liar who wanted to play double-or-quits with his mule.

The notary maintained that his old master was alive, and that the new lease was worthless. The judge, before whom the case was brought, could not come to a decision, and held that an inquiry should be made into the matter. And in the meantime the poor miserable miser of a father died of spite and rage and madness through losing such a mass of money, and being tricked by his own flesh and blood. And may the same fate befall those who burn the candle at both ends.

be a very great pleasure to me and pretty profitable to you to remain

VERBOQUET LE GENEREUX
16TH CENTURY

THE THREE DRUNKARDS

THERE were three gossips in a little Normandy village, neighbours
and great friends, who often told each other secrets of their household affairs. There was nothing done by one of their husbands
but news was at once carried to the houses of her companions.
In the end the three women all found themselves provided with
husbands of equal stupidity, and they were often able to have a
good time together in the market-place. There only remained one
drawback in their lives ; but this they found almost insupportable.
For on the days when the three friends set out to enjoy themselves
together, their husbands went to a tavern, and there drank so much
that they lost most of their good sense. Scarcely could they get back
home, and when each of them met his wife there was no pot, platter,
or stick that he did not use in greeting her.

So the good dames concluded one day to punish their men for their
drunkenness. The husbands went as usual to the tavern, and their
wives spied on them. While the men were drinking, three preaching
friars came in and asked for alms. The jolly topers, who were sitting
at the table with their backs to the fire, made room for the friars,
and they all began to see who could drink the most. And each put
such zest into the drinking that, when it grew late, they had much
trouble in getting back to their houses.

The first wife, seeing her husband so profoundly asleep that it
would have been easier to flay him than to wake him, took some
scissors and tonsured his crown like a monk's, and dressed him in
monastic garments which she was able to borrow. She then let him
sleep on in his frock till daybreak, when, being accustomed to
breakfast, he looked around for some food.

" How long you have slept, reverend father ! " said the woman in
pretended astonishment. " Had you not better rejoin the other
religious men of your order ? "

The husband, still dazed by his wine, did not look at his wife, and
yet grew angry with her. But she, like a woman sure of her ground,
went on in the same tone.

" Sir, out of pure devotion I gave you a lodging here for the night.

36

But I tell you that your companions have now departed, fearing that you would remain here alone, which would not be seemly and decent for a person in your way of life."

The husband, in utter astonishment, touched himself here and there, and, feeling his shaved head and his monk's frock, was terrified.

" Heavens ! isn't this me ? Isn't this Jean ? " he cried.

His wife continued to call him " sir," and to treat him with great reverence, and she managed him so well with the flat of her tongue that, being still half-drunk, he could only remember he had been drinking with some monks, and seeing himself thus clothed, he thought that by the vengeance of heaven he had been transformed into a friar. And so strongly did this mad opinion take hold of him that he asked his wife to point out the road the other monks had taken.

His wife replied that he could scarcely catch up with the other friars, but that out of pity she would pay his mass for him if he wished to say it. As the parish priest was aware of the trick the women were playing, and was helping them to cure their husbands of drunkenness, poor Jean, reduced to utter stupidity, was led by his wife to the church and clothed in the ornaments proper to a funeral service, and then conducted to an altar.

The second wife, who did not wish to fail in her part of the enterprise, began to flatter her husband as soon as he awoke, and revive his spirits.

" You know, my dear, this is a festival day ! Your gossip, Jean, so repents the time he has spent in evil ways that he has taken religious vows, and to-day he is saying his first mass, and by hearing it you will be infinitely benefited. Would you not like to confess your sins to him ? "

Poor Guillaume, amazed and half-unwell from drinking too much, began to lament his faults, and in this frame of mind came to the church. There, seeing his crony, Jean, ready to say his office, he took a handful of candles and knelt down and offered them, begging pardon for his mistakes.

The third wife, who desired to carry the deception to its highest point, had at daybreak shrouded her husband like a corpse and placed him on a bier, which was borne into the church. As Guillaume presented his offering, the dead man opened his eyes a little and caught a glimpse of Jean in the garb of a preacher. He was ready to laugh at the folly of his two old cronies ; but, feeling still the fumes of the night before and finding himself on a bier with lighted candles round him, he strongly doubted if he were alive. He dared not speak or move, and all three of them remained in this nightmare until the sun rising higher made them see more clearly what strange devotions can be produced by the fumes of good wine and the malice of women.

PAUL SCARRON

1610–1660

THE TWO JEALOUS LADIES

In the little town of La Flèche there were two most accomplished gentlemen who were very backward in taking wives, as often happens among persons of quality, according to the saying " Between those we would have and those we would not, we never marry." But the saying was at last crossed by both of these gentlemen. One of them called Monsieur de Fons-blanche, married a daughter of the family of Château-d'un, of humble origin, but very rich. The other, whose name was Monsieur du Lac, married a lady from the city of Chartres, who was not rich, but nevertheless exceeding beautiful, and of so good a family that she was related to several dukes, peers, and marshals of France.

These two gentlemen, who could share the town betwixt them, had always been good friends till after their marriage, when their two ladies looking enviously on each other, it quickly occasioned a rupture between the husbands. Madame de Fons-blanche was not, it is true, handsome in countenance, yet she had nevertheless a graceful mien, well shaped, had a great deal of wit, and was very obliging. Madame du Lac, as beautiful as she was, yet wanted address; she had wit indeed a great deal, but so ill-managed that she thereby rather rendered herself avoidable than acceptable. These two ladies were of the humour of most women nowadays, who never think they live great unless they have a score or two of beaux after them. This caused them to employ all the arts they had in making conquests, but therein du Lac succeeded much better than de Fons-blanche, for she had subdued all the youth of the town ; I mean among the quality, for she would by no means suffer any others to speak to her. This pride and affectation occasioned a great many murmurings against her, which at length broke out into open detraction, but nothing harmed her, for it is thought it rather contributed to than hindered her procuring new lovers.

Fons-blanche was not so desirous of having a great number of sparks ; she, nevertheless, had some, whom she managed with a great deal of address, and whereof there was one, a very handsome

38

young fellow, that had as much wit as she, and was one of the bravest youths of his time. This spark was her greatest favourite, but at length his diligence caused him to be suspected by the neighbours, and slander began to talk loud. It was here the rupture began between these ladies, who before had visited each other very civilly, nevertheless with a little jealous envy.

Du Lac began at last to slander Fons-blanche openly, to pry into her actions, and do all that lay in her power to ruin her reputation, especially about the aforesaid gentleman, whose name was Monsieur du Val-Rochet. This soon came to Fons-blanche's ears, who was extremely nettled at it, and said that, " If she had lovers, it was not by scores, as du Lac had, who every day gained new conquests by her impostures."

Du Lac hearing this, quickly returned her the like reflections. Whence you may imagine that these two women lived together in a town like a brace of demons. Some charitable people did all they could to reconcile them, but this proved in vain, for they could never be prevailed upon so much as to see each other. Du Lac thought the only way to offend Fons-blanche to the quick would be to get away her lover du Val-Rochet from her. She then caused Monsieur de Fons-blanche to be acquainted underhand that he was no sooner out of doors, which he was often, either hunting or visiting, but that du Val-Rochet called on his wife ; and further, that several persons of credit were ready to testify that they had seen him come out of her bedroom.

Monsieur de Fons-blanche, who had never yet had any suspicion of his wife, was nevertheless inclinable to reflect a little upon what he had heard, and in confusion, desired his lady to oblige him so far as to entertain du Val-Rochet's visits no longer. She seemed all obedience, nevertheless insinuated so many reasons why she might safely admit him, that he gave her liberty, and suffered her to act as before.

Du Lac perceiving this contrivance of hers had not had its desired effect, resolved to get some opportunity to talk with Val-Rochet herself. She was both fair and subtle, two qualities sufficient to surprise the wariest heart, though it had been never so much engaged. De Fons-blanche was extremely concerned at being like to lose her lover, but much more when she heard that Val-Rochet had spoken unhandsomely of her. This grief was augmented by her husband's death, which happened a little while after. She went into close mourning 'tis true, but still jealousy got the ascendant of her outward concern.

Her husband had been scarce buried fifteen days before she had a secret conference with Val-Rochet. I know not the subject of their discourse, but the event makes me pretty well able to guess at it, for in little more than a week after, their marriage was made public, so that in less than a month's time she had two husbands, a living and a dead. This seems to me to have been the most violent effect of jealousy imaginable ; for to deprive du Lac of her lover she both forfeited her modesty by marrying so soon, and forgave the unpardonable affront Val-Rochet had offered her.

Du Lac was almost ready to run mad when she first heard this news, and resolved forthwith to have him assassinated as he went on a journey to Brittany ; but which he being made acquainted with. she was prevented in that design.

Then she entered upon the strangest thought that ever jealousy could suggest, and that was, to set her husband and Val-Rochet together by the ears, which she brought about by her pernicious artifices. They quarrelled divers times, and at length came to a duel, which du Lac encouraged her husband in, being none of the wisest men in the world, that du Val-Rochet might have an opportunity to kill him, which she fancied no hard matter, and then she proposed to hang him out of the way for his pains.

But as fortune would have it, it happened quite otherwise ; for Val-Rochet, trusting to his skill in fencing, seemed to despise du Lac, thinking he durst not make a thrust at him, but therein he was extremely deceived ; for whilst he put himself out of guard, du Lac made a home thrust at him, and ran him through the body, whereof he instantly died.

This done, du Lac went home to his house, and acquainted his wife therewith, who was not only surprised, but concerned at so unexpected an accident. He after this fled away privately to a relation of his wife's, who, as I have told you before, had several persons of quality to her kindred, who laboured incessantly to obtain her husband's pardon from the King. Madame Fonsblanche was not a little astonished when she was first told that her husband was killed ; but coming afterwards to herself, she was advised to bury him quickly and privately, to prevent his body being arrested by the bailiffs.

Thus in less than six weeks' time Fons-blanche had been a widow twice. Du Lac not long after obtained his pardon, which was confirmed by the parliament of Paris, notwithstanding all the opposition the deceased person's widow could make.

This made her to entertain a wilder design than Madame du Lac had done before, and that was to stab du Lac as he walked in the market-place with some of his friends. For this purpose she provided herself a poniard, and marching up to him, attacked him so furiously that before he could get himself into a posture of defence, or have any of his friends turn about to help him, she had stabbed him mortally in two places, whereof he died three days after. His wife immediately got this virago seized and clapped up in prison. Her trial came on, and she was condemned to die, but her execution was respited by reason of her being with child ; nevertheless, not long after the stench of the prison did the work of the hangman, for she died of a disease caused thereby, after having been first delivered before her time, and her child, being baptized, died likewise soon after.

Madame du Lac began afterwards to reflect on what she had been the occasion of, and therefore forthwith resolved to turn a nun, which she did, after having put her affairs in order, in the nunnery of Almeneche, in the diocese of Sées, where she now continues, if she be not yet dead of her austerities, which she voluntarily inflicted on herself.

BISHOP FÉNELON
1651–1715

THE STORY OF ALIBEA

ABBAS, Shah of Persia, during his travels, left his court to wander through the country without being recognised, and see his people in all their natural liberty. Only one of his courtiers went with him.

" I do not know," said the King to him, " the real manners of men. All that approaches us is disguised. It is art and not simplicity of nature that we see. I wish to view the country, and look at the country folks who are so despised, though they are the true support of human society. I am tired of seeing courtiers who study me in order to take me by surprise in their flattery. I must go amongst ploughmen and shepherds who do not know me."

He passed through several villages where the people were dancing, and he was delighted to find, far away from the court, tranquil pleasures without expense. He had a meal in a hut, and as he was very hungry after walking more than usual, the coarse food he ate seemed to him more pleasant than all the exquisite dishes of his table.

Wandering through a field strewn with flowers, with a clear brook running by it, he saw a young shepherd playing the flute in the shadow of a great elm, close to his grazing sheep. The Shah went up to the lad and found him pleasant of face, with frank and simple bearing, in which there was a certain nobility of grace.

The rags with which the shepherd was covered did not lessen his beauty. The Shah thought at first it was some person of noble birth in disguise ; but he learnt from the shepherd that his father and mother lived in a neighbouring village, and that his name was Alibea.

The Shah talked with him, and found he had a firm and intelligent spirit. His eyes were lively and had nothing fierce or fiery in them. His voice was sweet and insinuating with touching tones. There was no coarseness in his face, and yet it had no soft or effeminate beauty. The shepherd, about sixteen years of age, did not know how he struck other men. He thought he looked and talked and spoke like other shepherds of his village ; but, without being educated, he had learnt all that a fine intelligence can teach those who listen to it.

The Shah, after a familiar talk, was charmed with the lad. He learnt from him in regard to the state of the people, all that kings never gather from the crowd of flatterers that surround them. From time to time he laughed at the ingenuousness of the boy, who was not at all tactful in his replies. It was a great novelty for the monarch to hear such natural speech. He signalled to the courtier not to reveal who he was ; for he feared that Alibea would at once lose his freedom and grace of manner if he learnt to whom he was speaking.

" I can see," he said, " that nature is not less beautiful in low conditions of life than in high conditions. Never has a son of a king seemed better born than this lad who looks after sheep. How happy should I be to have a son as handsome, as sensible, and as lovable ! He appears to me capable of filling any place, and if he is carefully taught he will surely be one day a great man. I wish to have him bred up by my side."

Alibea was taken to the court, and he was much surprised to learn that it was the great Shah whom he had pleased. He was taught to read and write and sing, and then he was given masters for the arts and the sciences that adorn the mind. At first, he was rather dazzled with the court, and his great change of fortune somewhat altered his feelings. His age and his favour joined together rather told against his wisdom and moderation. In place of his sheep crook and flute and shepherd's dress, he took a robe of purple, embroidered with gold, with a turban covered with precious stones. His beauty effaced that of the most handsome men at court. He learnt to handle the most serious affairs, and merited the trust of his master, who, knowing the exquisite taste of Alibea for all the magnificences of the palace, charged him at last with one of the highest duties in Persia. This was to watch over the jewels and precious articles of the crown.

Alibea wished to return to his village for a while. He lovingly roamed by all the places where he had danced and sung and played the flute with his companions. He helped his relatives and friends, and wished them, for their greatest happiness, never to leave their country life and never to know the unhappiness of an existence at court.

These unhappinesses he experienced. After the death of his good master Shah Abbas, his son, Shah Sophi, succeeded to the throne. Some courtiers of an envious and cunning nature found a way of prejudicing the new ruler against Alibea.

" He has abused the confidence of your father," they said. " He has massed immense treasures and stolen several things of high price entrusted to him."

Shah Sophi was both young and absolute in power. He did not need to be both to become a creature who was inattentive, credulous, and without caution. He had the vanity to wish to appear as a reformer of everything that his father had done better than he could. To get a pretext for deposing Alibea from his position, he asked him, following the advice of the envious courtiers, to bring him a sword adorned with diamonds of an immense price, which his grandfather had been wont to carry in his wars.

Shah Abbas had formerly taken from the weapon all its fine diamonds, and by good witnesses Alibea was able to prove that the thing had been done at the command of the late monarch, before the office of guardian of the royal jewels was given to Alibea. When his enemies found that this pretext would not serve to overthrow him, they advised Shah Sophi to order him to make, within a fortnight, an exact list of every precious thing entrusted to his care.

At the end of the fortnight the Shah demanded to see everything himself. Alibea opened all the doors, and showed everything that was in his keeping. Nothing was missing : all was right, well arranged, and preserved with the greatest care. The Shah was disappointed at finding throughout so much order and exactitude, and was almost inclined to take Alibea into favour again. But he perceived, at the end of a great gallery full of splendid articles, an iron door with three large locks.

" It is there," said the courtiers to him, " that Alibea has hidden all the costly things he had stolen."

" I wish to see what is behind this door ! " cried the Shah in sudden anger. " What have you put there ? Show it to me ! "

Alibea fell on his knees and begged him in the name of God not to take from him what was most precious to him in the world.

" It is not just," he said, "that I should lose in a moment all that remains to me, my only resource, after having worked so many years for your royal father. Take everything else away, if you will, but leave me this ! "

The Shah never doubted but that it was a treasure that Alibea had amassed by evil means. Speaking with still more determination he ordered that the door should be burst open. At last, Alibea, who had the keys, opened it himself. In the room there were found only the sheep crook, the flute, and the shepherd's dress which Alibea had worn in the old days, and which he often came to look at, for fear of forgetting himself in his new position.

" Behold," he said, " O great Shah, the precious remains of my ancient happiness ! Neither fate nor kingly power has been able to rob me of them. Behold my treasure, that I keep to enrich myself when you have reduced me to poverty ! Take all the rest : leave me these dear pledges of my early condition. Here are the true treasures that I shall never lack—simple innocent things, always sweet to those who know how to content themselves with the necessaries of life and are not tormented for the luxuries. Here are the treasures whose fruits are liberty and peace ! Here are the treasures that have never brought me a moment of care ! O delightful instruments of a simple and happy life, I love you only, and with you I would live and die ! What need was there that other deceptive glittering things should come and mislead me and trouble the quietness of my life ? I give them back to you, Grand Shah ! all these riches that I owe to your liberality. I will keep only that which I had when your father, by his favours, rendered me unhappy ! "

Hearing these words, the Shah understood the innocence of Alibea, and being indignant against the courtiers who had wished to overthrow him, he drove them away from him. Alibea became his chief minister, and was entrusted with the most secret affairs. But every day he came to look at his crook and flute and his shepherd's dress, which he always kept ready in his strong room to take up if inconstant fortune troubled his favour at court. He died in extreme old age, without having wished either to punish his enemies or to amass wealth ; and he left his relatives only enough to live in the position of shepherds, which he always believed to be the safest and the most happy.

THE ISLE OF PLEASURES

Bishop Fénelon

After having sailed for a long time over the Pacific, we saw in the distance an isle of sugar with mountains of stewed fruit, and rocks of candy and caramel, and streams of syrup flowing through the fields. The natives were very gluttonous ; they licked the paths as they walked along, and sucked their fingers after dipping them in the rivers. There were forests of liquorice and tall trees from which waffle cakes fell, and these the wind carried into the mouths of the voyagers, though their lips were scarcely parted.

As so many sweetnesses seemed to us insipid, we wished to go on to some other country where we could find food with a stronger taste. We were told that, ten leagues away, there was another island in which were found mines of ham, sausages, and peppered hashes. These things were dug out just as gold is dug from the mines of Peru. There were also brooks of onion sauce, and the walls of the houses were of pie-crust.

In stormy weather on this island it rains wine, and in fine weather the morning dew is a white wine like Greek wine. To reach this island, we placed on the shore of the land we were leaving a dozen men of prodigious fatness, who had been sent to sleep. They breathed so heavily in snoring that they filled our sail with a favourable wind.

Scarcely had we landed on the other island than we found on the shore a band of merchants who were selling appetites. For these were things the islanders often lost amid their pleasures of the table. There were also other persons who sold sleep. The price was regulated by the hour ; but some sleeps were dearer than others, in proportion to the dreams a man wished to have. The finest dreams were very costly.

I asked for the best that money could buy, and, feeling tired, I lay down to sleep. But hardly was I in my bed, when I heard a loud noise ; it terrified me, and I shouted for help. I was told that the earth had gaped open. I thought I was lost ; but the islanders reassured me, saying that the earth opened every night at a certain hour to pour out boiling streams of frothing chocolate and iced liqueurs of every kind. I rose in haste to get some : they were delicious.

Then I went to bed again, and in my sleep the world seemed to be made of crystal, and men nourished themselves as they pleased with perfumes. They could not walk without dancing, or speak but by singing : they had wings to travel the air and fins to sweep through the sea. These men, however, were like gun flints. You could not knock against them but they at once grew fiery. They were as inflammable as tinder, and I could not help laughing when I saw how easy it was to stir them up. I asked one of them why he was so touchy ; showing me his fist, he replied that he never gave way to anger.

As soon as I was awake, a merchant of appetites entered and asked me how much hunger I wanted, and if I would like to buy a relay of appetites that would enable me to pass the whole day in eating. I accepted the offer. For my money he gave me a dozen little bags of taffeta, which I fixed round me, and which were to serve me as stomachs to enable me to digest without trouble twelve great feasts in a single day. Scarcely had I put on the bags when I felt I was dying of hunger. I passed my time in a long delicious banquet. As soon as one repast was finished, hunger seized on me again, and I did not give it time to worry me. But, as I had a voracious appetite, the islanders remarked that I did not eat properly. They are distinguished by the exquisite delicacy and neatness of their meals.

By night I was tired of having passed the whole day at table, like a horse with his nose always in the manger. I resolved the next day to take a different course, and nourish myself only on fine fragrances. For breakfast I took some orange blossom perfume. At dinner a heavier nourishment was provided. I was given tuberoses to smell, and I had the scent of jonquils for collation. In the evening, I had for supper large baskets full of all sorts of fragrant flowers, to which were added some perfume stews. That night I had an attack of indigestion through having smelt so many nourishing odours. The next day I fasted as a relief from the fatigue of the pleasures of the table.

I was told that in the country there was a very singular town, and the people promised to take me there in a new kind of carriage. I was placed in a little wooden chair, very light and provided with great wings, and to this chair the people attached with silken cords four great birds as big as ostriches, but with wings proportioned to their bodies. These birds rose in their flight, and with the reins I turned them eastward, as I had been directed. I saw at my feet the high mountains, and we flew so rapidly that I could scarcely draw my breath as we swept through the waves of the air.

In an hour we arrived at the famous city. It is all of marble and three times as large as Paris. The whole town forms only a single house. There are twenty-four great courts, each of which is larger than the largest palace of the world. In the middle of these twenty-four courts there is a twenty-fifth, which is six times the size of each of the others. All the dwellings in this house are similar, for there is no inequality of condition among the inhabitants. There are no servants and no poor people. Everybody looks after himself, and has no one to wait on him. There are only the Wishes, which are little spirits, playful and fluttering, that give in a moment to each person all the he desires.

When I arrived I received one of these spirits, who attached himself to me and never let me want for anything. He scarcely gave me time to form my desires. I even began to be tired of the new wishes that this freedom of contenting every fancy excited in me. I understood by experience that it was better to do without superfluous things, than to be unceasingly full of new desires, without being able to stop and tranquilly enjoy a single pleasure.

The inhabitants of the city were polite and charming and obliging. They welcomed me as though I had been one of themselves. As soon as I wished to speak, they divined what I desired, and carried it out without waiting for me to explain in words. This surprised me, and I noticed that they never spoke among themselves. They read in each other's eyes all that they think, just as we do in a book. When they wish to hide their thought, they have only to close their eyes. They led me into a hall in which there was a music of perfumes. They arranged their perfumes as we arrange sounds. A certain assemblage of fragrances, some strong and the others weak, make a harmony that pleases the sense of smell, just as our concerts please the ear by the mingling of deep and high sounds.

In this country the women govern the men. They judge the lawsuits, and teach all sciences and carry on wars. The men powder and paint their faces and dress themselves up from morning to evening ; they spin and sew and work at embroidery, and are fearful of being beaten by their wives when they do not obey them. It is said that affairs were different a certain number of years ago. But the men, served by the Wishes, became so poor-spirited, so idle, and so ignorant, that the women were ashamed of letting themselves be governed by them. They met together to reform the evils of the commonwealth. They established public schools, where persons of their sex with most intelligence set themselves to study. They disarmed their husbands, who asked nothing better than to escape from fighting. They took away from them their judicial powers, watched over the public order, laid down laws and saw that they were kept, and thus saved the Republic, that otherwise would have been totally ruined by the frivolity and softness of the men.

Touched by this spectacle, and fatigued by so many feasts and amusements, I concluded that the pleasures of the senses, no matter how varied, how facile they are, degrade mankind, and do not make them happy. So I departed from these islands, so delightful in appearance, and, returning home, I found in a sober life, in moderate work, in pure manners, and in the practice of virtue, the health and happiness I had not been able to procure by a continuity of feasting and a variety of pleasures.

ALAIN-RENÉ LE SAGE
1668–1747

THE ADVENTURE OF DON POMPEYO DE CASTRO

FROM my boyish days, my passion was for a military life. Our own country being at peace, I went into Portugal; thence to Africa with the Duke of Braganza, who gave me a commission. I was a younger brother, with as slender a provision as most in Spain; so that my only chance was in attracting the notice of the commander-in-chief by my bravery. I was so far from deficient in my duty, that the Duke promoted me, step by step, to one of the most honourable posts in the service. After a long war, of which you all know the issue, I devoted myself to the court; and the King, on strong testimonials from the general officers, rewarded me with a considerable pension. Alive to that sovereign's generosity, I lost no opportunity of proving my gratitude by my diligence. I was in attendance as often as etiquette would allow me to offer myself to his notice. By this conduct I gained insensibly the love of that prince, and received new favours from his hands.

One day, when I distinguished myself in running at the ring, and in a bull-fight preceding it, all the court extolled my strength and dexterity. On my return home, with my honours thick upon me, I found there a note, informing me that a lady, my conquest over whom ought to flatter me more than all the glory I had gained that day, wished to have the pleasure of my company; and that I had only to attend in the evening, at a place marked out in the letter. This was more than all my public triumphs, and I concluded the writer to be a woman of the first quality. You may guess that I did not loiter by the way. An old woman in waiting, as my guide, conducted me by a little garden-gate into a large house, and left me in an elegant closet, saying: "Stay here, I will acquaint my mistress with your arrival." I observed a great many articles of value in the closet, which was magnificently illuminated; but this splendour only caught my attention as confirming me in my previous opinion of the lady's high rank. If appearances strengthened that conjecture, her noble and majestic air on her entrance left no doubt in my mind. Yet I was a little out in my calculation.

" Noble sir," said she, " after the step I have taken in your favour
it were impertinent to disown my partiality. Your brilliant actions
of to-day, in presence of the court, were not the inspirers of my
sentiments, they only urge forward this avowal. I have seen you
more than once, have inquired into your character, and the result
has determined me to follow the impulse of my heart. But do not
suppose that you are well with a duchess. I am but the widow of a
captain in the King's Guards ; yet there is something to throw a
radiance round your victory . . . the preference you have gained over
one of the first noblemen in the kingdom. The Duke d'Almeyda
loves me, and presses his suit with ardour, yet without success. My
vanity only induces me to bear his importunities."

Though I saw plainly, by this address, that I had got in with a
coquette, my presiding star was not a whit out of my good graces for
involving me in this adventure. Donna Hortensia, for that was the
lady's name, was just in the ripeness and luxuriance of youth and
dazzling beauty. Nay, more, she had refused the possession of her
heart to the earnest entreaties of a duke, and offered it unsolicited to
me. What a feather in the cap of a Spanish cavalier ! I prostrated
myself at Hortensia's feet, to thank her for her favours. I talked
just as a man of gallantry always does talk, and she had reason to be
satisfied with the extravagance of my acknowledgments. Thus we
parted the best friends in the world, on the terms of meeting every
evening when the Duke d'Almeyda was prevented from coming ; and
she promised to give me due notice of his absence. The bargain was
exactly fulfilled, and I was turned into the Adonis of this new Venus.

But the pleasures of this life are transitory. With all the lady's
precautions to conceal our private treaty of commerce from my
rival, he found means of gaining a knowledge, of which it concerned
us greatly to keep him ignorant ; a disloyal chambermaid divulged
the state secret. This nobleman, naturally generous, but proud, self-
sufficient, and violent, was exasperated at my presumption. Anger
and jealousy set him beside himself. Taking counsel only with his
rage, he resolved on an infamous revenge. One night when I was with
Hortensia, he waylaid me at the little garden-gate, with all his
servants provided with cudgels. As soon as I came out, he ordered
me to be seized, and beaten to death by these wretches. " Lay on,"
said he, " let the rash intruder give up the ghost under your chastisement ; thus shall his insolence be punished." No sooner had he
finished these words than his myrmidons assaulted me in a body,
and gave me such a beating as to stretch me senseless on the
ground, after which they hurried off with their master, to whom
this butchery had been a delicious pastime. I lay the remainder
of the night, just as they had left me. At daybreak some people
passed by, who, finding that life was still in me, had the humanity
to carry me to a surgeon. Fortunately my wounds were not

mortal; and, falling into skilful hands, I was perfectly cured in two months. At the end of that period I made my appearance again at court, and resumed my former way of life, except that I steered clear of Hortensia, who on her part made no further attempt to renew the acquaintance, because the Duke, on that condition, had pardoned her infidelity.

As my adventure was the town talk, and I was known to be no coward, people were astonished to see me as quiet as if I had received no affront; for I kept my thoughts to myself, and seemed to have no quarrel with any man living. No one knew what to think of my counterfeited insensibility. Some imagined that, in spite of my courage, the rank of the aggressor overawed me, and occasioned my tacit submission. Others, with more reason, mistrusted my silence, and considered my inoffensive demeanour as a cover to my revenge. The King was of opinion with these last, that I was not a man to put up with an insult, and that I should not be wanting to myself at a convenient opportunity. To discover my real intentions, he sent for me one day into his closet, where he said : " Don Pompeyo, I know what accident has befallen you, and am surprised, I own, at your forbearance. You are certainly acting a part."

" Sire," answered I, " how can I know whom to challenge ? I was attacked in the night by persons unknown : it is a misfortune of which I must make the best."

" No, no," replied the King, " I am not to be duped by these evasive answers. The whole story has reached my ears. The Duke d'Almeyda has touched your honour to the quick. You are nobly born, and a Castilian : I know what that double character requires. You cherish hostile designs. Admit me a party to your purposes ; it must be so. Never fear the consequences of making me your confidant."

" Since your Majesty commands it," resumed I, " my sentiments shall be laid open without reserve. Yes, sir, I meditate a severe retribution. Every man, wearing such a name as mine, must account for its untarnished lustre with his family. You know the unworthy treatment I have experienced ; and I purpose assassinating the Duke d'Almeyda, as a mode of revenge correspondent to the injury. I shall plunge a dagger in his bosom, or shoot him through the head, and escape, if I can, into Spain. This is my design."

" It is violent," said the King : " and yet I have little to say against it, after the provocation which the Duke d'Almeyda has given you. He is worthy of the punishment you destine for him. But do not be in a hurry with your project. Leave me to devise a method of bringing you together again as friends."

" Oh ! sir," exclaimed I with vexation, " why did you extort my secret from me ? What expedient can . . ."

" If mine is not to your satisfaction," interrupted he, " you may execute your first intention. I do not mean to abuse your confidence. I shall not implicate your honour ; so rest contented on that head."

I was greatly puzzled to guess by what means the King designed to terminate this affair amicably. But thus it was. He sent to speak with the Duke d'Almeyda in private.

"Duke," said he, "you have insulted Don Pompeyo de Castro. You are not ignorant that he is a man of noble birth, a soldier who has served with credit, and stands high in my favour. You owe him reparation."

"I am not of a temper to refuse it," answered the Duke. "If he complains of my outrageous behaviour, I am ready to justify it by the law of arms."

"Something very different must be done," replied the King : "a Spanish gentleman understands the point of honour too well to fight on equal terms with a cowardly assassin. I can use no milder term ; and you can only atone for the heinousness of your conduct by presenting a cane in person to your antagonist, and offering to submit yourself to its discipline."

"Oh heaven ! " exclaimed the Duke. "What ! sir, would you have a man of my rank degrade, debase himself before a simple gentleman and submit to be caned ! "

"No," replied the monarch, "I will oblige Don Pompeyo to promise not to touch you. Only offer him the cane, and ask his pardon : that is all I require from you."

"And that is too much, sir," interrupted the Duke d'Almeyda warmly ; "I had rather remain exposed to all the secret machinations of his resentment."

"Your life is dear to me," said the King ; "and I should wish this affair to have no bad consequences. To terminate it with less disgust to yourself, I will be the only witness of the satisfaction which I order you to offer to the Spaniard."

The King was obliged to stretch his influence over the Duke to the utmost before he could induce him to so mortifying a step. However, the peremptory monarch effected his purpose, and then sent for me. He related the particulars of his conversation with my enemy, and inquired if I should be content with the stipulated reparation. I answered " Yes," and gave my word that, far from striking the offender, I would not even accept the cane, when he presented it.

With this understanding, the Duke and myself at a certain hour attended the King, who took us into his closet. "Come," said he to the Duke, "acknowledge your fault, and deserve to be forgiven by humility of your contrition."

Then my antagonist made his apology, and offered me the cane in his hand.

"Don Pompeyo," said the monarch unexpectedly, "take the cane, and let not my presence prevent you from doing justice to your outraged honour. I release you from your promise not to strike the Duke."

"No, sir," answered I, "it is enough that he has submitted to the indignity of the offer : an offended Spaniard asks no more."

"Well, then ! " replied the King, "since you are content with this satisfaction, you may both of you at once assume the privilege of a gentlemanly quarrel. Measure your swords, and discuss the question honourably."

"It is what I most ardently desire," exclaimed the Duke d'Almeyda in a menacing tone ; "for that only is competent to make me amends for the disgraceful step I have taken."

With these words, he went away full of rage and shame ; and sent to tell me, two hours after, that he was waiting for me, in a retired place. I kept the appointment, and found his noblemen ready to fight lustily. He was not five-and-forty ; deficient neither in courage nor in skill ; so that the match was fair and equal.

"Come on, Don Pompeyo," said he, "let us terminate our difference here. Our hostility ought to be reciprocally mortal ; yours, for my aggression, and mine, for having asked your pardon."

These words were no sooner out of his mouth, than he drew upon me so suddenly, that I had no time to reply. He pressed very closely upon me at first, but I had the good fortune to put by all his thrusts. I acted on the offensive in my turn : the encounter was evidently with a man equally skilled in defence or in attack ; and there is no knowing what might have been the issue, if he had not made a false step in retiring, and fallen backwards. I stood still immediately, and said to the Duke, "Recover yourself."

"Why give me any quarter ? " he answered. "Your forbearance only aggravates my disgrace."

"I will not take advantage of an accident," replied I, "it would only tarnish my glory. Once more recover yourself, and let us fight it out."

"Don Pompeyo," said he rising, "after this act of generosity, honour allows me not to renew the attack upon you. What would the world say of me were I to wound you mortally ? I should be branded as a coward for having murdered a man, at whose mercy I had just before lain prostrate. I cannot therefore again lift my arm against your life, and I feel my resentful passions subsiding into the sweet emotions of gratitude. Don Pompeyo, let us mutually lay aside our hatred. Let us go still further ; let us be friends."

"Ah ! my lord, " exclaimed I, "so flattering a proposal I joyfully accept. I proffer you my sincere friendship ; and, as an earnest, promise never more to approach Donna Hortensia, though she herself should invite me."

"It is my duty," said he, "to yield that lady to you. Justice requires me to give her up, since her affections are yours already."

"No, no," interrupted I; "you love her. Her partiality in my favour would give you uneasiness; I sacrifice my own pleasures to your peace."

"Ah! too generous Castilian," replied the Duke, embracing me, "your sentiments are truly noble. With what remorse do they strike me! Grieved and ashamed, I look back on the outrage you have sustained. The reparation in the King's chamber seems now too trifling. A better recompense awaits you. To obliterate all remembrance of your shame, take one of my nieces whose hand is at my disposal. She is a rich heiress, not fifteen, with beauty beyond the attractions of mere youth."

I made my acknowledgments to the Duke in terms such as the high honour of his alliance might suggest, and married his niece a few days afterwards. All the court complimented this nobleman on having made such generous amends to an insulted rival; and my friends took part in my joy at the happy issue of an adventure which might have led to the most melancholy consequences. From this time, gentlemen, I have lived happily at Lisbon. I am the idol of my wife, and have not sunk the lover in the husband. The Duke d'Almeyda gives me new proofs of friendship every day; and I may venture to boast of standing high in the King of Portugal's good graces.

THE LINNET OF THE POPE

To be a woman and keep a secret are two things that never go together, and the least womanly woman is better able to keep her honour than a secret. You will say this is putting it too extravagantly, but I have a tale that will support my theory.

There were some nuns in a convent at Fontevrault, to which Pope John XXII. used to go pretty often to grant indulgences by way of raising revenue. It was a convent of excellent fame, where Satan could do nothing but lead the holy women into some slight peccadillo when they came to talk at the grille. For, as you know, the enemy of mankind can only get hold of nuns through their passion for chattering. The Holy Pastor came to them one day on his mule—which they kissed—and heaven knows how many indulgences were brought out ! Insatiable is the monastic tribe, and the nuns had got it into their heads to obtain the most fantastic of indults : they wished to obtain the right to confess each other, instead of going to a priest.

" Holy father," said the abbess, " speaking frankly as a woman, I must admit that there is little sincerity in the confessions we make to a man. With him we try to pass over a hundred little things, trifling mistakes, that we should blush to speak about to the other sex. For a man is often like to jest about the faults a nun accuses herself of."

" You want women confessors ! " said the Pope. " How can such a thing be possible ? I am sorry I must refuse your request, on one broad principle. This sacrament requires a great secrecy, and, as you know, the female race is over-talkative. Was it not a woman's love of chatter that first led to original sin ? Your sex cannot keep a secret. But if you like, I will test the matter and learn by my own experience if women have been defamed in this respect ? "

It was not the first time that the Abbess had worried His Holiness in regard to this affair, and he had made his preparations about the matter when he left Avignon. So he now took a little box, that he had carried on his mule, and handed it to the Abbess.

"Here," he said, "I will put this box in your hands to keep until I return to-morrow. Do not open it before I arrive, or you will not obtain the indult. If the box is intact to-morrow morning, I will grant your request."

He went away and all the nuns clustered round the mysterious box, crying :

"Let me touch it ! Let me see it ! "

They struggled to snatch it from each other, but happily no one attempted to open it, and the nuns went to bed, all worrying over what it was the box contained. Nobody slept very much, and the Abbess, especially, was almost sick with curiosity. At prayers the next morning everything went wrong. The convent was worried beyond bearing : for it does not take much to turn the head of a nun.

"Ah," said the Abbess to her anxious troop, " the Pope is trying to make us pine away in grief. What is this great secret he want to hide from us ? Why are we not good enough to have it revealed to us ? I must say he treats us nuns with no great honour ! Let us open the box just to be avenged on him. Who will be able to tell what we have done ? We can easily fasten it up again exactly as we found it."

At this speech every nun rejoiced. The Abbess opened the fatal box. What did she find in it ? A little linnet. The bird swiftly flew to the ceiling, and, singing, circled three times above their heads, and then flew out through a hole into the open air. The Abbess and her nuns heard a knock at the door, and the Holy Pontiff entered with a smile.

"Ah, there is my box ! " he cried. " Now we shall see if women can be trusted. For your indult was placed inside under seal. Oh, oh ! " he said, laughing, as he found the box open and peeped in, " your indult has flown away. Farewell, my discreet and trustworthy sisters ! There will be no woman confessor."

"So much the better," said one nun, softly. " I was not for the change. One man confessor is at least something."

" You want women confessors ! " said the Pope. How can such a thing be possible ? I am sorry I must refuse your request, on one broad principle. This sacrament requires a great secrecy, and as you know, the female race is over-talkative. Was it not a woman's love of chatter that first led to our troubles ? Your sex cannot keep a secret, but if you like, I will test the matter and learn by my own experience if women have been detained in this respect."

COMTE DE CAYLUS
1692–1763

THE CHAUDRON GIRLS

" My son," said my father to me one day, " you will become president of this salt granary, for nobody can tell who lives or dies. I hear you hang about the house of Madame Chaudron. She is a worthy woman ; I would not dispute it. It is not certain that she threw her husband down a well, as some people say. But though she has a good deal of society at her place, she has no money. Of course you prowl around her daughters, and at your age I should delight to flirt with the fair sex, especially as the Chaudron girls are as pretty as flowers and conduct themselves in a modest way. But money, my boy, is the main thing."

" I quite understand you, father," I replied.

And I went straightway into my study to consider things, thinking what I should do in the matter ; and, concluding that it was necessary to take a definite course of action, I put on my wig and went out.

I arrived at Madame Chaudron's ; as soon as I was seated and began to make my compliments—

" On what footing have you entered my house for the last three months ? " said Madame Chaudron, pointing to her three girls.

" I came here for a good reason," I said, somewhat astonished.

" Well," she continued, " you must be engaged to-day to her whom you choose for wife. I am not a mother to let false rumours get abroad about my girls."

Under this affront, I did not hesitate a moment.

" Madame," I said, " I am an honest man, and I will have no other wife but your second daughter, Babiche, whose hand I now ask of you in marriage. I told her I loved her when first I made her acquaintance. Now I will see my father on the matter."

I went at a run to find him, and in all filial affection I told him I had asked Babiche Chaudron in marriage. He looked at me between the eyes for a while.

" Did I not clearly forbid you to marry any of the Chaudron girls just about a quarter of an hour ago ? " he said. " They have

no money, and you know what money is, and what people will
say about her. Still I am your father, and I will approve the
marriage. Let us go to the mother.

So we went.

"My dear," he said, "my son is a fool, but I can't help having
the feelings of a father for him. Since he wants to do this foolish
thing, I suppose we must arrange the articles."

This matter was soon settled. We all had supper in the garden,
and by what happened there at the table you can see what pre-
destination is when the stars fight against a man. I sat between
Babiche and her eldest sister, and talked about the betrothal.

"I shall not say what I think," said the eldest Mademoiselle
Chaudron, "but if you mean to marry my sister Babiche, may this
wine poison you, if I do not become your wife instead of her!"

And she pleasantly tossed off a glass of red wine.

"You see, my son," said Madame Chaudron, "how the matter
stands. She is the eldest of the family, and rather than let her
second sister marry before her, she would do anything. What is
it that makes you prefer Babiche? Is it because you love her?
After you have been married to her less than a year, you will be
complaining to me about her!"

She was still speaking when—as by arrangement, though really
by chance—our notary, Monsieur Gandion, arrived.

"Your servant!" he said. "Here are the articles all drawn up.
But who is going to hold the handle of the frying-pan? In other
words, which of the young ladies is about to be married?"

My father all this time had seemed to be doing nothing, but he
was enjoying the society of the youngest Mademoiselle Chaudron,
to whom he listened without saying anything, because she was as
witty as she was pretty. Now he cried suddenly:

"She shall be my daughter-in-law, or I shall die through grief
at not being her father by marriage. You see," he continued,
"she has just said to me like that, that if she had a husband, he
should never die but by her hand. A pleasant wit like that can
only come from a fine intelligence, and I want her to marry my
son. Yes," he said to me, "beg Mademoiselle Babiche to
excuse you."

And this I did, saying:

"Mademoiselle, I beg you to pardon me and excuse me. It is
due to my not having reflected. But if I marry your youngest
sister, I shall make it a veritable pleasure to be your brother-
in-law."

"Sir," she replied, "I do not know how to be a shrew, and since
you use me in this fashion, I shall not say a word."

And with that, she gave me a blow with one hand, and broke a
pile of plates with the other, and went away.

" All that is only a sign of joy," said Madame Chaudron. " Don't let us enjoy ourselves any the less for that. Master Gandion, make out the contract! We will sign it to-morrow, and the wedding will take place on Sunday."

As we returned to spend the evening at my father's, we met on the road Sieur Bertrand's troop of play-actors, who were taking down their theatre. His eldest son, dressed up as a girl, took a violin and played us to the house.

" It is the custom," he said, " on an occasion like this, to kiss the young lady before we part."

And thereupon he embraced my betrothed. That put us all in a merry humour, and we invited him to come with his troop and dance with us. And this was done. About midnight, as I was going to dance the Forlande with my future bride—

" It is necessary for me to disguise myself," she said, " isn't it ? "

And she took the arm of young Bertrand and stealthily went away.

An hour afterwards, I asked myself where could she be. We all began to look for her. " Wherever has she got to ? We must find her ! " said everybody. We ranged the house. She was no more there than in my eye.

" It is some trick she is playing on us," said madame Chaudron, " that will make us laugh."

She called to her other two daughters, and hurried home ; but the youngest girl was not there. I went to bed. Next morning I awoke early, and leaving my father still snoring, for he had been overcome with wine at the ball, I went to the stable and took his mare and the road to Niort.

" They will know all the news there," I said to myself, " since the gazette is sold there."

On arriving, I saw in the market-place the theatre of Sieur Bertrand, and on the stage I recognised my betrothed. She was playing, I think, the part of Chiméne, for she wore a riding dress.

When the play was over, seeing Mademoiselle Chaudron leaving, arm in arm with young Bertrand, disguised as harlequin—

" Ha ! So I've found you at last," I said to her.

" Who is this insolent creature ? " she said. " I do not know you, my friend ! "

And with that, she made me a deep curtsey, and departed with the young actor.

THE LETTER

Comte de Caylus

Nor being a newsmonger, Madame, and liking only old reports about the wars and about politics, because they seem to me more truthful, I must turn to the events and stories of the town in order to keep my word with you. I will not answer for the impression that this tale will make on you, but I can assure you of its truth.

You know all the bonds that unite us, Alcidor and myself, so you will not think it strange that he should take me into his confidence. But judge of the astonishment he caused me by confessing to me that he was jealous! He is the last man I should have suspected of this weakness. His natural gaiety, his carelessness, and his knowledge of the world would have led me to think that he was stronger than I am in this respect. Yet he was jealous, but he took it like a gallant man.

"Spare me," he said, "all the commonplaces with which I used to cheer up any husband in my position. I have employed them on other men, and I know what they are worth. Just listen to me, and do not interrupt by trying to lighten my view of my wife's position."

So I promised to hear him in silence, and he continued :

"I will admit I am no longer in love with my wife. So it is not passion that blinds me. But I have still some sincere feelings for her, and I am hurt by her conduct. It is the kind of man she has chosen that upsets me. I imagined she had better taste. If I flattered myself I could hinder a woman of twenty-four years from following the movements of her heart, after I had ceased to love her, I should be a fool. Never shall I be capable of such an injustice. But counting on her discernment and her fine taste, I thought she would choose somebody like a gentleman, who would not compromise her—some one with a mind and character that I could welcome to my house. You see I was the most reasonable of husbands ! "

"I agree with you," I answered, " though it might be objected that supposing your wife has made a choice, it will be difficult for her to suit your taste in the matter as well as her own."

"That may be," said Alcidor. " Still it is not so much her choice of the Chevalier that angers me, as the affectation with which he speaks to her in my presence, and the desire he seems to have to wound me. The thing is got to such a point that many times I have need of all my self-control not to break out and make a scene. I am even pretty sure that my wife has noticed it. Yet it makes no change in her conduct. Her head is so turned that she goes out of her way to make things unpleasant for me."

My mouth was closed by the first words he had said to me. Still, I should have liked to tell him how surprised I was over the appearance of the Chevalier, whose vain and ridiculous character you well know. But to talk in this way was only to increase my friend's distress. He noticed how embarrassed I was, and saw the reason for it.

"Don't attempt to talk to me," he said. " I want no advice from you, though you would be better at it than any one else. I have only wished to relieve my feelings by showing you, my dear friend, the cruel situation in which I am placed. It is an insult the young brainless fop does to me : it is my honour he attacks— not the honour of the common mind—but that which even an enlightened man of some gallantry cannot relinquish."

He went on talking in the same manner all through our first conversation. That made it very embarrassing for me. After we had finished our walk, for he had led me to the Allées du Roule so as to make sure we should not be interrupted, you will guess, Madame, that my first idea was to have an interview with his wife. I wanted to tell her all I had learnt and warn her to be more careful, and to think a little on what she owes herself as well as her husband. But I could not find an opportunity. Alcidor never left the room, while I was with his wife, and it would have been worse than useless to speak to her in whispers in his presence. He would have begun to suspect me.

But I was a witness to the truth of all he had said concerning the conduct of the Chevalier. He was always at her side ; he spoke to her always in a low voice, and leered at her in a scandalous fashion. I do not know if Alcidor's admissions, and the fear I had of seeing him get beyond himself, led me to find all that happened before my eyes too much for any man to bear. But I know that I left the house, not only convinced of his patience and the justice of his complaint, but astonished at the indiscretions of the other pair. But I was more than ever resolved to speak to his wife at any cost. And I was about to call on her at noon the day before yesterday, thinking I should then be sure to find her alone, when my man brought Alcidor in to see me. His strange air—downcast, dismayed, and triumphant all at the same time—surprised me and disquietened me.

"What is the matter?" I said to him when my man had left the room. "I do not know what to think from your looks."

"I was right," he said in sorrowful satisfaction. "I can no longer doubt. The affair is settled and the Chevalier wins. I must admit," he continued, "that I did not think it had got beyond a flirtation. I thought a woman of character would have quickly been disgusted with a man of that sort. But he has won, and my wife will suffer for it. Affairs of this kind, conducted without any sort of brilliance, end in a clap of thunder. Read this," he said, giving me a letter, "and look at the address."

I saw that the name and address of the Chevalier were written without any attempt at secrecy.

"Heavens! what have you done?" I cried. "How did this letter get into your hands?"

I thought he had killed the Chevalier or murdered his wife.

"Don't be disturbed," he said, with great coolness. "Chance alone made me the possessor of it. I went out, about an hour ago, to see a man in the neighbourhood about some business. I did not use the carriage, but went on foot, dreaming and enjoying the fine weather, when a Savoyard asked me to look at the address on a letter he was carrying, and tell him where he would find it. Think what my feelings were when I recognised the handwriting of my wife! I told the Savoyard to follow me, and went into a café, where there were some writing materials."

"Well?" I said to him.

"God!" he said, "how I suffered in copying the letter—the most passionate a woman ever wrote! You can see how she is blinded by her mad feelings! She entrusted a letter of this importance to the first beggar that came her way! It was yesterday that the accursed Chevalier won her completely. Read it," he said, "read it, and see how I am attacked for entering my own house, and interrupting their courtship. But what I can't understand is that I did not perceive anything when they were talking together yesterday. They seemed to be continuing a dull sort of conversation that my arrival did not in the least interrupt. To finish my story," he continued, "I copied this terrible letter, kept the original, and gave the Savoyard some money to take the copy to the Chevalier. Now do you think my complaint is not well founded?"

It was then that I read the fatal letter, from which nothing that could wound the feelings of a husband was omitted. I did not want to give it back to him, and I was afraid to leave him in the condition in which he was. So I went with him to his wife. It was an awkward situation for me. Happily, we found her alone, and she greeted us with that frank and graceful air that you have remarked in her. But she did not keep it for long. For her husband overwhelmed her with the most offensive reproaches. The poor woman, trembling and amazed fell on the floor so stricken that she could not weep. I was sorry for her in spite of her faults, and went to her help.

"What, sir!" she said to me. "You stand by and see me treated in this way? Where am I? Were you not my friend?"

"I am willing that he should judge between us," exclaimed Alcidor.

I did all I could to arrive at some kind of compromise and put an end to the terrible scene. To some extent I succeeded. But an angry man will always continue to repeat himself, and Alcidor kept talking of the convincing evidence he had of the guilt of his wife. But she still protested her innocence with a firmness that astonished me; and, when the letter was mentioned, she still held to her position. So I began to think that, in spite of the difficulty, she had thought of some way of getting out of the matter: and then, as Alcidor pressed me more and more strongly, I was obliged to show the letter.

"This is not my writing," she said proudly, after she had looked at it. "How can Alcidor ever have thought so!"

Her husband was not struck by this reply. He regarded it as a confession of defeat on her part. And I will admit to you that I took the same view. Still I began to support her statement, having, it seemed to me, no other course. But I was quickly interrupted by her, and speaking to us both she said:

"I have always loved my husband. It was with much sorrow that I saw him grow cold to me. But with all his injustice he cannot say that I ever wearied him with any reproaches. I knew they were useless. The only fault I have committed is to have tried to win him back by the dangerous means of jealousy. I saw all the danger, but I thought I had avoided it by choosing a man who seemed to me incapable of wronging me in the minds of those who really knew me. The man himself, in fact, offered to carry out the plan I had formed. But when I saw yesterday what pain I was causing Alcidor, I told the servants I should not be at home if the Chevalier called again. I even gave this order in his presence, so that he should not pretend to be ignorant of my wishes. If your servants will deny that I gave this order, I will consent that you shall think me capable of having written this infamous letter. The handwriting, I admit, is like mine, but you," she said, looking with astonishing sternness at her husband, "should not have been deceived by so slight a resemblance. Do you mean still to tell me that this is my handwriting?"

"Oh, heavens!" said Alcidor, "I can see it now. You never wrote this!"

For some moments there was a silence, and as for myself I did not know where I was, when Alcidor, throwing himself at the feet of his wife, implored her to pardon him. And this she did, sweetly and nobly. I then wished to retire, but Alcidor begged me to stay for some time with his wife.

"This affair is not yet finished," she said to me with a smile. "Let him go on with it."

Alcidor went out in a quick, excited way, and as there was nothing to prevent me showing my curiosity, I begged his wife to satisfy it.

"To any one but you," she said, " I should not say anything of what I am about to tell you. Alcidor is still as much hurt in the depths of his soul as he was before he saw I had not written the letter."

"I do not understand it," I said.

"I will explain the mystery," she continued. "He is strongly attached to Céphise. You know how this woman always conducts herself? Very well! It is she who wrote the letter. Our hand-writings slightly resemble each other, and it was only my husband's jealousy that prevented him from at once seeing the difference. The likeness of the handwriting, the address to the Chevalier, all seemed to him to relate to me, while in fact it was all connected with Céphise."

"Now I understand," I said.

"But that is not all," she continued. "The Chevalier is madly in love with the woman. He pretended to attach himself to me, simply to draw Alcidor away from his loved one ; and you know why I pretended to listen to him. For the rest," she added, " you must stay with us. A man has need of a friend when he has just discovered the unfaithfulness of a woman. In one way, Alcidor is calmed down, but the discovery he has just made is perhaps just as upsetting in another way."

Our conversation was easily sustained. It was far from languishing for want of matter when Alcidor returned.

"I went to Céphise," he said, " to give her back her letter and break with her. Will you believe ? They would not let me in. Yet she was at home. I even saw the Chevalier's carriage. He, no doubt, received my copy of the letter, and, alarmed by the handwriting, he hastened to her to warn and advise her."

"I am delighted," I said, " with the way they are acting. They will see you no more, and you are happier than you deserve."

The trouble, however, is too recent to convince Alcidor of the justness of my remark. He still affects at times a nonchalance he is far from feeling. In the meantime, I neglect nothing to lead him from scorn to indifference for Céphise. She is a woman of no merit. His wife is excellent. She does not seek for any advantage over her husband, and she has no resentment for the unjust attack he made on her. She has wiped his wild words from her mind. I admire her and I console him. This, Madame, is my present occupation which I especially wanted to give you an account of, as it seemed to me connected with an adventure singular enough to entertain you for a moment.

VOLTAIRE
1694–1778

JEANNOT AND COLIN

MANY credible persons have seen Jeannot and Colin of the village of Issoire in Auvergne, a place famous all over the world for its college and its cauldron. Jeannot was the son of a very renowned mule-driver ; Colin owed his existence to an honest labourer in the neighbourhood, who cultivated the earth with the help of four mules, and who, after he had paid the poll-tax, the military-tax, the royal-tax, the excise-tax, the shilling-in-the-pound, the capitation, and the twentieths, did not find himself over-rich at the year's end.

Jeannot and Colin were very pretty lads for Auvergnians : they were remarkably attached to each other, and enjoyed together those little confidences, and those snug familiarities, which men always recollect with pleasure when they afterwards meet in the world.

The time dedicated to their studies was just upon the eve of elapsing, when a tailor brought Jeannot a velvet coat of three colours, with a Lyons waistcoat made in the first taste ; the whole was accompanied with a letter directed to Monsieur de la Jeannotiere. Colin could not help admiring the coat, though he was not at all envious of it ; but Jeannot immediately assumed an air of superiority which perfectly distressed his companion.

From this moment Jeannot studied no more ; he admired himself in the glass, and despised the whole world. Soon after a *valet-de-chambre* arrived post-haste, bringing a second letter, which was addressed to Monsieur the Marquis de la Jeannotiere ; it was an order from Monsieur the father, that Monsieur the son, should set out for Paris directly. Jeannot ascended the chaise and stretched out his hand to Colin with a smile of protection sufficiently dignified ; Colin felt his own insignificance and burst into tears : Jeannot departed in all his glory.

Those readers who like to be instructed as well as amused, must know that Monsieur Jeannot, the father, had very rapidly acquired a most immense fortune by business. Do you ask how it is one makes a great fortune ? It is because one is fortunate. Monsieur Jeannot was handsome, and so was his wife, who had still a certain

66

bloom about her. They came up to Paris on account of a law-suit, which ruined them; when fortune, who elevates and depresses mankind at will, presented them to the wife of a contractor for the army hospitals, a man of very great talent, who could boast of having killed more soldiers in one year than the cannon had blown up in ten.

Jeannot pleased the lady, and his wife pleased the contractor. Jeannot soon had his share in his patron's enterprise; and after-wards entered into other speculations. When once you are in the current of the stream, you have nothing to do but to leave your bark to itself; you will make an immense fortune without much difficulty. The mob on the bank, who see you scud along in full sail, open their eyes with astonishment; they are at a loss to conjecture how you came by your prosperity; they envy you at all events, and write pamphlets against you, which you never read. This is just what happened to Jeannot the father, who quickly became Monsieur de la Jeannotiere, and who, having purchased a marquisate at the end of six months, took Monsieur the Marquis his son from school, to introduce him into the fashionable world of Paris.

Colin, always affectionate, sent a letter of compliment to his old school-fellow, in which he wrote his "_these lines to congratulate_" him. The little Marquis returned no answer: Colin was perfectly ill with mortification.

The father and mother provided a tutor for the young Marquis. This tutor, who was a man of fashion, and who knew nothing, of course could teach nothing to his pupil. Monsieur wished his son to learn Latin; Madame wished him not: accordingly they called in as arbitrator an author, who was at that time celebrated for some very pleasing works. He was asked to dinner. The master of the house began by asking him:

"Monsieur, as you understand Latin, and are a courtier——"

"I, sir, understand Latin? not a word," replied the wit, "and very glad am I that I don't; for there is not a doubt but a man always speaks his own language the better when his studies are not divided between that and foreign languages: look at all our ladies, is not their vivacity more elegant than that of the men? Their letters, are they not written with a hundred times the anima-tion? Now all this superiority they possess from nothing else but their not understanding Latin."

"There now! was not I in the right?" said Madame: "I wish my son to be a wit: that he may make a figure in the world; and you see if he learns Latin he is inevitably lost. Are comedies or operas played in Latin? In a law-suit, does any one plead in Latin? Do we make love in Latin?"

Monsieur, dazzled by all this ratiocination, gave his judgment;

when it was finally determined that the young Marquis should not lose his time in becoming acquainted with Cicero, Horace, and Virgil. But then what was he to learn? for he must know something : could not he be shown a little geography?

"What would that serve?" replied the tutor : "when Monsieur the Marquis goes to any of his estates, won't the postillions know which way to drive him? They'll certainly take care not to go out of their way; one has no need of a quadrant to travel with; and a man may go from Paris to Auvergne very commodiously, without having the least idea of what latitude he is under."

"You are right," replied the father; "but I have somewhere heard of a very beautiful science, which is called astronomy, I think."

"The more's the pity then," cried the tutor; "does any one regulate himself by the stars in this world? and is it necessary that Monsieur the Marquis should murder himself by calculating an eclipse when he will find its very point of time in the almanack, a book which will teach him, moreover, the movable feasts and fasts, the age of the moon, and that of all the princesses in Europe." Madame was entirely of the tutor's opinion; the little Marquis was overjoyed; the father was very much undecided.

"What must my son learn then?" said he.

"To make himself agreeable : if," replied the friend whom they had consulted, "he knows but how to please, he knows everything; that is an art he can learn from his mother, without giving the least trouble either to that master or this.

At this speech Madame embraced the polite ignoramus, and said to him, "It is very plain, sir, that you are the most learned man in the whole world; my son will owe his entire education to you : however, I conceive that it will be as well if he should know a little of history."

"Alas! Madame, what is that good for?" replied he : "there is nothing either so pleasing or so instructive as the history of the day; all ancient history, as one of our wits observes, is nothing but a preconcerted fable; and as for modern, it is a chaos which no one can disintricate : what does it signify to Monsieur your son that Charlemagne instituted the twelve peers of France, and that his successor was a stutterer?"

"Nothing was ever better said," cried the tutor; "the spirits of children are overwhelmed with a mass of useless knowledge; but of all absurd sciences, that which, in my opinion, is the most likely to stifle the spark of genius is geometry. This ridiculous science has for its object surfaces, lines, and points, which have no existence in nature; ten thousand crooked lines are by the mere twist of imagination made to pass between a circle and a right line that touches it, although in reality it is impossible to draw a straw between them. In short, geometry is nothing but an execrable joke."

Monsieur and Madame did not understand too much of what the tutor said; but they were entirely of his opinion.

"A nobleman like Monsieur the Marquis," continued he, "ought not to dry up his brains with such useless studies; if at any time he has occasion for one of your sublime geometricians to draw the plan of his estates, can't money buy him a surveyor? or if he wishes to unravel the antiquity of his nobility, which rises to the most obscure times, can't he send for a Benedictine? And it is the same in every other art. A young lord, born under a lucky star, is neither painter, musician, architect, nor sculptor: but he makes all those arts flourish in proportion as his magnificence encourages them; and it is much better to patronise than to exercise them. Enough that Monsieur the Marquis has a taste; let artists work for him: it is in this we have so great reason to say that men of quality (I mean those who are very rich) know everything without having learned anything; because, in fact, they at least know how to judge of everything which they order and pay for."

The amiable ignoramus then took up the conversation.

"You have very justly remarked, Madame, that the great end of man is to rise in society: seriously, now, is it by science that success is to be obtained? Does any man in company even so much as think of talking about geometry? Is a man of fashion ever asked what star rose with the sun to-day? Who wishes to know, at supper, if the long-haired Clodia passed the Rhine?"

"Nobody, without doubt," exclaimed the Marchioness de la Jeannotiere, whose personal attractions had somewhat initiated her in the polite world; "and Monsieur my son ought not to cramp his genius by studying all this trash. But, after all, what shall he learn? for it is but right that a young lord should know how to shine upon occasion, as Monsieur my husband very justly observes. I remember hearing an old abbé say once, that the most delightful of all possible sciences was something, of which I have forgotten the name; but it begins with an h."

"With an h, Madame; it was not horticulture?"

"No, it was not horticulture he meant; it begins, I tell you, with an h and ends with a ry."

"Ah! I understand you, Madame, 'tis heraldry: heraldry is indeed a very profound science, but it has been out of fashion ever since the custom of painting arms on carriage doors was dropped. It was once the most useful thing in the world in a well-regulated state: but the study would have become endless; for nowadays there is not a hairdresser but has his coat of arms; and you know that whatever becomes common ceases to be esteemed."

At length after having examined the merits and demerits of every science, it was decided that Monsieur the Marquis should learn to dance.

Nature, which does everything, had bestowed on him a gift that quickly developed itself with a prodigious success ; it was an agreeable knack at singing ballads. The graces of youth joined to this superior talent made him looked upon as a young man of the greatest promise. He was beloved by the women ; and having his head always stuffed with songs, he manufactured them for his mistresses. He plundered *Bacchus* and *Cupid* to make one sonnet, the *Night* and the *Day* for another, the *Charms* and *Alarms* for a third ; but as he always found in his verses some feet too little or some too much, he was obliged to have them corrected at twenty shillings a song ; and thus he got a place in the *Literary Year*, by the side of the La Fares, the Chaulieus, the Hamiltons, the Sarrasins, and the Voitures of the day.

Madame the Marchioness now thought she should gain the reputation of being the mother of a wit ; and gave a supper to all the wits in Paris accordingly. The young man's brain was presently turned ; he acquired the art of speaking without understanding a single word he said, and perfected himself in the art of being good for nothing.

When his father saw him so eloquent, he began to regret, very sensibly, that he had not had his son taught Latin ; for in that case he could have bought him such a valuable place in the law. The mother, whose sentiments were less grovelling, wished to solicit a regiment for her son ; and in the meantime the son fell in love. Love is sometimes more expensive than a regiment : it cost him a great deal ; while his parents pinched themselves still more, in order to live among great lords.

A young widow of quality in their neighbourhood, who had but a very moderate fortune, had a great mind to resolve upon putting the vast riches of Monsieur and Madame de la Jeannotiere in a place of security, which she could easily do by appropriating them to her own use and marrying the young Marquis. She attracted him, suffered him to love her, gave him to understand that she was not indifferent to him, drew him in by degrees, enchanted, and vanquished him without much difficulty : sometimes she gave him praise, and sometimes advice, and quickly became the favourite both of his father and his mother. An old neighbour proposed their marriage ; the parents, dazzled with the splendour of the alliance, joyfully accepted the offer, and gave their only son to their intimate friend.

The young Marquis was thus about to marry a woman he adored, and by whom he himself was beloved ; the friends of his family congratulated him, and the marriage articles were just about to be settled, whilst all hands were working at their wedding clothes and songs.

He was one morning upon his knees before the charming wife with whom love, esteem, and friendship were about to present him; they were tasting in a tender and animated conversation the first fruits of their felicity, and were parcelling out a most delicious life, when a *valet-de-chambre* belonging to Madame the mother came up quite scared:

"Here is very different news," said he: "the bailiffs are ransacking the house of Monsieur and Madame; everything is laid hold of by the creditors; nay, they talk of seizing your persons; and so I made haste to come and be paid my wages."

"Let us see a little," said the Marquis, "what all this means what can this adventure be?"

"Go," said the widow, "and punish these rascals—go quickly."

He ran to the house; his father was already imprisoned; all the domestics had fled, each about his own business, but having first carried away everything they could lay hold on; his mother was alone, without protection, without consolation, drowned in tears; nothing remained but the recollection of her fortune, the recollection of her beauty, the recollection of her errors, and the recollection of her mad profuseness.

After the son had wept a long time with the mother, he ventured to say to her:

"Let us not despair; this young widow loves me to distraction, and is still more generous than rich, I can answer for her; I'll fly to her, and bring her to you."

He then returned to his mistress, and found her in a private interview with a very charming young officer.

"What! is it you, Monsieur de la Jeannotiere? what do you do here? is it thus you have abandoned your mother? Go to that unfortunate woman, and tell her that I wish her every happiness: I am in want of a chambermaid, and I will most undoubtedly give her the preference."

"My lad," said the officer, "you seem well-shaped enough, if you are inclined to enlist in my company, I'll give you every encouragement."

The Marquis, thunderstruck and bursting with rage, went in quest of his old tutor, lodged his troubles in his breast, and asked his advice. The tutor proposed to him to become a preceptor like himself.

"Alas!" said the Marquis, "I know nothing; you have taught me nothing, and are indeed the principal cause of all my misfortunes."

As he spoke this, he sobbed aloud.

"Write romances," said a wit who was present; "it is an excellent resource at Paris."

The young man, more desperate than ever, ran towards his

mother's confessor, who was a Theatin in great repute, troubling himself with the consciences of women of the first rank only. As soon as Jeannot saw him, he prostrated himself before him.

"Good God! Monsieur Marquis," said he, "where is your carriage? how does that respectable lady, the Marchioness your mother?"

The poor unfortunate youth related the disasters of his family and the farther he proceeded, the graver, the cooler, and the more hypocritical was the air of the Theatin.

"My son," said he, "it has pleased God to reduce you to this; riches serve but to corrupt the heart; God has therefore conferred a favour on your mother in bringing her to this miserable state.

"Yes, sir."

"Her election is thus rendered the more sure."

"But, father," resumed the Marquis, "in the meantime, is there no means of obtaining relief in this world?"

"Adieu! my son; there is a court-lady waiting for me."

The Marquis was ready to faint: he was treated in pretty much the same way by all his friends, and gained more knowledge of the world in half a day than he did all the rest of his life.

As he was thus plunged into the blackest despair, he saw advancing an old-fashioned sort of calash or tilt-cart, with leather curtains, which was followed by four enormous waggons well loaded. In the chaise was a young man coarsely clothed; he had a countenance round and fresh, breathing all the complacency of cheerfulness: his wife, a little brunette, fat, but not disagreeably so, was jolted in beside him; the vehicle did not move like the carriage of a *petit-maître*, but afforded the traveller sufficient time to contemplate the Marquis, motionless and abyssed in grief as he stood.

"Eh! good God!" cried the rider, "I do think that is Jeannot."

At his name the Marquis lifted up his eyes; the chaise stopped.

"It is too true, it is Jeannot," sighed the Marquis.

The fat little fellow made but one jump of it, and flew to embrace his old school-fellow. Jeannot recognised Colin; and shame and tears covered his face.

"You have abandoned me," said Colin; "but though you are a great lord, I will love you for ever."

Jeannot, confused and heart-broken, related to him with many sobs a part of his story.

"Come to the inn where I lodge and tell me the rest there," said Colin; "embrace my little wife, and then let's go and dine together."

They all three set forward on foot, their baggage following behind.

"What is the meaning of all this equipage? is it yours?" says Jeannot.

"Yes, it is all mine and my wife's. We are just arrived from the country, where I have the management of a good manufactory of tin and copper ; I have married the daughter of a rich dealer in utensils which are necessary both to great and small : we work hard ; God has prospered us : we have never changed our condition ; we are happy ; and we will assist our friend Jeannot. Be a Marquis no longer ; all the greatness in the world is not to be compared to a friend. You shall go back into the country with me, I will teach you our trade ; it is not very difficult ; I will make you my partner, and we will live merrily in the very corner of the earth where we were born."

The astonished Jeannot felt himself divided between grief and joy, between affection and shame ; and said to himself :

"All my fashionable friends have betrayed me, and Colin, whom I despised, alone comes to my relief."

What an instruction. The goodness of Colin's soul elicited from the breast of Jeannot a spark of nature which all the world had not yet stifled ; he felt himself unable to abandon his father and mother.

"We'll take care of your mother," said Colin ; "and as to your father, who is in prison, I understand those matters a little ; his creditors, when they see he has nothing to pay, will make up matters for a very trifle ; I'll undertake to manage the whole business."

Colin quickly released the father from prison : Jeannot returned to the country with his parents, who resumed their former profession ; he married a sister of Colin's, who, being of the same disposition as her brother, made him very happy ; and Jeannot the father, Jeannot the mother, and Jeannot the son, now saw that happiness was not to be found in vanity.

BABABEC AND THE FAKIRS

VOLTAIRE

WHEN I was in the city of Benares on the banks of the Ganges, the ancient home of the Brahmins, I endeavoured to gain some information. I understood Hindustani tolerably well ; I heard much, and noticed everything. I lodged with my correspondent Omri, the worthiest man I have ever known. He was of the religion of the Brahmins, and I have the honour to be a Mussulman ; yet we have never had high words on the subject of Mohammed and Brahma. We made our ablutions each on his own side, we drank

27*

of the same sherbet, and we ate of the same dish of rice, like a pair
of brothers.

One day we went together to the pagoda of Vishnu. We saw
there several groups of fakirs, some of whom were Janghis, that is
to say, fakirs devoted to contemplation, while the others were
disciples of the ancient gymnosophists, who led an active life.
They have, as every one knows, a learned language, which is that
of the most ancient Brahmins, and, written in this language, a
book which is called the Vedas. It is undoubtedly the most
ancient book in the whole of Asia, not excepting even the Zenda-
vesta.

I passed in front of a fakir who was reading this book.

" Ah ! wretched infidel ! " cried he, " you have made me lose
the number of vowels which I was counting ; and in consequence
of that my soul will have to pass into the body of a hare, instead
of going into that of a parrot, as I had good grounds for flattering
myself would be the case."

I gave him a rupee to console him. A few steps farther on, having
been so unfortunate as to sneeze, the noise that I made roused a
fakir who was in a trance.

" Where am I ? " said he ; " what a horrible fall I have had !
I can no longer see the tip of my nose ; the celestial light has
vanished." [1]

" If I am the cause," said I, " that you see at last beyond the
tip of your nose, here is a rupee to repair the damage that I have
committed ; so recover your celestial light."

Having thus got myself discreetly out of the scrape, I passed
on to the gymnosophists ; some of them there were who brought me
very nice little nails, to thrust into my arms and thighs in honour of
Brahma. I bought their nails, and used them to fasten down my
carpets. Others were dancing on their hands ; others were tumbling
on the slack rope ; others again kept hopping continually on one leg.
There were some loaded with chains, some who carried a pack-
saddle, and some who had their heads under a bushel ; yet they
were all eminent for their virtues. My friend Omri brought me
into the cell of one of the most famous of these philosophers, whose
name was Bababec. He was as naked as an ape, and had a big
chain round his neck, which must have weighed more than sixty
pounds. He was seated on a wooden chair, neatly furnished with
sharp little nails, which ran into him, and yet one would have
supposed that he was sitting on a velvet cushion. Many women
came to consult him as an oracle on family affairs, and it may be

---

[1] Voltaire has a note here : " When the fakirs wish to behold the celestial
light, an aspiration which is very general among them, they turn their eyes
towards the tip of the nose." Mr. Braid adopted a very similar process for
inducing hypnotism.

truly said that he enjoyed the very highest reputation. I heard the important conversation that Omri had with him.

"Do you think, father," said the former, "that after my soul has undergone the probation of seven transmigrations, I may be able to reach the abode of Brahma?"

"That depends," said the fakir; "what is your manner of life?"

"I endeavour," said Omri, "to be a good citizen, a good husband, a good father, and a good friend; I lend money without interest to the rich when they have occasion for it, I give it away to the poor, and I maintain peace among my neighbours."

"Do you ever sit on nails?" asked the Brahmin.

"Never, reverend father."

"I am sorry for it," replied the fakir; "you certainly will not enter the nineteenth heaven; and that is a pity."

"Very good," said Omri; "I am quite contented with my lot. What does it matter to me about the nineteenth or twentieth heaven, provided I do my duty during my pilgrimage, and am well received at the last stage? Is it not enough to be an honest man in this world, and then to be happy in the land of Brahma? Into which heaven do you expect to go, Mr. Bababec, with your nails and your chains?"

"Into the thirty-fifth," said Bababec.

"You are a droll fellow," replied Omri, "to expect a higher lodging than I; that expectation can only proceed from an inordinate ambition. You condemn those who seek for honours in this life, why do you aim at such great ones yourself in the next? Besides, on what do you found your expectation of having better treatment than I? Let me tell you that I give away in alms more in ten days than all the nails upon which you sit cost you in the course of ten years. What does it matter to Brahma that you pass your days stark naked, with a chain round your neck? That is a fine way of serving your country! I reckon that man is worth a hundred times more who sows pot-herbs, or plants trees, than the whole tribe of you and your fellows who look at the tips of their noses, or carry a pack-saddle to show the extreme nobility of their souls."

Having spoken thus, Omri soothed, coaxed, persuaded, and at last induced Bababec to leave his nails and his chain there and then, to come with him to his house, and to lead a respectable life. They scoured him well, they rubbed him all over with perfumed essences, they clothed him decently, and he lived for a fortnight in a thoroughly rational manner, confessing that he was a hundred times happier than before.

But he lost credit with the people, and the women came no more to consult him; so he left Omri and betook himself once more to his nails in order to recover his reputation.

L'ABBÉ BOURDELOT
17TH CENTURY

MONSIEUR OUFLE

A CHEERFUL man was M. Oufle, who loved a jovial evening with his friends, a glass of good wine, and a merry tale. A worthy man, too, was he, the most exemplary of husbands and the most indulgent of fathers,—but he had his weakness—which of us has not ?— and his weakness was weakness of intellect ; in short, he was a very good, a very respectable, a very kind-hearted man, but also a very silly one.

He regarded himself as a bit of a philosopher, and despised super- stition, yet for all that he was fidgeted if the salt-cellar were upset, alarmed if the knife and fork were crossed, and he would positively decline to make the thirteenth at dinner.

It was Carnival time, and M. Oufle invited all his own relations and his wife's relations to dinner. A pleasant evening they passed ; they ate and they drank, and they talked and they sang,—they ate till they were more than satisfied, drank till they were very merry, talked themselves dry, and sang themselves hoarse. Far be it from me to assert that any of the party had drunk more than he ought, but they had all grazed the line of moderation, and M. Oufle, being naturally light-headed, had become exceedingly " jolly."

When the relations withdrew, the children went to bed, Madame Oufle took her candle and departed with her lady's maid, and M. Oufle, for the sake of a little exercise, festooned up and down his chamber, whistling a plaintive melody, and whistling it out of tune.

This gentleman's eldest son, who had inherited all his father's amiable qualities, and his empty-headedness into the bargain, had slipped off from the paternal house by the back door, as soon as the guests began to leave, in a masquerading dress, and had betaken himself, after the manner of scapegraces, to a ball.

M. Oufle, having wearied of describing curves in his own room, opened the door and went upstairs, a process attended with diffi- culties which would have proved insuperable but for the assistance of the banisters. Arrived on the landing, M. Oufle observed his son's door open, so he walked into the room, impelled either by curiosity or by a desire for a little more conversation.

The son was, however, at that time dancing in the ball-room of a hotel two streets off.

M. Oufle, not finding the young man, sat himself down beside the bed, and began to overhaul the various masquerading dresses which his son had left out upon his chair. There was a neat suit of green and gold, intended as a forester's dress ; there was a costume of the time of François I., covered with spangles ; and last, but not least, there was a bearskin suit, so contrived that the wearer of it was covered with fur from head to foot, and looked precisely like a black bear escaped from a travelling caravan. M. Oufle turned this dress over and over, and its originality attracted his interest. He thought he should like to see whether it would fit his person ; he therefore arrayed himself in the habit, and found that it suited him to a T. Just then the idea entered his head that the opportunity of disabusing Madame Oufle of her superstitions had now presented itself. Madame Oufle was nearly as great a fool as her husband, and that is saying a good deal. She was infected with the vulgar belief in witchcraft and demonology, and believed implicitly that warlocks could transform themselves into wild beasts for the purpose of devouring children.

" Now," mused M. Oufle, " is a chance for me to eradicate these baneful superstitions from her mind. If she sees me in this dress, and takes me to be a werewolf, and when I show her the deception, she will never believe in the supernatural again."

Accordingly he walked to his wife's door and listened. The servant was still with her mistress, so M. Oufle retreated downstairs to the dining-room, intending to wait till his good lady was alone ; and that he might know when the maid was dismissed, he placed the door ajar.

Then, taking up a book, he seated himself before the fire. The book happened to be Bodin's *Dæmonomania*, and M. Oufle opened it at the chapter on Lycanthropy.

He read on, and the tales of werewolves floated in strange colours through his brain, till he fell asleep with his head on the table, and the book on his lap. And as he slumbered he dreamed of sorcerers being provided by the Evil One with wolf-skins which they were condemned to wear for seven years, and of Lycaon sentenced by Jove to run about in bestial form, till a piercing shriek and a crash brought him with a start to his feet.

The lady's maid, after having pinned her mistress's back hair into a heap, and fitted over it the nightcap, had left the chamber, and had come downstairs. As she passed the dining-room, she saw that there was still a light in it, and thinking that the candles had not been extinguished, she entered precipitately to put them out.

There in the dead of night she stood—and saw before her a monstrous black bear fast asleep before the fire, snoring loudly, with its head on the table and its snout up in the air, its hind paws upon the fender, a silk pocket-handkerchief over one knee, and a book on the lap. No wonder that she dropped her candle and screamed.

But the shriek which testified to her fear frightened M. Oufle out of the few senses he did possess. He sprang up, bewildered with his dreams, confused with the fumes of wine, and alarmed at the suddenness of his *reveil*. Opposite him was a pier-glass. He forgot entirely all the circumstances connected with the assumption of the bearskin, and with the last impressions produced by Bodin, and by his dream, stamped upon his brain, he jumped to the conclusion that he was bewitched, and that he had been changed into a werewolf. Full of this idea, he dashed past the terror-stricken maid ; and his wife, who had rushed to the landing, saw a frightful monster bounding down the stairs, uttering howls sufficiently loud to awake the dead, heard it unlock the front door and burst into the street. Thereupon, she fainted away.

M. Oufle, impelled by terror, ran along the street yelling for assistance ; he was naturally provided with a deep and sonorous bass voice, but his voice sounded hollow and fearful through his hideous vizor.

A few terrified people appeared in their nightcaps at the windows, only to run back and bury themselves trembling beneath the clothes.

A watchman who had started on his rounds came upon him suddenly as he turned a corner, and dropping his lanthorn beat a precipitate retreat.

In an adjoining street lived a fair damsel of considerable personal, but superior pecuniary, attractions, who was loved to distraction by a grocer's apprentice. The young man had made the lady's acquaintance as he served the shop, and had breathed his love over the cheeses he sold. His addresses had been countenanced by the beloved one, but were discouraged by the parents, who had not permitted the devoted youth to set foot within their doors. The apprentice had no other means open to him of testifying his devotion than by hiring a band of street musicians to perform at the rate of two francs an hour, during the silent watches of the night, below the window of the adored.

On the present occasion the band was performing the " Descent of Mars," when a discordant howl in their ears produced a sudden pause in their music not noted in their score, and the apparition of a monstrous bear running into the midst of them upon its hind legs, with ears and stumpy tail cocked up, produced such a panic among the sons of Orpheus, that they cast their instruments from them, and took to their heels. Not so the grocer's apprentice.

True love knows not fear. He flew to the door of his beloved and cast himself before it, determined to perish in her defence.

But the monster, without perceiving him, ran on repeating its dolorous howls.

The grocer's apprentice rose from the doorstep, dusted his coat, collected the scattered instruments, cast an amorous glance at the window of the adored, and retired home.

A party of students from the University were that evening going their rounds, performing feats of heroism, of which they might boast among their companions. These feats were not attended with much danger, and yet the achievement of them was an object of considerable ambition. They consisted simply in breaking lamps, and wrenching the knockers off doors.

Some people might think that the smashing of a street lamp was an operation within the scope of the most infantile abilities, and that the wrenching of a knocker from a door was neither a hazardous nor a very heroic act. But these people are entirely mistaken. The police occasionally interfere and capture one of those engaged in these acts, and, if captured it costs the student several francs to bribe the officer to let him escape.

Consequently, the ringing of a street bell at midnight is regarded by University men as an achievement equal to the bravest deed of a tried general, and the breaking off of a knocker is supposed to rank very much on a level with the proudest trophy of a blood-stained field.

On the night in question four valiant collegians were engaged on the hazardous undertaking of screwing up the door of a worthy citizen, an act of consummate ingenuity and sublime originality. Suddenly a wild and unearthly yell ringing through the hushed night broke upon their ears. Instantly the four students paused and turned pale. In another moment they saw a diabolical object moving rapidly down the street towards them. The young men shrank against the wall, each endeavouring to get behind the other, and reversing the proverb of the weakest going to the wall, for in their struggle the ablest-bodied secured that position, whilst the feeblest was the most exposed, and served as a screen to the others.

The approaching monster stood still for an instant, and they were able to observe him by the wan light of the crescent new moon, and the flickering oil lamp slung across the head of the street. A fearful object ! In their terror the screw-drivers dropped from their fingers. The noise attracted the creature's attention, and it ran up the steps towards them, articulating words in a hoarse tone, which they, in their alarm, were unable to catch. Suffice it to say that the sight of this monster coming within arm's length was too much for their courage ; with a shriek they burst past it, tumbling over each other, and rolling down the doorsteps, picked themselves up again and fled, palpitating, in four separate directions, calling for the police, imploring the aid of that august body which they had so long set at defiance.

What tales they related on the following morning to all the old ladies of their acquaintance it is not for me to record. One of the students broke his sword, and vowed that he had snapped it in his fight with the Daemon, another exhibited the bruises he had received in his fall as evidence of the desperate character of the conflict, a third wore his arm in a sling as though it had been broken in the encounter, and all agreed that the monster had fled from them, and not they from the monster.

The police! "Oh, horrors!" thought M. Oufle, "they have summoned the aid of the police. I shall be captured, be tried and sentenced, and burned at the stake as a werewolf."

The fear of this urged him to retreat stealthily homewards, keeping as much as possible in the shadows, lest any of the agents of justice should get sight of him, and carry him away to trial. If he could but reach home, he would implore his wife to stab him with a knife between the eyes, and draw some drops of blood, a sovereign cure for lycanthropy.

But poor M. Oufle's head was never very clear, and now it was in a thorough condition of bewilderment, so that he completely lost himself, and slunk about the streets in a disconsolate manner, vainly searching for his own domicile. His bewilderment became greater with every step he took; his confusion and alarm were not a little heightened by his stumbling over an elderly gentleman and leaving him apparently dead of fright on the pavement.

It did not mend matters when, hearing a *fiacre* drive by, he suddenly stepped towards it and asked the way of the driver,— for the coachman jumped off his seat in a paroxysm of terror, and the horses, equally frightened, ran away with the carriage, whilst the people inside screamed through the windows.

At last M. Oufle sat down on a doorstep and gave himself up to despair. The stake was before him, and his imagination conjured up all the horrors of his position, chained about the waist and dancing in the midst of the flames.

All at once, a familiar voice smote upon his ear—the voice of his eldest son. A ray of hope penetrated his breast. He rose from his seat and walked to meet his first born. That young gentleman was returning from the masquerade ball at which he had been figuring. He had imbibed a considerable amount of wine before he left home, and he had absorbed a little more during the pauses in the dance. He was accordingly scarcely sober, and as he returned home, he sang or talked to himself at the top of his voice. But now he saw something which sobered him instantaneously. This was nothing else than his own masquerading habit of bear's skin, which he had left hanging over the back of his chair, walking deliberately towards him, as though the spirit of the departed Bruin had retenanted his forsaken skin and was coming in the dead of night to demand a reckoning with him who had dared to use it as a Carnival habit.

He stood and looked at it with pale face and staring eyes, whilst a shudder ran through his frame.

If it had been within the limits of physical possibility, he would have sunk into his shoes. When he heard his own name articulated in hollow tones from the muzzle, he turned heel, and fled like the wind. In vain did M. Oufle call after him ; the louder he called, the faster fled the youth, and the distracted father was obliged to pursue his son.

The race was run with the utmost speed by both parties. The young man was urged on by terror lest the skin should overtake him, and M. Oufle dreaded losing sight of his son, lest he should at the same time lose all chance of regaining his home.

When M. Oufle le Jeune turned his white face over his shoulders, he saw the creature gaining upon him, and heard its hollow calls. He dodged from street to street, but he invariably saw the bear-skin double the corner and rush after him, turn where he would. It was in vain for him to hope to throw it out, and at last he ran straight for his home. This he had left by the garden. It was his custom to leave the house by the back door, and clamber over the garden rails, whenever he went out on his night expeditions, and now he made for the garden, hoping to climb the rails and escape through the door and lock it before the skin could overtake him.

He reached the railings. It was a difficult and delicate matter to surmount them with time at his disposal, but now that it was to be accomplished in no time at all, it was hazardous in the extreme. M. Oufle, junior, had reached the top, and was preparing to jump down, when a furry paw grasped his ankle and held him as though in a vice, for the monster proceeded to climb the railings, holding on to his leg. The poor youth vainly endeavoured to break away, he writhed and strained to be free ; holding the iron bars with his hands, he vociferated loudly for help. The creature reached the top and clasped him round the waist, whilst the hideous snout was poked close to his ear over his shoulder. Both leaped together, and were brought up with a jerk.

The rails were topped with sharp dart-heads, and one of these caught in the hide, so that M. Oufle and his son were suspended from it in mid air, the latter in the arms of his father. Both cried together for assistance ; the young man louder than ever when he heard the sonorous howls of his captor in his ear.

Lights appeared in the lower apartments at the back of the house, and presently the garden door was opened by a troop of terrified male and female servants, provided with blunderbusses, swords, and pistols. In the rear appeared Madame Oufle, half-dressed, but with her nightcap on her head.

The young man called to his mother, and the moment she saw the hope of the family dangling in the grasp of the monster, she fainted away again. There was an old man, a servant of the house, who claimed and exercised supreme authority in the household. He walked forward with a pistol in each hand ; and the youth cried to him to shoot the creature which clasped him through the head. In vain did M. Oufle shout to him to desist, his words were lost in the mask, and he would undoubtedly have received a couple of bullets through his head, had not the buttons of the dress just then given way with a burst, and slipped M. Oufle in a heap upon the ground, leaving the habit torn and dangling on the spike of the rails.

" Thank goodness ! " exclaimed M. Oufle, sitting up ; " the spell is off me."

" My father ! " cried the flower of the family.

" My husband ! " ejaculated the lady, recovering from her fainting fit.

" My master ! " exclaimed the grey-haired servant.

" Let us embrace all round," said M. Oufle.

L'ABBÉ BLANCHET
1707–1784

THE DEAN OF BADAJOZ

THE Dean of the cathedral of Badajoz was the most learned man in Spain. He knew more than all the doctors of Salamanca, and those of Coimbra and Alcala. He understood every dead and living tongue, and he was master of all sciences, human and divine. But unhappily he did not know magic, and he was inconsolable over it. He was told that there was a very skilful magician in Toledo, who was named Don Torribio. At once he saddled a good mule, and set out for Toledo, and alighted at the door of a pretty miserable house in which the great man was lodged.

"Sir," he said to the sorcerer, " I am the Dean of Badajoz. The learned men of Spain do me the honour of calling me their master ; but I come to beg from you a title more glorious—that of being your pupil. Deign to initiate me into the mysteries of your art, and count on a gratitude worthy of the benefit and of its author."

Don Torribio was not very polite, though he plumed himself on the fact of living with the best company of the under-world. He told the Dean that he must look elsewhere for a master of magic. He said he was tired of a profession in which he had gained only compliments and promises, and that he would no more dishonour himself by prostituting the occult sciences to ungrateful wretches.

"Ah, the ingratitude of men ! " cried the Dean. "What, Don Torribio, you have found some men without a sense of gratitude, and you would be so unjust as to confuse me with such monsters ! "

Then he poured out all that he had read about gratitude. With the sweetest of tones and the most honest air, he retailed all the virtuous sentiments that his memory could provide. He spoke so well that, after a moment's thought, the sorcerer avowed he could not refuse anything to a gallant man who knew by heart so many fine passages.

"Jacintha," he said to his servant, " put two partridges on the spit. I hope the Dean will do me the honour of staying to supper."

At the same time he took him by the hand and led him into

his study. There he touched his forehead, murmuring these three mysterious words, which I beg the reader not to forget :

" Ortobolan ! Pistafrier ! Onagriouf ! "

Then after other preparations, he began to explain to him with great clearness the prolegomena to the book on magic. The new pupil listened with such attention that he scarcely breathed. Then Jacintha entered, followed by a little man, booted up to the waist, who asked to speak to the Dean on a pressing matter. It was the postillion of his uncle, the Bishop of Badajoz, who had come to tell him that, a few hours after his departure, His Lordship had so violent an attack of apoplexy that his life was despaired of. The Dean swore with a good heart—softly, however, and without scandal —at the sickness, the sick man, and the courier who was taking up his time. He got rid of the postillion, telling him to return at once to Badajoz and that he would immediately follow. After that, he resumed his lesson as though there were not in the world either uncles or apoplexies.

Some days after, more news came from Badajoz ; but it was hardly worth while listening to. His uncle, the most reverend bishop, had gone to heaven to receive the reward of his virtues, and the chapter had elected the Dean to fill the vacant see. Don Torribio was present when the deputation arrived, and, as an able man, he profited by the occasion. Taking the new Bishop aside, he said he had a son, Don Benjamin, born with intelligence and good inclinations.

" But, my Lord," he said to his pupil, " my boy has no taste for occult science, and finding he would make a good priest, I let him study at the seminary. He is now one of the best of the clergy in Toledo, and I humbly entreat Your Lordship to resign the deanery of Badajoz to Benjamin, seeing you cannot keep it with the bishopric."

" Alas ! " said the prelate with an embarrassed air, " I shall always do all I can to favour you. But I must tell you I have expectations from a relative, an aged priest, who is only good enough to be a dean. If I do not give him this post, I shall upset all my family, for whom my love amounts to a weakness. But," he added in a more affectionate tone, " will you not come with me to Badajoz ? Will you have the cruelty to abandon me just at the moment when I am beginning to be able to help you ? Trust in me, my dear master, and let us go together, and think only of teaching your pupil. Rest easy about Don Benjamin. As soon as I can, I will do more for him than ever his father asks. A poor deanery in the depths of Estramadura is not a benefice that suits the son of a man like you."

So Don Torribio followed his illustrious pupil to Badajoz. He had splendid rooms in the episcopal palace, and he was respected by the whole diocese as the favourite of the Bishop as a sort of grand vicar.

Under the conduct of so skilful a master, the Bishop of Badajoz made rapid progress in the secret sciences. At first he gave himself up to them with an ardour that seemed excessive; but little by little he moderated this kind of intemperance and managed it so well that his studies in magic never interfered with his duties as a bishop. He held strongly to a maxim—which is very important for ecclesiastic sorcerers and for philosophers and men of letters—that it is not sufficient for them to frequent witches' dances, and arm their minds with all the most curious things in human knowledge; they must teach others the path of virtue, and make wholesome doctrines and sound morals flower in the souls of the faithful. It was by conducting his life on this wise principle that the learned bishop filled the whole of Christendom with the fame of his merits. And when he was thinking least about it, he was called to the archbishopric of Compostello.

The people and clergy of Badajoz grieved over an event that robbed them of so worthy a pastor; and as a last mark of respect the canons of the cathedral asked him to appoint his successor. Don Torribio was not asleep on such a fine occasion for placing his son. He asked for the bishopric from the new Archbishop, and it was with all the graces imaginable that his pupil refused him. He had such veneration for his dear master! He was so afflicted, so ashamed at having to refuse a thing that seemed quite simple! But what else could he do? Don Fernando de Lara, high constable of Castile, demanded this same see for his natural son. He had secret, important, and above all, long-standing obligations to the constable. So it was his duty to prefer an old benefactor to a recent one.

Don Torribio rather liked this equitable way of dealing with the matter. He saw by it that he would have to wait till his turn came, but that it would come surely on the first occasion. The magician was honest enough to believe in the tale about a long-standing obligation, and he rejoiced at being sacrificed to Don Fernando. There was nothing more to think about, except about preparing to depart, and they removed to Compostello. But it was scarcely worth the trouble, seeing how short a time they stayed there. For at the end of a few months, a messenger from the Pope came from Rome with a Cardinal's hat for the Archbishop, and with a letter in which His Holiness invited him to come and help him with his advice in the government of the Christian world. He was further permitted to bestow his mitre on any one he chose.

Don Torribio was not at Compostello when the courier from Rome arrived. He had gone to see his son, who was still the priest of a little parish in Toledo. But he returned quickly, and on his return he was not put to the trouble of asking for the vacant archbishopric.

The Cardinal ran to him with open arms.

" My dear master," he said, " I have two pieces of good news to
tell you instead of one. Your pupil is a Cardinal, and your son is soon
going to be one, or my position in Rome will be worth nothing. In
the meantime, I should like to make him archbishop of Compostello,
but wonder at his misfortune, or rather at mine! My mother,
whom we have left at Badajoz, has written me a cruel letter that
has upset all my plans. She wishes, at all cost, that I should take
for my successor the archdeacon of my old church, Don Pablas de
Salazar, her confessor and intimate friend. She threatens me she
will die with grief if I do not obey her, and I cannot doubt for an
instant that she will fail of her word. Put yourself in my place,
my dear master! Shall I kill my own mother ? "

Don Torribio was not a man to advise parricide. He applauded
the nomination of Don Pablas, and did not keep a grudge against
the mother of the Cardinal. This mother, if you want to know it,
was an old dame, almost imbecile, who lived with her cat and her
maid, and scarcely knew the name of her confessor. Was it really
she who insisted that the archbishopric should be given to Don
Pablas ? Was it not rather a Galician lady, a relative of this archdeacon, a young widow, very pious and very pretty, to whom the
prince of the church used to go very assiduously in search of edifica-
tion since he came to Compostello ?

However this may be, Don Torribio followed His Eminence to
Rome. And hardly had he arrived than the Pope died. It is easy
to foresee where this event will lead us. The conclave was held,
and all the voices of the Holy College were in favour of the Spanish
Cardinal. So behold him the Pope ! After the ceremonies of exaltation, Don Torribio was admitted to a private audience, and he wept
with joy at the feet of his dear pupil.   He humbly recalled his long
and faithful services, and reminded his disciple of his promises—
inviolable promises—that had been renewed just before the conclave.
He touched on the scarlet hat that His Holiness had cast off on
receiving the tiara, but instead of asking this hat for Don Benjamin
he ended on a note of such moderation that few person will understand it. He protested that he and his son had lost all ambitious
hopes, and that they would be well content if it pleased His
Holiness to grant them, with his benediction, a little pension
that would suffice for the modest needs of an ecclesiastic and a
philosopher.

During this little speech, the sovereign pontiff was asking himself
what he could do for his teacher. Could he not at length do without
him ? Did he not know as much magic as was needed by a Pope ?
Would it even be seemly for him to appear any more at the witches'
meetings, with their unbecoming etiquette ? All things considered,
he judged that Don Torribio was nothing but a useless and even

inconvenient man. This point decided, he was no longer troubled to find an answer.

" We have heard with grief," he said, " that under the pretext of occult sciences, you carry on an abominable commerce with the spirits of darkness and falsehood. This is why we exhort you, as a father, to expiate your crime by a penance proportionate to its enormity. We enjoin you to leave the lands of the Church in the space of three days, under pain of being handed over to the secular arm and the rigour of the flames."

Without disconcerting himself, Don Torribio repeated backwards the three mysterious words, which I hope the reader has not forgotten. And approaching the window, he cried :

" Jacintha ! Only put one partridge on the spit. The Dean will not stay to supper ! "

It was a thunderstroke for the pretended pope. He suddenly recovered from the kind of ecstasy into which the three magic words had thrown him when they were first pronounced. He saw that instead of being in the Vatican, he was still at Toledo in the study of Don Torribio. And he saw by the clock that it was not a complete hour since he had entered the magic room in which such beautiful dreams were woven. In less than an hour he had fancied he had become magician, bishop, archbishop, cardinal, pope ; and he found at the end of the affair he was only a dupe and a knave. All had been illusion, except the proofs he gave of the falseness of his evil heart. He went out without saying a word, found the mule where he had left it, and returned along the road to Badajoz without having learnt anything.

L'ABBÉ DE VOISENON
1708-1773

HE WAS WRONG

AND well! who is there that isn't? In this world we are surrounded by wrongs : they are necessary : they are the foundations of society : they make the mind lissom : they abate our self-love. A man who was always right would be insupportable. A man should be pardoned all his errors except that of being a bore : that alone is irreparable. When we bore our fellow-creatures we must live at home all alone. But I am wandering from my topic.

Let us pass to the story of Mondor. He was a young man with an unfortunate nature. He has a fine intelligence, a tender heart and a sweet soul. These are three great mistakes that are bound to produce many others.

In entering society he set himself chiefly to try to be always in the right. You will see how far that carried him. He struck up an acquaintance with a courtier and his wife : the lady found that Mondor had a fine intelligence, because he had a handsome figure ; the husband found that he had but a poor intellect, because he never agreed with any of his opinions.

The lady made many advances for the sake of the fineness of his intelligence : but as he was not in love with her, he did not perceive that she was paying him attentions. The husband begged him to look over a treatise on war which he had written—so at least he claimed. Mondor, after reading the work, said quite frankly that he thought the writer would make a good negotiator for a treaty of peace.

In these circumstances, the command of a regiment fell vacant. A little abortive Marquis found that the writer of the book on war had a transcendent genius, and he treated the wife of the writer as though she were a pretty woman. He obtained the regiment : the Marquis was made Colonel. Mondor was only a true man : he was in the wrong.

This adventure upset him : he lost all idea of making a fortune, and came to Paris to live quietly, and formed a plan for making friends there. Good heavens, how wrong it was of him! He thought he found a friend in the person of the young Alcipe.

Alcipe was amiable, with a decent air and the opinions of a sound man.

One day he came to Mondor with a sorrowful face. Mondor at once felt sorry for him : for there are no persons so foolish as those who have both intelligence and a good heart. Alcipe said that he had lost a hundred pounds. Mondor lent the money to him without a written acknowledgment. He thought by that he had won a friend. He was wrong ; he never saw him again.

He took up with some men of letters. They judged him capable of examining their pieces : it was easier to obtain an audience from him than from the public. There was one man in whom Mondor thought he recognised talent : he seemed worthy of real criticism : he read his work with attention : it was a comedy. He cut out some unnecessary details, showed that it wanted more solidity, asked the author to connect his scenes and make them rise one out of the other, to give the actors always a good situation, to make the dialogue full of character instead of a diamond-paste glitter of cheap epigrams, and to build up his characters and shade them finely instead of making them crudely contrast with each other. Such was the advice he gave, and the author corrected the piece in consequence. He found that Mondor was a bad adviser : the actors said that the piece was not capable of being played.

This disgusted Mondor with giving advice. The same author, whom he had tried to help, wrote another piece which was only a scrap-heap of unshaped and disconnected scenes. Mondor did not dare to advise him not to have it played : he was wrong. The piece was hissed off the stage. This threw him into a perplexity. If he gave advice, he was wrong ; if he did not give it, he was still wrong.

He renounced all commerce with the wits of the town, and mingled with men of learning. He found them almost as dull as persons who tried to be witty. They talked only when they had something to say : they were mostly silent. Mondor lost patience, and seemed to be only a giddy-minded creature. He made the acquaintance of some women of beauty—another mistake. He thought he was in a country nearer to the tropics. It was a land of lightning in which nearly all the fruit was burnt before it was ripe. He remarked that most of these women had only one idea, which they subdivided into little, shining, abstract thoughts. He perceived that all their art consisted in cutting up a little piece of wit. He saw how wrong he had been in seeking their society. He wished to reason about things and appeared awkward : he wished to shine as a wit and appeared heavy. In a word, he displeased, and felt it would not do to say to a young man : " Do you wish to get on with women ? Read the classic authors."

Of all men of the world Mondor was the most reasonable, and

he did not know what was the reasonable side to take. He felt
that a man does wrong less from taking a bad opening than from
taking a good one in a clumsy way. He had tried to be a courtier
and had broken his neck at it : he had tried to make friends and
had been duped in friendship : he had mingled with the wits and
had wearied of them : he had been bored with men of learning, and
he had bored the ladies whose society he sought.

He heard some vaunt the happiness of the man and woman
who truly loved each other. He thought the most sensible thing
to do was to fall in love : he planned to do it : this was precisely
the way of failing to know what love was. He studied all the
women he met : he weighed the graces and the talents of each, in
order to determine to love her who had one perfection more than
the others. He thought that love was a god with whom he could
trade.

In vain did he carry out this review ; in vain did he force himself
to fall in love. It was useless. One day, without thinking about
it, he was seized with a passion for a most ugly and capricious
woman : he congratulated himself on his choice. He saw, however,
that she was not beautiful : he was glad of it : he flattered himself
he would have no rivals. He was wrong. He did not know that
the uglier a woman is the more she flirts.

None of her mincing manners, none of her glances, none of her
little speeches but has its intention. She takes as much trouble
to make the most of her face as a farmer does to get a crop off a
poor soil. It succeeds with her ; the advances she makes flatter
the pride of the other sex, and the vanity of a man almost always
effaces the ugliness of a woman.

This Mondor learned by sad experience. He found himself
surrounded by competitors. He was disquietened by it : he was
wrong ; it led him into a much greater mistake, which was to
marry. He treated his wife with all possible consideration ; he
was wrong. She took his sweetness of character for weakness, and
harshly lorded it over him. He tried to quarrel ; he was wrong ;
it led him into the further mistake of a reconciliation. During the
reconciliations, he had two children—that is to say two mistakes.
He became a widower ; here he was in the right ; but he made
an error out of it, for he was so afflicted that he retired to his
country estates.

In the country he found a rich man who lived in arrogant
fashion ; he visited none of his neighbours ; Mondor thought he
was wrong. He showed as much affability as the other did
arrogance ; this was a great mistake. His house became the
haunt of small gentry who overwhelmed him without respite. He
envied the lot of his neighbour ; he saw too late that the misfortune
of being beset with folk is far more disagreeable than the mistake

of being feared. A suit was brought against him in regard to some rights of land. He preferred to give way to this unjust attack than to plead his case. He bore himself like a good fellow, gave a dinner to the other party and made a disadvantageous compromise ; he was wrong. Such a good way of making money attracted the attention of the parish. All his little neighbours tried to profit by his easy ways, and laid claim without any title to some imaginary right over his estate. He had to fight twenty law actions to avoid one.

That disgusted him ; he sold his lands ; he was wrong. He did not know what to do with his capital ; he was advised to finance a concert hall in a neighbouring large town. The director was a fine fellow who had become a lawyer in order to learn to be a connoisseur of music. The musical affair went into bankruptcy at the end of a year, in spite of the charming manners of the lawyer. This event ruined Mondor. He left the nothingness of all things here below ; he wished to become nothingness himself ; he became a monk and died of boredom ; that was his last error.

DENIS DIDEROT
1713–1784

THE TWO FRIENDS OF BOURBONNE

THERE were two men here, who might have been called the Orestes and Pylades of Bourbonne. One was named Olivier and the other Felix ; they were born the same day, in the same house, and from two sisters. The same milk fed them, for one of the sisters died in child-bed, and the other looked after both infants. They were brought up together, and they always separated from other boys. They loved each other as a man exists, as a man sees, without thinking about it. They felt it at every moment, but they never spoke about it. Once Olivier saved the life of Felix, who prided himself on being a great swimmer, and was almost drowned : neither of them remembered the incident. Many times Felix got Olivier out of some sorry scrape into which his impetuous character had carried him. Olivier never thought of thanking him ; they returned home without talking, or, on the way, they chatted about something else.

When they drew lots for the militia, the first fatal ticket was drawn by Felix, and Olivier said, " The other is for me ! " They served their time together, and came back to their village, dearer to each other than they had been before. This doesn't often happen in similar cases. For if reciprocal benefits cement a friendship based on intelligence, on the other hand they often add nothing to what I might call domestic and physical friendships. In one of the battles of our army, Olivier was in danger of having his head split open by a sabre stroke ; mechanically Felix sprang in front of him and received the stroke, and came back with his face marked with a large red scar. Some pretend that he was proud of this scar, but I do not believe it. At Hastembeck, Olivier brought Felix from a heap of dead on the battle-field, where he had fallen.

When they were questioned, the two friends sometimes spoke of the help each had received from the other, and never of that which they had given. And they never praised each other. Some time after their return from the wars, they fell in love, and, as chance led, they both loved the same girl. There was no rivalry between them. The first to see the passion of his friend retired from the wooing : this was Felix. Olivier married, and his friend, disgusted with life without knowing why threw himself into some dangerous trades. His last exploit was to become a smuggler.

You are not unaware that there are in France four tribunals at which smugglers are judged—Caen, Reims, Valence, and Toulouse—and that the most severe of the four is that of Reims presided over by Coleau, the most ferocious soul that nature has yet formed. Felix was caught with arms in his hand, and led before the terrible Coleau, and condemned to death, like five hundred other men who had preceded him. It was at night when Olivier learnt the fate of Felix. He rose up from the side of his wife, and without saying anything to her, went to Reims. He came before Judge Coleau, fell at his feet, and begged to be allowed to see and embrace his friend. Coleau looked at him in silence, and signed him to sit down. Olivier sat down. At the end of half an hour Coleau looked at his watch and said to Olivier :

"If you wish to see your friend while he is alive, you must make haste. He is on the way, and, if my watch is right, he will be hanged in less than ten minutes."

Transported with fury, Olivier leapt up, and with his cudgel caught Judge Coleau such a heavy blow on the neck that he stretched him out almost dead. Then running to the place of execution, shrieking, he struck down the executioner, attacked the police, and the populace, long indignant at these executions, broke out in riot. Felix was rescued by the mob, and got away. Olivier thought of following him, but a trooper of the horse police caught him on the flank with a lance. Olivier dragged himself as far as the gate of the town, but could not get any farther. Then some kindly waggoners lifted him on their cart and left him at the door of his house. The moment after he died.

"Wife, come and let me kiss you," he had just time to say. "I am done for, but Felix is saved ! "

Felix is still living. Escaping from the hands of justice, he threw himself into the forests of the province, the ways and by-ways of which he had learnt as a smuggler. Little by little he drew near to the house of Olivier, of whose death he was unaware.

In the depths of the wood was a charcoal-burner's hut that served as shelter to the smugglers. It was one of the places where they kept their goods and their arms. Here Felix came, not without running the risk of falling into an ambush, for the mounted police were following his trail. Some of his mates had brought news of his sentence at Reims, and the charcoal-burner and his woman thought Felix was a dead man when he appeared before them.

I will tell you the thing as it was told me from the charcoal-burner's wife, who died here a little while ago.

The children, wandering round the hut, were the first to see him. While he stopped to caress the youngest, who was his godchild, the others ran into the hut crying, " Felix ! Felix ! " The father and mother came out with joyful shouts ; but the wretched fugitive was so worn with fatigue and hunger that he had not the strength to reply, and he fell almost swooning in their arms. The good people helped him all they could, and gave him bread and wine and some vegetables, and he ate and fell asleep.

" Olivier ! Children do you know anything of Olivier ? " were his first words when he awoke.

" No ! " they answered him.

He told the story of his adventure at Reims, and passed the night and the following day in the hut. He sighed and called on Olivier, and thinking he was in prison at Reims, he wished to go there and die with him. It was not without much trouble that the charcoal-burner induced him to give up this plan.

In the middle of the second night, he took a gun, put a sabre under his arm, and called in a low voice to the charcoal-burner :

" Friend ! Take your axe and come with me."

" Where ? "

" What a question ! To Olivier's house."

They set out together, but, just as they left the forest, they were surrounded by a detachment of mounted police. I can only go by what the wife of the charcoal-burner told me. But it is unheard of that two men on foot should have been able to make a stand against a score of men on horseback. Apparently the police were scattered out, and they wished to take their man alive. However this may be, the fight was very fierce. There were five horses lamed and seven horsemen brought down with the axe or sabre. The poor charcoal-burner fell dead on the spot, with a bullet through his temple. Felix regained the forest, and as he is a man of incredible agility, he ran from one tree trunk to the other, and while running he charged his gun, fired, and gave a whistle. The continual whistles and gun-shots from different places at different intervals made the horsemen think that they had to do with a horde of smugglers, and, fearing an ambush, they quickly retreated.

Felix returned to the field of battle, and took the body of the charcoal-burner on his shoulder and carried him along the path to the hut, where the man's wife and children were still sleeping. He stopped at the door, he laid the corpse at his feet, and sat with his back against the tree and his face turned to the entrance to the hut. Such was the spectacle that awaited the charcoal-burner's wife when she came from the hovel. She awoke, and

did not find her husband by her side. She looked around for
Felix. He was not there. She arose, she came out, and, at the
sight awaiting her, she fell to the ground. The children ran out
and cried at what they saw. They threw themselves on their
father, they threw themselves on their mother. The poor woman,
recalled to her senses by the cries and movements of her children,
tore at her hair and dug her nails into her cheeks. Felix, motionless at the foot of the tree, his eyes closed, his head thrown back,
said, in a broken voice :

" Kill me ! " There was a moment's silence, and then the cries
and the moans went on ; again Felix said :

" Kill me, children, out of pity kill me ! "

Thus three days and three nights passed in grief. On the
fourth day Felix said to the woman :

" Take your wallet and put some bread in it and follow me."

After a long circuit over our mountains and through our forests
they came to Olivier's cottage, which lies, as you know, at the
end of the village, at the spot where the road divides into two
routes, one leading to Franche Comté and the other to Lorraine.
It was there that Felix found himself between the widows of two
men massacred for his sake.

" Where is Olivier ? " he brusquely said to his friend's wife.
From the silence of the woman, her mourning clothes, and her
tears he understood that Olivier was dead. He felt sick, and he
fell and struck his head against a trough in which bread was
kneaded. The two widows raised him up : his blood ran over
them, and while they were staunching the wound with their aprons,
he said to them :

" You are their wives, and yet you help me ! "

Then he swooned again, and when he recovered he said :

" Why did he not leave me ? Why did he come to Reims ?
Why didn't he let the thing go on ? "

Then he lost his head and madness came upon him, and he rolled
about the floor and tore his clothes. Drawing his sabre, he tried
to kill himself, but the two women sprang upon him, crying for
help. Neighbours rushed in and tied him up with ropes, and he
was bled seven or eight times. His fury fell with the weakening
of his strength, and he remained like a dead man for three or four
days, and then recovered his reason. In his first movement he
looked around him like a man awaking from a deep sleep.

" Where am I ? " he said. " Who are you, you women ? "

" I am the charcoal-burner's wife," said one.

" Ah, yes," he said, " I know you. But who is that other
woman ? "

Olivier's wife remained silent. Felix began to weep : he turned
his face to the wall.

" I am in Olivier's house . . . this is Olivier's bed . . . this woman, there . . . she was his wife ! Oh, my God ! "

But the women took such good care of him, they inspired him with so much pity, they prayed him so continually to live, they showed him in so touching a manner that he was their only resource, that he let himself be persuaded.

All the time he remained in this house he did not go to bed. He went out at night, wandering about the fields, rolling on the earth and calling out, " Olivier." One of the women always followed him and brought him back at daybreak.

There were several persons who knew that he was in Olivier's cottage, and among these persons were some who intended to betray him. The two widows warned him of the peril he was running. It was one afternoon ; he was sitting on a bench, his sabre across his knee, his elbows on the table, and his two hands over his eyes. At first he said nothing. Olivier's widow had a boy of sixteen to eighteen years, the charcoal-burner's wife a girl of fifteen.

" Go and look for your girl," he said to the charcoal-burner's widow, " and bring her here."

While she was away in the forest fetching her daughter, he sold some fields that he owned. The charcoal-burner's wife came back with her daughter, and the son of Olivier married the girl. Felix gave them the money he had got by his sale, and embraced them, and, weeping, asked them to forgive him. They went to live in a hut, where they still reside, and where they are now father and mother of children. The two widows lived together, and the children of Olivier had a father and two mothers. It is scarcely more than a year and a half since the charcoal-burner's wife died. Olivier's wife is still living.

One evening the two women were watching Felix—for there was always one of them who kept him in view—and they saw him burst into tears. He waved his arms in silence at the gate that separated him from them, and then began to pack his knapsack. The women said nothing to him, for they understood how urgent it was that he should depart. They supped together all three, without speaking. In the night Felix rose up ; the women could not sleep. He went towards the door on tiptoe. There he stopped, looked at the bed where the two women lay, wiped his eyes with his hands, and went out. The two women clasped their arms about each other, and spent the rest of the night in tears. No one knew where Felix had hidden, yet few weeks passed without him sending the widows some money. He has now gone to Prussia, where he serves in a regiment of the guards. It is said he is liked by his comrades, and that even the King has taken notice of him. Olivier's widow tells me he still sends her remittances.

THE
PLASTER OF DESGLANDS

Denis Diderot

Close to the house of Monsieur Desglands was a charming widow, who had several qualities similar to those of Ninon de Lenclos. Staid by intelligence, wanton by temperament, grieving in the morning for the folly of the night, she spent all her life in going from pleasure to remorse and from remorse to pleasure, without the habit of pleasure stifling her remorse, without the habit of remorse lessening her taste for pleasure. I got to know her in her last days, when she said she was finally escaping from her two great enemies. She never accepted the homage of a fool or a knave : her favours were always given to talent and worthiness. To say of a man that he had been one of her favourites was to say that he was a man of merit. As she knew her fickleness, she never promised to be faithful to anybody.

" I only gave one false pledge in my life," she said. " It was when I married."

If a man lost his feelings for her, or if she lost her passion for him, he still remained her friend. Never has there been a more striking example of the difference between probity and morals. You could not say she had any morals, and yet you were bound to admit it was difficult to find a more honest creature. The parish priest seldom saw her in church : but he always found her purse open to the poor. She said jestingly that law and religion were a pair of crutches that must not be taken away from those who had feeble legs. Women, who were afraid for her to meet their husbands, liked to see her among their children.

One day Desglands invited the lovely widow to dinner with some gentlemen of the country round about. The reign of Desglands was drawing to an end, and among his guests there was a man towards whom the fickle heart of the widow began to lean. They were at table, Desglands and his rival sitting side by side, opposite the lady. Desglands employed all the wit he had to enliven the conversation : he made the most gallant advances to the widow : but she was distracted and heard nothing, sitting with her eyes fixed on his rival. Desglands was holding an egg in his hand : a convulsive movement of jealousy took him : he clenched his hand and the

28

lightly-boiled egg splattered on the face of his neighbour, who raised his hand to strike back. Desglands gripped him by the wrist and whispered :

" Sir, I will take it as received."

There was a deep silence : the fair widow felt unwell. The meal was gloomy and short. On leaving the table, she had Desglands and his rival taken alone into another room. All that a woman could do to reconcile them she did. She pleaded, she wept, she fainted : she shook the hands of Desglands, she turned her eyes flooded with tears to the other man.

" And you love me ! " she said to one. " And you have loved me ! " she said to the other. " And yet you both wish to ruin me ! You want to make me a byword, the object of scorn and dislike to the whole province ! No matter which of you two takes the life of the other, I will never see him again. He cannot be my friend. My hate for him will finish only with my life."

Then she swooned again, and in swooning she said :

" You cruel men ! draw your swords and plunge them in my breast. If, while dying, I could see you embrace each other, I should die without regret ! "

Desglands and his rival did not stir, but their eyes were wet with tears. However, it was necessary to separate. The fair widow went home more dead than alive.

Next day Desglands paid a visit to his fickle charmer : he met his rival in her house. Who was most astonished ? It was the rival and the widow at seeing that Desglands had his right cheek covered by a great round patch of black taffeta.

" What is it ? " said the widow.

" It is nothing," said Desglands.

" A slight inflammation ? " said his rival.

" It will go away in time," said Desglands.

After a little conversation, Desglands left, and in leaving he made a sign to his rival which was well understood. For he too left, and they strolled away in opposite directions, and made a round, and met behind the gardens of the fair widow. There they fought their duel, and the rival of Desglands was left on the grass, seriously, but not mortally wounded. While he was being carried home, Desglands returned to the widow's house. He sat down and they talked again about the affair at the dinner.

" And what is the meaning," she asked, " of this enormous and ridiculous plaster that covers your cheek ? "

Desglands rose and looked at himself in the mirror.

" As a matter of fact," he said to himself, " I do find it now a little too large."

Taking the lady's scissors, he detached the taffeta from his cheek and cut off an inch or two, and replaced the black plaster.

" How does it look now ? " he said.

" An inch or two less ridiculous than before."

" It is always something," said Desglands.

His rival got better. There was a second duel, in which Desglands again won. So it went on for half a dozen duels. And after each combat, Desglands cut a little edge off the large, strange, black beauty-spot he wore on his cheek. The end of this adventure was the end of the fair widow. The trouble of it ruined her health that had always been somewhat weak and tottering.

And Desglands ?

One day, as we were walking together, he received a letter, and opened it and said :

" He was a very worthy man, but his death is hardly an affliction for me."

And at once he pulled off his cheek the rest of his black plaster that had been almost reduced, by frequent cuttings, to the size of an ordinary beauty-spot.

FRIAR CÔME AND THE CORPSE

Denis Diderot

HERE is an amusing little comedy that happened just outside my door. The scene of it is the hospital La Charité. Friar Côme, the famous surgeon of the Feuillants Order, had need of a corpse to make some experiments in cutting. He went to the Father attendant of the hospital :

" You have just come in time," said the attendant. " There you have, No. 46, a tall young fellow, who has no more than two hours of life left."

" Two hours ? " said Friar Côme. " That is not quite what I want. It is a bit too quick for me. I have to go to-night to Fontaine-bleau, and I shall not get back till to-morrow evening at seven at the earliest.

" Very well ! That does not matter," said the attendant to him. " You can go, and I will do all I can to keep him going for you."

Friar Côme went away, and the Father attendant called on the apothecary and ordered a good cordial for No. 46. The cordial worked wonderfully. The sick man slept for six hours. In the morning the attendant went to his bed and found him sitting up, coughing freely : hardly any fever, no more oppression, and not the least pain under the ribs.

"Ah ! Father," said the patient to him, "I do not know what you have given me, but you have put life in me again ! "

"Is that so ? "

"It is truth itself. Another dose like that and I am quit of my trouble."

"Yes. But what will Friar Côme say about it ? "

"What were you saying of Friar Côme ? "

"Nothing, nothing," answered the Father attendant, rubbing his chin with his hand, and looking somewhat disconcerted and disappointed.

"Father," said the sick man to him, "you look sulky. Are you angry because I've got better ? "

"No, no ! it is not that."

Yet from hour to hour, the attendant went to the bed of the sick man, and said to him :

"Well, my friend ! How are you getting on ? "

"Wonderfully well, Father."

"If this goes on," said the attendant, as he went back to his room, "I shall have done more than kept you going for Friar Côme."

And this was in fact what happened. In the evening Friar Côme came to make his experiments.

"Well," he said to the Father attendant, "where is my corpse ? "

"Your corpse ! There is not any ! "

"There is not any ! How's that ? "

"It is all your fault. Our man asked for nothing better than to die ; you are the cause that he has changed his mind. And now as a punishment you will have to wait. Why the mischief did you want to go to Fontainebleau ? If you had stayed here, I should never have thought of giving him the cordial that has cured him, and your experiment would have been carried out."

"Never mind," said Friar Côme. "It's no great misfortune. We must wait for another case."

CHARLES NODIER
1780–1844

THE LEGEND OF SISTER BEATRICE

Not far from the high summit of the Jura Mountains, and a little way down on its western slope, you can still see the ruins of the Convent of Our Lady of the Flowering Thorns. It lies at the end of a deep and narrow gorge that is sheltered to the north, and there every year the rarest flowers of the country are found. Half a league away, at the opposite end of the gorge, are the remains of an ancient manor house. Little is known about it, except that the last of the knights that took their name from the manor died in the conquest of the Tomb of Christ in the Holy Land without leaving an heir. His mourning widow did not desert the wild beautiful spot where the happiest days of her life had passed, but devoted herself to good works, and the fame of her piety and her benefactions is still remembered by the peasants. Having forgotten her name, they call her still the Holy Woman.

On one of those days when winter, drawing to an end, suddenly relaxes its harshness under the soft influences of a sky of springtime, the Holy Woman was walking at the end of the gorge, and to her surprise she found one of the hawthorn bushes covered with blossom. She at first thought it was the whiteness of fallen snow, and she was full of wondering delight on seeing it was really an innumerable multitude of beautiful little white stars with scarlet rays that crowned the bush with splendour. She took one of the sprays of flowering thorn and carried it home joyfully, and placed it in her oratory before an image of the Virgin Mary. And she felt so strange a joy in her soul, after making this simple offering to the Mother of God, that she resolved to go every day to the flowering bush and bring a new garland for the altar.

One evening, however, her care of the poor and the sick detained her much longer than usual. In vain she hastened to her wild garden : the night fell before she arrived. She was beginning to grow afraid of the darkness and the solitude, when a calm pure brightness, like that which falls from the sky at dawn, showed her all the flowering thorns, gleaming just ahead of her. She stopped for a moment, thinking that the light came from the camp fire of some wandering robbers. But rather than return without her garland for Our Lady, she collected her courage and stole on tiptoe toward the bush of white flowers, and with trembling hand took a branch, and returned down the road to the manor house without daring to look behind her.

All the night she thought on the strange light without finding any explanation of it. The following evening she went in the darkness to the hawthorns, accompanied by her old servant and her chaplain. The soft clear radiance still shone from the bushes ; and as they approached it seemed to become brighter and deeper. They fell on their knees. For it appeared to them there was something miraculous in the strange lovely radiance. Then the good priest arose, and singing a hymn, walked to the flowering thorns and, moving them aside, saw something that struck him with such wonder that he was overwhelmed with joy and gratitude. Amid the bushes was an image of the Virgin Mary, carved with artless simplicity from a piece of wood, and crudely coloured and clad in rough garments. From this image came the miraculous radiance that lighted up the hawthorns. Reciting the litany, he took the statue in his hands, and, followed by the lady and her servant, carried it to the oratory in the manor house. But in the morning the statue was not to be seen on the altar where it had been placed. Everybody wondered what had happened. All day long the lady of the manor grieved over the loss of the miraculous image. In the evening she went with all her people to the flowering thorns, and there, in the darkness, the radiant statue was again seen. The Mother of God had returned to her wild green dwelling-place, fragrant with the sweetness of her favourite flowers.

" Queen of the Angels ! " said the lady of the manor, " we can all see now that this is your chosen home, and here shall your church be built ! "

And soon afterwards a beautiful glorious temple was built around the sacred image. Kings came with an offering of a tabernacle of pure gold, and great lords enriched the church with their gifts. The fame of the miracles of Our Lady of the Flowering Thorns spread throughout Christendom, and from many lands a multitude of pious women gathered in the valley and formed themselves into a religious order. The Holy Woman was made Superior of the Convent, and after a long life of good works and sacrifices, she died in the service of Our Lady.

For two centuries after the death of the Holy Woman some young maiden of her race ever acted as sister custodian of the sacred tabernacle. She kept watch over it, and she alone was allowed to open the tabernacle on the solemn festivals when the miraculous image was displayed to the pilgrims. It was her duty to dust it every day and gather the offerings of flowers, chief among which was the flowering thorn, and weave them into a garland for the sacred statue.

At fifteen years of age, Beatrice was appointed by her family to enter the convent and become the sister custodian. As pure as her flowers was the lovely maid when she took her vows and entered on her gracious duties.

But there is an age, happy or unhappy, when the heart of a young girl understands that it is created to love, and Beatrice reached it. This need of her being, at first vague and restless, only made her duties dearer to her. Incapable then of explaining the secret movements that agitated her, she took them for the instinct of a religious fervour that accuses itself of not being sufficiently ardent, and believes itself wanting in sincerity unless it carries its love to enthusiasm and frenzy. The unknown object of her transports escaped from her recognition ; and among those that fell under the torrent emotions of her ingenuous soul, the Virgin Mary alone seemed to her worthy of that passionate adoration to which her life could scarcely suffice. The worship of the Divine Mother became the unique occupation of her thoughts, the only charm of her solitude ; it filled her with dreams of mysterious languors and ineffable transports. She was often seen lying before the tabernacle, praying and sobbing and wetting the altar-steps with her tears. The Queen of Heaven smiled, no doubt, from the height of her eternal throne, at this happy and tender mistake of innocence ; for the Holy Virgin loved Beatrice, and was pleased to be loved by her. And perhaps she had read in the heart of Beatrice that she would always be loved by her.

But an event happened about this time that lifted the veil under which the secret of Beatrice had long been concealed from herself. A young lord of the neighbourhood was attacked by robbers, and found almost dead in the forest. Indeed he scarcely showed any signs of life when the servants of the convent carried him into their infirmary. As the daughters of noble ladies were then always instructed from early childhood in the art of dressing wounds, Beatrice was sent by the other nuns to the help of the dying man. She used all the knowledge she had learnt of healing wounded men, but she relied more upon her prayers to Our Lady of the Flowering Thorns. Her long weary vigils by the bedside of the young lord, and the prayers she offered for him, effected all that she had hoped for. Raymond opened his eyes and recognised her.

" Ah," he cried, " Beatrice ! Is it you that I see again ? You that I loved from my boyhood ! You that the forgotten agreement between my father and yours once allowed me to hope I should wed ! By what unhappy hazard do I see you again, chained to a life that is not suited to you, and separated for ever from the brilliant world that you adorned ? Ah, if it were you yourself that chose this life of solitude and abnegation, it was because you did not know your own heart when you did it ! Beatrice, I swear to you, the vows you took in your ignorance are nothing either before God or before men ! Heaven has brought us together again to unite us in love for evermore ! Beatrice, it is your lover who implores you and who will guide you. You will become the wife of your Raymond as well as his sweetheart. Do not turn away with your eyes full of tears. Do not take your hands away that tremble in mine. No ! you will come with me, and you will never leave me ! "

Beatrice did not answer. Escaping from the enfeebled arms of the wounded knight, she staggered—bewildered, troubled, and panting—into the chapel, and fell at the feet of the Virgin, her consolation and her support. There she wept as she had done before : but it was no longer from a feeling unrecognised and without aim. Her passion was now more powerful than her piety, more powerful than her sense of shame, more powerful, alas ! than the Holy Virgin to whom she called in vain for help. Her tears this time were bitter and burning. The other nuns saw her lying for days outstretched and suppliant, but they were not astonished. For everybody in the convent knew her passionate devotion for Our Lady of the Flowering Thorns. Beatrice passed the rest of her time in the infirmary with the wounded knight, though he was now so far recovered that he scarcely needed her attention.

One evening, when the church was closed and all the sisters were retired in their cells, Beatrice came slowly into the choir and placed her lamp on the altar. With trembling hand she opened the door of the tabernacle, turning away as she did so, shivering and lowering her eyes, as though she feared the Queen of Heaven would strike her down with a glance. Then she threw herself on her knees and tried to pray, but the words died on her lips, or lost themselves in sobs. She enveloped her face in her veil and tried to calm herself, and in a last effort she broke out in wild confused words, without knowing if she were offering a prayer or a blasphemy.

" O, Heavenly Helper of my youth ! " she cried. " O, you that I have loved alone so long, O Mary, Divine Mary ! why have you abandoned me ? Why have you let your Beatrice fall a prey to the horrible passions of hell ? You know how I have fought against them, how I have struggled ! But now it is done with for ever. I can serve you no longer, for I am no longer worthy of my office. Far away from you must I go to hide my sin. Yet suffer me, O Mary, to worship you still ! Take pity on my tears. My senses have now betrayed me, but my soul at least still struggles against my passions. Receive the last of my prayers, and if my ancient service is worthy of any reward, send down death to the unfortunate woman at your altar before she can leave you."

Beatrice rose and approached with trembling body the miraculous image. She adorned it with new flowers, and taking those that were faded, she pressed them on her heart, and placed them in the blessed receptacle of her scapulary, so that she should never be separated from them. Then with a last glance at the tabernacle, she cried with terror and fled.

In the night, a horse-litter carried the handsome knight far from the convent, and a young nun, unfaithful to her vows, accompanied him. The first year passed in an intoxication of fulfilled passion. The world to Beatrice was a new spectacle, inexhaustible in delights. Love multiplied around her all the means of seduction that could perpetuate her error and achieve her ruin. She came out of dreams of pleasure only to awake amid the joy of feasts, the music of minstrels, and the play of the dancers. Her life was a wild festival in which the voice of her conscience vainly tried to make itself heard amid the clamours of the orgy. Still she had not quite forgotten Mary. More than once, in the preparation of her toilet, her scapulary had opened under her fingers. More than once she had let a glance and a tear fall on the withered flowers of the Virgin. Prayers had risen to her lips like a hidden flame beneath the ashes, but they had been extinguished under the kisses of her lover. Yet in her wildest moments something told her that a prayer might have saved her.

It was not long before she learnt that there is no lasting love except that which is refined by religion : that the love of our Lord and of Mary alone escapes from the changes of our feelings, and grows and strengthens as time goes on, while other loves quickly burn themselves away in the ashes of our heart. Yet Beatrice loved Raymond still, but a day came when she saw that Raymond loved her no longer. On this day she foresaw the more horrible day when she would be utterly abandoned by him for whom she had abandoned the altar, and this dreaded day arrived. Beatrice found herself with no support on earth, and, alas ! with no support in heaven. In vain she sought for solace in her memories and for comfort in her hopes. The flowers of the scapulary were as withered as those of her pleasures. The source of tears and prayers was dried up. The fate that Beatrice had made for herself was accomplished. The unfortunate woman accepted her ignominy. The higher one falls from the path of virtue the more terrible is the descent, and it was from a far height that Beatrice had fallen. She was at first frightened by her infamy, but she ended by taking it as a matter of course, because the spring of her soul was broken.

Fifteen years thus passed, and oh, what pleasures these fugitive years carried away with them !—innocence, modesty, youth and beauty and love, the roses of life that flower but once. And she could not keep that which would have repaid her for all other losses—

28*

her conscience. The jewels with which she had been adorned were a resource that was soon exhausted. She remained alone, derelict, an object of scorn to others as well as to herself, an example of shame and misery that mothers pointed out to their children to turn them from sin. She grew tired of living on pity, of receiving alms that even pious persons were often loath to give her, of being helped secretly by women who blushed at giving her a little bread. One day, wrapping herself in her rags, she determined to seek for food and shelter in some place where she was not known. She hoped to hide her infamy in her misery, and went away with nothing but the flowers she had once taken from the altar, and that now fell, one by one, in the dust beneath her dried lips.

Beatrice was still young, but shame and hunger made her look prematurely old. When her pale silent figure timidly implored help from passers-by, when her white and delicate hand was stretched out trembling to take their alms, there was no one who did not feel that she should have had another destiny on earth. The most indifferent persons stopped and looked at her with a glance that seemed to say, " Oh ! my daughter, how is it that you have fallen so low ? " But Beatrice never answered them : for she had long since lost the power to weep. She walked on and on ; her journey looked as though it would end only in death.

One day in particular she followed from dawn a hard and stony mountain-path, where there were no houses at which she could beg. She had for food only some roots torn from the clefts of the rocks. Her worn-out shoes tumbled from her bleeding feet. As, at night-fall, she felt that she would swoon from weariness and want of nourishment, she saw suddenly a long line of lights of a great building ahead of her. Collecting her remaining strength, she pushed forward. But at the silvery chime of a bell, that stirred in her heart a strange vague memory, all the lights went out, and around her were only night and silence. She still made a few more steps with outstretched arms, and her trembling hands struck against the closed door. There she leaned for a moment to take breath. She tried to hold on to the door so as not to fall. But her feeble fingers would not bear her ; they slipped under the weight of her body.

" Oh, Holy Virgin ! " she cried, " why did I leave you ! "

And she swooned on the doorstep. Such a night as this is an expiation for a whole life of disorders. The keen fresh air of dawn had scarcely begun to revive in her a confused and painful sense of life, when she saw that she was not alone. A woman knelt by her side, and raised her head carefully, and stared at her in an attitude of anxiety, waiting until she fully recovered her senses.

" Praise God for sending us so early such a case of misfortune and misery ! " said the good nun. " It is a happy augury to the glorious feast that we celebrate to-day. But how is it, my dear child, that you did not pull the bell ? The sisters would have welcomed you at any hour. Well, well ! do not try to talk now, poor lost lamb ! Drink this broth that I hastily heated as soon as I saw you. Taste this wine that will warm your body and remove the soreness from your limbs. Drink it all ; and now give me your cold little hands and let me warm them. Can you feel my breath on your fingers ? Oh, you will be well again soon ! "

Beatrice, touched with emotion, took the hands of the good nun and pressed them to her lips.

" I feel better already," she said to her, " and I am sure I am strong enough to go and thank God for his mercy in leading me to this holy house. But tell me first where I am ? "

" Where else could you be," said the nun, " if not at Our Lady of the Flowering Thorns. There is no other convent in these mountains less than five leagues away."

" Our Lady of the Flowering Thorns ! " cried Beatrice, with a look of joy, that at once gave way to signs of deep dismay. " Our Lady of the Thorns ! God have pity on me ! "

" What, my daughter ! do you not know our convent ? " said the nun. " You seem to come from a far country. I have never seen a woman wearing clothes like yours. But Our Lady of the Flowering Thorns does not limit her protection to the people of this land. If ever you have heard of her, you must know that she is good to all the world."

" I know her and I have served her," answered Beatrice. " But I come from a distant country, as you say, my Mother, and it is not astonishing that I did not at once recognise this home of peace and benediction. But there is the church, and there the convent and the hawthorns where I gathered so many flowers. Alas ! they are still blossoming. But I was so young when I saw them last. It was in the days," she continued, lifting her face to heaven with that resolute expression of self-sacrifice which comes of Christian remorse, " it was in the days when Sister Beatrice was the custodian of the holy chapel. Do you remember her, Mother ? "

" How could I forget her, my child, since Sister Beatrice has never ceased to be custodian of the tabernacle. She still lives among us to-day, and she will, I hope, remain for many years to come an example to all the community. After the protection of the Holy Virgin, we do not know a greater help to a holy life than she is."

" I was not speaking of her," said Beatrice, with a sad sigh. " I was speaking of the other Beatrice who occupied the same place sixteen years ago, and ended her life in sin."

" God will not punish you for your mad words," said the nun, drawing the beggar woman to her bosom. " Illness and distress have deranged your mind, and your memory is impaired. I have dwelt in this convent for more than sixteen years, and I have never known another custodian of the holy tabernacle than Sister Beatrice. And since you have decided to pray in the church while I prepare your bed, go, my daughter, to the altar. There you will see Beatrice. You will easily recognise her, for by Divine favour she has not lost in growing old a single grace of her youth. I will come for you very soon, and then I will not leave you until you are quite well and sound."

The nun went away into the cloisters. Tottering forward, Beatrice gained the church stairs, and knelt on the floor, and beat her head upon the stones. Then, growing bolder, she rose and stumbled from pillar to pillar, advancing as far as the rood screen, and there she again fell on her knees. Through the mist that covered her eyes, she had seen the sister custodian standing before the tabernacle.

Little by little the sister approached her, while making her usual round of holy duties, filling and trimming the dying lamps, and replacing the old garland of flowers by new blossoms. Beatrice could not believe her eyes. This sister was herself, not the woman that age and sin and despair had made her, but the girl that she had been in the innocent days of her youth. Was it an illusion produced by remorse ? Was it a miraculous punishment, anticipating those reserved for her by the anger of God ? In doubt she hid her head in her hand, and rested motionless against the bars of the screen, stammering the most tender of her ancient prayers. And yet the sister custodian continued to walk forward. Already the folds of her dress were brushing against the screen. Beatrice was so overpowered she dared not breathe.

" It is thee, dear Beatrice," said the sister, in a voice whose sweetness no human words can express. " I have no need to see thee to recognise thee, for thy prayers come to me now just as I used to hear them of old. Long have I waited for thee ; but, as I was sure of thy return, I took thy place on the day thou didst leave me, so that no one should perceive thy absence. Thou knowest now the worth of the pleasures and joys that seduced thee and thou wilt not leave again. What has happened will be known only to thee and me. Return then with confidence to the position thou hast among my daughters. Thou wilt find in thy cell, the way to which thou hast not forgotten, the habit thou didst leave there, and with it thou wilt clothe thyself again in thy early innocence, of which it is the emblem. This rare grace I owe to thy love, and I have obtained it on thy repentance. Farewell, sister custodian of Mary ! Love Mary as she has loved thee."

When Beatrice looked at her with eyes flooded with tears, when she stretched towards her her trembling arms in an act of gratitude broken by sobs, she saw the Holy Virgin mount the altar stairs, open the door of the tabernacle, and seat herself in heavenly glory, under her halo of gold and under her garland of flowering thorn.

Not without emotion did Beatrice come down from the choir. She visited her companions whose faith she had betrayed, and who, exempt from reproach, had grown old in the practice of an austere duty. She glided among her sisters, with bowed face, ready to humiliate herself at the first cry raised against her. In deep agitation of heart, she listened to their voices and heard nothing. As none of them had observed her departure, none of them remarked her return. She threw herself at the feet of the Holy Virgin, and it seemed to her that she was greeted with a smile. In the dreams of her life of illusions she had known nothing approaching such happiness as now was hers.

The Divine Festival of Mary—I think I have said that this happened on the Feast of the Assumption—was accomplished with a solemn calmness and intense ecstasy such as the community had never known before. Some saw miraculous lights playing around the tabernacle, others heard the songs of angels mingling in their chants, and stopped singing themselves to listen to the heavenly harmony. It seemed to the nuns that there was a great festival in heaven as well as in the Convent of Our Lady of the Flowering Thorns ; and by an event strange to the season of the year, all the hawthorns on the mountains burst again into blossom in the middle of August, so that, without as well as within, it was spring-time and fragrance. A soul had returned to the bosom of God, stripped of all the infirmities and all the ignominies of our condition, and there was great rejoicing in heaven.

Just for a moment the innocent joy of the nuns was obscured by one disquietude. A poor beggar woman, sick and weak and hungry, had been found at dawn at the door of the convent. The nun who saw her had tended her a little, and had then gone to prepare for her a warm soft bed, but when the bed was ready the woman could not be found. The unhappy creature had disappeared without leaving any trace. But it was thought that Sister Beatrice might have seen her in the church where she had gone to pray.

" Do not be disturbed, my sisters," said Beatrice, touched to tears by this tender solicitude, and pressing the nun who was looking for her to her bosom. " I saw the poor woman, and I know what has become of her. She is happy, my sisters—happier than she deserves, happier than ever you could hope she would be ! "

This answer quietened all anxiety ; but the nuns spoke of it a good deal, for it was the first harsh word that had come from the lips of the sister custodian. Thereafter, all the life of Beatrice passed like a single day, like the day promised in the future to the elect of the Lord, without tediousness, without regrets, or any emotions except those of piety to God and charity to men. She lived a century without seeming to grow old ; because it is only the evil passions of the soul that age the body. A good life is a perpetual youth. When Beatrice died, she fell asleep calmly in that light slumber of the grave that separates time from eternity. The Church honoured her memory by placing her in the ranks of the saints.

STENDHAL

(Marie-Henri Beyle)

1783–1842

THE PHILTRE

On a sombre, rainy night in the summer of 1823 a young lieutenant of the 96th Regiment, garrisoned at Bordeaux, withdrew from the café where he had lost nearly all his money. He cursed his folly, for he was poor.

He was walking quietly down one of the loneliest streets of the Lormond district, when suddenly he heard cries, and from a door that was noisily flung open, a woman escaped and ran and fell at his feet. So thick was the darkness he could not guess what was happening, save by the sounds about him. The men who were pursuing the woman, whoever they were, stopped in the doorway, apparently on hearing the steps of the young officer.

He listened a moment. The men spoke in whispers, but did not come up to him. Though the affair only filled him with disgust, Lieven thought it his duty to lift up the woman who had fallen before him.

He saw that she had only a chemise on. In spite of the profound darkness of the night—it was then about two o'clock in the morning —he dimly saw her long, unloosened hair. So it was a woman. The discovery by no means pleased him.

She seemed unable to walk without help. Lieven had need to call to mind his ideas of duty towards one's fellow-creatures, in order to prevent himself from leaving her. He saw himself appearing the next morning before a police magistrate. There would be jests from his fellow-officers, and satirical stories in the newspapers of the town.

"I must put her against the door of some house," he said to himself, "and ring the bell, and then get away as fast as I can."

He was preparing to do this, when he heard the woman moan some words in Spanish. He did not know a word of the language. Perhaps that was why the two very simple words that Leonora spoke stirred in him the most romantic feeling. He saw no longer a police magistrate, and a girl of the streets beaten by some drunken brutes. His imagination soared away into ideas of love and strange adventures.

Having lifted the woman up, Lieven began to speak to her and tried to console her. " But was she ugly ? " he asked himself. The doubt on this point brought his reason into play, and made him forget his romantic ideas. Lieven wished to get her to sit down on a doorstep ; she refused to do so.

" Let us go farther on," she said, with a foreign accent.

" Are you afraid of your husband ? " said Lieven.

" Alas ! I have left my husband, a most worthy man who worshipped me, for a lover who has treated me worse than a savage."

Lieven again forgot the police magistrate and all the unpleasant sequels to a night adventure.

" I have been robbed, sir," said Leonora, a few moments afterwards, " but I see I still have a little diamond ring. Perhaps some inn-keeper will give me shelter. But, sir, I should be the talk of the place, for I will admit to you I have only a chemise on me. Sir, I beg you, in the name of humanity, to find me some sort of room, and buy any kind of rough dress for me from some working woman. As soon as I was properly clad," she added, encouraged by the silence of the young officer, " you could take me to the door of some small inn. There I would cease to rely on your generosity, and beg you only to leave a most unhappy woman."

All this, spoken in bad French, was rather pleasant to Lieven.

" Madame," he answered, " I will do all that you want me. The main thing, however, for you and me is not to get ourselves arrested. I am Lieutenant Lieven of the 96th Regiment. If we meet a patrol, and the men are not of my regiment, they will take us to the guardhouse, where we shall have to pass the night ; and to-morrow you and I, madame, will be the talk of Bordeaux."

Lieven felt Leonora shiver as she leant on his arm.

" This horror of scandal is a good sign," he thought to himself. " Please take my coat," he said to the lady. " I will conduct you to my room."

" Oh, sir, sir. . . ."

" I will leave you absolute mistress of my room, and I will not appear there until to-morrow morning. But my orderly comes at six o'clock, and he is a man who will knock until the door is opened. I am a man of honour, madame. But is she pretty ? " he asked himself.

He opened the door of his house. The unknown lady almost fell at the bottom of the stairs, where she could not find the first step. Lieven spoke to her in whispers. She answered him also in a low voice.

" How dare you bring women into my house ! " cried the shrill-voiced, pretty landlady, coming out with a little lamp.

Lieven turned quickly towards his unknown lady, saw an admirable figure, and blew out the lamp.

" Silence, Madame Saucède, or to-morrow morning I leave you ! This lady is the wife of the Colonel, and I am not sleeping here to-night. Here are ten francs for you, if you keep a silent tongue in your head ! "

Lieven had reached the third floor ; at the door of his room he trembled.

" Enter, madame," he said to the lady. " There are phosphorus matches just by the clock. Light the candle, and make a good fire, and bolt the door from the inside. I respect you as if you were my sister, and when I come in the morning I will bring a dress."

" Jesus Maria ! " cried the lovely Spanish lady.

When Lieven knocked at the door the next morning, he was madly in love. In order not to wake his unknown lady too soon, he had had the patience to wait for his orderly at the door, and to go into a café and sign the papers brought to him. He had taken a room close by, and he brought clothes with him and also a mask.

" Thus, madame," he said through the door, " I shall not see you if you so desire."

The idea of the mask pleased the young Spanish woman, distracting her from her deep melancholy.

" You are so generous," she said, without opening the door, " that I will be bold enough to beg you to leave the parcel of clothing outside. When I hear you descend, I will take it."

" Adieu, madame," said Lieven, going away.

Leonora was so charmed by the promptitude with which he obeyed her that she said to him in almost the tones of the most tender friendship, " If you can, sir, come back in half an hour."

When he returned, Lieven found her masked ; but he saw she had lovely arms, a beautiful neck and delicate hands. He was delighted. He was a young man of good birth, who still had need to force himself to act with courage with women he loved. His tone was respectful, and he did the honours of his poor little room with such grace, that, turning round after having arranged the screen, he stood motionless with admiration before the most beautiful woman he had ever met. The foreign lady had taken off her mask. She had black eyes that seemed to speak. There was so much energy in them that they might have appeared hard in the ordinary circumstances of life. Despair gave them a little sympathy, and nothing was wanting to the beauty of Leonora. Lieven thought she was from eighteen to twenty years of age. There was a moment of silence. In spite of her deep grief, Leonora could not help remarking with some pleasure the rapture of the young officer, who seemed to her to move in good society.

" You are my benefactor," she said at last to him, " and in spite of your age and mine, I hope you will continue to respect me."

Lieven answered as the most passionate lover can ; but he was sufficiently master of himself to refrain from the pleasure of saying he loved her. Besides, the eyes of Leonora were so impressive, and she had so distinguished an air, despite the poorness of the dress she had just put on, that he had less trouble in acting prudently.

" One might as well be a complete ass," he said to himself.

He gave himself up to his shyness and to the heavenly pleasure of looking at Leonora, without saying anything to her. He could not have done better. Little by little the beautiful Spanish woman regained her confidence. It was very droll, sitting opposite one another and staring silently.

" I must get a hat like that of a working woman," she said, " which will hide my face. For, unhappily," she added, almost laughing, " I cannot use your mask in the street."

Lieven found a hat, and then took Leonora to the room he had rented for her. She redoubled his agitation and almost his happiness by saying to him :

" All this may end for me on the gallows ! "

" To serve you," said Lieven, with the greatest impetuosity, " I would throw myself in the fire. I have taken this room in the name of Madame Lieven, my wife."

" Your wife ! " said the Spanish girl, almost angry.

" You had to appear under this name or show a passport. And we have no passport."

The " we " gave him a thrill of happiness. He had sold the ring, or at least he gave the lady a hundred francs as its value. Lunch was brought in. She asked him to be seated.

" You have shown yourself the most generous of men," she said after lunch. " If you like you can leave me now. My heart will preserve an eternal gratitude for you."

" I will obey you," said Lieven, rising.

There was the pain of death in his heart. The unknown lady was very thoughtful, then she said :

" Remain. You are very young, but I need help, and where shall I find a man as generous as you are ? Besides, if you have a feeling for me of which I am unworthy, the story of my faults will soon make me lose your esteem, and take away all your interest in the most criminal of women. For, sir, I have done great wrong. I can complain of no one, and least of all of my husband, Don Gutier Ferrandez. He is one of those unhappy Spaniards who sought a refuge in France two years ago. We are both of us from Carthagena. But he is very rich and I am very poor.

" ' I am thirty years older than you, my dear Leonora,' he said to me, on the eve of our marriage, ' but I have some millions of money and I love you to madness. Look at the matter and decide for yourself. If my age makes the marriage disagreeable to you I will make your people think I am responsible for breaking it off.'

" That was four years ago. I was fifteen. What I felt most keenly then was the profound poverty into which my family had fallen in the Revolution. I did not love him, but I accepted him. Sir, I have need of your advice, for I do not know the ways of this country nor your language, as you can see. Did I not need your help so badly, I could not support the shame that is killing me. Last night, when you saw me driven from a poor tenement, you must have thought it was a woman of evil reputation whom you were helping. Sir, I am still worse than that. I am the most criminal and also the most unhappy of women," added Leonora, bursting into tears. " One of these days you will perhaps see me brought before your judges, and I shall be condemned to some ignominious punishment. Scarcely was I married when Don Gutier began to be jealous. Ah, heavens ! it was then without grounds. But no doubt he saw I had a bad charcter. I was so foolish as to be irritated by my husband's suspicions. Ah, unhappy woman ! "

" No matter what your crimes are," said Lieven, interrupting her, " I am devoted to you to death. But if we are likely to be pursued by the police, tell me about it quickly, so that I can arrange for your flight without loss of time."

" Flight ! " she said to him. " How can I travel in France ? My Spanish accent, my youth, my agitation, will lead to my arrest by the first policeman who asks for my passport. Doubtless the police of Bordeaux are searching for me at this moment. My husband will have promised them handfuls of gold if they succeed in finding me. Leave me, sir, abandon me ! I will speak more boldly to you. I adore a man who is not my husband—and what a man ! He is a monster. You will despise him. Yet he has only to send me a kind word, and I will fall, I will not say into his arms, but at his feet. In the depths of shame in which I find myself, I do not want at least to deceive my benefactor. I am an unhappy woman, sir, who admires you, who is very grateful to you, but never can I love you."

Lieven became very sad.

" Do not mistake my sudden grief, madame," he said in a feeble voice, " for an intention to leave you. I am thinking how you can avoid the pursuit of the police. Perhaps the best way is to remain concealed in Bordeaux. Later I can arrange for you to take the place of a woman of your age for whom I will book a passage on some ship."

The light died out of Lieven's eyes as he finished speaking.

"Don Gutier Ferrandez," continued Leonora, "became suspect to the party that tyrannises over Spain. He used to go for pleasure-trips on the sea. One day we found in the offing a French brig. We went on board, leaving behind all our property in Carthagena. My husband is still very rich. He has taken a fine mansion at Bordeaux and started in business again. But we live absolutely alone. He will not let me mix in French society. During the last year especially, under the pretext of political difficulties with the Liberals, I have not been allowed to pay two visits anywhere. My husband is the most generous of men, but he suspects all the world and takes a gloomy view of everything.

"Unhappily, he yielded a few months ago at my desire to have a box at the theatre. He chose the worst, and took a box just by the stage, so as not to expose me to the glances of the young men of the town. A troop of Neapolitan riders had just come to Bordeaux. . . . Ah! sir, how you are going to despise me!"

"Madame," replied Lieven, "I am listening to you with attention, but I think only of my misfortune. Your love is fixed for ever on a happier man."

"No doubt you have heard of the famous Mayral?" said Leonora, lowering her eyes.

"The Spanish circus-rider! Yes, all Bordeaux went to see him. He is a very smart, handsome chap."

"Alas! sir, I thought he was a man out of the common. He always looked at me as he rode. One day, passing under my box, from which my husband had just gone, he said, in Catalanian:

"'I am a captain in the army of the Marquesito and I adore you.'

"To be loved by a circus-rider! How shameful, sir! And it was still more shameful that I could think of it without shame. For some days I did not go to the show. I was very unhappy. One morning my chambermaid said to me: 'Senor Ferrandez has gone out; I beg you, madame, to read this letter.' And she hastened away, locking the door behind her. It was a love-letter from Mayral. He told me the story of his life, saying he was a poor officer forced by the direst need into a way of life that he offered to abandon for me. His true name was Don Roderigue Pimentel. I returned to the show. Little by little I believed in the misfortunes of Mayral: I received his letters with pleasure. Alas! I ended by answering them. I loved him with passion—a passion," she said, breaking again into tears, "that nothing can extinguish, not even the saddest of discoveries. I desired as much as he did an opportunity to speak to him. Yet I soon suspected that he was no Pimentel or officer of the army of the Marquesito. He had no pride, and I sometimes saw he was afraid I would laugh at him for being merely a circus-rider in a troop of acrobats.

"About two months ago, as we were starting for the show, my husband received the news that one of his ships had been wrecked near Royan.

"'I must go and see it to-morrow,' he said.

"This was unlike him, for usually he did not speak ten words a day. At the show, I gave Mayral a signal we had agreed upon, and while my husband was in the box, Mayral went to our house and took a letter I had left with our porter's wife. I saw Mayral return full of joy. I had had the weakness to write to him that I would see him the next night in the hall by the garden.

"My husband left at noon. It was splendid weather, and the heat was very great. In the evening, I said I would sleep in my husband's room, which was on the ground floor by the garden. At one in the morning, having opened the window, I was waiting for Mayral, when there was a sudden noise at the door. It was my husband. Half way on the road to Royan he had seen his ship quietly sailing up the Gironde towards Bordeaux.

"In entering, Don Gutier did not perceive my dreadful anxiety. He praised my idea of finding a cool room to sleep in, and lay down by my side. Think of my disquietude! Unhappily, the moonlight was very clear. Less than an hour afterwards, I saw Mayral come to the window. After the return of my husband, I had not thought of closing the glass door of the study next to the bedroom. It was wide open, and so was the door that led from the study into the room.

"In vain I tried, by movements of my head, to make Mayral understand that something had happened. I heard him enter the study, and he was soon close to the bed. Think of my terror! Everything could be seen as clearly as in daylight. Happily Mayral did not speak as he drew near.

"I showed him my husband sleeping by my side. He drew a dagger. Horrified, I half raised myself. He leaned over and said in my ear:

"'I see I come at an awkward hour. You may have found it pleasant to make a fool of a poor circus-rider, but this handsome gentleman is going to have a bad time.'

"'This is my husband,' I whispered, while with all my strength I held his hand.

"'I saw your husband go on the steamer to Royan this morning! An acrobat isn't such a fool as to believe that. Come and speak to me in the next room. I insist!—otherwise I will wake this fine gentleman. I am stronger and quicker and better armed, and I will show him that it is not good to jest with me. I want you, and he shall not have you'

"At this moment my husband awoke."

" ' Who is that speaking ? ' he cried, greatly disturbed.

" Mayral, who was holding me and speaking in my ear, lowered himself quickly. I stretched out my arm as though my husband's words had aroused me : I said several things to him that made Mayral clearly see it was my husband. At last Don Gutier, thinking he had been disturbed by a dream, went to sleep again. The blade of Mayral's dagger continued to gleam in the rays of the moon, which were now shining straight on the bed. I promised Mayral all he wanted, and at the end of an hour he went away.

" Will you believe me, sir, when I tell you that though the foolish action of Mayral made me see what sort of man he was, my passion for him did not diminish ? My husband, never going into society, passed all his time with me. Nothing was more difficult than the second interview that I had sworn to Mayral I would grant him. He wrote letters full of reproaches, and at the theatre he would not look at me. At last, sir, my fatal love carried me completely away.

" ' Come from the Exchange, when you see my husband there.' I wrote to him, ' I will hide you. Then if by any chance I get a moment of freedom I will see you ; and if my husband goes to the Exchange to-morrow, you can see me. Is not this a proof of my love and the injustice of your suspicions ? Think what I am exposing myself to ! '

" He replied that he always feared I should choose some one in good society, and make a fool of the poor Italian acrobat. One of his comrades had told some absurd tale about the matter. Eight days afterwards, my husband went to the Exchange ; Mayral came to me in broad daylight, climbing the garden wall. We had scarcely been three minutes together when my husband returned. Mayral went into my dressing-room ; but Don Gutier had only come back for some papers. Unfortunately, he had also a bag with some valuables. In an idle fit, he would not go down to his strong room, but put the gold in one of my chests in the dressing-room, and locked it, and for extra precaution, as he is very suspicious, he took away the key of my room. Mayral was furious. I could only speak to him through the door.

" My husband soon returned. After dinner, he compelled me to go out for a walk. He wanted to go to the theatre, and it was very late when we got home. All the doors of the house were closed with great care every evening, and my husband took all the keys. It was by the greatest hazard in the world that, profiting by my husband's first sleep, I managed to let Mayral out of the room. I got him into a little attic under the roof. It was impossible to let him out through the garden. Balls of wool had been stretched over it, and two or three porters were set on watch. Myral passed all the following day in the attic. Think of what I suffered ! Every instant I fancied I saw him coming down, dagger in hand, to murder my husband. He was capable of anything. The least noise in the house startled me.

"To crown my unhappiness, my husband did not go to the Exchange. At last, without having been able to speak for a minute to Mayral, I was able to let him escape through the garden, by giving each of the porters something to do. In passing, he broke the great mirror of the drawing-room with the handle of his dagger. He was furious.

"Here, sir, you will despise me as much as I despise myself. From this moment, I see now, Mayral loved me no longer. He thought I had made a fool of him. My husband was still very fond of me. Several times that day he kissed me and took me in his arms. Mayral, sick with pride rather than with love, fancied I had concealed him so that he could see these transports.

"He would not answer my letters; he would not even look at me at the show. You must be growing tired, sir, of this tale of infamies. Here is the worst and the most dastardly. It is eight days since the Neapolitan troop of riders announced its departure. Last Monday, mad with love for a man who for three weeks had not replied to my letters or looked at me, I left the house of the best of husbands, and, sir, in going away, I, who had brought as dowry only an unfaithful heart—I took the diamonds he gave me, and from his coffer I stole three or four rolls of five hundred francs, thinking that Mayral would be suspected at Bordeaux if he tried to sell diamonds."

At this part of her story, Leonora blushed deeply. Lieven was pale and desperate. Each word of Leonora's pierced his heart, and yet through the frightful perversity of his character, redoubled the passion that burnt in him. Beside himself, he took the hand of Donna Leonora, and she did not draw it away.

"What baseness it is in me," said Lieven to himself, "to play with her hand while she openly speaks to me of her love for another man. Only from disdain or absent-mindedness she lets me do it. I am the least delicate of men."

"Last Sunday, sir," continued Leonora, "towards two in the morning, after drugging my husband and the porter with laudanum, I fled. I came and knocked at the door of the house from which I was escaping when you passed. It is Mayral's.

"'Now will you believe I love you?' I said to him.

"I was wild with happiness. He seemed to me, even from the first, more astonished than loving. The next morning, when I showed him my diamonds and my gold, he resolved to leave the troop and fly with me to Spain. But heavens! I saw from his ignorance of the ways of my country, he was not a Spaniard. I was uniting myself for ever to a circus-rider! 'Well? What did it matter,' I thought, 'so long as he loves me? I feel he is the master

of my life. I shall be his servant, his faithful mate. He will follow
his trade. I am young, and if needs be, I will learn trick-riding.
If we fall in poverty in our old age, well ! in twenty years, I can die
by his side. I shall have nothing to complain of. I shall have had my
happiness.' What a mad fool I was ! " she said, interrupting herself.

" It must be admitted you were dying of weariness with your old
husband," said Lieven. " He would not let you mix with people of
your own position. This justifies you in my eyes. You were
nineteen and he was fifty-nine. How many wives live in high honour
in my country who have really done worse things than you, and have
none of your generous remorse ! "

Several phrases of this sort seemed to lighten the grief of Leonora.

" Sir," she continued, " I spent three days with Mayral. Yesterday evening he said to me :

" ' As the police may come and search my house, I will go and
deposit your gold and jewels with a good friend.'

" At one o'clock in the morning, when I was frightened to death
thinking he had fallen off his horse, he came in, gave me a kiss and
soon left the room again. Happily I used a light, though he forbade
me to do so. Some long time afterwards, as I was sleeping, a man
got in the bed. I knew at once it was not Mayral. I took a dagger,
and the coward was afraid and threw himself at my knees begging
for mercy.

" ' There's the guillotine for you if you touch me ! " he said.

" The baseness of the appeal shocked me. With what people had
I compromised myself ! I had the presence of mind to tell the man
I had relatives in Bordeaux, and that I would have him arrested
if he did not speak all the truth.

" ' Well,' he said, ' I have not stolen any of your gold or your
diamonds. Mayral has left Bordeaux with all the spoil. He has
gone off with the wife of our manager. He gave him twenty-five of
your fine louis to get the woman. He has given me two louis, and
there they are, unless you like to let me keep them. He gave me the
money to keep you here as long as possible, so that he could get
twenty or thirty hours' start.'

" ' Is he Spanish ? ' I asked.

" ' Spanish ? Him ? He comes from San Domingo, and he fled
from there after robbing and murdering his master.'

" ' Why did he come back this evening ? ' I said. ' Answer, or
my uncle will send you to the galleys ! '

" ' I hesitated to come here and keep you from going out. Mayral
said you were beautiful. He said it would be easy to take his
place, and it would avenge him for some trick you had played on
him. Then, as I still did not dare to, he brought the postchaise to
the door, and came up to kiss you, getting me to hide on the other
side of the bed.' "

Leonora's voice was stopped by sobs.

"The young acrobat who was with me," she went on, "was frightened, and gave me true and desolating information about Mayral. I was in despair. 'Perhaps he made me drink a philtre,' I said to myself, 'for I cannot hate him.' Amid all his infamies, sir, I cannot hate him. I feel I adore him!"

Donna Leonora stopped and remained thoughtful.

"Strangely blind!" said Lieven to himself. "A woman with such intelligence and believes in witchcraft!"

"At last," said Leonora, "the young man, seeing I was sunk in thought, began to be less afraid. He left me, and came back with one of his comrades. I was obliged to defend myself. The struggle was serious. Perhaps they wished to take my life. Finally I gained the door; but if you, sir, had not been there, they would probably have pursued me down the street."

The more Lieven saw Leonora maddened with love for Mayral, the more he adored her. She wept, and he kissed her hand. As he was speaking in veiled words of his love:

"Do you believe me, my true friend," she said to him, several days afterwards, "but I think if I could prove to Mayral that I had never tried to make him a dupe or play with him, perhaps he would love me?"

"I haven't much money," said Lieven. "I gamble out of boredom. But may be the banker at Bordeaux, to whom my father recommended me, will not refuse me fifteen or twenty louis. I will do all I can to get it. Do anything! With this money you can go to Paris."

Leonora flung her arms round his neck.

"My God! Why can't I love you? What! You will forgive my horrible folly?"

"To such a point that I would marry you with rapture, and pass my life with you, the happiest of men!"

"But if I meet Mayral, I feel myself weak and criminal enough to leave you, my benefactor, and fall at his feet."

Lieven reddened with anger.

"The only cure for me is to kill myself," he said, covering her with kisses.

"Ah! do not kill yourself, my friend," said Leonora.

He was never seen again. Leonora has entered the convent of the Ursulines.

THE JEW

STENDHAL

" I WAS then a very handsome man."

" But you are still remarkably striking."

" With what a difference ! I am forty-five. Then I was only thirty. It was in 1814. All I had were an uncommon figure and a rare beauty. For the rest I was a Jew, despised by you Christians, and by Jews as well. For I had been for a long time excessively poor."

" Men are very wrong in despising——"

" Don't put yourself to the cost of finding pretty phrases. This evening I feel disposed to talk, and when I do talk I am sincere. Our ship is going well ; the breeze is delightful ; to-morrow morning we shall be in Venice. . . . But to come back to the story of the curse about which we were speaking, and of my travels in France in 1814. I was very fond of money in 1814. It is the only passion I have ever known in myself.

" I spent my days in the streets of Venice with a little box, on the top of which some golden jewels were displayed ; but in a secret drawer I had cotton stockings, handkerchiefs, and other contraband English goods. One of my uncles, after the burial of my father, said to each of us—we were three—that there remained a capital only of five francs. This good uncle gave me a napoleon—twenty francs. In the night my mother decamped with twenty-one francs ; that left me only four francs. I stole from one of the neighbours a violin-case I knew she had put in the garret. I went and bought eight handkerchiefs of red cotton. They cost me ten sous ; I sold them for eleven. The first day I sold out all my stock four times. I hawked my handkerchiefs among the sailors by the arsenal. The merchant, astonished by my activity, asked me why I did not buy my goods by the dozen. It was a good half a league from his shop to the arsenal. I told him I only had four francs in the world, that my mother had stolen twenty-one francs from me. He gave me a very hard kick that lifted me out of the shop.

" Still, the next day I was back again. I had already sold the eight handkerchiefs the evening before. As it was a warm night I slept out of doors. I had lived, I had drunk Chio wine, and I had saved five sous out of my trade. That was the life I led from 1800 to 1814. I seemed to work under the blessing of God."

The Jew uncovered himself with a tender air.

"I was so good at the trade that several times I doubled my capital in a single day. Often I took a gondola and went to sell stockings to sailors on the ships. But, as soon as I had put by a little money, my mother and my sister found a pretext for making friends with me again, and robbing me. Once they took me to a jeweller's shop, put on a necklace and earrings, and went out, as for a moment, and never came back. The jeweller wanted fifty francs from me. I began to weep. I had only fourteen francs on me. I told him where my box was. He sent for it; but, while I was wasting time at the jeweller's, my mother had also gone off with the box. The jeweller gave me a good thrashing.

"When he was tired of beating me, I explained to him that if he would give me back my fourteen francs and lend me a little table drawer, in which I could fix a double bottom, I could certainly pay him back ten sous a day. And this is what I did. The jeweller ended by trusting me with earrings worth twenty francs; but he never allowed me to gain more than five sous on each piece.

"In 1805 I had a capital of a thousand francs. Then I considered that our law orders us to marry, and I thought of accomplishing my duty. I had the misfortune to fall in love with a Jewish girl named Stella. She had two brothers; one of them was quartermaster-sergeant among the French troops, and the other cashier at the paymaster's. They often pushed her at night out of the room they occupied in common, on the ground-floor on the side of San Paolo. I found her there one evening, weeping. Mistaking what she was, I offered to buy her ten sous' worth of Chio wine. Her tears increased. Telling her she was a fool, I walked on.

"But she struck me as very pretty. Next night, at the same hour—ten—my sales in Saint Mark's Place were finished, and I passed by the spot where I had met her. She was not there. Three days afterwards I was luckier. I had a long talk with her. She refused me with horror.

"'She has seen me go by with my box filled with jewels,' I thought. 'She wants me to make her a present of one of my necklaces, and that's what I won't do!'

"I resolved not to take the street any more. But in spite of myself, and almost without admitting it, I gave up drinking wine, and each day I set apart the money I thus saved. I was still more foolish not to use this money in trade. In that time, sir, I tripled my capital every week.

"When I had saved twelve francs—the price of my cheapest necklaces—I went several times down the street where Stella lived. At last I saw her. She rejected my gallant advances with indignation. In our talk I told her I had stopped drinking wine for three months to save the cost of one of my necklaces and offer it to her.

She did not reply, but asked my advice on a misfortune that had happened to her since she last saw me.

" Her brothers worked together at clipping any golden coins they could procure. (They plunged the sequins and napoleons in a bath of *aqua fortis*.) The quartermaster-sergeant had been put in prison ; and for fear of rousing suspicions, the cashier at the paymaster's would not take any steps to help him. Stella did not ask me to go to the citadel ; and for my part I never mentioned the place, but I begged her to wait for me the next evening. . . ."

" But we are still very far," I said, " from the curse that overcame you in France."

" You are right," said the Jew, " but I promise to finish in a few words the story of my marriage, or be silent. I don't know why I like to talk to-day of Stella.

" At some trouble, I got the quartermaster brother out of prison. They gave me the hand of their sister, and brought their father to Venice—a poor Jew of Innsbruck. I had rented some rooms, happily paid in advance, and had collected some bits of furniture there. My father-in-law went among all his relatives in the city announcing he was marrying his daughter. At last, after a year of anxieties, on the eve of the marriage, he made off with six hundred francs he had collected from his relatives. We were going, his daughter and he and I, to eat a salad at Murano. That was when he disappeared. Meanwhile, my two brothers-in-law stole every bit of the furniture in my room, and unfortunately the stuff was not all paid for.

" My credit was ruined. My brothers-in-law, whom folks had always seen with me, had told the merchants with whom I dealt that I was at Chiozzia, where I was selling anything I wanted. In a word, by all kinds of trickeries, they had stolen more than two hundred francs. I saw it was necessary to fly from Venice. I placed Stella as nursemaid with the jeweller who had trusted me with the necklaces. Early the next morning, having given Stella twenty francs, keeping only six myself, I fled.

" Never had I been so ruined. For I now seemed a thief. Happily, in my despair, I had the idea, on reaching Padua, to write the truth to the merchants of Venice from whom my wife's brothers had taken the goods. I learned next day there was an order out for my arrest, and the police of the kingdom of Italy were not to be trifled with.

" A famous lawyer of Padua had become blind. He wanted a valet to lead him about, but his misfortune made him so ill-tempered that he never kept a man more than a month. But I wagered with myself that I would not be driven out of his house. I entered his service, and the next day, as he was bored that nobody came to see him, I told him my story.

" ' If you do not protect me,' I said, ' I shall be arrested one of these days.'

" ' Arrest one of my servants ! ' he exclaimed, ' I should soon stop that ! '

" At last, sir, I won his favour. He went to bed early, and I obtained permission to do a little trade in the cafés of Padua, from eight o'clock, when he went to bed, to two o'clock in the morning, when the rich people left the cafés.

" I made two hundred francs in eighteen months. I asked to go. He told me that in his will he was leaving me a considerable sum of money, but that I must never leave his house.

" ' In that case,' I thought, ' why did you let me trade ? '

" I decamped. I paid my creditors at Venice. This brought me much honour. I married Stella. I taught her to trade. Now she can sell better than I can. At last I come to the story of my travels, and after that to the curse.

" I had more than a hundred louis capital. I must tell you the story of a new reconciliation with my mother, who stole from me again, and then got my sister to rob me. So I left Venice, seeing that, as long as I was there, I should be the dupe of my family. I settled at Zara, where I got on wonderfully. A Croatian captain, whom I had furnished with part of the clothes of his regiment, said to me one day :

" ' Filippo ! do you want to make a fortune ? We are going to France. Learn one thing ; that is, without seeming to be, I am the friend of Baron Bradal, the colonel of the regiment. Come with us as sutler. You will earn a good deal. But this business will only be a pretext. The colonel, with whom I seem to be on bad terms, has given me all the provisioning of the regiment. I want an intelligent man. You will suit me.'

" Now, you see, sir, I did not love my wife any more."

" What ! Poor Stella, to whom you had been so faithful ? "

" The fact is, sir, I loved nothing but money. Ah, I was very fond of that ! "

I began to laugh ; there was such true passion in his exclamation.

" I was made sutler to the regiment. I left Zara. After a march of forty-eight days we reached the Simplon. The five hundred francs I had brought with me had become already fifteen hundred francs, and besides I had a pretty covered cart and two horses. At the Simplon our sufferings began. I almost lost my life. I spent more than twenty-two nights sleeping in the open air in the cold."

" Ah," I said, " you were compelled to bivouac ! "

" I made each day fifty to sixty francs, but every night I was in danger of being frozen. At last the army got over the frightful mountain, and we arrived at Lausanne. There I entered into part-nership with Monsieur Perrin. Ah, the worthy man ! He was

a brandy merchant. I knew how to sell in six different languages,
while he was good at buying. Ah, the excellent man ! Only he
was too violent. When a Cossack would not pay for his drink, if
he was alone in the shop, Perrin thrashed him till he bled.

" ' But my friend,' I used to say to him, ' we are making a hundred francs a day. What does it matter if a drunkard does us out
of a couple of francs ? '

" ' I cannot help it,' he answered ; ' I do not like Cossacks.'

" ' You will get us murdered. Then, Monsieur Perrin, it will be
better to end our partnership.'

" The French vivandiers would not venture in our camp, for
no one paid them. We did splendid business. On reaching Lyons
we had fourteen thousand francs in our coffers. There, out of pity
for the poor French merchants, I went in for smuggling. There
was a great deal of tobacco outside Saint Clair gate. They came
and begged me to get it into the town. I told them to be patient
for a couple of days, until my friend the colonel was in command.
Then for five days I filled my covered cart with tobacco. The
Frenchmen at the gate grumbled, but did not dare to arrest me.
On the fifth day, one of them, who was drunk, attacked me. I
whipped on my horse, but the others stopped me. I was bleeding
all over, and demanded I should be led before the commander of
the guard. He belonged to our regiment, but would not recognise
me, and sent me to prison. While going to prison I gave two crowns
to my escort to lead me before my colonel. In the presence of the
soldiers he treated me very harshly and threatened to hang me.
As soon as we were alone he said :

" ' Cheer up ! to-morrow I will put another officer at the gate.
Instead of one cart, bring in two.'

" But I would not. I gave him two hundred sequins.

" ' What ! ' he said to me, ' do you take such a lot of trouble for
nothing ? '

" ' I am sorry for the poor merchants,' I replied.

" Our affairs—Perrin's and mine—went admirably as far as
Dijon. There, sir, in one night we lost more than twelve thousand
francs. The sales had been splendid. It was a grand review, and
we were the only vivandiers. We had a net gain of more than a
thousand francs. At midnight, when everybody was sleeping,
a cursed Croatian would not pay up. Perrin, seeing he was alone,
overwhelmed him with blows, and covered him with blood.

" ' You are mad,' I said. ' It is true this man has drunk six
francs' worth ; but if he has the strength to use his voice there will
be a row.'

" The Croatian tumbled like a dead man out of our shop, but he
was only stupefied. He began to shout. Some soldiers, bivouacking
close by, came up, and, finding him covered with blood, broke in

our door. Perrin tried to defend himself, and got eight sabre
wounds.

"'I am not guilty,' I said to the soldiers. 'He did it. Take me
to your colonel!'

"'We will not wake the colonel for you,' said one of the soldiers.

"In spite of my efforts, our unhappy shop was attacked by some
thousands of soldiers. The officers outside the mob could not get
through and use their authority. I thought that Perrin was dead:
I was in a pitiable condition myself. At last, sir, they pillaged us
of more than twelve hundred francs' worth of wine and brandy.

"At daybreak, I succeeded in escaping. My colonel gave me four
men to rescue Perrin if he were still alive. I found him in a guard-
room, and took him to a surgeon.

"'We must separate, my friend,' I said. 'You will end in getting
me killed.'

"But he insisted so much, that we started a second partnership,
paying some soldiers to guard our shop. In two months we made
twelve thousand francs each. Unhappily, Perrin killed in a duel one
of the soldiers who were guarding us.

"'You will get me killed,' I repeated, and I left him.

"I went to Lyons, where I bought watches and diamonds, which
were then cheap. For I am well up in all sorts of business. If you
dropped me into any country, with fifty francs in my pocket, in six
months I would have lived well and tripled my capital. I hid my
diamonds in a secret place I made in my cart. The regiment having
left for Valence and Avignon, I followed it after staying three days
in Lyons.

"But, sir, when I got to Valence at eight in the evening, it was
raining and dark. I knocked at the door of an inn. I was told there
was no room for a Cossack. I knocked again. They flung stones at
me from the upper window.

"'It is clear,' I said to myself, 'I shall die to-night in this accursed
town.'

"No one would answer: and no one would act as guide. I saw
that if I did not want to die, I should have to sacrifice some of my
goods. I gave a glass of brandy to the sentry. He was a Hungarian.
Hearing me speak his language, he took pity on me, and told me to
wait until he was relieved. I was perishing with cold: at last his
relief came. I treated the corporal and all the men, and they led me
to the commander. Ah, what a gentleman, sir! He called me in at
once. I explained to him that, out of hatred to the king, no inn-
keeper would give me a night's lodging for any money.

"'Very well,' he cried, 'they shall lodge you for nothing.'

"He gave me a fine billet for two nights, and four men were told
off to accompany me. I returned to the inn, where they had thrown
stones at me. I knocked twice. I said, in French, I had four men

with me, and we would break in the door if it were not opened. No answer. We found a great piece of wood and began to break down the door. It was half broken through when a man opened it angrily. He was a tall fellow—six feet high—with a sabre in one hand and a candle in the other. I thought there was going to be a row and my cart would be pillaged. So, though I had a lodging billet, I cried :

" ' I will pay in advance, sir, if you like.'

" ' Ah, it is you, Filippo ! ' cried the man, lowering his sabre and embracing me. ' What : don't you remember Bonnard, corporal of the twentieth regiment ? '

" I embraced him in turn, and sent the soldiers away. Bonnard had lodged with my father for six months at Vicenza.

" ' I am dying of hunger,' I said. ' For three days I have been wandering about Valence.'

" ' I will awaken my servant and soon get you a good supper.'

" He embraced me again, and was never tired of looking at me and questioning me. I went with him to the cellar, from which he brought an excellent wine that he kept in sand. As we were drinking while waiting for supper, a tall handsome girl of eighteen came in.

" ' Ah, you have got up ! ' said Bonnard. ' So much the better. Friend, this is my sister ! You must marry her ! You are a nice boy, and I will give her a dowry of six hundred francs.

" ' I am married already,' I said to him. ' I have a wife at Zara, where she is in business.'

" ' Let her go to the devil, with her business. Settle yourself in France—and marry the prettiest girl in the town.'

" Catherine was really very pretty. She looked at me in wonder.

" ' You are an officer ? ' she said, deceived by a fine pelisse bought at the review at Dijon.

" ' No, mademoiselle, I am a vivandier to the army, and I have made two hundred louis. I assure you there are not many of our officers with that money.' I had more than six hundred louis, but I am always very prudent.

" At last, will you believe it, sir ? Bonnard would not let me go any farther. He rented for me a little shop by the side of the guard-room, near the gate, where I did business with our soldiers. And though I did not follow the army any longer, there were days when I still made my ten francs. Bonnard was always saying to me : ' You must marry my sister.' Little by little Catherine got into the habit of coming to my little shop, and spending three or four hours there. At last, sir, I got madly in love with her. She was still more in love with me. But by God's grace we did not lose our senses.

" ' How can you want me to marry you ? ' I said to her. ' I am married.'

" ' Haven't you left your Italian wife all your stock ? Let her live on it at Zara, and you stay with us. Go into partnership with my brother, or keep your own business on. You are doing well and you will still do better.'

"I must tell you, sir, I was going in for banking business at Valence, and by buying good bills on Lyons, signed by men whom Bonnard knew, I sometimes made a hundred or a hundred and twenty francs a week in this way alone. So I remained in Valence until the autumn. I did not know what to do. I was dying to marry Catherine, and I had given her a dress and a hat from Lyons. When we went out walking together, her brother, she and I, everybody had their eyes on Catherine. She was really the most beautiful girl I have seen in my life.

"'If you will not marry me,' she would often say, 'I will be your servant. Only you must never leave me.'

"She went ahead of me to my shop, to save me the trouble of opening it. At last, sir, I was absolutely mad in love with her, and she was the same as regards me, but we were always good. At the end of autumn the allies left Valence.

"'The inn-keepers of this town might murder me,' I said to Bonnard. 'They know I have made some money here.'

"'Go if you will,' said Bonnard with a sigh. 'We will not force anybody. But if you will stay and marry my sister, I will give her half of my property, and if any one says anything about you, leave him to me.'

"Three times I put off the day of my departure. The last troops of the rear-guard were already at Lyons when I resolved to go. We spent the night weeping, Catherine, her brother, and myself. You see, sir, I lost my happiness by not remaining with this family. God would not permit me to be happy!

"At last I set off, the 7th of November 1814. I shall never forget that day. I could not guide my cart. I was obliged to engage a driver half-way between Valence and Vienne. The day after my departure, as I was harnessing my horse at Vienne, who should arrive at the inn?—Catherine! She at once folded me in her arms. She was known in the inn, and she pretended to have come to see an aunt of hers in the town.

"'I want to go with you as your servant,' she repeated, the tears rolling down her face. 'If you will not take me, I will throw myself in the Rhône.'

"All the people in the inn gathered round us. Catherine, who was as a rule so reserved and never said anything, talked and wept without restraint, and kissed me before them all. I got her quickly on my cart and drove away. A quarter of a league from the town I stopped.

"'Here we must say good-bye,' I said to her.

"She never spoke, and clutched her head in her hands with

29

convulsive movements. I was afraid. I saw she would throw
herself in the river, if I sent her back.

"'But I am married,' I repeated to her. 'Married before God,'
I said.

"'I know it quite well. I will be your servant.'

"Ten times I stopped my cart between Vienne and Lyons: but
she would not consent to leave me.

"'If I pass the bridge of the Rhône with her,' I said to myself,
'it will be the sign of the will of God.'

"At last, sir, without noticing it, I passed the bridge and reached
Lyons. At the inn they took us for husband and wife, and gave us
a single room. I started to trade in watches and diamonds, and
made ten francs a day; and, thanks to the admirable housekeeping
of Catherine, we lived on less than four. I took some rooms, which
we furnished very well. I then possessed thirteen thousand francs,
which in the banking business brought me in about eighteen
hundred francs. Never have I been so rich as in the year and a half
spent with Catherine. I was so rich that I bought a little pleasure-
carriage, and every Sunday we went for excursions outside the
town.

"A Jew of my acquaintance came to see me one day, and got me
to take him in my carriage some way from Lyons. There he said
suddenly to me:

"'Filippo, you have a wife and a son! they are unhappy.'

"Then he gave me a letter from my wife, and disappeared.
I came back alone to Lyons. The letter from my wife was filled
with reproaches that touched me much less than the idea of my
abandoned son. I saw from the letter that the business at Zara
was going on fairly well . . . but to abandon my son! The idea
hurt me.

"All that evening I did not speak. Catherine remarked it, but
she had such a good heart! Three weeks went by without her
asking me the reason of my sadness.

"'I have a son,' I said, when she at last spoke.

"'I guessed it,' she said to me. 'Let us go. I will be your
servant at Zara.'

"'Impossible. My wife knows everything. Look at her letter.'

"Catherine blushed very much at the insults my wife addressed
to her, at the tone of scorn with which, without knowing her, my
wife spoke of her. I embraced her, and did all I could to console
her, but, sir, the three months I spent at Lyons after that fatal
letter were hellish. I could not come to a decision.

"'If I set off at once!' I said to myself one night, with Catherine
sleeping by my side. As soon as the idea struck me, I felt a balm
spreading through my soul. 'It must be an inspiration from God!'
I said to myself. But then, as I looked at Catherine, I began to

say : ' What madness ! I cannot do that.'

" So the grace of God abandoned me, and I fell back into my bitter sorrowful mood. Without knowing what I did, I began to dress quietly, my eyes always fixed on Catherine. All my wealth was hidden in the bed. There were five hundred francs in a desk, for a payment she had to pay for a debt in my absence. I took this money ; I went to the coach-house where my cart was kept ; I hired a horse, and set off.

" At every moment I turned my head. ' Catherine will follow me,' I said to myself. ' If I see her, I am lost.'

" To get a little peace, I took the coach two leagues from Lyons. In my trouble I arranged with a carter to take my cart to chambéry : I evidently had no need of it. I can't remember any more what determined my actions. I felt all the bitterness of my loss on reaching Chambéry. I went to a notary and made a deed of gift of all my property at Lyons to Madame Catherine Bonnard, my wife. I thought of her honour, and of the gossip of neighbours.

" After the notary was paid and I came outside with my deed, I felt I should never have the strength to write to Catherine. I returned to the notary : he wrote a letter to her in my name, and one of his clerks came to the post and sent the letter off in my presence. In a dark tavern, I also had a letter written to Bonnard in Valence. He was informed in my name of the deed of gift, that amounted at least to thirteen thousand francs. He was also told that his sister was lying very ill at Lyons, and was expecting him. I sent this letter off myself. Never since have I heard anything of them.

" I found my cart at the foot of Mont Cenis. I cannot recall why I stuck to this vehicle, which was the immediate cause of my misfortunes. The true cause was no doubt some terrible curse that Catherine launched against me. Lively and passionate as she was, young (she was then just twenty), beautiful, innocent, for she had had no weakness except for me whom she wished to serve and honour as her husband, her voice probably reached to God in a prayer for my severe punishment.

" I bought a passport and a horse. I do not know how I stopped to think at the foot of Mont Cenis that there was a frontier there. I had an idea of doing a little smuggling with my five hundred francs. I bought some watches, which I concealed. Passing proudly before the custom-house officers, I was called to stop. Having done so much smuggling in my life, I carried my head high. The custom-house men went straight to my hiding-place in the cart : probably I had been betrayed by the watchmakers. They took my watches, and fined me besides a hundred crowns. I gave them fifty francs ; they let me go.

" This misfortune shook me up. In a moment I was reduced

from five hundred francs to a hundred francs. I could sell the horse and the cart, but it was a long way from Mont Cenis to Zara. As I was tormented by these sinister thoughts, a custom-house man ran up to me crying :

"'Dog of a Jew, you must give me twenty francs ! The others have tricked me, and given me five francs instead of ten, and I have had all the trouble of catching up to you.'

"It was almost dark ; the man was drunk ; and he insulted me, and seized me by the collar. Satan tempted me, and I stabbed him with my knife, and flung him into the torrent twenty feet below the road. It was the first crime of my life, and I said to myself, 'I am done for !'

"Nearing Suze, I heard a noise behind me. I put my horse at the gallop. He got his head, and I was not able to hold him back : the cart upset, and I broke my leg.

"'Catherine has cursed me,' I thought. 'Heaven is just. I shall be recognised and hanged in two months.'

"But, as you see, nothing of the sort happened."

AUGUSTIN EUGÈNE SCRIBE
1791–1861

THE PRICE OF A LIFE

JOSEPH, opening the door of the salon, came to tell us that the post-chaise was ready. My mother and my sister threw themselves into my arms. "There is yet time," said they. "It is not too late. Give up this journey and remain with us." I replied: "Mother, I am a gentleman. I am twenty years old, my country needs me, I must win fame; be it in the army, be it at court, I must be heard of, men must speak of me."

"And when you are far away, tell me, Bernard, what will become of me, your old mother?"

"You will be happy and proud to hear of your son's successes——"

"And if you are killed in some battle?"

"What matters it? What is life? Only a dream. One dreams only of glory at twenty, and when one is a gentleman; but do not fear, you will see me return to you in a few years, a colonel, a general, or, better still, with a fine position at Versailles."

"Indeed! When will that be?"

"It will come, and I shall be respected and envied by all—and then—every one will take off his hat to me—and then—I will marry my cousin Henriette, and I will find good husbands for my sisters, and we shall all live together tranquil and happy on my estates in Britanny."

"Why not do all that to-day, my son? Has not your father left you the finest fortune in the country? Where is there, for ten leagues around, a richer domain, or a more beautiful château than that of Roche-Bernard? Are you not loved and respected by your vassals? When you walk through the village, is there a single one who fails to salute you and take off his hat? Do not leave us, my son; remain here with your friends, near your sisters, near your old mother, whom perhaps you will not find here when you return. Do not waste in search of vainglory or abridge by cares and torments of all kinds the days which already go so swiftly. Life is sweet, my child, and the sun of Britanny is so bright!"

So saying she led me to the open window and pointed to the

133

beautiful avenues of my park ; the grand old chestnut trees were
in full bloom, and the air was sweet with the fragrance of the lilacs
and the honeysuckles, whose leaves sparkled in the sunlight.

All the house-servants awaited me in the anteroom. They were
so sad and quiet that they seemed to say to me : " Do not go,
young master, do not go."

Hortense, my eldest sister, pressed me in her arms, and my little
sister Amélie, who was in one corner of the room occupied in looking
at some engravings in a volume of La Fontaine, came to me, and
handing me the book, cried : " Read, read, my brother ! " It was
the fable of " The Two Pigeons."

But I repulsed them all and said : " I am twenty years old.
Je suis gentilhomme. I *must* in honour and glory. Let me go."

And I hastened to the courtyard, and got into the post-chaise,
when a woman appeared at the landing of the stairs. It was my
beautiful cousin Henriette ! She did not weep, she did not say a
word—but, pale and trembling, she could scarcely stand. She
waved me an adieu with her white handkerchief, then fell unconscious. I ran to her, raised her, put my arms around her, and
swore to her eternal love ; and the moment she recovered consciousness, leaving her in my mother's care, I ran to the chaise, and,
without turning my head, drove away.

If I had looked at Henriette I might have wavered. A few
moments afterward we were rolling along the grand route.

For a long while I thought of nothing but Henriette, my mother,
and my sisters, and all the happiness I had left behind me ; but
these thoughts were effaced in the measure that the towers of
Roche-Bernard faded from my view, and soon ambitious dreams of
glory spread over my spirit. What projects ! What castles in the
air ! What glorious deeds I performed in that chaise ! Riches,
honours, dignities, rewards of all kinds ! I refused nothing.
I merited them, and I accepted all ; at last, elevating myself as
I advanced on my journey, I was duke—governor of a province—
and no less a personage than a marshal of France when I arrived
in the evening at my destination. The voice of my valet, who
addressed me modestly as Monsieur le Chevalier, forced me to
abdicate for the time being, and I was obliged to return to the
earth and to myself.

The following day I continued my journey and dreamed the same
dreams, for the way was long. At last we arrived at Sédan, where
I expected to visit the Duc de C——, an old friend of our family.
He would (I thought) surely take me with him to Paris, where he
was expected at the end of the month, and then he would present
me at Versailles, and obtain for me, at the very least, a company of
dragoons.

I arrived in Sédan in the evening—too late to present myself at

the château of my friend (which was some distance from the city),
so I delayed my visit until the next day, and put up at the " Armes
de France," the best hotel in the place.

I supped at the table d'hôte and asked the way to take on the
morrow to the château of the Duc de C——.

" Any one can show you," said a young officer who sat near me,
" for it is well known the whole country round. It was in this
château that died a great warrior, a very celebrated man—Maréchal
Fabert ! " Then the conversation fell, as was natural between
young military men, on the Maréchal Fabert. They spoke of his
battles, his exploits, of his modesty, which caused him to refuse
letters of nobility and the collar of his order offered him by Louis
XIV. Above all, they marvelled at the good fortune which comes
to some men. What inconceivable happiness for a simple soldier
to rise to the rank of maréchal of France—he, a man of no family,
the son of a printer ! They could cite no other case similar to his,
and the masses did not hesitate to ascribe his elevation to supernatural causes. It was said that he had employed magic from his
childhood, that he was a sorcerer, and that he had a compact with
the devil ; and our old landlord, who had all the credulity of our
Breton peasants, swore to us that in this château of the Duc de
C——, where Fabert died, there had frequently been seen a black
man whom no one knew ; and that the servants had seen him enter
Fabert's chamber and disappear, carrying with him the soul of the
maréchal, which he had bought some years before, and which,
therefore, belonged to him ; and that even now, in the month of
May, on the anniversary of Fabert's death, one can see at night a
black man bearing a light, which is Fabert's soul.

This story amused us at dessert, and we gaily drank a bottle of
champagne to the familiar demon of Fabert, praying for his
patronage, and help to gain victories like those of Collioure and of
La Marfée.

The next day I arose early and set out for the château, which
proved to be an immense Gothic manor-house, having nothing very
remarkable about it. At any other time I would not have veiwed
it with any great interest ; but now I gazed at it with feelings of
curiosity as I recalled the strange story told us by the landlord of
the " Armes de France."

The door was opened by an old valet, and when I told him I
wished to see the Duc de C——, he replied that he did not know
whether his master was visible or not, or if he would receive me.
I gave him my name and he went away, leaving me alone in a very
large and gloomy hall, decorated with trophies of the chase and
family portraits. I waited some time, but he did not return. The
silence was almost oppressive ; I began to grow impatient and had
already counted two or three times all the family portraits, and all

the beams in the ceiling, when I heard a noise in the wainscot.

It was a door which the wind had blown open. I looked up, and perceived a very pretty boudoir lighted by two great casements and a glass door which opened on a magnificent park. I advanced a few steps into the apartment, and paused suddenly at a strange spectacle. A man (his back was turned to the door through which I had entered) was lying on a couch. He arose, and, without perceiving me, ran quickly to the window. Tears rolled down his cheeks and profound despair was imprinted on his features. He remained some time immovable, his head resting on his hands, then he commenced to walk with great strides across the room ; turning, he saw me, stopped suddenly, and trembled. As for myself, I was horror-struck, and dazed in consequence of my indiscretion. I wished to retire, and murmured some incoherent apologies

" Who are you ? What do you want ? " said he, in a deep voice, catching me by the arm.

I was very much frightened and embarrassed, but replied : " I am the Chevalier Bernard de la Roche-Bernard, and I have just arrived from Brittany."

" I know ! I know ! " said he, and, throwing his arms around me, he embraced me warmly, and leading me to the couch made me sit near him, spoke to me rapidly of my father and of all my family, whom he knew so well that I concluded that it was the master of the château.

" You are Monsieur de C——, are you not ? " asked I. He arose, looked at me with a strange glance, and replied : " I was, but I am no longer. I am no longer anybody." Then seeing my astonishment he said : " Not a word, young man, do not question me."

I replied, blushing : " If, Monsieur, I have witnessed, without wishing it, your chagrin and your sorrow, perhaps my devotion and my friendship can assuage your grief ? "

" Yes, yes, you are right ; not that you can change my condition, but you can receive, at least, my last wishes and my last vows. It is the only service that I ask of you."

He crossed the room, then came and sat down beside me, who agitated and trembling, awaited his words. They were somewhat grave and solemn, and his physiognomy, above all, had an expression that I had never before seen. His lofty brow, which I examined attentively, seemed marked by fate. His complexion was very pale, and his eyes were black, bright, and piercing ; and from time to time his features, altered by suffering, contracted under an ironical and infernal smile.

" That which I am about to relate to you," said he, will confound your reason, you will doubt, you will not believe me, perhaps ; even I often doubt still. I tell myself it cannot be ; but the proofs are too real ; and are there not in all that surrounds us, in our organisation even, many other mysteries that we are obliged to submit to, without being able to comprehend ? "

He paused a moment, as if to gather together his thoughts, passed his hand over his brow, and continued : " I was born in this château. I had two elder brothers to whom fell the wealth and honours of our house. I had nothing to expect, nothing to look forward to but an abbé's mantle ; nevertheless, ambitious dreams of glory and power fermented in my head and made my heart throb with anticipation. Miserable in my obscurity, eager for renown, I thought only of means to acquire it at any price, and these ideas made me insensible to all the pleasures and all the sweetness of life. To me the present was nothing ; I only existed for the future, and this future presented itself to me under a most sombre aspect. I reached my thirtieth year without having accomplished anything ;—then there arose in the capital literary lights whose brilliance penetrated even to our remote province. Ah ! thought I, if I could at least make for myself a name in the world of letters, that might bring renown, and therein lies true happiness. I had for a confidant of my chagrins an old servant, an aged negro, who had served in my family many years before my birth ; he was the oldest person on the estate, or for miles around, for no one could recall his first appearance, and the country folk said that he had known the Maréchal Fabert, was present at his death, and that he was an evil spirit."

At that name, I started with surprise ; the unknown paused and asked me the cause of my embarrassment.

" Nothing," said I ; but I could not help thinking that the black man must be the one spoken of by the old landlord of the " Armes de France " the previous evening.

M. de C—— continued :

" One day in Yago's presence (that was the old negro's name) I gave way to my feelings, bemoaned my obscurity, and bewailed my useless and monotonous life, and I cried aloud in my despair : ' I would willingly give ten years of my life to be placed in the first rank of our authors ! '

" ' Ten years,' said Yago, coolly ; ' that is much, it is paying very dear for so little a thing ; no matter, I accept your ten years ; remember your promise, I will surely keep mine.'

" I cannot describe to you my great surprise on hearing him speak thus. I believed that his mind had become enfeebled by the weight of years. I shrugged my shoulders and smiled, and took no further notice of him. Some days afterward I left home for Paris. There I found myself launched into the society of men of letters ; their example encouraged and stimulated me, and I soon published several works that were very successful, which I will not now describe. All Paris rushed to see me, the journals were filled with my praises. The new name I had taken became celebrated, and even recently, young man, you have admired my works."

Here another gesture of surprise on my part interrupted this recital. "Then you are not the Duc de C——? " cried I.

"No," replied he, coldly. And I asked myself: "A celebrated man of letters! Is this Marmontel? is it D'Alembert? is it Voltaire? "

The unknown sighed, a smile of regret and contempt spread over his lips, and he continued his recital.

"This literary reputation, which had seemed to me so desirable, soon failed to satisfy a soul so ardent as mine. I aspired to still higher successes, and I said to Yago (who had followed me to Paris and who kept close watch over me): 'This is not real glory, there is no veritable renown but that which one acquires in the career of arms. What is an author, a poet? Nothing! Give me a great general, or a captain in the army! Behold the destiny that I desire, and for a great military reputation I would willingly give ten more years of my life.'

"'I accept them,' replied Yago, quickly. 'I take them—they belong to me—do not forget it.'"

At this stage of his recital the unknown paused once more on seeing the alarm and incredulity that were depicted on my features.

"You remember, I warned you, young man," said he, "that you could not believe my story. It must seem to you a dream, a chimera—to me also;—nevertheless the promotions, the honours that I soon obtained, were no illusions. Those brave soldiers that I led into the thickest of the fight! Those brilliant charges! Those captured flags! Those victories which all France heard of; all that was *my* work—all that glory belonged to me! "

While he marched up and down the room with great strides, and spoke thus with warmth and with enthusiasm, astonishment and fear had almost paralysed my senses. "Who then is this person? " thought I. "Is it Coligny? is it Richelieu? is it the Maréchal de Saxe? "

From his state of exaltation my unknown had fallen again into the deepest dejection, and, approaching me, said with a sombre air: "Yago kept his promise; and when, later on, disgusted with the vain smoke of military glory, I aspired to that which is only real and positive in this world—when at the price of five or six years of existence I desired great riches, he gladly gave them to me. Yes, young man, I have possessed vast wealth, far beyond my wildest dreams—estates, forests, and châteaux. To-day, still, all this is mine, and in my power; if you doubt me—if you doubt the existence of Yago—wait here, he is coming, and you can see for yourself that which would confound your reason and mine were it not unfortunately too real."

The unknown approached the fireplace, looked at the timepiece, made a gesture of alarm, and said to me in a deep voice :

" This morning at daybreak I felt myself so weak and so feeble that I could scarcely rise. I rang for my *valet-de-chambre* ; it was Yago who appeared. ' What is this strange feeling ! ' asked I.

" ' Master, nothing but what is perfectly natural. The hour approaches, the moment arrives.'

" ' And what is it ? ' cried I.

" ' Can you not divine it ? Heaven has destined you sixty years to live ; you were thirty when I began to obey you.'

" ' Yago ! ' cried I in affright, ' do you speak seriously ? '

" ' Yes, master ; in five years you have spent in glory twenty-five years of life. You have sold them to me. They belong to me ; and these years that you have voluntarily given up are now added to mine.'

" ' What ! That, then, was the price of your services ? '

" ' Yes, and many others—for ages past—have paid more dearly ; for instance, Fabert, whom I protected also.'

" ' Be silent, be silent ! ' cried I ; ' this is not possible ; it cannot be true ! '

" ' As you please ; but prepare yourself ; for there only remains for you a brief half-hour of life.'

" ' You are mocking me ! '

" ' Not at all. Calculate for yourself. Thirty-five years you have had, and twenty-five years you have sold to me—total, sixty. It is your own count ; each one takes his own.' Then he wished to go away, and I felt my strength diminish. I felt my life leaving me.

" ' Yago ! Yago ! ' I cried feebly ; ' give me a few hours, a few hours more ! '

" ' No, no,' replied he, ' it would be taking away from myself, and I know better than you the value of life. There is no treasure worth two hours of existence.'

" I could scarcely speak ; my eyes were set in my head, and the chill of death congealed the blood in my veins. ' Very well ! ' said I with an effort, ' take back your gifts, for that which I have sacrificed all. Four hours more and I renounce my gold, my wealth—all this opulence that I have so much desired.'

" ' Be it so ; you have been a good master, and I am willing to do something for you. I consent.'

" I felt my strength come back, and I cried : ' Four hours— that is very little ! Yago ! Yago ! Four hours more and I renounce all my literary fame, all my works that have placed me so high in the world's esteem.'

" ' Four hours for that ! ' cried the negro with disdain ; ' it is too much. No matter. I cannot refuse your last request.'

" ' Not the last ! ' cried I clasping my hands before him. ' Yago !

Yago ! I supplicate you, give me until this evening. The twelve hours, the entire day, and all my exploits, my victories, all my military renown may all be effaced from the memory of men. This day, Yago, dear Yago ; this whole day, and I will be content ! '

" ' You abuse my kindness,' said he ; ' no matter, I will give you until sunset ; after that you must not ask me. This evening, then, I will come for you '—and he is gone," continued the unknown, in despairing accents—" and this day, in which I see you for the first time, is my last on earth."

Then, going to the glass door, which was open, and which led to the park, he cried : " Alas ! I will no longer behold the beautiful sky, these green lawns, the sparkling fountains ! I will never again breathe the balmy air of springtime. Fool that I have been ! These gifts that God has given to all of us ; these blessings, to which I was insensible, and of which I can only now, when it is too late, appreciate and comprehend the sweetness—and I might have enjoyed them for twenty-five years more !—and I have used up my life ! I have sacrificed it for what ? For a vain and sterile glory, which has not made me happy, and which dies with me ! Look ! " said he to me, pointing to some peasants who traversed the park, singing on their way to work. " What would I not give now to share their labours and their poverty ! But I have no longer anything to give, or to hope for here below, not even misfortune ! "

Just then a ray of sunlight (the sun of the month of May) shone through the casement and lit up his pale and distracted features. He seized my arm in a sort of delirium, and said to me :

" See ! see there ! is it not beautiful ? the sun !—and I must leave all this ! Ah ! at least I am still alive ! I will have this whole day—so pure, so bright, so radiant—this day which for me has no morrow ! " He then ran down the steps of the open door, and bounded like a deer across the park, and at a detour of the path he disappeared in the shrubbery, before I hardly realised that he was gone, or could detain him. To tell the truth, I would not have had the strength. I lay back on the couch, stunned, dazed, and weak with the shock of all I had heard. I arose and walked up and down the room, to assure myself that I was awake, that I had not been under the influence of a dream. Just then the door of the boudoir opened and a servant announced : " Here is my master, the Duc de C——."

A man of sixty years and of distinguished presence advanced toward me, and, giving me his hand, apologised for having made me wait so long.

" I was not in the château. I had gone to seek my younger brother, the Comte de C——, who is ill."

" And is he in danger ? " interrupted I.

"No, monsieur. Thanks to heaven," replied my host; "but in his youth ambitious dreams of glory exalted his imagination, and a serious illness that he has had recently (and which he deemed fatal) has upset his mind, and produced a sort of delirium and mental aberration, by which he persuades himself always that he has but one day to live. It is insanity."

All was explained to me.

"Now," continued the duke, "let us come to you, young man, and see what can be done for your advancement. We will depart at the end of the month for Versailles. I will present you at court."

I blushed and replied: "I appreciate your kindness, Monsieur le Duc, and I thank you very much; but I will not go to Versailles."

"What! would you renounce the court and all the advantages and promotions which certainly await you there?"

"Yes, Monsieur."

"But do you realise that with my influence you can rise rapidly, and that with a little assiduity and patience you can become distinguished in ten years?"

"Ten years lost!" I cried in terror.

"What!" replied he, astonished. "Ten years is not much to pay for fortune, glory, and honours? Come, come, my young friend. Come with me to Versailles."

"No, Monsieur le Duc. I am determined to return to Brittany, and I beg of you to receive my profound gratitude, and that of my family."

"What folly!" cried he.

And I, remembering what I had listened to, said: "It is wisdom!"

The next day I was en route, and with what exquisite delight did I behold my beautiful château of Roche-Bernard, the grand old trees in my park, and the bright sunshine of Brittany. I found again my vassals, my mother, my sisters, my fiancée, and my happiness, which I still retain, for one week later I married Henriette.

ALFRED DE VIGNY
1797-1863

NAPOLEON
AND POPE PIUS VII.

WE were at Fontainebleau. The Pope had just arrived. The Emperor had awaited him with great impatience as he desired the Holy Father to crown him. Napoleon received him in person, and they immediately entered the carriage—on opposite sides, at the same time, apparently with an entire neglect of etiquette, but this was only in appearance, for the movement was thoroughly calculated. It was so arranged that neither might seem to yield precedence or to exact it from the other. The ruse was characteristically Italian. They at once drove toward the palace, where all kinds of rumours were in circulation. I had left several officers in the room which preceded that of the Emperor ; and I was quite alone in his apartment.

I was standing looking at a long table, which was of Roman mosaic work, and which was absolutely loaded, covered with heaps of papers. I had often seen Napoleon enter and submit the pile of documents to a strange system of decision. He did not take the letters either by hazard or in order ; but when the number irritated him, he swept them off the table with his hand—striking right and left like a mower, until he had reduced the number to six or seven, which he opened.

Such disdainful conduct had moved me singularly. So many letters of distress and mourning cast underfoot as if by an angry wind ; so many useless prayers of widows and orphans having no chance except that of being spared by the consular hand ; so many groaning leaves, moistened by the tears of so many families trampled under his heel with as little compunction as if they were corpses on a battlefield—all these seemed to represent the fate of France. Although the hand that acted so ruthlessly was strong, it seemed always that such brutal strength was anything but admirable, and it seemed wrong that so much should be left to the caprice of such a man.

Moreover, had a little consideration been shown, Napoleon would have had so many more buttresses for his power and authority. I felt my heart rise against the man—but feebly, like the heart of one who was his slave. I thought of the letters which had been treated with such cruel contempt ; cries of anguish came from the envelopes ; and having read some of the petitions I constituted myself judge between the man and those who had sacrificed themselves so much for him, upon whose necks he was going to fasten the yoke tighter that very day. I was holding one of the papers in my hand, when the beating of the drums informed me of the arrival of Napoleon. Now you know that just as one always sees the flash from a cannon before one hears the report, one always saw him as he was heard to be approaching ; he was so active, and seemed to have so little time. When he rode into the courtyard of the palace, his attendants were scarcely able to keep up with him. The sentry had barely time to salute before the Emperor had got down from his horse and was hurrying up the staircase.

This time he had left the Pope in the carriage in order to be able to enter the palace alone, and had galloped on ahead. I heard the sound of his spurs at the same time as the drums. I had only just time enough to throw myself into an alcove where there was an old-fashioned high bedstead which was used by no one, and which was, fortunately, concealed by curtains.

The Emperor was in a state of great excitement, and strode about the room as if waiting for some one with great impatience. Having darted across the room several times, he went to the window and began to drum on the panes. A carriage rolled into the court ; he ceased beating a tattoo on the glass, and stamped with his foot as if the sight which he saw in the courtyard was anything but agreeable to him. Then he tore across the room to the door, which he opened for the Pope.

Pius VII. entered unattended. Bonaparte hastily closed the door after the old man with the care of a jailer. I will confess that I was in a state of mortal terror at being the third of the party. However, I remained motionless, listening eagerly to every word that was said.

The Pope was tall : his face was long, yellow, and had traces of great suffering, but bore the imprint of a goodness of soul and nobility of spirit which knew no bounds. He had fine, big, black eyes, and his mouth was sweetened by a smile which lent something spirituelle and vivacious to his countenance. It was a smile in which one could detect nothing of the cunning of the world, but which was full to overflowing of Christian goodness. On his head he wore a skull-cap, from under which escaped locks of his silver-streaked hair. A red velvet cloak hung negligently on his stooping shoulders, and his robe dragged at his feet. He entered slowly, with the calm and prudent step of an aged man, sank down into one of the big Roman armchairs, which were gilded and covered with eagles, lowered his eyes, and waited to hear what the other Italian had to say to him.

What a scene that was ! I can see it still. It was not the genius of the man which I noticed, but his character. Bonaparte was not then as you knew him afterward ; he had not grown gross— he had not the swollen face, the gouty legs, nor was he so ridiculously stout as he afterward became. Unfortunately, in art he is almost always represented by a sort of caricature, so that he will not be handed down to posterity as he really was. He was not ungainly then, but nervous and supple, lithe and active, convulsive in some of his gestures, in some gracious ; his chest was flat and narrow— in short, he looked just as I had seen him at Malta.

He did not stop stalking round the room when the Pope entered. He wandered round the chair of the latter like a cautious hunter ; then suddenly halting in front of Pius, he resumed a conversation which had been commenced in the carriage, and which he was evidently anxious to continue.

" I tell you again, Holy Father, I am not a free-thinker ; and I don't agree with those who are for ever reasoning about religious matters. I assure you that in spite of my old republicans I shall go to mass."

The last words he threw brusquely, as it were, in the Pope's face—incense of flattery undisguised. Then he suddenly stopped and examined the Pope's countenance to catch the result, which he seemed to expect to be great. The old man lowered his eyes and rested his hands on the heads of the eagles which formed the arms of the chair. He seemed to have assumed the attitude of a Roman statue purposely, as if wishing to express : " I resign myself to hearing all the profane things that he may choose to say to me ! "

Bonaparte took a turn round the room, and round the chair which was in the middle, and it was plain to be seen that he was not satisfied either with himself or with his adversary, and that he was reproaching himself for having resumed the conversation so rashly. So he began to talk more connectedly as he walked round the room, all the time watching narrowly the reflection of the pontiff's face in the mirror, and also eyeing him carefully in profile as he passed ; but not venturing to look him full in the face for fear of appearing too anxious about the effect of his words.

" There is one thing that hurts me very much, Holy Father," said he, " and that is that you consent to the coronation as you formerly consented to the Concordat—as if you were compelled to do so, and not as of free will. You sit there before me with the air of a martyr, resigned to the will of heaven, and suffering for the sake of your conscience. But that is not the fact. You are not a prisoner. You are as free as the air."

Pius VII. smiled and looked his interlocutor in the face. He realised that the despotic nature with which he had to contend was not satisfied with obedience unless one seemed willing, even anxious, to obey.

"Yes," continued Bonaparte, "you are quite free. You may return to Rome if you like. The road is open and no one will stop you."

Without uttering a word, the Pope sighed and raised his hand and his eyes to heaven ; then very slowly he lowered his eyes and studied the cross on his bosom attentively.

Bonaparte continued to walk round the room and to talk to his captive, his voice becoming sweeter and more wheedling.

"Holy Father, were it not for the reverence I have for you I should be inclined to say that you are a little ungrateful. You seem to ignore entirely the services which France has rendered you. As far as I am able to judge, the Council of Venice, which elected you Pope, was influenced somewhat by my campaign in Italy, as well as by a word which I spoke for you. I was very much troubled at the time that Austria treated you so badly. I believe that your Holiness was obliged to return to Rome by sea for fear of passing through Austrian territory.

He stopped for the answer of his silent guest ; Pius VII. made simply the slightest inclination of the head, and remained plunged in a melancholy reverie which seemed to prevent him from hearing Napoleon.

Bonaparte then pushed a chair near to that of the Pope. I started, for in seeking the chair he had come very near my hiding-place, he even brushed the curtains which concealed me.

"It was as a Catholic really that I was so afflicted about your vexations. I have never had much time to study theology, it is true, but I maintain a great faith in the Church. She has a wonderful vitality, Holy Father, although Voltaire did you some little harm, certainly. Now if you are only willing we can do a great deal of work together in the future."

He assumed a caressing, wheedling air of innocence.

"Really, I have tried to understand your motives, but I can't for the life of me see what objection you can have to making Paris your seat. I'll leave the Tuileries to you if you like. You'll find your room waiting for you there. I scarcely ever go there myself. Don't you see, Father, it is the capital of the world. I'll do whatever you want me to ; and really, after all, I am not as bad as I am painted. If you'll leave war and politics to me you may do as you like in ecclesiastical matters. In fact, I would be your soldier. Now wouldn't that be a grand arrangement ? We could hold our councils like Constantine and Charlemagne—I would open and dissolve them ; and then I would put the keys of the world into

your hands, for, as our Lord said : ' I came with a sword,' and I
would keep the sword ; I would only bring it to you for your
blessing after each new success of our arms."

The Pope, who until then had remained as motionless as an
Egyptian statue, slowly raised his head, smiled sadly, lifted his
eyes to heaven, and said, after a gentle sigh, as if he were confiding
the thought to his invisible guardian angel :

" Commediante ! "

Napoleon leaped from his chair like a wounded tiger. He was in
one of his " yellow tempers." At first he stamped about without
uttering a word, biting his lips till the blood came. He no longer
circled round his prey cautiously, but walked from end to end of the
room with firm resounding steps, and clinking his spurs noisily.
The room shook ; the curtains trembled like trees at the approach
of a storm ; I thought that something terrible would surely happen ;
my hair began to bristle, and I put my hand to my head unwittingly.
I looked at the Pope. He did not stir, but simply pressed the heads
of the eagles with his hands.

The storm burst violently.

" Comedian ! What ? I a comedian ? Indeed, I'll play some
comedies for you that will set you all a-weeping like women and
children ! Comedian, forsooth ! You are mistaken if you think that
you may insult me with impunity. My theatre is the world ; the
rôle that I play is the double one of master and actor ; I use all of
you as comedians, popes, kings, peoples, and the string by which
I work you—you my puppets—is fear. You would need to be a
much heavier man than you are, Signor Chiaramonti, to dare to
applaud or hiss me. Do you know that if it be my will you will
become a simple curé ? As for you and your tiara, France would
mock at you if I did not seem to be serious in saluting you.

" Only four years ago nobody dared speak of Christ. Had that
state of things continued who would have cared for the Pope,
I should like to know ? Comedian ! You gentlemen are a little too
ready at getting a foothold among us. And now you are dissatisfied because I am not such a fool as to sign away the liberties
of France as did Louis XIV. But you had better not sing to me
in that tune. It is I who hold you between my thumb and finger ;
it is I who can carry you from north to south and then back again
to the north like so many marionettes ; it is I who give you some
stability because you represent an old idea which I wish to
resuscitate ; and you have not enough wit to see that, and to act
as if you were not aware of the fact. Now I'll speak to you frankly.
Trouble your head with your own affairs and don't interfere in what
you don't understand and with what doesn't in the least concern
you. You seem to think that you are necessary, you set yourselves
up as if you were of some weight, and you dress yourselves in

women's clothes. But I'll let you know that you don't impose
on me with all that; and if you don't change your tactics very
soon I'll treat your robes as Charles XII. did that of the Grand
Vizier—I'll tear them with my spur."

Then he ceased. I scarcely dared breathe. I advanced my head
a little, not hearing his voice, to see if the poor old priest was dead
with fright. The same absolutely calm attitude, the same calm
expression on his face. For the second time he raised his eyes
to heaven, again he sighed, and smiled bitterly as he murmured:

" Tragediante ! "

Bonaparte was at the farther end of the room, leaning against a
marble chimney which was as high as he was tall. Like an arrow
shot out of a bow, he rushed straight at the old man ; I thought
he was going to kill him as he sat. But he suddenly stopped short,
seized a Sèvres vase on which the Capitol was painted, threw it on
the hearth and ground it under his heels. Then he remained
terribly quiet.

I was relieved, for I felt that his reason had got the better of his
temper. He became sad, and when he finally spoke in a deep voice,
it was evident that in the two words uttered by the Pope he had
recognised his true portrait.

" Miserable life ! " he said. Then he fell into reverie, and without
speaking tore the brim of his hat. When his voice again was heard
he was talking to himself :

" It's true. Tragedian or comedian, I am always playing a part—
all is costume and pose. How wearying it all is, and how belittling !
Pose ! pose ! always pose ! In one case full face, in another profile—
but invariably for effect. Always trying to appear what others
worship, so that I may deceive the fools, keeping them between
hope and fear. Dazzling them by bulletins, by prestige. Master
of all of them and not knowing what to do with them. That's
the simple truth after all.

" And to make myself so miserable through it all ! It really is too
much. For," continued he, sitting down in an armchair and crossing
his legs, " it bores me to death, the whole farce. As soon as I sit
down I don't know what to do with myself. I can't even hunt
for three days in succession at Fontainebleau with being weary of
it. I must always be moving and making others move. I speak
quite frankly. I have plans in my life which would require the
lives of forty emperors to carry out, and I make new ones every
morning and evening ; my imagination is always on the *qui vive* ;
but before I have carried out two of them I shall be exhausted in
body and mind ; for our poor lamp of life doesn't burn long enough.
And I must confess that if I could carry them out I should not
find that the world was one whit better than it is now ; but it
would be better though, for it would be united. I am not a

philosopher. I don't understand many theories. Life is too short to stop. As soon as I have an idea I put it into execution. Others will find reasons after me for praising me if I succeed and for abusing me if I fail. Differences of opinion are active—they abound in France—but I keep them down while I am alive—afterward—Well, no matter ! It is my business to succeed, and that I intend to do. Every day I make an Iliad by my actions—every day."

Thereupon he rose quickly. In that moment he was lively and natural, and was not thinking of posing as he afterward did in St. Helena ; he did not strive to make himself ideal or to pose for effect—he was himself outside of himself. He went back to the Pope, who had remained seated, and paced in front of him. Getting warmed up, he spoke with a dash of irony, at an incredible rate :

" Birth is everything. Those who come into the world poor and neglected are always desperate. That desperation turns to action or suicide according to character. When they have courage to attempt something as I have done, they raise the devil. But what else is to be done ? One must live. One must find one's place and make one's mark. I have carried everything before me like a cannon-ball—all the worse for those who happened to be in my way. But what else could I have done ? Each man eats according to his appetite, and I have an insatiable one.

" Do you know, Holy Father, at Toulon I had not wherewithal to buy myself a pair of epaulets, in place of which I had a mother and I don't know how many brothers on my shoulders. They are all satisfactorily settled at present. Josephine married me out of pity in spite of her old notary, who objected that I owned nothing but my cap and cape, and now we are going to crown her. The old man was right, though, as to what I possessed at that time. Imperial mantle ! Crown ! what does all that mean ? Is it mine ? Costume ! Actor's costume ! I will put them on for an hour and then I shall have had enough of them. Then I shall don my officer's uniform, and ' To horse ' ; all my life on horseback. I couldn't pass a single day resting, without being in danger of falling out of the chair. I am to be envied ? Eh !

" I repeat, Holy Father ; there are only two classes of men in the world : those who have and those who gain.

" Those who are in the first class rest, the others are restless. As I learnt that lesson at an early age and to some purpose I shall go a long way. There are only two men who have done anything before they were forty years old ; Cromwell and Jean-Jacques ; if you had given one a farm, and the other twelve hundred francs and his servant, they would neither have commanded nor preached nor written.

" There are workmen in buildings, in colours, in forms, and in

phrases; I am a workman in battles. It's my business. At the
age of thirty-five I have manufactured eighteen of them, which are
called 'Victories.' I must be paid for my work. And a throne is
certainly not extravagant payment. Besides, I shall always go
on working. You will see that all dynasties will date from mine,
although I am a mere parvenu. I am elected as you are, Holy
Father—and drawn from the multitude. On this point we can
well shake hands."

And, approaching the Pope, Napoleon held out his hand. Pius
took the hand which was offered to him, but shook his head sadly,
and I saw his fine eyes cloud with tears.

Bonaparte cast a hurried glance at the tears which he had wrung
from the old Pope, and I surprised even a rapid motion in the corners
of his mouth much resembling a smile of triumph. At that moment
his intensely powerful and overbearing nature seemed to me less
admirable than that of his saintly adversary; I blushed for all
my past admiration of Napoleon; I felt a sadness creep over me
at the thought that the grandest policy appears little when stained
by tricks of vanity. I saw that the Emperor had gained his end
in the interview by having yielded nothing and by having drawn
a sign of weakness from the Pope. He had wished to have the last
word, and without uttering another syllable, he left the room
as abruptly as he had entered.

I could not see whether he saluted the Pope or not, but I do not
think he did.

HONORÉ DE BALZAC
1799–1850

AN EPISODE OF THE REIGN OF TERROR

ABOUT eight o'clock on the evening of January 22, 1793, an aged woman was coming down the sharp descent of the Faubourg Saint-Martin that ends in front of the church of Saint-Laurent. Snow had fallen so heavily all day long that hardly a footfall could be heard. The streets were deserted. Fears that the silence around naturally enough inspired were increased by all the terror under which France was then groaning. So the old lady had thus far met with no one else. Her sight, which had long been failing, did not enable her to distinguish far off by the light of the street lamps some passers-by, moving like scattered shadows in the huge thoroughfare of the Faubourg. She went on bravely all alone in the midst of this solitude, as if her age were a talisman that could be relied on to preserve her from any mishap.

When she had passed the Rue des Morts she thought she perceived the heavy, firm tread of a man walking behind her. It occurred to her that it was not the first time she had heard this sound. She was alarmed at the idea that she was being followed, and she tried to walk faster in order to reach a fairly well-lighted shop, in the hope that, in the light it gave, she would be able to put to the test the suspicions that had taken possession of her.

As soon as she was within the circle of light projected horizontally by the shop-front, she quickly turned her head and caught a glimpse of a human form in the foggy darkness. This vague glimpse was enough for her. She tottered for a moment under the shock of terror that overwhelmed her, for she no longer doubted that she had been followed by the stranger from the first step she had taken outside her lodging. The longing to escape from a spy gave her strength. Without being able to think of what she was doing, she began to run—as if she could possibly get away from a man who must necessarily be much more agile than herself.

After running for a few minutes she reached a confectioner's shop, entered it, and fell, rather than sat, down upon a chair that stood in front of the counter. Even while she was raising the creaking latch, a young woman, who was busy with some embroidery, raised her eyes, and through the small panes of the half-window in the shop door recognised the old-fashioned violet silk mantle in which the old lady was wrapped. She hurriedly opened a drawer as if looking for something she was to hand over to her.

It was not only by her manner and the look on her face that the young woman showed she was anxious to get rid of the stranger without delay, as if her visitor were one of those there was no pleasure in seeing ; but, besides this, she allowed an expression of impatience to escape her on finding that the drawer was empty. Then, without looking at the lady, she turned suddenly from the counter, went towards the back shop, and called her husband, who at once made his appearance.

" Wherever have you put away . . . ? " she asked of him, with an air of mystery without finishing her question, but calling his attention to the old lady with a glance of her eyes.

Although the confectioner could see nothing but the immense black silk bonnet, trimmed with bows of velvet ribbon, that formed the strange visitor's headgear, he left the shop again, after having cast at his wife a look that seemed to say, " Do you think I would leave *that* in your counter . . . ? "

Surprised at the motionless silence of the old lady, the shop-woman turned and approached her, and as she looked at her she felt herself inspired with an impulse of compassion, perhaps not unmingled with curiosity. Although the woman's complexion showed an habitual pallor, like that of one who makes a practice of secret austerities, it was easy to see that a recent emotion had brought an unusual paleness to her face. Her head-dress was so arranged as to conceal her hair. No doubt it was white with age, for there were no marks on the upper part of her dress to show that she used hair powder. The complete absence of ornament lent to her person an air of religious severity. Her features had a grave, stately look. In these old times the manners and habits of people of quality were so different from those of other classes of society, that it was easy to distinguish one of noble birth. So the young woman felt convinced that the stranger was a *ci-devant*, an ex-aristocrat, and that she had belonged to the court.

" Madame . . ." she said to her with involuntary respect, forgetting that such a title was now forbidden.

The old lady did not reply. She kept her eyes fixed on the window of the shop as if she could distinguish some fearful object in that direction.

" What is the matter, citizeness ? " asked the shopkeeper, who had returned almost immediately.

And the citizen-confectioner roused the lady from her reverie by offering her a little cardboard box wrapped in blue paper.

" Nothing, nothing, my friends," she answered in a sweet voice. She raised her eyes to the confectioner's face as if to give him a look of thanks, but seeing the red cap on his head, she uttered a cry : " Ah, you have betrayed me ! "

The young woman and her husband replied by a gesture of horror at the thought, which made the stranger blush, perhaps at having suspected them, perhaps with pleasure.

" Pardon me," she said, with childlike gentleness. Then, taking a *louis d'or* from her pocket, she offered it to the confectioner : " Here is the price we agreed on," she added.

There is a poverty that the poor readily recognise. The confectioner and his wife looked at one another, silently turning each other's attention to the old lady, while both formed one common thought. This *louis d'or* must be her last. The lady's hands trembled as she offered the piece of money, she looked at it with a sadness that had no avarice in it, but she seemed to realise the full extent of the sacrifice she made. Starvation and misery were as plainly marked on her face as the lines that told of fear and of habits of asceticism. In her dress there were traces of old magnificence. It was of worn-out silk. Her mantle was neat though threadbare, with some carefully mended lace upon it. In a word, it was a case of wealth the worse for wear. The people of the shop, hesitating between sympathy and self-interest, began by trying to satisfy their consciences with words :

" But, citizeness, you seem to be very weak——"

" Would Madame like to take something ? " said the woman, cutting her husband short.

" We have some very good soup," added the confectioner.

" It is so cold to-night. Perhaps Madame has had a chill while walking ? But you can rest here and warm yourself for a while."

" We are not as black as the devil ! " exclaimed the confectioner.

Won by the tone of kindness that found expression in the words of the charitable shopkeepers, the lady let them know she had been followed by a stranger, and that she was afraid to go back alone to her lodgings.

" Is that all ? " replied the man in the red cap, " wait a little, citizeness."

He gave the *louis d'or* to his wife. . . . Then moved by that sort of gratitude that finds its way into the heart of a dealer when he has got an exorbitant price for some merchandise of trifling value, he went and put on his National Guard's uniform, took his hat, belted on his sword, and reappeared as an armed man. But his wife had had time to reflect. In her heart, as in so many more, reflection closed the open hand of benevolence. Anxious and fearful of seeing her husband involved in some bad business, the confectioner's wife tried to pull him by the skirt of his coat and stop him. But obeying his own charitable feelings the good fellow offered at once to escort the old lady.

" It seems that the man the citizeness is afraid of is still prowling about in front of our shop," said the young woman excitedly.

" I am afraid he is," put in the lady naïvely.

" What if he were a spy ? . . . if there were some plot ? . . . Don't go, and take back that box from her. . . ."

These words, whispered in the ear of the confectioner by his wife, froze the sudden courage that had inspired him.

" Well, I'll just say a few words to him, and rid you of him soon enough," exclaimed the shopkeeper, as he opened the door and slipped hurriedly out.

The old lady, passive as a child and almost stupefied by her fear, sat down again on the chair. The good shopkeeper was soon back. His face, naturally ruddy enough and further reddened by his oven fire, had suddenly become pallid. He was a prey to such terror that his legs shook and his eyes looked like those of a drunken man.

" Do you want to get our heads cut off, you wretch of an aristocrat ? " he cried out in a fury. " Come, show us your heels, and don't let us see you again, and don't reckon on my supplying you with materials for your plots ! "

As he ended, the confectioner made an attempt to take back from the old lady the little box which she had put into one of her pockets. But hardly had his bold hands touched her dress, than the stranger, preferring to risk herself amid the perils of the street without any other protector but God, rather than to lose what she had just bought, regained all the agility of youth. She rushed to the door, opened it briskly, and vanished from the sight of wife and husband as they stood trembling and astonished.

As soon as the stranger was outside she started off at a rapid walk. But her strength soon began to desert her, and she heard the spy, who had so pitilessly followed her, making the snow crackle as he crushed it with his heavy tread. She had to stop. He stopped. She did not dare to address him, or even to look at him—it might be on account of the fear that had seized upon her, or because she could not think what to say. Then she went on again walking slowly.

The man also slackened his pace so as to remain always just at the distance that enabled him to keep her in sight. He seemed to be the very shadow of the old woman. Nine o'clock struck as the silent pair once more passed by the church of Saint-Laurent.

It is a part of the nature of all minds, even of the weakest, to find a feeling of calm succeed to any violent agitation, for if our feelings are infinite, our organism has its limits. So the stranger, finding that her supposed persecutor did her no harm, was inclined to see in him some unknown friend, who was anxious to protect her. She summed up in her mind all the circumstances that had attended the appearance of the stranger, as if seeking for some plausible motives for this consoling opinion, and was then satisfied to recognise on his part a friendly rather than an evil purpose. Forgetful of the alarm, which this man had so short a time ago caused the confectioner, she now went on with a firm step into the upper part of the Faubourg Saint-Martin.

After walking for half an hour she came to a house situated near the point where the street, which leads to the Pantin barrier, branches off from the main line of the Faubourg. Even at the present day the neighbourhood is still one of the loneliest in all Paris. A north-east wind blowing over the Buttes Chaumont and Belleville whistled between the houses, or rather the cottages, scattered about this almost uninhabited valley, in which the enclosures were formed of fences built up of earth and old bones. The desolate place seemed to be the natural refuge of misery and despair.

The man, all eagerness in the pursuit of this poor creature, who was so bold as to traverse these silent streets in the night, seemed struck by the spectacle that presented itself to his gaze. He stood still, full of thought, in a hesitating attitude, in the feeble light of a street lamp, the struggling rays of which could hardly penetrate the fog. Fear seemed to sharpen the sight of the old lady, who thought she saw something of evil omen in the looks of the stranger. She felt her terror reawakening, and took advantage of the seeming hesitation that had brought the man to a standstill to slip through a shadow to the door of a solitary house ; she pushed back a spring latch, and disappeared in an instant like a ghost upon the stage.

The unknown man, without moving from where he stood, kept his eyes fixed on the house, the appearance of which was fairly typical of that of the wretched dwelling-places of this suburb of Paris. The tumble-down hovel was built of bricks covered with a coat of yellow plaster, so full of cracks that one feared to see the whole fall down in a heap of ruins before the least effort of the wind. There were three windows to each floor, and their frames, rotten with damp and warped by the action of the sun, suggested that the cold must penetrate freely into the rooms. The lonely house looked like some old tower that time has forgotten to destroy. A feeble gleam lit up the warped and crooked window-sashes of the garret window, that showed up the roof of this poor edifice, while all the rest of the house was in complete darkness.

Not without difficulty the old woman climbed the rough and clumsy stair, in ascending which one had to lean on a rope that took the place of a hand-rail. She gave a low knock at the door of the garret room, and hurriedly took her seat on a chair, which an old man offered to her.

"Hide yourself! hide yourself!" she said to him, "though we so seldom go out, our doings are known, our steps are spied upon. . . ."

"Is there anything new then?" asked another old woman, who was seated near the fire.

"That man, who has been prowling round the house since yesterday, followed me this evening. . . ."

At these words the three inmates of the hovel looked at each other, while they showed on their faces signs of serious alarm. Of the three the old man was the least agitated, perhaps because he was the most in danger. Under the weight of a great misfortune, or under the pressure of persecution, a brave man begins, so to say, by making the complete sacrifice of himself. He counts each day as one more victory won over fate. The looks of the two women fixed upon this old man made it easy to see that he was the one object of their keen anxiety.

"Why lose our trust in God, my sisters?" he said in a voice low but full of fervour; "we sang His praises in the midst of the cries of the murderers and of the dying at the convent of the Carmelites. If He willed that I should be saved from that butchery, it was no doubt to preserve me for some destiny that I must accept without a murmur. God guards His own, and He can dispose of them according to His will. It is of yourselves, and not of me, that we must think."

"No," said one of the old women, "what are our lives compared to that of a priest?"

"Once I saw myself outside of the Abbey of Chelles, I considered myself as a dead woman," said one of the two nuns—the one who had remained in the house.

"Here are the altar breads," said the other, who had just come in, offering the little box to the priest. "But . . ." she cried out, "I hear footsteps on the stairs!"

All three listened. . . The sound ceased.

"Do not be alarmed," said the priest, "if some one tries to get to see you. A person on whose good faith we can depend must by this time have taken all necessary steps to cross the frontier, in order to come here for the letters I have written to the Duc de Langeais and the Marquis de Beauséant, asking them to see what can be done to take you away from this wretched country, and the suffering and death that await you here."

"You are not going with us then?" exclaimed the two nuns in gentle protest, and with a look of something like despair.

"My place is where there are still victims," was the priest's simple reply.

They were silent, and gazed at their protector with reverent admiration.

"Sister Martha," he said, addressing the nun who had gone to get the altar breads, "this envoy of ours should answer 'Fiat voluntas' to the password 'Hosanna.'"

"There is some one on the stair!" exclaimed the other nun; and she opened a hiding-place constructed in the roof.

This time, in the deep silence, it was easy to catch the sound of the footsteps of some man, re-echoing on the stairs that were rough with lumps of hardened mud. The priest with some difficulty huddled himself into a kind of cupboard, and the nun threw some old clothes over him.

"You can shut the door," he said in a smothered voice.

The priest was hardly hidden away, when three knocks at the door made both the good women start. They were exchanging looks of inquiry without daring to utter a word. Both seemed to be about sixty years of age. Separated from the world for some forty years, they were like plants that are so used to the air of a hothouse that they die if one takes them out. Accustomed as they were to the life of the convent they had no idea of anything else. One morning their cloister had been broken open, and they had shuddered at finding themselves free. It is easy to imagine the state of nervous weakness the events of the Revolution had produced in their innocent minds. Unable to reconcile the mental habits of the cloister with the difficulties of life, and not fully understanding the circumstances in which they were placed, they were like children of whom every care had been taken till now, and who, suddenly deprived of their mother's care, pray instead of weeping. So face to face with the danger which they now saw before them, they remained silent and passive, knowing of no other defence but Christian resignation.

The man who had asked for admittance interpreted this silence in his own way. He opened the door and suddenly appeared in the room. The two nuns shuddered as they recognised the man who for some time had been prowling around their house and making inquiries about them. They remained motionless, looking at him with the anxious curiosity of untaught children who stare in silence at a stranger.

The man was tall in stature and heavily built. But there was nothing in his attitude, his general appearance, or the expression of his face to suggest that he was a bad character. Like the nuns, he kept quite still, and slowly cast his eyes round the room he had entered.

Two straw mats unrolled on the floor served for beds for the nuns. There was a table in the middle of the room, and there stood on it a brass candlestick, some plates, three knives, and a round loaf of bread. There was a very small fire in the grate. A few pieces of wood heaped up in a corner were a further sign of the poverty of these two recluses. One could see that the roof was in a bad state, for the walls, covered with a coat of very old paint, were stained with brown streaks that showed where the rain had leaked through. A reliquary, rescued no doubt from the sack of the Abbey of Chelles, served as an ornament to the mantelpiece. Three chairs, two boxes, and a shabby chest of drawers completed the furniture of the room. A door near the fireplace suggested that there was a second room beyond.

The individual who had in such an alarming way introduced himself to this poor household had soon taken mental note of all the contents of the little room. A feeling of pity could be traced upon his countenance, and he cast a kindly look upon the two women, and appeared to be at least as much embarrassed as they were. The strange silence that all three had kept so far did not long continue, for at last the stranger realised the timidity and inexperience of the two poor creatures, and said to them in a voice that he tried to make as gentle as possible :

" I do not come here as an enemy, citizenesses . . ." He stopped, as if recovering himself, and went on :

" Sisters, if any misfortune comes your way, believe me I have no part in it. . . . I have a favour to ask of you."

They still kept silence.

" If I am troubling you, if . . . if I am causing you pain, say so freely . . . and I will go away ; but be assured that I am entirely devoted to you ; that if there is any kindness I can do to you, you can claim it from me without fear ; and that I am perhaps the only one who is above the law, now that there is no longer a king. . . ."

There was such an air of truth in his words, that Sister Agatha— she of the two nuns who belonged to the noble family of Langeais, and whose manners seemed to indicate that in old times she had known the splendours of festive society and had breathed the air of the court—pointed with an alert movement to one of the chairs as if asking the visitor to be seated. The stranger showed something of pleasure mingled with sadness as he understood this gesture, but before taking the chair he waited till both the worthy ladies were seated.

" You have given a refuge here," he continued, " to a venerable priest, one of those who refused the oath, and who had a miraculous escape from the massacre at the Carmelites. . . ."

" Hosanna ! " . . . said Sister Agatha, interrupting the stranger, and looking at him with anxious curiosity.

" I don't think that is his name," he replied.

" But, sir, we have no priest here," said Sister Martha, eagerly.

" If that is so, you ought to be more careful and prudent,"

answered the stranger in a gentle tone, as he stretched out his hand to the table and took a breviary from it. " I don't suppose you know Latin, and . . ."

He said no more, for the extraordinary emotion depicted on the faces of the two poor nuns made him fear that he had gone too far. They were trembling, and their eyes filled with tears.

" Don't be alarmed," he said in a voice that seemed all sincerity, " I know the name of your guest, and your own names too, and for the last three days I have been aware of your distress and of your devoted care for the venerable Abbé de . . ."

" Hush ! " said Sister Agatha in her simplicity, putting a finger to her lips.

" You see, Sister, that if I had had in my mind the horrible idea of betraying you, I could have done so already, again and again. . . ."

Hearing these words, the priest extricated himself from his prison and came out again into the room.

" I could not possibly believe, sir," he said to the stranger, " that you were one of our persecutors, and I trust myself to you. What do you want of me ? "

The holy confidence of the priest, the nobility of mind that showed itself in his every look, would have disarmed even assassins. The mysterious man, whose coming had caused such excitement in this scene of resigned misery, gazed for a moment at the group formed by the three others ; then, taking a tone in which there was no longer any hesitation, he addressed the priest in these words :

" Father, I came to ask you to say a mass for the dead, for the repose of the soul . . . of one . . . of a sacred personage, whose body will never be laid to rest in consecrated ground. . . ."

The priest gave an involuntary shudder. The nuns, who did not yet understand to whom it was the stranger alluded, sat in an attitude of curiosity, their heads stretched forwards, their faces turned towards the two who were speaking together. The priest looked closely at the stranger, on whose face there was an unmistakable expression of anxiety, and also of earnest entreaty.

" Well," replied the priest, " come back this evening at midnight, and I shall be ready to celebrate the only rites for the dead that we may be able to offer up in expiation for the crime of which you speak. . . ."

The stranger started, but it seemed that some deep and soothing satisfaction was triumphing over his secret sorrow. After having respectfully saluted the priest and the two holy women, he took his departure, showing a kind of silent gratitude which was understood by these three generous souls.

About two hours after this scene the stranger returned, knocked softly at the door of the garret, and was admitted by Mademoiselle de Beauséant, who led him into the inner room of this poor place of refuge, where everything had been made ready for the ceremony.

Between two chimney-shafts that passed up through the room the nuns had placed the old chest of drawers, the antiquated outlines of which were hidden by a magnificent altar frontal of green watered silk. A large crucifix of ivory and ebony hung on the yellow-washed wall, contrasting so strongly with the surrounding bareness that the eye could not fail to be drawn to it. Four slender little tapers, which the sisters had succeeded in fixing on this improvised altar, by attaching them to it with sealing-wax, threw out a dim light, that was hardly reflected by the wall. This feeble illumination barely gave light to the rest of the room ; but, as it thus shone only on the sacred objects, it seemed like a light sent down from heaven on this unadorned altar. The floor was damp. The roof, which slanted down sharply on two sides, as is usual in garret rooms, had some cracks in it through which came the night wind—icy cold.

Nothing could be more devoid of all pomp, and nevertheless there was perhaps never anything more solemn than this mournful ceremony. A profound silence, in which one could have heard the least sound uttered on the highway outside, lent a kind of sombre majesty to the midnight scene. Finally, the greatness of the action itself contrasted so strongly with the poverty of its surroundings that the result was a feeling of religious awe.

On each side of the altar the two aged nuns knelt on the tiled floor without taking any notice of its deadly dampness, and united their prayers with those of the priest, who, robed in his sacerdotal vestments, placed on the altar a chalice of gold adorned with precious stones, a consecrated vessel that had been saved no doubt from the pillage of the Abbey of Chelles. Besides this chalice, a token of royal munificence, the wine and water destined for the Holy Sacrifice stood ready in two glasses, such as one would hardly have found in the poorest inn. For want of a missal the priest had placed a small prayer-book on the corner of the altar. An ordinary plate had been prepared for the washing of the hands, in this case hands all innocent and free from blood. There was the contrast of littleness with immensity ; of poverty with noble sublimity ; of what was meant for profane uses with what was consecrated to God.

The stranger knelt devoutly between the two nuns. But suddenly, as he noticed that, having no other means of marking that this was a mass offered for the dead, the priest had placed a knot of crape on the crucifix and on the base of the chalice, thus putting holy things in mourning, the stranger's mind was so mastered by some recollection that drops of sweat stood out upon his broad forehead. The four silent actors in the scene looked at each other mysteriously. Then their souls, acting and reacting on each other, inspired with one common thought, united them in devout sympathy. It seemed as if their minds had evoked the presence of the martyr whose remains the quicklime had burned away, and that his shade was present with them in all its kingly majesty. They were celebrating a requiem without the presence of the body of the departed. Under the disjointed laths and tiles of the roof four Christians were about to intercede with God for a King of France, and perform his obsequies though there was no coffin before the altar. There was the purest of devoted love, an act of wondrous loyalty performed without a touch of self-consciousness. No doubt, in the eyes of God, it was like the gift of the glass of water that ranks with the highest of virtues. All the monarchy was there, finding voice in the prayers of a priest and two poor women ; but perhaps the Revolution too was represented by that man, whose face showed too much remorse to leave any doubt that he was fulfilling a duty inspired by deep repentance.

Before he pronounced the Latin words, *Introibo ad altare Dei*, the priest, as if by an inspiration from on high, turned to the three who were with him as the representatives of Christian France, and said to them, as though to banish from their sight all the misery of the garret room :

" We are about to enter into the sanctuary of God ! "

At these words, uttered with deep devotion, a holy awe took possession of the stranger and the two nuns. Under the vast arches of St. Peter's at Rome these Christians could not have realised the majesty of God's Presence more plainly than in that refuge of misery ; so true is it that between Him and man all outward things seem useless, and His greatness comes from Himself alone. The stranger showed a really fervent devotion. So the same feelings united the prayers of these four servants of God and the King. The sacred words sounded like a heavenly music in the midst of the silence. There was a moment when the unknown man could not restrain his tears. It was at the *Pater Noster*, when the priest added this prayer in Latin which no doubt the stranger understood :

" *Et remitte scelus regicidis sicut Ludovicus eis remisit semetipse* (And forgive their crime to the regicides, as Louis himself forgave them.) "

The nuns saw two large tear-drops making lines of moisture down the strong face of the unknown, and falling to the floor.

The Office for the Dead was recited. The *Domine salvum fac regem*, chanted in a low voice, touched the hearts of these faithful Royalists, who thought how the child King, for whom at that moment they were imploring help of the Most High, was a captive in the hands of his enemies. The stranger suddered as he remembered that perhaps a fresh crime might be committed, in which he would no doubt be forced to have a share.

When the Office for the Dead was ended, the priest made a sign to the two nuns and they withdrew. As soon as he found himself alone with the stranger, he went towards him with a sad and gentle air, and said to him in a fatherly voice :

" My son, if you have imbrued your hands in the blood of the martyr King, confide in me. There is no fault that is not blotted out in God's eyes by a repentance as sincere and as touching as yours appears to be."

At the first words uttered by the priest the stranger gave way to an involuntary movement of alarm. But he recovered his self-control, and looked calmly at the astonished priest.

" Father," he said to him, in a voice that showed evident signs of emotion, " no one is more innocent than I am of the blood that has been shed. . . ."

" It is my duty to take your word for it," said the priest.

There was a pause, during which once more he looked closely at his penitent. Then, persisting in taking him for one of those timid members of the National Convention who abandoned to the executioner a sacred and inviolable head in order to save their own, he spoke once more in a grave tone :

" Consider, my son, that in order to be guiltless of this great crime it does not suffice merely to have had no direct co-operation in it. Those who, although they could have defended the king, left their swords in their scabbards, will have a very heavy account to render to the King of Heaven. . . . Oh, yes ! " added the old priest, shaking his head expressively from side to side. " Yes, very heavy ! . . . for in standing idle, they have made themselves the involuntary accomplices of this awful misdeed."

" Do you think," asked the man, as if struck with horror, " that even an indirect participation in it will be punished ? . . . Are we then to take it that, say, a soldier who was ordered to keep the ground at the scaffold is guilty ? . . ."

The priest hesitated. Pleased at the dilemma in which he had put this Puritan of Royalism, by placing him between the doctrine of passive obedience, which, according to the partisans of the monarchy, must be the essence of the military code, and the equally important doctrine, which was the sanction of the respect due to the person of the King, the stranger eagerly accepted the priest's hesitation as indicating a favourable solution of the doubts that seemed to harass him. Then, in order not to give the venerable theologian further time for reflection, he said to him :

" I would be ashamed to offer you any honorarium for the funeral service you have just celebrated for the repose of the soul of the King, and to satisfy my own conscience. One can only pay the price of what is inestimable by offering that which is also beyond price. Will you therefore condescend, sir, to accept the gift I make you of a sacred relic. . . . Perhaps the day will come when you will understand its value."

As he ceased speaking, the stranger held out to the priest a little box that was extremely light. The latter took it in his hands automatically, so to say, for the solemnity of the words of this man, the tone in which he spoke, the reverence with which he handled the box, had plunged him into a reverie of deep astonishment. Then they returned to the room where the two nuns were waiting for them.

" You are," said the stranger to them, " in a house the proprietor of which, the plasterer, Mucius Scaevola, who lives in the first storey, is famous in the quarter for his patriotism. But all the same he is secretly attached to the Bourbons. Formerly he was a huntsman to Monseigneur the Prince de Conti, and he owes his fortune to him. By staying here you are safer than anywhere else in France. Remain here, therefore. Certain pious souls will provide for your needs, and you can wait without danger for less evil times. A year hence, on January 21st " (as he pronounced these last words, he could not conceal an involuntary start), " if this poor place is still your refuge, I shall come back to assist once more with you at a mass of expiation."

He stopped without further explanation. He saluted the silent inhabitants of the garret, took in with a last look the signs that told of their poverty, and left the room.

For the two simple nuns such an adventure had all the interest of a romance. So when the venerable abbé had told them of the mysterious present so solemnly made to him by this man, they placed the box on the table, and the feeble light of the candle, shining on the three anxious faces, showed on all of them a look of indescribable curiosity. Mademoiselle de Langeais opened the box, and found in it a handkerchief of fine cambric soiled with perspiration. As they unfolded it they saw spots on it.

" They are blood stains," said the priest.

" It is marked with the royal crown ! " exclaimed the other sister.

With a feeling of horror the two sisters dropped the precious relic. For these two simple souls the mystery that surrounded the stranger had become something inexplicable. And, as for the priest, from that day he did not even attempt to find an explanation of it in his own mind.

It was not long before the three prisoners realised that notwithstanding the Terror an invisible hand was stretched out to protect them. At first firewood and provisions were sent in for them. Then the two nuns guessed that a woman was associated with their protector, for they were sent linen and clothes that would make it possible for them to go out without attracting attention by the aristocratic fashion of the dress they had been forced to wear till then. Finally Mucius Scaevola provided them with two " civic cards," certificates of good citizenship. Often by roundabout ways they received warnings, that were necessary for the safety of the priest, and they recognised that these friendly hints came so opportunely that they could only emanate from some one who was initiated into the secrets of the state. Notwithstanding the famine from which Paris was suffering, the refugees found rations of white bread left regularly at their garret door by invisible hands. However, they thought they could identify in Mucius Scaevola the mysterious agent of this beneficence, which was always as ingenious as it was well directed.

The noble refugees in the garret could have no doubt but that their protector was the same person who had come to assist at the mass of expiation on the night of January 22nd, 1793. He thus became the object of a very special regard on the part of all three. They hoped in him only, lived only thanks to him. They had added special prayers for him to their devotions ; morning and night these pious souls offered up petitions for his welfare, for his prosperity, for his salvation. They begged God to remove all temptations from him, to deliver him from his enemies, and to give him a long and peaceful life. Their gratitude was thus, so to say, daily renewed, but was inevitably associated with a feeling of curiosity that became keener as day after day went by.

The circumstances that had attended the appearance of the stranger were the subject of their conversations. They formed a thousand conjectures with regard to him, and it was a fresh benefit to them of another kind that he thus served to distract their minds from other thoughts. They were quite determined that on the night when, according to his promise, he would come back to celebrate the mournful anniversary of the death of Louis XVI. they would not let him go without establishing more friendly relations with him.

The night to which they had looked forward so impatiently came at last. At midnight the heavy footsteps of the unknown resounded on the old wooden stair. The room had been made ready to receive him ; the altar was prepared. This time the sisters opened the door before he reached it, and both hastened to show a light on the staircase. Mademoiselle de Langeais even went down a few steps in order the sooner to see their benefactor.

" Come," she said to him in a voice trembling with affection, " come . . . you are expected."

The man raised his head, and without replying cast a gloomy look at the nun. She felt as if a mantle of ice had fallen around her, and kept silence. At the sight of him the feeling of gratitude and of curiosity died out in all their hearts. He was perhaps less cold, less taciturn, less terrible than he appeared to these souls, whom the excitement of their feelings disposed to a warm and friendly welcome. The three poor prisoners realised that the man wished to remain a stranger to them, and they accepted the situation.

The priest thought that he noticed a smile, that was at once repressed, play upon the lips of the unknown, when he remarked the preparations that had been made for his reception. He heard mass and prayed. But then he went away after having declined, with a few words of polite refusal, the invitation that Mademoiselle de Langeais offered him to share with them the little supper that had been made ready.

After the 9th Thermidor—(the fall of Robespierre)—both the nuns and the Abbé de Marolles were able to go about in Paris without incurring the least danger. The old priest's first excursion was to a perfumer's shop at the sign of the *Reine des Fleurs*, kept by Citizen Ragon and his wife, formerly perfumers to the court, who had remained faithful to the royal family. The Vendéans made use of them as their agents for corresponding with the exiled princes and the royalist committee at Paris. The Abbé, dressed as the times required, was standing on the doorstep of the shop, which was situated between the Church of Saint Roch and the Rue des Frondeurs, when a crowd, which filled all the Rue Saint-Honoré, prevented him from going out.

" What is the matter ? " he asked Madame Ragon.

" It's nothing," she replied. " It's the cart with the executioner on the way to the Place Louis XV. Ah ! we saw it often enough last year. But to-day, four days after the anniversary of January 21st, one can watch that terrible procession go by without feeling displeasure."

" Why ? " said the abbé, " it is not Christian of you to talk thus."

" But it's the execution of the accomplices of Robespierre. They did their best to save themselves, but they are going in their turn where they sent so many innocent people ! "

The crowd was pouring past like a flood. The Abbé de Marolles, yielding to an impulse of curiosity, saw, standing erect on the cart, the man who three days before had come to hear his mass.

" Who is that ? " he said, " the man who . . ."

" It's the hangman," replied Monsieur Ragon, giving the executioner the name he bore under the monarchy.

" My dear, my dear," cried out Madame Ragon, " Monsieur l'Abbé is dying ! "

And the old lady seized a bottle of smelling salts with which to revive the aged priest from a fainting fit.

" No doubt," he said, " what he gave me was the handkerchief with which the King wiped his forehead as he went to martyrdom. . . . Poor man ! . . . The steel blade had a heart when all France was heartless ! . . ."

The perfumers thought that the poor priest was raving.

A PASSION IN THE DESERT

HONORÉ DE BALZAC

"IT is a terrible sight!" she exclaimed as we left the menagerie of Monsieur Martin.

She had just been witnessing this daring showman "performing" in the cage of his hyena.

"By what means," she went on, "can he have so tamed these animals as to be secure of their affection?"

"What seems to you a problem," I responded, interrupting her, "is in reality a fact of nature."

"Oh!" she exclaimed, with an incredulous smile.

"You think, then, that animals are devoid of passions?" I asked her. "You must know that we can teach them all the qualities of civilised existence."

She looked at me with an astonished air.

"But," I went on, "when I first saw Monsieur Martin, I confess that, like yourself, I uttered an exclamation of surprise. I happened to be standing by the side of an old soldier, whose right leg had been amputated, and who had come in with me. I was struck by his appearance. His was one of those intrepid heads, stamped with the seal of war, upon whose brows are written the battles of Napoleon. About this old soldier was a certain air of frankness and of gaiety which always gains my favour. He was doubtless one of those old troopers whom nothing can surprise; who find food for laughter in the dying spasms of a comrade, who gaily bury and despoil him, who challenge bullets with indifference— though their arguments are short enough—and who would hobnob with the devil. After keenly looking at the showman as he was coming from the cage, my neighbour pursed his lips with that significant expression of contempt which superior men assume to show their difference from the dupes. At my exclamation of surprise at Monsieur Martin's courage he smiled, and nodding with a knowing air, remarked, 'I understand all that.'

"'How?' I answered. 'If you can explain this mystery to me you will oblige me greatly.'

"In a few moments we had struck up an acquaintance, and went to dine at the first restaurant at hand. At dessert a bottle of champagne completely cleared the memory of this strange old soldier. He told his story, and I saw he was right when he exclaimed, ' I understand all that.'

When we got home, she teased me so, and yet so prettily, that I consented to write out for her the soldier's reminiscences.

The next day she received this episode, from an epic that might be called " The French in Egypt."

During the expedition undertaken in Upper Egypt by General Desaix, a Provençal soldier, who had fallen into the hands of the Maugrabins, was taken by these Arabs into the desert beyond the cataracts of the Nile. In order to put between them and the French army a distance to assure their safety, the Maugrabins made a forced march, and did not halt till night. They then camped by the side of a well, surrounded by a clump of palm trees, where they had before buried some provisions. Never dreaming that their prisoner would think of flight, they merely bound his hands, and all of them, after eating a few dates, and giving barley to their horses, went to sleep. When the bold Provençal saw his enemies incapable of watching him, he picked up a scimitar with his teeth, and then, with the blade fixed between his knees, cut the cords that lashed his wrists, and found himself at liberty. He at once seized a carbine and a dagger ; provided himself with some dry dates and a small bag of barley, powder and balls ; girded on the scimitar, sprang on a horse, and pressed forward in the direction where he fancied the French army must be found. Impatient to regain the bivouac, he so urged the weary horse that the poor beast fell dead, its sides torn with the spurs, leaving the Frenchman alone in the midst of the desert.

After wandering for some time amidst the sand with the desperate courage of an escaping convict, the soldier was forced to stop. Night was closing in. Despite the beauty of the Eastern night he had not strength sufficient to go on. Fortunately he had reached a height on the top of which were palm trees, whose leaves, for some time visible far off, had awakened in his heart a hope of safety. He was so weary that he lay down on a granite stone, oddly shaped like a camp-bed, and went to sleep without taking the precaution to protect himself in his slumber. He had sacrificed his life, and his last thought was a regret for having left the Maugrabins, whose wandering life began to please him, now that he was far from them and from all hope of succour.

He was awakened by the sun, whose pitiless rays falling vertically upon the granite made it intolerably hot. For the Provençal had been so careless as to cast himself upon the ground in the direction opposite to that on which the green majestic palm-tops threw their shadow. He looked at these solitary trees and shuddered ! They reminded him of the graceful shafts surmounted by long foils that distinguish the Saracenic columns of the Cathedral of Arles. He counted the few palms; and then looked about him. A terrible despair seized upon his soul. He saw a boundless ocean. The melancholy sands spread round him, glittering like a blade of steel in a bright light, as far as eye could see. He knew not whether he was gazing on an ocean or a chain of lakes as lustrous as a mirror. A fiery mist shimmered, in little ripples, above the tremulous landscape. The sky possessed an Oriental blaze, the brilliancy which brings despair, seeing that it leaves the imagination nothing to desire. Heaven and earth alike were all aflame. The silence was terrible in its wild and awful majesty. Infinity, immensity, oppressed the soul on all sides; not a cloud was in the sky, not a breath was in the air, not a movement on the bosom of the sand which undulated into tiny waves. Far away, the horizon was marked off, as on a summer day at sea, by a line of light as bright and narrow as a sabre's edge.

The Provençal clasped his arms about a palm tree as if it had been the body of a friend; then, sheltered by the straight and meagre shadow, he sat down weeping on the granite, and looking with deep dread upon the lonely scene spread out before his eyes. He cried aloud as if to tempt the solitude. His voice, lost in the hollows of the height, gave forth far off a feeble sound that woke no echo; the echo was within his heart!

The Provençal was twenty-two years old. He loaded his carbine.

"Time enough for that!" he muttered to himself, placing the weapon of deliverance on the ground.

Looking by turns at the melancholy waste of sand and at the blue expanse of sky, the soldier dreamed of France. With delight he fancied that he smelt the Paris gutters, and recalled the towns through which he had passed, the faces of his comrades, and the slightest incidents of his life. Then his Southern imagination made him fancy, in the play of heat quivering above the plain, the pebbles of his own dear Provence. But fearing all the dangers of this cruel mirage, he went down in the direction opposite to that which he had taken when he had climbed the hill the night before. Great was his joy on discovering a kind of grotto, naturally cut out of the enormous fragments of granite that formed the bottom of the hill. The remnants of a mat showed that this retreat had once been inhabited. Then, a few steps farther, he saw palm trees with a load of dates. Again the instinct which attaches man to life awoke within his heart. He now hoped to live until the passing of some Maugrabin; or perhaps he would soon hear the boom of cannon, for at that time Buonaparte was overrunning Egypt. Revived by this reflection, the Frenchman cut down a few bunches of ripe fruit, beneath whose weight the date trees seemed to bend, and felt sure, on tasting this unhoped-for manna, that the inhabitant of this grotto had cultivated the palm trees. The fresh and luscious substance of the date bore witness to his predecessor's care.

The Provençal passed suddenly from dark despair to well-nigh insane delight. He climbed the hill again ; and spent the remainder of the day in cutting down a barren palm tree, which the night before had served him for shelter.

A vague remembrance made him think of the wild desert beasts ; and, foreseeing that they might come to seek the spring which bubbled through the sand among the rocks, he resolved to secure himself against their visits by placing a barrier at the door of his hermitage. In spite of his exertions, in spite of the strength with which the fear of being eaten during sleep endued him, it was impossible for him to cut the palm to pieces in one day ; but he contrived to bring it down. When, towards evening, the monarch of the desert fell, the thunder of its crash resounded far, as if the mighty Solitude had given forth a moan. The soldier shuddered as if he had heard a voice that prophesied misfortune. But like an heir who does not long bewail the death of a relation, he stripped the tree of the broad, long, green leaves, and used them to repair the mat on which he was about to lie. At length, wearied by the heat and by his labours, he fell asleep beneath the red roof of his murky grotto.

In the middle of the night he was disturbed by a strange noise. He sat up ; in the profound silence he could hear a creature breathing—a savage respiration which resembled nothing human. Terror, intensified by darkness, silence, and the fancies of one suddenly awakened, froze his blood. He felt a sharp contraction of his scalp, when, as the pupils of his eyes dilated, he saw in the shadow two faint and yellow lights. At first he thought these lights were some reflection of his eyeballs, but soon, the clear brightness of the night helping him to distinguish objects in the grotto, he saw lying at two paces from him an enormous beast !

Was it a lion ?—a tiger ?—a crocodile ? The Provençal was not sufficiently educated to know the species of his enemy, but his terror was all the greater ; since his ignorance assisted his imagination. He bore the cruel torture of listening, of marking the caprices of this awful breathing, without losing a sound of it, or venturing to make the slightest movement. A smell as pungent as a fox's, but more penetrating, filled the grotto ; and when it entered his nostrils his terror passed all bounds ; he could no longer doubt the presence of the terrible companion whose royal den was serving him for bivouac. Presently the moon, now sinking, lighted up the den, and in the moon-rays gradually shone out a panther's spotted skin.

The lion of Egypt was sleeping, curled up like a great dog who is the peaceable possessor of a sumptuous kennel at a mansion door ; its eyes, which had been opened for one moment, were now closed again. Its face was turned towards the Frenchman.

A thousand troubled thoughts passed through the mind of the panther's prisoner. At first he thought of shooting it ; but there was not enough room between them to adjust his gun ; the barrel would have reached beyond the animal. And what if he awoke it ! This supposition made him motionless. Listening in the silence to the beating of his heart, he cursed the loud pulsations, fearing to disturb the sleep that gave him time to seek some means of safety. Twice he placed his hand upon his scimitar, with the intention of cutting off the head of his enemy ; but the difficulty of cutting through the short, strong fur compelled him to abandon the idea. To fail was certain death. He preferred the odds of conflict, and determined to await the daybreak. And daylight was not long in coming. The Frenchman was able to examine the panther. Its muzzle was stained with blood.

" It has eaten plenty," he reflected, without conjecturing that the feast might have been composed of human flesh ; " it will not be hungry when it wakes."

It was a female. The fur upon her breast and thighs shone with whiteness. A number of little spots like velvet looked like charming bracelets around her paws. The muscular tail was also white, but tipped with black rings. The upper part of her coat, yellow as old gold, but very soft and smooth, bore these characteristic marks, shaded into the form of roses, which serve to distinguish the panther from the other species of the genus *Felis*. This fearful visitor was snoring tranquilly in an attitude as graceful as that of a kitten lying on the cushions of an ottoman. Her sinewy blood-stained paws, with powerful claws, were spread beyond her head, which rested on them, and from which stood out the thin, straight whiskers with a gleam like silver wires.

If she had been imprisoned in a cage, the Provençal would assuredly have admired the creature's grace, and the vivid contrasts of colour that gave her garment an imperial lustre ; but at this moment he felt his sight grow dim at her sinister aspect. The presence of the panther, even sleeping, made him experience the effect which the magnetic eyes of the serpent are said to exercise upon the nightingale.

In the presence of this danger the courage of the soldier faltered, although without doubt it would have risen at the cannon's mouth. A desperate thought, however, filled his mind, and dried up at its source the chilly moisture which was rolling down his forehead. Acting as men do who, driven to extremities, at last defy their fate and nerve themselves to meet their doom, he saw a tragedy in this adventure, and resolved to play his part in it with honour to the last.

" Two days ago," he argued with himself, " the Arabs might have killed me."

30*

Considering himself as good as dead, he waited bravely, yet with restless curiosity, for the awaking of his enemy.

When the sun shone out, the panther opened her eyes suddenly ; then she spread out her paws forcibly, as if to stretch them and get rid of cramp. Then she yawned, showing an alarming set of teeth and an indented, rasp-like tongue. " She is like a dainty lady ! " thought the Frenchman, as he saw her rolling over with a gentle and coquettish movement. She licked off the blood that stained her paws and mouth, and rubbed her head with movements full of charm. " That's it ! Just beautify yourself a little ! " the Frenchman said, his gaiety returning with his courage. " Then we must say good morning ! " And he took up the short dagger of which he had relieved the Maugrabins.

At this moment the panther turned her head towards the Frenchman, and looked at him fixedly, without advancing. The rigidity of those metallic eyes, and their insupportable brightness, made the Provençal shudder. The beast began to move towards him. He looked at her caressingly, and fixing her eyes as if to magnetise her, he let her come close up to him ; then, with a soft and gentle gesture, he passed his hand along her body, from head to tail, scratching with his nails the flexible vertebrae that divide a panther's yellow back. The beast put up her tail with pleasure ; her eyes grew softer ; and when for the third time the Frenchman accomplished this self-interested piece of flattery, she broke into a purring like a cat. But this purr proceeded from a throat so deep and powerful that it re-echoed through the grotto like the peals of a cathedral organ. The Provençal, realising the success of his caresses, redoubled them, until the imperious beauty was completely soothed and lulled.

When he felt sure that he had perfectly subdued the ferocity of his capricious companion, whose hunger had been satisfied so cruelly the night before, he got up to leave the grotto. The panther let him go ; but when he had climbed the hill, she came bounding after him with the lightness of a sparrow hopping from branch to branch, and rubbed herself against the soldier's leg, arching her back after the fashion of a cat. Then looking at her guest with eyes whose brightness had grown less inflexible, she uttered that savage cry which naturalists have compared to the sound of a saw.

" What an exacting beauty ! " cried the Frenchman, smiling. He set himself to play with her ears, to caress her body, and to scratch her head hard with his nails. Then, growing bolder with success, he tickled her skull with the point of his dagger, watching for the spot to strike her. But the hardness of the bones made him afraid of failing.

The sultana of the desert approved the action of her slave by raising her head, stretching her neck, and showing her delight by the quietness of her attitude. The Frenchman suddenly reflected that

in order to assassinate this fierce princess with one blow he need
only stab her in the neck. He had just raised his knife for the
attempt, when the panther, with a graceful action, threw herself
upon the ground before his feet, casting him from time to time a look
in which, in spite of its ferocity of nature, there was a gleam of
tenderness.

The poor Provençal, with his back against a palm tree, ate his
dates, while he cast inquiring glances, now towards the desert for
deliverers, now upon his terrible companion, to keep an eye upon
her dubious clemency. Every time he threw away a date-stone, the
panther fixed her eyes upon the spot with inconceivable mistrust.
She scrutinised the Frenchman with a businesslike attention; but the
examination seemed favourable, for when he finished his poor meal,
she licked his boots, and with her rough, strong tongue removed the
dust incrusted in their creases.

" But when she becomes hungry ? " thought the Provençal.

Despite the shudder this idea caused him, the soldier began
examining with curiosity the proportions of the panther, certainly
one of the most beautiful specimens of her kind. She was three feet
high and four feet long, without the tail. This powerful weapon,
as round as a club, was nearly three feet long. The head—large
as that of a lioness—was distinguished by an expression of rare
delicacy ; true, the cold cruelty of the tiger dominated, but there
was also a resemblance to the features of a wily woman. In a word,
the countenance of the solitary queen wore at this moment an
expression of fierce gaiety, like that of Nero flushed with wine ;
she had quenched her thirst in blood, and now desired to play.

The soldier tried to come and go, and the panther let him, content
to follow him with her eyes, but less after the manner of a faithful
dog than of a great Angora cat, suspicious even of the movements of
its master. When he turned round he saw beside the fountain the
carcase of his horse ; the panther had dragged the body all that
distance. About two-thirds had been devoured. This sight reassured
the Frenchman. He was thus easily able to explain the absence of
the panther, and the respect which she had shown for him while he
was sleeping.

This first piece of luck emboldened him about the future. He
conceived the mad idea of setting up a pleasant household life,
together with the panther, neglecting no means of pacifying her and
of conciliating her good graces. He returned to her, and saw, to his
delight, that she moved her tail with an almost imperceptible
motion. Then he sat down beside her without fear, and began to
play with her ; he grasped her paws, her muzzle, pulled her ears,
threw her over on her back, and vigorously scratched her warm and
silky sides. She let him have his way, and when the soldier tried
to smooth the fur upon her paws she carefully drew in her claws,

which had the curve of a Damascus blade. The Frenchman, who kept one hand upon his dagger, was still thinking of plunging it into the body of the too-confiding panther; but he feared lest she should strangle him in her last convulsions. And besides, within his heart there was a movement of remorse that warned him to respect an inoffensive creature. It seemed to him that he had found a friend in this vast desert. Involuntarily he called to mind a woman whom he once had loved, whom he sarcastically had nicknamed " Mignonne," from her jealousy, which was so fierce that during the whole time of their acquaintance he went in fear that she would stab him. This memory of his youth suggested the idea of calling the young panther by this name, whose lithe agility and grace he now admired with less terror.

Towards evening he had become so far accustomed to his perilous position, that he almost liked the hazard of it. At last his companion had got into the habit of looking at him when he called in a falsetto voice " Mignonne."

At sundown Mignonne uttered several times a deep and melancholy cry.

" She has been properly brought up," thought the light-hearted soldier ; " she says her prayers ! " But it was, no doubt, her peaceful attitude which brought the jest into his mind.

" All right, my little pet ; I will let you get to sleep first," he said, relying on his legs to get away as soon as she was sleeping, and to seek some other shelter for the night.

The soldier waited with patience for the hour of flight, and when it came, set out full speed in the direction of the Nile. But he had only gone a quarter of a league across the sand when he heard the panther bounding after him, uttering at intervals that saw-like cry, more terrible even than the thudding of her leaps.

" Well ! " he said to himself, " she must have taken a fancy to me. Perhaps she has never yet met any one. It is flattering to be her first love ! " At this moment the Frenchman fell into a shifting quicksand, so dangerous to the traveller in the desert, escape from which is hopeless. He felt that he was sinking ; he gave a cry of terror. The panther seized him by the collar with her teeth, and spring backwards with stupendous vigour drew him from the gulf as if by magic.

" Ah ! Mignonne ! " cried the soldier, enthusiastically caressing her, " we are friends now for life and death. But no tricks, eh ? " and he retraced his steps.

Henceforth the desert was as though it had been peopled. It contained a being with whom he could converse, and whose ferocity had been softened for him, without his being able to explain so strange a friendship.

However great was his desire to keep awake and on his guard, he fell asleep. On awakening, Mignonne was no longer to be seen. He climbed the hill, and then perceived her afar off, coming along by leaps and bounds, according to the nature of these creatures, the extreme flexibility of whose vertebrae prevents their running.

Mignonne came up, her jaws besmeared with blood. She received the caresses of her companion with deep purrs of satisfaction. Her eyes, now full of softness, were turned, with even greater tenderness than the night before, to the Provençal, who spoke to her as to a pet.

"Ah! Beauty! you are a respectable young woman, are you not? You like petting, don't you? Are you not ashamed of yourself? You have been eating a Maugrabin! Well! they're animals, as you are. But don't you go and gobble up a Frenchman. If you do, I shall not love you!"

She played as a young pup plays with its master, letting him roll her over, beat and pet her; and sometimes she would coax him to caress her with a movement of entreaty.

A few days passed thus. This companionship revealed to the Provençal the sublime beauties of the desert. From the moment when he found within it hours of fear and yet of calm, a sufficiency of food, and a living creature who absorbed his thoughts, his soul was stirred by new emotions. It was a life of contrasts. Solitude revealed to him her secrets, and involved him in her charm. He discovered in the rising and the setting of the sun a splendour hidden from the world of men. His frame quivered when he heard above his head the soft whirr of a bird's wings—rare wayfarer; or when he saw the clouds—those changeful, man-coloured voyagers—mingle in the depth of heaven. In the dead of night he studied the effects of the moon upon the sea of sand, which the simoom drove in ever-changing undulations. He lived with the Oriental day; he marvelled at its pomp and glory; and often, after having watched the grandeur of a tempest in the plain, in which the sands were whirled in dry red mists of deadly vapour, he beheld with ecstasy the coming on of night, for then there fell upon him the benignant coolness of the stars. He heard imaginary music in the sky. Solitude taught him all the bliss of reverie. He spent whole hours in calling trifles to remembrance, in comparing his past life with his strange present. To his panther he grew passionately attached, for he required an object of affection. Whether by a strong effort of his will he had really changed the character of his companion, or whether, thanks to the constant warfare of the desert, she found sufficient food, she showed no disposition to attack him, and at last, in her perfect tameness, he no longer felt the slightest fear.

He spent a great part of his time in sleeping, but ever, like a spider in its web, with mind alert, that he might not let deliverance escape him, should any chance to pass within the sphere described by the horizon. He had sacrificed his shirt to make a flag, which he had hoisted to the summit of a palm tree stripped of leaves. Taught by necessity, he had found the means to keep it spread by stretching it with sticks, lest the wind should fail to wave it at the moment when the hoped-for traveller might be travelling the waste of sand.

It was during the long hours when hope abandoned him that he amused himself with his companion. He had learnt to understand the different inflexions of her voice. and the expression of her glances ; he had studied the varying changes of the spots that starred her robe of gold. Mignonne no longer growled, even when he seized her by the tuft with which her terrible tail ended, to count the black and white rings which adorned it, and which glittered in the sun like precious gems. It delighted him to watch the delicate soft lines of her snowy breast and graceful head. But above all when she was gambolling in her play he watched her with delight, for the agility, the youthfulness of all her movements filled him with an ever-fresh surprise. He admired her suppleness in leaping, climbing, gliding, pressing close against him, swaying, rolling over, crouching for a bound. But however swift her spring, however slippery the block of granite, she would stop short, without motion, at the sound of the word " Mignonne ! "

One day, in the most dazzling sunshine, an enormous bird was hovering in the air. The Provençal left his panther to examine this new visitor ; but after waiting for a moment the deserted sultana uttered a hoarse growl.

" Blessed if I don't believe that she is jealous ! " he exclaimed, perceiving that her eyes were once more hard and rigid. " A woman's soul has passed into her body, that is certain ! "

The eagle disappeared in air, while he admired afresh the rounded back and graceful outlines of the panther. She was as pretty as a woman. The blonde fur blended in its delicate gradations into the dull white colour of the thighs. The brilliant sunshine made this vivid gold, with spots of brown, take on a lustre indescribable. The Provençal and the panther looked at one another understandingly ; the beauty of the desert quivered when she felt the nails of her admirer on her skull. Her eyes gave forth a flash like lightning, and then she closed them hard.

" She *has* a soul," he cried, as he beheld the desert queen in her repose, golden as the sands, white as their blinding lustre, and, like them, fiery and alone.

" Well ? " she said to me, " I have read your pleading on behalf of animals. But what was the end of these two persons so well made to understand each other ? "

"Ah! They ended as all great passions end—through a misunderstanding. Each thinks the other guilty of a falsity, each is too proud for explanation, and obstinacy brings about a rupture."

"And sometimes in the happiest moments," she said, "a look, an exclamation, is enough! Well, what was the end of the story?"

"That is difficult to tell, but you will understand what the old fellow had confided to me, when, finishing his bottle of champagne, he exclaimed, 'I don't know how I hurt her, but she turned on me like mad, and with her sharp teeth seized my thigh. The action was not savage; but fancying that she meant to kill me I plunged my dagger into her neck. She rolled over with a cry that froze my blood; she looked at me in her last struggles without anger. I would have given everything on earth, even my cross—which then I had not won—to bring her back to life. It was as if I had slain a human being. And the soldiers who had seen my flag, and who were hastening to my succour, found me bathed in tears.

"'Well, sir,' he went on, after a moment's silence, 'since then I have been through the wars in Germany, Spain, Russia, France; I have dragged my carcase round the world; but there is nothing like the desert in my eyes! Ah! it is beautiful—superb!'

"'What did you feel there?' I inquired of him.

"'Oh! that I cannot tell you. Besides, I do not always regret my panther and my clump of palm trees. I must be sad at heart for that. But mark my words. In the desert there is everything and there is nothing.'

"'Explain yourself.'

"'Well!' he continued, with a gesture of impatience, 'it is God without man.'"

THE CONSCRIPT

Honoré de Balzac

One evening in the month of November 1793 the principal people of Carentan were gathered in the salon of Madame de Dey, at whose house the assembly was held daily. Some circumstances which would not have attracted attention in a large city, but which were certain to cause a flutter in a small one, lent to this customary meeting an unusual degree of interest. Two days before, Madame de Dey had closed her door to her guests, whom she had also excused herself from receiving on the preceding day, on the pretext of an indisposition. In ordinary times, these two occurences would have produced the same effect in Carentan that the closing of all the theatres would produce in Paris. In those days existence was to a certain extent incomplete. And in 1793 the conduct of Madame de Dey might have had the most deplorable results. The slightest venturesome proceeding almost always became a question of life or death for the nobles of that period.

In order to understand the intense curiosity and the narrow-minded cunning which enlivened the Norman countenances of all those people during the evening, but especially in order that we may share the secret anxiety of Madame de Dey, it is necessary to explain the rôle that she played at Carentan. As the critical position in which she found herself at that moment was undoubtedly identical with that of many people during the Revolution, the sympathies of more than one reader will give the needed touch of colour to this narrative.

Madame de Dey, the widow of a lieutenant-general and chevalier of the Orders, had left the court at the beginning of the emigration. As she possessed considerable property in the neighbourhood of Carentan, she had taken refuge there, hoping that the influence of the Terror would not be much felt so far from Paris. This prevision, based upon exact knowledge of the province, proved to be just. The Revolution did little devastation in Lower Normandy. Although, when Madame de Dey visited her estates formerly, she used to see only the noble families of the province, she had from policy thrown her house open to the leading *bourgeois* of the town and to the new authorities, striving to make them proud of their conquest of her, without arousing either hatred or jealousy in their minds. Gracious and amiable, endowed with that indescribable gentleness of manner which attracts without resort to self-abasement or to entreaties, she had succeeded in winning general esteem by the most exquisite tact, the wise promptings of which had enabled her to maintain her stand on the narrow line where she could satisfy the demands of that mixed society, without humiliating the self-esteem of the parvenus or offending that of her former friends.

About thirty-eight years of age, she still retained, not that fresh and buxom beauty which distinguishes the young women of Lower Normandy, but a slender and aristocratic beauty. Her features were small and refined, her figure slim and willowy. When she spoke, her pale face seemed to brighten and to take on life. Her great black eyes were full of suavity, but their placid, devout expression seemed to indicate that the active principle of her existence had ceased to be. Married in the flower of her youth to an old and jealous soldier, the falseness of her position in the centre of a dissipated court contributed much, no doubt, to cast a veil

of serious melancholy over a face on which the charm and vivacity
of love must formerly have shone bright.

Constantly obliged to restrain the ingenuous impulses of a woman,
at a time when she still feels instead of reflecting, passion had
remained unsullied in the depths of her heart. So it was that her
principal attraction was due to the youthful simplicity which at
intervals her face betrayed, and which gave to her ideas a naïve
expression of desire. Her aspect imposed respect, but there were
always in her bearing and in her voice symptoms of an outreaching
towards an unknown future, as in a young girl ; the most
unsusceptible man soon found himself falling in love with her,
and nevertheless retained a sort of respectful dread, inspired by her
courteous manners, which were most impressive. Her soul,
naturally great, and strengthened by painful struggles, seemed
to be too far removed from the common herd, and men realised
their limitations.

That soul necessarily demanded an exalted passion. So that
Madame de Dey's affections were concentrated in a single sentiment,
the sentiment of maternity. The happiness and pleasures of which
her married life had been deprived, she found in her excessive love
for her son. She loved him not only with the pure and profound
devotion of a mother, but with the coquetry of a mistress, the
jealousy of a wife. She was unhappy when separated from him,
anxious during his absence, could never see enough of him, lived
only in him and for him. In order to make men understand the
strength of this feeling, it will suffice to add that his son was not only
Madame de Dey's only child, but her last remaining relative, the
only living being to whom she could attach the fears, the hopes,
and the joys of her life. The late Count de Dey was the last scion
of his family, as she was the last heiress of hers.

Thus human schemes and interest were in accord with the noblest
cravings of the soul to intensify in the Countess's heart a sentiment
which is always strong in women. She had brought up her son
only with infinite difficulty, which had made him dearer than ever
to her. Twenty times the doctors prophesied his death ; but,
trusting in her presentiments and her hopes, she had the
inexpressible joy of seeing him pass through the dangers of childhood unscathed, and of exulting in the upbuilding of his constitution
in spite of the decrees of the faculty.

Thanks to constant care, her son had grown and had attained such
perfect development, that at twenty years of age he was considered
one of the most accomplished cavaliers at Versailles. Lastly—a
piece of good fortune which does not crown the efforts of all mothers
—she was adored by her son ; their hearts were bound together by
sympathies that were fraternal. Even if they had not been
connected by the decree of nature, they would have felt instinctively

for each other that affection of one being for another so rarely met with in life. Appointed sub-lieutenant of dragoons at eighteen, the young man had complied with the prevailing ideas of the requirements of honour at that period by following the princes when they emigrated.

Thus Madame de Dey, of noble birth, wealthy, and the mother of an émigré, was fully alive to the dangers of her painful situation. As she had no other aim than to preserve a great fortune for her son, she had renounced the happiness of accompanying him ; but, when she read the harsh laws by virtue of which the Republic daily confiscated the property of the émigrés at Carentan, she applauded herself for her courageous act. Was she not guarding her son's treasures at the peril of her life ?

Then, when she learned of the shocking executions ordered by the Convention, she slept undisturbed, happy to know that her only treasure was in safety, far from all perils and all scaffolds. She took pleasure in the belief that she had adopted the best course to save all his fortunes at once. Making the concessions to this secret thought which the disasters of the time demanded, without compromising her womanly dignity or her aristocratic beliefs, she enveloped her sorrows in impenetrable mystery. She had realised the difficulties which awaited her at Carentan. To go thither and assume the first place in society—was it not equivalent to defying the scaffold every day ? But, sustained by a mother's courage, she succeeded in winning the affection of the poor by relieving all sorts of misery indiscriminately, and made herself necessary to the rich by taking the lead in their pleasures.

She received the prosecuting attorney of the commune, the mayor, the president of the district, the public accuser, and even the judges of the Revolutionary Tribunal. The first four of these functionaries, being unmarried, paid court to her, in the hope of marrying her, whether by terrifying her by the injury which they had it in their power to do her, or by offering her their protection. The public accuser, formerly an attorney at Caen, where he had been employed by the Countess, tried to win her love by conduct full of devotion and generosity. A dangerous scheme ! He was the most formidable of all the suitors. He alone was thoroughly acquainted with the condition of his former client's large fortune. His passion was inevitably intensified by all the cravings of an avarice which rested upon almost unlimited power upon the right of life or death throughout the district.

This man, who was still young, displayed so much nobility in his behaviour that Madame de Dey had been unable as yet to make up her mind concerning him. But, scorning the danger that lay in a contest of wits with Normans, she employed the inventive genius and the cunning which nature has allotted to woman, to play those rivals against one another. By gaining time, she hoped to arrive safe and sound at the end of her troubles. At that time, the royalists in the interior of France flattered themselves that each day would see the close of the Revolution ; and that conviction was the ruin of a great many of them.

Despite these obstacles, the Countess had skilfully maintained her independence down to the day when, with incomprehensible imprudence, she had conceived the idea of closing her door. The interest which she inspired was so profound and so genuine that the people who came to her house that evening were greatly distressed when they learned that it was impossible for her to receive them. Then, with the outspoken curiosity which is a part of provincial manners, they inquired concerning the misfortune, the sorrow, or the disease which had afflicted Madame de Dey. To these questions, an old housekeeper called Brigitte replied that her mistress had shut herself into her room, and would not see anybody, not even her servants. The cloistral existence, so to speak, which the people of a small town lead, gives birth in them to such an unconquerable habit of analysing and commenting upon the actions of other people, that, after expressing their sympathy for Madame de Dey, without an idea whether she was really happy or unhappy, they all began to speculate upon the causes of her abrupt seclusion.

" If she were ill," said one curious individual, " she would have sent for the doctor ; but the doctor was at my house all day, playing chess. He said with a laugh that in these days there is but one disease, and that is unfortunately incurable."

This jest was put forward apologetically. Thereupon, men, women, old men, and maidens began to search the vast field of conjecture. Every one fancied that he caught a glimpse of a secret, and that secret engrossed the imaginations of them all. The next day, the suspicions became embittered. As life in a small town is open to all, the women were the first to learn that Brigitte had laid in more supplies than usual at the market. That fact could not be denied. Brigitte had been seen in the morning, in the square, and—a most extraordinary thing—she had bought the only hare that was offered for sale. Now the whole town knew that Madame de Dey did not like game. The hare became the starting-point for endless suppositions. When taking their daily walk, old men observed in the Countess's house a sort of concentrated activity which was made manifest by the very precautions which the servants took to conceal it. The valet was seen beating a rug in the garden ; on the day before, no one would have paid any heed to it ; but that rug became a link in the chain of evidence to support the romances which everybody was engaged in constructing. Every person had his own.

On the second day, when they learned that Madame de Dey

proclaimed that she was indisposed, the principal persons of Carentan met in the evening at the house of the Mayor's brother, an ex-merchant, a married man, of upright character and generally esteemed, and for whom the Countess entertained a high regard. There all the aspirants to the rich widow's hand had a more or less probable story to tell ; and each of them hoped to turn to his advantage the secret circumstances which forced her to compromise herself thus. The public accuser imagined a complete drama in which Madame de Dey's son was brought to her house by night.

The mayor favoured the idea of a priest who had not taken the oath, arriving from La Vendée and asking her for shelter ; but the purchase of a hare on Friday embarrassed the mayor greatly. The president of the district was strong in his conviction that it was a leader of Chouans or of Vendeans, hotly pursued. Others suggested a nobleman escaped from one of the prisons of Paris. In short, one and all suspected the Countess of being guilty of one of those acts of generosity which the laws of that day stigmatised as crimes, and which might lead to the scaffold. The public accuser said in an undertone that they must hold their tongues, and try to snatch the unfortunate woman from the abyss towards which she was rapidly precipitating herself.

" If you talk about this business," he added, " I shall be obliged to interfere, to search her house, and then——"

He did not finish his sentence, but they all understood his reticence.

The Countess's sincere friends were so alarmed for her that, during the morning of the third day, the procureur-syndic of the commune caused his wife to write her a note to urge her to receive as usual that evening. The old merchant, being bolder, called at Madame de Dey's house in the morning. Trusting in the service which he proposed to render her, he demanded to be shown to her presence, and was thunder-struck when he saw her in the garden, engaged in cutting the last flowers from the beds, to supply her vases.

" Doubtless she has been sheltering her lover," said the old man to himself, seized with compassion for the fascinating woman.

The strange expression on the Countess's face confirmed him in his suspicions. Deeply touched by that devotion so natural to a woman, and which always moves our admiration, because all men are flattered by the sacrifices which a woman makes for a man, the merchant informed the Countess of the reports which were current in the town, and of the dangerous position in which she stood.

" But," he said, as he concluded, " although there are some among our officials who are not indisposed to forgive you for an act of herosim of which a priest is the object, no one will pity you if they discover that you are sacrificing yourself to the affections of the heart."

At these words Madame de Dey looked at the old man with an expression of desperation and terror which made him shudder, old man though he was.

"Come," said she, taking his hand and leading him to her bedroom, where, after making sure that they were alone, she took from her bosom a soiled and wrinkled letter. "Read," she cried, making a violent effort to pronounce the word.

She fell into her chair as if utterly overwhelmed. While the old gentleman was feeling for his spectacles and wiping them, she fastened her eyes upon him and scrutinised him for the first time with curiosity ; then she said softly, in an altered voice :

"I trust you."

"Am I not sharing your crime ? " replied the old man, simply.

She started ; for the first time her heart found itself in sympathy with another heart in that little town. The old merchant suddenly understood both the distress and the joy of the Countess. Her son had taken part in the Granville expedition ; he wrote to his mother from prison, imparting to her one sad but sweet hope. Having no doubt of his success in escaping, he mentioned three days in which he might appear at her house in disguise. The fatal letter contained heartrending farewells in case he should not be at Carentan on the evening of the third day ; and he begged his mother to hand a considerable sum of money to the messenger, who had undertaken to carry that letter to her through innumerable perils. The paper shook in the old man's hand.

"And this is the third day ! " cried Madame de Dey, as she sprang to her feet, seized the letter, and began to pace the floor.

"You have been imprudent," said the merchant ; "why did you lay in provisions ? "

"Why, he may arrive almost starved, worn out with fatigue, and——"

She did not finish.

"I am sure of my brother," said the old man, "and I will go and enlist him on your side."

In this emergency the old tradesman recovered the shrewdness which he had formerly displayed in his business, and gave advice instinct with prudence and sagacity. After agreeing upon all that they were both to say and to do, the old man went about, on cleverly devised pretexts, to the principal houses of Carentan, where he announced that Madame de Dey, whom he had just seen, would receive that evening in spite of her indisposition. Pitting his shrewdness against the inborn Norman cunning, in the examination to which each family subjected him in regard to the nature of the Countess's illness, he succeeded in leading astray almost everybody who was interested in that mysterious affair. His first visit produced a marvellous effect.

He stated, in the presence of a gouty old lady, that Madame de Dey had nearly died of an attack of gout in the stomach ; as the famous Tronchin had once recommended her, in such a case, to place on her chest the skin of a hare, flayed alive, and to stay in bed and not move, the Countess, who had been at death's door two days before, having followed scrupulously Tronchin's advice, found herself sufficiently recovered to see those who cared to call on her that evening. That fable had a prodigious success, and the Carentan doctor, a royalist in secret, added to its effect by the air of authority with which he discussed the remedy. Nevertheless, suspicion had taken too deep root in the minds of some obstinate persons, or some philosophers, to be entirely dispelled ; so that, in the evening, those who were regular habitués of Madame de Dey's salon arrived there early ; some in order to watch her face, others from friendly regard ; and the majority were impressed by the marvellous nature of her recovery.

They found the Countess seated at the corner of the huge fire-place of her salon, which was almost as modestly furnished as those of the people of Carentan ; for, in order not to offend the sensitive self-esteem of her guests, she denied herself the luxury to which she had always been accustomed, and had changed nothing in her house. The floor of the reception-room was not even polished. She left old-fashioned dark tapestries on the walls, she retained the native furniture, burned tallow candles, and followed the customs of the town, espousing provincial life, and recoiling neither from the most rasping pettinesses nor the most unpleasant privations. But, realising that her guests would forgive her for any display of splendour which aimed at their personal comfort, she neglected nothing when it was a question of affording them enjoyment ; so that she always gave them excellent dinners. She even went so far as to make a pretence at miserliness, to please those calculating minds ; and after causing certain concessions in the way of luxurious living to be extorted from her, she seemed to comply with a good grace.

About seven o'clock in the evening, therefore, the best of the uninteresting society of Carentan was assembled at her house, and formed a large circle about the fireplace. The mistress of the house, sustained in her misery by the compassionate glances which the old tradesman bestowed upon her, submitted with extraordinary courage to the minute questionings, the trivial and stupid reasoning of her guests. But at every blow of the knocker at her door, and whenever she heard footsteps in the street, she concealed her emotion by raising some question of interest to the welfare of the province. She started noisy discussions concerning the quality of the season's cider, and was so well seconded by her confidant that her company almost forgot to watch her, her manner was so natural and her self-possession so imperturbable. The public accuser and one of the judges of the Revolutionary Tribunal sat silent, carefully watching every movement of her face and listening to every sound in the house, notwithstanding the uproar ; and on several occasions they asked her very embarrassing questions, which, however, the Countess answered with marvellous presence of mind. Mothers have such an inexhaustable store of courage ! When Madame de Dey had arranged the card-tables, placed everybody at a table of boston, reversis, or whist, she remained a few moments talking with some young people, with the utmost nonchalance, playing her part like a consummate actress. She suggested a game of loto—said that she alone knew where it was, and disappeared.

"I am suffocating, my poor Brigitte ! " she cried, wiping away the tears that gushed from her eyes, which gleamed with fever, anxiety, and impatience. "He does not come," she continued, looking about the chamber to which she had flown. "Here, I breathe again and I live. A few moments more, and he will be here ; for he still lives, I am certain ; my heart tells me so ! Do you hear nothing, Brigitte ? Oh ! I would give the rest of my life to know whether he is in prison or travelling through the country ! I would like not to think——"

She looked about again to make sure that everything was in order in the room. A bright fire was burning on the hearth ; the shutters were carefully closed ; the furniture glistened with cleanliness ; the way in which the bed was made proved that the Countess had assisted Brigitte in the smallest details ; and her hopes betrayed themselves in the scrupulous care which seemed to have been taken in that room, where the sweet charm of love and its most chaste caresses exhaled in the perfume of the flowers. A mother alone could have anticipated the desires of a soldier, and have arranged to fulfil them all so perfectly. A dainty meal, choice wines, clean linen, and dry shoes—in a word, all that was likely to be necessary or agreeable to a weary traveller was there set forth, so that he need lack nothing, so that the joy of home might make known to him a mother's love.

"Brigitte ? " said the Countess in a heartrending tone, as she placed a chair at the table, as if to give reality to her longings, to intensify the strength of her illusions.

"Oh ! he will come, madame ; he isn't far away. I don't doubt that he's alive and on his way here," replied Brigitte. "I put a key in the Bible and I held it on my fingers while Cottin read the Gospel of St. John ; and, madame, the key didn't turn."

"Is that a sure sign ? " asked the Countess.

" Oh ! it is certain, madame ; I would wager my salvation that he is still alive.   God can't make a mistake."

" Despite the danger that awaits him here, I would like right well to see him."

" Poor Monsieur Auguste ! " cried Brigitte ; " I suppose he is somewhere on the road, on foot ! "

" And there is the church clock striking eight ! " cried the Countess, in dismay.

She was afraid that she had remained longer than she ought in that room, where she had faith in the life of her son because she looked upon all that meant life to him.   She went downstairs ; but before entering the salon, she stood a moment in the vestibule, listening to see if any sound woke the silent echoes of the town. She smiled at Brigitte's husband, who was on sentry-duty, and whose eyes seemed dazed by dint of strained attention to the murmurs in the square and in the streets.   She saw her son in everything and everywhere.   In a moment she returned to the salon, affecting a jovial air, and began to play loto with some young girls ; but from time to time she complained of feeling ill, and returned to her chair at the fireplace.

Such was the condition of persons and things in the house of Madame de Dey, while, on the road from Paris to Cherbourg, a young man dressed in a dark carmagnole, the regulation costume at that period, strode along towards Carentan.   At the beginning of the conscription, there was little or no discipline.   The demands of the moment made it impossible for the Republic to equip all of its soldiers at once, and it was no rare thing to see the roads covered with conscripts still wearing their civilian dress.   These young men marched in advance of their battalions to the halting-places, or loitered behind, for their progress was regulated by their ability to endure the fatigue of a long march.

The traveller with whom we have to do was some distance in advance of the column of conscripts on its way to Cherbourg, which the Mayor of Carentan was momentarily expecting, in order to distribute lodging-tickets among them.   The young man walked with a heavy but still firm step, and his bearing seemed to indicate that he had long been familiar with the hardships of military life. Although the moon was shining on the pastures about Carentan, he had noticed some great white clouds which seemed on the point of discharging snow upon the country, and the fear of being surprised by a storm doubtless quickened his gait, which was more rapid than his weariness made comfortable.   He had an almost empty knapsack on his back, and carried in his hand a boxwood cane, cut from one of the high, broad hedges formed by that shrub around most of the estates in Lower Normandy.

The solitary traveller entered Carentan, whose towers, of fantastic aspect in the moonlight, had appeared to him a moment before. His steps awoke the echoes of the silent streets, where he met no one ; he was obliged to ask a weaver who was still at work to point out the Mayor's abode. That magistrate lived only a short distance away, and the conscript soon found himself safe under the porch of his house, where he seated himself on a stone bench, waiting for the lodging-ticket which he had asked for. But, being summoned by the Mayor, he appeared before him, and was subjected to a careful examination. The soldier was a young man of attractive appearance, who apparently belonged to some family of distinction. His manner indicated noble birth, and the intelligence due to a good education was manifest in his features.

" What is your name ? " the Mayor asked, with a shrewd glance at him.

" Julien Jussieu," replied the conscript.

" And you come from——? " said the magistrate, with an incredulous smile.

" From Paris."

" Your comrades must be far behind ? " continued the Norman in a mocking tone.

" I am three leagues ahead of the battalion."

" Doubtless some sentimental reason brings you to Carentan, citizen conscript ? " queried the Mayor, slyly. " It is all right," he added, imposing silence, with a wave of the hand, upon the young man, who was about to speak. " We know where to send you. Here," he said, handing him the lodging-ticket ; " here, *Citizen Jussieu.*"

There was a perceptible tinge of irony in the tone in which the magistrate uttered these last two words, as he held out a ticket upon which Madame de Dey's name was written. The young man read the address with an air of curiosity.

" He knows very well that he hasn't far to go, and when he gets outside, it won't take him long to cross the square," cried the Mayor, speaking to himself, while the young man went out. " He's a bold young fellow. May God protect him ! He has an answer for everything. However, if any other than I had asked to see his papers, he would have been lost ! "

At that moment the clock of Carentan struck half-past nine ; the torches were being lighted in Madame de Dey's ante-room, and the servants were assisting their masters and mistresses to put on their cloaks, their overcoats, and their mantles ; the card-players had settled their accounts and were about to withdraw in a body, according to the usual custom in all small towns.

" It seems that the public accuser proposes to remain," said a lady, observing that that important functionary was missing when they were about to separate to seek their respective homes, after exhausting all the formulas of leave-taking.

The redoubtable magistrate was in fact alone with the Countess, who waited in fear and trembling until it should please him to go.

" Citizeness," he said at length, after a long silence in which there was something horrible, " I am here to see that the laws of the Republic are observed."

Madame de Dey shuddered.

" Have you no revelations to make to me ? " he demanded.

" None," she replied in amazement.

" Ah, madame ! " cried the accuser, sitting down beside her and changing his tone, " at this moment, for lack of a word, either you or I may bring our heads to the scaffold. I have observed your temperament, your heart, your manners, too closely to share the error into which you have led your guests to-night. You are expecting your son, I am absolutely certain."

The Countess made a gesture of denial ; but she had turned pale, the muscles of her face had contracted, by virtue of the overpowering necessity to display a deceitful calmness, and the accuser's implacable eye lost none of her movements.

" Very well ; receive him," continued the revolutionary magistrate ; " but do not let him remain under your roof later than seven o'clock in the morning. At daybreak I shall come here armed with a denunciation which I shall procure."

She gazed at him with a stupefied air, which would have aroused the pity of a tiger.

" I shall prove," he said in a gentle tone, " the falseness of the denunciation by a thorough search, and the nature of my report will place you out of the reach of any future suspicion. I shall speak of your patriotic gifts, of your true citizenship, and we shall *all* be saved."

Madame de Dey feared a trap ; she did not move, but her face was on fire and her tongue was frozen. A blow of the knocker rang through the house.

" Ah ! " cried the terrified mother, falling on her knees. " Save him ! save him ! "

" Yes, let us save him," rejoined the public accuser, with a passionate glance at her ; " let us save him though it cost *us* our lives."

" I am lost ! " she cried, while the accuser courteously raised her.

" O madame ! " he replied, with a grand oratorical gesture, " I do not choose to owe you to any one but yourself."

" Madame, here he——" cried Brigitte, who thought that her mistress was alone.

At sight of the public accuser, the older servant, whose face was flushed with joy, became rigid and deathly pale.

"What is it, Brigitte?" asked the magistrate, in a mild and meaning tone.

"A conscript that the Mayor has sent here to lodge," replied the servant, showing the ticket.

"That is true," said the accuser, after reading the paper; "a battalion is to arrive here to-night."

And he went out.

The Countess was too anxious at that moment to believe in the sincerity of her former attorney to entertain the slightest suspicion; she ran swiftly upstairs, having barely strength enough to stand upright; then she opened the door of her bedroom, saw her son, and rushed into his arms, well-nigh lifeless.

"O my son, my son!" she cried, sobbing, and covering him with frenzied kisses.

"Madame——" said the stranger.

"Oh! it isn't he!" she cried, stepping back in dismay and standing before the conscript, at whom she gazed with a haggard expression.

"Blessed Lord God, what a resemblance!" said Brigitte.

There was a moment's silence, and the stranger himself shuddered at the aspect of Madame de Dey.

"Ah, monsieur!" she said, leaning upon Brigitte's husband, and feeling then in all its force the grief of which the first pang had almost killed her; "monsieur, I cannot endure to see you any longer; allow my servants to take my place and to attend to your wants."

She went down to her own apartments, half carried by Brigitte and her old servant.

"What, madame!" cried the maid, "is that man going to sleep in Monsieur Auguste's bed, wear Monsieur Auguste's slippers, eat the pie that I made for Monsieur Auguste? They may guillotine me, but I——"

"Brigitte!" cried Madame de Dey.

"Hold your tongue, chatterbox!" said her husband in a low voice; "do you want to kill madame?"

At that moment the conscript made a noise in his room, drawing his chair to the table.

"I will not stay here," cried Madame de Dey; "I will go to the greenhouse, where I can hear better what goes on outside during the night."

She was still wavering between fear of having lost her son and the hope of seeing him appear. The night was disquietingly silent. There was one ghastly moment for the Countess, when the battalion of conscripts marched into the town, and each man repaired to his lodging. There were disappointed hopes at every footstep and every sound; then nature resumed its terrible tranquillity. Towards

morning the Countess was obliged to return to her room. Brigitte,
who watched her mistress every moment, finding that she did not
come out again, went to her room and found the Countess dead.

"She probably heard the conscript dressing and walking about
in Monsieur Auguste's room, singing their cursed *Marseillaise* as if
he were in a stable!" cried Brigitte. "It was that which killed
her!"

The Countess's death was caused by a more intense emotion, and
probably by some terrible vision. At the precise moment when
Madame de Dey died at Carentan, her son was shot in Le Morbihan.
We might add this tragic story to the mass of other observations on
that sympathy which defies the law of space—documents which
some few solitary scholars are collecting with scientific curiosity, and
which will one day serve as basis for a new science, a science which
till now has lacked only its man of genius.

LA GRANDE BRETÈCHE

Honoré de Balzac

ABOUT one hundred yards from Vendôme, on the banks of the
Loire, there stands an old dark-coloured house, surmounted by
a very high roof, and so completely isolated that there is not in
the neighbourhood a single evil-smelling tannery or wretched inn,
such as we see in the outskirts of almost every small town. In
front of the house is a small garden bordering the river, in which the
boxwood borders of the paths, once neatly trimmed, now grow at
their pleasure. A few willows, born in the Loire, have grown as
rapidly as the hedge which encloses the garden, and half conceal
the house. The plants which we call weeds adorn the slope of the
bank with their luxuriant vegetation. The fruit-trees, neglected
for ten years, bear no fruit; their offshoots form a dense undergrowth. The espaliers resemble hornbeam hedges. The paths,
formerly gravelled, are overrun with purslane; but, to tell the truth,
there are no well-marked paths. From the top of the mountain
upon which hang the ruins of the old château of the Dukes of
Vendôme, the only spot from which the eye can look into this
enclosure, you would say to yourself that, at a period which it is
difficult to determine, that little nook was the delight of some
gentleman devoted to roses and tulips, to horticulture in short,
but especially fond of fine fruit. You espy an arbour, or rather

the ruins of an arbour, beneath which a table still stands, not yet entirely consumed by time. At sight of that garden, which is no longer a garden, one may divine the negative delights of the peaceful life which provincials lead, as one divines the existence of a worthy tradesman by reading the epitaph on his tombstone. To round out the melancholy yet soothing thoughts which fill the mind, there is on one of the walls a sun-dial, embellished with this commonplace Christian inscription : ULTIMAM COGITA. The roof of the house is terribly dilapidated, the blinds are always drawn, the balconies are covered with swallows' nests, the doors are never opened. Tall weeds mark with green lines the cracks in the steps ; the ironwork is covered with rust. Moon, sun, winter, summer, snow, have rotted the wood, warped the boards, and corroded the paint.

The deathly silence which reigns there is disturbed only by the birds, the cats, the martens, the rats and the mice, which are at liberty to run about, to fight, and to eat one another at their will. An invisible hand has written everywhere the word MYSTERY. If, impelled by curiosity, you should go to inspect the house on the street side, you would see a high gate, arched at the top, in which the children of the neighbourhood have made numberless holes. I learned later that that gate had been condemned ten years before. Through these irregular breaches you would be able to observe the perfect harmony between the garden front and the courtyard front. The same disorder reigns supreme in both. Tufts of weeds surround the pavements. Enormous cracks furrow the walls, whose blackened tops are enlaced by the countless tendrils of climbing plants. The steps are wrenched apart, the bell-rope is rotten, the gutters are broken. " What fire from heaven has passed this way ? What tribunal has ordered salt to be strewn upon this dwelling ? Has God been insulted here ? Has France been betrayed ? " Such are the questions which one asks one's self. The reptiles crawl hither and thither without answering. That empty and deserted house is an immense riddle the solution of which is known to no one.

It was formerly a small feudal estate and bore the name of La Grande Bretèche. During my stay at Vendôme, where Desplein had left me to attend a rich patient, the aspect of that strange building became one of my keenest pleasures. Was it not more than a mere ruin ? Some souvenirs of undeniable authenticity are always connected with a ruin ; but that abode, still standing, although in process of gradual demolition by an avenging hand, concealed a secret, an unknown thought ; at the very least, it betrayed a caprice. More than once, in the evening, I wandered in the direction of the hedge, now wild and uncared for, which surrounded that enclosure. I defied scratches, and made my way into that ownerless garden, that estate which was neither public nor private ; and I

remained whole hours there contemplating its disarray. Not even
to learn the story which would doubtless account for that extraordinary spectacle, would I have asked a single question of any
Vendômese gossip. Straying about there, I composed delightful
romances, I abandoned myself to little orgies of melancholy which
enchanted me.

If I had learned the cause of that perhaps most commonplace
neglect, I should have lost the unspoken poesy with which I
intoxicated myself. To me that spot represented the most diverse
images of human life darkened by its misfortunes ; now it was the air
of the cloister, minus the monks ; again, the perfect peace of the
cemetery, minus the dead speaking their epitaphic language ;
to-day, the house of the leper ; to-morrow, that of the Fates ; but
it was, above all, the image of the province, with its meditation,
with its hour-glass life. I have often wept there, but never laughed.
More than once I have felt an involuntary terror, as I heard above
my head the low rustling made by the wings of some hurrying dove.
The ground is damp ; you must beware of lizards, snakes, and toads,
which wander about there with the fearless liberty of nature ;
above all, you must not fear the cold, for, after a few seconds, you
feel an icy cloak resting upon your shoulders like the hand of the
Commendator on the neck of Don Juan. One evening I had
shuddered there ; the wind had twisted an old rusty weather-vane,
whose shrieks resembled a groan uttered by the house at the
moment that I was finishing a rather dismal melodrama, by which
I sought to explain to myself that species of monumental grief. I
returned to my inn, beset by sombre thoughts. When I had supped,
my hostess entered my room with a mysterious air, and said to me :

" Here is Monsieur Regnault, monsieur."

" Who is Monsieur Regnault ? "

" What ! monsieur doesn't know Monsieur Regnault ? That's
funny ! " she said, as she left the room.

Suddenly I saw a tall slender man, dressed in black, with his hat in
his hand, who entered the room like a ram ready to rush at his rival,
disclosing a retreating forehead, a small pointed head, and a pale
face, not unlike a glass of dirty water. You would have said that he
was the doorkeeper of some minister. He wore an old coat,
threadbare at the seams ; but he had a diamond in his shirt-frill
and gold rings in his ears.

" To whom have I the honour of speaking, monsieur ? " I asked
him.

He took a chair, seated himself in front of my fire, placed his hat
on my table, and replied, rubbing his hands :

" Ah ! it's very cold ! I am Monsieur Regnault, monsieur."

I bowed, saying to myself :

" Il Bondocani ! Look for him ! "

"I am the notary at Vendôme," he continued.

"I am delighted to hear it, monsieur," I exclaimed, "but I am not ready to make my will, for reasons best known to myself."

"Just a minute," he rejoined, raising his hand as if to impose silence upon me. "I beg pardon, monsieur, I beg pardon! I have heard that you go to walk sometimes in the garden of La Grande Bretèche."

"Yes, monsieur!"

"Just a minute," he said, repeating his gesture; "that practice constitutes a downright trespass. I have come, monsieur, in the name and as executor of the late Madame Comtesse de Merret, to beg you to discontinue your visits. Just a minute! I'm not a Turk, and I don't propose to charge you with a crime. Besides, it may well be that you are not aware of the circumstances which compel me to allow the finest mansion in Vendôme to fall to ruin. However, monsieur, you seem to be a man of education, and you must know that the law forbids entrance upon an enclosed estate under severe penalties. A hedge is as good as a wall. But the present condition of the house may serve as an excuse for your curiosity. I would ask nothing better than to allow you to go and come as you please in that house; but, as it is my duty to carry out the will of the testatrix, I have the honour, monsieur, to request you not to go into that garden again. Even I myself, monsieur, since the opening of the will, have never set foot inside that house, which, as I have had the honour to tell you, is a part of the estate of Madame de Merret. We simply reported the number of doors and windows, in order to fix the amount of the impost which I pay annually from the fund set aside for that purpose by the late countess. Ah! her will made a great deal of talk in Vendôme, monsieur."

At that, he stopped to blow his nose, the excellent man. I respected his loquacity, understanding perfectly that the administration of Madame de Merret's property was the important event of his life—his reputation, his glory, his Restoration. I must needs bid adieu to my pleasant reveries, to my romances; so that I was not inclined to scorn the pleasure of learning the truth from an official source.

"Would it be indiscreet, monsieur," I asked him, "to ask you the reason of this extraordinary state of affairs?"

At that question an expression which betrayed all the pleasure that a man feels who is accustomed to ride a hobby passed over the notary's face. He pulled up his shirt collar with a self-satisfied air, produced his snuff-box, opened it, offered it to me, and at my refusal, took a famous pinch himself. He was happy; the man who has no hobby has no idea of the satisfaction that can be derived from life. A hobby is the precise mean between passion and monomania. At that moment I understood the witty expression of Sterne in all its extent, and I had a perfect conception of the joy with which Uncle Toby, with Trim's assistance, bestrode his battle-horse.

" Monsieur," said Monsieur Regnault, " I was chief clerk to Master Roguin of Paris. An excellent office, of which you may have heard ? No ? Why, it was made famous by a disastrous failure. Not having sufficient money to practise in Paris, at the price to which offices had risen in 1816, I came here and bought the office of my predecessor. I had relatives in Vendôme, among others a very rich aunt, who gave me her daughter in marriage. Monsieur," he continued after a brief pause, " three months after being licensed by the Keeper of the Seals I was sent for one evening, just as I was going to bed (I was not then married), by Madame Comtesse de Merret, to come to her Château de Merret. Her maid, an excellent girl who works in this inn to-day, was at my door with madame countess's carriage. But, just a minute ! I must tell you, monsieur, that Monsieur Comte de Merret had gone to Paris to die, two months before I came here. He died miserably there, abandoning himself to excesses of all sorts. You understand ?—On the day of his departure madame countess had left La Grande Bretèche and had dismantled it. Indeed, some people declare that she burned the furniture and hangings, and all chattels whatsoever now contained in the estate leased by the said— What on earth am I saying ? I beg pardon, I thought I was dictating a lease.—That she burned them," he continued, " in the fields at Merret. Have you been to Merret, monsieur ? No ? " he said, answering his own question. " Ah ! that is a lovely spot ! For about three months," he continued, after a slight shake of the head, " monsieur count and madame countess led a strange life.

" They received no guests ; madame lived on the ground floor, and monsieur on the first floor. When madame countess was left alone, she never appeared except at church. Later, in her own house at her château, she refused to see the friends who came to see her. She was already much changed when she left La Grande Bretèche to go to Merret. The dear woman—I say ' dear,' because this diamond came from her ; but I actually only saw her once—the excellent lady, then, was very ill ; she had doubtless despaired of her health, for she died without calling a doctor ; so that many of our ladies thought that she was not in full possession of her wits. My curiosity was therefore strangely aroused, monsieur, when I learned that Madame de Merret needed my services. I was not the only one who took an interest in that story. That same evening, although it was late, the whole town knew that I had gone to Merret. The maid answered rather vaguely the questions that I asked her on the road ; she told me, however, that her mistress had received the sacrament from the curé of Merret during the day, and that she did not seem likely to live through the night.

" I reached the château about eleven o'clock ; I mounted the main staircase. After passing through divers large rooms, high and dark, and as cold and damp as the devil, I reached the state bed-chamber where the countess was. According to the reports that were current concerning that lady—I should never end, monsieur, if I should repeat all the stories that are told about her—I had thought of her as a coquette. But, if you please, I had much difficulty in finding her in the huge bed in which she lay. To be sure, to light that enormous wainscoted chamber of the old *régime*, where every-thing was so covered with dust that it made one sneeze simply to look at it, she had only one of those old-fashioned Argand lamps. Ah! but you have never been to Merret. Well, monsieur, the bed is one of those beds of the olden time, with a high canopy of flowered material. A small night-table stood beside the bed, and I saw upon it a copy of the *Imitation of Jesus Christ*, which, by the by, I bought for my wife, as well as the lamp. There was also a large couch for the attendant, and two chairs. Not a spark of fire. That was all the furniture. It wouldn't have filled ten lines in an inventory.

"Oh! my dear monsieur, if you had seen, as I then saw it, that huge room hung with dark tapestry, you would have imagined yourself transported into a genuine scene from a novel. It was icy cold; and, more than that, absolutely funereal," he added, raising his arm with a theatrical gesture and pausing for a moment. "By looking hard and walking close to the bed, I succeeded in discovering Madame de Merret, thanks to the lamp, the light of which shone upon the pillow. Her face was as yellow as wax, and resembled two clasped hands. She wore a lace cap, which revealed her lovely hair, as white as snow. She was sitting up, and seemed to retain that position with much difficulty. Her great black eyes, dulled by fever no doubt, and already almost lifeless, hardly moved beneath the bones which the eyebrows cover—these," he said, pointing to the arch over his eyes.—" Her brow was moist. Her fleshless hands resembled bones covered with tightly-drawn skin; her veins and muscles could be seen perfectly. She must have been very beautiful; but at that moment I was seized with in indefinable feeling at her aspect. Never before, according to those who laid her out, had a living creature attained such thinness without dying. In short, she was horrible to look at; disease had so wasted that woman that she was nothing more than a phantom. Her pale violet lips seemed not to move when she spoke to me. Although my profession had familiarised me with such spectacles, by taking me sometimes to the pillows of dying persons to take down their last wishes, I confess that the families in tears and despair whom I had seen were as nothing beside that solitary, silent woman in that enormous château.

"I did not hear the slightest sound, I could not detect the move-ment which the breathing of the sick woman should have imparted

to the sheets that covered her ; and I stood quite still, gazing
at her in a sort of stupor. It seems to me that I am there now.
At last her great eyes moved, she tried to raise her right hand
which fell back upon the bed, and these words came from her mouth
like a breath, for her voice had already ceased to be a voice ;
' I have been awaiting you with much impatience.'—Her cheeks
suddenly flushed. It was a great effort for her to speak, monsieur.
—' Madame,' I said. She motioned to me to be silent. At that
moment the old nurse rose and whispered in my ear : ' Don't speak ;
madame countess cannot bear to hear the slightest sound, and
what you said might excite her.'—I sat down. A few moments
later, Madame de Merret collected all her remaining strength to
move her right arm and thrust it, not without infinite difficulty,
beneath her bolster ; she paused for just a moment ; then she made
a last effort to withdraw her hand, and when she finally produced
a sealed paper, drops of sweat fell from her brow.—' I place my
will in your hands,' she said. ' Oh, *mon Dieu !* oh ! '—That was
all. She grasped a crucifix that lay on her bed, hastily put it to
her lips, and died. The expression of her staring eyes makes me
shudder even now, when I think of it. She must have suffered
terribly ! There was a gleam of joy in her last glance, a sentiment
which remained in her dead eyes.

" I carried the will away ; and when it was opened, I found that
Madame de Merret had appointed me her executor. She left all
her property to the hospital at Vendôme with the exception of a
few individual legacies. But these were her provisions with
respect to La Grande Bretèche : She directed me to leave her house,
for fifty years from the day of her death, in the same condition
as at the moment that she died ; forbidding any person whatsoever to
enter the rooms, forbidding the slightest repairs to be made, and
even setting aside a sum in order to hire keepers, if it should be
found necessary, to assure the literal execution of her purpose.
At the expiration of that period, if the desire of the testatrix has
been carried out, the house is to belong to my heirs, for monsieur
knows that notaries cannot accept legacies. If not, La Grande
Bretèche is to revert to whoever is entitled to it, but with the
obligation to comply with the conditions set forth in a codicil
attached to the will, which is not to be opened until the
expiration of the said fifty years. The will was not attacked ; and
so——"

At that, without finishing his sentence, the elongated notary
glanced at me with a triumphant air, and I made him altogether
happy by addressing a few compliments to him.

" Monsieur," I said, " you have made a profound impression
upon me, so I think I see that dying woman, paler than her sheets ;
her gleaming eyes terrify me ; and I shall dream of her to-night.

But you must have formed some conjecture concerning the provisions of that extraordinary will."

"Monsieur," he said with a comical reserve, "I never allow myself to judge the conduct of those persons who honour me by giving me a diamond."

I soon loosened the tongue of the scrupulous Vendômese notary, who communicated to me, not without long digressions, observations due to the profound politicians of both sexes whose decrees are law in Vendôme. But those observations were so contradictory and so diffuse that I almost fell asleep, despite the interest I took in that authentic narrative. The dull and monotonous tone of the notary, who was accustomed, no doubt, to listen to himself, and to force his clients and his fellow citizens to listen to him, triumphed over my curiosity.

"Aha! many people, monsieur," he said to me on the landing, "would like to live forty-five years more; but just a minute!" and with a sly expression, he placed his right forefinger on his nose, as if he would have said: "Just mark what I say."—"But to do that, to do that," he added, "a man must be less than sixty."

I closed my door, having been roused from my apathy by this last shaft, which the notary considered very clever; then I seated myself in my easy-chair, placing my feet on the andirons. I was soon absorbed in an imaginary romance à la Radcliffe, based upon the judicial observations of Monsieur Regnault, when my door, under the skilful manipulation of a woman's hand, turned upon its hinges. My hostess appeared, a stout red-faced woman, of excellent disposition, who had missed her vocation: she was a Fleming, who should have been born in a picture by Teniers.

"Well, monsieur," she said, "no doubt Monsieur Regnault has given you his story of La Grande Bretèche?"

"Yes, Mother Lepas."

"What did he tell you?"

I repeated in a few words the chilling and gloomy story of Madame de Merret. At each sentence my hostess thrust out her neck, gazing at me with the true innkeeper's perspicacity—a sort of happy medium between the instinct of the detective, the cunning of the spy, and the craft of the trader.

"My dear Madame Lepas," I added, as I concluded, "you evidently know more, eh? If not, why should you have come up here?"

"Oh! on an honest woman's word, as true as my name's Lepas——"

"Don't swear; your eyes are big with a secret. You knew Monsieur de Merret. What sort of a man was he?"

"Bless my soul! Monsieur de Merret was a fine man, whom you never could see the whole of, he was so long; an excellent

gentleman, who came here from Picardy, and who had his brains
very near his cap, as we say here. He paid cash for everything,
in order not to have trouble with anybody. You see, he was
lively. We women all found him very agreeable."

"Because he was lively ? " I asked.

"That may be," she said. "You know, monsieur, that a man
must have had something in front of him, as they say, to marry
Madame de Merret, who, without saying anything against the
others, was the loveliest and richest woman in the whole province.
She had about twenty thousand francs a year. The whole town
went to her wedding. The bride was dainty and attractive, a real
jewel of a woman. Ah ! they made a handsome couple at that
time ! "

"Did they live happily together ? "

"Oh, dear ! oh, dear ! yes and no, so far as any one could tell ;
for, as you can imagine, we folks didn't live on intimate terms
with them. Madame de Merret was a kind-hearted woman, very
pleasant, who had to suffer sometimes perhaps from her husband's
quick temper ; but although he was a bit proud, we liked him.
You see, it was his business to be like that ; when a man is noble,
you know——"

"However, some catastrophe must have happened, to make
Monsieur and Madame de Merret separate so violently ? "

"I didn't say there was any catastrophe, monsieur. I don't
know anything about it."

"Good ! I am sure now that you know all about it."

"Well, monsieur, I will tell you all I know. When I saw
Monsieur Regnault come up to your room, I had an idea that he
would talk to you about Madame de Merret in connection with
La Grande Bretèche. That gave me the idea of consulting with
monsieur, who seems to me a man of good judgment and incapable
of playing false with a poor woman like me, who never did anybody any harm, and yet who's troubled by her conscience. Up
to this time I've never dared to speak out to the people of this
neighbourhood, for they're all sharp-tongued gossips. And then,
monsieur, I've never had a guest stay in my inn so long as you
have, and to whom I could tell the story of the fifteen thousand
francs."

"My dear Madame Lepas," I said, arresting the flood of her
words, " if your confidence is likely to compromise me, I wouldn't
be burdened with it for a moment, for anything in the world."

"Don't be afraid," she said, interrupting me ; " you shall see."

This eagerness on her part made me think that I was not the
only one to whom my worthy hostess had communicated the secret
of which I dreaded to be the only confidant, and I listened.

"Monsieur," she began, "when the Emperor sent Spanish or

other prisoners of war here, I had to board, at the expense of the government, a young Spaniard who was sent to Vendôme on parole. In spite of the parole, he went every day to show himself to the subprefect. He was a Spanish grandee ! Nothing less ! He had a name in *os* and *dia*, something like Bagos de Férédia. I have his name written on my register ; you can read it if you wish. He was a fine young man for a Spaniard, who they say are all ugly. He was only five feet two or three inches tall, but he was well-built ; he had little hands, which he took care of—oh ! you should have seen ; he has as many brushes for his hands as a woman has for all purposes ! He had long black hair, a flashing eye, and rather a copper-coloured skin, which I liked all the same. He wore such fine linen as I never saw before on any one, although I have entertained princesses, and among others General Bertrand, the Duke and Duchess d'Abrantès, Monsieur Decazes, and the King of Spain. He didn't eat much ; but he had polite and pleasant manners, so that I couldn't be angry with him for it. Oh ! I was very fond of him, although he didn't say four words a day, and it was impossible to have the slightest conversation with him ; if any one spoke to him, he wouldn't answer ; it was a fad, a mania that they all have, so they tell me. He read his breviary like a priest, he went to mass and to the services regularly. Where did he sit ? We noticed that later : about two steps from Madame de Merret's private chapel. As he took his seat there the first time that he came to the church, nobody imagined that there was any design in it. Besides, he never took his face off his prayer-book, the poor young man ! In the evening, monsieur, he used to walk on the mountain, among the ruins of the château. That was the poor man's only amusement ; he was reminded of his own country there. They say that there's nothing but mountains in Spain.

"Very soon after he came here he began to stay out late. I was anxious when he didn't come home till midnight ; but we all got used to his whim ; he would take the key of the door, and we wouldn't wait for him. He lived in a house that we have on Rue de Casernes. Then one of our stablemen told us that one night, when he took the horses to drink, he thought he saw the Spanish grandee swimming far out in the river, like a real fish. When he came back, I told him to be careful of the eel-grass ; he seemed vexed that he had been seen in the water. At last, monsieur, one day, or rather one morning, we didn't find him in his room ; he hadn't come home. By hunting carefully everywhere, I found a writing in his table drawer, where there were fifty of the Spanish gold-pieces which they call *portugaises*, and which were worth about five thousand francs ; and then there were ten thousand francs' worth of diamonds in a little sealed box. His writing said that in case he didn't return, he left us this money and his diamonds, on condition that we would found masses to thank God for his escape and his salvation. In those days I still had my man, who went out to look for him. And here's the funny part of the story : he brought back the Spaniard's clothes, which he found under a big stone in a sort of a shed by the river, on the château side, almost opposite La Grande Bretèche.

"My husband went there so early that no one saw him ; he burned the clothes after reading the letter, and we declared, according to Count Férédia's wish, that he had escaped. The subprefect set all the gendarmerie on his track, but, bless my soul ! they never caught him. Lepas believed that the Spaniard had drowned himself. For my part, monsieur, I don't think it ; I think rather that he was mixed up in Madame de Merret's business, seeing that Rosalie told me that the crucifix that her mistress thought so much of that she had it buried with her, was made of ebony and silver ; now, in the early part of his stay here, Monsieur Férédia had one of silver and ebony, which I didn't see afterwards. Tell me now, monsieur, isn't it true that I needn't have any remorse about the Spaniard's fifteen thousand francs, and that they are fairly mine ? "

"Certainly. But did you never try to question Rosalie ? " I asked her.

"Oh ! yes, indeed, monsieur. But would you believe it ? That girl is like a wall. She knows something, but it's impossible to make her talk."

After conversing a moment more with me, my hostess left me beset by undefined and dismal thoughts, by a romantic sort of curiosity, a religious terror not unlike the intense emotion that seizes us when we enter a dark church at night and see a dim light in the distance under the lofty arches ; a vague figure gliding along, or the rustling of a dress or a surplice ; it makes us shudder. La Grande Bretèche and its tall weeds, its condemned windows, its rusty ironwork, its closed doors, its deserted rooms, suddenly appeared before me in fantastic guise. I tried to penetrate that mysterious abode, seeking there the kernel of that sombre story, of that drama which had caused the death of three persons. In my eyes Rosalie was the most interesting person in Vendôme. As I scrutinised her, I detected traces of some inmost thought, despite the robust health that shone upon her plump cheeks. There was in her some seed of remorse or of hope ; her manner announced a secret, as does that of the devotee who prays with excessive fervour, or that of the infanticide, who constantly hears her child's last cry. However, her attitude was artless and natural, her stupid smile had no trace of criminality, and you would have voted her innocent simply by glancing at the large handkerchief with red and blue squares which covered her vigorous bust, confined by a gown with white and violet stripes.

"No," I thought, "I won't leave Vendôme without learning the whole story of La Grande Bretèche. To obtain my end, I will become Rosalie's friend, if it is absolutely necessary."

"Rosalie ? " I said one evening.

"What is it, monsieur ? "

"You are not married ? "

She started slightly.

"Oh ! I sha'n't lack men when I take a fancy to be unhappy ! " she said, with a laugh.

She speedily overcame her inward emotion ; for all women, from the great lady down to the servant at an inn, have a self-possession which is peculiar to them.

"You are fresh and appetising enough not to lack suitors. But tell me, Rosalie, why did you go to work in an inn when you left Madame de Merret's ? Didn't she leave you some money ? "

"Oh, yes ! but my place is the best in Vendôme, monsieur."

This reply was one of those which judges and lawyers call dilatory. Rosalie seemed to me to occupy in that romantic story the position of the square in the middle of the chessboard ; she was at the very centre of interest and of truth ; she seemed to me to be tied up in the clue ; there was in that girl the last chapter of a romance ; and so, from that moment, Rosalie became the object of my attentions. By dint of studying the girl, I observed in her, as in all women to whom we devote all our thoughts, a multitude of good qualities : she was neat and clean, and she was fine-looking—that goes without saying ; she had also all the attractions which our desire imparts to women, in whatever station of life they may be. A fortnight after the notary's visit, I said to Rosalie one evening, or rather one morning, for it was very early :

"Tell me all that you know about Madame de Merret."

"Oh, don't ask me that, Monsieur Horace ! " she replied in alarm.

Her pretty face darkened, her bright colour vanished, and her eyes lost their humid, innocent light. But I insisted.

"Well," she rejoined, " as you insist upon it, I will tell you ; but keep my secret."

"Of course, of course, my dear girl ; I will keep all your secrets with the probity of a thief, and that is the most loyal probity that exists."

"If it's all the same to you," she said, " I prefer that it should be with your own."

Thereupon she arranged her neckerchief, and assumed the attitude of a story-teller ; for there certainly is an attitude of trust and security essential to the telling of a story. The best

stories are told at a certain hour, and at the table, as we all are now.
No one ever told a story well while standing, or fasting. But if it
were necessary to reproduce faithfully Rosalie's diffuse eloquence,
a whole volume would hardly suffice. Now, as the event of which
she gave me a confused account occupied, between the loquacity
of the notary and that of Madame Lepas, the exact position of the
mean terms of an arithmetical proportion between the two extremes,
it is only necessary for me to repeat it to you in a few words.
Therefore I abridge.

The room which Madame de Merret occupied at La Grande
Bretèche was on the ground floor. A small closet, about four feet
deep, in the wall, served as her wardrobe. Three months before
the evening, the incidents of which I am about to narrate, Madame
de Merret had been so seriously indisposed that her husband left
her alone in her room and slept in a room on the first floor. By
one of those chances which it is impossible to foresee, he returned
home, on the evening in question, two hours later than usual,
from the club to which he was accustomed to go to read the newspapers and to talk politics with the people of the neighbourhood.
His wife supposed that he had come home, and had gone to bed and
to sleep. But the invasion of France had given rise to a lively
discussion ; the game of billiards had been very close, and he had
lost forty francs, an enormous sum at Vendôme, where everybody
hoards money, and where manners are confined within the limits of
a modesty worthy of all praise, which perhaps is the source of a
true happiness of which no Parisian has a suspicion.

For some time past Monsieur de Merret had contented himself with
asking Rosalie if his wife were in bed ; at the girl's reply, always in
the affirmative, he went immediately to his own room with the
readiness born of habit and confidence. But on returning home
that evening, he took it into his head to go to Madame de Meret's
room, to tell her of his misadventure and perhaps also to console
himself for it. During dinner he had remarked that Madame de
Merret was very coquettishly dressed ; he said to himself as he
walked home from the club, that his wife was no longer ill, that
her convalescence had improved her ; but he perceived it, as
husbands notice everything, a little late. Instead of calling Rosalie,
who at that moment was busy in the kitchen, watching the cook
and the coachman play a difficult hand of *brisque*, Monsieur de
Merret went to his wife's room, lighted by his lantern, which he had
placed on the top step of the stairs. His footstep, easily recognised,
resounded under the arches of the corridor. At that instant that
he turned the knob of his wife's door, he fancied that he heard
the door of the closet that I have mentioned close ; but when
he entered, Madame de Merret was alone, standing in front of the
hearth. The husband naïvely concluded that Rosalie was in the

closet ; however, a suspicion, that rang in his ears like the striking of a lock, made him distrustful ; he looked at his wife and detected in her eyes something indefinable of confusion and dismay.

"You come home very late," she said.

That voice, usually so pure and so gracious, seemed to him slightly changed. He made no reply, but at that moment Rosalie entered the room. That was a thunderclap to him. He walked about the room, from one window to another, with a uniform step and with folded arms.

"Have you learned anything distressing, or are you ill ? " his wife timidly asked him, while Rosalie undressed her.

He made no reply.

"You may go," said Madame de Merret to her maid ; "I will put on my curl-papers myself."

She divined some catastrophe simply from the expression of her husband's face, and she preferred to be alone with him. When Rosalie was gone, or was supposed to be gone, for she stayed for some moments in the corridor, Monsieur de Merret took his stand in front of his wife, and said to her coldly :

"Madame, there is some one in your closet ? "

She looked at her husband calmly, and replied simply :

"No, monsieur."

That "no" tore Monsieur de Merret's heart, for he did not believe it ; and yet his wife had never seemed to him purer and more holy than she seemed at that moment. He rose to open the closet door ; Madame de Merret took his hand, stopped him, looked at him with a melancholy expression, and said in a voice strangely moved :

"If you find no one, reflect that all is at an end between us ! "

The indescribable dignity of his wife's attitude reawoke the gentleman's profound esteem for her, and inspired in him one of those resolutions which require only a vaster theatre in order to become immortal.

"No," he said, "I will not do it, Josephine. In either case, we should be separated for ever. Listen ; I know all the purity of your soul, and I know that you lead the life of a saint, and that you would not commit a mortal sin to save your life."

At these words, Madame de Merret looked at her husband with a haggard eye.

"See, here is your crucifix ; swear to me before God that there is no one there, and I will believe you, I will never open that door."

Madame de Merret took the crucifix and said :

"I swear it."

"Louder," said the husband, "and repeat after me : ' I swear before God that there is no one in that closet.' "

She repeated the words without confusion.

31*

"It is well," said Monsieur de Merret coldly. After a moment's silence: "This is a very beautiful thing that I did not know you possessed," he said, as he examined the crucifix of ebony encrusted with silver and beautifully carved.

"I found it at Duvivier's; when that party of prisoners passed through Vendôme last year, he bought it of a Spanish monk."

"Ah!" said Monsieur de Merret, replacing the crucifix on the nail. And he rang. Rosalie did not keep him waiting. Monsieur de Merret walked hastily to meet her, led her into the embrasure of the window looking over the garden, and said to her in a low voice:

"I know that Gorenflot wants to marry you, that poverty alone prevents you from coming together, and that you have told him that you would not be his wife until he found some way to become a master mason. Well, go to him, and tell him to come here with his trowel and his tools. Manage so as not to wake anybody in his house but him; his fortune will exceed your desires. Above all, go out of this house without chattering, or——"

He frowned. Rosalie started, and he called her back.

"Here, take my pass-key," he said.

"Jean!" shouted Monsieur de Merret in the corridor, in a voice of thunder.

Jean, who was both his coachman and his confidential man, left his game of *brisque* and answered the summons.

"Go to bed, all of you," said his master, motioning to him to come near. And he added, but in an undertone: "When they are all asleep, *asleep*, do you understand, you will come down and let me know."

Monsieur de Merret, who had not lost sight of his wife while giving his orders, calmly returned to her side in front of the fire, and began to tell her about the game of billiards and the discussion at the club. When Rosalie returned she found monsieur and madame talking most amicably. The gentleman had recently had plastered all the rooms which composed his reception-apartment on the ground floor. Plaster is very scarce in Vendôme, and the cost of transportation increases the price materially; so he had purchased quite a large quantity, knowing that he would readily find customers for any that he might have left. That circumstance suggested the design which he proceeded to carry out.

"Gorenflot is here, monsieur," said Rosalie in an undertone.

"Let him come in," replied the Picard gentleman aloud.

Madame de Merret turned pale when she saw the mason.

"Gorenflot," said her husband, "go out to the carriage-house and get some bricks, and bring in enough to wall up the door of this closet; you can use the plaster that I had left over to plaster the wall." Then beckoning Rosalie and the workman to him, he said in a low tone: "Look you, Gorenflot, you will sleep here to-night.

But to-morrow morning you shall have a passport to go abroad, to a city which I will name to you. I will give you six thousand francs for your journey. You will remain ten years in that city ; if you are not satisfied there, you can settle in another city, provided that it is in the same country. You will go by way of Paris, where you will wait for me. There I will give you a guarantee to pay you six thousand francs more on your return, in case you have abided by the conditions of our bargain. At that price you should be willing to keep silent concerning what you have done here to-night. As for you, Rosalie, I will give you ten thousand francs, which will be paid to you on the day of your wedding, provided that you marry Gorenflot ; but, in order to be married, you will have to be silent ; if not, no dower."

" Rosalie," said Madame de Merret, " come here and arrange my hair."

The husband walked tranquilly back and forth, watching the door, the mason, and his wife, but without any outward sign of injurious suspicion. Gorenflot was obliged to make a noise ; Madame de Merret seized an opportunity, when the workman was dropping some bricks, and when her husband was at the other end of the room, to say to Rosalie :

" A thousand francs a year to you, my dear child, if you can tell Gorenflot to leave a crack at the bottom.—Go and help him," she said coolly, aloud.

Monsieur and Madame de Merret said not a word while Gorenflot was walling up the door. That silence was the result of design on the husband's part, for he did not choose to allow his wife a pretext for uttering words of double meaning ; and on Madame de Merret's part, it was either prudence or pride. When the wall was half built, the crafty mason seized a moment when the gentleman's back was turned, to strike his pickaxe through one of the panes of the glass door.

At four o'clock, about daybreak, for it was September, the work was finished. The mason remained in the house under the eye of Jean, and Monsieur de Merret slept in his wife's chamber. In the morning, on rising, he said carelessly :

" Ah ! by the way, I must go to the mayor's office, for the passport."

He put his hat on his head, walked towards the door, turned back and took the crucifix. His wife fairly trembled with joy.

" He will go to Duvivier's," she thought.

As soon as the gentleman had left the room, Madame de Merret rang for Rosalie ; then, in a terrible voice, she cried :

" The pickaxe ; the pickaxe ! and to work ! I saw how Gorenflot understood last night ; we shall have time to make a hole, and stop it up."

In a twinkling Rosalie brought her mistress a sort of small axe, and she, with an ardour which no words can describe, began to demolish the wall. She had already loosened several bricks, when, as she stepped back to deal a blow even harder than the preceding ones, she saw Monsieur de Merret behind her ; she fainted.

" Put madame on her bed," said the gentleman coldly.

Anticipating what was likely to happen during his absence, he had laid a trap for his wife ; he had simply written to the mayor, and had sent a messenger to Duvivier. The jeweller arrived just as the disorder in the room had been repaired.

" Duvivier," asked Monsieur de Merret, " didn't you buy some crucifixes from the Spaniards who passed through here ? "

" No, monsieur."

" Very well, I thank you," he said, exchanging with his wife a tiger-like glance.—" Jean," he added, turning towards his confidential valet, " you will have my meals served in Madame de Merret's room ; she is ill, and I shall not leave her until she is well again."

The cruel man remained with his wife twenty days. During the first days, when there was a noise in the walled-up closet and Josephine attempted to implore him in behalf of the dying unknown, he replied, not allowing her to utter a word :

" You have sworn on the cross that there was no one there."

THE ATHEIST'S MASS

HONORÉ DE BALZAC

DOCTOR BIANCHON—a physician to whom science owes a beautiful physiological theory, and who, though still a young man, has won himself a place among the celebrities of the Paris School, a centre of light to which all the doctors of Europe pay homage—practised surgery before devoting himself to medicine. His early studies were directed by one of the greatest surgeons in France, the celebrated Desplein, who was regarded as a luminary of science. Even his enemies admitted that with him was buried a technical skill he could not bequeath to any successor. Like all men of genius he left no heirs. All that was peculiarly his own he carried to the grave with him.

The glory of great surgeons is like that of actors whose work exists only so long as they live, and of whose talent no adequate idea can be formed when they are gone. Actors and surgeons, and also great singers like those artists who increase tenfold the power of music by the way in which they perform it—all these are the heroes of a moment. Desplein is a striking instance of the similarity of the destinies of such transitory geniuses. His name, yesterday so famous, to-day almost forgotten, will live among the specialists of his own branch of science without being known beyond it.

But is not an unheard-of combination of circumstances required for the name of a learned man to pass from the domain of science into the general history of mankind? Had Desplein that universality of acquirements that makes of a man the expression, the type of a century? He was gifted with a magnificent power of diagnosis. He could see into the patient and his malady by an acquired or natural intuition, that enabled him to grasp the peculiar characteristics of the individual, and determined the precise moment, the hour, the minute, when he should operate, taking into account both atmospheric conditions and the special temperament of his patient. In order thus to be able to work hand in hand with Nature, had he studied the ceaseless union of organised and elementary substances contained in the atmosphere, or supplied by the earth to man, who absorbs and modifies them so as to derive from them an individual result? Or did he proceed by that power of deduction and analogy to which the genius of Cuvier owed so much?

However that may be, this man had made himself master of all the secrets of the body. He knew it in its past as in its future, taking the present for his point of departure. But did he embody in his own person all the science of his time, as was the case with Hippocrates, Galen and Aristotle? Did he lead a whole school towards new worlds of knowledge? No. And while it is impossible to deny to this indefatigable observer of the chemistry of the human body the possession of something like the ancient science of Magism—that is to say, the knowledge of principles in combination, of the causes of life, of life as the antecedent of life, and what it will be through the action of causes preceding its existence—it must be acknowledged that all this was entirely personal to him. Isolated during his life by egotism, this egotism was the suicide of his fame. His tomb is not surmounted by a pretentious statue proclaiming to the future the mysteries that genius has unveiled for it.

But perhaps the talents of Desplein were linked with his beliefs, and therefore mortal. For him the earth's atmosphere was a kind of envelope generating all things. He regarded the earth as an egg in its shell, and unable to solve the old riddle as to whether the egg or the hen came first, he admitted neither the hen nor the egg.

He believed neither in a mere animal nature giving origin to the race of man, nor in a spirit surviving him. Desplein was not in doubt. He asserted his theories. His plain open atheism was like that of many men, some of the best fellows in the world, but invincibly atheistic—atheists of a type of which religious people do not admit the existence. This opinion could harldy be otherwise with a man accustomed from his youth to dissect the highest of beings, before, during, and after life, without finding therein that one soul that is so necessary to religious theories. He recognised there a cerebral centre, a nervous centre, and a centre for the respiratory and circulatory system, and the two former so completely supplemented each other, that during the last part of his life he had the conviction that the sense of hearing was not absolutely necessary for one to hear, nor the sense of vision absolutely necessary for sight, and that the solar plexus could replace them without one being aware of the fact. Desplein, recognising these two souls in man, made it an argument for his atheism, without however assuming anything as to the belief in God. This man was said to have died in final impenitence, as many great geniuses have unfortunately died, whom may God forgive.

Great as the man was, his life had in it many " littlenesses " (to adopt the expression used by his enemies, who were eager to diminish his fame), though it would perhaps be more fitting to call them apparent contradictions. Failing to understand the motives on which high minds act, envious and stupid people at once seize hold of any surface discrepancies to base upon them an indictment, on which they straightway ask for judgment. If, after all, success crowns the methods they have attacked, and shows the coordination of preparation and result, all the same something will remain of these charges flung out in advance. Thus in our time Napoleon was condemned by his contemporaries for having spread the wings of the eagle towards England. They had to wait till 1822 for the explanation of 1804, and of the flat-bottomed boats of Boulogne.

In the case of Desplein, his fame and his scientific knowledge not being open to attack, his enemies found fault with his strange whims, his singular character. For he possessed in no small degree that quality which the English call " eccentricity." Now he would be attired with a splendour that suggested Crébillon's stately tragedy ; and then he would suddenly affect a strange indifference in the matter of dress. One saw him now in a carriage, now on foot. By turns sharp-spoken and kindly ; assuming an air of closeness and stinginess, but at the same time ready to put his fortune at the disposal of exiled professors of his science, who would do him the honour of accepting his help for a few days—no one ever gave occasion for more contradictory judgments. Although for the sake of obtaining a decoration that doctors were not allowed to canvass for, he was quite capable of letting a prayer-book slip out of his pocket when at court, you may take it that in his own mind he made a mockery of everything.

He had a deep disdain for men, after having caught glimpses of their true character in the midst of the most solemn and the most trivial acts of their existence. In a great man all his characteristics are generally in keeping with each other. If one of these giants has more talent than wit, it is all the same true that his wit is something deeper than that of one of whom all that can be said is that " He is a witty fellow." Genius always implies a certain insight into the moral side of things. This insight may be applied to one special line of thought, but one cannot see the flower without at the same time seeing the sun that produces it. The man who, hearing a diplomatist whom he was saving from death ask, " How is the Emperor ? " remarked, " The courtier is recovering, and the man will recover with him ! " was not merely a doctor or a surgeon, but was also not without a considerable amount of wit. Thus the patient, unwearying observation of mankind might do something to justify the exorbitant pretensions of Desplein, and make one admit that, as he himself believed, he was capable of winning as much distinction as a Minister of State as he had gained as a surgeon.

Amongst the problems that the life of Desplein presented to the minds of his contemporaries, we have chosen one of the most interesting, because the key to it will be found in the ending of the story, and will serve to clear him of many stupid accusations made against him.

Among all Desplein's pupils at the hospital, Horace Bianchon was one of those to whom he was most strongly attached. Before becoming a resident student at the Hôtel Dieu, Horace Bianchon was a medical student, living in the Quartier Latin in a wretched lodging-house, known by the name of the Maison Vauquer. There the poor young fellow experienced the pressure of that acute poverty, which is a kind of crucible, whence men of great talent are expected to come forth pure and incorruptible, like a diamond that can be subjected to blows of all kinds without breaking. Though the fierce fire of passion has been aroused, they acquire a probity that it cannot alter, and they become used to struggles that are the lot of genius, in the midst of the ceaseless toil, in which they curb desires that are not to be satisfied. Horace was an upright young man, incapable of taking any crooked course in matters where honour was involved ; going straight to the point ; ready to pawn his overcoat for his friends, as he was to give them his time and his long vigils. In a word, Horace was one of those friends who do not trouble themselves as to what they are to receive in return for what they bestow, taking it for granted that, when it comes to their turn, they will get more than they give. Most of his friends had for him that heart-felt respect which is inspired by unostentatious worth, and many of them would have been afraid to provoke his censure. But Horace manifested these good qualities without any pedantic display. Neither a puritan nor a preacher, he would in his simplicity enforce a word of good advice with any oath, and was ready for a bit of good cheer when the occasion offered. A pleasant comrade, with no more shyness than a trooper, frank and out-spoken—not as a sailor, for the sailor of to-day is a wily diplo-matist—but as a fine young fellow, who has nothing in his life to be ashamed of, he went his way with head erect and with a cheerful mind. To sum it all up in one word, Horace was the Pylades of more than one Orestes, creditors nowadays playing most real-istically the part of the Furies. He bore his poverty with that gaiety which is perhaps one of the chief elements of courage, and, like all those who have nothing, he contracted very few debts. As enduring as a camel, as alert as a wild deer, he was steadfast in his ideas and in his conduct.

The happiness of Bianchon's life began on the day when the famous surgeon became acquainted with the good qualities and the defects, which, each as well as the other, make Dr. Horace Bianchon doubly dear to his friends. When the teacher of a hospital class receives a young man into his inner circle, that young man has, as the saying goes, his foot in the stirrup. Desplein did not fail to take Bianchon with him as his assistant to wealthy houses, where nearly always a gratuity slipped into the purse of the student, and where, all unconsciously, the young provincial had revealed to him some of the mysteries of Parisian life. Desplein would have him in his study during consultations, and found work for him there. Sometimes he would send him to a watering-place as companion to a rich invalid,—in a word, he was preparing a professional connection for him. The result of all this was that after a certain time the tyrant of the operating theatre had his right-hand man. These two—one of them at the summit of professional honours and science, and in the enjoyment of an immense fortune and an equal renown, the other a modest cipher without fortune or fame— became intimate friends. The great Desplein told everything to his pupil. Bianchon came to know the mysteries of this tem-perament, half lion, half bull, that in the end caused an abnormal expansion of the great man's chest and killed him by enlargement of the heart. He studied the odd whims of this busy life, the schemes of its sordid avarice, the projects of this politician disguised as a man of science. He was able to forecast the disappointments that awaited the one touch of sentiment that was buried in a heart not of stone though made to seem like stone.

One day Bianchon told Desplein that a poor water-carrier in the

Quartier Saint-Jacques was suffering from a horrible illness caused by overwork and poverty. This poor native of Auvergne had only potatoes to eat during the hard winter of 1821. Desplein left all his patients. At the risk of breaking down his horse, he drove at full speed, accompanied by Bianchon, to the poor man's lodging, and himself superintended his removal to a private nursing home established by the celebrated Dubois in the Faubourg Saint-Denis. He went to attend to the man himself, and gave him, when he had recovered, money enough to buy a horse and a water-cart. The Auvergnat distinguished himself by an unconventional proceeding. One of his friends fell sick, and he at once brought him to Desplein, and said to his benefactor:

" I would not think of allowing him to go to any one else."

Overwhelmed with work as he was, Desplein grasped the water-carrier's hand and said to him:

" Bring them all to me."

He had this poor fellow from the Cantal admitted to the Hôtel Dieu, where he took the greatest care of him. Bianchon had on many occasions remarked that his chief had a particular liking for people from Auvergne, and especially for the water-carriers; but as Desplein took a kind of pride in his treatment of his poor patients at the Hôtel Dieu, his pupil did not see anything very strange in this.

One day when Bianchon was crossing the Place Saint-Sulpice he caught sight of his teacher going into the church about nine o'clock in the morning. Desplein, who at this period would not go a step without calling for his carriage, was on foot, and slipped in quietly by the side door in the Rue du Petit Lion, as if he was going into some doubtful place. The student was naturally seized by a great curiosity, for he knew the opinions of his master; so Bianchon too slipped into Saint-Sulpice and was not a little surprised to see the famous Desplein, this atheist, who thought very little of angels as beings who give no scope for surgery, this scoffer, humbly kneeling, and where? . . . in the Lady Chapel, where he heard a mass, gave an alms for the church expenses and for the poor, and remained throughout as serious as if he were engaged in an operation.

Bianchon's astonishment knew no bounds. " If," he said to himself, " I had seen him holding one of the cords of the canopy at a public procession on Corpus Christi I might just laugh at him; but at this time of day, all alone, without any one to see him, this is certainly something to set one thinking! "

Bianchon had no wish to appear to be playing the spy on the chief surgeon of the Hôtel Dieu, so he went away. It so happened that Desplein asked him to dine with him that day, not at his house but at a restaurant. Between the cheese and the dessert Bianchon, by cleverly leading up to it, managed to say something about the mass, and spoke of it as a mummery and a farce.

"A farce," said Desplein, "that has cost Christendom more bloodshed than all the battles of Napoleon, all the leeches of Broussais. It is a papal invention, that only dates from the sixth century. What torrents of blood were not shed to establish the feast of Corpus Christi, by which the Court of Rome sought to mark its victory in the question of the real presence, and the schism that has troubled the Church for three centuries ! The wars of the Count of Toulouse and the Albigenses were the sequel of that affair. The Vaudois and the Albigenses refused to recognise the innovation."

In a word Desplein took a pleasure in giving vent to all his atheistic ardour, and there was a torrent of Voltairian witticisms, or, to describe it more accurately, a detestable imitation of the style of the modern anti-clerical journalists.

"Hum ! " said Bianchon to himself, "what has become of my devotee of this morning ? "

He kept silent. He began to doubt if it was really his chief that he had seen at Saint-Sulpice. Desplein would not have taken the trouble to lie to Bianchon. They knew each other too well. They had already exchanged ideas on points quite as serious, and discussed systems of the nature of things, exploring and dissecting them with the knives and scapels of incredulity.

Three months went by. Bianchon took no further step in connection with the incident, though it remained graven in his memory. One day that year one of the doctors of the Hôtel Dieu took Desplein by the arm in Bianchon's presence, as if he had a question to put to him.

"Whatever do you go to Saint-Sulpice for, my dear master ? " he said to him.

"To see one of the priests there, who has caries in the knee, and whom Madame the Duchess of Angoulême did me the honour to recommend to my care," said Desplein.

The doctor was satisfied with this evasion, but not so Bianchon.

"Ah, he goes to see diseased knees in the church ! Why, he went to hear mass ! " said the student to himself.

Bianchon made up his mind to keep a watch on Desplein. He remembered the day, the hour, when he had caught him going into Saint-Sulpice, and he promised himself that he would be there next year on the same day and at the same hour, to see if he would catch him again. In this case the recurring date of his devotions would give ground for a scientific investigation, for one ought not to expect to find in such a man a direct contradiction between thought and action.

Next year, on the day and at the hour, Bianchon, who by this time was no longer one of Desplein's resident students, saw the surgeon's carriage stop at the corner of the Rue de Tournon and the Rue du Petit Lion. His friend got out, passed stealthily along by the wall of Saint-Sulpice, and once more heard his mass at the Lady altar. It was indeed Desplein, the chief surgeon of the hospital, the atheist at heart, the devotee at haphazard. The problem was getting to be a puzzle. The persistence of the illustrious man of science made it all very complicated. When Desplein had gone out Bianchon went up to the sacristan, who came to do his work in the chapel, and asked him if that gentleman was a regular attendant there.

" Well, I have been here twenty years," said the sacristan " and all that time M. Desplein has come four times a year to be present at this mass. He founded it."

" A foundation made by him ! " said Bianchon, as he went away. " Well, it is more wonderful than all the mysteries."

Some time passed by before Dr. Bianchon, although the friend of Desplein, found an opportunity to talk to him of this singular incident in his life. Though they met in consultation or in society, it was difficult to get that moment of confidential chat alone together, when two men sit with their feet on the fender, and their heads resting on the backs of their arm-chairs, and tell each other their secrets. At last, after a lapse of seven years, and after the Revolution of 1830, when the people had stormed the Archbishop's house, when Republican zeal led them to destroy the gilded crosses that shone like rays of light above the immense sea of house-tops, when unbelief side by side with revolt paraded the streets, Bianchon again came upon Desplein as he entered the church of Saint-Sulpice. The doctor followed him in, and took his place beside him, without his friend taking any notice of him, or showing the least surprise. Together they heard the mass he had founded.

" Will you tell me, my dear friend," said Bianchon to Desplein, when they left the church, " the reason for this monkish proceeding of yours ? I have already caught you going to mass three times, you of all men ! You must tell me the meaning of this mystery, and explain to me this flagrant contradiction between your opinions and your conduct. You don't believe in God and you go to mass ! My dear master, you are bound to give me an answer."

" I am like a good many devotees, men deeply religious to all appearance, but quite as much atheists as we can be, you and I."

And then there was a torrent of epigrams referring to certain political personages, the best known of whom presents us in our own time with a new edition of the *Tartuffe* of Molière.

" I am not asking you about all that," said Bianchon. " But I do want to know the reason for what you have just been doing here. Why have you founded this mass ? "

" My word ! my dear friend," said Desplein, " I am on the brink of the grave, and I may just as well talk to you about the early days of my life."

Just then Bianchon and the great man were in the Rue des Quatre Vents, one of the most horrible streets in Paris. Desplein pointed to the sixth storey of one of those high, narrow-fronted houses that stand like obelisks. The outer door opens on a passage, at the end of which is a crooked stair, lighted by small inner windows. It was a house with a greenish-coloured front, with a furniture dealer installed on the ground floor, and apparently a different type of wretchedness lodging in every storey. As he raised his arm with a gesture that was full of energy, Desplein said to Bianchon :

" I lived up there for two years ! "

" I know that. D'Arthez used to live there. I came there nearly every day when I was quite a young fellow, and in those days we used to call it ' the store bottle of great men ! ' Well, what comes next ? "

" The mass that I have just heard is connected with events that occurred when I was living in that garret in which you tell me D'Arthez once lived, the room from the window of which there is a line hanging with clothes drying on it, just above the flower-pot. I had such a rough start in life, my dear Bianchon, that I could dispute with any one you like the palm for suffering endured here in Paris. I bore it all, hunger, thirst, want of money, lack of clothes, boots, linen—all that is hardest in poverty. I have tried to warm my frozen fingers with my breath in that ' store bottle of great men,' which I should like to revisit with you. As I worked in the winter a vapour would rise from my head and I could see the steam of perspiration as we see it about the horses on a frosty day. I don't know where one finds the foothold to stand up against such a life. I was all alone, without help, without a penny to buy books or to pay the expenses of my medical education : without a friend, for my irritable, gloomy, nervous character did me harm.

" No one would recognise in my fits of irritation the distress, the struggles of a man who is striving to rise to the surface from his place in the very depths of the social system. But I can say to you, in whose presence I have no need to cloak myself in any way, that I had that basis of sound ideas and impressionable feelings, which will always be part of the endowment of men strong enough to climb up to some summit, after having long plodded through the morass of misery. I could not look for any help from my family or my native place beyond the insufficient allowance that was made to me. To sum it all up, at that time my breakfast in the morning was a roll that a baker in the Rue du Petit Lion sold cheaply to me because it was from the baking of yesterday or the day before, and which I broke up into some milk ; thus my morning meal did not cost me more than a penny. I dined only every second day, in a boardinghouse where one could get a dinner for eightpence. Thus I spent only fourpence-halfpenny a day.

" You know as well as I do what care I would take of such things as clothes and boots ! I am not sure that in later life we feel more trouble at the treachery of a colleague than we have felt, you and I, at discovering the mocking grimace of a boot-sole that is coming away from the sewing, or at hearing the rending noise of a torn coat-cuff. I drank only water. I looked at the cafés with the greatest respect. The Café Zoppi seemed to me like a promised land, where the Luculluses of the Quartier Latin had the exclusive right of entry. ' Shall I ever,' I used sometimes to ask myself, ' shall I ever be able to go in there to take a cup of coffee and hot milk, or to play a game of dominoes ? '

" Well, I brought to my work the furious energy that my poverty inspired. I tried rapidly to get a grasp of exact knowledge so as to acquire an immense personal worth in order to deserve the position I hoped to reach in the days when I would have come forth from my nothingness. I consumed more oil than bread. The lamp that lighted me during these nights of persistent toil cost me more than my food. The struggle was long, obstinate, without encouragement. I had won no sympathy from those around me. To have friends must one not associate with other young fellows, and have a few pence to take a drink with them, and go with them wherever students are to be found ? I had nothing. And no one in Paris quite realises that *nothing* is really *nothing*. If I ever had any occasion to reveal my misery I felt in my throat that nervous contraction that makes our patients sometimes imagine there is a round mass coming up the gullet into the larynx. Later on I have come across people who, having been born in wealth and never wanted for anything, knew nothing of that problem of the Rule of Three : A young man is to a crime as a five franc piece is to the unknown quantity X. These gilded fools would say to me :

" ' But why do you get into debt ? Why ever do you contract serious obligations ? '

" They remind me of that princess who, on hearing that the people were in want of bread, said : ' Why don't they buy sponge cakes ? ' I should like very much to see one of those rich men, who complains that I ask him for too high a fee when there has to be an operation—yes, I should like to see him all alone in Paris, without a penny, without luggage, without a friend, without credit, and forced to work his five fingers to the bone to get a living. What would he do ? Where would he go to satisfy his hunger ? Bianchon, if you have sometimes seen me bitter and hard, it was because I was then thinking at once of my early troubles and of the heartlessness, the selfishness of which I have seen a thousand instances in the highest circles ; or else I was thinking of the obstacles that hatred, envy, jealousy, calumny have raised up between me and success. In Paris, when certain people see you ready to put your foot in the stirrup, some of them pull at the skirt of your coat, others loosen the saddle-girth ; this one knocks a shoe off your horse, that one steals your whip ; the least treacherous of the lot is the one you see coming to fire a pistol at you point blank.

" You have talent enough, my dear fellow, to know soon enough the horrible, the unceasing warfare that mediocrity carries on against the man that is its superior. If one evening you lose twenty-five *louis*, next morning you will be accused of being a gambler, and your best friends will say that you lost twenty-five thousand francs last night. If you have a headache, you will be set down as a lunatic. If you are not lively, you will be set down as unsociable. If to oppose this battalion of pygmies you call up your own superior powers, your best friends will cry out that you wish to devour everything, that you claim to lord it and play the tyrant. In a word, your good qualities will be turned into defects, your defects will be turned into vices, and your virtues will be crimes. If you have saved some one, it will be said that you have killed him. If your patient reappears, it will be agreed that you have made sure of the present at the expense of his future ; though he is not dead, he will die. If you stumble, it will be a fall ! Invent anything whatever, and assert your rights, and you will be a difficult man to deal with, a sharp fellow, who does not like to see young men succeed. So, my dear friend, if I do not believe in God, I believe even less in man. Do you not recognise in me a Desplein that is quite different from the Desplein about whom every one speaks ill ? But we need not dig into that heap of mud.

" Well, I was living in that house, I had to work to be ready to pass my first examination, and I had not a farthing. You know what it is ! I had come to one of those crises of utter extremity when one says to oneself : ' I will enlist ! ' I had one hope. I was expecting from my native place a trunk full of linen, a present from some old aunts, who, knowing nothing of Paris, think about providing one with dress shirts, because they imagine that with thirty francs a month their nephew dines on ortolans. The trunk arrived while I was away at the Medical School. It had cost forty francs, carriage to be paid. The concierge of the house, a German cobbler, who lived in a loft, had paid the money and held the trunk. I took a walk in the Rue des Fosse-Saint-Germain-des-Prés and in the Rue de l'École de Médicine without being able to invent a stratagem which would put the trunk in my possession, without my being obliged to pay down the forty francs, which of course I meant to pay after selling the linen. My stupidity seemed a very fair sign to me that I was fit for no vocation but surgery. My dear friend, delicately organised natures, whose powers are exercised in some higher sphere, are wanting in that spirit of intrigue which is fertile in resources and shifts. Genius such as theirs depends on chance. They do not seek out things, they come upon them.

"At last, after dark, I went back to the house, just at the moment when my next-room neighbour was coming in, a water-carrier named Bourgeat, a man from Saint-Flour in Auvergne. We knew each other in the way in which two lodgers come to know each other, when both have their rooms on the same landing, and they can hear each other going to bed, coughing, getting up, and end by becoming quite used to each other. My neighbour informed me that the landlord, to whom I owed three months' rent, had sent me notice to quit. I must clear out next day. He himself was to be evicted on account of his business. I passed the most sorrowful night of my life.

"Where was I to find a porter to remove my poor belongings, my books? How was I to pay the porter and the concierge? Where could I go? With tears in my eyes I repeated these insoluble questions, as lunatics repeat their catchwords. I fell asleep. For the wretched there is a divine sleep full of beautiful dreams. Next morning, while I was eating my porringer full of bread crumbled into milk, Bourgeat came in, and said to me in bad French:

"'Mister Student, I'm a poor man, a foundling of the hospice of Saint-Flour, without father or mother, and not rich enough to marry. You are not much better off for relations, or better provided with what counts? Now, see here, I have down below a hand-cart that I have hired at a penny an hour. All our things can be packed on it. If you agree, we will look for a place where we can lodge together, since we are turned out of this. And after all, it's not the earthly paradise.'

"'I know it well, my good Bourgeat,' said I to him, 'but I am in a great difficulty. There's a trunk for me downstairs that contains linen worth a hundred crowns, with which I could pay the landlord and what I owe to the concierge, and I have not got as much as a hundred sous.'

"'Bah! I have found some bits of coin,' Bourgeat answered me joyfully, showing me an old purse of greasy leather. 'Keep your linen.'

"Bourgeat paid my three months, and his own rent, and settled with the concierge. Then he put our furniture and my box of linen on his hand-cart and drew it through the streets, stopping at every house that showed a 'Lodgings to Let' card. As for me I would go upstairs to see if the place to let would suit us. At noon we were still wandering about the Quartier Latin without having found anything. The rent was the great obstacle. Bourgeat proposed to me to have lunch at a wine-shop, at the door of which we left the hand-cart. Towards evening, in the Cour de Rohan off the Passage du Commerce, I found, under the roof at the top of a house, two rooms, one on each side of the staircase. We got them for a rent of sixty francs a year each. So there we were housed, myself and my humble friend.

"We dined together. Bourgeat, who earned some fifty sous a day, had saved about a hundred crowns. . . . He would soon be in a position to realise his ambition and buy a water-cart and a horse. When he found out how I was situated—and he wormed out my secrets with a depth of cunning and at the same time with a kindly good nature that still moves my heart to-day when I think of it—he renounced for some time to come the ambition of his life. Bourgeat had been a street seller for twenty-two years. He sacrificed his hundred crowns for my future."

At this point Desplein took a firm grip of Bianchon's arm.

"He gave me the money required for my examinations! This man understood, my friend, that I had a mission, that the needs of my intelligence came before his. He busied himself with me, he called me his 'little one,' he lent me the money I wanted to buy books; he came in sometimes quite quietly to watch me at my work; finally he took quite a motherly care to see that I substituted a wholesome and abundant diet for the bad and insufficient fare to which I had been condemned. Bourgeat, a man of about forty, had the features of a burgess of the middle ages, a full rounded forehead, a head that a painter might have posed as the model for a Lycurgus. The poor man felt his heart big with affection seeking for some object. He had never been loved by anything but a poodle, that had died a short time before, and about which he was always talking to me, asking if by any possibility the Church would consent to have prayers for its soul. His dog, he said, had been really like a Christian, and for twelve years it had gone to church with him, without ever barking, listening to the organ without so much as opening its mouth, and remaining crouched beside him with a look that made one think it was praying with him.

"This man transferred all his affection to me. He took me up as a lonely, suffering creature. He became for me like a most watchful mother, the most delicately thoughtful of benefactors, in a word the ideal of that virtue that rejoices in its own good work. When I met him in the street he gave me an intelligent look, full of a nobility that you cannot imagine; he would then assume a gait like that of a man who was carrying no burden; he seemed delighted at seeing me in good health and well dressed. It was such devoted affection as one finds among the common people, the love of the little shop-girl raised to a higher level. Bourgeat ran my errands. He woke me up in the night at the appointed hour. He trimmed my lamp, scrubbed our landing. He was a good servant as well as a good father to me, and as cleanly in his work

as an English maid. He looked after our housekeeping. Like
Philopoemen he sawed up our firewood, and he set about all his
actions with a simplicity in performing them that at the same
time preserved his dignity, for he seemed to realise that the end
in view ennobled it all.

"When I left this fine fellow to enter the Hôtel Dieu as a resident
student, he felt a kind of sorrowful gloom come over him at the
thought that he could no longer live with me. But he consoled
himself by looking forward to getting together the money that
would be necessary for the expenses of my final examination, and
he made me promise to come to see him on all my holidays.
Bourgeat was proud of me. He loved me for my own sake and
for his own. If you look up my essay for the doctorate you will
see that it was dedicated to him. In the last year of my indoor
course I had made enough money to be able to repay all I owed
to this worthy Auvergnat, by buying him a horse and a water-
cart. He was exceedingly angry at finding that I was thus depriving myself of my money, and nevertheless he was delighted at
seeing his desires realised. He laughed and he scolded me. He
looked at his water-barrel and his horse, and he wiped away a tear
as he said to me :

"' It's a pity ! Oh, what a fine water-cart ! You have done
wrong ! . . . The horse is as strong as if he came from Auvergne ! '

"He absolutely insisted on buying for me that pocket-case of
instruments mounted with silver that you have seen in my study,
and which is for me the most valued of my possessions. Although
he was enraptured with my first successes he never let slip a word
or a gesture that could be taken to mean, ' It is to me that this
man's success is due ! ' And nevertheless, but for him, I should
have been killed by my misery. The poor man broke himself
down for my sake. He had eaten nothing but bread seasoned with
garlic, in order that I might have coffee while I sat up at my work.
He fell sick. You may imagine how I passed whole nights at his
bedside. I pulled him through it the first time, but two years
after there was a relapse, and notwithstanding the most assiduous
care, notwithstanding the greatest efforts of science, he had to
succumb. No king was ever cared for as he was. Yes, Bianchon,
to snatch this life from death I tried unheard-of things. I wanted
to make him live long enough to allow him to see the results of
his work, to realise all his wishes, to satisfy the one gratitude that
had filled my heart, to extinguish a fire that burns in me even now !

"Bourgeat," continued Desplein, after a pause, with evident
emotion, "Bourgeat, my second father, died in my arms, leaving
me all he possessed by a will which he had made at a public notary's,
and which bore the date of the year when we went to lodge in the
Cour de Rohan. He had the faith of a simple workman. He loved

the Blessed Virgin as he would have loved his mother. Zealous Catholic as he was, he had never said a word to me about my own lack of religion. When he was in danger of death he begged me to spare nothing to obtain the help of the Church for him. I had mass said for him every day. Often in the night he expressed to me his fears for his future ; he was afraid that he had not lived a holy enough life. Poor man ! he used to work from morning to night. Who is heaven for, then, if there is a heaven ? He received the last sacraments like the saint that he was, and his death was worthy of his life.

" I was the only one who followed his funeral. When I had laid my one benefactor in the earth, I tried to find out how I could discharge my debt of gratitude to him. I knew that he had neither family nor friends, neither wife nor children. But he believed ! He had religious convictions, and had I any right to dispute them ? He had spoken to me timidly of masses said for the repose of the dead ; he did not seek to impose this duty on me, thinking that it would be like asking to be paid for his services to me. As soon as I could arrange for the endowment, I gave the Saint-Sulpice the sum necessary to have four masses said there each year. As the only thing that I could offer to Bourgeat was the fulfilment of his pious wishes, I go there in his name on the day the mass is said at the beginning of each quarter of the year, and say the prayers for him that he wished for. I say them in the good faith of one who doubts : ' My God, if there is a sphere where after their death you place those who have been perfect, think of good Bourgeat ; and if he has still anything to suffer, lay these sufferings on me, so that he may enter the sooner into what they call Paradise ! '" This, my dear friend, is all that a man who holds my opinions can allow himself. God must be good-hearted, and He will not take it ill on my part. But I swear to you, I would give my fortune for the sake of finding the faith of Bourgeat coming into my brain."

Bianchon, who attended Desplein in his last illness, does not venture to affirm, even now, that the famous surgeon died an atheist. Will not those who believe take pleasure in the thought that perhaps the poor Auvergnat came to open for him the gate of Heaven, as he had already opened for him the portals of that temple on earth, on the façade of which one reads : *To great men from their grateful motherland* ?

THE CHRIST IN FLANDERS

Honoré de Balzac

At a dimly remote period in the history of Brabant, communication between the Island of Cadzand and the Flemish coast was kept up by a boat which carried passengers from one shore to the other. Middelburg, the chief town in the island, destined to become so famous in the annals of Protestantism, at that time only numbered some two or three hundred hearths ; and the prosperous town of Ostend was an obscure haven, a straggling village where pirates dwelt in security among the fishermen and the few poor merchants who lived in the place.

But though the town of Ostend consisted altogether of some score of houses and three hundred cottages, huts, or hovels built of the driftwood of wrecked vessels, it nevertheless rejoiced in the possession of a governor, a garrison, a forked gibbet, a convent, and a burgomaster, in short, in all the institutions of an advanced civilisation.

Who reigned over Brabant and Flanders in those days ? On this point tradition is mute. Let us confess at once that this tale savours strongly of the marvellous, the mysterious, and the vague ; elements which Flemish narrators have infused into a story retailed so often to gatherings of workers on winter evenings, that the versions vary widely in poetic merit and incongruity of detail. It has been told by every generation, handed down by grandames at the fireside, narrated night and day, and the chronicle has changed its complexion somewhat in every age. Like some great building that has suffered many modifications of successive generations of architects, some sombre weather-beaten pile, the delight of a poet, the story would drive the commentator and the industrious winnower of words, facts, and dates to despair. The narrator believes in it, as all superstitious minds in Flanders likewise believe ; and is not a whit wiser nor more credulous than his audience. But as it would be impossible to make a harmony of all the different renderings, here are the outlines of the story ; stripped, it may be, of its picturesque quaintness, but with all its bold disregard of historical truth, and its moral teaching approved by religion—a myth, the blossom of imaginative fancy ; an allegory that the wise may interpret to suit themselves. To each his own pasturage, and the task of separating the tares from the wheat.

The boat that served to carry passengers from the Island of Cadzand to Ostend was upon the point of departure ; but before the skipper loosed the chain that secured the shallop to the little jetty where people embarked, he blew a horn several times to warn late lingerers, this being his last journey that day. Night was falling. It was scarcely possible to see the coast of Flanders by the dying fires of the sunset, or to make out upon the hither shore any forms of belated passengers hurrying along the wall of the dykes that surrounded the open country, or among the tall reeds of the marshes. The boat was full.

" What are you waiting for ? Let us put off ! " they cried.

Just at that moment a man appeared a few paces from the jetty, to the surprise of the skipper, who had heard no sound of footsteps. The traveller seemed to have sprung up from the earth, like a peasant who had laid himself down on the ground to wait till the boat should start, and had slept till the sound of the horn awakened him. Was he a thief ? or some one belonging to the custom-house or the police ?

As soon as the man appeared on the jetty to which the boat was moored, seven persons who were standing in the stern of the shallop hastened to sit down on the benches, so as to leave no room for the new-comer. It was the swift and instinctive working of the aristocratic spirit, an impulse of exclusiveness that comes from the rich man's heart. Four of the seven personages belonged to the most aristocratic families in Flanders. First among them was a young knight with two beautiful greyhounds ; his long hair flowed from beneath a jewelled cap ; he clanked his gilded spurs, curled the ends of his moustache from time to time with a swaggering grace, and looked round disdainfully on the rest of the crew.

A high-born damsel, with a falcon on her wrist, only spoke with her mother or with a churchman of high rank, who was evidently a relation. All these persons made a great deal of noise, and talked among themselves as though there were no one else in the boat ; yet close beside them sat a man of great importance in the district, a stout burgher of Bruges, wrapped about with a vast cloak. His servant, armed to the teeth, had set down a couple of bags filled with gold at his side. Next to the burgher came a man of learning, a doctor of the University of Louvain, who was travelling with his clerk. This little group of folk, who looked contemptuously at each other, was separated from the passengers in the forward part of the boat by the bench of rowers.

The belated traveller glanced about him as he stepped on board, saw that there was no room for him in the stern, and went to the bows in quest of a seat. They were all poor people there. At first sight of the bareheaded man in the brown camlet coat and trunk-hose and plain stiff linen collar, they noticed that he wore no ornaments, carried no cap nor bonnet in his hand, and had neither sword nor purse at his girdle, and one and all took him for a burgomaster sure of his authority, a worthy and kindly burgomaster like so many a Fleming of old times, whose homely features and characters have been immortalised by Flemish painters. The poorer passengers, therefore, received him with demonstrations of respect that provoked scornful tittering at the other end of the boat. An old soldier, inured to toil and hardship, gave up his place on the bench to the new-comer, and seated himself on the edge of the vessel, keeping his balance by planting his feet against one of those transverse beams, like the backbone of a fish, that hold the planks of a boat together. A young mother, who bore her baby in her arms, and seemed to belong to the working-class in Ostend, moved aside to make room for the stranger.

There was neither servility nor scorn in her manner of doing this ; it was a simple sign of the goodwill by which the poor, who know by long experience the value of a service and the warmth that fellowship brings, give expression to the openheartedness and the natural impulses of their souls ; so artlessly do they reveal their good qualities and their defects. The stranger thanked her by a gesture full of gracious dignity, and took his place between the young mother and the old soldier. Immediately behind him sat a peasant and his son, a boy ten years of age. A beggar woman, old, wrinkled, and clad in rags, was crouching, with her almost empty wallet, on a great coil of rope that lay in the prow. One of the rowers, an old sailor, who had known her in the days of her beauty and prosperity, had let her come in " for the love of God," in the beautiful phrase that the common people use.

" Thank you kindly, Thomas," the old woman had said. " I will say two *Paters* and two *Aves* for you in my prayers to-night."

The skipper blew his horn for the last time, looked along the silent shore, flung off the chain, ran along the side of the boat, and took up his position at the helm. He looked at the sky, and as soon as they were out in the open sea he shouted to the men : " Pull away, pull with all your might ! The sea is smiling at a squall, the witch ! I can feel the swell by the way the rudder works, and the storm in my wounds."

The nautical phrases, unintelligible to ears unused to the sound of the sea, seemed to put fresh energy into the oars ; they kept time together, the rhythm of the movement was still even and steady, but quite unlike the previous manner of rowing ; it was as if a cantering horse had broken into a gallop. The gay company seated in the stern amused themselves by watching the brawny arms, the tanned faces, and sparkling eyes of the rowers, the play of the tense muscles, the physical and mental forces that were being exerted to bring them for a trifling toll across the channel. So far from pitying the rowers' distress, they pointed out the men's faces to each other, and laughed at the grotesque expressions on the faces of the crew who were straining every muscle ; but in the fore part of the boat the soldier, the peasant, and the old beggar woman watched the sailors with the sympathy naturally felt by toilers who live by the sweat of their brow and know the rough struggle, the strenuous excitement of effort. These folk, moreover, whose lives were spent in the open air, had all seen the warnings of danger in the sky, and their faces were grave. The young mother rocked her child, singing an old hymn of the Church for a lullaby.

" If we ever get there at all," the soldier remarked to the peasant, " it will be because the Almighty is bent on keeping us alive."

" Ah ! He is the Master," said the old woman, " but I think it will be His good pleasure to take us to Himself. Just look at that light down there . . ." and she nodded her head as she spoke towards the sunset.

Streaks of fiery red glared from behind the masses of crimson-flushed brown cloud that seemed about to unloose a furious gale. There was a smothered murmur of the sea, a moaning sound that seemed to come from the depths, a low warning growl, such as a dog gives when he only means mischief as yet. After all, Ostend was not far away. Perhaps painting, like poetry, could not prolong the existence of the picture presented by sea and sky at that moment beyond the time of its actual duration. Art demands vehement contrasts, wherefore artists usually seek out Nature's most striking effects, doubtless because they despair of rendering the great and glorious charm of her daily moods ; yet the human soul is often stirred as deeply by her calm as by her emotion, and by silence as by storm.

For a moment no one spoke on board the boat. Every one watched that sea and sky, either with some presentiment of danger, or because they felt the influence of the religious melancholy that takes possession of nearly all of us at the close of the day, the hour of prayer, when all nature is hushed save for the voices of the bells. The sea gleamed pale and wan, but its hues changed, and the surface took all the colours of steel. The sky was almost overspread with livid grey, but down in the west there were long narrow bars like streaks of blood ; while lines of bright light in the eastern sky, sharp and clean as if drawn by the tip of a brush, were separated by folds of cloud, like the wrinkles on an old man's brow. The whole scene made a background of ashen greys and half-tints, in strong contrast to the bale-fires of the sunset. If written language might borrow of spoken language some of the bold figures of speech invented by the people, it might be said with the soldier that " the weather had been routed," or, as the peasant would say, " the sky glowered like an executioner." Suddenly a wind arose from the quarter of the sunset, and the skipper, who never took his eyes off the sea, saw the swell on the horizon line, and cried :

" Stop rowing ! "

The sailors stopped immediately, and let their oars lie on the water.

" The skipper is right," said Thomas coolly. A great wave caught up the boat, carried it high on its crest, only to plunge it, as it were, into the trough of the sea that seemed to yawn for them. At this mighty upheaval, this sudden outbreak of the wrath of the sea, the company in the stern turned pale, and sent up a terrible cry.

" We are lost ! "

" Oh, not yet ! " said the skipper calmly.

As he spoke, the clouds immediately above their heads were torn asunder by the vehemence of the wind. The grey mass was rent and scattered east and west with ominous speed, a dim uncertain light from the rift in the sky fell full upon the boat, and the travellers beheld each other's faces. All of them, the noble and the wealthy, the sailors and the poor passengers alike, were amazed for a moment by the appearance of the last comer. His golden hair, parted upon his calm serene forehead, fell in thick curls about his shoulders ; and his face, sublime in its sweetness and radiant with divine love, stood out against the surrounding gloom. He had no contempt for death ; he knew that he should not die. But if at the first the company in the stern forgot for a moment the implacable fury of the storm that threatened their lives, selfishness and their habits of life soon prevailed again.

" How lucky that stupid burgomaster is, not to see the risks we are all running ! He is just like a dog, he will die without a struggle," said the doctor.

He had scarcely pronounced this highly judicious dictum when the storm unloosed all its forces. The wind blew from every quarter of the heavens, the boat span round like a top, and the sea broke in.

" Oh ! my poor child ! My poor child ! . . . Who will save my baby ? " the mother cried in a heartrending voice.

" You yourself will save it," the stranger said.

The thrilling tones of that voice went to the young mother's heart and brought hope with them ; she heard the gracious words through all the whistling of the wind and the shrieks of the passengers.

" Holy Virgin of Good Help, who art at Antwerp, I promise thee a thousand pounds of wax and a statue, if thou wilt rescue me from this ! " cried the burgher, kneeling upon his bags of gold.

" The Virgin is no more at Antwerp than she is here," was the doctor's comment on this appeal.

" She is in heaven," said a voice that seemed to come from the sea.

" Who said that ? "

" 'Tis the devil ! " exclaimed the servant. " He is scoffing at the Virgin of Antwerp."

"Let us have no more of your Holy Virgin at present," the skipper cried to the passengers. " Put your hands to the scoops and bale the water out of the boat. And the rest of you," he went on, addressing the sailors, " pull with all your might ! Now is the time ; in the name of the devil who is leaving you in this world, be your own Providence ! Every one knows that the channel is fearfully dangerous ; I have been to and fro across it these thirty years. Am I facing a storm for the first time to-night ? "

He stood at the helm, and looked, as before, at his boat and at the sea and sky in turn.

" The skipper always laughs at everything," muttered Thomas.

"Will God leave us to perish along with those wretched creatures ? " asked the haughty damsel of the handsome cavalier.

" No, no, noble maiden. . . . Listen ! " and he caught her by the waist and said in her ear, " I can swim ; say nothing about it ! I will hold you by your fair hair and bring you safely to the shore ; but I can only save you."

The girl looked at her aged mother. The lady was on her knees entreating absolution of the Bishop, who did not heed her. In the beautiful eyes the knight read a vague feeling of filial piety, and spoke in a smothered voice.

" Submit yourself to the will of God. If it is His pleasure to take your mother to Himself, it will doubtless be for her happiness—in the other world," he added, and his voice dropped still lower. " And for ours in this," he thought within himself.

The Dame of Rupelmonde was lady of seven fiefs beside the barony of Gâvres.

The girl felt the longing for life in her heart, and for love that spoke through the handsome adventurer, a young miscreant who haunted churches in search of a prize, an heiress to marry, or ready money. The Bishop bestowed his benison on the waves, and bade them be calm ; it was all that he could do. He thought of his mistress, and of the delicate feast with which she would welcome him ; perhaps at that very moment she was bathing, perfuming herself, robing herself in velvet, fastening her necklace and her jewelled clasps, and the perverse Bishop so far from thinking of the power of Holy Church, of his duty to comfort Christians and exhort them to trust in God, that worldly regrets and lover's sighs mingled with the holy words of the breviary. By the dim light that shone on the pale faces of the company, it was possible to see their differing expressions as the boat was lifted high in air by a wave, to be cast back into the dark depths ; the shallop quivered like a fragile leaf, the plaything of the north wind in the autumn ; the hull creaked, it seemed ready to go to pieces. Fearful shrieks went up, followed by an awful silence

There was a strange difference between the behaviour of the folk in the bows and that of the rich or great people at the other end of the boat. The young mother clasped her infant tightly to her breast every time that a great wave threatened to engulf the fragile vessel ; but she clung to the hope that the stranger's words had set in her heart. Each time that her eyes turned to his face she drew fresh faith at the sight, the strong faith of a helpless woman, a mother's faith. She lived by that divine promise, the loving words from his lips ; the simple creature waited trustingly for them to be fulfilled, and scarcely feared the danger any longer.

The soldier, holding fast to the vessel's side, never took his eyes off the strange visitor. He copied on his own rough and swarthy features the imperturbability of the other's face, applying to this task the whole strength of a will and intelligence but little corrupted in the course of a life of mechanical and passive obedience. So emulous was he of a calm and tranquil courage greater than his own, that at last, perhaps unconsciously, something of that mysterious nature passed into his own soul. His admiration became an instinctive zeal for this man, a boundless love for and belief in him, such a love as soldiers feel for their leader when he has the power of swaying other men, when the halo of victories surrounds him, and the magical fascination of genius is felt in all that he does. The poor outcast was murmuring to herself :

" Ah ! miserable wretch that I am ! Have I not suffered enough to expiate the sins of my youth ? Ah ! wretched woman, why did you lead the gay life of a frivolous Frenchwoman ? Why did you devour the goods of God with churchmen, the substance of the poor with extortioners and fleecers of the poor ? Oh ! I have sinned indeed !—Oh my God ! my God ! let me finish my time in hell here in this world of misery."

And again she cried, " Holy Virgin, Mother of God, have pity upon me ! "

" Be comforted, mother. God is not a Lombard usurer. I may have killed people good and bad at random in my time, but I am not afraid of the resurrection."

" Ah ! master lancepesade, how happy those fair ladies are, to be so near to a bishop, a holy man ! They will get absolution for their sins," said the old woman. " Oh ! if I could only hear a priest say to me, ' Thy sins are forgiven ! ' I should believe it then."

The stranger turned towards her, and the goodness in his face made her tremble.

" Have faith," he said, " and you will be saved."

" May God reward you, good sir," she answered. " If what you say is true, I will go on pilgrimage barefooted to Our Lady of Loretto to pray to her for you and for me."

The two peasants, father and son, were silent, patient, and sub-

32

missive to the will of God, like folk whose wont it is to fall in instinctively with the ways of Nature like cattle. At the one end of the boat stood riches, pride, learning, debauchery, and crime—human society, such as art and thought and education and worldly interests and laws have made it ; and at this end there were terror and wailing, innumerable different impulses all repressed by hideous doubts—at this end, and at this only, the agony of fear.

Above all these human lives stood a strong man, the skipper ; no doubts assailed him, the chief, the king, the fatalist among them. He was trusting in himself rather than in Providence, crying, " Bale away ! " instead of " Holy Virgin ! " defying the storm, in fact, and struggling with the sea like a wrestler.

But the helpless poor at the other end of the wherry ! The mother rocking on her bosom the little one who smiled at the storm, the woman once so frivolous and gay, and now tormented with bitter remorse ; the old soldier covered with scars, a mutilated life the sole reward of his unflagging loyalty and faithfulness. This veteran could scarcely count on the morsel of bread soaked in tears to keep the life in him, yet he was always ready to laugh, and went his way merrily, happy when he could drown his glory in the depths of a pot of beer, or could tell tales of the wars to the children who admired him, leaving his future with a light heart in the hands of God. Lastly, there were the two peasants, used to hardships and toil, labour incarnate, the labour by which the world lives. These simple folk were indifferent to thought and its treasures, ready to sink them all in a belief ; and their faith was but so much the more vigorous because they had never disputed about it nor analysed it. Such a nature is a virgin soil, conscience has not been tampered with, feeling is deep and strong ; repentance, trouble, love, and work have developed, purified, concentrated, and increased their force of will a hundred times, the will—the one thing in man that resembles what learned doctors call the Soul.

The boat, guided by the well-nigh miraculous skill of the steersman, came almost within sight of Ostend, when, not fifty paces from the shore, she was suddenly struck by a heavy sea and capsized. The stranger with the light about his head spoke to this little world of drowning creatures :

" Those who have faith shall be saved ; let them follow me ! "

He stood upright, and walked with a firm step upon the waves. The young mother at once took her child in her arms, and followed at his side across the sea. The soldier too sprang up, saying in his homely fashion, " Ah ! *nom d'un pipe !* I would follow *you* to the devil " ; and without seeming astonished by it, he walked on the water. The old worn-out sinner, believing in the omnipotence of God, also followed the stranger.

The two peasants said to each other, " If they are walking on the sea, why should we not do as they do ? '' and they also arose and hastened after the others. Thomas tried to follow, but his faith tottered ; he sank in the sea more than once, and rose again, but the third time he also walked on the sea. The bold steersman clung like a remora to the wreck of his boat. The miser had had faith, and had risen to go, but he tried to take his gold with him, and it was his gold that dragged him down to the bottom. The learned man had scoffed at the charlatan and at the fools who listened to him ; and when he heard the mysterious stranger propose to the passengers that they should walk on the waves, he began to laugh, and the ocean swallowed him. The girl was dragged down into the depths by her lover. The Bishop and the older lady went to the bottom, heavily laden with sins, it may be, but still more heavily laden with incredulity and confidence in idols, weighted down by devotion, into which alms-deeds and true religion entered but little.

The faithful flock, who walked with a firm step high and dry above the surge, heard all about them the dreadful whistling of the blast ; great billows broke across their path, but an irresistible force cleft a way for them through the sea. These believing ones saw through the spray a dim speck of light flickering in the window of a fisherman's hut on the shore, and each one, as he pushed on bravely towards the light, seemed to hear the voice of his fellow crying, " Courage ! " through all the roaring of the surf ; yet no one had spoken a word—so absorbed was each by his own peril. In this way they reached the shore.

When they were all seated near the fisherman's fire, they looked round in vain for their guide with the light about him. The sea washed up the steersman at the base of the cliff on which the cottage stood ; he was clinging with might and main to the plank as a sailor can cling when death stares him in the face ; the MAN went down and rescued the almost exhausted seaman ; then he said, as he held out a succouring hand above the man's head :

" Good, for this once ; but do not try it again ; the example would be too bad."

He took the skipper on his shoulders, and carried him to the fisherman's door, knocked for admittance for the exhausted man ; then, when the door of the humble refuge opened, the Saviour disappeared.

The Convent of Mercy was built for sailors on this spot, where for long afterwards (so it was said) the footprints of Jesus Christ could be seen in the sand ; but in 1793, at the time of the French invasion, the monks carried away this precious relic, that bore witness to the Saviour's last visit to earth.

There at the convent I found myself shortly after the Revolution of 1830. I was weary of life. If you had asked me the reason of my despair, I should have found it almost impossible to give it, so languid had grown the soul that was melted within me. The west wind had slackened the springs of my intelligence. A cold, grey light poured down from the heavens, and the murky clouds that passed overhead gave a boding look to the land ; all these things, together with the immensity of the sea, said to me, " Die to-day or die to-morrow, still must we not die ? " And then——. I wandered on, musing on the doubtful future, on my blighted hopes. Gnawed by these gloomy thoughts, I turned mechanically into the convent church, with the grey towers that loomed like ghosts through the sea mists. I looked round with no kindling of the imagination at the forest of columns, at the slender arches set aloft upon the leafy capitals, a delicate labyrinth of sculpture. I walked with careless eyes along the side aisles that opened out before me like vast portals, ever turning upon their hinges. It was scarcely possible to see, by the dim light of the autumn day, the sculptured groinings of the roof, the delicate and clean-cut lines of the mouldings of the graceful pointed arches. The organ pipes were mute.

There was no sound save the noise of my own footsteps to awaken the mournful echoes lurking in the dark chapels. I sat down at the base of one of the four pillars that supported the tower, near the choir. Thence I could see the whole of the building. I gazed, and no ideas connected with it arose in my mind. I saw without seeing the mighty maze of pillars, the great rose-windows that hung like a network suspended as by a miracle in air above the vast doorways. I saw the doors at the end of the side aisles, the aerial galleries, the stained-glass windows framed in archways, divided by slender columns, fretted into flower forms and trefoil by fine filigree work of carved stone. A dome of glass at the end of the choir sparkled as if it had been built of precious stones set cunningly. In contrast to the roof with its alternating spaces of whiteness and colour, the two aisles lay to right and left in shadow so deep that the faint grey outlines of their hundred shafts were scarcely visible in the gloom. I gazed at the marvellous arcades, the scroll-work, the garlands, the curving lines, the arabesques interwoven and interlaced, and strangely lighted, until by sheer dint of gazing my perceptions became confused, and I stood upon the border-land between illusion and reality, taken in the snare set for the eyes, and almost light-headed by reason of the multitudinous changes of the shapes about me.

Imperceptibly a mist gathered about the carven stonework, and I only beheld it through a haze of fine golden dust, like the motes that hover in the bars of sunlight slanting through the air of a chamber. Suddenly the stone lacework of the rose-windows gleamed through this vapour that had made all forms so shadowy.

Every moulding, the edges of every carving, the least detail of the sculpture was dipped in silver. The sunlight kindled fires in the stained windows, their rich colours sent out glowing sparks of light. The shafts began to tremble, the capitals were gently shaken. A light shudder as of delight ran through the building, the stones were loosened in their setting, the wall-spaces swayed with graceful caution. Here and there a ponderous pier moved as solemnly as a dowager when she condescends to complete a quadrille at the close of a ball. A few slender and graceful columns, their heads adorned with wreaths of trefoil, began to laugh and dance here and there. Some of the pointed arches dashed at the tall lancet windows, who, like ladies of the Middle Ages, wore the armorial bearings of their houses emblazoned on their golden robes. The dance of the mitred arcades with the slender windows became like a fray at a tourney.

In another moment every stone in the church vibrated, without leaving its place ; for the organ-pipes spoke, and I heard divine music mingling with the songs of angels, an unearthly harmony, accompanied by the deep notes of the bells, that boomed as the giant towers rocked and swayed in their square bases. This strange Sabbath seemed to me the most natural thing in the world ; and I, who had seen Charles X. hurled from his throne, was no longer amazed by anything. Nay, I myself was gently swaying with a see-saw movement that influenced my nerves pleasurably in a manner of which it is impossible to give any idea. Yet in the midst of this heated riot, the cathedral choir felt cold as if it were a winter day, and I became aware of a multitude of women, robed in white, silent and impassive, sitting there. The sweet incense smoke that arose from the censers was grateful to my soul. The tall wax candles flickered. The lectern, gay as a chanter undone by the treachery of wine, was skipping about like a peal of Chinese bells.

Then I knew that the whole cathedral was whirling round so fast that everything appeared to be undisturbed. The colossal Figure on the crucifix above the altar smiled upon me with a mingled malice and benevolence that frightened me ; I turned my eyes away, and marvelled at the bluish vapour that slid across the pillars, lending to them an indescribable charm. Then some graceful women's forms began to stir on the friezes. The cherubs who up-held the heavy columns shook out their wings. I felt myself uplifted by some divine power that steeped me in infinite joy, in a sweet and languid rapture. I would have given my life, I think, to have prolonged these phantasmagoria for a little, but suddenly a shrill voice clamoured in my ears :

" Awake and follow me ! "

A withered woman took my hand in hers ; its icy coldness crept through every nerve. The bones of her face showed plainly through the sallow, almost olive-tinted wrinkles of the skin. The shrunken, ice-cold, old woman wore a black robe, which she trailed in the dust, and at her throat there was something white, which I dared not examine. I could scarcely see her wan and colourless eyes, for they were fixed in a stare upon the heavens. She drew me after her along the aisles, leaving a trace of her presence in the ashes that she shook from her dress. Her bones rattled as she walked, like the bones of a skeleton ; and as we went I heard behind me the tinkling of a little bell, a thin, sharp sound that rang through my head like the notes of a harmonica.

"Suffer ! " she cried, " suffer ! So it must be ! "

We came out of the church ; we went through the dirtiest streets of the town, till we came at last to a dingy dwelling, and she bade me enter in. She dragged me with her, calling to me in a harsh, tuneless voice like a cracked bell :

" Defend me ! defend me ! "

Together we went up a winding staircase. She knocked at a door in the darkness, and a mute, like some familiar of the Inquisition, opened to her. In another moment we stood in a room hung with ancient, ragged tapestry, amid piles of old linen, crumpled muslin, and gilded brass.

" Behold the wealth that shall endure for ever ! " said she.

I shuddered with horror ; for just then, by the light of a tall torch and two altar candles, I saw distinctly that this woman was fresh from the graveyard. She had no hair. I turned to fly. She raised her fleshless arm and encircled me with a band of iron set with spikes, and as she raised it a cry went up all about us, the cry of millions of voices—the shouting of the dead !

" It is my purpose to make thee happy for ever," she said. " Thou art my son."

We were sitting before the hearth, the ashes lay cold upon it ; the old shrunken woman grasped my hand so tightly in hers that I could not choose but stay. I looked fixedly at her, striving to read the story of her life from the things among which she was crouching. Had she indeed any life in her ? It was a mystery. Yet I saw plainly that once she must have been young and beautiful ; fair, with all the charm of simplicity, perfect as some Greek statute, with the brow of a vestal.

" Ah ! ah ! " I cried, " now I know thee ! Miserable woman, why hast thou prostituted thyself ?   In the age of thy passions, in the time of they prosperity, the grace and purity of thy youth were forgotten. Forgetful of thy heroic devotion, thy pure life, thy abundant faith, thou didst resign thy primitive power and thy spiritual supremacy for fleshly power. Thy linen vestments, thy couch of moss, the cell in the rock, bright with rays of the Light Divine, were forsaken ; thou hast sparkled with diamonds, and shone with the glitter of luxury and pride. Then, grown bold and insolent, seizing and overturning all things in thy course like a courtesan eager for pleasure in her days of splendour, thou hast steeped thyself in blood like some queen stupefied by empery. Dost thou not remember to have been dull and heavy at times, and the sudden marvellous lucidity of other moments ; as when Art emerges from an orgy ? Oh ! poet, painter, and singer, lover of splendid ceremonies and protector of the arts, was thy friendship for art perchance a caprice, that so thou shouldst sleep beneath magnificent canopies ?

"Was there not a day when, in thy fantastic pride, though chastity and humility were prescribed to thee, thou hadst brought all things beneath thy feet, and set thy foot on the necks of princes ; when earthly dominion, and wealth, and the mind of man bore thy yoke ? Exulting in the abasement of humanity, joying to witness the uttermost lengths to which man's folly would go, thou hast bidden thy lovers walk on all fours, and required of them their lands and wealth, nay, even their wives if they were worth aught to thee. Thou hast devoured millions of men without a cause ; thou hast flung away lives like sand blown by the wind from West to East. Thou hast come down from the heights of thought to sit among the kings of men. Woman ! instead of comforting men, thou hast tormented and afflicted them ! Knowing that thou couldst ask and have, thou hast demanded—blood ! A little flour surely should have contented thee, accustomed as thou hadst been to live on bread and to mingle water with thy wine. Unlike all others in all things, formerly thou wouldst bid thy lovers fast, and they obeyed. Why should thy fancies have led thee to require things impossible ? Why, like a courtesan spoiled by her lovers, hast thou doted on follies, and left those undeceived who sought to explain and justify all thy errors ? Then came the days of thy later passions, terrible like the love of a woman of forty years, with a fierce cry thou hast sought to clasp the whole universe in one last embrace—and thy universe recoiled from thee !

" Then old men succeeded to thy young lovers ; decrepitude came to thy feet and made thee hideous. Yet, even then, men with the eagle power of vision said to thee in a glance, ' Thou shalt perish ingloriously, because thou hast fallen away, because thou hast broken the vows of thy maidenhood. The angel with peace written on her forehead, who should have shed light and joy along her path, has been a Messalina, delighting in the circus, in debauchery, and abuse of power. The days of thy virginity cannot return ; henceforward thou shalt be subject to a master. Thy hour has come ; the hand of death is upon thee. Thy heirs believe that thou art rich ; they will kill thee and find nothing. Yet try at least to fling away this raiment no longer in fashion ; be once more as in the days of old !—Nay, thou art dead, and by thy own deed ! '

" Is not this thy story ? " so I ended. " Decrepit, toothless, shivering crone, now forgotten, going thy ways without so much as a glance from passers-by ! Why art thou still alive ? What doest thou in that beggar's garb, uncomely and desired of none ? Where are thy riches ?—for what were they spent ? Where are thy treasures ?—what great deeds hast thou done ? "

At this demand, the shrivelled woman raised her bony form, flung off her rags, and grew tall and radiant, smiling as she broke forth from the dark chrysalid sheath. Then like a butterfly, this diaphanous creature emerged, fair and youthful, clothed in white linen, an Indian from creation issuing her palms. Her golden hair rippled over her shoulders, her eyes glowed, a bright mist clung about her, a ring of gold hovered above her head, she shook the flaming blade of a sword towards the spaces of heaven.

" See and believe ! " she cried.

And suddenly I saw, afar off, many thousands of cathedrals like the one that I had just quitted ; but these were covered with pictures and with frescoes, and I heard them echo with entrancing music. Myriads of human creatures flocked to these great buildings, swarming about them like ants on an ant-heap. Some were eager to rescue books from oblivion or to copy manuscripts, others were helping the poor, but nearly all were studying. Up above this countless multitude rose giant statues that they had erected in their midst, and by the gleams of a strange light from some luminary as powerful as the sun, I read the inscriptions on the bases of the statues—Science, History, Literature.

The light died out. Again I faced the young girl. Gradually she slipped into the dreary sheath, into the ragged cere-cloths, and became an aged woman again. Her familiar brought her a little dust, and she stirred it into the ashes of her chafing-dish, for the weather was cold and stormy ; and then he lighted for her, whose palaces had been lit with thousands of wax-tapers, a little cresset, that she might see to read her prayers through the hours of night.

" There is no faith left in the earth ! . . ." she said.

In such a perilous plight did I behold the fairest and the greatest, the truest and most life-giving of all Powers.

" Wake up, sir, the doors are just about to be shut," said a hoarse voice. I turned and beheld the beadle's ugly countenance ; the man was shaking me by the arm, and the cathedral lay wrapped in shadows as a man is wrapped in his cloak.

" Belief," I said to myself, " is Life ! I have just witnessed the funeral of a monarchy, now we must defend the Church."

EL VERDUGO

HONORÉ DE BALZAC

MIDNIGHT had just sounded from the belfry tower of the little town of Menda. A young French officer, leaning over the parapet of the long terrace at the farther end of the castle gardens, seemed to be unusually absorbed in deep thought for one who led the reckless life of a soldier ; but it must be admitted that never were the hour, the scene, and the night more favourable to meditation.

The blue dome of the cloudless sky of Spain was overhead ; he was looking out over the coy windings of a lovely valley lit by the uncertain starlight and the soft radiance of the moon. The officer, leaning against an orange tree in blossom, could also see, a hundred feet below him, the town of Menda, which seemed to nestle for shelter from the north wind at the foot of the crags on which the castle itself was built. He turned his head and caught sight of the sea ; the moonlit waves made a broad frame of silver for the landscape.

There were lights in the castle windows. The mirth and movement of a ball, the sounds of the violins, the laughter of the officers and their partners in the dance were borne towards him, and blended with the far-off murmur of the waves. The cool night had a certain bracing effect upon his frame, wearied as he had been by the heat of the day. He seemed to bathe in the air, made fragrant by the strong, sweet scent of flowers and of aromatic trees in the gardens.

The castle of Menda belonged to a Spanish grandee, who was living in it at that time with his family. All through the evening the elder daughter of the house had watched the officer with such a wistful interest that the Spanish lady's compassionate eyes might well have set the young Frenchman dreaming. Clara was beautiful ; and although she had three brothers and a sister, the broad lands of the Marqués de Légañès appeared to be sufficient warrant for Victor Marchand's belief that the young lady would have a splendid dowry. But how could he dare to imagine that the most fanatical believer in blue blood in all Spain would give his daughter to the son of a grocer in Paris ? Moreover, the French were hated. It was because the Marquis had been suspected of an attempt to raise the country in favour of Ferdinand VII. that General G——, who governed the province, had stationed Victor Marchand's battalion in the little town of Menda to overawe the neighbouring districts, which received

32*

the Marqués de Légañès' word as law. A recent despatch from
Marshal Ney had given ground for fear that the English might ere
long effect a landing on the coast, and had indicated the Marquis as
being in correspondence with the Cabinet in London.

In spite, therefore, of the welcome with which the Spaniards had
received Victor Marchand and his soldiers, that officer was always on
his guard. As he went towards the terrace, where he had just
surveyed the town and the districts confided to his charge, he had
been asking himself what construction he ought to put upon the
friendliness which the Marquis had invariably shown him, and how
to reconcile the apparent tranquillity of the country with his
General's uneasiness. But a moment later these thoughts were
driven from his mind by the instinct of caution and very legitimate
curiosity. It had just struck him that there was a very fair number
of lights in the town below. Although it was the Feast of Saint
James, he himself had issued orders that very morning that all
lights must be put out in the town at the hour prescribed by military
regulations. The castle alone had been excepted in this order.
Plainly here and there he saw the gleam of bayonets, where his own
men were at their accustomed posts ; but in the town there was a
solemn silence, and not a sign that the Spaniards had given themselves up to the intoxication of a festival. He tried vainly for a
while to explain this breach of the regulations on the part of the
inhabitants ; the mystery seemed but so much the more obscure
because he had left instructions with some of his officers to do
police duty that night, and make the rounds of the town.

With the impetuosity of youth, he was about to spring through a
gap in the wall preparatory to a rapid scramble down the rocks,
thinking to reach a small guard-house at the nearest entrance into
the town more quickly than by the beaten track, when a faint sound
stopped him. He fancied that he could hear the light footstep of a
woman along the gravelled garden walk. He turned his head and
saw no one ; for one moment his eyes were dazzled by the wonderful
brightness of the sea, the next he saw a sight so ominous that he
stood stock-still with amazement, thinking that his senses must be
deceiving him. The white moonbeams lighted the horizon, so that
he could distinguish the sails of ships still a considerable distance out
at sea. A shudder ran through him ; he tried to persuade himself
that this was some optical delusion brought about by chance effects
of moonlight on the waves ; and even as he made the attempt, a
hoarse voice called to him by name. The officer glanced at the gap
in the wall ; saw a soldier's head slowly emerge from it, and knew
the grenadier whom he had ordered to accompany him to the castle.

" Is that you, Commandant ? "

" Yes. What is it ? " returned the young officer in a low voice.
A kind of presentiment warned him to act cautiously.

"Those beggars down there are creeping about like worms ; and, by your leave, I came as quickly as I could to report my little reconnoitring expedition."

"Go on," answered Victor Marchand.

"I have just been following a man from the castle who came round this way with a lantern in his hand. A lantern is a suspicious matter with a vengeance ! I don't imagine that there was any need for that good Christian to be lighting tapers at this time of night. Says I to myself, ' They mean to gobble us up ! ' and I set myself to dogging his heels ; and that is how I found out that there is a pile of faggots, sir, two or three steps away from here."

Suddenly a dreadful shriek rang through the town below, and cut the man short. A light flashed in the Commandant's face, and the poor grenadier dropped down with a bullet through his head. Ten paces away a bonfire flared up like a conflagration. The sounds of music and laughter ceased all at once in the ballroom ; the silence of death, broken only by groans, succeeded to the rhythmical murmur of the festival. Then the roar of cannon sounded from across the white plain of the sea.

A cold sweat broke out on the young officer's forehead. He had left his sword behind. He knew that his men had been murdered, and that the English were about to land. He knew that if he lived he would be dishonoured ; he saw himself summoned before a court-martial. For a moment his eyes measured the depth of the valley ; the next, just as he was about to spring down, Clara's hand caught his.

"Fly !" she cried. "My brothers are coming after me to kill you. Down yonder at the foot of the cliff you will find Juanito's Andalusian. Go !"

She thrust him away. The young man gazed at her in dull bewilderment ; but obeying the instinct of self-preservation, which never deserts even the bravest, he rushed across the park in the direction pointed out to him, springing from rock to rock in places unknown to any save the goats. He heard Clara calling to her brothers to pursue him ; he heard the footsteps of the murderers ; again and again he heard their balls whistling about his ears ; but he reached the foot of the cliff, found the horse, mounted, and fled with lightning speed.

A few hours later the young officer reached General G——'s quarters, and found him at dinner with the staff.

"I put my life in your hands !" cried the haggard and exhausted Commandant of Menda.

He sank into a seat, and told his horrible story. It was received with an appalling silence.

"It seems to me that you are more to be pitied than to blame," the terrible General said at last. "You are not answerable for the

Spaniard's crimes, and unless the Marshal decides otherwise, I acquit you."

These words brought but cold comfort to the unfortunate officer. " When the Emperor comes to hear about it ! " he cried.

" Oh, he will be for having you shot," said the General, " but we shall see. Now we will say no more about this," he added severely, " except to plan a revenge that shall strike a salutary terror into this country, where they carry on war like savages."

An hour later a whole regiment, a detachment of cavalry, and a convoy of artillery were upon the road. The General and Victor marched at the head of the column. The soldiers had been told of the fate of their comrades, and their rage knew no bounds. The distance between headquarters and the town of Menda was crossed at a well-nigh miraculous speed. Whole villages by the way were found to be under arms ; every one of the wretched hamlets was surrounded, and their inhabitants decimated.

It so chanced that the English vessels still lay out at sea, and were no nearer the shore, a fact inexplicable until it was known afterwards that they were artillery transports which had outsailed the rest of the fleet. So the townsmen of Menda, left without the assistance on which they had reckoned when the sails of the English appeared, were surrounded by French troops almost before they had had time to strike a blow. This struck such terror into them that they offered to surrender at discretion. An impulse of devotion, no isolated instance in the history of the Peninsula, led the actual slayers of the French to offer to give themselves up ; seeking in this way to save the town, for from the General's reputation for cruelty it was feared that he would give Menda over to the flames, and put the whole population to the sword. General G—— took their offer, stipulating that every soul in the castle from the lowest servant to the Marquis should likewise be given up to him. These terms being accepted, the General promised to spare the lives of the rest of the townsmen, and to prohibit his soldiers from pillaging or setting fire to the town. A heavy contribution was levied, and the wealthiest inhabitants were taken as hostages to guarantee payment within twenty-four hours.

The General took every necessary precaution for the safety of his troops, provided for the defence of the place, and refused to billet his men in the houses of the town. After they had bivouacked, he went up to the castle and entered it as a conqueror. The whole family of Légañès and their household were gagged, shut up in the great ballroom, and closely watched. From the windows it was easy to see the whole length of the terrace above the town.

The staff was established in an adjoining gallery, where the General forthwith held a council as to the best means of preventing the landing of the English. An aide-de camp was despatched to

Marshal Ney, orders were issued to plant batteries along the coast, and then the General and his staff turned their attention to their prisoners. The two hundred Spaniards given up by the towns-folk were shot down then and there upon the terrace. And after this military execution, the General gave orders to erect gibbets to the number of the prisoners in the ballroom in the same place, and to send for the hangman out of the town. Victor took advantage of the interval before dinner to pay a visit to the prisoners. He soon came back to the General.

" I am come in haste," he faltered out, " to ask a favour."

" *You !* " exclaimed the General, with bitter irony in his tones.

" Alas ! " answered Victor, " it is a sorry favour. The Marquis has seen them erecting the gallows, and hopes that you will com-mute the punishment for his family ; he entreats you to have the nobles beheaded."

" Granted," said the General.

" He further asks that they may be allowed the consolation of religion, and that they may be unbound ; they give you their word that they will not attempt to escape."

" That I permit," said the General, " but you are answerable for them."

" The old noble offers you all that he has if you will pardon his youngest son."

" Really ! " cried the Commander. " His property is forfeit already to King Joseph." He paused ; a contemptuous thought set wrinkles in his forehead, as he added, " I will do better than they ask. I understand what he means by that last request of his. Very good. Let him hand down his name to posterity ; but when-ever it is mentioned, all Spain shall remember his treason and its punishment ! I will give the fortune and his life to any one of the sons who will do the executioner's office. . . There, don't talk any more about them to me."

Dinner was ready. The officers sat down to satisfy an appetite whetted by hunger. Only one among them was absent from the table—that one was Victor Marchand. After long hesitation he went to the ballroom, and heard the last sighs of the proud house of Légañês. He looked sadly at the scene before him. Only last night, in this very room, he had seen their faces whirled past him in the waltz, and he shuddered to think that those girlish heads, with those of the three young brothers, must fall in a brief space by the executioner's sword. There sat the father and mother, their three sons and two daughters, perfectly motionless, bound to their gilded chairs. Eight serving men stood with their hands tied behind them. These fifteen prisoners, under sentence of death, exchanged grave glances ; it was difficult to read the thoughts that filled them from their eyes, but profound resignation and regret that their enterprise should have failed so completely was written on more than one brow.

The impassive soldiers who guarded them respected the grief of their bitter enemies. A gleam of curiosity lighted up all faces when Victor came in. He gave orders that the condemned prisoners should be unbound, and himself unfastened the cords that held Clara a prisoner. She smiled mournfully at him. The officer could not refrain from lightly touching the young girl's arm ; he could not help admiring her dark hair, her slender waist. She was a true daughter of Spain, with a Spanish complexion, a Spaniard's eyes, blacker than the raven's wing beneath their long curving lashes.

" Did you succeed ? " she asked, with a mournful smile, in which a certain girlish charm still lingered.

Victor could not repress a groan. He looked from the faces of the three brothers to Clara, and again at the three young Spaniards. The first, the oldest of the family, was a man of thirty. He was short, and somewhat ill made ; he looked haughty and proud, but a certain distinction was not lacking in his bearing, and he was apparently no stranger to the delicacy of feeling for which in olden times the chivalry of Spain was famous. His name was Juanito. The second son, Felipe, was about twenty years of age ; he was like his sister Clara ; and the youngest was a child of eight. In the features of the little Manuel a painter would have discerned something of that Roman steadfastness which David has given to the children's faces in his Republican *genre* pictures. The old Marquis, with his white hair, might have come down from some canvas of Murillo's. Victor threw back his head in despair after this survey ; how should one of these accept the General's offer ! nevertheless he ventured to intrust it to Clara. A shudder ran through the Spanish girl, but she recovered herself almost instantly, and knelt before her father.

" Father," she said, " bid Juanito swear to obey the commands that you shall give him, and we shall be content."

The Marquesa trembled with hope, but as she lent towards her husband and learned Clara's hideous secret, the mother fainted away. Juanito understood it all, and leapt up like a caged lion. Victor took it upon himself to dismiss the soldiers, after receiving an assurance of entire submission from the Marquis. The servants were led away and given over to the hangman and their fate. When only Victor remained on guard in the room, the old Marqués de Légañès rose to his feet.

" Juanito," he said. For all answer Juanito bowed his head in a way that meant refusal ; he sank down into his chair, and fixed tearless eyes upon his father and mother in an intolerable gaze. Clara went over to him and sat on his knee ; she put her arms about him, and pressed kisses on his eyelids, saying gaily :

" Dear Juanito, if you but knew how sweet death at your hands will be to me ! I shall not be compelled to submit to the hateful touch of the hangman's fingers. You will snatch me away from the evils to come and . . Dear, kind Juanito, you could not bear the thought of my belonging to any one—well, then ? "

The velvet eyes gave Victor a burning glance ; she seemed to try to awaken in Juanito's heart his hatred for the French.

" Take courage," said his brother Felipe, " or our well-nigh royal line will be extinct."

Suddenly Clara sprang to her feet. The group round Juanito fell back, and the son who had rebelled with such good reason was confronted with his aged father.

" Juanito, I command you ! " said the Marquis solemnly.

The young Count gave no sign, and his father fell on his knees ; Clara, Manuel, and Felipe unconsciously followed his example, stretching out suppliant hands to him who must save their family from oblivion, and seeming to echo their father's words.

" Can it be that you lack the fortitude of a Spaniard and true sensibility, my son ? Do you mean to keep me on my knees ? What right have you to think of your own life and of your own sufferings ?—Is this my son, madam ? " the old Marquis added, turning to his wife.

" He will consent to it," cried the mother in agony of soul. She had seen a slight contraction of Juanito's brows which she, his mother, alone understood.

Mariquita, the second daughter, knelt, with her slender clinging arms about her mother ; the hot tears fell from her eyes, and her little brother Manuel upbraided her for weeping. Just at that moment the castle chaplain came in ; the whole family surrounded him and led him up to Juanito. Victor felt that he could endure the sight no longer, and with a sign to Clara he hurried from the room to make one last effort for them. He found the General in boisterous spirits ; the officers were still sitting over their dinner and drinking together ; the wine had loosened their tongues.

An hour later, a hundred of the principal citizens of Menda were summoned to the terrace by the General's orders to witness the execution of the family of Légañès. A detachment had been told off to keep order among the Spanish townsfolk, who were marshalled beneath the gallows whereon the Marquis's servants hung ; the feet of those martyrs of their cause all but touched the citizen's heads. Thirty paces away stood the block ; the blade of a scimitar glittered upon it, and the executioner stood by in case Juanito should refuse at the last.

The deepest silence prevailed, but before long it was broken by the sound of many footsteps, the measured tramp of a picket of soldiers, and the jingling of their weapons. Mingled with these came other noises—loud talk and laughter from the dinner-table where the officers were sitting ; just as the music and the sound of the dancer's feet had drowned the preparations for last night's treacherous butchery.

All eyes turned to the castle, and beheld the family of nobles coming forth with incredible composure to their death. Every brow was serene and calm. One alone among them, haggard and overcome, leant on the arm of the priest, who poured forth all the consolations of religion for the one man who was condemned to live. Then the executioner, like the spectators, knew that Juanito had consented to perform his office for a day. The old Marquis and his wife, Clara and Mariquita, and their two brothers knelt a few paces from the fatal spot. Juanito reached it, guided by the priest. As he stood at the block the executioner plucked him by the sleeve, and took him aside, probably to give him certain instructions. The confessor so placed the victims that they could not witness the executions, but one and all stood upright and fearless, like Spaniards, as they were.

Clara sprang to her brother's side before the others.

" Juanito," she said to him, " be merciful to my lack of courage. Take me first ! "

As she spoke, the footsteps of a man running at full speed echoed from the walls, and Victor appeared upon the scene. Clara was kneeling before the block ; her white neck seemed to appeal to the blade to fall. The officer turned faint, but he found strength to rush to her side. " The General grants you your life if you will consent to marry me," he murmured.

The Spanish girl gave the officer a glance full of proud disdain.

" Now, Juanito ! " she said in her deep-toned voice.

Her head fell at Victor's feet. A shudder ran through the Marquesa de Légañès, a convulsive tremor that she could not control, but she gave no other sign of her anguish.

" Is this where I ought to be, dear Juanito ? Is it all right ? " little Manuel asked his brother.

" Oh, Mariquita, you are weeping ! " Juanito said when his sister came.

" Yes," said the girl ; " I am thinking of you, poor Juanito ; how unhappy you will be when we are gone."

Then the Marquis's tall figure approached. He looked at the block where his children's blood had been shed, turned to the mute and motionless crowd, and said in a loud voice as he stretched out his hands to Juanito :

" Spaniards ! I give my son a father's blessing. Now, *Marquis*, strike ' without fear ' ; thou art ' without reproach.' "

But when his mother came near, leaning on the confessor's

arm—" She fed me from her breast ! " Juanito cried, in tones that
drew a cry of horror from the crowd. The uproarious mirth of
the officers over their wine died away before that terrible cry. The
Marquesa knew that Juanito's courage was exhausted ; at one
bound she sprang to the balustrade, leapt forth, and was dashed
to pieces on the rocks below. A cry of admiration broke from the
spectators. Juanito swooned.

" General," said an officer, half drunk by this time, " Marchand
has just been telling me something about this execution ; I will
wager that it was not by your orders—— "

" Are you forgetting, gentlemen, that in a month's time five
hundred families in France will be in mourning, and that we are
still in Spain ? " cried General G——. " Do you want us to leave
our bones here ? "

But not a man at the table, not even a subaltern, dared to
empty his glass after that speech.

In spite of the respect in which all men hold the Marqués de
Légañès, in spite of the title of *El Verdugo* (the executioner) conferred upon him as a patent of nobility by the King of Spain, the
great noble is consumed by a gnawing grief. He lives a retired life,
and seldom appears in public. The burden of his heroic crime
weighs heavily upon him, and he seems to wait impatiently till
the birth of a second son shall release him, and he may go to join
the Shades that never cease to haunt him.

A SEASHORE DRAMA

Honoré de Balzac

Young men almost always have a pair of compasses with which
they delight to measure the future ; when their will is in accord
with the size of the angle which they make, the world is theirs.
But this phenomenon of moral life takes place only at a certain age.
That age, which in the case of all men comes between the years of
twenty-two and twenty-eight, is the age of noble thoughts, the age
of first conceptions, because it is the age of unbounded desires, the
age at which one doubts nothing ; he who talks of doubt speaks
of impotence. After that age, which passes as quickly as the season
for sowing, comes the age of execution. There are in a certain sense

two youths : one during which one thinks, the other during which one acts ; often they are blended, in men whom nature has favoured, and who, like Caesar, Newton, and Bonaparte, are the greatest among great men.

I was reckoning how much time a thought needs to develop itself ; and, compasses in hand, standing on a cliff a hundred fathoms above the ocean, whose waves played among the reefs, I laid out my future, furnishing it with works, as an engineer draws fortresses and palaces upon vacant land. The sea was lovely ; I had just dressed after bathing ; I was waiting for Pauline, my guardian angel, who was bathing in a granite bowl full of white sand, the daintiest bath-tub that Nature ever designed for any of her sea-fairies. We were at the extreme point of Le Croisic, a tiny peninsula of Britanny ; we were far from the harbour, in a spot which the authorities considered so inaccessible that the customs officers almost never visited it. To swim in the air after swimming in the sea ! Ah ! who would not have swum into the future ? Why did I think ? Why does evil happen ? Who knows ? Ideas come to your heart, or your brain, without consulting you. No courtesan was ever more whimsical or more imperious than is conception in an artist ; it must be caught, like fortune, by the hair, when it comes. Clinging to my thought, as Astolpho clung to his hippogriff, I galloped through the world, arranging everything therein to suit my pleasure.

When I looked about me in search of some omen favourable to the audacious schemes which my wild imagination advised me to under-take, a sweet cry, the cry of a woman calling in the silence of the desert, the cry of a woman coming from the bath, refreshed and joyous, drowned the murmur of the fringe of foam tossed constantly back and forth by the rising and falling of the waves in the inden-tations of the shore. When I heard that note, uttered by the soul, I fancied that I had seen on the cliff the foot of an angel, who, as she unfolded her wings, had called to me : " Thou shalt have success ! " I descended, radiant with joy and light as air ; I went bounding down, like a stone down a steep slope. When she saw me, she said to me : " What is the matter ? " I did not answer, but my eyes became moist. The day before, Pauline had under-stood my pain, as she understood at that moment my joy, with the magical sensitiveness of a harp which follows the variations of the atmosphere. The life of man has some glorious moments ! We walked silently along the shore. The sky was cloudless, the sea without a ripple ; others would have seen only two blue plains, one above the other ; but we who understood each other without need of speech, we who could discover between those two swaddling-cloths of infinity the illusions with which youth is nourished, we pressed each other's hand at the slightest change which took place either in the sheet of water or in the expanse of air ; for we took those trivial phenomena for material interpretations of our twofold thought.

Who has not enjoyed that unbounded bliss in pleasures, when the soul seems to be released from the bonds of the flesh, and to be restored as it were to the world whence it came ? Pleasure is not our only guide in those regions. Are there not times when the sentiments embrace each other as of their own motion, and fly thither, like two children who take each other's hands and begin to run without knowing why or whither ? We walked along thus.

At the moment that the roofs of the town appeared on the horizon, forming a greyish line, we met a poor fisherman who was returning to Le Croisic. His feet were bare, his canvas trousers were ragged on the edges, with many holes imperfectly mended ; he wore a shirt of sail-cloth, wretched list suspenders, and his jacket was a mere rag. The sight of that misery distressed us—a discord, as it were, in the midst of our harmony. We looked at each other, to lament that we had not at that moment the power to draw upon the treasury of Abu-l-Kásim. We saw a magnificent lobster and a crab hanging by a cord which the fisherman carried in his right hand, while in the other he had his nets and his fishing apparatus. We accosted him, with the purpose of buying his fish, an idea which occurred to both of us, and which expressed itself in a smile, to which I replied by slightly pressing the arm which I held and drawing it closer to my heart. It was one of those nothings which the memory afterward transforms into a poem, when, sitting by the fire, we recall the time when that nothing moved us, the place where it happened, and that mirage, the effects of which have never been defined, but which often exerts an influence upon the objects which surround us, when life is pleasant and our hearts are full.

The loveliest places are simply what we make them. Who is the man, however little of a poet he may be, who has not in his memory a boulder that occupies more space than the most famous landscape visited at great expense ? Beside that boulder what tempestuous thoughts ! there, a whole life mapped out ; here, fears banished ; there, rays of hope entered the heart. At that moment, the sun, sympathising with these thoughts of love and of the future, cast upon the yellowish sides of that cliff an ardent beam ; some mountain wild-flowers attracted the attention ; the tranquillity and silence magnified that uneven surface, in reality dark of hue, but made brilliant by the dreamer ; then it was beautiful, with its meagre vegetation, its warm-hued camomile, its Venus's hair, with the velvety leaves. A prolonged festivity, superb decorations, placid exaltation of human strength ! Once before, the Lake of Bienne, seen from Île St.-Pierre, had spoken to me thus ; perhaps the cliff of Le Croisic would be the last of those delights. But, in that case, what would become of Pauline?

"You have had fine luck this morning, my good man," I said to the fisherman.

"Yes, monsieur," he replied, stopping to turn towards us the tanned face of those who remain for hours at a time exposed to the reflection of the sun on the water.

That face indicated endless resignation; the patience of the fisherman, and his gentle manners. That man had a voice without trace of harshness, kindly lips, no ambition; an indefinably frail and sickly appearance. Any other type of face would have displeased us.

"Where are you going to sell your fish?"

"At the town."

"How much will you get for the lobster?"

"Fifteen sous."

"And for the crab?"

"Twenty sous."

"Why so much difference between the lobster and the crab?"

"The crab is much more delicate, monsieur; and then it's as cunning as a monkey, and don't often allow itself to be caught."

"Will you let us have both for a hundred sous?" said Pauline.

The man was thunderstruck.

"You shan't have them!" I said laughingly; "I will give ten francs. We must pay for emotions all that they are worth."

"Very well," she replied, "I propose to have them; I will give ten francs two sous."

"Ten sous."

"Twelve francs."

"Fifteen francs."

"Fifteen francs fifty," she said.

"One hundred francs."

"One hundred and fifty."

I bowed. At that moment we were not rich enough to carry the bidding any farther. The poor fisherman did not know whether he ought to be angry as at a practical joke, or to exult; we relieved him from his dilemma by giving him the name of our landlady and telling him to take the lobster and the crab to her house.

"Do you earn a living?" I asked him, in order to ascertain to what cause his destitution should be attributed.

"With much difficulty and many hardships," he replied. "Fishing on the seashore, when you have neither boat nor nets, and can fish only with a line, is a risky trade. You see, you have to wait for the fish or the shell-fish to come, while the fishermen with boats can go out to sea after them. It is so hard to earn a living this way, that I am the only man who fishes on the shore. I pass whole days without catching anything. The only way I get anything is when a crab forgets himself and goes to sleep, as this one did, or a lobster is fool enough to stay on the rocks. Sometimes, after a high sea, the wolf-fish come in, and then I grab them."

"Well, take one day with another, what do you earn ? "

"Eleven or twelve sous. I could get along with that if I were alone ; but I have my father to support, and the poor man can't help me, for he's blind."

At that sentence, uttered with perfect simplicity, Pauline and I looked at each other without a word.

"You have a wife or a sweetheart ? "

He cast at us one of the most pitiful glances that I ever saw, as he replied :

"If I had a wife, then I should have to let my father go : I couldn't support him, and a wife and children too."

"Well, my poor fellow, how is it that you don't try to earn more by carrying salt to the harbour, or by working in the salt marshes ? "

"Oh ? I couldn't do that for three months, monsieur. I am not strong enough ; and if I should die, my father would have to beg. What I must have is a trade that requires very little skill and a great deal of patience."

"But how can two people live on twelve sous a day ? "

"Oh, monsieur, we eat buckwheat cakes, and barnacles that I take off the rocks."

"How old are you ? "

"Thirty-seven."

"Have you ever been away from here ? "

"I went to Guérande once, to draw my lot in the draft, and I went to Savenay, to show myself to some gentlemen who measured me. If I had been an inch taller I should have been drafted. I should have died on the first long march, and my poor father would have been asking alms to-day."

I had thought out many dramas ; Pauline was accustomed to intense emotions, living with a man in my condition of health ; but neither of us had ever listened to more touching words than those of that fisherman. We walked some distance in silence, both of us measuring the silent depths of that unknown life, admiring the nobility of that self-sacrifice which was unconscious of itself ; the strength of his weakness surprised us ; that unconscious generosity made us small in our own eyes. I saw that poor creature, all instinct, chained to that rock as a galley-slave is chained to his ball, watching for twenty years for shell-fish to support himself, and sustained in his patience by a single sentiment. How many hours passed on the edge of that beach ! how many hopes crushed by a squall, by a change of weather ! He hung over the edge of a granite shelf, his arms stretched out like those of an Indian fakir, while his father, sitting on a stool, waited in silence and darkness for him to bring him the coarsest of shell-fish and of bread, if the sea were willing.

" Do you ever drink wine ? " I asked him.

" Three or four times a year."

" Well, you shall drink some to-day, you and your father, and we will send you a white loaf."

" You are very kind, monsieur."

" We will give you your dinner if you will guide us along the shore as far as Batz, where we are going, to see the tower which overlooks the basin and the coast between Batz and Le Croisic."

" With pleasure," he said. " Go straight ahead, follow the road you are now on ; I will overtake you after I have got rid of my fish and my tackle."

We nodded simultaneously, and he hurried off towards the town, light at heart. That meeting held us in the same mental situation in which we were previously, but it had lowered our spirits.

" Poor man ! " said Pauline, with that accent which takes away from a woman's compassion whatever there may be offensive in pity ; " does it not make one feel ashamed to be happy when one sees such misery ? "

" Nothing is more cruel than to have impotent desires," I replied.

" Those two poor creatures, father and son, will no more know how keen our sympathy is than the world knows how noble their lives are ; for they are laying up treasures in heaven."

" What a wretched country ! " she said, as she pointed out to me, along a field surrounded by a loose stone wall, lumps of cow-dung arranged symmetrically. " I asked some one what those were. A peasant woman, who was putting them in place, answered that she was *making wood*. Just fancy, my dear, that when these blocks of dung are dried, these poor people gather them, pile them up, and warm themselves with them. During the winter they are sold, like lumps of peat. And what do you suppose the best paid dressmaker earns ? Five sous a day," she said, after a pause ; " but she gets her board."

" See," I said to her, " the winds from the ocean wither or uproot everything ; there are no trees ; the wrecks of vessels that are beyond use are sold to the rich, for the cost of transportation prevents them from using the firewood in which Britanny abounds. This province is beautiful only to great souls ; people without courage could not live here ; it is no place for anybody except poets or barnacles. The storehouse for salt had to be built on the cliff, to induce anybody to live in it. On one side, the sea ; on the other, the sands ; above, space."

We had already passed the town and were within the species of desert which separates Le Croisic from the village of Batz. Imagine, my dear uncle, a plain two leagues in length, covered by the gleaming sand that we see on the seashore. Here and there a few rocks raised their heads, and you would have said that they were gigantic beasts lying among the dunes. Along the shore there is an occasional reef, about which the waves play, giving them the aspect of great white roses floating on the liquid expanse and coming to rest on the shore. When I saw that plain bounded by the ocean on the right, and on the left by the great lake that flows in between Le Croisic and the sandy heights of Guérande, at the foot of which there are salt marshes absolutely without vegetation, I glanced at Pauline and asked her if she had the courage to defy the heat of the sun, and the strength to walk through the sand.

"I have on high boots ; let us go thither," she said, pointing to the tower of Batz, which circumscribed the view by its enormous mass, placed there like a pyramid, but a slender, indented pyramid, so poetically adorned that it allowed the imagination to see in it the first ruins of a great Asiatic city. We walked a few yards and sat down under a rock which was still in the shadow ; but it was eleven o'clock in the morning, and that shadow, which ceased at our feet, rapidly disappeared.

"How beautiful the silence is," she said to me ; "and how its intensity is increased by the regular plashing of the sea on the beach ! "

"If you choose to abandon your understanding to the three immensities that surround us, the air, the water, and the sand, listening solely to the repeated sound of the flow and the outflow," I replied, "you will not be able to endure its language ; you will fancy that you discover therein a thought which will overwhelm you. Yesterday, at sunset, I had that sensation ; it prostrated me "

"Oh, yes, let us talk," she said, after a long pause. "No orator can be more terrible than this silence. I fancy that I have discovered the causes of the harmony which surrounds us," she continued. "This landscape, which has only three sharp colours, the brilliant yellow of the sand, the blue of the sky, and the smooth green of the sea, is grand without being wild, it is immense without being a desert, it is changeless without being monotonous ; it has only three elements, but it is diversified."

"Women alone can express their impressions thus," I replied ; "you would drive a poet to despair, dear heart, whom I divined so perfectly."

"The excessive noonday heat imparts a gorgeous colour to those three expressions of infinity," replied Pauline, laughing. "I can imagine here the poesy and the passion of the Orient."

"And I can imagine its despair."

" Yes," she said ; " that dune is a sublime cloister."

We heard the hurried step of our guide ; he had dressed himself in his best clothes. We said a few formal words to him ; he evidently saw that our frame of mind had changed, and, with the reserve that misfortune imparts, he kept silent. Although we pressed each other's hands from time to time, to advise each other of the unity of our impressions, we walked for half an hour in silence, whether because we were overwhelmed by the heat, which rose in shimmering waves from the sand, or because the difficulty of walking absorbed our attention. We walked on, hand in hand, like two children ; we should not have taken a dozen steps if we had been arm in arm. The road leading to Batz was not marked out ; a gust of wind was enough to efface the footprints of horses or the wheel-ruts ; but our guide's practised eye recognised the road by the droppings of cattle or of horses. Sometimes it went down towards the sea, sometimes rose towards the upland, at the caprice of the slopes, or to skirt a rock. At noon we were only half-way.

" We will rest there," said I, pointing to a promontory formed of rocks high enough to lead one to suppose that we should find a grotto there.

When I spoke, the fisherman, who had followed the direction of my finger, shook his head and said :

" There's some one there ! People who go from Batz to Le Croisic, or from Le Croisic to Batz, always make a détour in order not to pass that rock."

The man said this in a low voice, and we divined a mystery.

" Is he a thief and assassin ? "

Our guide replied only by a long-drawn breath which increased our curiosity.

" But will anything happen to us if we pass by there ? "

" Oh no ! "

" Will you go with us ? "

" No, monsieur."

" We will go then, if you assure us that we shall be in no danger."

" I don't say that," replied the fisherman hastily ; " I say simply that the man who is there won't say anything to you, or do any harm to you. Oh, bless my soul ! he won't so much as move from his place ! "

" Who is he pray ? "

" A man ! "

Never were two syllables uttered in such a tragic tone. At that moment we were twenty yards from that reef, about which the sea was playing ; our guide took the road which skirted the rocks ; we went straight ahead, but Pauline took my arm. Our guide quickened his pace in order to reach the spot where the two roads met again at the same time that we did. He evidently supposed that, after seeing the man, we would quicken our pace. That circumstance kindled our curiosity, which then became so intense that out hearts throbbed as if they had felt a thrill of fear. Despite the heat of the day and the fatigue caused by walking through the sand, our hearts were still abandoned to the indescribable langour of a blissful harmony of sensations ; they were filled with that pure pleasure which can only be described by comparing it to the pleasure which one feels in listening to some lovely music, like Mozart's *Andiano mio ben.* Do not two pure sentiments, which blend, resemble two beautiful voices singing ? In order fully to appreciate the emotion which seized us, you must share the semi-voluptuous condition in which the events of that morning had enveloped us. Gaze for a long while at a turtle-dove perched on a slender twig, near a spring, and you will utter a cry of pain when you see a hawk pounce upon it, bury its steel claws in its heart, and bear it away with the murderous rapidity that powder communicates to the bullet.

When we had walked a yard or two across the open space that lay in front of the grotto, a sort of platform a hundred feet above the ocean, and sheltered from its rage by a succession of steep rocks, we were conscious of an electric shock not unlike that caused by a sudden noise in the midst of the night. We had spied a man seated on a boulder of granite, and he had looked at us. His glance, like the flash of a cannon, came from two bloodshot eyes, and his stoical immobility could be compared only to the unchanging posture of the masses of granite which surrounded him. His eyes moved slowly ; his body, as if it were petrified, did not move at all. After flashing at us that glance which gave us such a rude shock, he turned his eyes to the vast expanse of the ocean, and gazed at it, despite the dazzling light which rose therefrom, as the eagles are said to gaze at the sun, without lowering the lids, which he did not raise again. Try to recall, my dear uncle, one of those old druidical oaks, whose gnarled trunk, newly stripped of its branches, rises fantastically above a deserted road, and you will have an accurate image of that man. He had one of those shattered herculean frames, and the face of Olympian Jove, but ravaged by age, by the hard toil of the seafaring man, by grief, by coarse food, and blackened as if struck by lightning. As I glanced at his calloused, hairy hands, I saw chords which resembled veins of iron. However, everything about him indicated a robust constitution. I noticed a large quantity of moss in a corner of the grotto, and upon a rough table, hewn out by chance in the midst of the granite, a broken loaf covering an earthen jug. Never had my imagination, when it carried me back to the deserts where the first hermits of Christianity lived, conceived a face more grandly religious or more appallingly penitent than was the face of that man.

Even you, who have listened to confessions, my dear uncle, have perhaps never met with such sublime remorse; but that remorse was drowned in the waves of prayer, the incessant prayer of silent despair. That fisherman, that sailor, that rude Breton, was sublime by virtue of some unknown sentiment. But had those eyes wept? Had that statuelike hand struck its fellow-man? Was that stern forehead, instinct with pitiless uprightness, on which, however, strength had left those marks of gentleness which are the accompaniment of all true strength—was that forehead, furrowed by wrinkles, in harmony with a noble heart? Why was that man among the granite? Why the granite in that man? Where was the man? Where was the granite? A whole world of thoughts rushed through our minds. As our guide had anticipated, we had passed in silence, rapidly; and when he met us, we were tremulous with terror, or overwhelmed with amazement. But he did not use the fulfilment of his prediction as a weapon against us.

"Did you see him?" he asked.

"Who is that man?" said I.

"They call him *The Man of the Vow*."

You can imagine how quickly our two faces turned toward our fisherman at those words! He was a simple-minded man; he understood our silent question; and this is what he said, in his own language, the popular tone of which I shall try to retain:

"Madame, the people of Le Croisic, like the people of Batz, believe that that man is guilty of something, and that he is doing a penance ordered by a famous priest to whom he went to confess, a long way beyond Nantes. Other people think that Cambremer— that's his name—has an evil spell that he communicates to everybody who passes through the air he breathes. So a good many people, before they pass that rock, look to see what way the wind is. If it's from *galerne*," he said, pointing towards the west, "they wouldn't go on, even if it was a matter of searching for a piece of the true Cross; they turn back, because they're frightened. Other people, the rich people of Le Croisic, say that he's made a vow, and that's why he's called *The Man of the Vow*. He is always there night and day; never comes out.

"These reports about him have some appearance of sense. You see," he added, turning to point out a thing which we had not noticed, "he has stuck up there, on the left, a wooden cross, to show that he has put himself under the protection of God, the Blessed Virgin, and the saints. Even if he hadn't consecrated himself like that, the fear everybody has of him would make him as safe there as if he were guarded by soldiers. He hasn't said a word since he shut himself up there in the open air; he lives on bread and water that his brother's daughter brings him every morning—a little maid of twelve years, that he's left his property to ; and she's a pretty thing, as gentle as a lamb, a nice little girl and very clever. She has blue eyes as long as that," he said, holding up his thumb, " and a cherub's head of hair.

" When any one says to her : ' I say, Pérotte ' (that means Pierrette amongst us," he said, interrupting himself : " she is consecrated to St. Pierre ; Cambremer's name is Pierre, and he was her godfather), ' I say, Pérotte, what does your uncle say to you ? ' ' He don't say anything,' she'll answer, ' not anything at all, nothing ! ' ' Well, then, what does he do to you ? ' ' He kisses me on the forehead Sundays ! ' ' Aren't you afraid of him ? ' ' Why no, he's my godfather.' He won't let any one else bring him anything to eat. Pérotte says that he smiles when she comes ; but that's like a sunbeam in a fog, for they say he's as gloomy as a fog."

" But," I said, " you arouse our curiosity without gratifying it. Do you know what brought him here ? Was it grief, was it repentance, was it insanity, was it crime, was it—— ? "

" Oh ! only my father and I know the truth of the thing, Monsieur. My dead mother worked for a judge to whom Cambremer told the whole story, by the priest's order ; for he wouldn't give him absolution on any other condition, according to what the people at the harbour said. My poor mother overheard what Cambremer said, without meaning to, because the judge's kitchen was right next to his study, and she listened. She's dead, and the judge who heard him is dead. My mother made father and me promise never to tell anything to the people about here ; but I can tell you that the night my mother told it to us, the hair on my head turned grey."

" Well, tell us, my fine fellow ; we will not mention it to anybody."

The fisherman looked at us, and continued thus :

" Pierre Cambremer, whom you saw yonder, is the oldest of the Cambremers, who have always been sailors, from father to son ; that's what their name says—the sea has always bent under them. The man you saw was a boat fisherman. So he had boats and went sardine-fishing ; he went deep-sea fishing too, for the dealers. He'd have fitted out a vessel and gone after cod, if he hadn't been so fond of his wife ; a fine woman she was, a Brouin from Guérande ; magnificent girl, and she had a big heart. She was so fond of Cambremer that she'd never let her man leave her any longer than he had to, to go after sardines. They used to live over there— look ! " said the fisherman, ascending a hillock to point to an islet in the little inland sea between the dunes, across which we were walking, and the salt marshes of Guérande. " Do you see that house ? That was his.

" Jacquette Brouin and Cambremer never had but one child, a boy ; and they loved him like—like what shall I say ?—indeed, like people love their only child ; they were mad over him. If their little Jacques had put dirt in the saucepan, saving your presence, they'd have thought it was sugar. How many times we've seen 'em at the fair, buying the prettiest fallals for him ! It was all nonsense—everybody told 'em so. Little Cambremer, seeing that he was allowed to do whatever he wanted to, became as big a rogue as a red ass.

" When any one went to the elder Cambremer and told him : ' Your boy nearly killed little So-and-so,' he'd laugh and say : ' Bah ! he'll make a fine sailor ! he'll command the king's fleet.' And when somebody else said : ' Pierre Cambremer, do you know that your boy put out the little Pougaud girl's eye ? ' Pierre said : ' He'll be fond of the girls ! ' He thought everything was all right. So my little scamp, when he was ten years old, used to be at everybody, and amuse himself cutting off hens' heads, cutting pigs open in short, he rolled in blood like a polecat. ' He'll make a famous soldier ! ' Cambremer would say ; ' he's got a taste for blood.' I remember all that, you see," said the fisherman.

" And so did Cambremer too," he continued after a pause. " When he got to be fifteen or sixteen years old, Jacques Cambremer was—what shall I say ?—a shark. He used to go to Guérande to enjoy himself, or to Savenay to make love to the girls. Then he began to steal from his mother, who didn't dare to say anything to her husband. Cambremer was so honest that he'd travel twenty leagues to pay back two sous, if he had been overpaid in settling an account. At last the day came when his mother was stripped clean. While his father was away fishing, the boy carried off the sideboard, the dishes, the sheets, the linen, and left just the four walls ; he'd sold everything to get money to go to Nantes and raise the devil. The poor woman cried for whole days and nights. She couldn't help telling the father about that, when he came home ; and she was afraid of the father—not for herself, oh no ? When Pierre Cambremer came home and found his house furnished with things people had lent his wife, he said :

" ' What does all this mean ? '

" The poor woman was nearer dead than alive.

" ' We've been robbed,' said she.

" ' Where's Jacques ? '

" ' Jacques is on a spree.'

" No one knew where the villain had gone.

" ' He goes on too many sprees ! ' said Pierre.

" Six months later, the poor man learned that his son was in danger of falling into the hands of justice at Nantes. He went there on foot ; made the journey faster than he could have gone by sea

got hold of his son, and brought him back here. He didn't ask him :
' What have you been doing ? ' He just said to him :

" ' If you don't behave yourself here with your mother and me
for two years, going fishing and acting like an honest man, you'll
have an account to settle with me ! '

" The idiot, counting on his father's and mother's stupidity, made
a face at him. At that Pierre fetched him a crack that laid Master
Jacques up in bed for six months. The poor mother almost died of
grief. One night, when she was sleeping peacefully by her husband's
side, she heard a noise, got out of bed, and got a knife-cut on her arm.
She shrieked and some one brought a light. Pierre Cambremer
found his wife wounded ; he thought that a robber did it—as if
there was any such thing in our province, where you can carry ten
thousand francs in gold from Le Croisic to St.-Nazaire, without fear,
and without once being asked what you've got under your arm !
Pierre looked for Jacques, but couldn't find him.

" In the morning, the little monster had the face to come home
and say that he'd been to Batz. I must tell you that his mother
didn't know where to hide her money. Cambremer always left his
with Monsieur Dupotet at Le Croisic. Their son's wild ways had
eaten up crowns by the hundred, francs by the hundred, and louis
l'or ; they were almost ruined, and that was pretty hard for folks
who used to have about twelve thousand francs, including their
island. No one knew what Cambremer paid out at Nantes to clear
his son. Bad luck raised the deuce with the family. Cambremer's
brother was in a bad way and needed help. To encourage him,
Pierre told him that Jacques and Pérotte (the younger Cambremer's
daughter) should marry.

" Then he employed him in the fishing, so that he could earn his
living ; for Joseph Cambremer was reduced to living by his work.
His wife had died of a fever, and he had had to pay for a wet-nurse
for Pérotte. Pierre Cambremer's wife owed a hundred francs to
different people on the little girl's account, for linen and clothes, and
for two or three months' wages for that big Frelu girl, who had a
child by Simon Gaudry, and who nursed Pérotte. Mère Cambremer
had sewed a Spanish coin into the cover of her mattress, and marked
: : ' For Pérotte.' She had had a good education ; she could
write like a clerk, and she'd taught her son to read ; that was the
ruin of him. No one knew how it happened, but that scamp of a
Jacques scented the gold, stole it and went off to Le Croisic on a
spree.

" As luck would have it, Goodman Cambremer came in with his
boat. As he approached the beach, he saw a piece of paper floating ;
he picked it up and took it to his wife, who fell flat when she recognised her own written words. Cambremer didn't say anything, but
he went to Le Croisic, and found out that his son was playing

billiards ; then he sent for the good woman who keeps the café, and said :

" ' I told Jacques not to spend a gold-piece that he'll pay you with ; I'll wait outside ; you bring it to me, and I'll give you silver for it.'

" The good woman brought him the money. Cambremer took it, said : ' All right ! ' and went home. The whole town heard about that. But here's something that I know, and that other people only suspect in a general way. He told his wife to clean up their room, which was on the ground floor ; he made a fire on the hearth, lighted two candles, placed two chairs on one side of the fireplace and a stool on the other. Then he told his wife to put out his wedding clothes and to get into her own. When he was dressed, he went to his brother and told him to watch in front of the house and tell him if he heard any noise on either of the beaches, this one or the one in front of the Guérande salt marshes. When he thought that his wife was dressed, he went home again, loaded a gun, and put it out of sight in the corner of the fireplace. Jacques came at last ; it was late he had been drinking and playing billiards till ten o'clock ; he had come home by the point of Carnouf. His uncle heard him hailing crossed to the beach in front of the marsh to fetch him, and rowed him to the island without a word. When he went into the house his father said to him :

" ' Sit down there,' pointing to the stool. ' You are before your father and mother, whom you have outraged, and who have got to try you.'

" Jacques began to bellow, because Cambremer's face was working in a strange way. The mother sat as stiff as an oar.

" ' If you call out, if you move, if you don't sit on your stool as straight as a mast, I'll shoot you like a dog,' said Pierre, pointing his gun at him.

" The son was dumb as a fish ; the mother didn't say anything.

" ' Here,' said Pierre to his son, ' is a paper that was wrapped round a Spanish gold-piece ; the gold-piece was in your mother's bed ; nobody else knew where she had put it ; I found the paper on the water as I was coming ashore ; you gave this Spanish gold-piece to Mother Fleurant to-night, and your mother can't find hers in her bed. Explain yourself ! '

" Jacques said that he didn't take the money from his mother and that he had had the coin ever since he went to Nantes.

" ' So much the better,' said Pierre. ' How can you prove it ?

" ' I had it before.'

" ' You didn't take your mother's ? '

" ' No.'

" ' Will you swear it by your everlasting life ? '

" He was going to swear ; his mother looked up at him and said :

" ' Jacques, my child, be careful ; don't swear, if it isn't true. You may mend your ways and repent ; there's time enough still.'

" And she began to cry.

" ' You're neither one thing nor the other,' he said, ' and you've always wanted to ruin me.'

" Cambremer turned pale, and said :

" ' What you just said to your mother will lengthen your account. Come to the point ! Will you swear ? '

" ' Yes.'

" ' See,' said Pierre, ' did your piece have this cross which the sardine-dealer who paid it to me had made on ours ? '

" Jacques sobered off, and began to cry.

" ' Enough talk,' said Pierre. ' I don't say anything about what you've done before this. I don't propose that a Cambremer shall be put to death on the public square at Le Croisic. Say your prayers, and make haste ! A priest is coming to confess you.'

" The mother went out, so that she needn't hear her son's sentence. When she had left the room, Cambremer the uncle arrived with the rector of Piriac ; but Jacques wouldn't say anything to him. He was sly ; he knew his father well enough to be sure that he wouldn't kill him without confession.

" ' Thank you, monsieur ; excuse us,' said Cambremer to the priest, when he saw that Jacques was obstinate. ' I meant to give my son a lesson, and I ask you not to say anything about it.—If you don't mend your ways,' he said to Jacques, ' the next time will be the last, and I'll put an end to it without confession.'

" He sent him off to bed. The boy believed what he had heard, and imagined that he could arrange matters with his father. He went to sleep. The father sat up. When he saw that his son was sound asleep, he stuffed his mouth with hemp and tied a strip of canvas over it very tight ; then he bound his hands and feet. Jacques stormed and wept blood, so Cambremer told the judge. What could you expect ! The mother threw herself at the father's feet.

" ' He has been tried,' he said ; ' you must help me put him in the boat.'

" She refused. Cambremer took him to the boat all alone, laid him in the bottom, tied a stone round his neck, and rowed abreast of the rock where he is now. Then the poor mother, who had got her brother-in-law to bring her over here, cried : ' Mercy ! ' All in vain ; it had the effect of a stone thrown at a wolf. The moon was shining ; she saw the father throw their son into the water, the son to whom her heart still clung ; and as there wasn't any

wind, she heard a splash, then nothing more, not a sound or a
bubble ; the sea's a famous keeper, I tell you ! When he came
ashore here to quiet his wife, who was groaning, Cambremer found
her about the same as dead. The two brothers couldn't carry her,
so they had to put her in the boat that had just held the son, and
they took her home, going round through Le Croisic passage. Ah !
La Belle Brouin, as they called her, didn't last a week. She died
asking her husband to burn the accursed boat. He did it, too.
As for him, he was like a crazy man ; he didn't know what he
wanted, and he staggered when he walked, like a man who can't
carry his wine. Then he went off for ten days, and when he came
back he planted himself where you saw him, and since he's been
there he hasn't said a word."

The fisherman took only a moment or two in telling us this
story, and he told it even more simply than I have written it.
The common people make few comments when they tell a story ;
they select the point that has made an impression on them, and
interpret it as they feel it. That narrative was as sharp and
incisive as a blow with an axe.

" I shall not go to Batz," said Pauline, as we reached the upper
end of the lake.

We returned to Le Croisic by way of the salt marshes, guided
through their labyrinth by a fisherman who had become as silent
as we. The current of our thoughts had changed. We were both
absorbed by depressing reflections, saddened by that drama which
explained the swift presentiment that we had felt at the sight of
Cambremer. We both had sufficient knowledge of the world to
divine all that our guide had not told us of that triple life. The
misfortunes of those three people were reproduced before us as if
we had seen them in the successive scenes of a drama, to which
that father, by thus expiating his necessary crime, had added the
dénouement. We dared not look back at that fatal man who
terrified a whole province.

A few clouds darkened the sky ; vapours were rising along the
horizon. We were walking through the most distressingly desolate
tract of land that I have even seen ; the very soil beneath our feet
seemed sickly and suffering—salt marshes, which may justly be
termed the scrofula of the earth. There the ground is divided
into parcels of unequal size, all enclosed by enormous heaps of grey
earth, and filled with brackish water, to the surface of which the
salt rises. These ravines, made by the hand of man, are subdivided
by causeways along which workmen walk, armed with long rakes
with which they skim off the brine, and carry the salt to round
platforms built here and there, when it is in condition to pile
For two hours we skirted that dismal chess-board, where the salt
is so abundant that it chokes the vegetation, and where we saw no

other living beings than an occasional *paludier*—the name given to the men who gather the salt.

These men, or rather this tribe of Bretons, wear a special costume : a white jacket not unlike that worn by brewers. They intermarry, and there has never been an instance of a girl of that tribe marrying anybody except a *paludier*. The ghastly aspect of those swamps, where the surface of the mire is neatly raked, and of that greyish soil, which the Breton flora hold in horror, harmonised with the mourning of our hearts. When we reached the place where we were to cross the arm of the sea which is formed by the eruption of the water into that basin, and which serves doubtless to supply the salt marshes with their staple, we rejoiced to see the meagre vegetation scattered along the sandy shore. As we crossed, we saw, in the centre of the lake, the islet where the Cambremers lived ; we looked the other way.

When we reached our hotel, we noticed a billiard-table in a room on the ground floor ; and, when we learned that it was the only public billiard-table in Le Croisic, we prepared for our departure that night. The next day we were at Guérande. Pauline was still depressed, and I could already feel the coming of the flame that is consuming my brain. I was so cruelly tormented by my visions of those three lives that she said to me :

" Write the story, Louis ; in that way you will change the nature of this fever."

So I have written it down for you, my dear uncle ; but it has already destroyed the tranquillity that I owed to the sea-baths and to our visit here.

FACINO CANE

Honoré de Balzac

I was living in a small street of which doubtless you do not even know the name, the Rue des Lesdiguières. It begins at the Rue St. Antoine opposite the fountain near the Place de la Bastille, and runs into the Rue de la Cerisaie. The love of learning had flung me into a garret where I worked during the night, and I passed the day in a neighbouring library, the *Bibliothèque de Monsieur*. I lived frugally. I had accepted all those conditions of a monastic life that are so necessary to workers. When it was fine I barely allowed myself a walk on the Boulevard Bourdon. One passion-only drew me away from my studious habits, but was not even that a sort of study ? I would go out to observe the manners of the Faubourg, its inhabitants and their characters.

As badly dressed as the workmen themselves and careless about keeping up an appearance, I did not make them in any way suspicious of me. I could mingle freely with them, and watch them making their bargains and quarrelling amongst themselves as they left their work. With me the power of observation had already become intuitive. It penetrated to the soul, without leaving the body out of account : or rather, it grasped so well the outer details, that it went at once beyond them ; it gave me the power of living the life of the individual on whom I brought it to bear, thus permitting me in fancy to substitute myself for him as the dervish in the *Arabian Nights* took the body and soul of the persons over whom he pronounced certain words.

When between eleven o'clock and midnight I met a workman and his wife returning together from the Ambigu Comique, I amused myself by following them from the Boulevard du Pont-aux-Choux as far as the Boulevard Beaumarchais. These good people would talk at first of the piece they had just seen. From one thing to another they would get on to their own affairs. The mother would be dragging her child by the hand without heeding either its complaints or its questions. The pair would reckon up the money that would be paid them next day, and spend it in twenty different ways. Then came household details ; complaints as to the excessive price of potatoes, or about the length of the winter and the dearness of peat fuel ; strong representations as to the amount owing to the baker ; and at last disputes that became a bit angry, and in which the character of each came out in picturesque expressions.

While listening to these people I could enter into their life ; I felt myself with their rags on my back ; I walked with my feet in their broken shoes ; their desires, their needs all came into my soul, or my soul passed into theirs. It was the dream of one who was still wide awake. With them I grew angry against the foremen of the workshops who tyrannised over them, or against the bad custom that forced them to come again and again to ask in vain for their pay. To get away from my ordinary occupations, to become some one else by this over excitation of my mental faculties, and to play this game at my will—this was my recreation. To what do I owe this gift ? Is it a kind of second sight ? or is it one of those powers the abuse of which would lead to insanity ? I have never investigated the sources of this faculty of mine ; I possess it and I make use of it, that is all.

I need only tell you that in those days I had analysed the elements of that heterogeneous mass called " the people," so that I could

estimate their good and bad qualities. Already I knew all that was
to be learned from that famous Faubourg, that nursery of Revolutions, which gives shelter at once to heroes, inventors, and practical
scientists, and knaves and scoundrels,—to virtues and vices, all
huddled together by misery, stifled by poverty, drowned in wine,
wasted by strong drink. You would never imagine how many
unknown adventures, how many forgotten dramas belong to that city
of sorrow. How many horrible and beautiful things ! For imagination
would never go so far as the reality that is hidden there, and that
no one can go there and discover. One has to go down to too great
a depth if one is to find out those wonderful scenes of living tragedy
or comedy, masterpieces that chance has brought into being.

I know not why I have so long kept untold the story that I am
going to relate to you ; it is one of those strange tales that are laid
by in the bag from which memory draws them out at haphazard
like the numbers of a lottery. I have plenty of others quite as
singular as this one, buried away in the same fashion ; but they
will have their turn, believe me.

One day my housekeeper, a working-man's wife, came and asked
me to honour with my presence the wedding of one of her sisters. In
order to enable you to understand what sort of a wedding it would
be I must tell you that I used to pay forty sous a month to this poor
creature, who came in every morning to make my bed, polish my
shoes, brush my clothes, sweep the room, and get my breakfast
ready. For the rest of her time she went to turn the handle of a
mangle, and by this hard work earned ten sous a day. Her husband,
a cabinet-maker, earned four francs.

But, as their household included three children, they could barely
pay for the bread they ate. I have never come across more real
respectability than that of this man and wife. Five years after I
had left the neighbourhood Dame Vaillant came to wish me a
happy name day, and brought me a bunch of flowers and some
oranges as presents—she who had never been in a position to save
ten sous. Poverty had drawn us together. I was never able to
pay her more then ten francs, often borrowed for the occasion.
This will explain my promise to go to the wedding ; I counted on
taking an unobtrusive part in the rejoicings of these poor people.

The feast and the dance were both held at a wine shop in the Rue
de Charenton, in a large room on the first storey. It was lighted
with lamps with tin reflectors ; the paper showed grease spots at
the level of the tables, and along the walls there were wooden
benches. In this room some eighty people, dressed in their Sunday
clothes, decked out with flowers and ribbons, all full of the holiday
spirit, danced with flushed faces as if the world was coming to an
end. The happy pair kissed each other amid a general outbreak
of satisfaction, and one heard " Eh ! eh ! " and " Ah ! ah ! "

pronounced in a tone of amusement, that all the same was more
respectable than the timid ogling of young women of a better class.
Every one manifested a rough and ready pleasure that had in it
something infectious.

But neither the general aspect of the gathering, nor the wedding,
nor anything of the kind, has really to do with our story. Only I
want you to keep in mind the quaint setting of it all. Imagine to
yourself the shabby shop, with its decorations of red paint,
smell the odour of the wine, listen to the shouts of delight,
keep to the Faubourg, in the midst of these workers, these old
men, these poor women abandoning themselves to one night of
pleasure.

The orchestra was made up of three blind men from the Hospice des
Quinze-Vingts ; the first was the violin, the second the clarionet, and
the third the flageolet. All three were paid one lump sum of seven
francs for the night. At this price, of course, they gave us neither
Rossini nor Beethoven ; they played what they liked and what they
could, and with a charming delicacy of feeling no one found fault
with them for it ! Their music was such a rough trial to my ears, that,
after a glance at the audience, I looked at the trio of blind men, and
recognising the uniform of the hospice, I felt from the first disposed
to be indulgent. These artists were seated in the deep bay of a
window, and thus in order to be able to distinguish their features
one had to be near them.

I did not at once come close to them ; but when I approached
them I cannot say how it was, but all was over with me, I forgot
the marriage and the music ; my curiosity was excited to the
highest pitch, for my soul passed into the body of the clarionet
player. The violin and the flageolet had both commonplace
features, the well-known face of the blind, with its strained look,
all attention and seriousness ; but that of the clarionet player was
one of those phenomenal faces that make the artist or the philosopher
stop at once to look at them.

Imagine a plaster mask of Dante, lighted up with the red glare
of an Argand-lamp, and crowned with a forest of silver-white hair.
His blindness added to the bitter sorrowful expression of this
splendid face, for one could imagine the dead eyes were alive again ;
a burning light seemed to shine out from them, the expression of
a single ceaseless desire that had set its deep marks on the rounded
forehead, which was scored by wrinkles like the lines of an old wall.
The old man was blowing away at haphazard, without paying the
least attention to time or tune, his fingers rising and falling, and
moving the old keys through mere mechanical habit. He did
not trouble about making what is called in the slang of the orchestra
" quacks," and the dancers took no more notice of this than the
two comrades of my Italian did—for I made up my mind that he

must be an Italian, and an Italian he was.   There was something
noble and commanding to be seen in this aged Homer, who kept
all to himself some Odyssey destined to forgetfulnes.   It was a
nobility so real that it still triumphed over his obscurity ; an
air of command so striking that it rose superior to his
poverty.

None of the strong feelings that lead a man to good as well as
to evil, that make of him a convict or a hero, were wanting to this
splendidly outlined face, with its sallow Italian complexion, and the
shadows of the iron-grey eyebrows that threw their shade over the
deep cavities in which one would tremble at seeing the light of
thought appear once more, as one fears to see brigands armed with
torch and dagger show themselves at the mouth of a cavern.   There
was a lion in that cage of flesh, a lion of which the fury had uselessly
spent itself on the iron of its bars.   The fire of despair had burned
out among its ashes, the lava had cooled ; but rifts, fallen rocks,
and a little smoke told of the violence of the eruption, the ravages
of the fire.   These ideas called up by the aspect of the man were
as warmly pictured in my mind, as they were coldly marked upon
his face.

In the interval between each dance the violin and the flageolet,
becoming seriously occupied with a bottle and glasses, hung their
instruments to a button of their reddish tunics, and stretched out a
hand to a little table standing in the bay of the window, on which
were their refreshments.   They always offered the Italian a full
glass, which he could not have got unaided, for the table was behind
his chair.   Each time the clarionet thanked them with a friendly
nod of his head.   Their movements were carried out with that
precision which always seems so astonishing in the case of the
blind folk from the Quinze-Vingts, and which seems to make one
think they can see.   I drew near to the three blind men to listen
to them, but when I stood near them they somehow scrutinised
me, and doubtless failing to recognise the workman type in me,
they said not a word.

" From what country are you, you who play the clarionet ? "

" From Venice," answered the blind man, with a slight Italian
accent.

" Were you born blind, or were you blinded by . . ."

" By a mishap," he replied sharply ; " a cursed amaurosis in
my eyes."

" Venice is a beautiful city.   I have always had an idea of going
there."

The face of the old man became animated, its furrows rose and
fell, he was strongly moved.

" If I went there with you, you would not lose your time," said
he to me.

" Don't talk of Venice to him," said the violin to me, " or our Doge will start his story. Besides that he has already two bottles under his belt, the old prince ! "

" Come, let us be getting on, Père Canard," said the flageolet.

All three began to play ; but all the time that they were going through the four parts of the quadrille the Venetian was sizing me up ; he guessed the extraordinary interest I took in him. His face lost its cold expression of sadness. Some hope or other brightened all his features—played like a blue flame in the wrinkles of his face. He smiled as he wiped his forehead—that forehead with its bold and terrible look ; finally he became quite gay, like a man who is getting up on his hobby.

" What is your age ? " I asked him.

" Eighty-two years."

" How long have you been blind ? "

" It will soon be fifty years," he replied, in a tone which suggested that his regret was not only for the loss of his sight, but also for some great power of which he had been deprived.

" But why do they call you the Doge ? " I asked him.

" Ah ! that's a joke," he said ; " I am a patrician of Venice, and I could have been a Doge as well as any one else."

" What is your name then ? "

" Here," he said, " I am old Canet. My name has never appeared otherwise on the local registers. But in Italian it is Marco Facino Cane, Prince of Varese."

" What ! Are you descended from the famous condottiere, Facino Cane, whose conquests passed into the possession of the Dukes of Milan ? "

" É vero (that's true)," said he. " In those times the son of Cane, to escape being killed by the Visconti, took refuge in Venice, and had his name inscribed in the Golden Book of nobility. But now neither the Book nor any of the House of Cane is left ! "

And he made a startling gesture to signify his feeling that patriotism was dead, and his disgust for human affairs.

" But if you were a Senator of Venice, you must have been rich. How did you come to lose your fortune ? "

At this question he raised his head, turning to me as if regarding me with a movement full of truest tragedy, and replied to me :

" In the midst of misfortunes ! "

He no longer thought of drinking ; with a wave of his hand he refused the glass of wine which the old flageolet player offered him at this moment, then he bowed down his head.

These details were not of a kind to put an end to my curiosity. During the quadrille that the three instruments played in mechanical style, I watched the old Venetian noble with the feelings that devour a man of only twenty. I saw Venice and the Adriatic, and I saw its ruin in this ruined face. I was moving about in that city so beloved of its inhabitants. I went from the Rialto to the Grand Canal, from the Riva degli Schiavoni to the Lido ; I came back to its cathedral so sublime in its originality ; I looked up at the windows of the Casa d'Oro, each of which has different ornaments ; I contemplated its old palaces, so rich in marbles—in a word, all those wonders that move the student's feelings all the more when he can colour them with his fancy, and does not spoil the poetry of his dreams by the sight of the reality.

I traced backward the course of the life of this scion of the greatest of the condottieri, seeking out in it the traces of his misfortunes and the causes of the deep physical and moral degradation that made the sparks of greatness and nobility that shone again at that moment seem all the finer. Our thoughts were no doubt in mutual accord, for I believe that blindness makes mental communication much more rapid, by preventing the attention from dispersing itself on external things. I had not long to wait for a proof of our bond of feeling. Facino Cane stopped playing, rose, came to me and said, "Come out," in a way that produced on me the effect of an electric shock. I gave him my arm and we went away.

When we were in the street, he said to me :

"Will you take me to Venice, guide me there ? Will you have confidence in me ? You will be richer than the ten richest firms of Amsterdam or London ; richer than the Rothschilds ; in a word, rich as the *Arabian Nights.*"

I thought the man was mad. But there was in his voice a power that I obeyed. I let him lead me, and he took me in the direction of the ditches of the Bastille, as if he still had the use of his eyes. He sat down on a stone in a very lonely place, where, since then, the bridge has been built under which the Canal Saint Martin passes to the Seine. I took my place on another stone facing the old man whose white hairs glittered like threads of silver in the moonlight. The silence, hardly disturbed by such stormy sounds as reached us from the Boulevards, the brightness of the night, all helped to make the scene something fantastic.,

"You talk of millions to a young man, and you think that he would hesitate to endure a thousand ills to secure them ! Are you not making a jest of me ? "

"May I die without confession," said he fiercely, " if what I am about to tell you is not true ! I was once a young man of twenty as you are now. I was rich. I was handsome. I was a noble. I began with the first of all follies—love. I loved as men no longer love, going so far as to hide in a chest at the risk of being stabbed, without

having received anything else but the promise of a kiss. To die for
her seemed to me worth a whole life. In 1760 I fell in love with one
of the Vendramini, a girl of eighteen, married to a certain Sagredo,
one of the richest of the Senators, a man of thirty years, madly
devoted to his wife. My love and I, we were as innocent as two
little cherubs when the husband surprised us talking love together.
I was unarmed ; he was armed, but he missed me. I sprang on him,
I strangled him with my two hands, twisting his neck like a chicken's.
I wanted to go away with Bianca, but she would not go with me.
That's what women are like ! I went away alone. I was condemned
in my absence, my property was confiscated for the benefit of my
heirs ; but I had carried off with me my diamonds, five pictures by
Titian rolled up, and all my gold. I went to Milan, where I was not
molested, for my affair did not interest the State.

" One little remark before going on," he said, after a pause.
" Whether it is true or not that a woman's fancies influence her
child before its birth, it is certain that my mother had a passion for
gold while she was expecting mine. I have a monomania for gold,
the satisfaction of which is so necessary for my very life, that in
whatever circumstances I have been, I have never been without some
gold in my possession. I am always handling gold. When I was
young I always wore jewels, and I always carried about with me
two or three hundred ducats."

As he said these words he took two ducats out of his pocket and
showed them to me.

" I can smell gold. Although I am blind, I stop in front of the
jewellers' shops. This passion was my ruin. I became a gambler,
to have the enjoyment of gold. I was not a swindler ; I was
swindled. I ruined myself. When I had no longer any of my fortune
left I was seized with a wild longing to see Bianca again. I returned
secretly to Venice. I found her once more ; I was happy for six
months, hidden with her, supported by her. I had a delightful
thought of thus living my life to the end. Her hand was sought by
the Proveditore of the Republic. He guessed he had a rival ; in
Italy they can almost smell them ; he spied on us, and surprised us
together, the coward ! You can imagine what a sharp fight there was.
I did not kill him, but I wounded him seriously. That adventure
broke off my happiness. Since that day I never found any one like
Bianca. I have had many pleasures. I lived at the court of
Louis XV. in the midst of the most famous women, but nowhere
did I find the characteristics, the graces, the love of my fair
Venetian.

" The Proveditore had his followers. He called them. The palace
was surrounded. I defended myself, hoping to die before the eyes of
my dear Bianca, who helped me to kill the Proveditore. Formerly
this woman had refused to share my flight ; now, after six months of

happiness, she was ready to die my death, and received several
blows. Entangled in a big cloak that they threw over me, I was
rolled in it, carried to a gondola and conveyed to the dungeons of the
Pozzi. I was only twenty-two years old then, and I held so fast
to the fragment of my broken sword, that to get it from me they
would have had to cut off my wrist. By a strange chance, or rather
inspired by a thought for the future, I hid this bit of steel in a corner,
in case it might be of use to me. I was given medical care. None of
my wounds was mortal. At twenty-two one can recover from
anything. I was doomed to die by decapitation, but I pretended to
be ill in order to gain time. I believed that I was in a dungeon next
to the canal. My plan was to escape by making a hole through the
wall and swimming across the canal at the risk of drowning
myself.

" Here are some of the reasons on which I based my hopes :

" Whenever the jailer brought me my food I read, by the light he
carried, inscriptions scrawled upon the walls, such as, ' Towards the
palace,' ' Towards the canal,' ' Towards the underground passage,'
and at last succeeded in making out a general plan of the place.
There were some small difficulties about it, but they could be
explained by the actual state of the Palace of the Doges, which
is not completed. With the cleverness that the desire to regain
one's liberty gives one, by feeling with my fingers the surface of
a stone, I succeeded in deciphering an Arabic inscription, by
which the writer of the words intimated to his successors that
he had loosened two stones in the lowest course of masonry, and
dug beyond them eleven feet of a tunnel. In order to continue
his task it was necessary to spread over the floor of the dungeon
itself the little bits of stone and mortar produced by the work
of excavation.

" Even if my keepers or the inquisitors had not felt quite easy in
their minds on account of the very structure of the building, which
made only an external surveillance necessary, the arrangement of
the Pozzi dungeons, into which one descends by a few steps, made it
possible gradually to raise the level of the floor without its being
noticed by the jailers. The immense amount of work he had done
had proved to be superfluous, at least for the man who had undertaken it, for the fact that it had been left unfinished told of the death
of the unknown prisoner. In order that his zeal might not be useless
for ever, it was necessary that some future prisoner should know
Arabic ; but I had studied Eastern languages at the Armenian
convent of Venice. A sentence written on the back of one of the
stones told the fate of this unfortunate man, who had died the victim
of his immense riches, which Venice had coveted, and of which she
had taken possession. It took me a month to arrive at any result.
Whilst I was at work, and during the intervals when I was over-

33*

whelmed with fatigue, I heard the sound of gold, I thought I could see gold before me, I was dazzled by diamonds ! . . . Oh ! just wait.

"One night, my piece of steel, now blunted, came upon wood. I sharpened my broken fragment of a sword and made a hole in the wood. In order to work I used to drag myself along like a serpent on my stomach, and I stripped so as to dig like a mole, with my hands out in front of me, stretched on the stones I had already burrowed through. In two days I was to appear before my judges, so during this night I meant to make a last effort. I cut through the wood, and my blade struck against nothing beyond it.

"Imagine my surprise when I put my eye to the hole ! I had penetrated the wainscot of an underground room, in which a dim light allowed me to see a great heap of gold. The Doge and one of the Council of Ten were in this cellar. I heard their voices. From their talk I gathered that here was the secret hoard of the Republic, the gifts of the Doges, and the reserves of booty known as the 'share of Venice,' and levied on the produce of over-sea expeditions.

"I was saved !

"When next the jailer came, I proposed to him to assist me to escape, and to go away with me, taking off with us all that we could carry. There was no reason to hesitate, and he agreed. A ship was about to sail for the Levant. Every precaution was taken. Bianca lent her aid to the plans I dictated to my accomplice. In order not to arouse suspicion Bianca was to rejoin us only at Smyrna. In a single night the hole was enlarged, and we climbed down into the secret treasury of Venice. What a night ! I saw four huge casks full of gold. In the room before that, silver was in the same profusion, piled up in two heaps, leaving a path in the middle by which to pass through the room, with the coins sloping up in piles on each side till they reached a height of five feet at the walls. I thought the jailer would go mad.

"He sang, he danced, he laughed, he cut capers among the gold. I threatened to strangle him if he wasted our time or made a noise. In his joy he did not at first notice a table on which were the diamonds. I threw myself upon it so cleverly that I was able, unseen by him, to fill with them my sailor's jacket and the pockets of my trousers. Mon Dieu ! but I did not take one-third of them. Under this table there were ingots of gold. I persuaded my comrade to fill as many sacks as we could carry with gold, pointing out to him that this was the only way in which our plunder would not lead to our being discovered abroad.

"'Pearls, jewels, and diamonds would only lead to our being recognised,' I said to him.

"Whatever might be our eagerness for it, we could not take away more than two thousand pounds of gold, and this required six journeys through the prison to get it to the gondola. The sentinel at the water gate had been won over at the price of a sack of ten pounds of gold. As for the two gondoliers, they were under the impression that they were serving the Republic. We made our start at day-break. When we were in the open sea, and when I remembered that night, when I recalled all the sensations I had felt, and when I saw again in imagination that vast treasure house, where, according to my estimate, I was leaving thirty millions in silver, twenty millions in gold, and many millions in diamonds, pearls, and rubies, there came upon me something like a fit of madness—I had the gold fever.

" We arranged to be put ashore at Smyrna, and there we at once embarked for France. When we were getting on board of the French ship Heaven did me the favour of ridding me of my accomplice. At the moment I did not realise the full result of this ill-natured stroke of chance, at which I rejoiced exceedingly. We were so utterly unnerved, that we had remained in a half-dazed condition without saying a word to each other, waiting till we were in safety to enjoy ourselves as we wished. It is not surprising that this rogue had his head a bit turned. You will see later on how God punished me !

" I did not feel I was safe till I had sold two-thirds of my diamonds in London and Amsterdam, and exchanged my gold dust for notes that could be cashed. For five years I hid myself in Madrid. Then, in 1770, I came to Paris under a Spanish name, and had a most brilliant career there. Bianca had died. But in the midst of my enjoyments, and when I had a fortune of six million francs at my command, I was struck with blindness. I have no doubt that this infirmity was the result of my stay in the dungeon, and of my toils when I burrowed through the stone, though perhaps my mania for seeing gold implied an abuse of the power of sight that predestined me to the loss of my eyes.

" At this time I was in love with a woman to whom I intended to unite my lot. I had told her the secret of my name. She belonged to a powerful family, and I hoped for everything from the favour shown me by Louis XV. I had put my trust in this woman, who was the friend of Madame du Barry. She advised me to consult a famous oculist in London. But after we had stayed some months in that city, the woman gave me the slip one day in Hyde Park, after having robbed me of all my fortune, and left me without any resource. For being obliged to conceal my real name, which would hand me over to the vengeance of Venice, I could not appeal to any one for help. I was afraid of Venice.

" My infirmity was taken advantage of by spies with whom this woman had surrounded me. I spare you the story of adventures worthy of Gil Blas. Then came your Revolution. I was forced to become an inmate of the Quinze-Vingts Hospice, where this creature arranged for my admission, after having kept me for two years at the Bicêtre Asylum as a lunatic. I have never been able to kill her, for I could not see to do it, and I was too poor to hire another hand. If before I lost Benedetto Capri, my jailer, I had questioned him as to the position of my dungeon, I might have ascertained exactly where the treasure lay, and returned to Venice when the Republic was annihilated by Napoleon. . . .

"However, notwithstanding my blindness, let us go back to Venice! I will rediscover the door of the prison, I shall see the gold through its walls, I shall smell it even under waters beneath which it is buried. For the events that overthrew the power of Venice were of such a kind that the secret of this treasure must have died with Vendramino, the brother of Bianca, a Doge who I hoped would have made my peace with the Council of Ten. I wrote letters to the First Consul, I proposed an arrangement with the Emperor of Austria, but every one turned me away as a madman! Come, let us start for Venice, let us start even if we have to beg our way! We shall come back millionaires. We will repurchase my property and you shall be my heir. You will be Prince of Varese!"

In my astonishment at these revelations, which in my imagination assumed all the aspect of a poem, and looking at this grey head, and the dark waters of the ditches of the Bastille, stagnant water like that of the Venetian canals, I made no reply. Facino Cane concluded doubtless that I judged him as all the rest had done with a scornful pity, and he made a gesture that expressed all the philosophy of despair.

The narration had perhaps carried him back to his days of happiness at Venice. He seized his clarionet and played in a melancholy tone a Venetian air, a barcarolle, and, as he played, he regained the skill of his first years, the talent of a patrician lover. It was something like the lament by the rivers of Babylon. But gold soon reasserted its mastery.

"That treasure!" he said to me, "I always see it, as in a waking dream. I walk about in the midst of it. The diamonds sparkle, and I am not as blind as you think. The gold and the diamonds illuminate my darkness, the night of the last Facino Cane, for my title goes to the Memmi. Mon Dieu! the murderer's punishment has begun soon enough! Ave Maria. . . ."

He recited some prayers which I could not hear.

"We shall go to Venice!" I said to him, when he rose.

"I have found a man, then!" he exclaimed, and his face lighted up.

I gave him my arm and took him home. At the door of the Quinze-Vingts he grasped my hand, while some of the guests from the wedding party passed on their way home with deafening shouts.

" Shall we start to-morrow ? " said the old man.

" As soon as we have a little money."

" But we can go on foot. I will beg alms. I am strong, and one feels young when one sees gold in front of one."

Facino Cane died that winter after two months of lingering illness. The poor fellow had a catarrh.

VICTOR HUGO
1802–1885

CLAUDE GUEUX

CLAUDE GUEUX was a poor workman, living in Paris about eight years ago, with his mistress and child. Although his education had been neglected, and he could not even read, the man was naturally clever and intelligent, and thought deeply over matters. Winter came with its attendant miseries—want of work, want of food, want of fuel. The man, the woman, and the child were frozen and famished. The man turned thief. I know not what he stole. What signifies, as the result was the same ? To the woman and child it gave three days' bread and warmth ; to the man, five years' imprisonment. He was taken to Clairvaux—the abbey now converted into a prison, its cells into dungeons, and the altar itself into a pillory. This is called progress.

Claude Gueux, the honest workman, who turned thief from force of circumstances, had a countenance which impressed you—a high forehead somewhat lined with care, dark hair already streaked with grey, deep-set eyes beaming with kindness, while the lower part clearly indicated firmness mingled with self-respect. He rarely spoke, yet there was a certain dignity in the man which commanded respect and obedience. A fine character, and we shall see what society made of it.

Over the prison workshop was an inspector, who rarely forgot that he was the gaoler also to his subordinates, handing them the tools with one hand, and casting chains upon them with the other. A tyrant, never using even self-reasoning ; with ideas against which there was no appeal ; hard rather than firm, at times he could even be jocular—doubtless a good father, a good husband, really not vicious, but *bad*. He was one of those men who never can grasp a fresh idea, who apparently fail to be moved by any emotion ; yet with hatred and rage in their hearts look like blocks of wood, heated on the one side but frozen on the other. This man's chief characteristic was obstinacy ; and so proud was he of this very stubbornness that he compared himself with Napoleon— an optical delusion, like taking the mere flicker of a candle for a star. When he had made up his mind to a thing, however absurd, he would carry out that absurd idea. How often it happens, that, when a catastrophe occurs, if we inquire into the cause we find it originated through the obstinacy of one with little ability but having full faith in his own powers.

Such was the inspector of the prison workshop at Clairvaux—a man of flint placed by society over others, who hoped to strike sparks out of such material ; but a spark from a like source is apt to end in a conflagration.

The inspector soon singled out Claude Gueux, who had been numbered and placed in the workshop, and, finding him clever, treated him well. Seeing Claude looking sad (for he was ever thinking of her he termed his wife), and being in a good humour, by way of pastime to console the prisoner he told him the woman had become one of the unfortunate sisterhood, and had been reduced to infamy ; of the child nothing was known.

After a time Claude had accustomed himself to prison rule, and by his calmness of manner and a certain amount of resolution clearly marked in his face, he had acquired a great ascendency over his companions, who so much admired him that they asked his advice, and tried in all ways to imitate him. The very expression in his eyes clearly indicated the man's character ; besides, is not the eye the window of the soul, and what other result could be anticipated than that the intelligent spirit should lead men with few ideas, who yield to the attraction as the metal does to the lodestone ? In less than three months Claude was the virtual head of the workshop, and at times he almost doubted whether he was king or prisoner, being treated something like a captive Pope, surrounded by his Cardinals.

Such popularity ever has its attendant hatred ; and though beloved by the prisoners, Claude was detested by the gaolers. To him two men's rations would have been scarcely sufficient. The inspector laughed at this, as his own appetite was large ; but what would be mirth to a duke, to a prisoner would be a great misfortune. When a free man, Claude Gueux could earn his daily four-pound loaf and enjoy it ; but as a prisoner he daily worked, and for his labour received one pound and a half of bread and four ounces of meat : it naturally followed that he was always hungry.

He had just finished his meagre fare, and was about to resume his labours, hoping in work to forget famine, when a weakly-looking young man came toward him, holding a knife and his untasted rations in his hand, but seemingly afraid to address him.

" What do you want ? " said Claude, roughly.

" A favour at your hands," timidly replied the young man.

" What is it ? " said Claude.

" Help me with my rations ; I have more than I can eat."

For a moment Claude was taken aback, but without further ceremony he divided the food in two and at once partook of one-half.

"Thank you," said the young man; "allow me to share my rations with you every day."

"What is your name?" said Claude.

"Albin."

"Why are you here?" added Claude.

"I robbed."

"So did I," said Claude.

The same scene took place daily between this man old before his time (he was only thirty-six) and the boy of twenty, who looked at the most seventeen. The feeling was more like that of father and son than one brother to another; everything created a bond of union between them—the very toil they endured together, the fact of sleeping in the same quarters and taking exercise in the same courtyard. They were happy, for were they not all the world to each other? The inspector of the workshop was so hated by the prisoners that he often had recourse to Claude Gueux to enforce his authority; and when a tumult was on the point of breaking out, a few words from Claude had more effect than the authority of ten warders. Although the inspector was glad to avail himself of this influence, he was jealous all the same, and hated the superior prisoner with an envious and implacable feeling—an example of might over right, all the more fearful as it was secretly nourished. But Claude cared so much for Albin that he thought little about the inspector.

One morning as the warders were going their rounds one of them summoned Albin, who was working with Claude, to go before the inspector.

"What are you wanted for?" said Claude.

"I do not know," replied Albin, following the warder.

All day Claude looked in vain for his companion, and at night, finding him still absent, he broke through his ordinary reserve and addressed the turnkey. "Is Albin ill?" said he.

"No," replied the man.

"How is it that he has never put in an appearance to-day?"

"His quarters have been changed," was the reply.

For a moment Claude trembled, then calmly continued, "Who gave the order?"

"Monsieur D——." This was the inspector's name.

On the following night the inspector, Monsieur D——, went his rounds as usual. Claude, who had perceived him from the distance, rose, and hastened to raise his woollen cap and button his grey woollen vest to the throat—considered a mark of respect to superiors in prison discipline.

" Sir," said Claude, as the inspector was about to pass him, " has Albin really been quartered elsewhere ? "

" Yes," replied the inspector.

" Sir, I cannot live without him. You know the rations are insufficient for me, and Albin divided his portion with me. Could you not manage to let him resume his old place near me ? "

" Impossible ; the order cannot be revoked."

" By whom was it given ? "

" By me."

" Monsieur D——," replied Claude, " on you my life depends."

" I never cancel an order once given."

" Sir, what have I ever done to you ? "

" Nothing."

" Why, then," cried Claude, " separate me from Albin ? "

" Because I do," replied the inspector, and with that he passed on.

Claude's head sank down, like the poor caged lion deprived of his dog ; but the grief, though so deeply felt, in no way changed his appetite—he was famished. Many offered to share their rations with him, but he steadily refused, and continued his usual routine in silence—breaking it only to ask the inspector daily, in tones of anguish mingled with rage, something between a prayer and a threat, these two words : " And Albin ? "

The inspector simply passed on, shrugging his shoulders ; but had he only observed Claude he would have seen the evident change, noticeable to all present, and he would have heard these words, spoken respectfully but firmly :

" Sir, listen to me ; send my companion to me. It would be wise to do so, I can assure you. Remember my words ! "

On Sunday he had sat for hours in the courtyard, with his head bowed in his hands, and when a prisoner called Faillette came up laughing, Claude said : " I am judging some one."

On October 25, 1831, as the inspector went his rounds, Claude, to draw his attention, smashed a watch-glass he had found in the passage. This had the desired effect.

" It was I," said Claude. " Sir, restore my comrade to me."

" Impossible," was the answer.

Looking the inspector full in the face, Claude firmly added : " Now, reflect ! To-day is the 25th of October ; I give you till the 4th of November."

A warder remarked that Claude was threatening Monsieur D——, and ought at once to be locked up.

" No, it is not a case of blackhole," replied the inspector, smiling disdainfully ; " we must be considerate with people of this stamp."

The following day Claude was again accosted by one of the prisoners named Pernot, as he was brooding in the courtyard.

" Well, Claude, you are sad indeed ; what are you pondering over ? "

" I fear some evil threatens that good Monsieur D——," answered Claude.

Claude daily impressed the fact on the inspector how much Albin's absence affected him, but with no result save four-and-twenty hours' solitary confinement.

On the 4th of November he looked round his cell for the little that remained to remind him of his former life. A pair of scissors, and an old volume of the *Émile*, belonging to the woman he had loved so well, the mother of his child—how useless to a man who could neither work nor read !

As Claude walked down the old cloisters, so dishonoured by its new inmates and its fresh whitewashed walls, he noticed how earnestly the convict Ferrari was looking at the heavy iron bars that crossed the window, and he said to him : " To-night I will cut through these bars with these scissors," pointing to the pair he still held in his hand.

Ferrari laughed incredulously, and Claude joined in the mirth. During the day he worked with more than ordinary ardour, wishing to finish a straw hat, which he had been paid for in advance by a tradesman at Troyes—M. Bressier.

Shortly before noon he made some excuse to go down into the carpenters' quarters, a storey below his own, at the time the warders were absent. Claude received a hearty welcome, as he was equally popular here as elsewhere.

" Can any one lend me an axe ? " he said.

" What for ? "

Without exacting any promises of secrecy he at once replied : " To kill the inspector with to-night."

Claude was at once offered several ; choosing the smallest, he hid it beneath his waistcoat and left. Now, there were twenty-seven prisoners present, and not one of those men betrayed him ; they even refrained from talking upon the subject among themselves, waiting for the terrible event which must follow.

As Claude passed on, seeing a young convict of sixteen yawning idly there, he strongly advised him to learn how to read. Just then Faillette asked what he was hiding.

Claude answered unhesitatingly : " An axe to kill Monsieur D—— to-night ; but can you see it ? "

" A little," said Faillette.

At seven o'clock the prisoners were locked in their several work-shops. It was then the custom for the warders to leave them, until the inspector had been his rounds.

In Claude's workshop a most extraordinary scene took place, the only one of the kind on record. Claude rose and addressed his companions, eighty-four in number, in the following words :

" You all know Albin and I were like brothers. I liked him at first for sharing his rations with me, afterwards because he cared for me. Now I never have sufficient, though I spend the pittance I earn in bread. It could make no possible difference to the inspector, Monsieur D——, that we should be together ; but he chose to separate us simply from a love of tormenting, for he is a bad man. I asked again and again for Albin to be sent back, without success ; and when I gave him a stated time, the 4th November, I was thrust into a dungeon. During that time I became his judge, and sentenced him to death on November the 4th. In two hours he will be here, and I warn you I intend to kill him. But have you anything to say ? "

There was a dead silence. Claude then continued telling his comrades, the eighty-four thieves, his ideas on the subject—that he was reduced to a fearful extremity, and compelled by that very necessity to take the law into his own hands ; that he knew full well he could not take the inspector's life without sacrificing his own, but that as the cause was a just one he would bear the consequences, having come to this conclusion after two months' calm reflection ; that if they considered resentment alone hurried him on to such a step they were at once to say so, and to state their objections to the sentence being carried out.

One voice alone broke the silence which followed, saying, " Before killing the inspector, Claude ought to give him a chance of relenting."

" That is but just," said Claude, " and he shall have the benefit of the doubt."

Claude then sorted the few things a poor prisoner is allowed, and gave them to the comrades he mostly cared for after Albin, keeping only the pair of scissors. He then embraced them all—some not being able to withhold their tears at such a moment. Claude continued calmly to converse during this last hour, and even gave way to a trick he had as a boy, of extinguishing the candle with a breath from his nose. Seeing him thus, his companions afterward owned that they hoped he had abandoned his sinister idea. One young convict looked at him fixedly, trembling for the coming event.

" Take courage, young fellow," said Claude, gently ; " it will be but the work of a minute."

The workship was a long room with a door at both ends, and with windows each side overlooking the benches, thus leaving a pathway up the centre for the inspector to review the work on both sides of him. Claude had now resumed his work—something like Jacques Clement, who did not fail to repeat his prayers.

As the clock sounded the last quarter to nine, Claude rose and placed himself near the entrance, apparently calm. Amid the most profound silence the clocks struck nine ; the door was thrown open, and the inspector came in as usual alone, looking quite jovial and self-satisfied, passing rapidly along, tossing his head at one ; grinding words out to another, little heeding the eyes fixed so fiercely upon him. Just then he heard Claude's step, and turning quickly around said ;

"What are you doing here ? Why are you not in your place ? " just as he would have spoken to a dog.

Claude answered respectfully, " I wish to speak to you, sir."

"On what subject ? "

"Albin."

"Again ! "

"Always the same," said Claude.

"So then," replied the inspector, walking along, " you have not had enough with twenty-four hours in the blackhole."

Claude, following him closely, replied : "Sir, return my companion to me ! "

"Impossible ? "

"Sir," continued Claude, in a voice which would have moved Satan, " I implore you to send Albin back to me ; you will then see how I will work. You are free, and it would matter but little to you ; you do not know the feeling of having only one friend. To me it is everything, encircled by the prison walls. You can come and go at your pleasure ; I have but Albin. Pray let him come back to me ! You know well he shared his food with me. What can it matter to you that a man named Claude Gueux should be in this hall, having another by his side called Albin ? You have but to say ' Yes,' nothing more. Sir, my good sir, I implore you in the name of Heaven to grant my prayer ! "

Claude, overcome with emotion, waited for the answer.

"Impossible ! " replied the inspector, impatiently ; "I will not recall my words. Now go, you annoyance ! " And with that he hurried on toward the outer door, amid the breathless silence maintained by the eighty-four thieves.

Claude, following and touching the inspector, gently asked :

"Let me at least know why I am condemned to death. Why did you separate us ? "

"I have already answered you : because I chose," replied the inspector.

With that he was about to lift the latch, when Claude raised the axe, and without one cry the inspector fell to the ground, with his skull completely cloven from three heavy blows dealt with the rapidity of lightning. A fourth completely disfigured his face, and Claude, in his mad fury, gave another and a useless blow ; for the inspector was dead.

Claude, throwing the axe aside, cried out, " Now for the other ! "

The other was himself; and taking the scissors, *his wife's*, he plunged them into his breast. But the blade was short, and the chest was deep, and vainly he strove to give the fatal blow. At last, covered with blood, he fell fainting across the dead. Which of the two would be considered the victim?

When Claude recovered consciousness he was in bed, surrounded by every care and covered with bandages. Near him were Sisters of Charity, and a recorder, ready to take down his deposition, who with much interest inquired how he was. Claude had lost a great deal of blood; but the scissors had done him a bad turn, inflicting wounds not one of which was dangerous: the only mortal blows he had struck were on the body of Monsieur D——. Then the interrogator commenced.

"Did you kill the inspector of the prison workshops at Clairvaux?"

"Yes," was the reply.

"Why did you do so?"

"Because I did."

Claude's wounds assumed a more serious aspect, and he was prostrated with a fever which threatened his life. November, December, January, February passed, in nursing and preparations, and Claude in turn was visited by doctor and judge—the one to restore him to health, the other to glean the evidence needful to send him to the scaffold.

On the 16th of March, 1832, perfectly cured, Claude appeared in court at Troyes, to answer the charge brought against him. His appearance impressed the court favourably; he had been shaved and stood bareheaded, but still clad in prison garb. The court was well guarded by a strong military guard, to keep the witnesses within bounds, as they were all convicts.

But an unexpected difficulty occurred: not one of these men would give evidence; neither questions nor threats availed to make them break their silence, until Claude requested them to do so. Then they in turn gave a faithful account of the terrible event; and if one, from forgetfulness or affection for the accused, failed to relate the whole facts, Claude supplied the deficiency. At one time the women's tears fell fast.

The usher now called the convict Albin. He came in trembling with emotion and sobbing painfully, and threw himself into Claude's arms. Turning to the Public Prosecutor, Claude said:

"Here is a convict who gives his food to the hungry," and stooping, he kissed Albin's hand.

All the witnesses having been examined, the counsel for the prosecution then rose to address the court. "Gentlemen of the jury, society would be utterly put to confusion if a public prosecution did not condemn great culprits like him, who," etc.

After the long address by the prosecution, Claude's counsel rose. Then followed the usual pleading for and against, which ever takes place at the criminal court.

Claude in his turn gave evidence, and every one was astonished at his intelligence ; there appeared far more of the orator about this poor workman than the assassin. In a clear and straightforward way he detailed the facts as they were—standing proudly there, resolved to tell the whole truth. At times the crowd was carried away by his eloquence. This man, who could not read, would grasp the most difficult points of argument, yet treat the judges with all due deference. Once Claude lost his temper, when the counsel for the prosecution stated that he had assassinated the inspector without provocation.

" What ! " cried Claude, " I had no provocation ? Indeed ! A drunkard strikes me—I kill him ; then you would allow there was provocation, and the penalty of death would be changed for that of the galleys. But a man who wounds me in every way during four years, humiliates me for four years, taunts me daily, hourly, for four years, and heaps every insult on my head—what follows ? You consider I had no provocation ! I had a wife for whom I robbed—he tortured me about her. I had a child for whom I robbed—he taunted me about this child. I was hungry, a friend shared his bread with me—he took away my friend. I begged him to return my friend to me—he cast me into a dungeon. I told him how much I suffered—he said it wearied him to listen. What then would you have me do ? I took his life ; and you look upon me as a monster for killing this man, and you decapitate me ; then do so."

Provocation such as this the law fails to acknowledge, because the blows leave no marks to show.

The judge then summed up the case in a clear and impartial manner, dwelling on the life Claude had led, living openly with an improper character ; then he had robbed, and ended by being a murderer. All this was true. Before the jury retired, the judge asked Claude if he had any questions to ask, or anything to say.

" Very little," said Claude. " I am a murderer, I am a thief ; but I ask you, gentlemen of this jury, why did I kill ? Why did I steal ? "

The jury retired for a quarter of an hour, and according to the judgment of these twelve countrymen—*gentlemen of the jury*, as they are styled—Claude Gueux was condemned to death. At the very outset several of them were much impressed with the name of Gueux (vagabond), and that influenced their decision.

When the verdict was pronounced, Claude simply said : " Very well ; but there are two questions these gentlemen have not answered. Why did this man steal ? What made him a murderer ? "

He made a good supper that night, exclaiming, " Thirty-six years have now passed me." He refused to make any appeal until the last minute, but at the instance of one of the sisters who nursed him he consented to do so. She in her fulness of heart gave him a five-franc piece.

His fellow-prisoners, as we have already noticed, were devoted to him, and placed all the means at their disposal to help him to escape. They threw into his dungeon, through the air-hole, a nail, some wire, the handle of a pail : any one of these would have been enough for a man like Claude to free himself from his chains. He gave them all up to the warder.

On the 8th of June, 1832, seven months and four days after the murder, the recorder of the court came, and Claude was told that he had but one hour more to live, for his appeal had been rejected.

" Indeed," said Claude, coldly ; " I slept well last night, and doubtless I shall pass my next even better."

First came the priest, then the executioner. He was humble to the priest, and listened to him with great attention, regretting much that he had not had the benefit of religious training, at the same time blaming himself for much in the past. He was courteous in his manner to the executioner ; in fact he gave up all—his soul to the priest, his body to the executioner.

While his hair was being cut, some one mentioned how the cholera was spreading, and Troyes at any moment might become a prey to this fearful scourge. Claude joined in the conversation, saying, with a smile, " There is one thing to be said—I have no fear of the cholera ! " He had broken half of the scissors—what remained he asked the jailor to give to Albin ; the other half lay buried in his chest. He also wished the day's rations to be taken to his friend. The only trifle he retained was the five franc piece that the sister had given him, which he kept in his right hand after he was bound.

At a quarter to eight the dismal procession usual in such cases left the prison. Pale, but with a firm tread, Claude Gueux slowly mounted the scaffold, keeping his eyes fixed on the crucifix the priest carried—an emblem of the Saviour's suffering. He wished to embrace the priest and the executioner, thanking the one and pardoning the other ; the executioner simply repulsed him. Just before he was bound to the infernal machine he gave the five-franc piece to the priest, saying, " For the poor."

The hour had scarcely struck its eight chimes when this man, so noble, so intelligent, received the fatal blow which severed his head from his body.

A market-day had been chosen for the time of execution, as there would be more people about ; for there are still in France small towns that glory in having an execution. The guillotine that day

remained, inflaming the imagination of the mob to such an extent
that one of the tax-gatherers was nearly murdered. Such is the
admirable effect of public executions !

We have given the history of Claude Gueux's life, more to solve
a difficult problem than for aught else. In his life there are two
questions to be considered—before his fall and after his fall. What
was his training and what was the penalty ? This must interest
society generally ; for this man was well gifted, his instincts were
good. Then what was wanting ? On this revolves the grand
problem which would place society on a firm basis.

What Nature has begun in the individual, let society carry out. Look
at Claude Gueux. An intelligent and most noble-hearted man,
placed in the midst of evil surroundings, he turned thief. Society
placed him in a prison where the evil was yet greater, and he ended
with becoming a murderer. Can we really blame him, or ourselves ?—questions which require deep thought, or the result will
be that we shall be compelled to shirk this most important subject.
The facts are now before us, and if the government gives no thought
to the matter, what are the rulers about ? . . .

JENNY

VICTOR HUGO

I

IT was night. The cabin, poor, but warm and cosy, was full of a
half-twilight, through which the objects of the interior were but
dimly visible by the glimmer of the embers which flickered on the
hearth and reddened the dark rafters overhead. The fisherman's
nets were hanging on the wall. Some homely pots and pans
twinkled on a rough shelf in the corner. Beside a great bed with
long, falling curtains, a mattress was extended on a couple of old
benches, on which five little children were asleep like cherubs in
a nest. By the bedside, with her forehead pressed against the
counterpane, knelt the children's mother. She was alone. Outside
the cabin the black ocean, dashed with stormy foam-flakes, moaned
and murmured, and her husband was at sea.

From his boyhood he had been a fisherman. His life, as one may
say, had been a daily fight with the great waters ; for every day the
children must be fed, and every day, rain, wind, or tempest, out
went his boat to fish. And while, in his four-sailed boat, he plied
his solitary task at sea, his wife at home patched the old sails, mended
the nets, looked to the hooks, or watched the little fire, where the

fish-soup was boiling. As soon as the five children were asleep, she fell upon her knees and prayed to Heaven for her husband in his struggle with the waves and darkness. And truly such a life as his was hard. The likeliest place for fish was a mere speck among the breakers, not more than twice as large as his own cabin—a spot obscure, capricious, changing on the moving desert, and yet which had to be discovered in the fog and tempest of a winter night, by sheer skill and knowledge of the tides and winds. And there— while the gliding waves ran past like emerald serpents, and the gulf of darkness rolled and tossed, and the straining rigging groaned as if in terror—there, amidst the icy seas, he thought of his own Jenny ; and Jenny, in her cottage, thought of him with tears.

She was thinking of him then and praying. The sea-gull's harsh and mocking cry distressed her, and the roaring of the billows on the reef alarmed her soul. But she was wrapped in thoughts— thoughts of their poverty. Their little children went bare-footed winter and summer. Wheatbread they never ate ; only bread of barley. Heavens ! the wind roared like the bellows of a forge, and the sea-coast echoed like an anvil. She wept and trembled. Poor wives whose husbands are at sea ! How terrible to say, " My dear ones—father, lover, brothers, sons—are in the tempest." But Jenny was still more unhappy. Her husband was alone— alone without assistance on this bitter night. Her children were too little to assist him. Poor mother ! Now she says, " I wish they were grown up to help their father." Foolish dream ! In years to come, when they are with their father in the tempest, she will say with tears, " I wish they were but children still."

II

Jenny took her lantern and her cloak. " It is time," she said to herself, " to see whether he is coming back, whether the sea is calmer, and whether the light is burning on the signal-mast." She went out. There was nothing to be seen—barely a streak of white on the horizon. It was raining, the dark, cold rain of early morning. No cabin window showed a gleam of light.

All at once, while peering round her, her eyes perceived a tumble-down old cabin which showed no sign of light or fire. The door was swinging in the wind ; the worm-eaten walls seemed scarcely able to support the crazy roof, on which the wind shook the yellow, filthy tufts of rotten thatch.

" Stay," she cried, " I am forgetting the poor widow whom my husband found the other day alone and ill. I must see how she is getting on."

She knocked at the door and listened. No one answered. Jenny shivered in the cold sea-wind.

" She is ill. And her poor children ! She has only two of them ; but she is very poor, and has no husband."

She knocked again, and called out, "Hey, neighbour!" But the cabin was still silent.

"Heaven!" she said, "how sound she sleeps, that it requires so much to wake her."

At that instant the door opened of itself. She entered. Her lantern illumined the interior of the dark and silent cabin, and showed her the water falling from the ceiling as through the openings of a sieve. At the end of the room an awful form was lying: a woman stretched out motionless, with bare feet and sightless eyes. Her cold white arm hung down among the straw of the pallet. She was dead. Once a strong and happy mother, she was now only the spectre which remains of poor humanity, after a long struggle with the world.

Near the bed on which the mother lay, two little children—a boy and a girl—slept together in their cradle, and were smiling in their dreams. Their mother, when she felt that she was dying, had laid her cloak across their feet and wrapt them in her dress, to keep them warm when she herself was cold.

How sound they slept in their old, tottering cradle, with their calm breath and quiet little faces! It seemed as if nothing could awake these sleeping orphans. Outside, the rain beat down in floods, and the sea gave forth a sound like an alarm bell. From the old creviced roof, through which blew the gale, a drop of water fell on the dead face, and ran down it like a tear.

III

What had Jenny been about in the dead woman's house? What was she carrying off beneath her cloak? Why was her heart beating? Why did she hasten with such trembling steps to her own cabin, without daring to look back. What did she hide in her own bed, behind the curtain? What had she been stealing?

When she entered the cabin, the cliffs were growing white. She sank upon the chair beside the bed. She was very pale; it seemed as if she felt repentance. Her forehead fell upon the pillow, and at intervals, with broken words, she murmured to herself, while outside the cabin moaned the savage sea.

"My poor man! O Heavens, what will he say? He has already so much trouble. What have I done now? Five children on our hands already! Their father toils and toils, and yet as if he had not care enough already, I must give him this care more. Is that he? No, nothing. I have done wrong—he would do quite right to beat me. Is that he? No! So much the better. The door moves as if someone were coming in; but no. To think that I should feel afraid to see him enter!"

Then she remained absorbed in thought, and shivering with the cold, unconscious of all outward sounds, of the black cormorants, which passed shrieking, and of the rage of wind and sea.

All at once the door flew open, a streak of the white light of morning entered, and the fisherman, dragging his dripping net, appeared upon the threshold, and cried, with a gay laugh, " Here comes the Navy."

" You ! " cried Jenny ; and she clasped her husband like a lover, and pressed her mouth against his rough jacket.

" Here I am, wife," he said, showing in the firelight the good-natured and contented face which Jenny loved so well.

" I have been unlucky," he continued.

" What kind of weather have you had ? "

" Dreadful."

" And the fishing ? "

" Bad. But never mind. I have you in my arms again, and I am satisfied. I have caught nothing at all, I have only torn my net. The deuce was in the wind to-night. At one moment of the tempest I thought the boat was foundering, and the cable broke. But what have you been doing all this time ? "

Jenny felt a shiver in the darkness.

" I ? " she said, in trouble. " Oh, nothing ; just as usual. I have been sewing. I have been listening to the thunder of the sea, and I was frightened."

" Yes ; the winter is a hard time. But never mind it now."

Then, trembling as if she were going to commit a crime :

" Husband ! " she said, " our neighbour is dead. She must have died last night, soon after you went out. She has left two little children, one called William and the other Madeline. The boy can hardly toddle, and the girl can only lisp. The poor, good woman was in dreadful want."

The man looked grave. Throwing into a corner his fur cap sodden by the tempest : " The deuce," he said, scratching his head. " We already have five children ; this makes seven. And already in bad weather we have to go without our supper. What shall we do now ? Bah, it is not my fault ; it's God's doing. These are things too deep for me. Why has He taken away their mother from these mites ? These matters are too difficult to understand. One has to be a scholar to see through them. Such tiny scraps of children ! Wife, go and fetch them. If they are awake, they must be frightened to be alone with their dead mother. We will bring them up with ours. They will be brother and sister to our five. When God sees that we have to feed this little girl and boy besides our own, He will let us take more fish. As for me, I will drink water. I will work twice as hard. Enough. Be off and bring them ! But what is the matter ? Does it vex you ? You are generally quicker than this."

His wife drew back the curtain.

" Look ! " she said.

PROSPER MÉRIMÉE
1803-1870

THE TAKING OF THE REDOUBT

A FRIEND of mine, a soldier, who died in Greece of fever some years since, described to me one day his first engagement. His story so impressed me that I wrote it down from memory. It was as follows :—

I joined my regiment on September 4. It was evening. I found the colonel in the camp. He received me rather brusquely, but having read the general's introductory letter he changed his manner, and addressed me courteously.

By him I was presented to my captain, who had just come in from reconnoitring. This captain, whose acquaintance I had scarcely time to make, was a tall, dark man, of harsh, repelling aspect. He had been a private soldier, and had won his cross and epaulettes upon the field of battle. His voice, which was hoarse and feeble, contrasted strangely with his gigantic stature. This voice of his he owed, as I was told, to a bullet which had passed completely through his body at the battle of Jena.

On learning that I had just come from college at Fontainebleau, he remarked, with a wry face, " My lieutenant died last night."

I understood what he implied—" It is for you to take his place, and you are good for nothing."

A sharp retort was on my tongue, but I restrained it.

The moon was rising behind the redoubt of Cheverino, which stood two cannon-shots from our encampment. The moon was large and red, as is common at her rising ; but that night she seemed to me of extraordinary size. For an instant the redoubt stood out coal-black against the glittering disk. It resembled the cone of a volcano at the moment of eruption.

An old soldier, at whose side I found myself, observed the colour of the moon.

" She is very red," he said. " It is a sign that it will cost us dear to win this wonderful redoubt."

I was always superstitious, and this piece of augury, coming at that moment, troubled me. I sought my couch, but could not sleep. I rose, and walked about awhile, watching the long line of fires upon the heights beyond the village of Cheverino.

When the sharp night air had thoroughly refreshed my blood I went back to the fire. I rolled my mantle round me, and I shut my eyes, trusting not to open them till daybreak. But sleep refused to visit me. Insensibly my thoughts grew doleful. I told myself that I had not a friend among the hundred thousand men who filled that plain. If I were wounded, I should be placed in hospital, in the hands of ignorant and careless surgeons. I called to mind what I had heard of operations. My heart beat violently, and I mechanically arranged, as a kind of rude cuirass, my handkerchief and pocket-book upon my breast. Then, over-powered with weariness, my eyes closed drowsily, only to open the next instant with a start at some new thought of horror.

Fatigue, however, at last gained the day. When the drums beat at daybreak I was fast asleep. We were drawn up in rank. The roll was called, then we stacked our arms, and everything announced that we should pass another uneventful day.

But about three o'clock an aide-de-camp arrived with orders. We were commanded to take arms.

Our sharp-shooters marched into the plain. We followed slowly, and in twenty minutes we saw the outposts of the Russians falling back and entering the redoubt. We had a battery of artillery on our right, another on our left, but both some distance in advance of us. They opened a sharp fire upon the enemy, who returned it briskly, and the redoubt of Cheverino was soon concealed by volumes of thick smoke. Our regiment was almost covered from the Russians' fire by a piece of rising ground. Their bullets (which besides were rarely aimed at us, for they preferred to fire upon our cannoneers) whistled over us, or at worst knocked up a shower of earth and stones.

Just as the order to advance was given, the captain looked at me intently. I stroked my sprouting moustache with an air of unconcern; in truth, I was not frightened, and only dreaded lest I might be thought so. These passing bullets aided my heroic coolness, while my self-respect assured me that the danger was a real one, since I was veritably under fire. I was delighted at my self-possession, and already looked forward to the pleasure of describing in Parisian drawing-rooms the capture of the redoubt of Cheverino.

The colonel passed before our company. "Well," he said to me, "you are going to see warm work in your first action."

I gave a martial smile, and brushed my cuff, on which a bullet, which had struck the earth at thirty paces distant, had cast a little dust.

It appeared that the Russians had discovered that their bullets did no harm, for they replaced them by a fire of shells, which began to reach us in the hollows where we lay. One of these, in its explosion, knocked off my shako and killed a man beside me.

"I congratulate you," said the captain, as I picked up my shako. "You are safe now for the day."

I knew the military superstition which believes that the axiom *non bis in idem* is as applicable to the battlefield as to the courts of justice. I replaced my shako with a swagger.

"That's a rude way to make one raise one's hat," I said, as lightly as I could. And this wretched piece of wit was, in the circumstances, received as excellent.

"I compliment you," said the captain. "You will command a company to-night; for I shall not survive the day. Every time I have been wounded the officer below me has been touched by some spent ball; and," he added, in a lower tone, "all their names began with P."

I laughed sceptically; most people would have done the same; but most would also have been struck, as I was, by these prophetic words. But, conscript though I was, I felt that I could trust my thoughts to no one, and that it was my duty to seem always calm and bold.

At the end of half an hour the Russian fire had sensibly diminished. We left our cover to advance on the redoubt.

Our regiment was composed of three battalions. The second had to take the enemy in flank; the two others formed the storming party. I was in the third.

On issuing from behind the cover, we were received by several volleys, which did but little harm. The whistling of the balls amazed me. "But after all," I thought, "a battle is less terrible than I expected."

We advanced at a smart run, our musketeers in front. All at once the Russians uttered three hurrahs—three distinct hurrahs—and then stood silent, without firing.

"I don't like that silence," said the captain. "It bodes no good."

I began to think our people were too eager. I could not help comparing, mentally, their shouts and clamour with the striking silence of the enemy.

We quickly reached the foot of the redoubt. The palisades were broken and the earthworks shattered by our balls. With a roar of "Vive l'Empereur!" our soldiers rushed across the ruins.

I raised my eyes. Never shall I forget the sight which met my view. The smoke had mostly lifted, and remained suspended, like a canopy, at twenty feet above the redoubt. Through a bluish mist could be perceived, behind their shattered parapet, the Russian Grenadiers, with rifles lifted, as motionless as statues. I can see them still—the left eye of every soldier glaring at us, the right hidden by his lifted gun. In an embrasure, at a few feet distant, a man with a fusee stood by a cannon.

I shuddered. I believed that my last hour had come.

"Now for the dance to open!" cried the captain. These were the last words I heard him speak.

There came from the redoubt a roll of drums. I saw the muzzles lowered. I shut my eyes; I heard a most appalling crash of sound, to which succeeded groans and cries. Then I looked up, amazed to find myself still living. The redoubt was once more wrapped in smoke. I was surrounded by the dead and wounded. The captain was extended at my feet; a ball had carried off his head, and I was covered with his blood. Of all the company, only six men, except myself, remained erect.

This carnage was succeeded by a kind of stupor. The next instant the colonel, with his hat on his sword's point, had scaled the parapet with a cry of " Vive l'Empereur ! " The survivors followed him. All that succeeded is to me a kind of dream. We rushed into the redoubt, I know not how; we fought hand to hand in the midst of smoke so thick that no man could perceive his enemy. I found my sabre dripping blood; I heard a shout of " Victory " ; and, in the clearing smoke, I saw the earthworks piled with dead and dying. The cannons were covered with a heap of corpses. About two hundred men in the French uniform were standing, without order, loading their muskets or wiping their bayonets. Eleven Russian prisoners were with them.

The colonel was lying, bathed in blood, upon a broken cannon. A group of soldiers crowded round him. I approached them.

"Who is the oldest captain? " he was asking of a sergeant.

The sergeant shrugged his shoulders most expressively.

"Who is the oldest lieutenant? "

"This gentleman, who came last night," replied the sergeant, calmly.

The colonel smiled bitterly.

"Come, sir," he said to me, "you are now in chief command. Fortify the gorge of the redoubt at once with waggons, for the enemy is out in force. But General C—— is coming to support you."

"Colonel," I asked him, "are you badly wounded? "

"Pish, my dear fellow ! The redoubt is taken ! "

MATEO FALCONE

Prosper Mérimée

GOING out of Porto-Vecchio and turning north-west, towards the interior of the island, you see the land rise pretty sharply, and, after a three hours' walk along winding paths, obstructed by great lumps of rock, and sometimes cut by ravines, you reach the edge of a most extensive bush country—the *mâquis*. The *mâquis* is the home of the Corsican shepherds and of whoever is in trouble with the police. You must know that the Corsican peasant, to save himself the trouble of manuring, sets fire to a stretch of wood ; if the flames spread further than is necessary, so much the worse ; but whatever happens, he is sure of a good harvest from sowing on this ground, fertilised by the ashes of the trees it bore. When the corn has been gathered (they leave the straw, which would be a trouble to collect), the tree roots, which have stayed in the ground without wasting away, put forth very heavy shoots in the following spring, which in a few years reach a height of seven or eight feet. It is this species of close thicket that they call the *mâquis*. It is made up of different kinds of trees and shrubs mixed and entangled as God wills. Only with a hatchet in his hand can a man open himself a way through, and there are *mâquis* so thick and bushy that the wild rams themselves are unable to penetrate them.

If you have killed a man, go into the *mâquis* of Porto-Vecchio, and you will live there in safety, with a good gun, powder and shot ; you must not forget a brown cloak with a hood to it, that will serve as covering and mattress. The shepherds give you milk, cheese, and chestnuts, and you will have nothing to fear from the law, or the dead man's relations, except when you have to go down into the town to renew your stock of ammunition.

Mateo Falcone, when I was in Corsica, had his house half a league's distance from the *mâquis*. He was a fairly rich man in the countryside ; living as a gentleman, that is to say, without doing anything, on the produce of his flocks, that shepherds, a kind of nomads, pastured here and there over the mountains. When I saw him, two years after the incident I am about to relate to you, he seemed to me fifty years old at most. Imagine a man small but sturdy, with crisp hair, black as jet, large quick eyes, and a complexion the colour of boot-leather. His skill with the gun passed for extraordinary, even in his country, where there are so many good shots. For example, Mateo would never fire at a wild ram with buck-shot ; at a hundred and twenty paces, he would bring it down with a bullet in the head or the shoulder as he chose. He used his weapon as easily at night as in the day-time, and I heard this proof of his skill, that will perhaps seem incredible to those who have not travelled in Corsica. At eighty paces, a lighted candle was placed behind a piece of transparent paper as big as a plate. He aimed. The candle was blown out, and, after a minute in the most absolute darkness, he fired and pierced the paper three times out of four.

With such transcendent merit, Mateo Falcone had won a great reputation. Men said he was as good a friend as he was a dangerous enemy : obliging too, and charitable, he lived at peace with everybody in the neighbourhood of Porto-Vecchio. But it was said of him that, at Corte, whence he had taken his wife, he had disembarrassed himself in the most vigorous manner of a rival accounted as redoubtable in war as in love ; at least, to Mateo was attributed a certain shot that had surprised his rival shaving before a little mirror hung in his window. The affair was hushed up, and Mateo married. His wife Giuseppa had given him first three girls (at which he was enraged) and finally a boy, whom he called Fortunato, the hope of his family, heir to the name. The daughters were well married : their father could count at need on the poniards and carbines of his sons-in-law. The son was only ten years old, but already promised well.

One autumn day, Mateo went out early with his wife to visit one of his flocks in a clearing in the *mâquis*. Little Fortunato wanted to accompany him, but the clearing was too far away ; besides, it was very necessary that some one should stay to guard the house ; the father refused ; we shall see if he had not good reason to regret it.

He had been away some hours, and little Fortunato was tranquilly stretched in the sun, looking at the blue mountains, and thinking that next Sunday he would be going to dinner in the town, at the house of his uncle the Corporal, when he was suddenly interrupted in his meditations by the sound of a gun. He stood up and turned to the side of the plain whence the sound came. Other gunshots followed, fired at irregular intervals, and always nearer and nearer ; at last, a man appeared in the path leading from the plain to Mateo's house, a pointed cap on his head, like those worn by the mountaineers, bearded, in tatters, dragging himself with difficulty, leaning on his gun. He had just received a bullet in the thigh.

The man was an outlaw, who, having set off by night to get powder in the town, had fallen on the way into an ambuscade of Corsican light infantry. After a vigorous defence, he had succeeded in making good his retreat, hotly pursued, and firing from rock to rock. But he had not much start of the soldiers, and his wound made it impossible for him to reach the *mâquis* before being caught up.

He came up to Fortunato, and said :

" You are Mateo Falcone's son ? "

" Yes."

" I am Gianetto Sanpiero. The yellow collars are after me. Hide me, for I can go no further."

" And what will my father say, if I hide you without his leave ? "

" He will say you have done right."

" Who knows ? "

" Hide me quickly ; they are coming."

" Wait till my father comes back."

" Wait ! Confound it ! They will be here in five minutes. Come, hide me, or I'll kill you."

Fortunato answered him with the utmost calm :

" Your gun is not loaded, and there are no cartridges in your bandolier."

" I have my dagger."

" But will you run as quick as I ? "

He made a bound and put himself out of reach.

" You are not the son of Mateo Falcone. Will you let me be arrested in front of your house ?

The child seemed touched.

" What will you give me if I hide you ? " he said, coming nearer.

The bandit rummaged in a leather pouch that hung at his belt, and took out a five-franc piece that he had no doubt kept to buy powder. Fortunato smiled at the sight of the piece of silver ; he seized it and said to Gianetto :

" Fear nothing."

Instantly he made a great hole in a hayrick placed near the house. Gianetto squatted down in it, and the child covered him up so as to leave him a little air to breathe, and yet so that it was impossible to suspect that a man was concealed in the hay. He bethought himself too of an ingenious piece of savage cunning. He fetched a cat and her little ones, and established them on the hayrick, to make believe that it had not been stirred for some time. Then, noticing traces of blood on the path close to the house, he covered them carefully with dust, and, that done, lay down again in the sun with the utmost tranquillity.

Some minutes later, six men in brown uniform with yellow collars, commanded by an adjutant, were before Mateo's door. The adjutant was distantly connected with Falcone. (It is well known that in Corsica degrees of relationship are counted farther than elsewhere.) His name was Tiodoro Gamba : he was a man of energy, much feared by the bandits, many of whom he had already run down.

" Good-day, little cousin," said he, accosting Fortunato. " How you have grown ! Did you see a man pass by just now ? "

" Oh, I am not yet as big as you, cousin," the child answered with a simple air.

" That will come. But tell me, haven't you seen a man go by ? "

" Have I seen a man go by ? "

" Yes ; a man with a pointed cap, and a waistcoat worked in red and yellow ? "

" A man with a pointed cap, and a waistcoat worked in red and yellow ? "

" Yes ; answer quickly, and do not repeat my questions."

" This morning, Monsieur the Curé went past our door on his horse Piero. He asked me how papa was, and I told him. . . ."

" Ah, you young scamp, you are playing the fool ! Tell me at once which way Gianetto went ; he is the man we are after, and I am sure he took this path."

" Who knows ! "

" Who knows ? I know you have seen him."

" Does one then see passers-by when one is asleep ? "

" Rogue, you were not asleep ; the gunshots woke you up."

" So you think, cousin, that your carbines make so much noise ? My father's rifle makes much more."

" May the devil take you, cursed scamp that you are ! I am very sure you have seen Gianetto. Perhaps you have even hidden him. Come, mates, into the house with you, and see if our man is not there. He was only going on one foot, and he has too much sense, the rascal, to try and reach the *mâquis* limping. Besides, the traces of blood stop here."

" And what will papa say ? " asked Fortunato, chuckling ; " what will he say when he hears that his house was entered while he was out ? "

" Rogue ! " said Adjutant Gamba, taking him by the ear, " do you know that, if I like, I can make you change your tune ? Perhaps if I give you a score of blows with the flat of the sword, you will speak at last."

And Fortunato went on chuckling.

" My father is Mateo Falcone," he said with emphasis.

" Do you know, little scamp, that I can take you off to Corte or to Bastia ? I will put you to sleep in a cell, on straw, with irons on your feet, and I will have your head cut off unless you say where is Gianetto Sanpiero."

The child broke into a laugh at this ridiculous threat. He said again :

" My father is Mateo Falcone."

" Adjutant," said one of the troopers under his breath, " do not let us get into trouble with Mateo."

It was clear that Gamba was embarrassed. He spoke in a low voice to his men, who had already gone through the house. It was not a long business, for a Corsican's cottage is made up of a single square room. The furniture consists of a table, benches, chests, household utensils, and the weapons of the chase. Meanwhile, little Fortunato stroked his cat, and seemed to find a malicious enjoyment in the discomfiture of the troopers and his cousin.

A soldier came up to the hayrick. He saw the cat, and carelessly stuck a bayonet in the hay, shrugging his shoulders, as if he felt he were taking a ridiculous precaution. Nothing stirred ; and the child's face did not betray the slightest emotion.

The adjutant and his men cursed their luck ; they were already looking seriously towards the plain, as if ready to go back whence they had come, when their leader, convinced that threats would make no impression on Falcone's son, wished to make a final attempt, and try the effect of caresses and gifts.

" Little cousin," said he, " you seem to be a wide-awake young rogue ! You will go far. But you are playing a risky game with me ; and, if it were not for fear of troubling my cousin Mateo, devil take it, if I would not carry you off with me."

" Bah ! "

" But, when my cousin returns, I shall tell him the whole story, and he will give you the whip till the blood comes, for telling lies."

" How do you know ? "

" You will see. . . . But look here. . . . Be a good boy, and I will give you something."

" As for me, cousin, I will give you a piece of advice ; and that is, that if you dawdle any longer, Gianetto will be in the *mâquis*, and it will take a smarter fellow than you to go and look for him there."

The adjutant pulled a silver watch out of his pocket, worth a good ten crowns ; and, noticing that little Fortunato's eyes glittered as they looked at it, dangled the watch at the end of its steel chain, and said :

" Scamp ! you would be glad enough to have a watch like this hanging from your neck ; you would walk in the streets of Porto-Vecchio, proud as a peacock ; and people would ask you, ' What time is it ? ' and you would say to them, ' Look at my watch.' "

" When I am big, my uncle the Corporal will give me a watch."

" Yes ; but your uncle's son has one already . . . not as fine as this it is true . . . and yet he is younger than you."

The child sighed.

" Well, would you like the watch, little cousin ? "

Fortunato, ogling the watch out of the corners of his eyes, was like a cat to whom one offers a whole chicken. The cat dares not put a claw on it, feeling that one is laughing at him, and turns away his eyes from time to time, so as not to succumb to the temptation ; but he licks his lips continually ; and seems to say to his master, " What a cruel joke this is ! "

And yet, Adjutant Gamba seemed to be making a real offer of the watch. Fortunato did not put out his hand, but said, with a bitter smile :

" Why are you laughing at me ? "

" By God ! I am not laughing. Only tell me where is Gianetto, and the watch is yours."

Fortunato allowed an incredulous smile to escape him ; and, fixing his black eyes on those of the adjutant, tried to read in them the good faith he sought for in the words.

" May I lose my epaulettes," cried the adjutant, " if I do not give you the watch on that condition ! My fellows are witnesses, and I cannot unsay it."

As he spoke, he brought the watch nearer and nearer till it almost touched the pale cheek of the child, whose face showed clearly how covetousness and the respect due to hospitality were contending in his soul. His bare breast heaved convulsively, and he seemed almost choking. Meanwhile the watch swung, and twisted, and sometimes touched the tip of his nose. At last, little by little, his right hand rose towards the watch ; he touched it with the tip of his fingers ; its whole weight was in his hand, without the adjutant, however, letting go the end of the chain . . . the face was blue . . . the case newly burnished . . . it seemed all on fire in the sun. . . . The temptation was too strong.

Fortunato lifted his left hand also, and indicated with his thumb, over his shoulder, the hayrick on which he leant. The adjutant instantly understood. He dropped the end of the chain. Fortunato felt himself sole possessor of the watch. He leapt with the agility of a deer, and put ten paces between himself and the hay-rick, that the troopers immediately set to work to bring down.

It was not long before they saw the hay stir ; a bleeding man came out of it, with a dagger in his hand ; but, when he tried to get on his feet, his congealed wound prevented him from standing upright. He fell. The adjutant flung himself upon him and wrested away his poniard. Immediately he was strongly bound, in spite of his resistance.

Gianetto, laid on the ground, and tied up like a bundle of sticks, turned his head towards Fortunato, who had come up again.

" Son of . . . ! " he said, with more scorn than anger.

The child threw him the piece of silver he had had from him, feeling that he no longer deserved it ; but the proscribed man did not seem to notice the action. He said very tranquilly to the adjutant :

" My dear Gamba, I cannot walk ; you will have to carry me to the town."

" You were running just now, quicker than a young goat," retorted the cruel victor ; " but be easy : I am so glad to have got you, I would carry you a league on my back without feeling the weight. Anyhow, comrade, we will make you a litter with branches and your cloak, and we shall find horses at the farm of Crespoli."

" Good," said the prisoner ; " you will put a little straw on the litter, won't you, to make me more comfortable."

While the troopers were busy, some in making a sort of stretcher with branches of a chestnut-tree, others in dressing Gianetto's wound, Mateo Falcone and his wife appeared suddenly at the bend of a path that led to the *mâquis*. The woman was in front, bending heavily under the weight of a huge sack of chestnuts, while her husband strutted along, carrying nothing but a gun in his hand, and another slung on his back. It is beneath the dignity of a man to carry any other burden than his weapons.

Mateo's first thought on seeing the soldiers was that they had come to arrest him. But why this idea ? Had Mateo then some quarrel with the law ? Not at all. He enjoyed a good reputation. He was " well spoken of " as the saying is ; but he was a Corsican and a mountaineer, and there are few Corsican mountaineers who, if they look well into their memories, do not find there some peccadillo, a gunshot or a dagger-blow, or other bagatelle. Mateo had a clearer conscience than most ; for it was ten years since he had aimed his gun at a man ; but he was prudent nevertheless, and got ready to make a good defence, if need be.

" Wife," said he, to Giuseppa, " put down your sack, and be ready."

She instantly obeyed. He gave her the gun from his bandolier, which might have inconvenienced him. He cocked the one he had in his hand, and advanced slowly towards his house, keeping along the trees by the side of the path, and ready, at the slightest sign of hostility, to throw himself behind the biggest trunk, whence he would be able to fire from cover. His wife walked at his heels, holding his spare gun and his cartridge-box. It is the business of a good wife, in case of battle, to load her husband's weapons.

The adjutant, on the other side, was considerably troubled at seeing Mateo advance in this manner, with measured steps, his gun ready, and his finger at the trigger.

" If by chance," he thought, " Mateo should be a relation of Gianetto, or a friend, and should wish to defend him, the bullets of his two guns will reach two of us, as sure as a letter by post, and, if he should aim at me in spite of our relationship . . . ! "

In the difficulty he made a very courageous resolve, and that was to go forward to meet Mateo by himself and tell him about the matter, accosting him as an old acquaintance ; but the short distance that separated him from Mateo seemed terribly long.

" Hola there, old comrade," he cried, " how are you, old man ? It is I, Gamba, your cousin."

Mateo, without answering a word, had stopped, and, as the other spoke, slowly raised the barrel of his gun, so that at the moment when the adjutant came up to him it was pointed to the sky.

" Good-day, brother," [1] said the adjutant, holding out his hand. " It is a very long time since I last saw you."

" Good-day, brother."

" I had come to give good-day to you in passing, and to my cousin Pepa. We have made a long march to-day ; but we must not complain of being tired, for we have made a famous capture.

---

[1] *Buon giorno, fratello*, is the ordinary Corsican greeting.

We have just got hold of Gianetto Sanpiero."

" God be praised," cried Giuseppa ; " he robbed us of a milch-goat last week."

These words rejoiced Gamba.

" Poor devil," said Mateo, " he was hungry."

" The rogue defended himself like a lion," pursued the adjutant, a little taken aback ; " he killed one of my troopers, and, not content with that, broke Corporal Chardon's arm ; but that is no great harm, he was only a Frenchman. . . . Then he had hidden himself so well that the devil could not have discovered him. Without my little cousin Fortunato, I should never have been able to find him."

" Fortunato ! " cried Mateo.

" Fortunato ! " repeated Giuseppa.

" Yes, Gianetto had hidden himself under that hayrick over there ; but my little cousin showed me the trick. I shall tell his uncle the Corporal, and he will send him a fine present for his pains. And his name and yours shall be in the report that I send to the Public Prosecutor."

" Curse it ! " said Mateo, very low.

They had come up to the soldiers. Gianetto was already laid on his litter, ready to start. When he saw Mateo with Gamba he smiled an odd smile ; then, turning towards the door of the house, he spat on the threshold, and said :

" The house of a traitor."

Only a man ready to die would have dared to apply the name of traitor to Falcone. A good dagger thrust, that would leave no need of a second, would have instantly avenged the insult. But Mateo's only movement was to put his hand to his forehead like a stunned man.

Fortunato had gone into the house on seeing the arrival of his father. He soon reappeared with a bowl of milk, which he presented with downcast eyes to Gianetto.

" Keep off ! " shouted the bandit with a voice of thunder.

Then, turning to one of the troopers :

" Let's have a drink, comrade," he said.

The soldier put his flask in his hands, and the bandit drank the water given him by a man with whom he had just been exchanging gunshots. Then he asked that his hands should be fastened crossed on his breast, instead of tied behind his back.

" I like," said he, " to lie at my ease."

They did their best to satisfy him ; then the adjutant gave the signal for the start, said " Good-bye " to Mateo, who did not answer, and went down at a smart pace towards the plain.

Ten minutes passed before Mateo opened his mouth. The child looked uneasily, now at his mother, and now at his father, who, leaning on his gun, considered him with an expression of concentrated rage.

" You begin well," said Mateo at last, in a voice calm, but terrifying to those who knew the man.

" Father ! " cried the child, coming nearer, with tears in his eyes as if to throw himself at his knees.

But Mateo shouted at him :

" Out of my presence ! "

And the child stopped short, and sobbed, motionless, a few steps from his father.

Giuseppa came up. She had just noticed the watch-chain, one end of which hung out of Fortunato's shirt.

" Who gave you that watch ? " she asked sternly.

" My cousin, the adjutant."

Falcone seized the watch, and, flinging it violently against a stone, broke it in a thousand pieces.

" Woman," said he, " is this child mine ? "

The brown cheeks of Giuseppa became brick red.

" What are you saying, Mateo ? Do you know to whom you are speaking ? "

" Well, this child is the first of his race to be a traitor."

The sobs and chokes of Fortunato redoubled, and Falcone kept his lynx eyes always fixed upon him. At last he struck the ground with the butt of his gun, then threw it across his shoulder, and took once more the path to the *mâquis*, shouting to Fortunato to follow him. The child obeyed.

Giuseppa ran after Mateo and caught him by the arm.

" He is your son," she said in a trembling voice, fixing her black eyes on her husband's as if to read what was passing in his soul.

" Leave me," answered Mateo ; " I am his father."

Giuseppa kissed her son and went weeping back into the cottage. She threw herself on her knees before an image of the Virgin, and prayed fervently. Meanwhile Falcone walked some two hundred paces along the path, and did not stop until he went down into a small ravine. He felt the earth with the butt of his gun, and found it soft and easy to dig. The place seemed suitable to his purpose.

" Fortunato, go up to that big rock."

The child did as he was told, and then knelt.

" Say your prayers."

" Father, my father, do not kill me."

" Say your prayers ! " repeated Mateo in a terrible voice.

The child, stammering and sobbing, recited the *Pater* and the *Credo*. The father responded *Amen* in a loud voice at the end of each prayer.

" Are those all the prayers you know ? "

" Father, I know the *Ave Maria*, too, and the litany my aunt taught me."

" It is very long, but never mind."

The child finished the litany in a stifled voice.

" Have you done ? "

" O father, have mercy ! forgive me ! I will not do it again !
I will beg my cousin the Corporal ever so hard that Gianetto may
be pardoned ! "

He was still speaking ; Mateo had cocked his gun, and took aim,
saying :

" May God forgive you ! "

The child made a desperate effort to get up and embrace his
father's knees ; but he had not the time. Mateo fired, and
Fortunato fell stone-dead.

Without throwing a glance at the corpse, Mateo took the path
to his house, to get a spade for the digging of his son's grave. He
had only gone a few yards when he met Giuseppa, running, alarmed
by the gunshot.

" What have you done ? " she cried.

" Justice."

" Where is he ? "

" In the ravine. I am going to bury him. He died a Christian ;
I will have a mass sung for him. Let them tell my son-in-law,
Tiodoro Bianchi, to come and live with us."

TAMANGO

Prosper Mérimée

Captain Ledoux was a good sailor. He had begun by being
a simple seaman, and then assistant helmsman. At the battle
of Trafalgar he had his left hand smashed by a splinter of wood ;
he lost his hand, and was discharged with good certificates.
Repose hardly suited him, and, when an opportunity of re-em-
barkation presented itself, he served as second lieutenant on board
a privateer. The money he got from some prizes made it possible
for him to buy books and study the theory of navigation, of whose
practice he had already a perfect understanding. In time he
became captain of a private lugger, with three guns and a crew of
sixty men, and the coasting sailors of Jersey have not yet forgotten his exploits.

The peace made him miserable : he had amassed a small fortune
during the war, and had hoped to increase it at the expense of the

English. He was obliged to offer his services to peaceable merchants; and, since he had the reputation of a resolute and experienced man, he was readily entrusted with a ship. When the slave-trade was forbidden, and it was necessary, in order to carry it on, not only to elude the vigilance of the French customs-officers, which was not very difficult, but also, a more risky affair, to escape the English cruisers, Captain Ledoux became a valuable man to the merchants in ebony.

Very different from most sailors who have languished, as he had, a long time in subordinate positions, he had not that profound horror of innovation, and that spirit of routine, that they too often carry into the higher ranks. On the contrary, Captain Ledoux had been the first to advise his owner to use iron tanks to hold water and keep it sweet. On his boat, the handcuffs and chains with which slave-ships are provided were made after a new system, and carefully varnished to protect them from rust. But what brought him most credit among the slave merchants was the building, that he personally superintended, of a brig designed for the trade, a clean sailer, narrow, long like a ship of war, and able none the less to accommodate a very large number of blacks. He called her the *Esperance*. It was his idea that the 'tween decks, narrow and shut in as they were, should be only three feet four inches in height. He maintained that this size allowed slaves of a reasonable height to be comfortably seated; and what need have they of getting up?

"When they get to the colonies," said Ledoux, "they will be only too long on their feet."

The negroes, arranged in two parallel lines, with their backs against the sides of the vessel, left an empty space between their feet, used, in all other slave-ships, for moving about. Ledoux thought of placing other negroes in this space, lying at right angles to the rest. In this way his ship held ten more blacks than any other of the same tonnage. It would have been strictly possible to place yet more, but one must have some humanity, and leave a nigger at least a space five feet long and two broad in which to disport himself during a voyage of six weeks and more. "For, after all," said Ledoux to his owner, to justify this liberal allowance, "the niggers are men like the whites."

The *Esperance* left Nantes on a Friday, as superstitious people have since remarked. The inspectors, who made a scrupulous examination of the brig, did not discover six big cases full of chains, handcuffs, and those irons that are called, for some reason or other, "bars of Justice." Nor were they at all astonished at the enormous provision of water that the *Esperance* was to carry, although, according to her papers, she was only going as far as Senegal, to trade there in wood and ivory. The voyage is not a long one, it is true, but there is no harm in taking precautions. If one should be surprised by a calm, what would become of one without water ?

The *Esperance*, then, sailed on a Friday, well fitted and equipped throughout. Ledoux would, perhaps, have liked masts a little more solid ; however, he could not complain, since the building has been under his own direction. His voyage to the African coast was fortunate in every way. He cast anchor in the river of Joale (I believe) at a time when the English cruisers were not watching that part of the coast. The native merchants came immediately on board. The moment could not have been more favourable. Tamango, a famous warrior and man-seller, had just brought a great quantity of slaves to the coast, and was getting rid of them cheaply, as a man who knew that it was in his power to re-stock the market as soon as his goods should become scarce.

Captain Ledoux went ashore and paid his call on Tamango. He found him with two of his wives, some lesser merchants and overseers, in a straw hut that had been hastily built for him. Tamango had dressed himself out to receive the white captain. He was clad in an old blue military tunic, still bearing the corporal's stripes ; but on each shoulder hung two epaulettes fastened to the same button, flapping, one before and one behind. Since he had no shirt, and the tunic was a little short for a man of his height, a considerable strip of black skin, which looked like a large belt, appeared between the white facings of the tunic and his drawers of Guinea cloth. A big cavalry sabre was hung from a cord at his side, and he held in his hands a fine double-barrelled gun of English make. Thus equipped, the African warrior believed that he surpassed in elegance the most accomplished dandy in Paris or London.

Captain Ledoux observed him silently for some time, while Tamango, throwing a chest like a grenadier on parade before a strange general, enjoyed the impression he thought he was making on the white man. Ledoux, after examining him like a connoisseur, turned to his second in command, and said :

" There's a rascal I should sell for a thousand crowns, if I could get him safe and sound to Martinique."

They sat down, and a sailor who knew a little of the negro language served as interpreter. After the first polite compliments had been exchanged, a boy brought a basket of bottles of brandy. They drank, and the captain, to put Tamango in a good humour, made him a present of a pretty copper powder-flask decorated with a portrait of Napoleon in relief. When the present had been accepted with suitable gratitude, they left the hut and sat down in the shade before the brandy bottles. Tamango made a sign for the slaves he had to sell to be brought before them.

They appeared in a long string, their bodies bent with weariness and terror, each one with his neck in a six-foot fork, whose points were fastened with a wooden bar close behind his head.   When they are to get on the move, one of the overseers takes the handle of the first slave's fork on his shoulder ; this slave looks after the fork of the man immediately behind him ; the second carries the fork of the third slave ; and so on.   When they are to halt, the leader of the file sticks the pointed handle of his fork in the ground, and the whole column comes to a stand.   There is obviously no use in thinking of escape by flight, when one carries a great stick six feet long fastened to one's neck.

The captain shrugged his shoulders as each slave, male or female, passed before him ; he found the men weakly, the women too young or too old, and complained of the decay of the black race.

" It is degenerating in every way," he would say ; " once things were very different. The women were five feet six inches tall, and four of the men could have turned the capstan of a frigate by themselves to lift the main anchor."

However, in the midst of his criticism, he made a first choice of the sturdiest and most handsome blacks. He was willing to pay for these at the ordinary rates, but he demanded a great reduction on the others. Tamango, on his side, was looking after his interests, praising his merchandise, and speaking of the scarcity of men, and the perils of the trade. He finished by setting a price, I do not know what, on the slaves that the white captain wished to take on board.

As soon as the interpreter had put Tamango's proposition into French, Ledoux almost fell backwards with surprise and indignation : then, muttering some terrible oaths, he got up, as if to break off all treaty with so unreasonable a man. Then Tamango begged him to stay, and succeeded with difficulty in getting him to sit down again. Another bottle was opened, and the discussion recommenced. It was now the black's turn to find the white man's offers unreasonable and absurd. For a long time they shouted, and argued, and drank prodigious quantities of brandy, but the brandy had very different effects on the two contracting parties. The more the Frenchman drank, the lower the prices he offered ; the more the African drank, the more he lessened his demands.

In this way, at the end of the basket, they came to an agreement. Some cheap cotton, some powder, some flints, three casks of brandy, and fifty guns in bad repair, were given in exchange for one hundred and sixty slaves. The captain, in order to confirm the bargain, clapped his hand in that of the more than half-drunken black, and the slaves were instantly handed over to the French sailors, who hurried to remove their wooden forks, and to substitute collars and handcuffs of iron ; a good example of the superiority of European civilisation.

There still remained a score and a half of slaves ; they were children, old men, and sick women.   The ship was full.

Tamango, who did not know what to do with this trash, offered to sell them to the captain at a bottle of brandy apiece.   The offer was tempting.   Ledoux remembered that at the representation of " The Sicilian Vespers," at Nantes, he had seen a good number of big fat men enter a pit that was already full, and yet succeed in finding sitting room, by virtue of the compressibility of the human body.   He took the twenty slenderest slaves of the thirty.

Then Tamango asked only a glass of brandy apiece for the ten who were left.   Ledoux remembered that in public conveyances children only pay for and only occupy half places.   He accordingly took three children, but declared that he had no mind to burden himself with a single other black.   Tamango, seeing that he had still seven slaves on his hands, took his gun, and aimed at the woman who came first : she was the mother of the three children.

" Buy, or I kill her," he said to the white ; " a little glass of brandy, or I fire."

" And what the devil do you want me to do with her ? " asked Ledoux.

Tamango fired, and the slave fell dead on the ground.

" Another ! " cried Tamango, aiming at a broken-down old man ; " a glass of brandy, or else . . ."

One of his wives pulled his arm aside, and the shot went at random.   She had just recognised, in the old man her husband was about to kill, a *guru*, or magician, who had foretold that she was to be Queen.

Tamango, infuriated with the brandy, was beside himself when he saw his wishes opposed.   He struck his wife roughly with the butt of his gun ; then, turning to Ledoux :

" See here," he said, " I give you this woman."

She was pretty.   Ledoux looked at her smiling, and took her by the hand.

" I shall find a place to put her," said he.

The interpreter was a humane man.   He gave Tamango a cardboard snuff-box, and asked for the six slaves who were left.   He freed them from their forks, and let them go where they thought fit.   They immediately made off, some this way, some that, not knowing in the least how they were to get back to their country, two hundred leagues from the coast.

Meanwhile the captain said good-bye to Tamango, and busied himself in getting his cargo as quickly as possible on board.   It was imprudent to stay long up river ; the cruisers might reappear, and he meant to set sail the next day.   As for Tamango, he lay down on the grass in the shade, to sleep off the effects of the brandy.

When he awoke, the vessel was already under sail, and going down the river.   Tamango, whose head was still muddled by the debauch of the day before, asked for his wife, Ayché. They told him she had had the misfortune to displease him, and that he had given her as a present to the white captain, who had taken her on board. Tamango, stupefied at this news, smote his head, then took his gun, and, since the river made several turns before emptying itself in the sea, ran by the shortest road to a little bay half a league from the mouth. There he hoped to find a canoe in which he could overtake the brig, whose voyage would be retarded by the twistings of the river. He was not mistaken ; he had just time to throw himself into a canoe and join the slave-ship.

Ledoux was surprised to see him, and still more so to hear him ask for the return of his wife.

" A thing once given is not to be taken back," he replied.

And he turned his back on him.

The black insisted, offering to give back some of the things he had had in exchange for the slaves. The captain broke into a laugh, and said that Ayché was a very good woman, and that he meant to keep her. At this poor Tamango wept floods of tears, and uttered cries of misery as piercing as those of a poor wretch under a surgical operation. One minute he was running about the deck calling for his beloved Ayché, and the next he was beating his head on the planks as if to kill himself. Unmoved throughout, the captain, pointing to the land, made signs that it was time for him to leave. Tamango persisted. He offered even his golden epaulettes, his gun, and his sabre. All was in vain.

During this discussion, the lieutenant of the *Esperance* said to the captain :

" We lost three slaves last night, so we have some room. Why not take this sturdy rogue, who is worth in himself alone more than the three who are dead ? " Ledoux reflected that Tamango would sell for a good thousand crowns ; that this voyage, which seemed likely to be very profitable, would probably be his last ; and that, finally, since his fortune was made and he was giving up the slave-trade, it did not much matter to him whether he left a good or evil reputation on the coast of Guinea. Besides, there was absolutely no one on the shore, and the African warrior was entirely at his mercy. All that had to be done was to remove his weapons ; for it would have been dangerous to lay a hand on him while they were still in his possession. Ledoux accordingly asked for his gun, as if to examine it, and make sure it was worth as much as the beautiful Ayché. In testing the triggers, he was careful to let the powder fall from the priming. The lieutenant, for his part, got possession of the sabre ; and, when Tamango had been thus disarmed, two strong sailors flung themselves upon him, knocked him down, and proceeded to bind him. The black's resistance was heroic.

Recovering from his first surprise, he made a long struggle with

the two sailors, in spite of the disadvantages of his position. Thanks
to his prodigious strength, he succeeded in getting to his feet. With
a blow of the fist he grounded the man who was holding him by the
neck ; he left a bit of his coat in the hand of the other sailor, and
rushed like a madman at the lieutenant to snatch away his sabre.
The lieutenant struck him on the head with it, and gave him a large
wound, though not very deep. Tamango fell a second time. They
instantly bound him securely, hand and foot. While he was
struggling, he uttered cries of rage, and flung himself about like a
wild boar taken in the nets ; but, when he saw that all resistance
was useless, he shut his eyes, and did not make another movement.
His powerful, rapid breathing was the only sign that he was still
alive.

" My word ! " cried Captain Ledoux, " the blacks he sold will
have a good laugh when they see him a slave in his turn. They will
see by this there is a Providence above."

Meanwhile poor Tamango was bleeding to death. The charitable
interpreter, who had saved the lives of six slaves the day before,
came up to him, bound his wound, and gave him a few words of
consolation. I do not know what he could say to him. The black
remained motionless as a corpse. Two sailors had to carry him below
like a package, to the place that was to be his. For two days he
would neither eat nor drink ; he was scarcely seen to open his eyes.
His comrades in captivity, lately his prisoners, saw his appearance
in their midst with dull astonishment. Such was the fear with
which he still inspired them, that not one of them dared to jeer at
the misery of him who had caused their own.

Favoured with a good wind from the land, the vessel speedily
slipped away from the African coast. Free already from anxiety
about the English cruisers, the captain no longer thought of anything but the enormous profits awaiting him in the colonies towards
which he was making his way. His ebony wood was keeping sound.
No contagious diseases. Only twelve niggers, and they of the
feeblest, had died from heat ; a mere bagatelle. He took the
precaution of making all his slaves come on deck every day, so that
his human cargo should suffer as little as possible from the fatigues
of the voyage. Turn by turn, a third of the poor wretches had an
hour in which to take in their provision of air for the whole day.
A part of the crew, armed to the teeth, mounted guard over them
for fear of a revolt ; care was taken besides never entirely to remove
their irons. Sometimes a sailor, who knew how to play the fiddle,
regaled them with a concert. It was odd then to see all those black
figures turn towards the musician, lose by degrees their expression
of dull despair, burst into laughter, and (when their chains allowed
them) clap their hands. Exercise is necessary for health ; and so
another of the salutary practices of Captain Ledoux was to set his

slaves frequently dancing, as one makes horses prance, when they are on board ship for a long voyage.

" Now then, my children, dance, be happy," thundered the captain, cracking an enormous coach-whip.

And immediately the poor blacks leapt and danced.

Tamango's wound kept him below hatches for some time. He appeared at last on deck ; and first, proudly lifting his head in the midst of the timorous crowd of slaves, he threw a glance, sad but calm, over the immense stretch of water surrounding the boat ; then he lay down, or rather let himself fall on the deck, without even caring to arrange his irons so as to be as little uncomfortable as possible. Ledoux was seated on the quarter-deck, tranquilly smoking his pipe. Ayché, without irons, dressed in an elegant robe of blue cotton, her feet in pretty morocco-leather slippers, was carrying a tray of liqueurs in her hand, ready to pour him out a drink. It was clear that she held a high position in the captain's service. A black, who detested Tamango, signed to him to look in that direction. Tamango turned, saw her, uttered a cry, and, leaping up, ran towards the quarter-deck before the sailors on guard could prevent so enormous a breach of naval discipline.

" Ayché ! " he thundered, and Ayché screamed with terror. " Do you believe there is no MAMA-JUMBO in the country of the white men ? "

The sailors were already running up with lifted clubs ; but Tamango folded his arms, and, as if indifferent, went quietly back to his place, while Ayché, bursting into tears, seemed petrified by the mysterious words.

The interpreter explained what was this terrible Mama-Jumbo, whose mere name produced such terror.

" It is the nigger's Bogey Man," he said. " When a husband is afraid lest his wife should do what plenty of wives do in France as well as in Africa, he threatens her with Mama-Jumbo. I have seen Mama-Jumbo myself, and fathomed the trick ; but the blacks . . . the blacks are such fools they understand nothing. Imagine that one evening, while the women are amusing themselves with a dance, a *folgar*, as they call it in their gibberish, suddenly a strange music is heard, coming from a little wood, very thick and very dark. They see no one to make it ; all the musicians are hidden in the wood. There are reed flutes, and wooden tabours, *balafos*, and guitars made from the halves of gourds. They are all playing a tune to bring the devil on earth. The women no sooner hear that tune than they start trembling ; they would make off, but their husbands hold them back : they know well what is coming next. All at once there comes out of the wood a great white figure as high as our topmast, with a head as big as a bushel measure, eyes as large as hawse-holes, and a mouth like the devil's, with fire inside. The thing walks slowly,

slowly ; and it never goes more than half a cable's length from the wood. The women cry :

" ' Behold Mama-Jumbo ! '

" They bawl like oyster-women. Then their husbands say :

" ' Now then, you jades, tell us if you have behaved yourselves ; if you lie, there is Mama-Jumbo to eat you all raw."

" There are some who are foolish enough to confess, and then their husbands beat them to a jelly."

" And so what was this white figure, this Mama-Jumbo ? " the captain asked.

" Oh, it was a wag muffled up in a big white sheet, carrying, instead of a head, a hollowed pumpkin furnished with a lighted candle, on the end of a long pole. It was nothing more cunning than that, but it needs no great expense of cleverness to deceive the blacks. With all that, the Mama-Jumbo is a good invention, and I wish my wife believed in it."

" As for mine," said Ledoux, " if she is not frightened of Mama-Jumbo, she is afraid of Martin-Rod ; and she knows, too, how I would give it her if she played me some trick. We are not long-suffering in the family of Ledoux, and although I have only one hand left, it still makes pretty good play with a rope's end. As for your joker down there, who talks of Mama-Jumbo, tell him to behave himself, and not frighten this little woman here, or I will have his back so flayed that his hide will no longer be black, but as red as a raw beefsteak."

With these words the captain went down to his cabin, summoned Ayché, and tried to console her : but neither caresses, nor even blows, for one loses patience at last, could bring the beautiful negress to reason ; she wept floods of tears. The captain went on deck again in a bad temper, and scolded the officer of the watch over the manœuvre he was ordering at the time.

That night, when almost all the crew were fast asleep, the men of the watch heard first a low song, solemn, lugubrious, coming from the 'tween decks, and then a woman's scream, horribly piercing. Immediately afterwards the coarse voice of Captain Ledoux, swearing and threatening, and the noise of his terrible whip resounded throughout the ship. An instant later, all was silent again. The next day Tamango appeared on deck with a scarred face, but an air as proud, as resolute as before.

Ayché had no sooner seen him than, leaving the quarter-deck, where she was sitting beside the captain, she ran swiftly to Tamango, knelt before him, and said in accents of utter despair :

" Forgive me, Tamango, forgive me ! "

Tamango watched her fixedly for a minute ; then, noticing that the interpreter was some way off :

" A file ! " he said.

And he lay down on the deck, turning his back on Ayché. The captain scolded her sharply, even gave her a blow or two, and forbade her to speak to her ex-husband; but he was far from suspecting the meaning of the short words they had exchanged, and asked no questions on the subject.

Meanwhile Tamango, shut up with the other slaves, exhorted them night and day to make a generous attempt to regain their liberty. He spoke to them of the small numbers of the white men, and pointed out the continually increasing carelessness of their guards; then, without explaining himself exactly, he said that he would know how to take them back to their country, boasted his knowledge in the occult sciences, with which the blacks are much taken up, and threatened with the vengeance of the devil those who should refuse to help him in his scheme. In his harangues he used only the Berber dialect, known to the greater part of the slaves, but not understood by the interpreter. The reputation of the orator, the habit the slaves were in of fearing and obeying him, came marvellously to the aid of his eloquence, and the blacks begged him to fix a day for their deliverance long before he himself believed he was in a position to effect it.

He replied vaguely to the conspirators that the time was not come, and that the devil, who was appearing to him in his dreams, had not yet warned him, but that they should hold themselves in readiness for the first signal. However, he lost no opportunity of experimenting on the watchfulness of his guards. On one occasion, a sailor, leaving his gun leaning on the parapet, was amusing himself by watching a troop of flying-fish that were following the vessel; Tamango took the gun and began to handle it, copying with grotesque gesture the movements he had seen made by soldiers at drill. The gun was taken from him after an instant; but he had learnt that he could touch a weapon without awaking immediate suspicion; and, when the time should come for making use of one, he would be a bold man who should try to wrest it from his hands.

One day Ayché threw him a biscuit, making him a signal that he alone understood. The biscuit contained a little file; on this instrument depended the success of the conspiracy. Tamango was very careful at first not to show the file to his companions; but, when night was come, he began to murmur unintelligible words that he accompanied with bizarre gestures. He grew by degrees so excited as to cry aloud. To hear the varied intonations of his voice, one would have said he was engaged in a lively conversation with an invisible person. The slaves all trembled, not doubting but that the devil was at that very moment in the midst of them. Tamango put an end to the scene with a cry of joy.

"Comrades," said he, "the spirit I have conjured up has at last given me what he had promised, and I have in my hand the instrument of our deliverance. Now you need nothing but a little courage to set yourselves at liberty.''

He made those who were near him touch the file, and the imposture, stupid as it was, found credence among men still stupider.

After long expectation the great day of vengeance and liberty arrived. The conspirators, bound to each other by a solemn oath, had settled their plan after mature deliberation. The most determined, with Tamango at their head, when it was their turn to go on deck, were to possess themselves of the weapons of the guards ; others were to go to the captain's cabin and get hold of the guns that were stored there. Those who had succeeded in filing their irons were to commence the attack ; but, in spite of the stubborn work of many nights, the greater number of slaves were still unable to take an active part in the engagement. Accordingly, three sturdy blacks had been entrusted with the killing of the man who carried the manacle-key in his pocket, after which they were to go instantly and free their chained companions.

On that day Captain Ledoux was in a delightful temper ; contrary to his usual practice, he pardoned a ship's boy who had deserved a thrashing. He complimented the officer of the watch on his navigation, told the crew he was pleased with them, and announced that at Martinique, where they would shortly arrive, each man was to receive a bonus. All the sailors, full of agreeable ideas, were mentally planning the spending of this gratuity. They were thinking of brandy and the coloured women of Martinique, when Tamango and the other conspirators were made to come on deck.

They had been careful so to file their irons that they should not seem severed, and yet that the slightest effort should suffice to break them. Besides, they made such a jingling with them that any one who heard them would have said they were carrying a double weight. After taking breaths of air for some time, they joined hands and danced, while Tamango chanted the war-song of his family, that he sang in other times before going into battle. When the dance had gone on for some time Tamango, as if overcome by fatigue, lay down full length at the feet of a sailor who was carelessly leaning on the parapet of the ship ; all the conspirators did the same. In this way each sailor was surrounded by several blacks.

All at once, as soon as he had noiselessly broken his irons, Tamango loosed a great shout that was to serve as a signal, seized the sailor who was close to him violently by the legs, upset him, and putting a foot on his stomach, wrested his gun from him, and made use of it to kill the officer of the watch. Simultaneously each sailor of the watch was assailed, disarmed, and instantly slaughtered. A war-cry rose throughout the ship. The boat-swain, who had the key of the irons, was one of the first to fall. Then a crowd of blacks poured out on the decks. Those who could not find weapons seized the capstan bars, or the oars of the sloop. From that moment the crew of Europeans was lost. However, a few sailors rallied on the quarter-deck; but they lacked arms and resolution.

Ledoux was still alive and had lost none of his courage. Observing that Tamango was the soul of the conspiracy, he thought that if he could kill him he could make quick work of his accomplices. He accordingly ran to meet him, sabre in hand, calling him with loud shouts. Tamango instantly rushed upon him. He held a gun by the end of the barrel, and was using it like a club. The two leaders met on one of the gangways, a narrow passage communicating between the forecastle and the after-deck. Tamango struck the first blow. The white avoided it by a nimble movement of the body. The butt struck the deck, and broke, and the shock was so violent that the gun escaped from Tamango's hands. He was defenceless, and Ledoux, with a smile of diabolic joy, prepared to run him through; but Tamango was as agile as his country's panthers. He threw himself into his adversary's arms, and gripped the hand with which he was holding the sabre. The one struggled to retain the weapon, the other to wrest it away. In this furious wrestle both fell; but the African was underneath. Undismayed, he squeezed his adversary with his full strength, and bit him in the throat with such violence that the blood spurted out as if under the teeth of a lion. The sabre slipped from the captain's weakening grip. Tamango seized it; then, getting up, his mouth all bloody, he drove it again and again through his already half-dead enemy.

The victory was no longer in suspense. The few sailors who were left tried to beg pity from the rebels; but all, even the interpreter, who had never done them any harm, were pitilessly massacred. The lieutenant died with honour. He had gone aft to one of those little cannon that turn on a pivot and are charged with grapeshot. He managed the gun with his left hand, and defended himself so well with a sword in his right that he brought round him a crowd of blacks. Then, pressing the trigger of the gun, he made a broad road paved with dead and dying, through the midst of the dense mass. An instant later he was cut to pieces.

When the corpse of the last white had been slashed and cut to pieces, and flung into the sea, the blacks, satiated with vengeance, looked up at the sails of the vessel, which, steadily filled by a fresh breeze, seemed to be still in the service of their oppressors, and taking the conquerors, in spite of their triumph, towards the land of slavery.

"Then nothing has been done," they thought bitterly. "Will that great fetish of the white men be willing to take us back to our country, we who have spilled the blood of his masters?"

Some said that Tamango would know how to make him obey. Tamango was instantly summoned with loud shouts.

He did not hurry to make his appearance. He was found standing in the poop cabin, resting one hand on the captain's bloody sabre, and absently offering the other to his wife Ayché, who was kissing it, kneeling before him. The joy of victory did not lessen a dark anxiety that was betrayed in his whole manner. Less clownish than the others, he better understood the difficulties of his position.

He appeared at last on deck, affecting a calm that he did not feel. Urged by a hundred confused voices to direct the course of the vessel, he went up to the helm with slow steps, as if to postpone for a little the moment that, for himself and for the others, was to decide the extent of his power.

In the whole vessel there was not one black, however stupid, who had not noticed the influence that a certain wheel and the box placed in front of it exercised on the movements of the ship; but there was always a great mystery for them in this mechanism. Tamango examined the compass for a long time, moving his lips, as though he were reading the characters he saw traced there; then he put his hand to his forehead and took the thoughtful attitude of a man making a mental calculation. All the blacks crowded round him, mouths gaping, eyes wide open, following his slightest gesture. At last, with the mixture of fear and hardihood that is given by ignorance, he gave a violent jerk to the steering wheel.

Like a generous courser rearing under the spur of an imprudent horseman, the good ship *Espérance* bounded over the waves at this unheard-of manœuvre. One would have said that in her indignation she wished to engulf herself and her ignorant pilot. The proper connection between the positions of the sails and the rudder being rudely broken, the vessel heeled over so violently that she seemed on the point of sinking. Her long yards were plunged in the sea. Many men were knocked down; some fell overboard. Presently the ship rose proudly from the surge, as if to make one more fight with destruction. The wind redoubled its force, and, all at once, with a horrible noise, the two masts fell, broken a few feet above the deck, covering the ship with wreckage and a heavy network of ropes.

The horrified negroes fled below the hatches, shrieking with terror; but, since the wind no longer found purchase, the vessel righted and abandoned herself to the gentle tossing of the waves. Then the more courageous of the blacks came again on the decks and cleared them of the wreckage that encumbered them. Tamango remained motionless, resting his elbow on the binnacle, hiding his face in his folded arms. Ayché was with him, but dared not say a word to him. Little by little the blacks came up to them ; a murmur rose, which presently changed into a storm of reproaches and insults.

" Traitor ! impostor ! " they cried, " you are the cause of all our misfortunes ; it was you who sold us to the white men, it was you who urged us to revolt against them. You had boasted to us of your knowledge, you had promised to take us back to our country. We believed you, fools that we were, and behold, we have all had a narrow escape from death because you offended the white man's fetish."

Tamango proudly lifted his head, and the negroes about him shrank back afraid. He picked up two guns, signed to his wife to follow him, and walked towards the forepart of the vessel. There he made himself a rampart with empty casks and planks ; he settled himself in this species of entrenchment, from which protruded the menacing bayonets of his two guns. They left him in peace. Among the rebels, some were weeping ; others, raising their hands to heaven, invoked their fetishes and those of the white men ; some, on their knees before the compass, whose perpetual motion was a marvel to them, prayed to it to take them to their country ; some lay in gloomy dejection on the deck. In the midst of these despairing men should be pictured women and children howling with fright, and a score of wounded begging the help that no one thought of giving them.

Suddenly a nigger appeared on the deck, his face radiant. He announced that he had just found the place where the white men kept their brandy ; his joy and his manner were a sufficient proof that he had that moment tried it. This news suspended for the moment the poor wretches' cries. They ran to the storeroom and glutted themselves with liquor. An hour later they were to be seen leaping and laughing on the deck, abandoning themselves to all the extravagances of the most brutal drunkenness. Their dances and songs were accompanied by the groans and sobs of the wounded. In this way passed the rest of the day and all the night.

In the morning, on waking up, fresh despair. A great number of wounded had died during the night. The ship was surrounded by floating corpses. The sea was rough and the sky clouded. A council was held. Some novices in the magic art, who had not dared to speak of their knowledge before Tamango, offered their services one after another. Each vain attempt added to their discouragement. At last they spoke again of Tamango, who had not yet left his barricade. After all he was the wisest amongst them, and he alone could take them from the horrible situation in which he had placed them. An old man approached him with offers of peace. He begged him to come and give his advice ; but Tamango, stern as Coriolanus, was deaf to his prayers. At night, in the midst of the disorder, he had provided himself with biscuits and salt meat. He seemed determined to live alone in his retreat.

There was still the brandy. That at least gives forgetfulness of the sea, slavery, and approaching death. One sleeps, and dreams of Africa, and sees the gum-tree forests, the straw-covered huts, and the baobabs, whose shade covers a whole village. The orgy of the day before began again. In this way many days went by. Their life was made up of shrieking and groaning and tearing their hair, and then getting drunk and sleeping. Many died of drink ; some flung themselves in the sea, or stabbed themselves to death.

One morning Tamango left his stronghold, and came as far as the stump of the mainmast.

"Slaves," said he, "the Spirit has appeared unto me in a dream, and revealed the means of taking you hence and bringing you back to your country. Your ingratitude should make me abandon you ; but I have pity on the cries of these women and children. I forgive you : listen to me."

All the blacks bent their heads respectfully, and gathered round him.

"The whites," Tamango went on, "alone know the words of power that move these big houses of wood ; but we can guide as we will these light boats that are not unlike those of our own country."

He pointed to the sloop and the other boats of the brig.

"Let us fill them with food, embark, and row with the wind ; my Master and yours will make it blow towards our country."

They believed him. Never was project more insane. Ignorant of the use of the compass, under an unfamiliar sky, he could do nothing but wander at random. According to his notions, he imagined that if he rowed straight ahead, he would reach at least some land inhabited by black men, for the black men possess the earth, and the white men live in their ships. He had heard his mother say that.

Soon all was ready for the embarkation ; but the sloop and one small boat were all that were fit for use. There was not enough room for the eighty negroes still alive. They had to abandon all the wounded and sick. The greater number of these asked them to kill them before leaving.

The two boats, launched with infinite difficulty, and laden beyond measure, left the ship in a choppy sea that threatened to swamp them every moment. The little boat got away first. Tamango and Ayché had taken their places in the sloop, which, heavier built and laden, lagged considerably behind. They could still hear the plaintive cries of some poor wretches left on board the brig, when a fair-sized wave took the sloop broadside on, and filled her with water. The little boat saw their disaster, and her rowers redoubled their efforts, for fear of having to pick up some of the wrecked. Almost all in the sloop were drowned. A dozen only were able to regain the vessel. Of this number were Tamango and Ayché. When the sun set, they saw the small boat disappear below the horizon ; but no one knows what became of it.

Why should I weary the reader with a disgusting description of the tortures of hunger ? About twenty persons in a small space, now tossed by a stormy sea, now roasted by a burning sun, quarrel day by day over the scanty remains of their provisions. Each scrap of biscuit costs a battle, and the weak die, not because the strong kill them, but because they leave them to their death. At the end of a few days there was no longer a living thing on the brig *Esperance* but Tamango and his wife Ayché.

. . . .

One night the sea was rough, the wind blew, and the darkness was such that one could not see the prow of the vessel from the poop. Ayché was lying on a mattress in the captain's cabin, and Tamango was sitting at her feet. For a long time there had been silence between them.

" Tamango," said Ayché at last, " all that you suffer, you suffer because of me."

" I do not suffer," he answered bluntly, and threw on the mattress, besides his wife, the half biscuit that remained to him.

" Keep it for yourself," she said, gently refusing the biscuit ; " I am not hungry any more. Besides, why eat ? Is not my hour come ? "

Tamango got up without reply, went tottering on deck, and sat down at the foot of a broken mast. With his head bowed on his breast, he whistled the song of his family. Suddenly a great shout sounded through the noise of wind and sea. A light appeared. He heard other shouts and a big black vessel slipped swiftly by his own ; so near that the yards passed over his head. He saw only two faces lit by a lantern hung from a mast. These men shouted once again before their ship, carried along by the wind, disappeared into the darkness. Undoubtedly the look-out men had seen the wrecked vessel ; but the storm prevented them from tacking about. The next day there was not a sail on the horizon. Tamango lay down on his mattress and closed his eyes. His wife Ayché had died that night.

. . . .

I do not know how long afterwards an English frigate, the *Bellona*, sighted a ship, dismasted and apparently deserted by her crew. When a sloop was sent alongside, there was found a dead negress and a nigger so fleshless and emaciated that he was like a mummy. He was unconscious, but had still a breath of life. The surgeon took him in hand and nursed him, and when the *Bellona* reached Kingstown, Tamango was in perfect health. They asked him for his story. He told them what he knew of it. The planters of the island wanted him hanged as a rebel negro ; but the governor, who was a humane man, interested himself in him, and found his actions justifiable, since after all he had only exerted the legitimate right of self-defence ; and since those he had killed were only Frenchmen. They gave him his liberty, that is to say, set him to work for the Government ; but he had six sous a day and his food. He was a very fine-looking man. The colonel of the 75th saw him, and took him to make a cymbal-player of him in the regimental band. He learnt a little English ; but he scarcely spoke. Instead he drank rum and grog in inordinate quantities. He died in hospital of inflammation of the lungs.

THE BLUE ROOM

Prosper Mérimée

A young man was walking with an agitated air about the railway station. He had blue glasses, and although he had not a cold in his head, he kept putting his handkerchief to his nose. In his left hand he held a little black bag, containing, as I learnt later, a silk dressing-gown and some Turkish trousers.

From time to time he went to the entrance and looked up and down the street ; then he drew out his watch and studied the timetable. It was an hour before the train went ; but there are some folk who are always afraid of being late. The train was not one of those that busy people take—few first class carriages. And the hour it went was not that which allows business men to leave as soon as their work is done, and arrive in time for dinner at their country-houses. When the passengers began to show themselves, a Parisian would have seen by their air that they were farmers or little traders of the suburbs.

Still, each time any one entered the station, each time a cab stopped at the gate, the heart of the young man in blue glasses swelled out like a balloon ; his knees trembled ; his bag almost fell from his hand ; and his glasses nearly tumbled from his nose, on which, it might be said in passing, they were placed wrong side round.

It was still worse when, after a long wait, there appeared through a side door, coming precisely from the only point that was not subjected to continual observation, a woman clad in black, with a thick veil over her face, holding in her hand a bag of brown morocco, containing, as I afterwards discovered, a wonderful dressing-gown and a pair of blue satin slippers. The woman and the young man came towards each other, looking to the right and the left, but never before them. They came together, touched hands, and stayed for some minutes without saying a word panting, trembling, overcome by one of those poignant emotions, for which I would give a hundred years of philosophic meditations.

"Léon," said the young woman—I have forgotten to say she was young and pretty—" Léon, what happinesss! Never should I have known you in those blue glasses! "

"What joy! " said Léon. " I should have never recognised you under that black veil! "

"What joy! " she continued. "Let us get our seats quick. If the train started without us! . . . (And she squeezed his arm.) Nobody guesses what is happening. At this moment I am with Clara and her husband, going to their country-house, where I ought to-morrow to say good-bye! . . . And," she added laughing and lowering her head, " it is just an hour since I went away with Clara, and to-morrow, . . . after having passed the last evening with her . . . (again she squeezed his arm), to-morrow, in the morning, she will leave me at the station, where I shall find Ursule, whom I have sent on ahead at my aunt's. . . . Oh! I have thought out everything! Let us get our tickets. . . . It is impossible we should be found out! Oh! If they want to know our names at the end? I have already forgotten. . . ."

"Monsieur and Madame Duru."

"No! not Duru. There was a shoemaker at the boarding-school with that name."

"Then, Dumont? . . ."

"Daumont! "

"Very well! But they will not question us! "

A bell rang, the door of the waiting-room opened, and the young woman, always carefully veiled, darted into a carriage with her young companion. For the second time the bell rang, a porter shut the door of their compartment.

"We are alone! " they cried joyfully.

But at that very moment a man of about fifty, dressed all in black, with a broad serious face, entered the carriage and settled down in a corner. The engine whistled and the train set off. The young couple, withdrawing as far as they could from their inconvenient neighbour, began to talk in whispers, and, as an extra precaution, in English.

" Sir," said the other passenger, in the same language and with a much purer English accent, " if you want to talk secrets, you had better not use English before me. I am an Englishman. Sorry to trouble you ; but in the other compartment there was only one man, and as a matter of principle I never travel with a single man. He looked to me like a Judas. And this might have tempted him."

He pointed to his travelling-bag that he had thrown on a cushion before him.

" If I can't sleep, I will read."

And he did loyally try to sleep. Opening his bag, he took out a travelling-cap, put it on his head, and kept his eyes shut for some minutes. Then opening them with a movement of impatience, he groped in his bag for spectacles, then for a Greek book. At last he began to read very attentively. In getting the book out of the bag he had overturned many things, all thrown in anyhow. Among other articles he drew out was a pretty thick bundle of Bank of England notes, placed them on the seat in front of him, and before putting them back in the bag he showed them to the young man and asked him if he could change bank-notes at a certain town.

" Probably. It is on the way to England," said Léon.

It was to this town that the young couple were going. There is a little hotel there, fairly clean, where travellers usually stay only on Saturday evening. It is pretended that the rooms are good ; but the landlord and his servants are not far enough removed from Paris to keep a really good inn. Léon had come across the place some time before, when he was not wearing blue glasses, and after the account he gave of it, his sweetheart felt she would like to see it.

Besides, on this day, she was in such a frame of mind that the walls of a prison would have seemed to her full of charm if she had been shut in there with Léon. However, the train went on, the Englishman read his Greek without turning to look at his companions, who chatted in such whispers that only lovers could have understood. Perhaps I shall not surprise my readers by admitting that they were eloping lovers. And what was really deplorable was that they were not married, and there were great difficulties in the way of their marriage.

They reached their stopping-place. The Englishman was the first to alight. While Léon was helping his sweetheart to get out of the carriage without showing her ankles, a man darted from a neighbouring compartment on to the platform. He was pale, even yellow, with sunken, bloodshot eyes and a straggling beard— quite a criminal in appearance. His suit was clean but thread-worn. His frock-coat once black, now grey at the elbows and at the back, was buttoned to the chin, probably to hide a waistcoat still shabbier. He came up to the Englishman, and in a very humble voice :

" Uncle ! " he said to him.

" Leave me alone, you wretch," cried the Englishman, his grey eye lighting up with anger, as he began to walk out of the station.

" Don't drive me to despair," said the other man, in a tone at once sorrowful and threatening.

" Will you be good enough to look after my bag a moment ? " said the old Englishman, throwing his bag at the feet of Léon.

Seizing the arm of the man who had accosted him, he pushed him in a corner, where he hoped he would not be overheard, and there he spoke to him for a moment in a very harsh voice. Then, taking from his pocket some papers, he put them in the hand of the man who had called him uncle. The man took the papers without any thanks, and almost at once went away and disappeared.

There is only one hotel in the town, so you must not be astonished that, at the end of a few minutes, all the characters in this truthful tale met again there. In France every traveller who has the luck to have a well-dressed woman on his arm is sure of obtaining the best room in all the hotel : thus is it established that we are the most polished nation in Europe.

If the room given to Léon was the best, it would be rash to conclude that it was excellent. There was a great wooden bed, with curtains of chintz, on which was printed in violet the magical story of Pyramus and Thisbe. The walls were covered with a painted paper representing a view of Naples, and crowded with figures. Unhappily, idle and indiscreet travellers had added moustaches and pipes to all the figures, male and female ; and many foolish remarks in prose and verse were written in pencil on the sky and on the sea. Against this background hung several engravings : *Louis Philippe swearing to the Charta of* 1830 ; *The First Meeting of Julie and Saint Preux ;* the *Regrets* and the *Hope of Happiness* after Dubuffe. This room was called the Blue Room, because the two arm-chairs to the right and left of the fire-place were in Dutch velvet of this colour. But for many years past they had been hidden under coverings of grey, glazed cloth with amaranth frills.

While the maids of the hotel gathered round the young lady and offered her their services, Léon, who was not wanting in good sense, even when in love, went to the kitchen to order dinner. He had to use all his eloquence and resort to bribery to get the promise of a private dinner ; but greatly was he disconcerted when he learnt that in the big dining-room adjoining the Blue Room the officers of the 3rd Hussars, who were about to relieve the officers of the 3rd Light Infantry, were joining the latter that very day in a farewell dinner that would take place with much cordiality.

The landlord swore by all his gods that, apart from the gaiety natural to all French soldiers, the Hussars and the Light Infantry were noted in the town for their gentleness and their good conduct, and that their presence would not inconvenience Madame in the least, the custom of the officers being to end the dinner before midnight.

As Léon went back to the Blue Room, worried over this affair, he saw that the old Englishman had taken the room next to his. The door was open. The Englishman, sitting before a table on which were placed a glass and a bottle, looked at the ceiling with deep attention, as though he were counting the flies that were walking there.

"What does it matter who our neighbours are?" said Léon to himself. "The Englishman will soon be drunk, and the soldiers will have gone away before midnight."

In entering the Blue Room his first care was to make sure that the communicating doors were properly closed and locked. On the side of the Englishman there was a double door; the wall was thick. On the side of the Hussars the partition was thinner; but the door had a lock and key. After all, it was a more effectual barrier against curiosity than the curtains of a cab are; and how many people think they are isolated from the world in a cab!

Certainly the richest imagination cannot picture a more complete happiness than that of two young lovers who, after long waiting, find themselves alone, far from the eyes of jealous and curious people, so that they can relate at leisure their bygone troubles and relish the delights of a perfect meeting. But the devil always finds some means of pouring his drop of bitterness into the cup of felicity. While eating a pretty poor dinner in the Blue Room, composed of some dishes stolen from the banquet of the officers, Léon and his lady had to suffer a good deal from the conversation that those gentlemen held in the neighbouring room. Their talk turned on matters that had nothing to do with strategy and tactics, and I cannot possibly report it.

It was a long string of coarse stories, accompanied by outbursts of laughter in which it was sometimes difficult for our lovers not to take part. Léon's sweetheart was not a prude, but there are some things a woman does not like to hear, even in company with the man she loves. The situation became more and more embarrassing; and when the officers were beginning their dessert, Léon went down to the kitchen to beg the landlord to tell the gentlemen there was a sick lady in the next room, and to ask them to have the politeness to make a little less noise.

The landlord, as always happens in army dinners, was quite flurried, and did not know what to say. For at the moment when Léon gave him the message for the officers, a waiter asked him for champagne for the Hussars, and a maid for a bottle of port for the Englishman.

" I told him we had no port," she added.

" You are a fool. I keep every kind of wine. I will find him his bottle of port ! Bring me a bottle of ratafia, a bottle of fifteen, and a decanter of brandy."

After having manufactured the port in a turn of the hand, the landlord entered the dining-room and gave the message from Léon. It first excited a furious storm. Then a bass voice, that dominated all the others, demanded what kind of woman they had for a neighbour.

" My faith, messieurs," said the landlord, " she is very pretty and she is very shy. Marie Jeanne says she has a wedding ring. So it may be a bride who has come here for her honeymoon, as they sometimes do."

" A bride ! " shouted forty voices. " She must come and drink with us. We will toast her health, and teach her husband his duties ! "

At these words there was a great clanking of spurs, and our couple trembled, thinking that their room was going to be taken by storm. But suddenly a voice stayed the movement. Evidently it was one of the chiefs that spoke. He reproached the officers with their impoliteness, and told them to sit down, and speak decently without shouting. Then he added some words in too low a voice to be heard in the Blue Room. They were received with deference, but not without exciting a certain restrained hilarity.

From this moment there was a comparative silence in the officers' room, and our loving pair blessed the salutary effects of discipline, and began to talk together with more ease. But after so much upset, it took some time to recover those tender emotions which anxieties, the fatigues of travelling, and above all the coarse merriment of their neighbours, had greatly troubled. At their age, however, the thing is not very difficult, and they soon forgot all the unpleasantness of their adventurous expedition, and began to think only of its pleasures.

They fancied they had made peace with the Hussars. Alas ! it was only a truce. The moment when they were least expecting it, when they were thousands of leagues away from this sublunary world, behold ! twenty-four bugles, sustained by several trombones, poured out the air known to French soldiers, " Ours is the victory ! " How could any one resist such a tempest ? The poor lovers were much to be pitied.

No, not very much. For in the end the officers came out of the dining-room, defiling before the door of the Blue Room with much clank of sabres and spurs, and shouting one after the other, " Good-night, madame, the bride."

Then all sound ceased. No, I am mistaken. The Englishman came out into the corridor and cried :

" Waiter, bring me another bottle of that same port ! "

Calmness settled at last on the little inn. The night was sweet, the moon at full. From time immemorial lovers have delighted to look at our satellite. Léon and his lady opened their window, that looked on a little garden, and breathed with joy the cool air, fragrant with the scent of clematis. They did not remain at the window very long. A man was walking in the garden, his head bowed, his arms crossed, a cigar in his mouth. Léon thought he recognised the nephew of the Englishman who loved the good wine of Portugal.

I hate useless details, and besides I am not obliged to tell the reader all that took place, hour by hour, in the inn. So I will only say that the candle, burning on the mantelpiece in the Blue Room, was more than half consumed, when, in the bedroom of the Englishman, hitherto silent, a strange noise was heard, such as a heavy body might produce in its fall. And with this noise there mingled a sort of cracking, not less strange, followed by a stifled cry and several indistinct words, resembling a curse. The young couple in the Blue Room were startled. Perhaps they had been aroused by the fall ; for on both of them the mysterious noise produced an almost sinister impression.

" It is our Englishman dreaming," said Léon, trying to smile. He wished to reassure his companion, but he shivered involuntarily. Two or three minutes afterwards, a door was opened in the corridor, very carefully it seemed, then it was shut very quietly. Some one could be heard walking slowly and uneasily, who, to all appearance, was trying to pass without being heard.

" What a cursed place ! " cried Léon.

" Ah, it is like heaven ! . . . " said the young lady, letting her head fall on Léon's shoulder. " I am so sleepy. . . ."

She sighed and fell asleep again almost at once. But Léon was worried, and his imagination began to dwell on several things that, in another frame of mind, he would have passed over. The sinister figure of the Englishman's nephew was recalled to his memory. There was hatred in the glance he gave his uncle, whilst speaking to him with humility, no doubt because he was asking for money. What could be easier than for a man, still young and vigorous, and desperate besides, to climb from the garden to the window of the next room ? . . . Moreover, he was staying in the inn, since he was walking in the garden at night. Perhaps . . . even probably . . . indubitably, he knew that there was a thick bundle of bank-notes in his uncle's bag. . . . And that heavy blow, like a club falling on a bald head ! . . . that stifled cry ! . . . that frightful oath, and then the creeping steps afterwards ! The nephew had the air of a murderer. . . . But a hotel full of officers is not a good place for a murderer. No doubt this Englishman, like a prudent man, had locked his door, especially knowing what sort of fellow was hanging about. He mistrusted him, since he did not want to go up to him with his bag in his hand. . . . But why think of such hideous things when you are so happy ?

That was what Léon said to himself. In the middle of his thoughts, which I refrain from analysing at length, and which came to him almost as confused as the visions of a dream, he had his eyes fixed mechanically on the communicating door between the Blue Room and the Englishman's room.

In France the doors do not shut well. Between this one and the floor there was an opening of nearly half an inch. Suddenly, through this opening, scarcely lighted by the reflection from the waxed floor, there appeared something blackish, flat, resembling the blade of a knife, for the edge, touched by the light from the candle, showed a thin brilliant line. This moved slowly in the direction of a little slipper of blue satin, thrown indiscreetly a little way from the door. Was it some insect like a centipede ? . . . No ; it was not an insect, it had no fixed shape. . . . Two or three brown trails, each with its line of light at the edge, penetrate into the Blue Room. Their movement quickens, owing to the slope of the floor ; they advance rapidly, and begin to touch the little slipper. No more doubt ! It is a liquid, and its colour can now be seen distinctly by the light of the candle—it is blood ! And while Léon, motionless, stared with horror at the frightful thing, the young lady slept on peacefully, and her regular breath warmed the neck and shoulder of the terrified man.

The care that Léon had taken to order dinner as soon as he arrived at the inn is sufficient to prove that he had a good head on his shoulders and was able to look ahead. He did not belie his character on this occasion. He made no movement, and all the force of his mind bent in an effort to come to some decision in the presence of the frightful misfortune that threatened him.

I imagine that most of my readers, and especially my lady readers, full themselves with the spirit of heroism, will blame Léon for his inactivity and his lack of courage. He ought, I shall be told, to have run to the Englishman's room and arrested the murderer. At the very least, he should have pulled his bell and aroused the people of the inn. To this I must answer, first, that in French inns the bell-rope is only an ornament in the bedrooms : there is no apparatus in metal attached to the other end of the cord. I will also add, respectfully but firmly, that, if it is wrong to let an Englishman die in the next room, it is not at all praiseworthy to sacrifice to an old foreigner the young and pretty woman who is sleeping with her head on your shoulder. What would have happened if Léon had shouted out and awakened everybody in the inn ? Gendarmes, a magistrate and his clerk would soon have arrived. Before asking him what he had seen or heard, these gentlemen are so inquisitive by profession that they would have started by asking Léon :

" What is your name ?   Where are your papers ?   And madame ? Why are you staying together in this Blue Room ?   You will both have to appear before the court of assize and give evidence that, on such a date, at such an hour at night, you have been witnesses to such and such things."

Now, it was precisely this idea of the magistrate and the police that first presented itself to the mind of Léon. There are some problems in life that are difficult to solve. Is it better to let an unknown foreigner be murdered, or lose and bring dishonour upon a beloved woman ?   Léon did what most men would have done in his place. He did not stir. With his eyes fixed on the blue slipper, and the little red stream that touched it, he remained for some time as though he was fascinated, while a cold sweat came on his forehead, and his heart beat in his breast enough to break it open. A crowd of horrible thoughts and odd images beset him, and an inner voice said to him every minute, " In an hour everything will be known, and it is your fault ! "   However, through continually asking himself, " Whatever shall I do in this affair ? " a man often ends by finding some rays of hope.

" If we leave this accursed hotel," said Léon to himself, " before they discover what has happened in the next room, perhaps we shall be able to cover up our traces. Nobody knows us here. They have only seen me in blue glasses, and they have never seen her without her veil. We are only two steps from the station, and in an hour we shall be far away from this town."

Then, as he had well studied the time-table in arranging his elopement, he remembered that a train to Paris passed at eight o'clock. Soon after that, he and his lady would be lost in the immensity of that city, that hides so many criminals. Who could there discover two innocent persons ?   But if any one entered the Englishman's room before eight o'clock ? All the problem was there.

Well convinced there was nothing else he could do, he made a desperate effort to shake off the drowsiness that had long been gaining on him. But at his first movement his companion awoke and kissed him. At the touch of his icy cheek she gave a little cry.

" What is the matter ? " she said anxiously. " Your forehead is like marble."

" It is nothing," he replied in a shaky voice. " I heard a noise in the next room."

Getting out of bed, he took the blue slipper away, and placed an armchair before the communicating door, so as to hide from his sweetheart the frightful stream which, having now ceased to spread, formed a large pool on the floor. Then he opened the door and

35

listened in the corridor. He even dared to try the door of the Englishman's room. It was locked. There was already some stir in the inn. The day was dawning. Some stablemen were grooming the horses in the yard, and, on the second floor, an officer was coming downstairs with clanking spurs. He was going to see that the horses were properly looked after.

Léon returned to the Blue Room, and, with circumlocutions and euphemisms, and all the precautions that love could suggest, he told his lady in what situation they were.

It was dangerous to remain, and dangerous to go too soon, and still more dangerous to wait in the inn until the discovery was made in the next room. It is useless to describe the fright caused by this information; the tears that followed it; the wild proposals that were made; how many times the two unhappy creatures threw themselves in each others arms, saying, " Pardon me ! " " Pardon me ! " Each blamed themselves. They promised to die together ; for the young lady was sure they would be found guilty of the murder of the Englishman ; and as they were not certain they would be permitted to kiss on the scaffold, they stifled each other with embraces, and watered each other with their tears.

At last, having said many absurdities and many loving things, they recognised, in the midst of a thousand kisses, that Léon's plan of departing by the eight o'clock train was the only practical one. But there were still two mortal hours to pass. At each step in the corridor they trembled in all their limbs. Each squeak of a boot announced to them the arrival of the police. Their little luggage was packed in the twinkling of an eye. The young lady wished to burn the blue slipper in the fire-place, but Léon took it and after wiping it on the under bedclothes, he kissed it, and put it in his pocket. He was surprised to find it had a vanilla fragrance : his lady liked the same perfume as the Empress Eugénie.

Already everybody was awake in the inn. They could hear the waiters laughing, the maids singing, the soldiers brushing the officers' clothes. Seven o'clock chimed. Léon wished to get his love to take a cup of coffee but she declared her throat was so tight that she would die if she tried to drink anything. Léon, putting on his blue glasses, went down to pay his bill. The landlord begged his pardon for the noise that had been made. He still could not understand it, for the officers were always so quiet. Léon assured him he had heard nothing, and had slept excellently.

" Now your neighbour in the other room," continued the landlord, " cannot have inconvenienced you, for he has not made much noise. I wager he is still sleeping like the dead."

Léon leant heavily against the desk to prevent himself from falling, and his lady, who had resolved to come with him, clutched his arm, pressing her veil over her eyes.

"It is an English lord," went on the landlord pitilessly. "He always wants the best of everything. Ah, he is a gentleman ! But all the English are not like him. There is another here who is a mean rascal. He finds everything too dear—the room and the dinner. He wanted me to give him a hundred and fifty francs for a Bank of England note of five pounds. But is it good ? Here, sir, you ought to know that, for I heard you speaking English with Madame. Is it a good one ? "

He held out a five pound bank-note. On one of the corners was a little red stain that Léon understood.

"I think it is quite good," he said in a strangled voice.

"Oh, you have plenty of time," continued the landlord. "The train is not due till eight o'clock, and it is always late. Won't you sit down, madame ? you seem tired."

At this moment a plump maid entered.

"Some warm water, quick," she said, " for the tea of milord ! Get a sponge also ! He has broken his bottle of port and all his room is flooded."

Léon let himself fall into a chair ; his companion did the same. A strong desire to laugh took them both, and they had some trouble not to give way. The young lady shook him joyfully by the hand.

"Decidedly," said Léon to the landlord, " we will not go till the afternoon. Prepare a really good lunch for us at twelve."

THE
GAME OF BACKGAMMON

Prosper Mérimée

THE motionless sails hung glued against the masts ; the sea was smooth as a mirror ; the heat was stifling, the calm hopeless. On a sea-voyage the means of entertainment at command of a vessel's guests are soon exhausted. People know each other too well after passing four months together in a wooden house of a hundred and twenty feet in length. When you see the first lieutenant approaching, you know at once that he will talk to you of Rio de Janeiro, where he has just been ; then of the famous Essling Bridge that he saw built by the Marine Guards, of whom he was one. At the end of a fortnight you know even the expressions he affects, the punctuations of his phrases, the different intonations of his voice. When has he ever neglected a melancholy pause after the first occurrence in his tale of the words " The Emperor " . . . ? " If you had see him then ! ! ! " (three points of exclamation) he invariably adds. And the episode of the trumpeter's horse, and the cannon-ball that ricochetted and carried away a cartridge-case with seven thousand five hundred francs' worth of gold and jewels, etc. etc. !—The second lieutenant is a great politician ; he comments every day on the last number of the *Constitutionnel* that he brought away with him from Brest ; or, if he leave the sublimities of politics for a descent to literature, will regale you with the plot of the last vaudeville he saw played. Good heavens ! . . .

The Marine Commissioner had a very interesting story. How he delighted you the first time he described his escape from the hulks of Cadiz ! But, at the twentieth repetition, upon my honour, it was unbearable. And the ensigns, and the midshipmen ! The memory of their conversations makes the hair rise on my head. The captain is usually the least tiresome person on board. In his quality of autocrat he is in a state of secret hostility against his whole staff ; he annoys, and sometimes is oppressive ; but there is a certain pleasure in cursing at him. If he has a passion for scolding his subordinates, they have the pleasure of seeing their superior look ridiculous, and that is a consolation.

On the vessel in which I had embarked the officers were the best men in the world, all good fellows, friendly as brothers, but each one more tedious than the last. The captain was the mildest of men, and (an exception) no busybody. It was always with regret that he exerted his absolute authority. None the less the voyage seemed long to me, and especially this calm which overtook us when only a few days from sight of land . . . !

One day after dinner, that our enforced idleness had made us protract as long as was humanly possible, we were all assembled on the deck watching the monotonous but always majestic spectacle of a sunset over the sea. Some were smoking, others reading, for the twentieth time, one of the thirty volumes of our dreary library ; all were yawning till the tears came. An ensign, seated beside me, was amusing himself with all the gravity befitting a serious business, by dropping point downwards on the deck the dirk usually carried by marine officers in undress uniform.

It was an amusement of sorts, and it needed some skill to make the point stick quite perpendicularly in the wood. Wishing to imitate the ensign, and having no dirk of my own, I wanted to borrow the captain's, but he refused me. He was oddly fond of the weapon, and it would have annoyed him to see it serve for so futile an amuse-ment. The dirk had once belonged to a brave officer who had unfortunately died in the last war. . . . I guessed that a story was to follow, and was not mistaken. The captain began without waiting to be pressed ; as for the officers about us, since each one of them knew Lieutenant Roger's misfortunes by heart, they made an immediate and prudent retreat. Here is something like the captain's tale :—

Roger, when I met him, was my senior by three years ; he was a lieutenant, I an ensign. I assure you he was one of the best officers in our corps ; good-hearted too, witty, well educated, talented—in a word, a delightful young man. He was, unfortunately, a little proud and sensitive ; this was due, I think, to the fact that he was illegitmate, and that he feared lest his birth should lose him respect in society ; but, to tell the truth, of all his faults, the greatest was a violent and continual desire of standing first wherever he happened to be. His father, whom he had never seen, made him an allowance that would have been more than sufficient for his needs, if Roger had not been generosity itself. Everything he had was at the disposal of his friends. When he had just touched his quarter's money, he would say to any one who went to see him with a sad and careworn face, " Well, comrade, and what is the matter with you ? You don't seem able to make much of a noise when you slap your pockets ; come now, here is my purse, take what you want, and come and have dinner with me."

There came to Brest a young and very pretty actress called Gabrielle, who was not long in making her conquests among the naval and military officers. She was not a regular beauty, but she had a figure, fine eyes, a little foot, and a fairly saucy way with her ; and all that is very pleasing when one is in the latitude of twenty to twenty-five. It was said too that she was the most capricious creature of her sex, and her manner of playing did not give the lie to her reputation. One day she would play entrancingly, and one would have called her a *comédienne* of the first order ; the next, in the same piece, she would be cold, insensible, repeating her words like a child saying its catechism. What especially interested us young men was an anecdote current about her. It appeared that she had been kept in great magnificence in Paris by a senator, who, as they say, was mad on her. One day this man put his hat on in her presence ; she asked him to take it off, and even complained that he was lacking in respect for her. The senator laughed, shrugged his shoulders, and said, settling himself in a chair, " At least I can be at ease in the house of a woman I pay." A heavy blow, delivered by the white hand of Gabrielle, instantly paid him for his reply, and sent his hat to the other side of the room. Thenceforward complete rupture. Bankers and generals had made considerable offers to the lady ; but she had refused them all, and become an actress, in order, as she put it, to live in independence.

When Roger saw her and heard the story he decided that she was made for him, and, with the rather brutal frankness of which we sailors are accused, he took these means of showing her how deeply he was smitten by her charms. He bought the most beautiful and rarest flowers that he could find at Brest, made a bouquet of them that he tied with a fine pink ribbon, and very carefully arranged in the knot a roll of twenty-five napoleons ; it was all he possessed at the moment. I remember I went in the wings with him during an interval. He made Gabrielle a very short compliment on the grace with which she wore her dress, offered her the bouquet, and asked if he might come and see her at her house. All this was said in three words.

So long as Gabrielle only saw the flowers, and the handsome young man who presented them, she smiled on him, accompanying her smile with one of the most gracious of bows ; but when she had the bouquet in her hands, and felt the weight of the gold, her face changed more swiftly than the sea lifted by a tropical hurricane ; and certainly she was scarcely less malicious, for she threw the bouquet and the napoleons with all her strength at the head of my poor friend, who carried the marks on his face for over a week. The manager's bell sounded, and Gabrielle went on and played at random.

Roger picked up his bouquet and his roll of money with a very abashed air, went to a café to offer the bouquet (without the money) to the girl behind the bar, and tried, in drinking punch, to forget his cruel lady. He did not succeed ; and, in spite of the annoyance he felt at being unable to show himself with his black eye, he became madly amorous of the choleric Gabrielle. He wrote her twenty letters a day, and what letters ! submissive, tender, respectful— letters one could have sent to a princess. The first were sent back to him unopened ; the rest received no reply. Roger, however, kept up some hope, until we found that the orange-seller of the theatre was wrapping up his oranges in Roger's love-letters, given him, with refined malice, by Gabrielle. This was a terrible blow to our friend's pride. However, his passion did not weaken. He spoke of demanding the actress in marriage, and when told that the Minister of Marine would never give his consent, he declared he would blow out his brains.

While things were so, it happened that the officers of a line regiment, in garrison at Brest, wanted Gabrielle to repeat a vaude-ville couplet, which she refused from pure caprice. The officers and the actress were both so obstinate that the former hissed till the curtain was lowered, and the latter left the place. You know what the pit is like in a garrison town. It was agreed between the officers that the next day and the days following the culprit should be hissed without mercy, and that she should not be allowed to play a single part until she had apologised with sufficient humility to expiate her crime. Roger had not been present at this per-formance ; but he learnt the same evening of the scandal that had set the whole theatre in an uproar, and so of the projects of vengeance plotted for the morrow. His decision was instantly made.

The next day, when Gabrielle appeared, hoots and hisses enough to split the ears came from the officers' benches. Roger, who had placed himself purposely quite close to the brawlers, stood up and addressed the noisiest in terms so outrageous that all their anger was instantly turned upon himself. Then, with great sang-froid, he took his note-book from his pocket, and wrote down the names that were shouted to him from all sides ; he would have made appointments to do battle with the whole regiment, if a great number of naval officers had not interfered from *esprit de corps* and drawn challenges from the greater part of his adversaries. The tumult was truly terrific.

The whole garrison was confined for several days ; but, when we were again at liberty, there was a terrible account to settle. There were threescore of us on the field. Roger alone fought with three officers successively ; he killed one of them, and grievously wounded the other two, without receiving a scratch. I was less fortunate : a cursed lieutenant, who had been a fencing-master, gave me a great sword-thrust in the chest, from which I nearly died. That duel, or rather battle, was a fine spectacle, I assure you. The navy had the advantage throughout, and the regiment was obliged to leave Brest.

You may well think that our superior officers did not forget the author of the quarrel. For fifteen days there was a sentinel at his door.

When he was no longer under arrest, I left the hospital and went to see him. What was my surprise, on entering his quarters, to see him seated at lunch with Gabrielle. They looked as if they had had for some time a perfect understanding. Already they were calling each other " thou," and drinking out of the same glass. Roger presented me to his lady-love as his best friend, and told her how I had been wounded in the species of skirmish whose first cause had been herself. That brought me a kiss from the fair lady. This girl had altogether martial inclinations.

They spent three months together, perfectly happy, not separated for a moment. Gabrielle seemed madly in love with him, and Roger avowed that he had not known what love was before knowing Gabrielle.

A Dutch frigate came into the harbour. The officers gave us a dinner. We drank freely of all sorts of wine ; and, when the table had been cleared, not knowing what to do, for these gentlemen spoke very bad French, we began to play. The Dutchmen seemed to have plenty of money ; and their first lieutenant especially wished to play for stakes so high that not one of us cared to have a game with him. Roger, who did not usually play, thought it his business, this being so, to sustain the honour of his country. He played accordingly, and agreed to whatever the Dutch lieutenant proposed. He won at first, then lost. After some alternations of winning and losing, they separated without advantage on either side. We dined the Dutch officers in return. We played again. Roger and the lieutenant took up their battle. In short, during several days, they made appointments at the café or on board, trying all sorts of games, mostly backgammon, and always increasing their stakes, so that they came to be playing for twenty-five napoleons a game. It was a huge sum for poor officers like us: more than two months' pay! At the end of a week Roger had lost all the money he possessed, and three or four thousand francs borrowed right and left.

You are right in suspecting that Roger and Gabrielle had ended by setting up a common household and a common purse; that is to say, Roger, who had just touched a big share of prize-money, had contributed ten or twenty times as much as the actress. However, he always considered that this sum belonged principally to his lady, and he had kept only fifty napoleons for his personal expenses. He had had, none the less, to use this reserve in order to go on playing. Gabrielle did not make the slightest protest.

The household wealth went the same way as his pocket-money. Soon Roger was reduced to playing for his last twenty-five napoleons. He applied himself horribly; and the game was long and well fought. There came a moment when Roger, holding the dice-box, had but one chance to win; I think he needed the six four. The night was advanced. An officer who had watched their play for a long time had ended by falling asleep in a chair. The Dutchman was tired and sleepy; besides he had drunk a great deal of punch. Roger alone was well awake, and a prey to the most violent despair. He trembled as he threw the dice. He threw them so roughly on the board that the shock brought a candle to the floor. The Dutchman turned first towards the candle, that had just covered his new trousers with wax, and then looked at the dice. They showed six and four. Roger, pale as death, took the twenty-five napoleons. They went on playing. The luck became favourable to my unfortunate friend, who, however, made mistake after mistake, and played as if he wished to lose. The Dutch lieutenant grew wild, doubled, and tenfold increased the stakes; always he lost. I think I see him still; a big, phlegmatic blonde, with a face that seemed made of wax. He rose at last, after losing forty thousand francs, that he paid without his face betraying the slightest emotion.

Roger said:

"What we have done this evening does not count, you were half asleep; I do not want your money."

" You are joking," replied the stolid Dutchman ; " I played very well, but the dice have been against me. I am sure of being able to beat you always, and give you four holes (48 points). Good-night ! "

And he left him.

We learnt the next day that, made desperate by his losses, he had blown out his brains in his cabin, after drinking a bowl of punch.

The forty thousand francs won by Roger were spread on a table, and Gabrielle contemplated them with a smile of satisfaction.

" Behold us quite rich," said she ; "what shall we do with all this money ? "

Roger said nothing in reply ; he seemed stupefied since the Dutchman's death.

" We must do a thousand mad things," Gabrielle continued ; " money so easily gained must be spent in the same fashion. Let us buy a carriage and look down on the Maritime Prefect and his wife. I would like to have diamonds and Cashmeres. Ask for leave of absence, and let us go to Paris ; here we shall never come to the end of such a lot of money."

She stopped to look at Roger, who with his eyes fixed on the floor, resting his head in his hands, had not heard her, and seemed to be turning over in his mind the most sinister ideas.

" What the devil is the matter with you, Roger ? " she cried, putting a hand on his shoulder. " I believe you are sulky with me ; I cannot get a word from you."

" I am very unhappy," he said at last with a stifled sigh.

" Unhappy ! God forgive me, you are not feeling remorseful over plucking that fat *mynheer* ? "

He lifted his head and looked at her with haggard eyes.

" What does it matter ? " she pursued, " what does it matter that he took the thing tragically and blew out what few brains he had ? I do not pity players who lose ; and his money is certainly better in our hands than in his own ; he would have spent it in drinking and smoking, while we, we are going to commit a thousand extravagances, each one more elegant than the one before."

Roger walked up and down the room, his head bowed on his breast, his eyes half shut and filled with tears. You would have pitied him if you had seen him.

" Do you know," said Gabrielle, " that any one who did not know your romantic sensibilities might well believe you had cheated ? "

" And if that were the truth ? " he cried in a hollow voice, stopping before her.

" Bah ! " she answered, smiling, " you are not clever enough to cheat at play."

" Yes, I cheated, Gabrielle ; I cheated, like the wretch I am."

She knew from his emotion that what he said was only too true :

35*

she sat down on a sofa, and stayed some time without speaking.

" I would rather," she said at last in a voice deeply moved, " I would rather you had killed ten men than cheated at play."

There was a mortal silence for half an hour. The two of them were seated on the same sofa, and did not look at each other a single time. Roger rose first, and said " Good-night " to her, in a fairly calm voice.

" Good-night," she replied, drily and coldly.

Roger told me afterwards that he would have killed himself that very day, if he had not feared that our comrades would guess the reason of his suicide. He did not wish his memory sullied.

The next day Gabrielle was as gay as usual ; you would have said she had already forgotten the confidences of the night before. As for Roger, he had become sombre, fanciful, morose ; he scarcely left his room, avoided his friends, and often spent whole days without saying a word to his mistress. I attributed his unhappiness to an honourable but excessive sensibility, and I made several attempts to console him. but he drily repulsed me, affecting a great indifference towards his unfortunate partner. One day he even made a violent attack on the Dutch nation, and wanted to persuade me that there was not a single respectable man in Holland. Secretly, however, he tried to find out the family of the Dutch lieutenant ; but no one could give him any information about them.

Six weeks after that unhappy game of backgammon, Roger found a note in Gabrielle's room, written by a midshipman, who seemed to be thanking her for favours she had shown him. Gabrielle was untidiness itself, and the note in question had been left by her upon her mantelpiece. I do not know if she had been unfaithful, but Roger thought so, and his rage was terrific. His love and a remnant of pride were the only sentiments that could still attach him to life, and the stronger of them was about to be thus suddenly destroyed. He overwhelmed the proud actress with insults, and, violent as he was, I do not know how he kept himself from striking her.

" Doubtless," he said, " this puppy has given you plenty of money ? It is the only thing you care for, and you would grant yours favours to the dirtiest common sailor, provided he could pay for them."

" Why not ? " the actress coldly replied. " Yes : I would take pay from a sailor, but . . . *I would not steal from him.*"

Roger uttered a cry of rage. He drew his dagger, trembling, and for a moment looked with wild eyes at Gabrielle ; then, pulling himself together, he threw the weapon at his feet, and left the room so as not to yield to the temptation that obsessed him.

The same evening I passed very late by his lodgings, and seeing a light in his windows, I went in to borrow a book from him. I

found him very busy writing. He did not disturb himself, and
seemed scarcely to perceive my presence in his room. I sat down
by his desk and observed his features : they were so altered that
any other than I would have had difficulty in recognising him.
Suddenly I saw on the desk a letter already sealed and addressed
to myself. I instantly opened it. Roger told me that he was
about to put an end to his days, and entrusted me with various
commissions. While I read, he went on writing without taking
any notice of me ; he was making his farewells to Gabrielle. . . .
You can guess my astonishment, and what I had to say to him,
overwhelmed as I was by his resolve.

"What, you mean to kill yourself, you who are so happy ? "

"My friend," said he, sealing his letter, "you know nothing ;
you do not know me ; I am a rogue : I am so despicable that a
courtesan insults me ; and I am so sensible of my baseness that
I have not the strength to fight against it."

Then he told me the story of the game of backgammon, and all
that you know already. As I listened, I was at least as moved as
he ; I did not know what to say to him ; I gripped his hands, I
had tears in my eyes, but I could not speak. At last I had the idea
of suggesting that he could not reproach himself with having
voluntarily been the Dutchman's undoing, and that after all he
had made him lose by his . . . cheating . . . only twenty-five
napoleons.

"Then," he cried, with bitter irony, "I am a little thief and not a
great one. And, with all my ambition, to be no more than a pick-
pocket ! "

And he shouted with laughter.

I wept.

Suddenly the door opened ; a woman came in and threw herself
in his arms ; it was Gabrielle.

"Forgive me," she cried, straining him to herself. "Forgive
me. I know well I love no one but you. I love you better now
than if you had not done the thing for which you reproach yourself. If you like, I will steal ; I have already stolen. . . . Yes,
I have stolen, I stole a gold watch . . . . What worse could one do ? "

Roger shook his head with an air of incredulity ; but his forehead
seemed to lighten.

"No, my poor child," he said, gently repulsing her, "there is
no help for it ; I must kill myself. I suffer too much ; I cannot
bear up against my misery."

"Eh, well ! if you mean to die, Roger, I shall die with you.
What is life to me without you ! I am brave, I have fired guns ;
I will kill myself just like any one else. Besides I have played in
tragedy, I am in the habit of doing it. She had tears in her eyes
when she began, but this last idea made her laugh, and Roger

himself smiled. " You laugh, my officer," she cried, clapping her hands and kissing him ; " you will not kill yourself ! "

And she went on kissing him, now weeping, now laughing, now swearing like a sailor ; for she was not one of those women who are frightened by a coarse word.

Meanwhile I had got possession of Roger's pistols and dirk, and I said to him :

" My dear Roger, you have a sweetheart and a friend who love you. Believe me, you can yet find some happiness in this world." I went out after embracing him, and left him alone with Gabrielle.

I think we should only have succeeded in postponing his sombre plans, if he had not received a billet from the Minister, appointing him first lieutenant on board a vessel that was to go cruising in the Indies, after passing through the English squadron blockading the port. It was a risky business. I made him see that it was better to die nobly from an English bullet than to put an inglorious end to his days without doing any good to his country. He promised to live. He distributed half the forty thousand francs among disabled seamen and the widows and children of sailors. He gave the rest to Gabrielle, who first swore only to use the money in good works. She had a real intention of keeping her word, poor girl ; but her enthusiasms were of short duration. I learnt afterwards that she gave some thousands of francs to the poor. She bought chiffons with the rest.

We embarked, Roger and I, on a fine frigate, *La Galatée* ; our men were brave, well drilled, well disciplined ; but our commander was an ignoramus who thought himself a Jean Bart, because he swore better than an army captain, because he murdered the French language, and because he had never studied the theory of his profession, whose practice he understood sufficiently badly. However, luck was good to him at first. We got happily off the roads, thanks to a breeze that compelled the blockading squadron to take to the open sea, and we began our cruise by burning an English corvette and one of the Company's vessels off the coast of Portugal.

We sailed slowly towards the Indian seas, set back by contrary winds and the bad navigation of our captain, whose lack of skill added to the dangers of our cruise. Now chased by superior strengths, now pursuing merchant vessels, we did not pass a single day without some new adventure. But neither the hazardous life we were living, nor the troubles of the frigate's routine that fell to his share, could distract Roger from the melancholy thoughts that pursued him without respite. He, who was once the most zealous and brilliant officer in our port, now contented himself with the mere performance of his duty. As soon as his work was done he shut himself up in his cabin, without books and without paper; he spent whole hours lying in his bunk, and the poor wretch could not sleep.

One day, observing his dejection, I bethought myself of saying to him :

" Great Heavens, my dear fellow, you are grieving over a small matter. You have tricked a fat Dutchman out of twenty-five napoleons ; well, and you have remorse enough for a million. Now tell me, when you were the lover of the Prefect's wife at ——, were you remorseful then ? Yet she was worth more than twenty-five napoleons."

He turned over on his mattress without answering.

I went on.

" After all, your crime, since you say it was a crime, had an honourable motive, and was due to a lofty soul."

He turned his head and looked furiously at me.

" Yes, for anyhow, if you had lost, what would have become of Gabrielle ? Poor girl, she would have sold her last shirt for you. . . . If you had lost she would have been reduced to misery. . . . It was for her, for love, that you cheated. There are men who kill for love . . . who kill themselves. . . . You, my dear Roger, did more. For a man of our kind there is more courage in stealing, to put it clearly, than in suicide."

" Perhaps now," said the captain, breaking off in his story, " I seem absurd to you. I assure you that in that moment my friendship for Roger gave me an eloquence I do not possess to-day and, devil take it if I did not speak in good faith, speaking so to him, and if I did not believe all I said. Ah ! I was young then ! "

" My friend," he said, seeming to make a great effort to command himself, " you think me better than I am. I am a low-down rogue. When I cheated that Dutchman, I thought only of getting twenty-five napoleons, that was all. I did not think of Gabrielle, and that is why I scorn myself. . . . For me to value my honour at less than twenty-five napoleons ! What abasement ! Yes ; I should be happy if I could say, ' I stole to save Gabrielle from misery.' . . . No ! . . . No ! I did not think of her. I was not a lover at that moment. . . . I was a gambler. . . . I was a thief. . . . I stole money to have it myself . . . and that deed has so brutalised and debased me that now I have no longer courage or love. . . . I live, and I no longer think of Gabrielle. . . . I am a done man."

He seemed so wretched that if he had asked me for my pistols to kill himself, I believe I should have given them him.

A certain Friday—day of ill omen—we sighted a big English frigate, the *Alcestis*, who gave chase to us. She carried fifty-eight guns, and we had only eight-and-thirty. We hoisted all sail to escape her ; but her speed was greater than ours, and she gained on us every moment ; it was clear that before night we should be forced into an unequal combat. Our captain called Roger to his cabin, where they were a good quarter of an hour consulting together. Roger came up on deck again, took me by the arm, and led me aside.

"In two hours from now," he said, "the engagement will begin; that brave man who is trotting up and down the quarter-deck has lost his head. There were two courses open to him: the first, the more honourable, was to let the enemy catch us up, and then tackle her vigorously, throwing a hundred sturdy rascals aboard her; the other course, not bad, but rather cowardly, was to lighten ourselves by throwing some of our cannon into the sea. Then we could have closely hugged the African coast that we shall sight over there to larboard. The English, for fear of running aground, would have been forced to let us escape; but our —— captain is neither a coward nor a hero; he is going to let himself be destroyed from afar by cannon-shot, and, after some hours of battle, will honourably lower his flag. So much the worse for you; the hulks of Portsmouth await you. As for me, I have no intention of seeing them."

"Perhaps," I said, "our first shots will do such damage to the enemy that she will be obliged to give up the chase."

"Listen; I do not mean to be a prisoner, I want to have myself killed; it is time that I should make an end of things. If by bad luck I am only wounded, give me your word that you will throw me into the sea. That is the proper death-bed for a good sailor like me."

"What madness," I cried, "and what sort of a job are you giving me?"

"You will be fulfilling the duty of a good friend. You know that I must die. You should remember, I only consented not to kill myself, in the hope of being killed. Come, promise me this: if you refuse, I am going to ask the favour from the boatswain, who will not."

After reflecting a little, I said:

"I give you my word to do what you want, only if you are wounded to death, without hope of recovery. In that case, I agree to spare you your sufferings."

"I shall be wounded to death, or killed."

He offered me his hand, and I gripped it firmly. He was calmer after that, and indeed his face shone with a certain martial gaiety.

Towards three o'clock in the afternoon the enemy's bow guns began to make play in our rigging. We furled some of our sails; we presented our broadside to the *Alcestis*, and kept up a steady fire to which the English vigorously replied. After about an hour's fighting, our captain who did nothing at the right moment, wanted to try and board. But we had already many dead and wounded, and the rest of our crew had lost their keenness; finally, we had suffered sorely in our rigging, and our masts were badly damaged. At the moment when we spread sail to come up to the English ship our mainmast, with no longer anything to hold it, fell with a horrible crash. The *Alcestis* profited by the confusion into which this accident instantly threw us. She came up by our poop, giving us her whole broadside at half the range of a pistol ; she raked our unlucky frigate from stern to stem, and we were only able to reply with two small guns. At this moment I was close to Roger, who was busy having the shrouds cut that still held the fallen mast. I felt him forcibly grip my arm ; I turned round and saw him knocked over on the deck, and covered with blood. He had just received a charge of grape-shot in the stomach.

The captain ran to him.

" What is to be done, lieutenant ? " he cried.

" We must nail our flag to the stump of the mast, and scuttle the ship."

The captain left him at once, not finding this advice very much to his taste.

" Come," said Roger, " remember your promise."

" This is nothing," I said. " You can recover from it."

" Throw me overboard," he cried, cursing horribly, and seizing me by the skirts of my coat ; " you can see that I cannot recover ; throw me in the sea ; I do not want to see our flag struck."

Two sailors came up to carry him to the cockpit.

" To your guns, you rogues," he shouted ; " load with grape-shot, and aim at the deck. And you, if you do not keep your word, I curse you, and I hold you the most cowardly and the vilest of all men ! "

His wound was certainly mortal. I saw the captain call a midshipman, and command him to strike our colours.

" Give me a hand-shake," I said to Roger.

At the very moment when our flag was lowered——

.   .   .   .

" Captain, a whale to the larboard," an ensign interrupted, running up.

" A whale ? " cried the captain, transported with joy, leaving his tale where it was. " Sharp now, lower the long-boat ! lower the yawl ! lower all the long-boats ! Harpoons, ropes, etc., etc."

I was unable to learn how poor Lieutenant Roger died.

THE ETRUSCAN VASE

PROSPER MÉRIMÉE

AUGUSTE SAINT-CLAIR was not popular in what is called Society ; principally because he only tried to please those who pleased him. He sought them out, and fled the others. Besides, he was absent-minded and indolent. One evening, as he was leaving the Théâtre Italien, the Marquise A—— asked him how Mademoiselle Sontag had sung. " Yes, madame," replied Saint-Clair, smiling pleasantly and thinking of something quite different. It was impossible to attribute this ridiculous reply to timidity ; for he spoke to a great lord, to a great man, or even to a fashionable woman, with the same aplomb with which he would have entertained an equal. The Marquise decided that Saint-Clair was a prodigy of impertinence and stupidity.

Madame B—— asked him to dinner one Monday. She talked a great deal to him ; and, as he left the house, he declared he had never met a more delightful woman. Now Madame B—— was in the habit of collecting wit for a month at other people's houses, and spending it at her own in a single evening. Saint-Clair saw her again on the Thursday of the same week. This time he was a little bored. A third visit decided him never to show himself again in her drawing-room. Madame B—— declared that Saint-Clair was a young man with no manners, and of the worst form.

He had been born with a tender and loving heart ; but, at an age when impressions that last for a lifetime are too easily taken, his too expansive sensibility had made him the butt of his comrades. He was proud, ambitious ; he held to his opinions with childlike tenacity. From that time he studied to hide all the outward signs of what he regarded as an unworthy weakness. He achieved his end ; but his victory cost him dear. He could hide from others the feelings of his too sensitive soul, but in imprisoning them in himself he made them a hundred times more cruel. In Society he won the sad reputation of an indifferent and careless man ; and in solitude his restless imagination made torments for him, the more frightful in that he would confide them to nobody.

It is true that it is difficult to find a friend. Difficult ! Is it possible ? Have two men existed who did not hide a secret from each other ? Saint-Clair scarcely believed in friendship, and the fact was obvious. The young people of Society found him cold and reserved.

He never asked them for their secrets ; and for them, all his thoughts and most of his actions were hidden in mystery. The French love to talk of themselves ; so that Saint-Clair was, in spite of himself, the depositary of plenty of confidences. His friends—and the word means the people he saw twice a week—complained of his distrust of them ; it is a fact that the man who, unasked, shares his secret with us, is usually offended if he does not learn our own. People think there should be reciprocity in indiscretion.

"He is buttoned up to the chin," said one day the handsome Major Alphonse de Thémines. "I could never put the slightest trust in that devil of a Saint-Clair."

"I think him something of a Jesuit," replied Jules Lambert. "Some one told me on his word of honour he had twice met him coming out of Saint-Sulpice. No one knows what he is thinking. I can never be at ease with him."

They separated. Alphonse met Saint-Clair on the Boulevard Italien walking along with bent head, blind to everybody. Alphonse stopped him, took him by the arm, and before they had reached the Rue de la Paix, had told him the whole story of his affair with Madame ——, whose husband was so jealous and so brutal.

The same evening Jules Lambert lost his money at cards. He went and danced. While dancing, he elbowed a man who, having also lost all his money, was in a very bad temper. The result was an exchange of words, and arrangements for a meeting. Jules begged Saint-Clair to be his second, and on the same occasion borrowed money from him, which he has so far forgotten to repay.

After all, Saint-Clair was genial enough. His faults harmed nobody but himself. He was obliging, often delightful, scarcely ever a bore. He had travelled much, read much, and only spoke of his travels and his reading when pressed. Besides, he was big, and well made ; his face was noble and intellectual ; it was almost always too grave, but his smile was open and full of kindness.

I was forgetting an important point. Saint-Clair was attentive to all women, and sought their conversation more than that of men. Did he love ? It was difficult to say. Only, if love did touch this cold being, it was known that the pretty Countess Mathilde de Coursy was the woman he preferred. She was a young widow at whose house he was a regular visitor. There were the following data from which to conclude their intimacy : first, the almost ceremonious politeness of Saint-Clair towards the Countess, and vice versâ ; secondly, his foible of never pronouncing her name in public—or, if he were forced to speak of her, never with the slightest praise ; thirdly, before Saint-Clair had been introduced to her, he had been a passionate lover of music, and the Countess had a similar fondness for painting. Since they had met their tastes had changed.

Lastly, when the Countess had been at a watering-place the year before, Saint-Clair had set off six days after her.

.   .   .   .   .   .

My duty as historian compels me to declare that one night in the month of July, a few minutes before dawn, the park-gate of a country-house opened, and a man came out, with all the precautions of a thief afraid of being surprised. The country-house belonged to Madame de Coursy, and the man was Saint-Clair. A woman wrapped in a pelisse accompanied him as far as the gate and leaned through it to see him the longer, as he went off down the path under the park wall. Saint Clair stopped, looked circumspectly about him, and made a sign with his hand for the woman to go in. In the brightness of the summer night he could distinguish her pale face still motionless in the same place. He retraced his steps, came up to her, and took her tenderly in his arms. He wanted to make her promise to go in ; but he had still a hundred things to say to her. Their talk had lasted ten minutes when they heard the voice of a peasant going out to work in the fields. A kiss was taken and returned, the gate was closed, and Saint-Clair, with one bound, was at the end of the path.

He followed a road that seemed well known to him. Sometimes he almost leapt for joy, and ran, striking the bushes with his cane ; sometimes he stopped or walked slowly, looking at the sky, tinting now with purple in the east. Indeed any one who had seen him would have taken him for a lunatic delighted to have broken from his cage. After half an hour's walk he was at the door of a lonely little house he had rented for the season. He unlocked the door and went in, threw himself on a big sofa, and there, with eyes fixed and lips curved in a gentle smile, gave himself up to thoughts and daydreams. His imagination brought him none but ideas of happiness. " How happy I am ! " he kept saying to himself every moment. " At last I have met a heart that understands my own ! . . . Yes, I have found my ideal. . . . I have at the same time a *friend* and a beloved. . . . What character ! . . . What passion of soul ! . . . No, she has loved no one before me. . . ." Soon, since vanity slips always into the affairs of this world, " she is the most beautiful woman in Paris," he thought. And his imagination went over all her charms at once. " She has chosen me from all. . . . She had the flower of Society for admirers. That Colonel of Hussars, so handsome, so brave—and not too much of a fop . . . that young author who makes such pretty water-colours, and plays ' proverbs ' so well. . . . That Russian Lovelace who was through the Balkan Campaign and served under Diébitch . . . above all, Camille T——, with his undoubted wit, his fine manners, and a handsome sabre-cut on his forehead . . . she has shown the door to the lot of them. And I . . . ! " Then came his refrain : " How happy I am ! How happy

I am ! " And he got up and opened the window, unable to breathe ;
alternately he walked up and down, and tossed upon his sofa.

Happy and unhappy lovers are amost equally dull. One of my
friends, who was often in one or other case, found no other way of
getting a listener than to give me an excellent luncheon, during
which he was free to talk of his loves ; but it was an absolute
condition that the conversation should be changed after the coffee.

Since I cannot give a lunch to all my readers, I will spare them the
amorous musings of Saint-Clair. Besides, one cannot live for ever in
the clouds. Saint-Clair was tired ; he yawned, stretched his arms,
and saw that it was full daylight ; he had to think of sleeping. When
he woke, he saw from his watch that he had scarcely time to dress
and run up to Paris, where he had been invited to a luncheon-
dinner with several young fellows of his acquaintance.

. . . .

Another bottle of champagne had just been uncorked ; I leave the
reader to decide how many had already been drunk. Let it suffice
him to know that the moment had arrived, which comes pretty
early at a bachelor luncheon, when everybody wants to speak at
the same time, and when the strong heads begin to grow anxious
about the weak.

" I wish," said Alphonse de Thémines, who never lost an opportunity of speaking of England, " I wish it were the fashion in Paris
as in London, for each man to call a toast to his sweetheart. In
that way we should really know whose are the sighs of our friend
Saint-Clair." As he spoke he filled his own glass and those of his
neighbours.

Saint-Clair, a little embarrassed, was about to reply ; but Jules
Lambert was before him.

" I strongly approve of the custom," said he, " and I adopt it."
He raised his glass : " To all the milliners of Paris ! I except only
those over thirty, the one-eyed, the one-legged, etc."

" Hurrah ! Hurrah! " shouted the young Anglophiles.

Saint-Clair stood up, his glass in his hand.

" Gentlemen," he said, " my heart is not so comprehensive as that
of our friend Jules, but it is more constant. And there is the more
merit in my constancy in that I have been separated for a long time
from the lady of my thoughts. I am sure you will approve my choice,
even if you are not already my rivals. To Judith Pasta, gentlemen !
May we soon see once again the first *tragédienne* of Europe ! "

Thémines wanted to object to this toast, but the applause prevented him. Saint-Clair, having parried the thrust, thought himself
quit of the business for the day.

The talk turned on the theatre. Dramatic criticism served as a
means of transition to politics. From the Duke of Wellington they
passed to English horses, and from English horses to women, by a

chain of ideas easy to follow, since young men find, first a fine horse, and secondly a pretty mistress, the two possessions most to be desired.

Then they discussed the methods of obtaining these desirable objects. Horses are bought, and one also buys women ; but we do not speak of that kind. Saint-Clair, after modestly pleading his lack of experience in the delicate subject, observed that the first step towards pleasing a woman was to be singular, and different from the others. But was there a general formula for singularity ? He did not think so.

" According to your view," said Jules, " a lame man or a hunchback is more likely to please than a straight fellow built like everybody else ? "

" You push things rather far," Saint-Clair replied : " but I accept, if necessary, all the consequences of my proposition. For instance, if I were a hunchback, I should not blow my brains out, and I should decide to make conquests. In the first place, I should pay my addresses to two kinds of women only, to those of a real sensibility, or to those, and there are plenty of them, who pretend to an original character, eccentrics, as they say in England. I should paint for the former the horror of my position, the cruelty of nature towards me ; I should try to set them pitying my lot, and contrive to let them suspect me capable of a passionate love. I should kill a rival in a duel, and poison myself with a feeble dose of laudanum. After a few months they would no longer notice my hump, and then it would be my business to watch for the first access of tenderness. As for the women who pretend to originality, their conquest is easy. You have only to persuade them that it is a firmly established rule that no hunchback can have a love affair, and they will be instantly anxious to prove it by an exception."

" What a Don Juan ! " cried Jules.

" Let us break our legs, gentlemen," said Colonel Beaujeu, " since we have the ill luck not to be born with humpbacks ! "

" I agree absolutely with Saint-Clair," said Hector Roquantin, who was only three and a half feet high. " One sees every day the most beautiful and fashionable women giving themselves to men whom you fine fellows would never suspect."

" Hector, get up, I beg you, and ring for wine," said Thémines with the most natural air imaginable.

The dwarf rose, and every one smiled, remembering the fable of the fox who had lost his tail.

" As for me," said Thémines, taking up the conversation, " the longer I live, the clearer I see that passable looks," and he threw a complacent glance in the mirror that was opposite him, " passable looks, and taste in dress, make the great singularity that conquers the most cruel " ; and he flipped a breadcrumb from the lapel of his coat.

"Bah!" cried the dwarf, "a handsome face and clothes by Staub win you the women you keep for eight days and are bored by at the second meeting. But for love, for what is called love, something else is needed. . . . You want——"

"See here," interrupted Thémines, "would you like a decisive example? You all knew Massigny, and you know what sort of a man he was. The manners of an English stable-boy, and the conversation of his horse. But he was as handsome as Adonis, and wore his cravat like Brummel. Taking him altogether, he was the biggest bore I have ever known."

"He tried to kill me with dulness," said Colonel Beaujeu. "Imagine: I had to travel two hundred leagues with him."

"Did you know," asked Saint-Clair, "that he caused the death of that poor Richard Thornton whom you knew?"

"But surely," replied Jules, "he was killed by brigands near Fondi?"

"Certainly; but you shall see that Massigny was at least an accomplice in the crime. Several travellers, Thornton among them, had arranged to go to Naples, all together, for fear of the brigands. Massigny wanted to join the party. As soon as Thornton knew it, he went on, for horror, I suppose, at the idea of having to spend some days with him. He set out alone, and you know the rest."

"Thornton was right," said Thémines; "of two deaths he chose the easier. Any one would have done the same in his place." He paused, and continued: "You grant me then that Massigny was the most tedious man on earth?"

"Granted!" There was a shout of acclamation.

"Let us not reduce anybody to despair," said Jules; "let us make an exception of . . . especially when he is expounding his political plans."

"You will also grant me," pursued Thémines, "that Madame de Coursy is a woman of brains, if ever there was one."

There was a moment's silence. Saint-Clair bent his head, and thought that all eyes were upon him.

"Who questions it?" he said at last, still leaning over his plate, apparently examining with great interest the flowers painted on the porcelain.

"I maintain," said Jules, raising his voice, "I maintain that she is one of the three most delightful women in Paris."

"I knew her husband," said the colonel. "He often showed me charming letters from his wife."

"Auguste," put in Hector Roquantin, "you must introduce me to the Countess. They say you count for something there."

"At the end of the autumn," murmured Saint-Clair, "when she comes back to Paris. . . . I . . . I think she does not entertain in the country."

" Will you listen to me ? " cried Thémines.

There was silence again. Saint-Clair fidgeted on his chair like a prisoner in a Court of Justice.

" You had not seen the Countess three years ago, Saint-Clair ; you were then in Germany," Alphonse de Thémines went on with relentless calm. " You can have no idea of what she was in those days ; beautiful, fresh as a rose, lively too, and gay as a butterfly. Well, among her numerous admirers, who do you think was honoured with her favour ? Massigny ! The stupidest of men, and the dullest, turned the head of the cleverest of women. Do you think a hunchback could have done as much ? No, believe me, have a handsome face and a good tailor, and be bold."

Saint-Clair was in an atrocious position. He was going to give the narrator a formal contradiction ; but fear of compromising the Countess held him back. He would have liked to say something in her favour ; but his tongue was frozen. His lips trembled with rage, and he searched his head in vain for some roundabout means of starting a quarrel.

" What ! " cried Jules with surprise, " Madame de Coursy gave herself to Massigny ! Frailty, thy name is woman ! "

" The reputation of a woman is a thing of such small importance ! " said Saint-Clair, in a dry, scornful voice. " One may pull it to pieces to make a little sport, and——"

As he spoke, he remembered with horror a certain Etruscan vase that he had seen a hundred times on the Countess's maintelpiece in Paris. He knew it had been a present from Massigny on his return from Italy ; and, damning circumstance ! the vase had been brought from Paris to the country. Every evening, when she took off her bouquet, Mathilde placed it in the Etruscan vase.

The words died on his lips : he saw no longer but one thing, thought no longer but of one thing—the Etruscan vase.

" A fine proof ! " a critic will say. " To think of suspecting one's mistress for so small a thing as that ! "

Have you been in love, master Critic ?

Thémines was in too good a temper to be offended at the tone Saint-Clair had taken in speaking to him.

He replied lightly, with an air of good fellowship :

" I only repeat what the world said. It was taken as truth while you were in Germany. But I scarcely know Madame de Coursy ; it is eighteen months since I went to her house. It is possible that people were mistaken, and that Massigny was telling me a yarn. To return to what we were considering : I should be none the less right, even if the example I have just quoted should prove to be false. You all know that France's most brilliant woman, she whose works——"

The door opened, and Théodore Neville came in. He had just returned from Egypt.

"Théodore! Back so soon!" He was overwhelmed with questions.

"Have you brought back a real Turkish costume?" asked Thémines.

"Have you an Arab horse, and an Egyptian groom?"

"What sort of a man is the Pasha?" asked Jules. "When will he make himself independent? Have you seen heads cut off with single sabre blows?"

"And the dancing girls!" said Roquantin. "Are Cairo women beautiful?"

"Did you see General L——?" asked Colonel Beaujeu. "How has he organised the Pasha's army? Did Colonel C—— give you a sword for me?"

"And the Pyramids? And the cataracts of the Nile? And the statue of Memnon? Ibrahim Pasha? etc." All spoke at once; Saint-Clair thought of nothing but the Etruscan vase.

Théodore seated himself cross-legged, for he had taken to the habit in Egypt and had not been able to lose it in France, waited till the questioners had tired themselves out, and spoke as follows, so fast as not to be easily interrupted:

"The Pyramids! I tell you, they are a regular humbug. They are not nearly so high as one thinks. The Minister at Strasbourg is only four metres lower. I am full up with antiquities. Don't speak of them. The mere sight of a hieroglyph would make me faint. There are so many travellers who busy themselves with these things! My object was to study the appearances and manners of all that bizarre crowd that fills the streets of Alexandria and Cairo—Turks, Bedouins, Copts, Fellahs, Megrabis. I made some hurried notes when I was in quarantine. What an infamy that is! I hope none of you believe in contagion. As for me, I calmly smoked my pipe in the midst of three hundred plague-stricken people. Ah! colonel, you would see some fine cavalry there, well mounted. I will show you some superb weapons I brought back. I have a *djerid* that belonged to the famous Mourad Bey. Colonel, I have a *yataghan* for you, and a *khandjar* for Auguste. You shall see my *metchla*, my *burnous*, my *haick*. Do you know, I could have brought some women back if I had wanted. Ibrahim Pasha sent so many from Greece, that they are to be had for the asking . . . but on account of my mother. . . . I talked a lot with the Pasha. He is a clever man, my word, and no bigot. You would scarcely believe how learned he is in our affairs. I tell you he knows of the slightest mysteries of our Cabinet. I drew from his conversation the most precious information as to the state of the parties in France. . . . At present he is much busied with statistics. He subscribes to all our newspapers. Do you know, he is a determined Bonapartist! He talks of nothing but Napoleon. ' Ah,' he said to me, ' what a great man was Bounabardo!' *Bounabardo*, that is their name for Bonaparte."

" Giourdina, that is to say, Jordan," mumured Thémines beneath his breath.

" At first," Théodore went on, " Mohammed Ali was very reserved with me. You know all Turks are very mistrustful. He took me for a spy, damme! or a Jesuit. He has a horror of Jesuits. But, after a visit or two, he saw that I was a traveller, unprejudiced, and curious to learn on the spot the customs, manners, and politics of the Orient. Then he unbent and spoke to me with an open heart. At my last audience, which was the third he gave me, I took the liberty of saying, ' I do not understand why your Highness does not make himself independent of the Porte.' ' My God!' said he, ' I should like to; but I am afraid that the Liberal papers, which govern everything in your country, would not support me when once I had proclaimed the independence of Egypt.' He is a handsome old man, with a fine white beard and never a laugh. He gave me some excellent preserves; but, of all I gave him, what pleased him most was the collection of uniforms of the Imperial Guard, by Charlet."

" Is the Pasha romantic? " asked Thémines.

" He bothers himself little with books; but you know that Arabian literature is wholly romantic. They have a poet called Melek Ayatalne-fous-Ebn-Esraf, who recently published some *Meditations* beside which those of Lamartine would seem to be classical prose. On my arrival in Cairo I hired a teacher of Arabic, with whom I set myself to read the Koran. Although I had only a few lessons I learnt enough to understand the sublime beauties of the Prophet's style, and to realise how bad are all our translations. Look, would you like to see Arabic writing? This word in gold letters is *Allah*, that is to say, God."

He showed as he spoke a very dirty letter that he had taken from a purse of perfumed silk.

" How long did you stay in Egypt? " asked Thémines.

" Six weeks."

And the traveller went on, describing everything, from cedar to hyssop.

Saint-Clair went out almost immediately after his arrival, and took the road to his country house. The impetuous gallop of his horse prevented him from following out his ideas. But he knew vaguely that his happiness in this world had been destroyed for ever, and that he could blame nothing for it but a dead man and an Etruscan vase.

Arriving home, he threw himself on the sofa where, the night before, he had made that lingering and delicious analysis of his happiness. The idea he had most lovingly caressed had been that his mistress was not a woman like another, that she had not loved, and could never love, but him alone. And now this beautiful dream disappeared before the mournful, cruel reality. " I possess a fine woman ; that is all. She is clever. Then she is the more to blame, for being able to love Massigny ! . . . It is true, she loves me now . . . with all her soul . . . as she can love. To be loved like Massigny ! . . . She has submitted to my attentions, my whims, my importunities. But I have been mistaken. There was no sympathy between our hearts. Massigny or me, it is all one to her. He was handsome, she loved him for his good looks. I sometimes amuse her. ' Well, we will love Saint-Clair,' she says to herself, ' since the other is dead. And if Saint-Clair dies, or grows wearisome, we shall see.' "

I firmly believe the devil watches invisible by an unhappy wretch so torturing himself. It is an amusing sight for the enemy of mankind, and when the victim feels his wounds are closing, Satan is there to open them again.

Saint-Clair thought he heard a voice that murmured in his ears,

> " The singular honour
> of being successor . . ."

He sat up and looked wildly about him. How happy he would have been to find some one in his room. He would undoubtedly have torn him to pieces.

The clock struck eight. The Countess expected him at half-past. What if he were to miss the appointment ! " Indeed, why see Massigny's mistress again ? " He lay down again on the sofa, and closed his eyes. " I want to sleep," he said. He lay still for half a minute, and then jumped to his feet and ran to the clock to see how the time was going. " How I wish it were half-past eight," he thought, " then it would be too late to set out." In his heart, he did not feel he had the courage to stay at home ; he wanted a pretext. He would have been glad to be very ill. He walked up and down in his room, sat down, took a book, but could not read a syllable. He set himself before his piano, and had not the energy to open it. He whistled, looked at the clouds, and wanted to count the poplars before his windows. Finally he returned to consult the clock, and saw that he had not succeeded in passing three minutes. " I cannot help loving her," he said, grinding his teeth and stamping his foot. " She rules me, and I am her slave, as Massigny was before me. Ah well, wretched fellow, obey, since you have not the heart to break a chain you hate ! "

He took his hat and went hurriedly out.

When we are carried away by a passion, we find some consolation for our self-esteem, in contemplating our weakness from the height of our pride. " It is true, I am feeble," one says, " but if I wished ! "

He went leisurely up the path that led to the park-gate, and from a long way off saw a white figure that showed against the deep colour of the trees. She fluttered a handkerchief in her hand, as if to signal to him. His heart beat violently, and his knees trembled ; he had not the strength to speak, and had become so timid that he feared lest the Countess should read his ill-humour in his face.

He took the hand she offered him, kissed her forehead, because she threw herself in his arms, and followed her to her rooms, mute, stifling with difficulty the sighs that seemed ready to burst his chest.

A single candle lit the Countess's boudoir. They sat down. Saint-Clair noticed his friend's coiffure ; a single rose in her hair. He had brought her the day before a fine English engraving, after Leslie's " Duchess of Portland " (her hair is dressed in this way), and had said but these words, " I like that simple rose better than all your elaborate coiffures." He did not like jewellery, and thought like that lord who brutally said : " With decked-out women and caparisoned horses the devil himself would have nothing to do."

Last night, playing with a pearl necklace belonging to the Countess (for he always wanted something in his hands while talking), he had said : " Jewels are only good to hide defects. You, Mathilde, are too pretty to wear them." This evening, the Countess, who remembered his lightest words, had put off rings, necklaces, earrings, and bracelets. He noticed footgear first in a woman's dress, and, like many men, he was a little mad on this point. A heavy shower had fallen before sundown. The grass was still drenched ; yet the Countess had walked across the wet lawn in silk stockings and black satin slippers. . . . What if she were to be ill ?

" She loves me," said Saint-Clair to himself.

And he sighed over his folly, and looked at Mathilde, smiling in spite of himself, divided between his ill-humour and the pleasure of seeing a pretty woman trying to please him by all those little nothings that lovers hold so valuable.

As for the Countess, her radiant face expressed a mixture of love and playful mischief that made her still more lovable. She took something that was in a Japanese lacquer box, and offering her little hand closed, hiding the thing it held.

" The other evening," she said, " I broke your watch. Here it is, mended."

She gave him the watch, and looked at him tenderly, mischievously, biting her lower lip, as if to keep from laughing. Great God, but how beautiful her teeth were ! How they shone white on the vivid red of her lips ! (A man looks very foolish when he takes coldly a pretty woman's coaxings.)

Saint-Clair thanked her, took the watch, and was going to put it in his pocket.

" Look now," she went on, " open it, and see if it is properly mended. You who are so learned, and have been to the Polytechnic School, ought to see that."

" I did not learn very much there," said Saint-Clair.

And he absently opened the watch-case. What was his surprise ! A miniature portrait of Madame de Coursy had been painted on the inside of the case. How could he sulk further ? His forehead lightened. He thought no more of Massigny ; he remembered only that he was with a charming woman and that this woman adored him.

. . . .

" The lark, that harbinger of dawn," began to sing, and long strips of pale light furrowed the eastern clouds. It was the hour when Romeo said farewell to Juliet ; the classic parting hour of lovers.

Saint-Clair was standing by a mantelpiece, the key of the park in his hand, his eyes fixed attentively on the Etruscan vase of which we have already spoken. He still felt spiteful towards it, in the bottom of his heart. But he was in a good-humour, and the very simple idea that Thémines might have lied began to come into his head. While the Countess, who meant to accompany him as far as the park-gate, was wrapping a shawl round her head, he lightly struck the odious vase with the key, gradually increasing the force of the blows, until it seemed likely he would soon be making it fly to pieces.

" Oh ! take care ! take care ! " cried Mathilde, " you are going to break my beautiful Etruscan vase ! "

And she snatched the key from his hands.

Saint-Clair was very dissatisfied, but patient. He turned his back on the mantelpiece, so as not to succumb to the temptation, and, opening his watch, set himself to examine the portrait he had just been given.

" Who is the painter ? " he asked.

" Monsieur R——. Massigny introduced him to me. (Massigny discovered after his journey to Rome that he had an exquisite taste for the Fine Arts, and became the Mæcenas of all the young artists.) Really, I think the portrait is like me, though a little flattering."

Saint-Clair would have liked to hurl the watch against the wall, which would have made mending a difficult matter. He restrained himself, however, and put it in his pocket ; then, observing that it was already day, he begged Mathilde not to accompany him, crossed the park with long strides, and in a moment, was alone in the fields.

" Massigny! Massigny! " he cried with concentrated rage, " shall I always be meeting you! . . . Doubtless the painter who made the portrait, painted another for Massigny! . . . Fool that I was! I believed for a moment that I was loved with a passion like my own . . . and that because she dresses her hair with a rose, and wears no jewels. . . . She has a cabinet full of them. . . . Massigny, who only saw the dress of women, was so fond of jewels! Yes, she is good-natured, it must be admitted. She knows how to accommodate herself to the tastes of her lovers. Curse it! I would a hundred times rather she were a courtesan, and sold herself for money. Then at least I should be able to believe that she loves me, since she is my mistress, and I do not pay her."

Presently a still more painful idea occurred to him. In a few weeks the Countess would be out of mourning. Saint-Clair was to marry her as soon as her year of widowhood should be over. He had promised. Promised? No. He had never spoken of it. But that had been his intention, and the Countess had known it. For him, that was as good as an oath. Yesterday he would have given a throne to hasten the moment when he should be able publicly to acknowledge his affection ; now, he trembled at the bare idea of uniting his lot with that of Massigny's old mistress.

" And yet, I owe it to her," he said, " and it shall be. No doubt she thought, poor woman, that I knew of her old intrigue. They say it was public property. And then, too, she does not know me. . . . She cannot understand me. She thinks I only love her as Massigny loved her.

Then, not without pride, he said :

" For three months she has made me the happiest of men. That happiness is well worth the sacrifice of my whole life."

He did not go to bed, but rode all morning in the woods. In a pathway of the wood of Verrières he saw a man on a fine English horse who called him by name from a distance and came instantly up to him. It was Alphonse de Thémines. To one in Saint-Clair's state of mind solitude was particularly agreeable ; and the meeting with Thémines turned his ill-humour into choking rage. Thémines either did not notice it, or else took a roguish pleasure in provoking him. He talked, laughed and joked, without noticing that he met with no response. Saint-Clair, seeing a narrow byway, instantly turned his horse into it, hoping the tormentor would not follow him : but he was mistaken ; tormentors do not so readily leave their prey. Thémines turned, and quickened his pace to draw level with Saint-Clair, and to go on more comfortably with the conversation.

I said the byway was narrow. The horses could scarcely walk abreast ; it was not surprising that Thémines, excellent horseman as he was, should graze Saint-Clair's feet in passing beside him. Saint-Clair, whose rage had reached its utmost limit, could no longer control himself. He rose in his stirrups and smartly switched Thémines' horse over the nose.

" What the devil is the matter with you, Auguste ? " shouted Thémines. " Why do you hit my horse ? "

" Why do you follow me ? " replied Saint-Clair in a terrible voice.

" Are you out of your senses, Saint-Clair ? Do you forget that you are talking to me ? "

" I know very well I am talking to a coxcomb."

" Saint-Clair ! . . . I think you are mad. . . . Listen : to-morrow you will apologise to me or pay for your impertinence."

" Till to-morrow, then, sir."

Thémines pulled up his horse ; Saint-Clair urged his, and soon disappeared in the wood.

At that moment he felt calmer. He had the weakness of believing in presentiments. He thought he would be killed next morning, and that that was a proper solution of his difficulty. One more day to spend ; to-morrow no more anxieties, no more torments. He went home, sent his servant with a note to Colonel Beaujeu, wrote some letters, then dined with a good appetite, and punctually at half-past eight was at the little gate of the park.

" What is the matter with you to-day, Auguste ? " said the Countess. " You are strangely gay, and yet, with all your jokes, you cannot make me laugh. Yesterday you were just a little dull, and I, I was gay. To-day we have changed parts. . . . I have a frightful headache."

" Dearest, I admit it ; yes, I was very tedious yesterday. But to-day I have had fresh air and exercise ; I am marvellously well."

" As for me, I got up late ; I slept on this morning, and had tiresome dreams."

" Ah ! Dreams ? Do you believe in dreams ? "

" What folly ! "

" I believe in them : I guess you had a dream announcing some tragic event."

" Heavens ! I never remember my dreams. However, I recollect. . . . I saw Massigny in my dreams ; so you see it was nothing very amusing."

" Massigny ! I should have thought, on the contrary, you would have been delighted to see him again."

" Poor Massigny ! "

" Poor Massigny ? "

" Auguste, tell me, I beg you, what is the matter with you to-night ? There is something fiendish in your smile. You look as if you were laughing at yourself."

" Ah ! Now you are treating me as badly as the old dowagers treat me, your friends."

" Yes, Auguste, to-day you are wearing the expression

you have with people you do not like."

" Naughty one ! Come, give me you hand."

He kissed her hand with ironic gallantry, and they looked stead-fastly at each other for a minute. Saint-Clair lowered his eyes first, and cried :

" How difficult it is to live in this world without getting a reputa-tion for wickedness. . . . One would have to talk of nothing but the weather, or sport, or else discuss with your old friends the reports of their charitable committees."

He took a paper from the table.

" See, here is your laundress's bill. Let us talk of this, my angel, and then you will not say I am wicked."

" Really, Auguste, you astonish me——"

" This spelling reminds me of a letter I found this morning. I must tell you that I set my papers in order, for I am tidy now and again. And so I came across a love-letter from a dressmaker, with whom I was in love when I was sixteen. She had her own way of writing each word, and always the most complicated. Her style is worthy of her spelling. Well, since in those days I was something of a coxcomb, I did not think it suited my dignity to have a mistress who could not write like a Sévigné. I left her abruptly. To-day, re-reading the letter, I perceived that this dressmaker must have been very much in love with me."

" Indeed ! a woman whom you kept ? "

" In great magnificence : on fifty francs a month. But my guardian did not make me too generous an allowance, for he used to say that a young man with money ruins himself and ruins others."

" And the woman ? What became of her ? "

" How do I know ? . . . She probably died in a hospital."

" Auguste. . . . If that were so, you would not speak so carelessly."

" If you must know the truth, she married a respectable man ; and I gave her a little dowry when I came of age."

" How good you are ! . . . But why do you like to seem wicked ? "

" Oh yes, I am very good. . . . The more I think of it, the more I am persuaded that this woman really loved me. . . . But in those days I did not know how to distinguish a true feeling under a ridiculous form."

" You should have brought me your letter. I should not have been jealous. We women have more intuition than you, and we see at once from the style of a letter whether the author is speaking honestly or is pretending a passion he does not feel."

" And yet how often you let yourselves be duped by fools and coxcombs ! "

As he spoke he was looking at the Etruscan vase, and his eyes and voice had a sinister expression that Mathilde did not notice.

" Come now ! You men, you all want to pass as Don Juans. You imagine you are making dupes when often you are only meeting Doña Juana, still wilier than yourselves."

" I understand that, with your fine intellects, you ladies tell a fool a league away. At the same time, I have no doubt that our friend Massigny, a fool and a coxcomb, died blameless and a martyr."

" Massigny ? He was not too much of a fool ; and then, there are foolish women. I must tell you a story about Massigny. . . . But, tell me, have I not told you it before ? "

" Never," replied Saint-Clair in a trembling voice.

" Massigny fell in love with me on his return from Italy. My husband knew him, and introduced him to me as a man of wit and taste. They were made for each other. Massigny was very attentive from the first ; he gave me, as his own, water-colours he had bought at Schroth's, and talked music and painting to me with a tone of the most diverting superiority. One day he sent me an amazing letter. He told me, among other things, that I was the most respectable woman in Paris ; for which reason he wanted to be my lover. I showed the letter to my cousin Julie. We were both mad in those days, and we resolved to play him a trick. One evening we had some visitors, among others Massigny. My cousin said to me : " I am going to read you a declaration of love I received this morning." She took the letter and read it amidst bursts of laughter. . . . Poor Massigny ! "

Saint-Clair fell on his knees with a cry of joy. He seized the Countess's hand, and covered it with kisses and tears. Mathilde was surprised to the last degree, and thought at first that he was ill. Saint-Clair could say nothing but " Forgive me ! Forgive me ! " At last he rose. He was radiant. At that moment he was happier than on the day when for the first time Mathilde had said to him, " I love you."

" I am the most idiotic and most culpable of men," he cried ; " for the last two days I have suspected you . . . and I did not ask you for an explanation———"

" You suspected me ! . . . And of what ? "

" I am a wretch ! . . . They told me you had loved Massigny, and——"

" Massigny ! " and she began to laugh ; then, becoming instantly grave again, " Auguste," she said, " you can be mad enough to have such suspicions, and hypocrite enough to hide them from me ! "

There were tears in her eyes.

" I implore you, forgive me."

" How should I not forgive you, dearest ? But first let me swear to you———"

" Oh ! I believe you, I believe you. Tell me nothing."

" But, in Heaven's name, what motive could make you suspect such an improbability ? "

" Nothing, nothing at all but my cursed head . . . and . . . you see, that Etruscan vase that I knew Massigny had given you."

The Countess clasped her hands with astonishment; then, laughing aloud, she cried:

"My Etruscan vase! My Etruscan vase!"

Saint-Clair could not help laughing himself, while big tears ran down his cheeks. He seized Mathilde in his arms and said:

"I will not loose you till you have forgiven me."

"Yes, I forgive you, madman that you are!" said she, kissing him tenderly. "You make me very happy to-day: this is the first time I have seen you weep, and I believed you had no tears."

Then, escaping from his arms, she seized the Etruscan vase, and broke it in a thousand pieces on the floor. (It was a rare and irreplaceable specimen. There was a painting on it in three colours of a fight between a Lapithe and a Centaur.)

For some hours Saint-Clair was the most ashamed of men, and the happiest.

.   .   .   .

"Well," said Roquantin to Colonel Beaujeu, whom he met in the evening at Tortoni's, "the news is true?"

"Too true, my friend," replied the Colonel sadly.

"Tell me how it happened."

"Oh! Very properly. Saint-Clair began by telling me he was in the wrong, but that he wished to draw Thémines' fire before apologising. I could but think he was right. Thémines wished it decided by lot who should fire first. Saint-Clair demanded that it should be Thémines. Thémines fired: I saw Saint-Clair turn round where he stood, and fall stone-dead. I have noticed before in many soldiers struck by a bullet this strange twisting round before death."

"It is very odd," said Roquantin. "And what did Thémines do?"

"Oh! What must be done on such occasions. He threw his pistol on the ground with an air of regret. He threw it with such force that he smashed the hammer. It was an English pistol, by Manton; I doubt if there is a gunsmith in Paris who could make him another."

.   .   .   .

The Countess saw nobody for three years; winter and summer, alike, she stayed in her country-house, scarcely leaving her room, and waited on by a mulatto woman who knew of her relations with Saint-Clair, and to whom she did not say two words a day. At the end of three years her cousin Julie came back from a long journey; she forced her way in, and found poor Mathilde so thin and pale that she thought she was looking on the corpse of the the woman she had left beautiful and full of life. She succeeded with difficulty in drawing her from her retreat, and in taking her to Hyères. The Countess languished there for three or four months, and then died of a consumption caused by domestic trouble; so Doctor M—— said, who attended her.

ALEXANDRE DUMAS
1803–1870

ZODOMIRSKY'S DUEL

I

At the time of this story our regiment was stationed in the dirty little village of Valins, on the frontier of Austria.

It was the 4th of May in the year 182–, and I, with several other officers, had been breakfasting with the Aide-de-Camp in honour of his birthday, and discussing the various topics of the garrison.

"Can you tell us without being indiscreet," asked Sub-Lieutenant Stamm of Andrew Michaelovitch, the aide-de-camp, "what the Colonel was so eager to say to you this morning?"

"A new officer," he replied, "is to fill the vacancy of captain."

"His name?" demanded two or three voices.

"Lieutenant Zodomirsky, who is betrothed to the beautiful Mariana Ravensky."

"And when does he arrive?" asked Major Belayef.

"He *has* arrived. I have been presented to him at the Colonel's house. He is very anxious to make your acquaintance, gentlemen, and I have therefore invited him to dine with us. But that reminds me, Captain, you must know him," he continued, turning to me, "you were both in the same regiment at St. Petersburg."

"It is true," I replied. "We studied there together. He was then a brave, handsome youth, adored by his comrades, in every one's good graces, but of a fiery and irritable temper."

"Mademoiselle Ravensky informed me that he was a skilful duellist," said Stamm. "Well, he will do very well here; a duel is a family affair with us. You are welcome, Monsieur Zodomirsky. However quick your temper, you must be careful of it before me, or I shall take upon myself to cool it."

And Stamm pronounced these words with a visible sneer.

"How is it that he leaves the Guards? Is he ruined?" asked Cornet Naletoff.

"I have been informed," replied Stamm, "that he has just inherited from an old aunt about twenty thousand roubles. No, poor devil! he is consumptive."

"Come, gentlemen," said the Aide-de-Camp, rising, "let us

36   353

pass to the saloon and have a game of cards. Koloff will serve dinner whilst we play."

We had been seated some time, and Stamm, who was far from rich, was in the act of losing sixty roubles, when Koloff announced :
"Captain Zodomirsky."

"Here you are, at last !" cried Michaelovitch, jumping from his chair. "You are welcome."

Then turning to us, he continued : "These are your new comrades, Captain Zodomirsky ; all good fellows and brave soldiers."

"Gentlemen," said Zodomirsky, "I am proud and happy to have joined your regiment. To do so has been my greatest desire for some time, and if I am welcome, as you courteously say, I shall be the happiest man in the world."

"Ah! good day, Captain," he continued, turning to me and holding out his hand, "We meet again. You have not forgotten an old friend, I hope !"

As he smilingly uttered these words, Stamm, to whom his back was turned, darted at him a glance full of bitter hatred. Stamm was not liked in the regiment ; his cold and taciturn nature had formed no friendship with any of us. I could not understand his apparent hostility towards Zodomirsky, whom I believed he had never seen before.

Some one offered Zodomirsky a cigar. He accepted it, lit it at the cigar of an officer near him, and began to talk gaily to his new comrades.

'Do you stay here long ?" asked Major Belayef.

"Yes, monsieur," replied Zodomirsky. "I wish to stay with you as long as possible," and as he pronounced these words he saluted us all round with a smile. He continued : "I have taken a house near that of my old friend Ravensky, whom I knew at St. Petersburg. I have my horses there, an excellent cook, a passable library, a little garden, and a target ; and there I shall be quite as a hermit, and happy as a king. It is the life that suits me."

"Ha! you practise shooting !" said Stamm, in such a strange voice, accompanied by a smile so sardonic, that Zodomirsky regarded him in astonishment.

"It is my custom every morning to fire twelve balls," he replied.

"You are very fond of that amusement, then ?" demanded Stamm, in a voice without any trace of emotion ; adding, "I do not understand the use of shooting, unless it is to hunt with."

Zodomirsky's pale face was flushed with a sudden flame. He turned to Stamm, and replied in a quiet but firm boice, "I think monsieur, that you are wrong in calling it lost time to learn to shoot with a pistol ; in our garrison life an imprudent word often leads to a meeting between comrades, in which case he who is known for a good shot inspires respect among those indiscreet persons who amuse themselves in asking useless questions."

"Oh! that is not a reason, Captain. In duels, as in everything else, something should be left to chance. I maintain my first opinion, and say that an honourable man ought not to take too many precautions."

"And why?" asked Zodomirsky.

"I will explain to you," replied Stamm. "Do you play at cards, Captain?"

"Why do you ask that question?"

"I will try to render my explanation clear, so that all will understand it. Every one knows that there are certain players who have an enviable knack, whilst shuffling the pack, of adroitly making themselves master of the winning card. Now, I see no difference myself, between the man who robs his neighbour of his money and the one who robs him of his life." Then he added, in a way to take nothing from the insolence of his observation, "I do not say this to you, in particular, Captain, I speak in general terms."

"It is too much as it is, monsieur!" cried Zodomirsky. "I beg Captain Alexis Stephanovitch to terminate this affair with you." Then, turning to me, he said, "You will not refuse me this request?"

"So be it, Captain," replied Stamm quickly. "You have told me yourself you practise shooting every day, whilst I practise only on the day I fight. We will equalise the chances. I will settle details with Monsieur Stephanovitch."

Then he rose and turned to our host.

"*Au revoir*, Michaelovitch," he said. "I will dine at the Colonel's." And with these words he left the room.

The most profound silence had been kept during this altercation; but as soon as Stamm disappeared, Captain Pravdine, an old officer, addressed himself to us all.

"We cannot let them fight, gentlemen," he said.

Zodomirsky touched him gently on his arm.

"Captain," he said, "I am a new-comer amongst you; none of you know me. I have yet, as it were, to win my spurs; it is impossible for me to let this quarrel pass without fighting. I do not know what I have done to annoy this gentleman, but it is evident that he has some spite against me."

"The truth of the matter is that Stamm is jealous of you, Zodomirsky," said Cornet Naletoff. "It is well known that he is in love with Mademoiselle Ravensky."

"That, indeed, explains all," he replied. "However, gentlemen, I thank you for your kind sympathy in this affair from the bottom of my heart."

"And now to dinner, gentlemen!" cried Michaelovitch. "Place yourselves as you choose. The soup, Koloff; the soup!"

Everybody was very animated. Stamm seemed forgotten ; only Zodomirsky appeared a little sad. Zodomirsky's health was drunk ; he seemed touched with this significant attention, and thanked the officers with a broken voice.

"Stephanovitch," said Zodomirsky to me, when dinner was over, and all had risen, " since M. Stamm knows you are my second and has accepted you as such, see him, and arrange everything with him ; accept all his conditions ; then meet Captain Pravdine and me at my rooms. The first who arrives will wait for the other. We are now going to Monsieur Ravensky's house."

" You will let us know the hour of combat ? " said several voices.

" Certainly, gentlemen. Come and bid a last farewell to one of us."

We all parted at the Ravensky's door, each officer shaking hands with Zodomirsky as with an old friend.

II

Stamm was waiting for me when I arrived at his house. His conditions were these—Two sabres were to be planted at a distance of one pace apart ; each opponent to extend his arm at full length and fire at the word " *Three*." One pistol alone was to be loaded.

I endeavoured in vain to obtain another mode of combat.

" It is not a victim I offer to M. Zodomirsky," said Stamm, " but an adversary. He will fight as I propose, or I will not fight at all ; but in that case I shall prove that M. Zodomirsky is brave only when sure of his own safety."

Zodomirsky's orders were imperative. I accepted.

When I entered Zodomirsky's rooms they were vacant ; he had not arrived. I looked round with curiosity. They were furnished in a rich but simple manner, and with evident taste. I drew a chair near the balcony and looked out over the plain. A storm was brewing ; some drops of rain fell already, and thunder moaned.

At this instant the door opened, and Zodomirsky and Pravdine entered. I advanced to meet them.

" We are late, Captain," said Zodomirsky, " but it was un-avoidable."

" And what says Stamm ? " he continued.

I gave him his adversary's conditions. When I had ended, a sad smile passed over his face ; he drew his hand across his forehead and his eyes glittered with feverish lustre.

" I had forseen this," he murmured. " You have accepted, I presume ? "

" Did you not give me the order yourself ? "

" Absolutely," he replied.

Zodomirsky threw himself in a chair by the table, in which position he faced the door. Pravdine placed himself near the window, and I near the fire. A presentiment weighed down our spirits. A mournful silence reigned.

Suddenly the door opened and a woman muffled in a mantle which streamed with water, and with the hood drawn over her face, pushed past the servant, and stood before us. She threw back the hood, and we recognised Mariana Ravensky!

Pravdine and I stood motionless with astonishment. Zodomirsky sprang towards her.

" Great Heavens! what has happened, and why are you here? "

" Why am I here, George? " she cried. " Is it *you* who ask me, when this night is perhaps the last of your life? Why am I here? To say farewell to you. It is only two hours since I saw you, and not one word passed between us of to-morrow. Was that well, George? "

" But I am not alone here," said Zodomirsky in a low voice. " Think, Mariana. Your reputation—your fair fame—— "

" Are you not all in all to me, George? And in such a time as this, what matters anything else? "

She threw her arm about his neck and pressed her head against his breast.

Pravdine and I made some steps to quit the room.

" Stay, gentlemen," she said, lifting her head. " Since you have seen me here, I have nothing more to hide from you, and perhaps you may be able to help me in what I am about to say." Then, suddenly flinging herself at his feet—

" I implore you, I command you, George," she cried, " not to fight this duel with Monsieur Stamm. You will not end two lives by such a useless act! Your life belongs to me; it is no longer yours. George, do you hear? You will not do this."

" Mariana! Mariana! in the name of heaven do not torture me thus! Can I refuse to fight? I should be dishonoured—lost! If I could do so cowardly an act, shame would kill me more surely than Stamm's pistol."

" Captain," she said to Pravdine, " you are esteemed in the regiment as a man of honour; you can, then, judge about affairs of honour. Have pity on me Captain, and tell him he *can* refuse such a duel as this. Make him understand that it is not a duel, but an assassination; speak, speak, Captain, and if he will not listen to me, he will to you."

Pravdine was moved. His lips trembled and his eyes were dimmed with tears. He rose, and, approaching Mariana, respectfully kissed her hand, and said with a trembling voice:

" To spare you any sorrow, Mademoiselle, I would lay down my life; but to counsel M. Zodomirsky to be unworthy of his uniform by refusing this duel is impossible. Each adversary, your betrothed as well as Stamm, has a right to propose his conditions.

But whatever be the conditions, the Captain is in circumstances
which render this duel absolutely necessary. He is known as a
skilful duellist ; to refuse Stamm's conditions were to indicate that
he counts upon his skill."

"Enough, Mariana, enough," cried George. "Unhappy girl !
you do not know what you demand. Do you wish me, then, to fall
so low that you yourself would be ashamed of me ? I ask you, are
you capable of loving a dishonoured man ? "

Mariana had let herself fall upon a chair. She rose, pale as a
corpse, and began to put her mantle on.

"You are right, George, it is not I who would love you no more,
but you who would hate me. We must resign ourselves to our fate.
Give me you hand, George ; perhaps we shall never see each other
again. To-morrow ! to-morrow ! my love."

She threw herself upon his breast, without tears, without sobs,
but with a profound despair.

She wished to depart alone, but Zodomirsky insisted on leading
her home.

Midnight was stroking when he returned.

"You had better both retire," said Zodomirsky as he entered.
" I have several letters to write before sleeping. At five we must be
at the rendezvous."

I felt so wearied that I did not want telling twice. Pravdine
passed into the saloon, I into Zodomirsky's bedroom, and the master
of the house into his study.

The cool air of the morning woke me. I cast my eyes upon the
window, where the dawn commenced to appear. I heard Pravdine
also stirring. I passed into the saloon, where Zodomirsky immediately joined us. His face was pale but serene.

"Are the horses ready ? " he inquired.

I made a sign in the affirmative.

"Then let us start," he said.

We mounted into the carriage and drove off.

III

"Ah," said Pravdine all at once, "there is Michaelovitch's
carriage. Yes, yes, it is he with one of ours, and there is Naletoff,
on his Circassian horse. Good ! the others are coming behind. It is
well we started so soon."

The carriage had to pass the house of the Ravenskys. I could
not refrain from looking up ; the poor girl was at her window,
motionless as a statue. She did not even nod to us.

"Quicker ! quicker ! " cried Zodomirsky to the coachman.
It was the only sign by which I knew that he had seen Mariana.

Soon we distanced the other carriages, and arrived upon the place
of combat—a plain where two great pyramids rose, passing in this

district by the name of the " Tomb of the Two Brothers." The first rays of the sun darting through the trees began to dissipate the mists of night.

Michaelovitch arrived immediately after us, and in a few minutes we formed a group of nearly twenty persons. Then we heard the crunch of other steps upon the gravel. They were those of our opponents. Stamm walked first, holding in his hand a box of pistols. He bowed to Zodomirsky and the officers.

" Who gives the word to fire, gentlemen ? " he asked.

The two adversaries and the seconds turned towards the officers, who regarded them with perplexity.

No one offered. No one wished to pronounce that terrible " Three," which would sign the fate of a comrade.

" Major," said Zodomirsky to Belayef, " will you render me this service ? "

Thus asked, the Major could not refuse, and he made a sign that he accepted.

" Be good enough to indicate our places, gentlemen," continued Zodomirsky, giving me his sabre and taking off his coat, " then load, if you please."

" That is useless," said Stamm, " I have brought the pistols ; one of the two is loaded, the other has only a gun-cap."

" Do you know which is which ? " said Pravdine.

" What does it matter ? " replied Stamm, " Monsieur Zodomirsky will choose."

" It is well," said Zodomirsky.

Belayef drew his sabre and thrust it in the ground midway between the two pyramids. Then he took another sabre and planted it before the first. One pace alone separated the two blades. Each adversary was to stand behind a sabre, extending his arm at full length. In this way each had the muzzle of his opponent's pistol at six inches from his heart. Whilst Belayef made these preparations Stamm unbuckled his sabre, and divested himself of his coat. His seconds opened his box of pistols, and Zodomirsky, approaching, took without hesitation the nearest to him. Then he placed himself behind one of the sabres.

Stamm regarded him closely ; not a muscle of Zodomirsky's face moved, and there was not about him the least appearance of bravado, but of the calmness of courage.

" He is brave," murmured Stamm.

And taking the pistol left by Zodomirsky he took up his position behind the other sabre, in front of his adversary.

They were both pale, but whilst the eyes of Zodomirsky burned with implacable resolution, those of Stamm were uneasy and shifting. I felt my heart beat loudly.

Belayef advanced. All eyes were fixed on him.

"Are you ready, gentlemen ? " he asked.

"We are waiting, Major," replied Zodomirsky and Stamm together, and each lifted his pistol before the breast of the other.

A death-like silence reigned. Only the birds sang in the bushes near the place of combat. In the midst of his silence the Major's voice resounding made every one tremble.

"One."

"Two."

"*Three.*"

Then we heard the sound of the hammer falling on the cap of Zodomirsky's pistol. There was a flash, but no sound followed it.

Stamm had not fired, and continued to hold the mouth of his pistol against the breast of his adversary.

"Fire ! " said Zodomirsky, in a voice perfectly calm.

"It is not for you to command, Monsieur," said Stamm, " it is I who must decide whether to fire or not, and that depends on how you answer what I am about to say."

"Speak, then ; but in the name of heaven speak quickly."

"Never fear, I will not abuse your patience."

We were all ears.

"I have not come to kill you, Monsieur," continued Stamm, " I have come with the carelessness of a man to whom life holds nothing, whilst it has kept none of the promises it has made to him. You, Monsieur, are rich, you are beloved, you have a promising future before you : life must be dear to you. But fate has decided against you : it is you who must die and not I. Well Monsieur Zodomirsky, give me your word not to be so prompt in the future to fight duels, and I will not fire."

"I have not been prompt to call you out, Monsieur," replied Zodomirsky in the same calm voice ; " you have wounded me by an outrageous comparison, and I have been compelled to challenge you. Fire, then ; I have nothing to say to you."

"My conditions cannot wound your honour," insisted Stamm. Be our judge, Major," he added, turning to Belayef. " I will abide by your opinion ; perhaps M. Zodomirsky will follow my example."

" M. Zodomirsky has conducted himself as bravely as possible ; if he is not killed, it is not his fault." Then, turning to the officers round, he said :

"Can M. Zodomirsky accept the imposed condition ? "

"He can ! he can ! " they cried, " and without staining his honour in the slightest."

Zodomirsky stood motionless.

"The Captain consents," said old Pravdine, advancing. "Yes, in the future he will be less prompt."

"It is you who speak, Captain, and not M. Zodomirsky," said Stamm.

" Will you affirm my words, Monsieur Zodomirsky ? " asked Pravdine, almost supplicating in his eagerness.

" I consent," said Zodomirsky, in a voice scarcely intelligible.

" Hurrah ! hurrah ! " cried all the officers enchanted with this termination. Two or three threw up their caps.

" I am more charmed than any one," said Stamm, " that all has ended as I desired. Now, Captain, I have shown you that before a resolute man the art of shooting is nothing in a duel, and that if the chances are equal a good shot is on the same level as a bad one. I did not wish in any case to kill you. Only I had a great desire to see how you would look death in the face. You are a man of courage ; accept my compliments. The pistols were not loaded." Stamm, as he said these words, fired off his pistol. There was no report !

Zodomirsky uttered a cry which resembled the roar of a wounded lion.

" By my father's soul ! " he cried, " this is a new offence, and more insulting than the first. Ah ! it is ended, you say ? No, Monsieur, it must recommence, and this time the pistols shall be loaded, if I have to load them myself."

" No, Captain," replied Stamm tranquilly, " I have given you your life, I will not take it back. Insult me if you wish, I will not fight with you."

" Then it is with me whom you will fight, Monsieur Stamm," cried Pravdine, pulling off his coat. " You have acted like a scoundrel ; you have deceived Zodomirsky and his seconds, and, in five minutes if your dead body is not lying at my feet, there is no such thing as justice."

Stamm was visibly confused. He had not bargained for this.

" And if the Captain does not kill you, I will ! " said Naletoff.

" Or I ! " " Or I ! " cried with one voice all the officers.

" The devil ! I cannot fight with you all," replied Stamm. " Choose one amongst you, and I will fight with him, though it will not be a duel, but an assassination."

" Reassure yourself, Monsieur," replied Major Belayef, " we will do nothing that the most scrupulous honour can complain of. All our officers are insulted, for under their uniform you have conducted yourself like a rascal. You cannot fight with all ; it is even probable you will fight with none. Hold yourself in readiness, then. You are to be judged. Gentlemen, will you approach ? "

We surrounded the Major, and the fiat went forth without discussion. Every one was of the same opinion.

Then the Major, who had played the *rôle* of president, approached Stamm, and said to him :

" Monsieur, you are lost to all the laws of honour. Your crime was premeditated in cold blood. You have made M. Zodomirsky pass through all the sensations of a man condemned to death, whilst you were perfectly at ease, you who knew that the pistols were not loaded. Finally, you have refused to fight with the man whom you have doubly insulted."

"Load the pistols! load them!" cried Stamm, exasperated. "I will fight with any one!"

But the Major shook his head with a smile of contempt.

"No, Monsieur Lieutenant," he said, "you will fight no more with your comrades. You have stained your uniform. We can no longer serve with you. The officers have charged me to say that, not wishing to make your deficiencies known to the Government, they ask you to give in your resignation on the cause of bad health. The surgeon will sign all necessary certificates. To-day is the 3rd of May: you have from now to the 3rd of June to quit the regiment."

"I will quit it, certainly; not because it is your desire, but mine," said Stamm, picking up his sabre and putting on his coat.

Then he leapt upon his horse, and galloped off towards the village, casting a last malediction to us all.

We all pressed round Zodomirsky. He was sad; more than sad, gloomy.

"Why did you force me to consent to this scoundrel's conditions, gentlemen?" he said. "Without you, I should never have accepted them."

"My comrades and I," said the Major, "will take all the responsibility. You have acted nobly, and I must tell you in the name of us all, M. Zodomirsky, that you are a man of honour." Then turning to the officers: "Let us go, gentlemen, we must inform the Colonel of what has passed."

"We mounted into the carriages. As we did so we saw Stamm in the distance galloping up the mountain side from the village upon his horse. Zodomirsky's eyes followed him.

"I know not what presentiment torments me," he said, "but I wish his pistol had been loaded, and that he had fired."

He uttered a deep sigh, then shook his head, as if with that he could disperse his gloomy thoughts.

"Home," he called to the driver.

We took the same route that we had come by, and consequently again passed Mariana Ravensky's window. Each of us looked up, but Mariana was no longer there.

"Captain," said Zodomirsky, "will you render me a service?"

"Whatever you wish," I replied.

"I count upon you to tell my poor Mariana the result of this miserable affair."

"I will do so. And when?"

"Now. The sooner the better. Stop!" cried Zodomirsky to the coachman. He stopped and I descended, and the carriage drove on.

Zodomirsky had hardly entered when he saw me appear in the

doorway of the saloon. Without doubt my face was pale, and wore a look of consternation, for Zodomirsky sprang towards me, crying :

" Great heavens, Captain ! What has happened ? "

I drew him from the saloon.

" My poor friend, haste, if you wish to see Mariana alive. She was at her window ; she saw Stamm gallop past. Stamm being alive, it followed that you were dead. She uttered a cry, and fell. From that moment she has never opened her eyes."

" Oh, my presentiments ! " cried Zodomirsky, " my presentiments ! " and he rushed, hatless and without his sabre, into the street.

On the staircase of Mlle. Ravensky's house he met the doctor, who was coming down.

" Doctor," he cried, stopping him, " she is better, is she not ? "

" Yes," he answered, " better, because she suffers no more."

" Dead ! " murmured Zodomirsky, growing white, and supporting himself against the wall. " Dead ! "

" I always told her, poor girl ! that, having a weak heart, she must avoid all emotion——"

But Zodomirsky had ceased to listen. He sprang up the steps, crossed the hall and the saloon, calling like a madman :

" Mariana ! Mariana ! "

At the door of the sleeping chamber stood Mariana's old nurse, who tried to bar his progress. He pushed by her, and entered the room.

Mariana was lying motionless and pale upon her bed. Her face was calm as if she slept. Zodomirsky threw himself upon his knees by the bedside, and seized her hand. It was cold, and in it was clenched a curl of black hair.

" My hair ! " cried Zodomirsky, bursting into sobs.

" Yes, yours," said the old nurse, " your hair that she cut off herself on quitting you at St. Petersburg. I have often told her it would bring misfortune to one of you."

If any one desires to learn what became of Zodomirsky, let him inquire for Brother Vassili, at the Monastery of Troitza.

The holy brothers will show the visitor his tomb. They know neither his real name, nor the causes which, at twenty-six, had made him take the robe of a monk. Only they say, vaguely, that it was after a great sorrow, caused by the death of a woman whom he loved.

MARCEAU'S PRISONER

Alexandre Dumas

I

On the evening of the 15th of December 1793 a traveller, pausing on the summit of the mountain at the foot of which rolls the river Moine, near the village of Saint-Crépin, would have looked down upon a strange spectacle.

He would have perceived thick volumes of smoke rising from the roofs and windows of cottages, succeeded by fierce tongues of flame, and in the crimson glare of the increasing conflagration the glitter of arms. A Republican brigade of twelve or fifteen hundred men had found the village of Saint-Crépin abandoned, and had set it in a blaze. Apart from the rest stood a cottage, which had been left untouched by the flames. At the door were stationed two sentinels. Inside, sitting at a table, was a young man, who appeared to be from twenty to twenty-two years old. His long fair hair waved round his clear-cut features, and his blue mantle, but half concealing his figure, left revealed the epaulettes of a general. He was tracing on a map by the light of a lamp the route his soldiers must follow. This man was General Marceau.

" Alexandre," he said, turning to his sleeping companion, " wake up ; an order has arrived from General Westermann," and he handed the despatch to his colleague.

" Who brought the order ? "

" Delmar, the people's representative."

" Very good. Where do these poor devils assemble ? "

" In a wood a league and a half from this place. It is here upon the map."

Then orders, given in a low voice, broke up the group of soldiers extended round the ashes which had once been a village. The line of soldiers descended the roadway which separates Saint-Crépin from Montfaucon, and when, some seconds after, the moon shone forth between two clouds upon the long lines of bayonets, they seemed to resemble a great black serpent with scales of steel gliding away into the darkness.

They marched thus for half an hour, Marceau at their head. The study he had made of the localities prevented him from missing the route, and after a quarter of an hour's further march they perceived before them the black mass of the forest. According to their instructions, it was there that the inhabitants of some villages and the remnants of several armies were to assemble to hear mass; altogether about eighteen hundred Royalists.

The two generals separated their little troop into several parties, with orders to surround the forest. As they advanced thus in a circle, it seemed that the glade which formed the centre of the forest was lighted up. Still approaching, they could distinguish the glare of torches, and soon, as objects became more distinct, a strange scene burst upon their sight.

Upon an altar, roughly represented by some piles of stones, stood the *curé* of the village of Sainte-Marie-de-Rhé, chanting the mass; grouped around him was a circle of old men grasping torches, and, upon their knees, women and children were praying. Between the Republicans and this group a wall of soldiers was placed. It was evident that the Royalists had been warned.

They did not wait to be attacked, but opened fire at once upon their assailants, who advanced without firing a single shot. The priest still continued chanting the mass. When the Republicans were thirty paces from their enemies the first rank knelt down; three lines of barrels were lowered like corn before the wind; the volley burst forth. The light gleamed upon the lines of the Royalists and some shots struck the women and children kneeling at the foot of the altar. For an instant wails of distress arose. Then the priest held up his crucifix, and all was silent again.

The Republicans, still advancing, fired their second discharge, and now neither side had time to load; it was a hand-to-hand fight with bayonets, and all advantage was on the side of the well-armed Republicans. The Royalists gave way; entire ranks fell. The priest, perceiving this, made a sign. The torches were extinguished, and all was darkness. Then followed a scene of disorder and carnage, where each man struck with blind fury, and died without asking for pity.

"Mercy! mercy!" cried a heartrending voice, suddenly, at Marceau's feet, as he was about to strike. It was a young boy without weapons. "Save me, in the name of Heaven!" he cried.

The General stooped and dragged him some paces from the affray, but as he did so the youth fainted. Such excess of terror in a soldier astonished Marceau; but, notwithstanding, he loosened his collar to give him air. His captive was a girl!

There was not an instant to lose. The Convention's orders were imperative; all Royalists taken with or without weapons, whatever their age or sex, must perish upon the scaffold. He placed the young girl at the foot of a tree, and ran towards the skirmish. Amongst the dead he perceived a young Republican officer, whose figure appeared to him about the same as that of his prisoner. He stripped him quickly of his coat and hat, and returned with them to the girl. The freshness of the night had revived her.

" My father ! my father ! " were her first words. " I have abandoned him ; he will be killed ! "

" Mademoiselle Blanche ! " suddenly whispered a voice behind the tree, " the Marquis de Beaulieu lives ; he is saved." And he who had said these words disappeared like a shadow.

" Tinguy, Tinguy ! " cried the girl, extending her arms towards the spot where he had stood.

" Silence ! a word will denounce you," said Marceau ; " and I wish to save you. Put on this coat and hat and wait here."

He returned to his soldiers, gave orders for them to retire upon Chollet, left his companion in command, and came back to his prisoner. Finding her ready to follow him, he directed their steps to the road where his servant waited with horses. The young girl sprang into the saddle with all the grace of a practised rider. Three-quarters of an hour after they galloped into Chollet. Marceau, with his little escort, took his way to the Hôtel Sans Culotte. He engaged two rooms, and conducted the young girl to one of them, advising her, at the same time, to take some rest after the fearful night she had endured. Whilst she slept, Marceau determined on the course he would take to save her. He would take her himself to Nantes, where his mother lived. He had not seen her for three years, and it would be natural enough for him to ask permission for leave of absence. As dawn began to break he entered General Westermann's house. His demand was accorded at once, but it was necessary that his permission should be signed by Delmar. The General promised to send him with the certificate, and Marceau returned to the hotel to snatch a few moments of repose.

Marceau and Blanche were about to sit down to breakfast when Delmar appeared in the doorway. He was one of Robespierre's agents, in whose hands the guillotine was more active than intelligent.

" Ah ! " he said to Marceau, " you wish to leave us already, citizen, but you have done this night's work so well I can refuse you nothing. My only regret is that the Marquis de Beaulieu escaped. I had promised the Convention to send them his head."

Blanche stood erect and pale like a statue of terror. Marceau placed himself before her.

" But we will follow his track. Here is your permission," he added ; " you can start when you choose. But I cannot quit you without drinking to the health of the Republic." And he sat down at the table by the side of Blanche.

They were beginning to feel more at ease, when a discharge of musketry burst upon their ears. The General leapt to his feet and rushed to his arms, but Delmar stopped him.

" What noise is that ? " asked Marceau.

" Oh, nothing ! " replied Delmar. " Last night's prisoners being shot." Blanche uttered a cry of terror. Delmar turned slowly and looked at her.

" Here is a fine thing," he said. " If soldiers tremble like women, we shall have to dress up our women as soldiers. It is true you are very young," he continued, catching hold of her and scanning her closely, " you will get used to it in time."

" Never, never ! " cried Blanche, without dreaming how dangerous it was for her to manifest her feelings before such a witness. " I could never get used to such horrors."

" Boy," he replied, loosing her, " do you think a nation can be regenerated without spilling blood ? Listen to my advice ; keep your reflections to yourself. If ever you fall into the hands of the Royalists they will give you no more mercy than I have done to their soldiers." And saying these words he went out.

" Blanche," said Marceau, " do you know, if that man had given one gesture, one sign, that he recognised you, I would have blown his brains out ? "

" My God ! " she said, hiding her face in her hands, " when I think that my father might fall into the hands of this tiger, that if he had been made a prisoner, this night, before my eyes—— It is atrocious. Is there no longer pity in this world ? Oh ! pardon, pardon," she said, turning to Marceau, " who should know that better than I ? "

At this instant a servant entered and announced that the horses were ready.

" Let us start, in the name of Heaven ! " she cried ; " there is blood in the air we breathe here."

" Yes, let us go," replied Marceau, and they descended together.

II

Marceau found at the door a troop of thirty men whom the General-in-Chief had ordered to escort them to Nantes.

As they galloped along the high-road, Blanche told him her history : how, her mother being dead, she had been brought up by her father ; how her education, given by a man, had accustomed her to exercises which, on the insurrection breaking out, had become so useful to her in following her father.

As she finished her story, they saw twinkling before them in the mist the lights of Nantes. The little troop crossed the Loire, and some seconds after Marceau was in the arms of his mother. A few words sufficed to interest his mother and sisters in his young companion. No sooner had Blanche manifested a desire to change her dress than the two young girls led her away, each disputing which should have the pleasure of serving her as lady's-maid. When Blanche re-entered, Marceau stared in astonishment. In her first costume he had hardly noticed her extreme beauty and gracefulness, which she had now resumed with her woman's dress. It is true, she had taken the greatest pains to make herself as pretty as possible ; for one instant before her glass she had forgotten war, insurrection, and carnage. The most innocent soul has its coquetry when it first begins to love.

Marccau could not utter a word, and Blanche smiled joyously, for she saw that she appeared as beautiful to him as she had desired.

In the evening the young *fiancé* of Marceau's sister came, and there was one house in Nantes—one only, perhaps—where all was happiness and love, surrounded, as it was, by tears and sorrow.

And now, from this time forth, a new life began for Marceau and Blanche. Marceau saw a happier future before him, and it was not strange that Blanche should desire the presence of the man who had saved her life. Only from time to time as she thought of her father tears would pour from her eyes, and Marceau would reassure her, and to distract her thoughts would tell her of his first campaign ; how the school-boy had become a soldier at fifteen, an officer at seventeen, a colonel at nineteen, and a general at twenty-one.

Nantes at this time writhed under the yoke of Carrier. Its streets ran with blood, and Carrier, who was to Robespierre what the hyæna is to the tiger, and the jackal to the lion, gorged himself with the purest of this blood. No one bore a reputation more blameless than that of the young general, Marceau, and no suspicion had as yet attacked his mother or sisters. And now the day fixed for the marriage of one of these young girls arrived.

Amongst the jewels that Marceau had sent for, he chose a necklace of precious stones, which he offered to Blanche.

She looked at it first with all the coquetry of a young girl ; then she closed the box.

" Jewels are out of place in my situation," she said. " I cannot accept it whilst my father, hunted from place to place, perhaps begs a morsel of bread for his food and a granary for his shelter."

Marceau pressed her in vain. She would accept nothing but an artificial red rose which was amongst the jewels.

The churches being closed, the ceremony took place at the village hotel. At the door of the hotel a deputation of sailors awaited the young couple. One of these men, whose face appeared familiar to Marceau, held in his hand two bouquets. One he gave to the young bride, and, advancing towards Blanche, who regarded him fixedly, he presented her with the other.

" Tinguy, where is my father ? " said Blanche, growing very pale.

" At Saint-Florent," replied the sailor. " Take this bouquet. There is a letter inside."

Blanche wished to stop him, to speak to him, but he had disappeared. She read the letter with anxiety. The Royalists had suffered defeat after defeat, giving way before devastation and

famine. The Marquis had learnt everything through the watchfulness of Tinguy. Blanche was sad. This letter had cast her back
again into all the horrors of war. During the ceremony a stranger
who had, he said, affairs of the utmost importance to communicate
to Marceau had been ushered into the saloon. As Marceau entered
the room, his head bent towards Blanche, who leant upon his arm,
he did not perceive him. Suddenly he felt her tremble. He looked
up. Blanche and he were face to face with Delmar. He approached
them slowly, his eyes fixed on Blanche, a smile upon his lips. With
his forehead beaded with cold sweat, Marceau regarded him as
Don Juan regarded the statue of the commandant.

" You have a brother, citizeness ? " he said to Blanche.   She
stammered. Delmar continued :

" If my memory and your face do not deceive me, we breakfasted
together at Chollet. How is it I have not seen you since in the ranks
of the Republican army ? "

Blanche felt as if she were going to fall, for the eye of Delmar
pierced her through and through. Then he turned to Marceau ; it
was Delmar's turn to tremble. The young general had his hand
upon the hilt of his sword, which he gripped convulsively. Delmar's
face resumed its habitual expression ; he appeared to have totally
forgotten what he was about to say, and taking Marceau by the arm
he drew him into the niche of a window, and talked to him a few
minutes about the situation in La Vendée, and told him he had come
to consult with Carrier on certain rigorous measures about to be
inflicted on the Royalists. Then he quitted the room, passing
Blanche, who had fallen cold and white into a chair, with a bow and
a smile.

Two hours after Marceau received orders to rejoin his army,
though his leave of absence did not expire for fifteen days. He
believed this to have some connection with the scene which had just
passed. He must obey, however ; to hesitate were to be lost.

Marceau presented the order to Blanche. He regarded her sadly.
Two tears rolled down her pale cheeks, but she was silent.

" Blanche," he said, " war makes us murderous and cruel ; it is
possible that we shall see each other no more." He took her hand.
" Promise me, if I fall, that you will remember me sometimes, and
I promise you, Blanche, that if between my life and death I have the
time to pronounce one name—one alone—it shall be yours."
Blanche was speechless for tears, but in her eyes were a thousand
promises more tender than that which Marceau demanded. With
one hand she pressed Marceau's, and pointed with the other to his
rose, which she wore in her hair.

" It shall never leave me," she said.

An hour after he was on the road to rejoin his army. Each step
he took on the road they had journeyed together recalled her to his

mind, and the danger she ran appeared more menacing now that he was away from her side. Each instant he felt ready to rein in his horse and gallop back to Nantes. If Marceau had not been so intent upon his own thoughts he would have perceived at the extremity of the road and coming towards him a horseman who, after stopping an instant to assure himself he was not mistaken, had put his horse at a gallop and joined him. He recognised General Dumas. The two friends leapt from their horses and cast themselves into each other's arms. At the same instant a man, his hair streaming with perspiration, his face bleeding, his clothing rent, sprang over the hedge and, half fainting, fell at the feet of the two friends, exclaiming :

" She is arrested ! "

It was Tinguy.

" Arrested ! Who ? Blanche ! " cried Marceau.

The peasant made an affirmative sign. He could no longer speak. He had run five leagues, crossing fields and hedges in his flight to join Marceau.

Marceau stared at him stupidly.

" Arrested ! Blanche arrested ! " he repeated continually, whilst his friend applied his gourd full of wine to the clenched teeth of the peasant.

" Alexandre," cried Marceau, " I shall return to Nantes ; I must follow her, for my life, my future, my happiness, all is with her ! " His teeth chattered violently, and his body trembled convulsively.

" Let him beware who has dared to put his hand on Blanche, I love her with all the strength of my soul ; existence is no longer possible for me without her. Oh, fool that I was to leave her ! Blanche arrested ! And where has she been taken ? "

Tinguy, to whom this question was addressed, commenced to recover. " To the prison of Bouffays," he answered.

The words were hardly out of his mouth when the two friends were galloping back to Nantes.

Marceau knew he had not an instant to lose : he directed his steps at once to Carrier's house. But neither menaces nor prayers could obtain an interview from the deputy of the " Mountain."

Marceau turned away quietly ; he appeared in the interval to have adopted a new project, and he prayed his companion to await him at the gate of the prison with horses and a carriage.

Before Marceau's name and rank the prison gates were soon opened, and he commanded the gaoler to conduct him to the cell where Blanche was enclosed. The man hesitated ; but, on Marceau repeating his desire in a more imperative tone, he obeyed, making him a sign to follow him.

" She is not alone," said his guide, as he unlocked the low-arched door of a cell whose sombre gloom made Marceau shudder, " but she will not be troubled long with her companion ; he is to be guillotined to-day." Saying these words he closed the door on Marceau, and determined to keep as quiet as possible concerning an interview which would be so compromising to him.

Still dazzled from his sudden passage from day to darkness, Marceau groped his way into the cell like a man in a dream. Then he heard a cry, and the young girl flung herself into his arms. She clung to him with inarticulate sobs and convulsive embraces.

" You have not abandoned me, then," she cried. " They arrested me, dragged me here ; in the crowd which followed I recognised Tinguy. I cried out ' Marceau ! Marceau ! ' and he disappeared. Now you have come, you will take me away, you will not leave me here ? "

" I wish I could tear you away this moment, if it were at the price of my life ; but it is impossible. Give me two days, Blanche, but two days. Now I wish you to answer me a question on which your life and mine depend. Answer me as you would answer to God. Blanche, do you love me ? "

" Is this the time and place for such a question ? Do you think these walls are used to vows of love ? "

" This *is* the moment, for we are between life and death. Blanche, be quick and answer me ; each instant robs us of a day, each hour, of a year. Do you love me ? "

" Oh ! yes, yes ! " These words escaped from the young girl's heart, who, forgetting that no one could see her blushes, hid her head upon his breast.

" Well ! Blanche, you must accept me at once for your husband."

The young girl trembled.

" What can be your design ? "

" My motive is to tear you from death ; we will see if they will send to the scaffold the wife of a Republican general."

Then Blanche understood it all ; but she trembled at the danger to which he must expose himself to save her. Her love for him increased, and with it her courage rose.

" It is impossible," she said firmly.

" Impossible ! " interrupted Marceau ; " what can rise between us and happiness, since you have avowed you love me ? Listen, then, to the reason which has made you reject your only way of escape. Listen, Blanche ! I saw you and loved you ; that love has become a passion. My life is yours, your fate is mine ; happiness or death, I will share either with you ; no human power can separate us, and if I quitted you, I have only to cry ' *Vive le roi !* ' and your prison gates will reopen, and we will come out no more except together. Death upon the same scaffold, that will be enough for me."

" Oh, no, no ; leave me, in the name of Heaven, leave me ! "

" Leave you ! Take heed what you say, for if I quit this prison without having the right to defend you, I shall seek out your father—your father whom you have forgotten, and who weeps for you—and I shall say to him : ' Old man, she could have saved herself, but she has not done so ; she has wished your last days to be passed in mourning, and her blood to be upon your white hair. Weep, old man, not because your daughter is dead, but because she did not love you well enough to live.' "

Marceau had repulsed her, and she had fallen on her knees beside him, and he, with his teeth clenched, strode to and fro with a bitter laugh ; then he heard her sob, the tears leapt to his eyes, and he knelt before her.

" Blanche, by all that is most sacred in the world, consent to become my wife ! "

" You must, young girl," interrupted a strange voice, which made them tremble and rise together. " It is the only way to preserve your life. Religion commands you, and I am ready to bless your union." Marceau turned astonished, and recognised the *curé* of Sainte-Marie-de-Rhé, who had made part of the gathering which he had attacked on the night when Blanche became his prisoner.

" Oh, my father," he cried, seizing his hand, " obtain her consent !"

" Blanche de Beaulieu," replied the priest, with solemn accents, " in the name of your father, whom my age and friendship give me the right of representing, I command you to obey this young man."

Blanche seemed agitated with a thousand different emotions ; at last she threw herself into Marceau's arms.

" I cannot resist any longer," she said. " Marceau, I love you, and I will be your wife." Their lips joined ; Marceau was at the height of joy ; he seemed to have forgotten everything. The priest's voice broke in upon their ecstasy.

" We must be quick," he said, " for my moments are numbered."

The two lovers trembled ; this voice recalled them to earth. Blanche glanced around the cell with apprehension.

" What a moment," she said, " to unite our destinies ! Can you think a union consecrated under vaults so sombre and lugubrious can be fortunate and happy ? "

Marceau shuddered, for he himself was touched with superstitious terror. He drew Blanche to that part of the cell where the daylight struggling through the crossed bars of a narrow air-hole rendered the shadows less thick, and there, falling on their knees, they awaited the priest's blessing. As he extended his arms above them and pronounced the sacred words, the clash of arms and the tread of soldiers was heard in the corridor.

Blanche cast herself in terror into Marceau's arms.

" Can they have come to seek me already ? " she cried. " Oh, my love, how frightful death is at this moment ! " The young General threw himself before the door, a pistol in each hand. The astonished soldiers drew back.

" Reassure yourselves," said the priest ; " it is I whom they seek. It is I who must die."

The soldiers surrounded him.

" My children," he cried, in a loud voice, addressing himself to the young pair. " On your knees ; for with one foot in the tomb I give you my last benediction, and that of a dying person is sacred." He drew, as he spoke, a crucifix from his breast, and extended it towards them ; himself about to die, it was for them he prayed.

There was a solemn silence.

Then the soldiers surrounded him, the door closed, and all disappeared.

Blanche threw her arms about Marceau's neck.

" Oh, if you leave me, and they come to seek me, and you are not here to aid me ! Oh, Marceau, think of me upon the scaffold far from you, weeping, and calling you, without response ! Oh, do not go ! do not go ! I will cast myself at their feet : I will tell them I am not guilty, that, if they will leave me in prison with you all my life, I will bless them ! "

" I am sure to save you, Blanche ; I answer for your life. In less than two days I shall be here with your pardon, and then, instead of a prison and a cell, a life of happiness, a life of liberty and love ! "

The door opened, the gaoler appeared. Blanche clung more closely to her lover's breast, but each instant was precious, and he gently unwound her arms from about him, and promised to return before the close of the second day.

" Love me for ever," he said, rushing out of the cell.

" For ever," said Blanche, half fainting, and showing him in her hair the red rose that he had given her. Then the door closed upon him like the gate of the Inferno.

III

Marceau found his companion waiting for him at the porter's lodge. He called for ink and paper.

" What are you about to do ? " asked his friend.

" I am going to write to Carrier, to demand a respite of two days, and to tell him his own life depends on Blanche's."

" Wretched man ! " cried his friend, snatching the unfinished letter away from him. " You threaten him, you who are in his power, you who have set his orders to rejoin your army at defiance. Before an hour passes you will be arrested, and what then can you do for yourself or her ? "

Marceau let his head fall between his hands, and appeared to reflect deeply.

" You are right," he cried, rising suddenly ; and he drew his friend into the street.

A group of people were gathered round a post-chaise.

" If this evening is hazy," whispered a voice at Marceau's ear, " I do not know what would prevent twenty strong fellows from entering the town and freeing the prisoners. It is a pity that Nantes is so badly guarded."

Marceau trembled, turned, and recognised Tinguy, darted a glance of intelligence at him, and sprang into the carriage.

" Paris ! " he called to the postilion, and the horses darted forward with the rapidity of lightning. At eight o'clock the carriage entered Paris.

Marceau and his friend separated at the square of the Palais Egalité, and Marceau took his way alone on foot through the Rue Saint-Honoré, descended at the side of Saint-Roch, stopped at No. 366, and asked for Robespierre. He was informed that he had gone to the Théâtre de la Nation. Marceau proceeded there, astonished to have to seek in such a place the austere member of the Committee of Public Welfare. He entered, and recognised Robespierre half hidden in the shadow of a box. As he arrived outside the door he met him coming out. Marceau presented himself, and gave him his name.

" What can I do for you ? " said Robespierre.

" I desire an interview with you."

" Here, or at my house ? "

" At your house."

" Come, then."

And these two men, moved by feelings so opposite, walked along side by side, Robespierre indifferent and calm, Marceau passionate and excited. This was the man who held within his hands the fate of Blanche.

They arrived at Robespierre's house, entered, and ascended a narrow staircase, which led them to a chamber on the third floor. A bust of Rousseau, a table, on which lay open the *Contrat Social* and *Emile*, a chest of drawers, and some chairs, completed the furniture of the apartment.

" Here is Cæsar's palace," said Robespierre, smiling ; " what have you to demand from its president ? "

" The pardon of my wife, who is condemned to death by Carrier."

" Your wife condemned to death by Carrier ! The wife of

Marceau, the well-known Republican! the Spartan soldier! What is Carrier then doing at Nantes?"

Marceau gave him an account of the atrocities which Carrier was superintending at Nantes.

"See how I am always misunderstood," cried Robespierre, with a hoarse voice, broken by emotion. "Above all, where my eyes cannot see, nor my hand arrest. There is enough blood being spilt that we cannot avoid, and we are not at the end of it yet."

"Then give me my wife's pardon."

Robespierre took a leaf of white paper.

"What was her name?"

"Why do you wish to know that?"

"It is necessary in cases of identity."

"Blanche de Beaulieu."

Robespierre let his pen fall.

"What? The daughter of the Marquis de Beaulieu, the chief of the Royalists of La Vendée. How is it that she is *your* wife?"

Marceau told him all.

"Young fool and madman!" he said. "Must you——"

Marceau interrupted him: "I ask from you neither insults nor abuse. I ask for her life. Will you give it me?"

"Will family ties, love's influence, never lead you to betray the Republic?"

"Never."

"If you find yourself armed, face to face with the Marquis de Beaulieu?"

"I will fight against him as I have already done."

"And if he falls into your hands?"

Marceau reflected an instant:

"I will bring him to you, and you shall be his judge."

"You swear it to me?"

"Upon my honour."

Robespierre took up his pen and finished writing.

"There is your wife's pardon," he said. "You can depart."

Marceau took his hand and wrung it with force. He wished to speak, but tears choked his utterance; and it was Robespierre who said to him:

"Go! there is not an instant to lose. *Au revoir!*"

Marceau sprang down the stairs and into the street, and ran toward the Palais-Egalité, where his carriage waited.

From what a weight his heart was freed! What happiness awaited him! What joy after so much grief! His imagination plunged into the future, and he saw the moment when, appearing on the threshold of the prison-cell, he would cry:

" Blanche, you are saved ! You are free ! Before us lies a life of love and happiness."

Yet from time to time a vague uneasiness tormented him ; a sudden chill struck cold upon his heart. He spurred on the postilions by lavish promises of gold, and the horses flew along the road. Everything seemed to partake of the feverish agitation of his blood. In a few hours he had left Versailles, Chartres, Le Mans, La Flèche behind him. They were nearing Angers, when suddenly, with a terrible crash, the carriage heeled over on its side, and he fell. He rose hurt and bleeding, separated with his sabre the traces which bound one of the horses, and, leaping on its back, reached the next post ; and, taking a fresh horse, rapidly continued his course.

And now he has crossed Angers, he perceives Nigrande, reaches Varade, passes Ancenis ; his horse streams with foam and blood. He gains Saint-Donatien, then Nantes—Nantes, which encloses his life, his happiness ! Some seconds after he passes the gates, he is in the town, he reins in his horse before the prison of Bouffays. He has arrived. What matters all their troubles now ? He calls :

" Blanche, Blanche ! "

The gaoler appears and replies :

" Two carts have just left the prison. Mademoiselle de Beaulieu was in the first."

With a curse upon his lips, Marceau springs to the ground, and rushes with the hustling crowd towards the great square. He comes up with the last of the two carts ; one of the prisoners inside recognises him. It is Tinguy.

" Save her ! save her ! " he cries out, " for I have failed ! "

Marceau pushes on through the crowd ; they hustle him, they press around him, but he hurls them out of his path. He arrives upon the place of execution. Before him is the scaffold. He flourishes aloft the scrap of paper, crying :

" A pardon ! a pardon ! "

At that instant the executioner, seizing by its long, fair hair the head of a young girl, held it up before the terrified crowd.

Suddenly from the midst of that silent crowd a cry was heard—a cry of anguish, in which there seemed to have been gathered all the forces of human agony. Marceau had recognised between the teeth of this uplifted head the red rose which he had given to his young bride.

A BAL MASQUÉ

ALEXANDRE DUMAS

I SAID that I was in to no one ; one of my friends forced admission. My servant announced Mr. Anthony R———. Behind Joseph's livery I saw the corner of a black frock-coat ; it is probable that the wearer of the frock-coat, from his side, saw a flap of my dressing-gown ; impossible to conceal myself.

"Very well ! Let him enter," I said out loud. "Let him go to the devil," I said to myself.

While working it is only the woman you love who can disturb you with impunity, for she is always at bottom interested in what you are doing.

I went up to him, therefore, with the half-bored face of an author interrupted in one of those moments of sorest self-mistrust, while I found him so pale and haggard that the first words I addressed to him were these :

"What is the matter ? What has happened to you ? "

"Oh ! Let me take breath," said he. "I'm going to tell you all about it, besides, it's a dream perhaps, or perhaps I am mad."

He threw himself into an arm-chair, and let his head drop between his hands.

I looked at him in astonishment ; his hair was dripping with rain ; his shoes, his knees, and the bottom of his trousers were covered with mud. I went to the window ; I saw at the door his servant and his cabriolet ; I could make nothing out of it all.

He saw my surprise.

"I have been to the cemetery of Père-Lachaise," said he.

"At ten o'clock in the morning ? "

"I was there at seven—a cursed bal masqué ! "

I could not imagine what a bal masqué and Père-Lachaise had to do with one another. I resigned myself, and turning my back to the mantelpiece began to roll a cigarette for him between my fingers with the phlegm and the patience of a Spaniard.

While he was coming to the point I hinted to Anthony that I, for my part, was commonly very susceptible to attentions of that kind.

He made me a sign of thanks, but pushed my hand away.

Finally, I bent over to light the cigarette for myself : Anthony stopped me.

"Alexandre," he said to me, "listen, I beg of you."

" But you have been already a quarter of an hour and have not told me anything."

" Oh ! it is a most strange adventure."

I got up, placed my cigarette on the mantelpiece, and crossed my arms like a man resigned ; only I began to believe, as he did, that he was fast becoming mad.

" You remember the ball at the Opéra, where I met you ? " he said to me after a moment's silence.

" The last one, where there were at least two hundred people ? "

" The very same. I left you with the intention of abandoning myself to one of those varieties of which they spoke to me as being a curiosity even in the midst of our curious times ; you wished to dissuade me from going ; a fatality drove me on. Oh ! you, why did you not see it all, you who have the knack of observation ? Why were not Hoffman or Callot there to paint the picture as the fantastic burlesque thing kept unrolling itself beneath my eyes ? Unsatisfied and in melancholy mood I walked away, about to quit the Opéra ; I came to a hall that was overflowing and in high spirits : corridors, boxes, parterre. Everything was obstructed. I made a tour of the room ; twenty masks called me by name and told me theirs.

" These were all leaders—aristocrats and merchants—in the undignified disguise of pierrots, of postilions, of merry-andrews, or of fishwives. They were all young people of family, of culture, of talent ; and there, forgetful of family, talent, breeding, they were resurrecting in the midst of our sedate and serious times a soirée of the Regency. They had told me about it, and yet I could not have believed it !—I mounted a few steps, and leaning against a pillar, half hidden by it, I fixed my eyes on that sea of human beings surging beneath me. Their dominoes, of all colours, their motley costumes, their grotesque disguises formed a spectacle resembling nothing human. The music began to play. Oh, it was then these gargoyle creatures stirred themselves to the sound of that orchestra whose harmony reached me only in the midst of cries, of laughs, of hootings ; they hung on to each other by their hands, by their arms, by their necks ; a long coil formed itself, beginning with a circular motion, the dancers, men and women, stamping with their feet, made the dust break forth with a noise, the atoms of which were rendered visible by the wan light of the lustres ; turning at ever-increasing speed with bizarre postures, with unseemly gestures, with cries full of abandonment ; turning always faster and still faster, swaying and swinging like drunken men, yelling like lost women, with more delirium than delight, with more passion than pleasure ; resembling a coil of the damned doing infernal penance under the scourge of demons !

" All this passed beneath my eyes, at my feet. I felt the wind of their whirling past ; as they rushed by each one whom I knew flung a word at me that made me blush. All this noise, all this humming, all this confusion, all this music went on in my brain as well as in the room ! I soon came to the point of no longer knowing whether that which I had before my eyes was a dream or reality ; I came to the point of asking myself whether it was not I who was mad and they who were sane ; I was seized with a weird temptation to throw myself into the midst of this pandemonium, like Faust through the Witches' Sabbath, and I felt that I, too, would then have cries, postures, laughs like theirs. Oh ! from that to madness there is but one step. I was appalled ; I flung myself out of the room, followed even to the street door by shrieks that were like those cries of passion that come out of the caverns of the fallow deer.

" I stopped a moment under the portico to collect myself ; I did not wish to venture into the street ; with such confusion still in my soul I might not be able to find my way ; I might, perhaps, be thrown under the wheels of some carriage I had not seen coming. I was as a drunken man might be who begins to recover sufficient reason in his clouded brain to recognise his condition, and who, feeling the will return but not the power, with fixed eyes and staring, leans motionless against some street post or some tree on the public promenade.

" At that moment a carriage stopped before the door, a woman alighted or rather shot herself from the doorway.

" She entered beneath the peristyle, turning her head from right to left like one who had lost her way ; she was dressed in a black domino, had her face covered by a velvet mask. She presented herself at the door.

" ' Your ticket,' said the door-keeper.

" ' My ticket ? ' she replied. ' I have none.'

" ' Then get one at the box-office.'

" The domino came back under the peristyle, fumbled nervously about in all her pockets.

" ' No money ! ' she cried. ' Ah ! this ring—a ticket of admission for this ring,' she said.

" ' Impossible,' replied the woman who was distributing the cards ; ' we do not make bargains of that kind.'

" And she pushed away the brilliant, which fell to the ground and rolled to my side.

" The domino remained still without moving, forgetting the ring, sunk in thought.

" I picked up the ring and handed it to her.

" Through her mask I saw her eyes fixed on mine.

" ' You must help me to get in,' she said to me ; ' you must, for pity's sake.'

" ' But I am going out, madame,' I said to her.

" ' Then give me six francs for this ring, and you will render me a service for which I shall bless you my life long.'

" I replaced the ring on her finger ; I went to the box-office, I took two tickets. We re-entered together.

" As we arrived within the corridor I felt that she was tottering. Then with her second hand she made a kind of ring around my arm.

" ' Are you in pain ? ' I asked her.

" ' No, no, it is nothing,' she replied, ' a dizziness, that is all.'

" She hurried me into the hall.

" We re-entered into that giddy madhouse.

" Three times we made the tour, breaking our way with great difficulty through the waves of masks that were hurling themselves one upon the other ; she trembling at every unseemly word that came to her ear ; I blushing to be seen giving my arm to a woman who would thus put herself in the way of such words ; then we returned to the end of the hall.

" She fell upon a sofa. I remained standing in front of her, my hand leaning on the back of her seat.

" ' Oh ! this must seem to you very bizarre,' she said, ' but not more so than to me, I swear to you. I have not the slightest idea of all this ' (she looked at the ball), ' for even in my dreams I could not imagine such things. But they wrote me, you see, that he would be here with a woman, and what sort of a woman should it be who could come to a place like this ? '

" I made a gesture of surprise ; she understood.

" ' But *I* am here, you wish to ask, do you not ? Oh ! but for me that is another thing : I, I am looking for him ; I, I am his wife. As for these people, it is madness and dissipation that drives them hither. But I, I, it is jealousy infernal ! I have been everywhere looking for him ; I have been all night in a cemetery ; I have been to a public execution ; and yet, I swear to you, as a young girl I have never once gone into the street without my mother ; as a wife I have never taken one step out of doors without being followed by a lackey ; and yet here I am, the same as all these women who are so familiar with the way ; here I am giving my arm to a man whom I do not know, blushing under my mask at the opinion he ought to have of me ! I know all this !—Have you ever been jealous, monsieur ? '

" ' Unhappily,' I replied to her.

" ' Then you will forgive me, for you understand. You know that voice that cries out to you " Do ! " as in the ear of a madman ; you have felt that arm that pushes one into shame and crime, like the arm of fate. You know that at such a moment one is capable of everything, if one can only get vengeance.'

" I was about to reply ; all at once she rose, her eyes fastened on two dominoes that were passing in front of us at that moment.

" ' Silence ! ' she said.

" And she hurried me on following in their footsteps. I was thrown into the middle of an intrigue of which I understood nothing ; I could feel all the threads vibrating, but could take hold of none of them by the end ; but this poor wife seemed so troubled that she became interesting. I obeyed like a child, so imperious is real feeling, and we set ourselves to follow the two masks, one of which was evidently a man, the other a woman. They spoke in a low voice ; the sounds reached our ears with difficulty.

" ' It is he ! ' she murmured ; ' it is his voice ; yes, yes, that is his figure——'

" The latter of the two dominoes began to laugh.

" ' That is his laugh,' said she ; ' it is he, monsieur, it is he ! The letter said true, O, mon Dieu, mon Dieu ! '

" In the meanwhile the two masks kept on, and we followed them always. They went out of the hall, and we went out after them ; they took the stairs leading to the boxes, and we ascended in their footsteps ; they did not stop till they came to the boxes in the centre ; we were like their two shadows. A little closed box was opened ; they entered it ; the door again closed upon them.

" The poor creature I was supporting on my arm frightened me by her excitement. I could not see her face, but crushed against me as she was, I could feel her heart beating, her body shivering, her limbs trembling. There was something uncanny in the way there came to me such knowledge of unheard of suffering, the spectacle of which I had before my very eyes, of whose victim I knew nothing, and of the cause of which I was completely ignorant. Nevertheless, for nothing in this world would I have abandoned that woman at such a moment.

" As she saw the two masks enter the box and the box close upon them, she stopped still a moment, motionless, and as if overwhelmed. Then she sprang forward to the door to listen. Placed as she was, her slightest movement would betray her presence and ruin her ; I dragged her back violently by the arm, I lifted the latch of the adjoining box, I drew her in after me, I lowered the grille and pulled the door to.

" ' If you wish to listen,' I said to her, ' at least listen from here.'

" She fell upon one knee and flattened her ear against the partition, and I—I held myself erect on the opposite side, my arms crossed, my head bent and thoughtful.

" All that I had been able to observe of that woman seemed to me to indicate a type of beauty. The lower part of her face, which was not concealed by her mask, was youthful, velvety, and round ; her lips were scarlet and delicate ; her teeth, which the black velvet mask falling just above them made appear still whiter, were small, separated, and glistening ; her hand was one to be modelled, her figure to be held between the fingers ; her black hair, silky, escaped in profusion from beneath the hood of her domino, and the foot of a child, that played in and out under her skirt, looked as if it should have trouble in balancing her body, all lithe, all graceful, all airy as it was.

" Oh ! what a marvellous piece of perfection must she be ! Oh ! he that should hold her in his arms, that should see every faculty of that spirit absorbed in loving him, that should feel the beating of her heart against his, her tremblings, her nervous palpitations, and that should be able to say, ' All of this, all of this, comes of love, of love for me, for me alone among all the millions of men, for me, angel predestined ! Oh ! that man !—that man ! '

" Such were my thoughts, when all at once I saw that woman rise, turn toward me, and say to me in a voice broken and fierce :

" ' Monsieur, I am beautiful, I swear it ; I am young, I am but nineteen. Until now I have been white as an angel of the Creation— ah, well—' she threw both arms about my neck, ' —ah, well, I am yours—take me ! '

" At the same instant I felt her lips pressed close to mine, and the effect of a bite, rather than that of a kiss, ran shuddering and dismayed through my whole body ; over my eyes passed a cloud of flame.

" Ten minutes later I was holding her in my arms, in a swoon, half dead and sobbing.

" Slowly she came to herself ; through her mask I made out how haggard were her eyes ; I saw the lower part of her pale face, I heard her teeth chatter one upon the other, as in the chill of a fever. I see it all once more.

" She remembered all that had taken place, and fell at my feet.

" ' If you have any compassion,' she said to me, sobbing, ' any pity, turn away your eyes from me, never seek to know me ; let me go and forget me. I will remember for two ! '

" At these words she rose again ; quickly, like a thought that escapes us, she darted toward the door, opened it, and coming back again, ' Do not follow me, in heaven's name, monsieur, do not follow me ! ' she said.

" The door pushed violently open, closed again between her and me, stole her from my sight, like an apparition. I have never seen her more !

" I have never seen her more ! And ever since, ever since the six months that have glided by, I have sought her everywhere, at balls, at spectacles, at promenades. Every time I have seen from a distance a woman with a lithe figure, with a foot like a child's, with black hair, I have followed her, I have drawn near to her, I have looked into her face, hoping that her blushes would betray her. Nowhere have I found her again, in no place have I seen her again

—except at night, except in my dreams! Oh! there, there she reappears; there I feel her, I feel her embraces, her biting caresses so ardent, as if she had something of the devil in her; then the mask has fallen and a face more grotesque appeared to me at times blurred as if veiled in a cloud; sometimes brilliant, as if circled by an aureole; sometimes pale, with a skull white and naked, with eyes vanished from the orbits, with teeth chattering and few.

"In short, ever since that night, I have ceased to live; burning with mad passion for a woman I do not know, hoping always, and always disappointed at my hopes. Jealous without the right to be so, without knowing of whom to be jealous, not daring to avow such madness, and all the time pursued, preyed upon, wasted away, consumed by her."

As he finished these words he tore a letter from his breast.

"Now that I have told you everything," he said to me, "take this letter and read it."

I took the letter and read:

"Have you perhaps forgotten a poor woman who has forgotten nothing and who dies because she cannot forget?

"When you receive this letter I shall be no more. Then go to the cemetery of Père-Lachaise, tell the concierge to let you see among the newest graves one that bears on its stone the simple name 'Marie,' and when you are face to face with that grave, fall on your knees and pray."

"Ah, well!" continued Anthony, "I received that letter yesterday, and I went there this morning. The concierge conducted me to the grave, and I remained two hours on my knees there, praying and weeping. Do you understand? She was there, that woman. Her flaming spirit had stolen away; the body consumed by it had bowed, even to breaking, beneath the burden of jealousy and of remorse; she was there, under my feet, and she had lived, and she had died for me unknown; unknown! —and taking a place in my life as she had taken one in the grave: unknown!—and burying in my heart a corpse, cold and lifeless, as she had buried one in the sepulchre—Oh! Do you know anything to equal it? Do you know any event so appalling? Therefore, now, no more hope. I will see her again never. I would dig up her grave that I might recover, perhaps, some traces wherewithal to reconstruct her face; and I love her always! Do you understand, Alexandre? I love her like a madman; and I would kill myself this instant in order to rejoin her, if she were not to remain unknown to me for eternity, as she was unknown to me in this world."

With these words he snatched the letter from my hands, kissed it over and over again, and began to weep like a little child.

I took him in my arms, and not knowing what to say to him, I wept with him.

ACKNOWLEDGMENTS

To Messrs. GEORGE BELL & SONS, LTD., London,
In arrangement with whom the translation of Voltaire's " Bababec and the Fakirs," from the volume of *Voltaire's Tales* in Bohn's Library, is here used.

To Messrs. T. C. & E. C. JACK, London and Edinburgh,
For the translations of Balzac's " Episode under the Terror " and " Facino Cane," and for the translations of Prosper Mérimée's " Mateo Falcone," " Tamango," " The Game of Backgammon," and " The Etruscan Vase," all here reprinted by arrangement from the Balzac and Mérimée volumes in Messrs. Jack's series of *The World's Story-Tellers*.

To Messrs. GEORGE NEWNES, LTD., London,
For permission to reprint, by arrangement, from the *Strand Magazine*, the translations of Balzac's " A Passion in the Desert," Victor Hugo's " Jenny," Mérimée's " Taking of the Redoubt," Dumas' " Zodomirsky's Duel," and " Marceau's Prisoner."

To Messrs. PUTNAM'S SONS, London and New York,
By arrangement with whom the translations by George Burnham Ives of Balzac's " The Conscript," " La Grande Bretèche," and " A Seashore Drama " are here reprinted from their series of *Little French Masterpieces*.

To Messrs. J. M. DENT & SONS, LTD., London,
For the use of their Copyright translations of Balzac's " The Christ in Flanders " and " El Verdugo " from *Everyman's Library*.

IV
FRENCH

THE
Masterpiece Library of Short Stories

The Thousand Best Complete Tales of all Times and all Countries

Selected by

AN INTERNATIONAL BOARD OF EMINENT CRITICS

Sir William Robertson Nicoll, LL.D.

Sir Arthur Quiller-Couch   Sir Frederick Wedmore
Clement Shorter   Sir Edmund Gosse, C.B., LL.D.
George Saintsbury, LL.D.   W. P. Trent, LL.D.
Richard le Gallienne   Carl Van Doren
Brander Matthews, Litt.D.   Thomas Seccombe

Edited by

Sir J. A. Hammerton

IV.   FRENCH

LONDON
THE EDUCATIONAL BOOK COMPANY LIMITED

THE
Masterpiece Library
of Short Stories

The Thousand Best Complete
Tales of all Times and
all Countries

Selected by
AN INTERNATIONAL BOARD
OF EMINENT EDITORS

Sir William Robertson Nicoll, LL.D.

[list of editors — illegible]

Edited by
Sir J. A. Hammerton

IV. FRENCH

London
THE EDUCATIONAL BOOK COMPANY LIMITED

Contents to Volume IV

THE FRENCH STORY-TELLERS

From George Sand to Émile Zola

FROM George Sand to Émile Zola, the modern short story was written by the French with perfect art. It is true that Maupassant and other later writers had something of importance to contribute; but the moulds into which they cast their materials were fashioned by their predecessors. In fact, the most brilliant of the later men were professed disciples of the writers of the period at which we have now arrived. These writers were widely different in outlook, style, and subject-matter. Some of them were wildly and fantastically romantic; others were violently and harshly realistic. But they all knew how to write a *conte*, and how to bring out the special qualities of this new fine flower of literature. Much of the credit for the extraordinary success of the modern French short story is due to the good taste of the French newspaper public. They required in their journals a finer literary quality than was found in the daily newspapers of other countries. The mere collection of news did not interest them; they wanted to be moved, entertained, and charmed, rather than to be instructed. The more popular prints relied on the serial novel as their principal attraction; the more distinguished journals found in the short story an artistic and satisfying literary side-dish. Provided the short story of the day was good, the leading article brilliant, and the chronicle of town gossip piquant and witty, it did not matter about the news.

GEORGE SAND

In these favouring circumstances, the contemporaries of Mérimée proceeded to develop the brief prose tale with amazing fecundity and skill. In America, about the same time, Poe had also worked out in an original way both the practice and theory of the new literary form; but the American people did not then fully appreciate the worth of Poe's wonderful creations. So it was left almost entirely to French writers to elaborate the qualities and define the scope of the new kind of fiction. Thus it is that the art of the modern short story became a

French art. Even George Sand, that wild woman writer of genius who turned her love-affairs into novels in which there was more vehemence of spirit than lasting literary quality, could write a short story like her " Marquise " with an instinctive feeling for the true form of the *conte*. She does not explain and analyse the character of the old noblewoman who fell in love with an actor ; she merely suggests the strange depths of passion in the cold, cynical, aged beauty. She leaves the imagination of the reader vibrating of its own power to the hints she gives. There is seen the art of the short story !

JULES JANIN

Jules Janin, one of the admiring critics who helped George Sand to win fame, was the glory of the *Journal des Débats*—one of the greatest French newspapers. Janin was one of those wizards of the pen who could do anything ; according to Thackeray, he translated Sterne and other English novelists without troubling to learn a word of English ! He was brilliance incarnate, and he wrote as he talked, in an improvisation of wit and whimsy and extravagant good sense. He was a born actor who gesticulated on paper instead of on the stage : one of the princes of Bohemia, in the days when the Quartier Latin was what it now merely pretends to be. His tale of " The Vendean Marriage," with its telling situations and picturesque colouring, is an admirable example of his broad, free, dashing style.

ÉMILE SOUVESTRE

Émile Souvestre was another newspaper writer with a fine talent for literature. As he saw it, " the journalist continues, in a new form and for other purposes, the work of the wandering minstrels of the Middle Ages ! It is from him that the people ask exciting stories to delight their hours of leisure. The briefness of these hours makes it necessary that the tales shall be short ; for they are usually read at the family gathering in the evening, and everybody likes to break up at bedtime with a complete impression, which can only be given by a short story." Souvestre was a Breton who had a long struggle in Paris before he won fame by his *Philosopher under the Roof*, from which we have taken the touching, quiet sketch of " Uncle Maurice." He was a man who tried to find in the study of the lives of the humble, in their simple pleasures and deep sorrows, the truth of feeling and sense of religion that he missed in the fashionable society of his age. His studies of Breton ways and customs made his picturesque native land famous throughout the world.

ALFRED DE MUSSET

A strange tenderness and love of simplicity can also be traced in the work of Alfred de Musset, who was really a most complex creature. He tells the story of his own life in " The White Blackbird "—one of the most delightful allegories in any literature. The unusual kind of bird represents genius, and especially the genius of the author. The common blackbird hen who makes herself seem white by means of paste and flour is probably George Sand, with whom Musset lived for a little while at Venice. They were two egoists who did not get on well together ; but Musset was finely sincere amid his extravagances of manner. If Hugo is the eagle of modern French lyrical poetry, Musset is the nightingale, and his prose is almost as good as his verse. The charming little story of " Camille " has a sweetness about it which shows that Musset—who died in his prime from absinthe drinking—was a fine fellow at heart.

THÉOPHILE GAUTIER

Théophile Gautier—who found his inspiration in an underdone steak—pretended to be the wildest of the Romantic school. But romance was only a matter of clothes with him—his famous scarlet waistcoat is the only romantic thing about him. He was a healthy, imperturbable man who lived with his eyes. His imagination was entirely visual : he never allowed his feelings to colour his art. But what a magnificent painter in words he was ! He had only one beloved book—the dictionary, and he continually dredged it for strange terms and novel epithets. He is the pure artist in French literature, and the inventor of the phrase, " art for art's sake." In " The Mummy's Foot " and " The Pavilion on the Lake " his glittering descriptive power and his exquisite care for form are finely displayed. The translation of the first tale is by Lafcadio Hearn, who learnt much of his art from Gautier. In " The Nest of Nightingales " the fantastic quality has a softer charm.

OCTAVE FEUILLET

In the work of Octave Feuillet the force of the romantic movement has weakened. He began with graceful essays in sentimentality, written, however, in a masterly diction. Then he got more life and reality into his studies of fashionable society, of which his " Circe " is a happy illustration. It is one of the first examples of the new dialogue form of stories, in which a dramatic structure is used purely for the purpose of narration. He was the favourite novelist of the Second Empire, but it was after the disasters of the war with Prussia that Feuillet rose to the full height of his power, and drew the admiration of so fastidious a critic as Walter Pater. His brief sketch of " Saving the Flag " is one of the finest things of its kind. It is a masterpiece of quiet intensity.

CONSTANT GUÉROULT—LÉO LESPÈS

Constant Guéroult is a writer of a lower order. He began at the age of thirty as a novelist of the sensational school, but he had some flashes of inspiration, and in one of these he wrote his remarkable study of the mind of a murderer, " After the Crime." Léo Lespès was a man of the same school. He was one of the founders of the *Petit Journal*, which gained its great circulation largely owing to his contributions. His brilliant little stories, of which " The Mirror " is a charming example, were the delight of a large public, but he is now scarcely known outside his own country. His picture of the lovely blind girl who finds a mirror in her sweetheart is a touching essay in sentiment.

CHAMPFLEURY

The next writer, Champfleury, would have nothing to do with sentiment. He wanted to develop the sombre side of Balzac's view of modern society, and become the first novelist of the purely realistic school. This, in point of date, he is : but in regard to literary merit he has been so completely eclipsed by Flaubert, Zola and Maupassant that his longer tales are quite forgotten. He lives now by a few short stories that he wrote for mere amusement : for in them he displays a genuine gift of humorous observation which is worth more than his strained attempts at realism. His " Great Find of Monsieur Bretoncel " is a little classic of humour ; and the briefer " Monsieur Tringle " is quite as sensibly funny.

GUSTAVE FLAUBERT

Champfleury is followed by the man who smothered his serious work—Gustave Flaubert. Flaubert is the supreme writer of the realistic school. He anticipated and excelled Zola in the rigorous study of the darker facts of life : he formed and shaped the genius of his young friend, Maupassant : and his influence can be traced in the best work of Tolstoi and other foreign novelists. A big, fair-haired Norman, consumed with a passion for the finest effects in literary art, Flaubert united in himself all the chief lines of activity in modern French literature. Pure romance attracted him as much as the realistic study of life did. He was above all things an artist, ready to model in the clay of realism, or the marble of classicism, or the golden bronze of romance. Were it not for their great length, all his three famous novelettes would be included in our collection ; but as they exceed the limits of the true short story, we have been compelled to choose only one of them—the picturesque, romantic evocation of mediæval life and thought, " St. Julian the Hospitaller."

BAUDELAIRE

With the work of Charles Baudelaire, the influence of Poe, the only great short-story writer outside France, began to tell on the French mind. Baudelaire was inspired both by Poe and De Quincey, but at the same time he retained a fine strange originality of his own, and exercised in turn a considerable influence on Swinburne and later English writers. He was a bundle of raw nerves with a ferocious contempt for modern civilisation, and he became one of the chief spirits of anarchism in modern literature. His two short stories, " An Heroic Death " and " The Cord," are studies in that new kind of cruel, cold-blooded irony which led Victor Hugo to say that Baudelaire had invented a new kind of shudder. Baudelaire was really a pessimist, amusing himself at the expense of humanity, but as an artist he was admirable alike in poetry and prose.

HENRI MÜRGER

Baudelaire, however, was not representative of the spirit of his age. Never were the French more gay and light-hearted than in the middle of the nineteenth century, when their country had recovered from the exhaustion of the Napoleonic era. It was agitated with new movements in art and literature and politics, and the young men in the Quartier Latin in Paris were brimming over with zest for life and love of art. Henri Mürger, the son of a Paris hall-porter of a house inhabited by famous writers, painters, and singers, entered the world of literature with the help of some of his father's tenants. Passing his life in the happy-go-lucky Bohemian society of the capital, Mürger swiftly rose to fame at the age of twenty-six, by his brilliant picture of this society—his *Vie de Bohème*, from which we have taken two short stories, "Francine's Muff" and "The Passage of the Red Sea." The first shows the pathos of life in Bohemian Paris : the second its gaiety, sparkle, and glitter. "It is a delightful life," said Mürger, "but a terrible one."

AUGUSTE VITU—THÉODORE DE BANVILLE

In Auguste Vitu's "Second Violin" we have an excellent example of the little, well-turned romances, by means of which the inhabitants of Bohemia managed, now and then, to earn a little money. The art with which it is written is not a personal quality ; by this time every Frenchman with any bent to literature could write a short story with an instinct for this new literary form. The short story was no longer a delightful experiment ; it was a tradition. Every writer tried his hand at it. Serious historians, like Renan and Taine, were almost as good at it as was a professional short-story writer like Théodore de Banville. Banville wrote some hundreds of brilliant *contes*, and there is such an equality of craftsmanship about all his work that it is difficult to decide which to select. In his prose as in his verse, Banville was the accomplished artist, more interested in technique than in life. Had he only felt more deeply, he might have rivalled the greatest of his contemporaries, for he had an amazing control of his instrument. His "Transposition" is an effective study of the superstition of the transmigration of souls, and his "First Love" is a striking piece of work, with a depth of thought in it unusual in Banville, while his tale of "The Cab" shows how finely ironical he could be. A good many French short-story writers of the present day owe to Banville more than they care to confess. His numerous volumes of half-forgotten short stories have been a mine of inspiration to other writers.

DUMAS THE YOUNGER

So great was the vogue of the short story that even the most brilliant playwright of the period, Alexandre Dumas the younger—son of the creator of the *Three Musketeers*—was compelled to see what he could do in the new art of fiction. His "Hanging at La Piroche" is not only a remarkably fine tale, but it is a lesson in the kind of writing required in the short story. The younger Dumas was always a lay preacher ; he invented the problem play that Ibsen perfected, and, like Mr. Bernard Shaw, he generally wrote a preface to each of his plays, in which he discussed some literary or social doctrine. The discussion with which he begins his story contains some sound literary advice, and the story itself has an unusual and surprising plot that is handled with quiet and assured mastery. Dumas was too good a playwright to use a dramatic construction in the short story. He gets his effect by a more subtle and leisurely style of narration.

ERCKMANN-CHATRIAN

Émile Erckmann and Alexandre Chatrian, two Alsatian friends who wrote together under their hyphenated names, are among the best short-story writers in France. They wrote together for thirty years, composing stories, legends, and plays about their native country, with a fine strong personal feeling that made their work read like the production of a single mind. One of their plays, *The Polish Jew*, known in English as *The Bells*, gave Sir Henry Irving his weirdest and most powerful part ; but it is by two or three of their novels and half a dozen of their short stories that Erckmann-Chatrian have won a high place in literature. Their fantastic ghost story, " My Inheritance," is as full of thought as it is of picturesqueness and humour. " Uncle Bernard's Shell " is a tender, charming tale of home life in the Alsatian mountains. Then in " The Papers of Madame Jeannette " we have one of the best tales of the French Revolution ever written, while " The Inventor " anticipates the weirdly scientific stories of Mr. H. G. Wells.

EDMOND ABOUT—GUSTAVE DROZ

If Edmond About had kept his short stories within the limits in which Erckmann-Chatrian worked, he would be more largely represented in this volume. For About is equal to Mérimée as a writer of tales. He is one of the wittiest of Frenchmen and a keen observer of manners and characters. Most of his works, however, are something between a novel and a short story ; they are in fact novelettes ; but his admirable genius is well displayed in his entertaining story, " Which was the Madman ? " with its surprising and dramatic revolution in the situation of the two men. Gustave Droz is another French writer of high reputation, from whom we have chosen only one short tale, " The Sempstress's Story." Droz, however, is rather monotonous in subject matter. He was in love with babies, and in middle age he turned from art to literature in order to write about them in a series of tales that won a remarkable popularity.

ANDRÉ THEURIET

André Theuriet is a fine novelist with a wider range. In his long novels he depicts French peasant life in fresh, limpid, delicate colours, in which his passion for the countryside is admirably expressed. But, as his " Sentimental Journey " shows, he is also keenly interested in the feelings of men and women, and there is a curious tone of irony in the conclusion to this idyll of railway travel. In " La Bretonne " he touches one of the sombre depths of life in a country town. With all his delicacy and love of beauty Theuriet did not turn away from the darker facts of life ; he tried to interpret them.

LUDOVIC HALÉVY

Ludovic Halévy never tried to interpret anything. Son of the famous Jewish composer, Élie Halévy, Ludovic enjoyed life to the full under the Second Empire, and wrote the librettos to Offenbach's gaily brilliant burlesques. Halévy was a fine light wit, with a scholarly style that won him a seat in the French Academy. "The Grand Marriage " is a work of his old age, written with the verve of youth, and his "Dream " is one of the most audacious pictures of life beyond the grave that has been composed. It is worthy of Voltaire, who was probably also a Frenchman of Jewish origin.

GABORIAU—VILLIERS DE L'ISLE-ADAM

Émile Gaboriau is better known as a weaver of detective romances than as a short-story writer. The tragic title of his tale of " The Accursed House " is, however, a joke on the reader. For the story is a delightful and entertaining satire on the owners of Paris tenements, with their inconvenient habit of raising the rents of their flats. The veritable master of the story of mystery and terror is Count Villiers de l'Isle-Adam, the descendant of one of the most ancient noble families in Europe, who died in poverty in a Paris hospital in 1889. Villiers is equal to Poe, and his style is better than the American's. His "Torture by Hope " is taken from his *Cruel Tales*, which is one of the classics of the modern French short story.

ERNEST DAUDET—ARMAND SILVESTRE

Ernest Daudet is somewhat overshadowed by the fame of his younger brother, and most of his life has been spent in historical studies. But in his earlier short stories, such as " The Vengeance of the Admiral," he displays a power of invention as remarkable as that of the younger Daudet, though he lacks the grace and flexibility of style of Alphonse Daudet. Of Armand Silvestre there is little to be said, in spite of the beauty and power of his tale of " The Storm." Silvestre was a young man of genius—poet as well as prose writer—who tumbled into the mud of Paris and wallowed there. His early work is full of life and charm and loveliness. He might have been one of the glories of French literature, but became one of its shames. The work he might have done was carried out by Alphonse Daudet, the most delightful writer of short stories in the world. There have been men more powerful in genius than he, but none with equal exquisiteness, subtlety, and flower-like perfection. The trouble with Daudet is not to find his best stories, but to discover some grounds for omitting a large number of them. For there might be at least fifty of his *contes* that deserve to be included in any collection of " the thousand best " short stories. The selection made by the Editorial Board for the present work was one of its many difficulties, but it would certainly be impossible to bring together in the space here given to Daudet a better or more representative set of his stories.

ALPHONSE DAUDET

Alphonse Daudet can make a story out of nothing. How slight is the foundation of " The Pope's Mule " ! Just an old country saying, going back to the times when the Popes had removed from Rome to Avignon. Yet what a work of art he makes of it ! " The Goat of

Monsieur Seguin " is another delicious omelette of literature, in which the lightness and grace of the maker's hand count for everything. "Old Folks " is a touching example of Daudet's pathos, where he smiles through his tears. The sight of two taverns standing opposite in a hamlet in Provence, one bright and bustling with business, the other decayed and silent, inspires him with the wonderful little drama of "The Two Inns." Then in "The Elixir of Father Gaucher " we have a little jewel of humour—real humour, not French wit. Quite as good in the same way is Daudet's story of his own childhood, "The Pope is Dead." Many of these tales were composed in an old mill in Provence, from which Daudet used to send a weekly sketch to Paris. Collected together under the title of *Letters from my Mill!* these sketches were at once recognised as a work of immortal beauty. In the opinion of many good judges, these early stories of Daudet's native province are superior in worth to the long novels he wrote when he settled in Paris.

His short stories of Paris life, however, are as good in their way as his sketches of Provence. Most of them turn on the Siege of Paris and the subsequent outbreak of the Commune. "The Little Pies " is a delicious comedy in a tragic setting. "The Siege of Berlin " is a strange, touching sketch of the end of one of the soldiers of the great Napoleon. "The Boy Spy " is one of the smallest and greatest of Daudet's works : and "Belisaire's Prussian " is a horrible savage thing, in which Daudet's own anger against the Germans is expressed. But in the quiet, moving sketch entitled "Mothers " his fine power of sympathy revives, and in the famous "Last Lesson "—the greatest of all his stories, long or short—his intense patriotism is conveyed with incomparable art, and a telling reticence of emotion. In the apparently artless words of a child the deep despair that Frenchmen felt in 1871 is brought out with such power that we forget that the thing is literature. It seems life itself. There is more conscious art in the two lovely poems in prose, "The Death of the Dauphin " and "The Magistrate in the Fields." But they are pearls of literary art. "At the Palais de Justice " is a love story of an unusual kind, and "The Beneficent God of Chemille " is such a mixture of loveliness, humour, and seriousness, that only the inimitable Daudet could have written it.

ÉMILE ZOLA

It is strange to find Émile Zola, the most brutal of the realists, writing stories comparable with those Daudet wrote in happy mood from his mill. "The Shoulders of the Marquise," "The Paradise of Cats," and "The Legend of Little Blue Riding-Hood " are quite unlike Zola's more famous novels. They were written in 1874, about five years after the appearance of Daudet's tales, when Zola was still uncertain of his way and undecided in aim. But if only for their unusual delicacy and lightness and grace they deserve to be remembered.

E. W.

THE MARQUISE

THE Marquise de R—— never said brilliant things, although it is the fashion in French fiction to make every old woman sparkle with wit. Her ignorance was extreme in all matters which contact with the world had not taught her, and she had none of that nicety of expression, that exquisite penetration, that marvellous tact, which belong, it is said, to women who have seen all the different phases of life and society ; she was blunt, heedless, and sometimes very cynical. She put to flight every idea I have formed concerning the noble ladies of the olden times, yet she was a genuine Marquise and had seen the Court of Louis XV. But as she was an exceptional character, do not seek in her history for a study of the manners of any epoch.

I found much pleasure in the society of the lady. She seemed to me remarkable for nothing much except her prodigious memory for the events of her youth and the masculine lucidity with which she expressed her reminiscences. For the rest, she was, like all aged persons, forgetful of recent events and indifferent to everything in which she had any present personal concern.

Her beauty had not been of that piquant order which, though lacking in splendour and regularity, still gives pleasure in itself ; she was not one of those women taught to be witty, in order to make as favourable an impression as those who are so by nature. The Marquise undoubtedly had had the misfortune to be beautiful. I have seen her portrait, for, like all old women, she was vain enough to hang it up for inspection in her apartments. She was represented in the character of a huntress nymph, with a low satin waist painted to imitate tiger-skin, sleeves of antique lace, bow of sandal-wood, and a crescent of pearl lighting up her hair.

It was an admirable painting, and, above all, an admirable woman —tall, slender, dark, with black eyes, austere and noble features, unsmiling, deep red lips, and hands which, it was said, had thrown the Princess de Lamballe into despair. Without lace, satin or powder, she might indeed have seemed one of those beautiful, proud nymphs fabled to appear to mortals in the depths of the forest or upon the solitary mountain-sides, only to drive them mad with passion and regret.

Yet the Marquise had made few acquaintances ; according to her own account she had been thought dull and frivolous. The roués of that time cared less for the charms of beauty than for the allurements of coquetry ; women infinitely less admired than she had robbed her of all her adorers, and, strange enough, she had seemed indifferent to her fate. The little she told me of her life made me believe that her heart had had no youth, and that a cold selfishness had paralysed all its faculties. Still, her old age was adorned by several sincere friends, and she gave alms without ostentation.

One evening I found her even more communicative than usual ; there was much of sadness in her voice.

" My child," she said, " the Vicomte de Larrieux has just died of the gout. It is a great sorrow to me, for I have been his friend these sixty years."

" What was his age ? " I asked.

" Eighty-four. I am eighty, but not so infirm as he was, and I can hope to live longer. N'importe ! Several of my friends have gone this year, and although I tell myself that I am younger and stronger than any of them, I cannot help being frightened when I see my contemporaries dropping off around me."

" And these," said I, " are the only regrets you feel for poor Larrieux, a man who worshipped you for sixty years, who never ceased to complain of your cruelty, yet never revolted from his allegiance ? He was a model lover : there are no more such men."

" My dear child," answered the Marquise, " I see that you think me cold and heartless. Perhaps you are right ; judge for yourself. I will tell you my whole history, and, whatever opinion you may have of me, I shall, at least, not die without having made myself known to some one.

" When I was sixteen I left St. Cyr, where I had been educated, to marry the Marquis de R——. He was fifty, but I dared not complain, for every one congratulated me on this splendid match, and all my portionless companions envied my lot.

" I was never very bright, and at that time I was positively stupid ; the education of the cloister had completely benumbed my faculties. I left the convent with a romantic idea of life and of the world, stupidly considered a merit in young girls, but which often results in the misery of their whole lives. As a natural consequence, the experience brought me by my brief married life was lodged in so narrow a mind that it was of no use to me. I learned, not to understand life, but to doubt myself.

" I was a widow before I was seventeen, and as soon as I was out of mourning I was surrounded by suitors. I was then in all the splendour of my beauty, and it was generally admitted that there was neither face nor figure that could compare with mine ; but my husband, an old, worn-out, dissipated man, who had never shown me anything but irony and disdain, and had married me only to secure an office promised with my hand, had left me such an aversion to marriage that I could never be brought to contract new ties. In my ignorance of life I fancied that all men resembled him, and that in a second husband I should find M. de R——'s hard heart, his pitiless irony, and that insulting coldness which had so deeply humiliated me.

"This terrible entrance into life had dispelled for me all the illusions of youth. My heart, which perhaps was not entirely cold, withdrew into itself and grew suspicious. I was foolish enough to tell my real feelings to several women of my acquaintance. They did not fail to tell what they had learned, and without considering the doubts and anguish of my heart, boldly declared that I despised all men. There is nothing men will resent more readily than this ; my lovers soon learned to despise me, and continued their flatteries only in the hope of finding an opportunity to hold me up to ridicule. I saw mockery and treachery written upon every forehead, and my misanthropy increased every day. About this time there came to Paris from the Provinces a man who had neither talent, strength, nor fascination, but who possessed a frankness and uprightness of feeling very rare among the people with whom I lived. This was the Vicomte de Larrieux. He was soon acknowledged to be my most favoured lover.

"He, poor fellow, loved me sincerely in his soul. His soul ! Had he a soul ? He was one of those hard, prosaic men who have not even the elegance of vice or the glitter of falsehood. He was struck only by my beauty ; he took no pains to discover my heart.

"This was not disdain on his part, it was incapacity. Had he found in me the power of loving, he would not have known how to respond to it. I do not think there ever lived a man more wedded to material things than poor Larrieux. He ate with delight, and fell asleep in all the arm-chairs ; the remainder of the time he took snuff. He was always occupied in satisfying some appetite. I do not think he had one idea a day.

"And yet, my dear friend, will you believe it ? I never had the energy to get rid of him ; for sixty years he was my torment. Constantly offended by my repulses, yet constantly drawn to me by the very obstacles I placed in the way of his passion, he had for me the most faithful, the most undying, the most wearisome love that ever man felt for woman."

"I am surprised," said I, " that in the course of your life you never met a man capable of understanding you, and worthy of converting you to real love. Must we conclude that the men of to-day are superior to those of other times ? "

"That would be a great piece of vanity on your part," she answered, smiling. "I have little reason to speak well of the men of my own time ; yet I doubt, too, whether you have made much progress ; but I will not moralise. The cause of my misfortune was entirely within myself. I had no tact, no judgment. A women as proud as I was should have possessed a superior character, and should have been able to distinguish at a glance many of the insipid, false, insignificant men who surrounded me. I was too ignorant, too narrow-minded for this. As I lived on I acquired more judgment and have learned that several of the objects of my hatred deserved far other feelings."

"And while you were young," I rejoined, "were you never tempted to make a second trial ? Was this deep-rooted aversion never shaken off ? It is strange."

The Marquise was silent, then hastily laying her gold snuff-box on the table—"I have begun my confession," said she, "and I will acknowledge everything. Listen. Once, and only once, I have loved, with a love as passionate and indomitable as it was imaginative and ideal. For you see, my child, you young men think you understand women, but you know nothing about them. If many old women of eighty were occasionally to tell you the history of their loves, you would perhaps find that the feminine soul contains sources of good and evil of which you have no idea. And now, guess what was the rank of the man for whom I entirely lost my head—I, a Marquise, and prouder and haughtier than any other."

"The King of France, or the Dauphin, Louis XIV."

"Oh, if you go on in that manner, it will be three hours before you come to my lover. I prefer to tell you at once—he was an actor."

"A king, notwithstanding, I imagine."

"The noblest, the most elegant that ever trod the boards. You are not amazed ? "

"Not much. I have heard that such ill-sorted passions were not rare, even when the prejudices of caste in France were more powerful than they are to-day."

"Those ill-sorted passions were not tolerated by the world, I can assure you. The first time I saw him I expressed my admiration to the Comtesse de Ferrières, who happened to be beside me, and she answered : ' Do not speak so warmly to any one but me. You would be cruelly taunted were you suspected of forgetting that in the eyes of a woman of rank an actor can never be a man.'

"Madame Ferrières' words remained in my mind, I know not why. At the time this contemptuous tone of hers seemed to me absurd, and this fear of committing myself a piece of malicious hypocrisy.

"His name was Lelio ; he was by birth an Italian, but spoke

French admirably. He may have been thirty-five, although on the stage he often seemed less than twenty. He played Corneille ; after this he played Racine, and in both he was admirable."

" I am surprised," said I, interrupting the Marquise, " that his name does not appear in the annals of dramatic talent."

" He was never famous," she answered, " and was appreciated neither by the court nor the town. I have heard that he was outrageously hissed when he first appeared. Afterward he was valued for his feeling, his fire, and his efforts at correct elocution. He was tolerated and sometimes applauded, but, on the whole, he was always considered an actor without taste.

" In those days tragedy was played ' properly ' ; it was necessary to die with taste, to fall gracefully, and to have an air of good breeding, even in the case of a blow. Dramatic art was modelled upon the usage of good society, and the diction and gestures of the actors were in harmony with the hoops and hair powder, which even then disfigured *Phèdre*.[1] I have never appreciated the defects of this school of art. I bravely endured it twice in the week, for it was the fashion to like it ; but I listened with so cold and constrained an air that it was generally said I was insensible to the charms of fine poetry.

" One evening, after a rather long absence from Paris, I went to the Comédie Française to see *Le Cid*.[2] Lelio had been admitted to this theatre during my stay in the country, and I saw him for the first time. He played Rodrigue. I was deeply moved by the very first tone of his voice. It was penetrating rather than sonorous, but vibrating and strongly accentuated. His voice was much criticized. That of the Cid was supposed to be deep and powerful, just as all the heroes of antiquity were supposed to be tall and strong. A king who was but five feet six inches could not wear the diadem ; it would have been contrary to the decrees of taste. Lelio was small and slender. His beauty lay not in the features, but in the nobleness of his forehead, the irresistible grace of his attitude, the careless ease of his movements, the proud but melancholy expression of his face.

" The word charm should have been invented for him ; it belonged to all his words, to all his glances, to all his motions. It was indeed a charm which he threw around me. This man, who stepped, spoke, moved without system or affectation, who sobbed with his heart as much as with his voice, who forgot himself to become identified with his passion ; this man in whom the body seemed wasted and shattered by the soul, and a single one of whose glances contained all the life I failed to find in real life, exercised over me a really magnetic power.

" I alone could follow and understand him, and he was for five years my king, my life, my love. To me he was much more than a

[1] *Phèdre*, a Tragedy by Racine.
[2] *Le Cid*, a Tragedy by Corneille.

man. His was an intellectual power which formed my soul at its
will. Soon I was unable to conceal the impression he made on me.
I gave up my box at the Comédie Française in order not to betray
myself. I pretended I had become pious, and in the evening went to
pray in the churches ; instead of that I dressed myself as a working
woman and mingled with the common people that I might listen to
him unconstrained.

"At last I bribed one of the employees of the theatre to let me
occupy a little corner where no one could see me and which I reached
by a side corridor. As an additional precaution I dressed myself as
a schoolboy. When the hour for the theatre sounded in the large
clock in my drawing-room I was seized with violent palpitations.
While my carriage was getting ready I tried to control myself ; and if
Larrieux happened to be with me I was rude to him, and threatened
to send him away. I must have had great dissimulation and great
tact to have hidden all this for five years from Larrieux, the most
jealous of men, and from all the malicious people about me.

"I must tell you that instead of struggling against this passion
I yielded to it with eagerness, with delight. It was so pure ! Why
should I have blushed for it ? It gave me new life ; it initiated me
into all the feelings I had wished to experience ; it almost made me
a woman. I was proud to feel myself thrill and tremble. The first
time my dormant heart beat aloud was to me a triumph. I learned to
pout, to love, to be faithful and capricious. It was remarked I grew
handsomer every day, that my dark eyes softened, that my smile
was more expressive, that what I said was truer and had more
meaning than could have been expected.

"I have just told you that when I heard the clock strike I trembled
with joy and impatience. Even now I seem to feel the delicious
oppression which used to overwhelm me at the sound of that clock.
Since then, through the vicissitudes of fortune, I have come to find
myself very happy in the possession of a few small rooms in the
Marais. Well, of all my magnificent house, my aristocratic *faubourg*,
and my past splendour I regret only that which could have recalled
to me those days of love and dreams. I have saved from the general
ruin a few pieces of furniture which I look upon with as much
emotion as if the hour for the theatre were about to strike now, and
my horses were pawing at the door. Oh ! my child, never love as
I loved ; it is a storm which death alone can quell.

"Then I learned to take pleasure in being young, wealthy, and
beautiful. Seated in my coach, my feet buried in furs, I could see
myself reflected in the mirror in front of me. The dress of that time,
which has since been so laughed at, was of extraordinary richness and
splendour. When arranged with taste and modified in its exaggeration, it endowed a beautiful woman with dignity, with a softness, the
grace of which the portraits of that time could give you no idea. A

woman, clothed in its panoply of feathers, of silks, and flowers, was obliged to move slowly. I have seen very fair women in white robes with long trains of watered silk, their hair powdered and dressed with white plumes, who might without exaggeration have been compared to swans.

"Despite all Rousseau has said, those enormous folds of satin, that profusion of muslin which enveloped a slender little body as down envelops a dove, made us resemble birds rather than wasps. Long wings of lace fell from our arms, and our ribbons, purses, and jewels were variegated with the most brilliant colours. Balancing ourselves in our little high-heeled shoes, we seemed to fear to touch the earth, and walked with the disdainful circumspection of a little bird on the edge of a brook.

"At the time of which I am speaking blonde powder began to be worn and gave the hair a light and soft colour. This method of modifying the crude shades of the hair gave softness to the face, and an extraordinary brilliance to the eyes. The forehead was completely uncovered, its outline melted insensibly into the pale shades of the hair. It thus appeared higher and prouder, and gave all women a majestic air. It was the fashion, too, to dress the hair low, with large curls thrown back and falling on the neck. This was very becoming to me, and I was celebrated for the taste and magnificence of my dress. I sometimes wore red velvet with grebe-skin, sometimes white satin edged with tiger-skin, sometimes lilac damask shot with silver, with white feathers and pearls in my hair.

"Thus attired I would pay a few visits until the hour for the second piece at the theatre, for Lelio never came on in the first. I created a sensation wherever I appeared, and, when I again found myself in my carriage, I contemplated with much pleasure the reflected image of the woman who loved Lelio, and might have been loved by him. Until then, the only pleasure I had found in being beautiful lay in the jealousy I excited. But from the moment that I loved I began to enjoy my beauty for its own sake. It was all I had to offer Lelio as a compensation for the triumphs which were denied him in Paris, and I loved to think of the pride and joy this poor actor, so misjudged, so laughed at, would feel were he told that the Marquise de R—— had dedicated her heart to him.

"These the dreams, however, were as brief as they were beautiful. As soon as my thoughts assumed some consistency, as soon as they took the form of any plan whatever, I had the fortitude to suppress them, and all the pride of rank reasserted its empire over my soul. You seem surprised at this. I will explain it by and by.

"About eight o'clock my carriage stopped at the little Church of the Carmelites near the Luxembourg, and I sent it away, for I was supposed to be attending the religious lectures which were given there at that hour. But I only crossed the church and the garden and

came out on the other street. I went to the garret of the young
needle-woman named Florence, who was devoted to me. I locked
myself up in her room, and joyfully laid aside all my adornments to
don the black square-cut coat, the sword and wig of a young college
professor.

" Tall, with my dark complexion and inoffensive glances, I really
had the awkward hypocritical look of a little priestling who had
stolen in to see the play   I took a hackney-coach, and hastened to
hide myself in my little box at the theatre. Then my joy, my
terror, my trembling ceased. A profound calm come upon me and
I remained until the raising of the curtain as if absorbed in expectation of some great solemnity.

" As the vulture in his hypnotic circling surrounds the partridge
and holds him panting and motionless, so did the soul of Lelio, that
great soul of a poet and tragedian, envelop all my faculties, and
plunge me into a torpor of admiration. I listened, my hands clasped
upon my knees and my chin upon the front of the box, and my
forehead bathed in perspiration ; I hardly breathed ; the crude
light of the lamps tortured my eyes, which, tired and burning, were
fastened on his every gesture, his every step. His feigned motions,
his simulated misfortune, impressed me as if they were real. I could
hardly distinguish between truth and illusion. To me, Lelio was
indeed Rodrigue, Bajazet, Hippolyte. I hated his enemies. I
trembled at his dangers ; his sorrows drew from me floods of tears,
and when he died I was compelled to stifle my emotions in my
handkerchief.

" Between the acts I sat down at the back of my box ; I was as
one dead until the meagre tone of the orchestra warned me that the
curtain was about to rise again. Then I sprang up, full of strength
and ardour, the power to feel, to weep. How much freshness, poetry,
and youth there was in that man's talent ! That whole generation
must have been of ice not to have fallen at his feet.

" And yet, although he offended every conventional idea, although
he could not adapt his taste to that silly public, although he
scandalized the women by the carelessness of his dress and deport-
ment, and displeased the men by his contempt for their foolish
actions, there were moments when, by an irresistible fascination, by
the power of his eye and his voice, he held the whole of this ungrateful
public as if in the hollow of his hand, and compelled it to applaud
and tremble.

" This happened but seldom, for the entire spirit of the age cannot
be suddenly changed ; but when it did happen, the applause was
frantic. It seemed as if the Parisians, subjugated by his genius,
wished to atone for all their injustice. As for me, I believed that this
man had at most a supernatural power, and that those who most
bitterly despised him were compelled to swell his triumph in spite

of themselves. In truth, at such times the Comédie Française seemed smitten with madness, and the spectators, on leaving the theatre, were amazed to remember that they had applauded Lelio. As for me, I seized the opportunity to give full play to my emotion ; I shouted, I wept, I passionately called his name. Happily for me, my weak voice was drowned in the storm which raged about me.

"At other times he was hissed when he seemed to me to be sublime, and then I left the theatre, my heart full of rage. Those nights were the most dangerous for me. I was violently tempted to seek him out, to weep with him, to curse the age in which we lived, and to console him by offering him my enthusiasm and love.

"One evening as I left the theatre by the side passage which led to my box, a small, slender man passed in front of me, and turned into the street. One of the stage-carpenters took off his hat and said : ' Good evening, Monsieur Lelio.'

"Eager to obtain a nearer view of this extraordinary man, I ran after him, crossed the street, and, forgetting the danger to which I exposed myself, followed him into a café. Fortunately, it was not one in which I was likely to meet any one of my own rank.

"When, by the light of the smoky lamp, I looked at Lelio, I thought I had been mistaken and had followed another man. He was at least thirty-five, sallow, withered, and worn out. He was badly dressed, he looked vulgar, spoke in a hoarse, broken voice, shook hands with the meanest wretches, drank brandy, and swore horribly.

"It was not until I had heard his name repeated several times that I felt sure that this was the divinity of the theatre, interpreter of the great Corneille. I could recognize none of those charms which had so fascinated me, not even his glance, so bright, so ardent, and so sad. His eyes were dull, dead, almost stupid ; his strongly-accentuated pronunciation seemed ignoble when he called to the waiter, or talked of gambling and taverns. He walked badly, he looked vulgar, and the paint was only half wiped from his cheeks. It was no longer Hippolyte—it was Lelio. The temple was empty ; the oracle was dumb ; the divinity had become a man, not even a man—an actor.

"He went out, and I sat stupefied, without even presence of mind enough to drink the hot spiced wine I had called for. When I remembered where I was, and perceived the insulting glances which were heaped upon me, I became frightened. It was the first time I had ever found myself in such an equivocal position, and in such immediate contact with people of that class.

"I rose and tried to escape, but forgot to pay my reckoning. The waiter ran after me ; I was terribly ashamed ; I was obliged to return, enter into explanations at the desk, and endure all the mocking and suspicious looks which were turned upon me.

"When I left I thought I was followed. In vain I looked for a hackney-coach ; there were none remaining in front of the theatre. I constantly heard heavy steps echoing my own. Trembling, I turned my head, and recognized a tall, ill-looking fellow whom I had noticed in one corner of the café, and who had very much the air of a spy or something worse. He spoke to me ; I do not know what he said ; I was too much frightened to hear, but I had still presence of mind enough to rid myself of him. I struck him in the face with my cane, and, leaving him stunned at my audacity, I shot away swift as an arrow, and did not stop till I reached Florence's little garret.

"When I awoke the next morning in my own bed, with its wadded curtains and coronal of pink feathers, I almost thought I had dreamed, and felt greatly mortified when I recollected the dis-illusions of the previous night. I thought myself thoroughly cured of my love, and I tried to rejoice at it, but in vain. I was filled with a mortal regret, the weariness of life again entered my heart, the world had not a pleasure which could charm me.

"Evening came, but brought no more beneficial emotions. Society seemed to me stupid. I went to church and listened to the evening lecture with a determination of becoming pious ; I caught cold, and came home quite ill. I remained in bed several days. The Comtesse de Ferrières came to see me, assured me that I had no fever, that lying still made me ill, that I must amuse myself, go out, go to the theatre. She compelled me to go with her to see *Cinna*.[1]

"'You no longer go to the theatre,' said she to me ; 'your health is undermined by your piety, and the dulness of your life. You have not seen Lelio for some time ; he has improved, and he is now some-times applauded. I think he may some day become very tolerable.'

"I do not know why I allowed myself to be persuaded. How-ever, as I was completely disenchanted with Lelio, I thought I no longer ran any risk in braving his fascinations in public. I dressed myself with excessive brilliance, and, in a court proscenium box, fronted a danger in which I no longer believed.

"But the danger was never more imminent. Lelio was sublime, and I had never been more in love with him. My recent adventure seemed but a dream. I could not believe that Lelio was other than he seemed upon the stage. In spite of myself, I yielded to the terrible agitations into which he had the power of throwing me. My face was bathed in tears, and I was compelled to cover it with my hand-kerchief.

"In the disorder of my mind I wiped off my rouge and my patches, and the Comtesse de Ferrières advised me to retire to the back of my box, for my emotion was creating a sensation in the house. I fortunately had had the skill to make every one believe it was the playing of Mlle. Hippolyte Clairon which affected me so deeply.

[1] *Cinna*, a Tragedy by Corneille.

She was, in my own opinion, a very cold and formal actress, too superior perhaps for her profession, as it was then understood ; but her manner of saying ' Tout beau,' in *Cinna,* had given her a great reputation. It must be said, however, that when she played with Lelio she outdid herself. Although she took pains to proclaim her share in the fashionable contempt for his method of acting, she assuredly felt the influence of his genius.

" That evening Lelio noticed me, either on account of my dress or my emotion ; for I saw him, when he was not acting, bend over one of the spectators, who, at that epoch, sat upon the stage, and inquire my name. I guessed his question by the way both looked at me.

" My heart beat almost to suffocation, and I noticed during the play that Lelio's eyes turned several times toward me. What would I not have given to hear what the Chevalier de Bretillac, whom he had questioned, had said to him about me ! Lelio's face did not indicate the nature of the information he had received, for he was obliged to retain the expression suited to his part. I knew this Bretillac very slightly, and I could not imagine whether he would speak well or ill of me.

" That night I understood for the first time the nature of the passion which enchained me to Lelio. It was a passion purely intellectual, purely ideal. It was not he I loved, but those heroes of ancient times whose sincerity, whose fidelity, whose tenderness he knew how to portray ; with him and by him I was carried back to an epoch of forgotten virtues. I was bright enough to think that in those days I should not have been misjudged and hated, and that I should not have been reduced to loving a phantom of the footlights.

" Lelio was to me but the shadow of the Cid, the representative of that antique chivalric love now ridiculed in France. My Lelio was a fictitious being who had no existence outside the theatre. The illusions of the stage, the glare of the footlights, were a part of the being whom I loved. Without them he was nothing to me, and faded like a story before the brightness of day. I had no desire to see him off the boards ; and should have been in despair had I met him. It would have been like contemplating the ashes of a great man.

" One evening as I was going to the Carmelite church with the intention of leaving it by the passage door, I perceived that I was followed, and became convinced that henceforth it would be almost impossible to conceal the object of my nocturnal expeditions. I decided to go publicly to the theatre. Lelio saw me and watched me ; my beauty had struck him, my sensibility flattered him. His attention sometimes wandered so much as to displease the public. Soon I could no longer doubt. He was madly in love with me.

" My box had pleased the Princess de Vaudemont. I gave it up to her, and took for myself a smaller one, less in view of the house

and better situated. I was almost upon the stage, I did not lose
one of Lelio's glances ; and he could look at me without its being
seen by the public. But I no longer needed to catch his eye in
order to understand all his feelings. The sound of his voice, his
sighs, the expression which he gave to certain verses, certain words,
told me that he was speaking to me. I was the happiest and
proudest of women, for then it was the hero, not the actor, who
loved me.

" I have since heard that Lelio often followed me in my walks and
drives ; so little did I desire to see him outside of the theatre that I
never perceived it. Of the eighty years I have passed in this world,
those five are the only ones in which I really lived.

" One day I read in the *Mercure de France* the name of a new actor
engaged at the Comédie Française to replace Lelio, who was about
to leave France.

" This announcement was a mortal blow to me. I could not
conceive how I should exist when deprived of these emotions, this
life of passion and storm. This event gave an immense development to my love, and was well-nigh my ruin.

" I no longer struggled with myself ; I no longer sought to stifle
all thoughts contrary to the dignity of my rank. I regretted that he
was not what he appeared on the stage ; I wished him as young and
handsome as he seemed each night before the footlights, that I
might sacrifice to him all my pride, all my prejudices.

" While I was in this state of irresolution, I received a letter in an
unknown hand. It is the only love-letter I have ever kept. Though
Larrieux has written me innumerable protestations, and I have
received a thousand perfumed declarations from a hundred others,
it is the only real love-letter that was ever sent me."

The Marquise rose, opened with a steady hand an inlaid casket,
and took from it a crumpled, worn-out letter, which I read with
difficulty :

" MADAME—I am certain you will feel nothing but contempt for
this letter, you will not even deem it worthy of your anger. But,
to a man falling into an abyss, what matters one more stone at the
bottom ? You will think me mad, and you will be right. You will
perhaps pity me, for you will not doubt my sincerity. However
humble your piety may have made you, you will understand the
extent of my despair ; you must already know *how much evil and
how much good your eyes can do.* . . .

" You must know this already, madame ; it is impossible that
the violent emotions I have portrayed upon the stage, my cries of
wrath and despair, have not twenty times revealed to you my
passion. You cannot have lighted all these flames without being
conscious of what you did. Perhaps you played with me as a tiger

with his prey ; perhaps the spectacle of my folly and my tortures was your pastime. But no ; to think so were to presume too much. No, madame, I do not believe it ; you never thought of me. You felt the verses of the great Corneille, you identified these with the noble passions of tragedy ; that was all.

" And I, madman that I was, I dared to think that my voice alone sometimes awoke your sympathies, that my heart echoed in yours, that between you and me there was something more than between me and the public. Oh, my madness was arrant, but it was sweet ! Leave me my illusions, madame ; what are they to you ? Do you fear that I should boast of them ? By what right should I do so, and who would believe me ? I should only make myself a laughing-stock of sensible people. Leave me this conviction ; it has given me more joy than the severity of the public has caused me sorrow. Let me bless you, let me thank you upon my knees, for the sensibility which I have discovered in your soul, and which no one else has ever shown me ; for the tears which I have seen you shed for my fictitious sorrows, and which have often raised my inspiration almost to delirium ; for the timid glances which sought, at least it seemed so, to console me for the coldness of my audience. Oh, why were you born to pomp and splendour ! Why am I an obscure and nameless artist ! Why have I not riches and the favour of the public, that I might exchange them for a name, for one of those titles which I have hitherto disdained, and which, perhaps, would permit me to aspire as high as you are placed !

" Once I deemed the distinctions conferred upon talent superior to all others. To what purpose, thought I, is a man a Chevalier or a Marquis but to be the sillier, the vainer, and the more insolent ? I hated the pride of men of rank, and thought that I should be sufficiently avenged for their disdain if my genius raised me above them. Dreams and delusions all ! My strength has not equalled my mad ambition. I have remained obscure ; I have done worse— I have touched success, and allowed it to escape me. I thought myself great, and I was cast down to the dust ; I imagined that I was almost sublime, and I was condemned to be ridiculous. Fate took me —me and my audacious dreams—and crushed me as if I had been a reed ! I am a most wretched man ! But I committed my greatest folly when I cast my eyes beyond that row of lights which marked between me and the rest of society an invisible line of separation. It is to me a circle of Popilius. I, an actor, I dared to raise my eyes and fasten them upon a beautiful woman—upon a woman, young, lovely, and of high rank ; for you are all this, madame, and I know it. The world accuses you of coldness and of exaggerated piety. I alone understand you. Your first smile, your first tear, sufficiently disproved the absurd fable which the Chevalier de Bretillac repeated against you.

"But then what a destiny is yours! What fatality weighs upon you as upon me, that in the midst of society so brilliant, which calls itself so enlightened, you should have found only the heart of a poor actor to do you justice. Nothing will deprive me of the sad and consoling thought that, had we been born in the same rank, you would have been mine in spite of my rivals, in spite of my inferiority. You would have been compelled to acknowledge that there is in me something greater than their wealth, and their titles—the power of loving you.   LELIO."

"This letter," continued the Marquise, "was of a character very unusual at the time it was written, and seemed to me, notwithstanding some passages of theatrical declamation at the beginning, so powerful, so true, so full of only bold passion, that I was overwhelmed by it. The pride which still struggled within me faded away. I would have given all the remaining days I had to live one hour of such love.

"I answered in these words, as nearly as I can remember:

"'I do not accuse you, Lelio; I accuse destiny. I do not pity you alone; I pity myself also. Neither pride nor prudence shall make me deny you the consolation of believing that I have felt a preference for you. Keep it, for it is the only one I can offer you. I can never consent to see you.'

"Next day I received a note which I hastily read and threw into the fire, to prevent Larrieux from seeing it, for he came suddenly upon me while I was reading it. It read thus:

"'MADAME—I must see you or I must die. Once—once only, but for a single hour, if such is your will. Why should you fear an interview since you trust my honour and my prudence. Madame, I know who you are; I am well aware of your piety and of the austerity of your life. I am not fool enough to hope for anything but a word of compassion, but it must fall from your own lips. My heart must receive it and bear it away, or my heart must break.

LELIO.'

"I believed implicitly in the humility, in the sincerity of Lelio. Besides, I had ample reason to trust my own strength. I resolved to see him. I had completely forgotten his faded features, his low-bred manners, his vulgar aspect; I recollected only the fascination of his genius, his letters, and his love. I answered:

"'I will see you. Find some secure place, but hope for nothing but for what you have asked. Should you seek to abuse my trust, you would be a villain, and I should not fear you.'

"Answer:

"'Your trust would save you from the basest of villains. You will see, Madame, that Lelio is not unworthy of it. Duke —— has often been good enough to offer me the use of his house in the Rue de Valois Deign to go thither after the play.'

" Some explanations and directions as to the locality of the house followed. I received this note at four o'clock. The whole negotiation had occupied but a day. I had spent it in wandering through the house like one distracted ; I was in a fever. This rapid succession of events bore me along as in a dream.

" When I had made the final decision, when it was impossible to draw back, I sank down upon my ottoman, breathless and dizzy.

" I was really ill. A surgeon was sent for ; I was bled. I told my servants not to mention my indisposition to any one ; I dreaded the intrusion of officious advisers, and was determined not to be prevented from going out that night.

" I threw myself upon my bed to await the appointed hour, and gave orders that no visitors should be admitted. The blood-letting had relieved and weakened me ; I sank into a great depression of spirits. All my illusions vanished with the excitement which had accompanied my fever. Reason and memory returned ; I remembered my disenchantment in the coffee-house, and Lelio's wretched appearance there ; I prepared to blush for my folly, and to fall from the height of my deceitful visions to a bare and despicable reality. I no longer understood how it had been possible for me to consent to exchange my heroic and romantic tenderness for the revulsion of feeling which awaited me, and the sense of shame which would henceforth poison all my recollections. I bitterly regretted what I had done ; I wept my illusions, my love, and that future of pure and secret joys which I was about to forfeit. Above all, I mourned for Lelio, whom in seeing I should for ever lose, in whose love I had found five years of happiness, and for whom in a few hours I should feel nothing but indifference.

" In the paroxysm of my grief I violently wrung my arms ; the vein reopened, and I had barely time to ring for my maid, who found me in a swoon in my bed. A deep and heavy sleep, against which I struggled in vain, seized me. I neither dreamed nor suffered ; I was as one dead for several hours. When I again opened my eyes my room was almost dark, my house silent ; my waiting-woman was asleep in a chair at the foot of my bed. I remained for some time in such a state of numbness and weakness that I recollected nothing.

" Suddenly my memory returned, and I asked myself whether the hour and the day of rendezvous were passed, whether I had slept an hour or a century ; whether I had killed Lelio by breaking my word. Was there yet time ? I tried to rise, but my strength failed me. I struggled for some moments as if in a nightmare. At last I summoned all the forces of my will. I sprang to the floor, opened the curtains, and saw the moon shining upon the trees of my garden. I ran to the clock ; the hands marked ten. I seized my maid and waked her : ' Quinette, what day of the week is it ? '

38

"She sprang from her chair, screaming, and tried to escape from me, for she thought me delirious; I reassured her and learned that I had only slept three hours. I thanked God. I asked for a hackney-coach. Quinette looked at me in amazement. At last she became convinced that I had the full use of my senses, transmitted my order, and began to dress me.

"I asked for my simplest dress; I put no ornaments in my hair, I refused to wear my rouge. I wished above all things for Lelio's esteem and respect, for they were far more precious to me than his love. Nevertheless, I was pleased when Quinette, who was much surprised at this new caprice, said, examining me from head to foot: 'Truly, madame, I know not how you manage it. You are dressed in a plain white robe, without either train or pannier; you are ill and as pale as death; you have not even put on a patch; yet I never saw you so beautiful as to-night. I pity the men who will look upon you!'

"'Do you think me so very austere, my poor Quinette?'

"'Alas, madame, every day I pray Heaven to make me like you; but up to this time——'

"'Come, simpleton, give me my mantle and muff.'

"At midnight I was in the house in the Rue de Valois. I was carefully veiled, a sort of valet de chambre received me; he was the only human being to be seen in this mysterious dwelling. He led me through the windings of a dark garden to a pavilion buried in silence and shadow. Depositing his green silk lantern in the vestibule, he opened the door of a large dusky room, showed me by a respectful gesture and with a most impassive face a ray of light proceeding from the other extremity, and said, in a tone so low that it seemed as if he feared to awaken the sleeping echoes: 'Your ladyship is alone, no one else has yet come. Your ladyship will find in the summer parlour a bell which I will answer if you need anything.' He disappeared as if by enchantment, shutting the door upon me.

"I was terribly frightened; I thought I had fallen into some trap. I called him back. He instantly reappeared, and his air of stupid solemnity reassured me. I asked him what time it was, although I knew perfectly well, for I had sounded my watch twenty times in the carriage. 'It is midnight,' answered he, without raising his eyes.

"I now resolutely entered the summer parlour, and I realised how unfounded were my fears when I saw that the doors which opened upon the garden were only of painted silk. Nothing could be more charming than this boudoir; it was fitted up as a concert-room. The walls were of stucco as white as snow, and the mirrors were framed in unpolished silver. Musical instruments of unusually rich material were scattered about, upon seats of white velvet, trimmed with pearls. The light came from above through leaves of alabaster, which formed a dome. This soft, even light might have been mistaken for that of the moon. A single statue of white marble stood in the middle of the room ; it was an antique and represented Isis veiled, with her finger upon her lips. The mirrors which reflected us, both pale and draped in white, produced such an illusion upon me that I was obliged to distinguish my finger from hers.

"Suddenly the silence was interrupted ; the door was opened and closed, and light footsteps sounded upon the floor. I sank into a chair more dead than alive, for I was about to see Lelio shorn of the illusions of the stage. I closed my eyes, and inwardly bade them farewell before I reopened them.

"But how much was I surprised ! Lelio was beautiful as an angel. He had not taken off his stage dress, and it was the most elegant I had ever seen him wear. His Spanish doublet was of white satin, his shoulder and garter knots of cherry ribbons, and a short cloak of the same colour was thrown over his shoulder. He wore an immense ruff of English lace ; his hair was short and unpowdered, partially covered by a cap with white feathers and a diamond rose. In this costume he had just played Don Juan in Molière's *Festin de Pierre*. Never had I seen him so beautiful, so young, so poetical, as at that moment. Velasquez would have worshipped such a model.

"He knelt before me. I could not help stretching out my hand to him, he seemed so submissive, so fearful of displeasing me. A man sufficiently in love to tremble before a woman was rare in those times, and this one was thirty-five and an actor.

"It seemed to me then, it seems to me still, that he was in the first bloom of youth. In his white dress he looked like a young page ; his forehead had all the purity, his heart all the ardour of a first love. He took my hands and covered them with kisses. My senses seemed to desert me ; I caressed his burning forehead, his stiff, black hair, and the brown neck which disappeared in the soft whiteness of his collar. He wept like a woman ; I was overwhelmed with surprise.

"I wept delicious tears. I compelled him to raise his head and look at me. How splendid, how tender were his eyes ! How much fascination his warm, true soul communicated to the very defects of his face, and the scars left upon it by time and toil ! When I saw the premature wrinkles upon his beautiful forehead, when I saw the pallor of his lips, the languor of his smile, my heart was melted. I felt that I must needs weep for his griefs, his disappointments, the labours of his life. I identified myself with him in all his sorrows, even that of his long, hopeless love for me, and I had but one wish— to compensate him for the ills he had suffered.

"My dear Lelio, my great Rodrigue, my beautiful Don Juan ! He spoke to me, he told me how from a dissipated actor I had made him a man full of life and ardour ; how I had raised him in his own eyes, and restored to him the illusions of his youth ; he spoke of his respect, his veneration for me, of his contempt for the species of love which was then in fashion. Never did a man with more penetrating eloquence speak to the heart of a woman ; never did Racine make love utter itself with such conviction of its own truth, such poetry, such strength. Everything elevated and profound, everything sweet and fiery which passion can inspire, lay in his words, his face, his eyes, his caresses. Alas ! did he deceive himself ! Was he playing a part ? "

" I certainly do not think so," I cried, looking at the Marquise. She seemed to grow young as she spoke ; and, like the fairy Urgela, to cast off her hundred years. I know not who has said that a woman's heart has no wrinkles.

" Listen to the end," said she. " I threw my arms around his neck ; I shivered as I touched the satin of his coat, as I breathed the perfume of his hair. My emotion was too violent and I fainted.

" He recalled me to myself by his prompt assistance. I found him still kneeling at my feet. ' Pity me, kill me,' cried he. He was paler and far more ill than I.

" ' Listen, Lelio,' said I. ' Here we separate for ever, but let us carry from this place a whole future of blissful thoughts and adored memories. I swear, Lelio, to love you till my death. I swear it without fear, for I feel that the snows of age will not have the power to extinguish this ardent flame.'

" Lelio knelt before me ; he did not implore me, he did not reproach me ; he said that he had not hoped for so much happiness as I had given him, and that he had no right to ask for more. Nevertheless, as he bade me farewell, his despair, the emotion which trembled in his face, terrified me. I asked him if he would not find happiness in thinking of me, if the ecstasy of our meeting would not lend its charm to all the days of his life, if his past and future sorrows would not be softened each time he recalled it. He roused himself to promise, to swear all I asked. He again fell at my feet and passionately kissed my dress. I made a sign and he left me. The carriage I had sent for came.

" The automatic servant of the house knocked three times outside to warn me. Lelio despairingly threw himself in front of the door : he looked like a spectre. I gently repulsed him and he yielded. I crossed the threshold, and as he attempted to follow me, I showed him a chair in the middle of the room, underneath the statue of Isis. He sat down in it. A passionate smile wandered over his lips, his eyes sent out one more flash of gratitude and love. He was still beautiful, still young, still a grandee of Spain.

" After a few steps, when I was about to lose him for ever, I turned back and looked at him once more. Despair had crushed him. He was old, altered, frightful. His body seemed paralysed. His stiffened lips attempted an unmeaning smile. His eyes were glassy and dim ; he was now only Lelio, the shadow of a lover and a prince."

The Marquise paused ; then, while her aspect changed like that of a ruin which totters and sinks, she added : " Since then I have not heard him mentioned."

The Marquise made a second and a longer pause ; then, with the terrible fortitude which comes with length of years, which springs from the persistent love of life or the near hope of death, she said with a smile : " Well, do you not now believe in the ideality of the eighteenth century ? "

JULES JANIN
1804–1874

THE VENDEAN MARRIAGE

So you have never heard the circumstances of Monsieur
Baudelot de Dairval's marriage, the man who died four years
ago, and was so mourned by his wife that she died a week later
herself, good lady ?   Yet it is a story worth telling.

It happened in Vendée, and the hero, a Vendean, brave, young,
daring, and of fine family, died tranquilly in his bed without ever
suspecting that there would be a second rising in Vendée.

Baudelot de Dairval was the grandson of that César Baudelot who
is mentioned in the Memoirs of the Duchess of Orleans, own mother
of the regent Louis Philippe.   This woman, who has thrown such
contempt on the greatest names of France, could not help praising
César de Baudelot.   Saint-Simon, sceptic and mocker, but good
fellow withal, also spoke highly of him.   So you'll understand that
bearing such a name young Henri was not backward in the first rising
in Vendée, in protesting, arms in hand, against the excesses of the
Revolution.   Baudelot was a Vendean simply because a man of his
name and nature could be nothing else.   He fought like his associates,
neither more nor less.   He was the friend of Cathelmeau and of all
the others.   He took part in those battles of giants ; fighting stoutly
in the battle, and then laughing and singing as soon as he no longer
heard the cries of the wounded.   What wars, what wild tempests
were ever like those ?   But it is not my business to tell again the
story so often told.

But I want to tell you that one day, surprised at a farm by a
detachment of the Republican Blues, Baudelot unexpectedly called
together his troop.   " My friends," said he " this farm is surrounded.
You must all escape !   Take with you the women and children.
Rejoin our chief, Cathelmeau.   As for me, I'll stay and defend the
gate.   I certainly can hold it alone for ten minutes.   Those three
thousand out there would massacre us all.   Good-bye, good-bye,
my brave fellows !   Don't forget me !   It's my turn to-day.
You'll get yourselves killed to-morrow ! "

In those exceptional times and in that exceptional war, nothing
seemed astonishing.   Men did not even think of those rivalries in

heroism so frequent in civilised warfare. In such a struggle of extermination there was no time to pose for sublimity of soul. Heroism was quite unaffected. So Baudelot's soldiers judged for themselves that their chief spoke sensibly, and obeyed as simply as he had commanded. They withdrew by the roof, taking away the women and children. Baudelot remained at the door making noise enough for forty, haranguing, disputing and discharging his gun. One would have thought a whole regiment ready to fire was stationed there, and the Blues held themselves on the alert. Baudelot remained on the defensive as long as he had any voice. But when that failed and he thought his troop must have reached a place of safety, he tired of the warlike feint. He felt ill at ease at thus commanding the absent ; and keeping quiet, he merely propped up the door as it was shaken from outside. This lasted several minutes, then the door cracked, and the Blues began to fire through the fissures. Baudelot was not wounded, and as his meal had been interrupted, he returned to the table and tranquilly ate some bread and cheese, and emptied a pitcher of country wine, thinking meanwhile that this was his last repast !

Finally the Blues forced the door and rushed in. It took them some minutes to clear away obstructions, and to recognise each other in the smoke of their guns. These soldiers of the Republic hunted eagerly with look and sword for the armed troop which had withstood them so long. Judge their surprise at seeing only a tall, very handsome young man, calmly eating black bread moistened with wine. Dumb with astonishment the conquerors stopped and leaned on their guns, and thus gave Henri Baudelot time to swallow his last mouthful.

" To your health, gentlemen ! " he said, lifting his glass to his lips. " The garrison thanks you for the respite you have granted." At the same time he rose, and going straight to the Captain, said : " Monsieur, I am the only person in this house. I am quite ready for death."

Then he kept quiet, and waited. To his great surprise he was not shot at once. Perhaps he had fallen into the hands of recruits so little exercised as to delay twenty-four hours before killing a man. Perhaps his captors were moved by his coolness and fine bearing, and were ashamed at setting three hundred to kill one. We must remember that in that sad war there were French feelings on both sides.

So they contented themselves with tying his hands and leading him, closely watched, to a manor on the outskirts of Nantes, which once an attractive country-seat, had now become a kind of fortress. Its master was no other than the chief of the Blues, who had captured Baudelot. This Breton, a gentleman although a Blue, had been one of the first to share the enthusiasm of the revolutionaries. He was one of those nobles so heroic to their own injury, who renounced in a day fortunes, their coats of arms, and their own names, forgetting both what they had promised their fathers and what they owed to their sons, equally oblivious of past and future, and unfortunate victims of the present. But we will not reproach them, for either they died under the stroke of the Revolution, or lived long enough to see that all their sacrifices were vain.

Baudelot de Dairval was confined in the donjon, or, rather, in the pigeon-house of his conqueror. The doves had been expelled to give place to Chouan captives. Still covered with shining slates, still surmounted by its creaking weather-cock, this prison had retained a calm, gracious air, and it had not been thought necessary to bar the openings by which the pigeons came and went. A little straw had been added to the usual furniture.

At first the dovecote of a country manor struck him as a novel prison. He decided that as soon as his hands were free he would compose a romance upon it, with a guitar accompaniment. While thus thinking, he heard a violin and other instruments playing a joyful march. By piling up the straw against the wall and leaning on it with his elbow, Baudelot could look out of one of the openings. He saw a long procession of young men and pretty women in white gowns, preceded by village fiddlers, and all merry and joyous. As it passed at the foot of the dovecote, a pretty girl looked up attentively. She was fair, slender and dreamy-looking. Baudelot felt that she knew of the prisoner, and he began to whistle the air of Richard, " In an Obscure Tower," or something of the kind. For this young man was versed in all kinds of accomplishments, equally skilful with sword and guitar, an adept at horsemanship, a fine dancer, a true gentleman of wit and sword, such as are manufactured no more.

The wedding procession passed, or, at least, if not a wedding it was a betrothal, and Baudelot stopped singing. He heard a sound at his prison door ; some one entered.

It was the master of the house himself. He had been a Marquis under Capet, now he called himself simply Hamelin. He was a Blue, but a decent soul enough. The Republic ruled him body and soul ; he lent his sword and his castle. But he had not become cruel or wicked in its service. The morning of this very day, Captain Hamelin, for so he had been appointed by the Republic, learning that some Chouans were at his farm, had headed a detachment of Blues and postponed his betrothal. You know how he had seized Baudelot. As soon as the Chouan was in keeping the Captain had returned to his betrothal feast, and this is the reason why he did not shoot the prisoner at once or take him to Nantes.

Captain Hamelin was not so thorough a Blue as to have quite forgotten the hospitable old customs of Bretagne soil. Therefore, while his friends were sitting down to table, he felt it incumbent to call upon his captive.

" Can I do anything for you, monsieur ? " he asked.

" Monsieur," said Baudelot, bowing, " I should like the use of at least one of my hands."

" Your hands shall be unbound, monsieur," answered Hamelin, " if you will promise not to try to escape. But before you promise, remember that at six o'clock to-morrow morning you will surely be taken to Nantes."

" And shot at eight o'clock just as surely ? " asked Baudelot.

Captain Hamelin was silent.

" Very well, monsieur," said Baudelot. " Unbind my hands, and unless I'm delivered, I give my word as a gentleman and a Christian to stay here like a pigeon with clipped wings."

Captain Hamelin could not help smiling at his prisoner's allusion, and untied his hands.

" Now," said Baudelot, stretching his arms like a man stiff from sleep, " now, monsieur, I thank you, and am truly your servant until to-morrow. It will not be my fault if my gratitude does not last longer ! "

Captain Hamelin said : " If you have any last arrangements— a will to make, for instance—I will send you writing materials." He was touched, for he was not a Breton for nothing.

Seeing this, Baudelot took his hand. " Do you know," he said sadly, " that simple word ' will ' wounds me more than the words ' death at Nantes ! ' It recalls that all my friends are dead. There is no one to whom I can bequeath my name, my sword, my love and my hate, and these are all I have left. Yet, it must be sweet to dispose of a fortune, to be generous even beyond the tomb ; and while writing last benefits, to imagine the tears of joy and sorrow they will cause. That is sweet and honourable, isn't it, Captain ? I must not think of it."

" I will send you some dinner," said Hamelin. " This is my day of betrothal, and my table is better provided than usual. My fiancée herself shall serve you, monsieur."

In one of the highest apertures of his cage, Baudelot saw a daisy which had been sown there by one of the first occupants of the dovecote. The pretty flower swayed joyously in the wind, and he gathered it and offered it to the Captain.

" It is our custom at home, Captain, to offer the bride a gift. Be so good as to give yours this little flower, which has blossomed in my domain. And now, good-night. I have kept you from your love long enough. May God remember your kindness toward me ! Good-bye. Best wishes ! Send me some supper, for I'm hungry and need rest."

And they separated with friendly looks.

Dinner was brought the young Vendean by a pretty Breton girl with white teeth, rosy lips, and the pensive air which befitted a shy

country maiden who had already seen so many proscripts. She
served him zealously, and gave him no peace if he did not eat of this
or that dish, drink this or that wine. It was a magnificent repast.
The dovecote grew fragrant. It was almost like the time when the
winged occupants of the tower gathered crumbs from the feast.
As the girl was pouring champagne, Baudelot said to her :

" What is your name, my child ? "

" My name is Marie," she answered.

" The same as my cousin's, " went on the young man ; " and how
old are you, Marie ? "

" Seventeen years," said Marie.

" The age of my cousin," said Baudelot, and as he thought of his
pretty cousin butchered by the executioner, his heart almost failed
him. But he blushed to weep before this child in whose eyes tears
were gathering, and as he could not speak, he held out his glass. But
the glass was full, and in the last rays of the sun the champagne
sparkled joyously, for wine sparkled and spring bloomed even during
the Terror. Seeing that his glass was full, Baudelot said :

" You have no glass, Marie ? "

" I am not thirsty," said Marie.

" Oh ! " said Baudelot, " this bright wine does not like to be drunk
by a man alone. It is convivial by nature, and rejoices to be among
boon companions. It is the great support of the Fraternity of which
you have heard so much, my poor Marie, and which men really
comprehend so little. Be friendly ; dip your lips in my glass, my
pretty Breton, if you would have me drink champagne once more
before I die," and he lifted the glass to Marie's lips. She held them
out, but at the words to " die " her heart overflowed, and copious
tears rolled into the joyous wine.

" To your health, Marie ! " said Baudelot, and drank both wine
and tears.

Just then they heard the horn, the hautboys, and the violins.
" What's that ? " said the young man, setting down his glass. " God
bless me, it's a ball ! "

" Alas ! " said Marie, " alas ! yes, it's a ball. My young mistress
did not want dancing, but her lover and her father insisted. She is
very unhappy this evening."

" Oh ! " said the young Vendean, " my good Marie, if you are as
kind as I think, you'll do something for me ! Go, run, fly, tell your
mistress that Count Baudelot de Dairval, Colonel of Light Horse,
requests permission to pay her his respects. Or, no ; find my host,
not his bride, and tell him that his prisoner is very dull, that the
noise of the ball will prevent his sleeping, that the night will be long
and cold, that it's a charity to snatch an unhappy young man from
the sad thought of his last night, that I beg him, in Heaven's name,
to let me attend his ball. Tell him he has my word of honour not to

try to escape. Tell him all that, Marie ; and tell him whatever else comes into your heart and mind. Speak loud enough for your mistress to hear and be interested ; and, thanks to you, Marie, I'm sure he will yield. Then, child, if I am invited, send your master's valet. Tell him to bring me clean linen and powder. There must be some powder still left in the castle. Tell him to bring me one of his master's coats, and get them to lend me my sword just for the evening. I will not unsheath it. So, Marie, go, child ! " And the prisoner hurried her off and held her back in a way to make one both laugh and cry.

A few minutes later Captain Hamelin's valet appeared in the dove-cote. He was a good old fellow, faithful to powder and to all the other customs. Although a member of the municipal council, he was an honest man, devoted to Monsieur Robespierre only because he alone in all republican France had dared to continue powder, ruffles, and embroidered vest.

He brought a complete suit, which Captain Hamelin had ordered when younger and a Marquis, to visit the court and see the King when there was a court and a King. This suit was very rich and hand-some, the linen very white, the shoes very fine. Baudelot's host had forgotten nothing, not even the perfumes and cosmetics of an aristocrat. Baudelot entrusted his head to the valet, who adorned it complaisantly, not without profound sighs of regret. Baudelot was young and handsome, but had not been groomed for some time. Therefore, when he saw himself dressed, curled, and fresh shaven, his eyes animated by a good meal and by the music in the distance, he could not help smiling with self-content and recalling his beautiful nights at masked balls and at operas with the Comte de Mirabeau.

He lacked only his sword, which was given him at the door with a reminder of his promise. It was night when he crossed the garden to the ballroom.

All the most beautiful republican ladies of the province were there. But, you know, women are not so revolutionary that they do not feel aristocratic sympathy for a young and handsome gentleman who is to be shot on the morrow.

To return to our story. The betrothal ball had begun. The fiancée was Mademoiselle de Mailly, grand-niece of the beautiful De Mailly, so beloved of Madame de Maintenon. She was a sad young blonde, evidently unhappy at dancing and marrying in that period of proscription. She was one of those strong spirits which seem weak until a certain fatal hour has sounded, when apparent weakness becomes invincible energy. The heroine replaces the little girl, and the ruins of a whole world could not intimidate her, who, until then, trembled at the least sign of displeasure.

Eleanor de Mailly was then very dejected. The friends of her childhood imitated her silence and despondency. Never before was a Breton feast so gloomy. Nothing went as it should, neither dance

nor dancers, and there was general lack of ease. The young men did
not even try to please the pretty girls, and when the ball had scarcely
begun every one wished it would end.

Suddenly the door into the great hall opened, and every one looked
that way. There entered a pretty courtier, a lost type, a handsome
officer, smiling and well dressed. He had the dress and graceful
bearing of old times. This apparition was in charming contrast
with the dulness of the gathering. The men and women who
were bluest at heart were delighted to find with them this remnant
of the old French society so suddenly blotted out, alas! And,
indeed, it was charming to see this young proscript, whom death
on the morrow awaited, entering into this republican company,
recalling its gaiety, and thinking of nothing but to be agreeable
and please the ladies, faithful to the end to his calling of French
gentleman!

His entrance took only a minute. Once in the room, he gave
himself up to the ball and went to invite the first woman he saw.
It was the fair-haired girl whom he had noticed in the garden.
She accepted without hesitation, remembering that republican
death, the most unpleasant of all deaths, was offering her partner
a bloody hand. When the men saw Baudelot dancing, doomed
as he was, they blushed at their own lack of ardour. All the women
were invited to dance at once, and accepted in order to see Baudelot
nearer. So, thanks to the victim, the ball grew nearly gay.

Baudelot heartily shared this convulsive pleasure. His smile was
not forced ; his dance was light and graceful. He alone was
genuinely entertained. The others amused themselves in very
terror, and became almost delirious at sight of this beautiful youth,
who was king of the festival far more than the bridegroom. Animated by such passion, terror, and bloody interest, the ball took
possession of all. Baudelot was everywhere, saluting old ladies,
like the King of France, and young ones with joy and admiration,
talking to men in the mad language of youth and of nature mixed
with wit.

The more he yielded to this frank and natural gaiety, the more
he forgot that the night was advancing with frightful rapidity.
And the later it grew the more the women trembled in their hearts
at the thought that he must really die, for they were near the epoch
of old French honour, which made Baudelot's presence at the ball
the sign that there was no hope for him. They knew his word
bound him faster than iron chains could have done. They knew
that both Baudelot and Hamelin were doing right. Baudelot's
pleasure did no wrong to the committee of public safety. As you
may imagine, then, looks and smiles were very tender, and more
than one sigh escaped at sight of the handsome proscript. As for
him, drunk with success, he had never been so full of love and

passion. So when he went to dance for the third time with the queen of the ball, the fair-haired fiancée, he felt her little hand trembling, and trembled in his turn.

For when he glanced at her she was pale and exhausted.

" What is the matter, Eleanor ? " he asked. " What is the matter, madame ? Out of pity for your partner, do not tremble and grow so pale ! "

Then turning toward the window curtains, which were moving to the dance music, she pointed out the dawning light.

" It is morning," she said.

" Ah, well ! " said Baudelot, " what does it matter ? It is morning. I have passed the most beautiful night of my life I have seen you and loved you and been able to tell you I love you, for you know the dying don't lie. And now, good-bye, Eleanor, good-bye ! Be happy and accept the blessing of the Chouan ! "

It was the custom in Britanny, at the end of the last square dance, to kiss the lady on the forehead. The dance finished, Baudelot pressed his lips to Eleanor's brow. She grew faint and stood motionless, her brow supported by his lips. Then she recovered herself, and Baudelot led her to a seat. She made him sit down beside her, and said :

" Listen, you must go. Listen, they are harnessing the horses to take you to Nantes. Listen, in two hours you will be dead. Fly, then ! If you wish, I will go with you. Then they will say you fled out of love, not from fear. Listen, if you will not escape alone, or with me, I will throw myself under the wheels of the carriage, and you will pass over my broken body ! "

She said this in a low tone, without looking at him, and almost smiling, as though speaking of another ball.

Baudelot did not listen, but he looked at her with a joy in his heart such as he never before felt.

" How I love her ! " he said to himself. He answered : " You know very well that is impossible, Eleanor. Oh, yes ; if I were free you should have no husband but me, but I do not belong either to myself or to you. So good-bye, beautiful angel, and if you love me give me back the wild flower I sent you from my prison. Give it back, Eleanor. The little flower has been on your breast, it will help me to die."

At that moment Eleanor looked like death. There was a solemn silence. The music had stopped, and daylight was filling the room.

Suddenly there was a great noise of horses and riders. It seemed to come from Nantes, and all the women moved spontaneously to protect Baudelot with their bodies, but his own soldiers appeared to deliver him. They were in the garden ; they forced their way into the house, crying :

" Baudelot ! Baudelot ! "

They were astonished enough to find their young leader not loaded with irons, but surrounded by handsomely dressed ladies and himself adorned as they had never beheld him.

Baudelot's first question was :

" Gentlemen, did you enter the pigeon-house ? "

" Yes," was the answer. " That's where we began, Captain. Neither you nor the pigeons will find it again. The pigeon-house is torn down."

" Then," said Baudelot, drawing his sword, " I am released from my word. Thanks, my brave fellows ! "

Then he took off his hat.

" Madame," he said very gently, " receive the humble gratitude of the captive."

He asked for a carriage.

" One is already harnessed, Captain," said one of his soldiers. " The owner of the house tells us it was to take you to Nantes."

Just then Baudelot noticed Hamelin bound with the fetters he himself had worn.

" Service for service, Captain," he said ; " only, instead of untying your cords, allow me to cut them. No one shall wear them again."

Then, as he saw Eleanor recovering herself, he continued :

" Captain Hamelin, this period of civil war and spilled blood is too sad for betrothals. One can't tell whether there will be prisoners to watch in the morning or enemies to receive in the evening. Postpone your marriage, I beg of you. See, your fiancée herself wishes you to do so. My noble young lady, allow the poor Chouan to escort you back to your home at Mailly, will you not ? "

And soon all the young Chouans galloped away, rejoicing to have delivered their Captain, and glorious in the rising sun. Poor fellows, they had so little time left, most of them, for the sunshine !

There are men who seem immortal whatever they do. Baudelot de Dairval was not killed although he did not leave Vendée for an hour. When his country was less inundated with blood he married Eleanor de Mailly, and Captain Hamelin witnessed the wedding contract.

ÉMILE SOUVESTRE
1806–1854

UNCLE MAURICE

THE destinies of men are like the dawn; some rise raying out a thousand gleams, others are drowned in sombre clouds. That of my Uncle Maurice was of the unfortunate sort. He came into the world so puny that it was thought he would die; but in spite of his prediction, that could almost be called a hope, he continued to live, suffering and deformed. His childhood was without joy. Bullied because of his weakness, mocked because of his ugliness, the little hunchback vainly tried to make friends. Everybody passed him by, pointing their finger at him.

Still his mother remained to him, and it was to her that the boy brought all the love that was scorned elsewhere. Happy in this refuge, he reached the age when a man takes his place in life, and he had to be content with a position disdained by his companions. His scholarship should have opened all careers to him; he became receiver at one of the little city toll-gates. Enclosed in this dwelling-space of a few feet he had no other distraction, between his calculations and his entries, than reading and visits from his mother. On fine summer days she came to work at the door of the hut, in the shadow of the vines planted by Maurice. Even when she was silent, her presence was a solace to the hunchback. He heard the click of her long knitting-needles; he saw her sweet, sad profile, recalling so many ordeals bravely supported; and from time to time he could touch the bent shoulders with a caressing hand and exchange a smile.

This consolation was soon taken away from him. His old mother fell ill, and at the end of a few days there was no hope for her. Maurice, desperate at being left alone on earth, gave himself up to the wildest grief. Kneeling down by the bed of the dying woman, he called to her in the most tender way, and pressed her in his arms, as if he were struggling to keep the life in her. His mother tried with an effort to caress him and speak to him; but her hands

431

were cold and her voice was gone. She could only touch her boy's forehead with her lips and sigh, before her eyes closed for ever. Some friends tried to lead Maurice from the room, but he would not go, and leant over the motionless body on the bed.

"Dead!" he cried. "Dead, my mother! You never left me. You alone loved me. What is there left for me in the world?"

"God!" said a stifled voice.

Maurice looked around in terror. For he was alone in the room with his dead mother. Had she spoken with her last breath? He did not try to understand; but the answer he had received guided him for the rest of his life.

It was soon after the loss of his mother that I began to know him. I often went to see him at the little toll-gate. He entered into my childish games, and told me his best stories, and let me gather his flowers. Disinherited of all the graces that attract others, he was very kind to all who came to him. He was afraid to make any advances, but always eagerly welcomed a new acquaintance; and when he was mocked he submitted with a patient sweetness, and what grief he felt he never showed.

No other official was so honest, intelligent, and eager for work. But the men who could have helped him to a better position were dismayed by his deformity. Deprived of protectors, he saw his merits go always unrecognised. His superiors thought that they showed him favour enough in allowing him to keep the humble job by which he lived. He dwelt in a suburb, in an old house divided into tenements and peopled by workmen as poor as he was, but less lonely. Only one of his neighbours lived alone in a little attic, where the wind and the rain came through the roof. She was a young girl, pale, silent, without beauty, and with little besides her patient poverty to recommend her. She was never seen to speak to another woman, and no song ever cheered her garret. Wrapped in a long shabby cloak, like a kind of shroud, she worked without interest and without distraction. Her look of weariness touched Uncle Maurice. He tried to get into conversation with her. She answered in a friendly way, but very briefly. It was easy to see that her loneliness and her silent life were more pleasing to her than the friendly services of the hunchback. So he understood it and became silent.

But Toinette's needle was scarcely able to feed her, and at last she could get no work. Maurice learnt that the girl was starving, and that the shop-keepers refused to allow her to buy things on credit. He at once went to the tradesmen and arranged to pay them secretly for everything Toinette had from them. Things went on thus for some months; the young needle-woman continued without work, and became at last alarmed at the debts she had run up with the shop-keepers. She went to them to see if she could come to some arrangement, and in the explanation that followed she learnt what had been done for her. Her first action was to hasten to Uncle Maurice and thank him on her knees for his goodness. Her habitual coldness gave way to an inexpressible flow of feeling ; it seemed that gratitude had melted the ice over her numbed heart.

Freed from the embarrassment of his secret work of friendship, the little hunchback was able to carry on his good work openly and with more effect. For Toinette became to him a sister, whom he had the right to care for and watch over. It was the first time, since the death of his mother, that any one had come into his life. The girl received his services with a sort of reserved emotion. All the efforts of Maurice could not dissipate her deep sadness. She appeared touched by his kindness ; she thanked him at times with much feeling ; but there all intimate confidences stopped. Leaning over her closed heart, the little hunchback could not read anything there. Indeed he was not anxious to ; giving himself up entirely to the happiness of being no longer alone, he accepted Toinette as her long troubles had made her ; he loved her thus, and wished for no more than to be with her.

Insensibly this idea occupied his mind until it effaced all others. The girl was, like himself, without relations ; habit had softened in her sight the ugliness of the little man ; she seemed to look at him with pitying affection. What more could she expect ? Till then, the hope of winning a companion for life had been repressed by Maurice as a dream ; but chance seemed to have so worked as to make a reality of it. After many hesitations he grew bold and decided to speak to her.

It was in the evening ; the little hunchback, trembling with emotion, went to the garret. As he entered, he seemed to hear a strange voice pronouncing the name of the girl. He pushed the door open eagerly, and saw Toinette weeping and leaning on the shoulder of a young man in the dress of a sailor. At the sight of my uncle, she quickly recovered herself and ran to him and cried :

" Ah, come ! come ! Look, I thought he was dead ! It is Julien, my betrothed ! "

Maurice drew back, his knees giving way under him. He understood everything in a single word. He felt as though the earth were opening beneath him, and that his heart was going to break. But then he seemed to hear the same voice that had spoken to him by the death-bed of his mother, and he pulled himself together and recovered his strength. He went part of the way with Toinette and Julien after their marriage when they set off together ; and after having wished them all the happiness that had been refused to himself, he returned with a resigned soul to the old house in the suburb. There it was he ended his life, abandoned by men, but not, as he said, by his Father. Everywhere he felt the divine presence, and it consoled him for everything else. When he died, it was with a smile, and like an exile setting out for his own country. He who had comforted him in life knew how to make him the great gift of death.

ALFRED DE MUSSET
1810–1857

THE WHITE BLACKBIRD

I

How glorious but how painful it is in this world to be an exceptional blackbird! I am not a fabulous creature, and Monsieur de Buffon has described me. But, alas! I am extremely rare, and very difficult to find. Would to Heaven I were quite an impossibility!

My father and mother were two good folks, who had lived for a number of years in the depth of an old, retired garden in the Marais district of Paris. It was an exemplary household. While my mother, sitting in a thick bush, laid her eggs regularly three times a year, and brooded them while she slumbered, my father, still very neat and petulant in spite of his great age, foraged around her all the day, with patriarchal piety, and brought her fine insects which he seized delicately by the tip of the tail, so as not to disgust his wife. And when night fell, he never missed, when the weather was fine, to regale her with a song that was the delight of the neighbourhood. Never a quarrel, never a cloud, had disturbed this happy union.

Scarcely had I come into the world than, for the first time in his life, my father got in a bad humour. Though I was still only a doubtful grey, he recognised in me neither the colour nor the shape of his numerous posterity.

"There's a dirty child," he would sometimes say, looking at me crossly; "that urchin must thrust himself into all the rubbish and dirt he meets, to get so ugly and muddy!"

"Good gracious, my dear!" said my mother, always rolled in a ball in an old bowl in which she had made her nest, "don't you see it is his youth? In your young days, weren't you a charming good-for-nothing? Let our little blackbird grow bigger, and you will see how handsome he is. He is one of the best I have ever laid."

But while taking my part, my mother was under no delusion.

435

She saw my fatal plumage shoot, and it seemed to her a monstrosity. But she did as do all mothers, who like their children for the very thing in which nature has ill-treated them, as though it were their fault or as though they fought in advance against the injustice that must fall on their offspring.

When the time came for my first moult, my father looked at me very attentively, and became quite pensive. While my feathers were still coming out, he treated me pretty kindly, and even gave me feeding paste, when he saw me shivering almost naked in a corner. But as soon as my poor, chill winglets began to be re-covered with down, he grew so angry at each white feather he saw, that I feared he would keep plucking me for the rest of my days. Alas ! I had no mirror ; I was unaware of the reason of his fury, and I asked myself why the best of fathers was so savage towards me.

One day a ray of sunshine and my new plumes made me, in spite of myself, joyful of heart. As I fluttered between the trees I began, for my misfortune, to sing. At the first note he heard, my father leaped in the air like a rocket.

" What is that I hear there ? " he cried. " Is that how a black-bird whistles ? Is that how I whistle ? Is it whistling ? "

And swooping down close to my mother with a most terrible look :

" Unhappy woman ! " he said. " What is this that has been laid in your nest ? "

At these words my indignant mother rushed from her bowl, not without hurting her foot. She wished to speak, but her sobs suffocated her ; she fell to earth half-fainting. I saw her about to expire. Frightened and trembling with terror, I flung myself at my father's knees.

" Oh ! my father," I said to him, " if I whistle wrong, if I am badly feathered, do not let my mother be punished for it. Is it her fault if nature has refused me a voice like yours ? Is it her fault if I have not your fine yellow beak and your handsome black coat in the French fashion, that gives you the air of a church-warden about to swallow an omelette ? If heaven has made a monster of me, and if some one must suffer for it, let me at least be the only unhappy one ! "

" That is not the question," said my father. " What is the meaning of the absurd manner in which you permit yourself to whistle ? Who taught you to whistle thus against all the customs and all the rules ? "

" Alas, sir," I humbly replied, " I have whistled as well as I could, feeling gay because it was fine weather, and perhaps because I had eaten too many flies."

" No one whistles that way in my family," said my father, quite beside himself. " For ages we have whistled from father to son, and learn that when I make my voice heard at evening, there is an old gentleman on the first floor, and a shop-girl in the attic, who open their windows to listen to me. Isn't it enough I have before my eyes the frightful colour of your stupid feathers that give you a powdered look like a clown at a fair ? If I wasn't the most peaceful of blackbirds, I would have plucked you naked a hundred times, neither more nor less, like a pullet in a farmyard ready for the spit ! "

" Very well," I cried, revolted by my father's injustice, " if this is how things stand, sir, never mind ! I will disappear from your sight. I will free you from the presence of this unhappy white tail, by which you pull me all day long. I will depart, sir. There will be quite enough children to console you in your old age, since my mother lays three times a year. Far from you I shall hide my misery, and perhaps," I added sobbing, " perhaps I shall find in the neighbouring kitchen garden, or in the gutters, some worms or some spiders to maintain my mournful life."

" As you like," said my papa, far from melting at this oration. " So long as I never see you again. You are not my son. You are not a blackbird."

" What am I then, sir, if you please ? "

" I know nothing about it. But you are not a blackbird."

After these terrifying words my father went away with slow steps. My mother rose up sadly, and limped to finish weeping in her bowl. For myself, confused and desolate, I flew away as best I could, and went, as I had announced, to perch on the gutter of a neighbouring house.

II

My father had the inhumanity to leave me for several days in this mortifying situation. With all his violence, he had a kind heart, and by the side glances he gave me, I saw he would have liked to pardon and recall me. My mother, above all, continually raised her eyes to me with tender looks, and even risked at times sending me a plaintive cry. But my horrible white feathers inspired them, in spite of themselves, with a repugnance and affright for which I clearly saw there was no remedy.

" I am not a blackbird," I repeated to myself ; and indeed, while washing in the morning and mirroring myself in the water of the gutter, I saw only too clearly how little I resembled my family. " Oh, heavens ! " I cried. " Teach me then what I am ! "

One night it was raining in torrents, and I was about to fall asleep, worn out with hunger and grief, when I saw a bird perching by me, wetter, paler, and thinner than I should have thought it possible to be. He was just about my colour, as far as I could judge through the rain that flooded us ; he scarcely had on his body enough feathers to clothe a sparrow, and yet he was bigger than I. He seemed to me at first a very poor, beggarly creature, but he preserved, in spite of the storm that beat on his almost bald forehead, an air of haughtiness that charmed me. Modestly I made him a deep bow, which he answered by a peck that almost threw me into the gutter. Seeing me scratch my ear and withdraw without trying to reply to him in his own language :

" Who are you ? " he asked in a voice as hoarse as his head was bald.

" Alas, my lord ! " I answered (fearing another thrust), " I do not know. I thought I was a blackbird, but I have been convinced that I am not."

The singularity of my reply and my air of sincerity interested him. He came closer and got me to relate my story, which I did with all the sadness and all the humility that became my position and the frightful weather.

" If you were a pigeon like me," he said, when I had done, " the silly nonsense you worry over would not trouble you for a moment. We pigeons travel ; that is our life, and we have our love affairs, but I do not know who is my father. To cleave the air, to sweep through space, to see mountains and plains far below us, to breathe the azure of the heavens, to dart like an arrow at a goal that never escapes us—that is our pleasure and our existence. I can travel farther in one day than a man can in ten ! "

" On my word, sir," I said, growing bolder, " you are a gipsy bird ! "

" That's another matter that doesn't trouble me," he continued. " I have no country. I know only three things—travel, my wife, my little ones. Where my wife is, there is my motherland."

" But what is that hanging from your neck ? It looks like an old bit of curl paper."

" These are papers of importance," he said, bridling up. " I am going to Brussels this trip, and taking to a banker there some news that will knock Government stock down one franc seventy-eight centimes ! "

" Good heavens ! " I cried, " what a fine life you lead, and Brussels, I am sure, must be a town worth seeing ! Could you not take me with you ? Since I am not a blackbird, I may be a racing pigeon."

" If you were one," he answered, " you would have returned the peck I gave you just now.

" Very well, sir, I will return it. Don't let us get on bad terms over such a little thing. Look ! Morning is breaking and the weather clearing up. In pity, let me come with you. I am abandoned. I have nothing left in the world. If you refuse me, nothing remains but to drown myself in this gutter."

" Very well," he said. " Let us be off ! Follow me if you can."

I threw a last glance on the garden where my mother was sleeping. A tear flowed from my eye ; the wind and the rain bore it away. I opened my wings, and I departed.

III

My wings, I have said, were still not very strong. While my leader went like the wind, I panted along by his side. I kept up for some time, but soon I had such a fit of giddiness that I felt near to swooning.

" Will it take us much longer ? " I asked in a weak voice.

" No," he replied, " we are at Bourget. We have only another sixty leagues to do."

I tried to pluck up courage, not wishing to look like a half-drowned chicken, and I flew for another quarter of an hour, but then I was quite done up.

" Sir," I again stammered out, " couldn't we stop a moment ? I am tormented with thirst, and if we perched on a tree—— "

" Go to the devil ! You are only a blackbird," said the pigeon angrily.

And without deigning to turn his head, he kept on his mad flight. As for me, dazed and unable to see, I fell into a wheat-field. I do not know how long the swoon lasted. When I recovered consciousness, the first thing that came into my head were the last words of the pigeon. " You are only a blackbird," he said to me. " Oh, my dear parents," I thought, " you must, therefore, have been mistaken. I will return home. You will recognise in me your true and legitimate child, and let me take my place again in the nice little heap of leaves under my mother's bowl."

I made an effort to rise ; but the fatigue of the flight, and the pain I felt from my fall, paralysed my limbs. Scarcely had I got on my feet, when I was overcome with weakness, and fell back on my side. The frightful thought of death had already come into my mind, when, through the cornflowers and the poppies, I saw two charming persons coming towards me on tiptoe. One was a pretty little magpie hen, admirably dappled, and extremely coquettish ; the other was a turtle-dove with rose-coloured plumage. The dove stopped a few steps away with a fine air of modesty and compassion for my misfortune, but the magpie came skipping up in the most delightful way in the world.

" Good heavens ! poor child ! what are you doing there ? " she asked me in a playful, silvery voice.

" Alas ! Madame the Marquise," I replied, for I saw at once she was a noble lady. " I am a poor wretch of a traveller whose coachman has left him on the road, and I am on the way to die of hunger."

" By our Lady ! What is that you say ? " she exclaimed.

And she at once began to flutter here and there on the bushes that surrounded us, coming and going from one side to the other, bringing me a quantity of berries and fruits, which she placed in a little heap by me, going on with her questions all the time.

" But who are you ? Where do you come from ? What an extraordinary adventure ! Where are you going ? Travelling alone, and so young ! Just out of your first moult ? What are your parents doing ? Where are they ? How did they let you go in this condition ? It is enough to raise all the feathers on one's head ! "

While she was speaking, I raised myself a little on one side, and ate with a good appetite. The turtle dove stood still, looking at me always with an eye of pity. However, she remarked that I turned my head with a languishing air and she saw that I was thirsty. Of the rain that fell in the night a drop still remained on a leaf of pimpernel. She timidly gathered this drop of water in her beak, and brought it to me cool and fresh. Certainly if I had not been very unwell, so reserved a hen would not have allowed herself such a bold act.

At that time I did not know what love was, but my heart beat violently. Divided between two diverse emotions, I was over-come by an inexplicable charm. My cup-bearer was so sweet and tender, and my serving-maid so gay and bright, that I should have liked to continue eating thus for all eternity. Unhappily, there is a limit even to the appetite of a convalescent. The meal over and my strength recovered, I satisfied the curiosity of the little magpie, and told her my misfortunes with as much sincerity as I had related them the night before to the pigeon. The magpie listened to me with more attention than might have been expected from her, and the turtle-dove gave me some charming marks of her depth of feeling. But when I touched on the capital point that brought about my trouble, that is to say, my ignorance of what sort of bird I was :

" Are you jesting ? " cried the magpie. " You a blackbird ! You a pigeon ! For shame ! You are a magpie, my dear boy, and a very pretty magpie," she added, giving me a flick of her wing that was like a tap from a fan.

" But, Madame," I replied, " it seems to me that for a magpie, I am of such a colour, if you will pardon me——"

" A Russian magpie, my dear, you are a Russian magpie ! Don't you know that they are all white ? Poor boy, what innocence ! "

" But, Madame," I continued, " how could I be a Russian magpie born in the Marais in Paris in an old broken bowl ? "

" Ah ! the dear child ! You belong to the invasion of 1814, my dear. Do you think that you are the only one ? Trust in me and do not bother. I want to lead you away at once, and show you the loveliest things on earth."

" Where, Madame, please ? "

" In my green palace, my darling. You will see the life we lead there. After you have been a magpie for a quarter of an hour, you will not want to hear about anything else. A hundred of us are there—none of the coarse village magpies that go begging on the highways—but all noble and belonging to good society, slim, smart, and no bigger than a fist. None of us has more or less than seven black marks and five white marks. It is an unchangeable thing, and we scorn the rest of the world. It is true you want the black marks, but the fact that you are a Russian will suffice to get you admitted.

" Our life is made up of two things—chatter and dress. From morn till noon we get ourselves up, and from noon to night we prattle. Each of us perches on the highest and oldest tree possible. In the middle of the forest rises an immense oak, uninhabited, alas ! It was the dwelling-place of the late King Pie X., and there we go in pilgrimage, sighing very deeply. But except for this slight grief, we pass the time admirably. Our ladies are no more prudish than our husbands are jealous, but our pleasures are pure and honest because our hearts are as noble as our language is free and gay. In haughtiness we have no equal, and if a jay or some other cad chances to mingle with us, we pluck him without pity.

" Yet we are the best souls in the world ; and the sparrows, tom-tits, and goldfinches that live in the undergrowth, always find us ready to help them and feed them, and defend them. Nowhere is there more chatter than among us, and nowhere less backbiting. We do not lack some old pious pies who pass the whole day in prayer, but the giddiest of our young gossips can pass by the severest old dowager without fearing a peck. In a word, we life for pleasure, honour, chatter, glory, and dress ! "

" How attractive that all is, Madame," I replied. " I should certainly be very ill-bred if I did not obey the wishes of a lady like you. But before I have the honour to follow you, allow me, I pray, to say a word to this good turtle-dove here. Fair lady," I continued, turning to the turtle-dove, " speak to me frankly, I beg you. Do you think I am truly a Russian magpie ? " At this question the turtle-dove lowered her head and became both pale and red, like the ribbons of Lolotte.

" But, sir," she said, " I do not know if I can——"

" Speak," I cried, " in the name of heaven ! I had no intention of offending you. Quite the contrary. You both seem to me so charming that I swear on the spot to offer my heart and my foot to either of you who will accept them, at the very moment I know whether I am a magpie or something else. For in looking at you," I added in a whisper, " I feel I am something of a turtle-dove, and it gives me a strange feeling."

"Indeed," said the turtle-dove, with a deeper blush, "I do not know if it is the reflection of the sunlight falling on you through these poppies, but your plumage seems to have a slight tint——"

She did not dare to say more.

"Oh, what perplexity!" I cried, "how can I know where I stand? How can I give my heart to one of you when it is so cruelly torn apart? Oh, Socrates, how admirable a precept, but hard to follow, you gave us when you said, ' Know thyself!'"

Since the day when my unhappy song had upset my father, I had made no use of my voice. In this moment it struck me I could employ it as a means to discern the truth. "Great Scott!" I thought, "since my father put me outside the door after the first verse, it is pretty certain that the second will produce some effect on these ladies!" So, giving a polite bow, as though asking for an indulgence by reason of the wetting I had received from the rain, I began first to whistle, then to warble, then to execute runs, and at last to sing with a full throat like a Spanish muleteer when he has got his breath.

As I sang the little magpie hen moved away from me with an air of surprise that soon became stupefaction, and then passed to a feeling of fright accompanied by profound boredom. She made circles round me like a cat round a bit of hot fat that has just burnt her, but which she still wants to taste again. Seeing the effect of my experiment, and wishing to push it to the end, the more impatience the Marquise showed, the more I sang myself hoarse. For twenty-five minutes she resisted my melodies; at last, being unable to contain herself, she flew off with a loud noise to her palace of verdure. As for the turtle-dove, she, from the beginning, had almost fallen fast asleep.

"What an admirable effect of music!" I thought. "Oh, Paris! Oh, my mother's bowl! More than ever am I bent on returning to you."

At the moment when I started to leave, the turtle-dove opened her eyes.

"Farewell," she said, "O pretty and wearisome stranger! My name is Gourouli. Do not forget me!"

"Lovely Gourouli," I replied, "you are good and sweet and charming. I would I could live and die for you. But you are rose-coloured; so such happiness is not for me."

IV

The sad effects produced by my song did not fail to sadden me. "Alas! music, alas! poetry," I said when I was going back to Paris, "how few are the hearts that understand you!"

While making these reflections I struck my head against that of a bird who was flying in an opposite direction. The shock was so unforeseen and heavy, that we both fell on the top of a tree which, by good luck, was underneath us. After recovering a little I looked at the strange bird in expectation of a quarrel. I was surprised to see that he was white. In fact he had a larger head than mine, and on the forehead a kind of tuft that gave him an air of an heroic comedian. Moreover, he carried his tail high in the air in a very magnanimous way. For the rest, he did not seem at all disposed to fight. We greeted each other civilly, and made mutual excuses, and then entered into conversation. I took the liberty of asking his name and his country.

" You do not recognise me ? " he said. " I am astonished ! Are you not one of us ? "

" In truth, sir," I replied, " I do not know what I am. Everybody asks me the same thing. There must be a wager on the matter."

" You are joking," he said. " Your plumage suits you too well for me to pass over a brother bird. You infallibly belong to that illustrious and venerable race known as white cockatoos ! "

" Faith ! that is possible and it would be a great honour for me. But go on speaking as if I were not, and condescend to inform me whom I have the glory of meeting."

" I am," replied the unknown bird, " the great poet Kacatogan. I have gone on great travels, sir, on arid excursions, and cruel peregrinations. It was not yesterday that I began to rhyme, and my muse knows what misfortune is. I have hummed under Louis XVI., I have brawled for the Republic, I have nobly sung the Empire. I have discreetly praised the Restoration. I have even made an effort in these later days, and submitted myself, not without pain, to the requirements of this tasteless age. I have thrown off piquant epigrams, sublime hymns, graceful dithyrambs, pious elegies, long-haired dramas, frizzled romances, powdered farces, and bald-headed tragedies. In a word, I flatter myself with having added to the temple of the Muses some graceful festoons, some sombre battlements, and some ingenious arabesques. What can you expect ? I am an old man. But I still rhyme with vigour, sir, and, such as you see me now, I was thinking out a poem of not less than six pages when you raised a bump on my forehead. Anyhow, if I can help you in any way, I am quite at your service."

" Indeed, sir, you can," I replied, " for you see me at this moment in a great poetical difficulty. I dare not say I am a poet, far less a great poet like you," making him a bow, " but I have received from nature a gift of song that I must show whenever I feel happy or sorrowful. To tell you the whole truth, I am quite ignorant of all the rules of singing."

" I have forgotten them," said Kacatogan ; " don't trouble about that."

"But a shameful thing has happened to me," I went on. "On those who hear it my voice produces pretty much the same effect as that of a certain Jean de Nivelle on . . . You know what I mean!"

"I know," said Kacatogan. "I know from experience this odd effect. The cause is mysterious, but the effect is incontestable. I have never been able to find the remedy. In younger days I was much upset when they always hissed me, but now I do not trouble about it. The dislike, I think, arises from the fact that the public reads the works of other writers and thus becomes distracted."

"I think like you, sir," I said ; "but you will agree that it is hard for a person with good intentions, to see everybody run away as soon as he opens his throat. Would you mind listening to me, and giving me your frank opinion?"

"Willingly, I am all ears."

I at once began to sing, and I had the satisfaction of seeing that Kacatogan neither fled nor fell asleep. He looked at me fixedly, and from time to time he inclined his head with an air of approbation, and murmured in a flattering way. But I soon perceived he was not listening, but thinking out his poem. As I was taking breath, he suddenly interrupted me.

"At last I have found that rhyme!" he said, smiling and shaking his head. "It is the sixty thousand seven hundred and fourteenth that has come from this brain! Yet they have the impudence to say I am growing old. I must go and read it to some good friends. I must go and read it to them, and we shall see what they will say of it!"

Speaking thus he flew away, and disappeared without seeming to remember that he had met me.

V

Left alone and disappointed, I had nothing better to do than to profit by the remaining daylight and fly swiftly to Paris. Unhappily I did not know the route. My flight with the pigeon had hardly been agreeable enough to leave me with a clear memory of it. So, instead of going quite straight, I turned leftwards to Bourget, and, overtaken by the night, I was obliged to seek for lodging in Morfontaine Wood. Everybody had gone to bed when I arrived. The magpies and the jays, who are the worst sleepers on earth, were wrangling on all sides. In the bushes the sparrows were squalling and scrambling over each other. By the water-side two herons gravely walked along, perched on their high stilts, in an attitude of meditation, patiently waiting for their wives. Enormous crows, half asleep, squatted heavily on the top of the highest tree, and through their noses said their evening prayers. Lower down the amorous tomtits still ran after each other in the undergrowth, while a chubby woodpecker pushed his family from behind to make them enter the hollow in a tree.

Squadrons of tree-sparrows came from the fields, dancing in the air like puffs of smoke, and flinging themselves on a sapling, which they entirely covered. The finches, the warblers, the red-breasts arranged themselves lightly on the branches like crystals on a chandelier. All round was the sound of voices, speaking with great distinctness. " Get along, my wife ! " " Get along, my daughter ! " " Come, my sweet ! " " This way, my love ! " " Here I am, my dear ! " " Good-night, my darling ! " " Good-bye, my friend ! " " Sleep well, my children ! " What a position for a bachelor to sleep in such an inn. I was tempted to join some birds of my size and beg a shelter from them. " In the night," I thought, " all birds are black ; and besides, how could I harm anybody by sleeping in all politeness close to them ? "

I went first to a ditch where some starlings had gathered. They were making their evening toilette with particular care, and I remarked that most of them had gilded wings and polished feet ; they were the dandies of the forest. They were pretty good fellows and honoured me with no attention. But their talk was so empty, they spoke with such fatuity of their amours and trickeries, and provoked each other so much, that I could not put up with it.

I went and perched on a branch where half a dozen birds of different species stood in a row. I modestly took the last place at the end of the bough, hoping I should not be interfered with. Unfortunately, my neighbour was an old hen dove, stiff as a rusted vane. At the moment I approached, the scanty feathers covering her bones were the object of her solicitude. She pretended to clean them ; but she was too much afraid of dragging one of them out. She merely went over them to see if any more were missing. I scarcely touched her with the tip of the wing, but she rose up majestically.

" What are you doing, sir ? " she said, tightening her beak with quite a British prudeness. And striking out with her elbow, she threw me down with a vigour that would have done honour to a porter.

I fell in the heather where a plump wood-hen was sleeping. My mother herself, in her bowl, had not such an air of beatitude. She was so round, so spread out, so well settled on her triple stomach, that you would have taken her for a pie of which the crust had been eaten. I crept furtively close to her. " She will not awake," I said, " and in any case such a motherly creature will not be very angry." She was not. Half opening her eyes, she said with a light sigh, " You worry me, my little one. Go away."

At the same instant I heard some one calling me. It was some thrushes, who, from the top of a mountain ash, motioned to me to come to them. " There at last are some good souls ! " I thought.

They were all hens, and they made place for me laughing like mad things, and I thrust myself eagerly in their feathery group, like a love-letter in a muff. But it was not long before I discerned that these ladies had eaten more grapes than was reasonable. They could scarcely hold on to the branches, and their low jests, their claps of laughter, and their loose songs compelled me to leave.

I began to despair, and was going to sleep in a solitary corner, when a nightingale broke into song. Everybody remained silent. Alas! how pure his voice was. He gave sweetness even to sorrow! Far from troubling the slumber of any one, his harmonies seemed like a lullaby. No one thought of making him keep silent; nobody thought it wrong for him to sing his song at such an hour; his father did not beat him; his friends did not fly from him!

" I alone," I cried, " am forbidden to be happy! Flee from this cruel world! Better to seek a path through the shadows at the risk of being swallowed by some owl, than let myself be lacerated by the sight of other persons' happiness! "

In this vein I set out, and for some hours wandered at hazard. In the first glow of dawn I perceived the towers of Notre Dame. In the twinkling of an eye I reached Paris, and it was not long before I saw our garden. Quicker than lightning I flew there. Alas, it was empty! I called my parents in vain. The tree where my father perched, the bush of my mother, the beloved bowl—all had disappeared. The axe had destroyed everything. In place of the avenue of foliage where I was born, there were only a hundred faggots of firewood.

VI

I sought my parents in all the neighbouring gardens; but it was trouble lost. They had no doubt fled for shelter to some distant part of the town, and I could never get any news of them. Overcome with frightful sadness, I perched on the gutter from which the anger of my father had first exiled me. There I spent days and nights deploring my existence. I did not sleep; I scarcely ate; I was nearly dying of grief.

" Thus," I said aloud, " I am not a blackbird, since my father pulled my feathers out; nor a pigeon, since I tumbled on the way when I wanted to go to Belgium; nor a Russian magpie, since the little Marquise stopped up her ears as soon as I opened my mouth: nor a turtle-dove, since Gourouli, the good Gourouli herself, snored like a monk when I sang; nor a parrot, since Kacatogan would not deign to listen to me; nor any sort of bird whatever, since at Morfontaine they let me sleep all alone. Yet I have feathers on my body. Here are my feet and here are my wings. I am not a monster —witness Gourouli and the little Marquise herself, who found me to their liking. By what inexplicable mystery are these wings and feathers and feet formed into a mass to which nobody can give a name ? Should I not be by chance——"

I was interrupted by two housewives quarrelling in the street. "Bless me !" said one of them, "if you bring it off, I will make you a present of a white blackbird !"

"Just heavens !" I cried. "There I am ! Oh, Providence ! I am the son of a blackbird, and I am white ; I am a white blackbird !"

I must admit that this discovery modified many of my ideas. Instead of continuing my lamentations, I began to bridle up and stalk proudly along the gutter, regarding everything with a victorious air.

"It is something," I said to myself, "to be a white blackbird. You don't find that by following a donkey. How vain it was for me to grieve that I could not meet others like me ! It is the fate of genius. I wished to flee the world but I must astonish it. Since I am this unparalleled bird, whose existence vulgar souls deny, I am in duty bound to carry myself as such, neither more nor less than like a Phœnix, and contemn the rest of the feathered creatures. I must buy the memoirs of Alfieri and the poems of Lord Byron ; this substantial nourishment will inspire me with a noble pride, without counting that which God has already given me. Yes, I want to add, if it can be, to the prestige of my birth. Nature has made me rare ; I will make myself mysterious. It shall be a favour, a glory even to see me. In fact," I whispered, "if I were to show myself frankly for money ?

"Shame ! What an unworthy thought ! I want to write a poem like Kacatogan, not in one chant, but in twenty-four, like all the great men. No ! It is not enough. There shall be forty-eight chants, with notes and an appendix. The universe must learn that I exist. I shall not fail, in my poem, to deplore my isolation ; but I will do so in such a way that the happiest people will envy me. Since heaven has refused me a mate, I will say terrible things about the wives of others. I will prove that everything is sour, except the grapes I eat. The nightingales must look to themselves. I shall demonstrate that, as surely as two and two make four, their sorrowful songs make one sick, and their stuff is worth nothing. I must find an enterprising publisher of the new school. I first want to create a strong literary position. I mean to have round me a court composed, not only of journalists, but of veritable men of letters, and even of literary women. I shall write a part for Madame Rachel, and, if she will not play it, I will announce, with the sound of trumpets, that her talent is much inferior to that of an old provincial actress. I shall go to Venice, and in the midst of this enchanted city I shall rent on the Grand Canal the fine palace of Mocenigo that costs four pounds and fivepence a day.

" There I shall draw inspiration from the memories the author of *Lara* must have left behind him. From the depth of my solitude I will flood the world with a deluge of poems in Spenserian stanzas, in which I will comfort my great soul. I will make all the tomtits sigh, all the turtle-doves croon, all the geese shall melt in tears, and the old owls shall shriek. But as regards my person, I shall show myself inexorable and inaccessible to love. In vain will they urge and implore me to take pity on the unhappy creatures carried away by my sublime chants. To all that I shall answer, ' Bah ! ' Oh, excess of glory ! My manuscripts shall sell for their weight in gold, my books shall cross the seas ; fame, fortune shall follow me everywhere. Alone I shall seem indifferent to the murmurs of the crowd that encircles me. In a word, I shall be a perfect white blackbird, a veritable eccentric poet, feasted, looked after, admired, envied, but quite discontented and intolerable."

VII

It took me no more than six weeks to produce my first work. It was, as I had promised myself, a poem in forty-eight chants. There were certainly some roughnesses in it, owing to the prodigious fecundity with which it had been written ; but I thought that the public of our day, accustomed to the fine literature that is printed at the bottom of newspapers, would not reproach me with them.

I had a success worthy of myself ; that is to say, without a parallel. The subject of my work was myself. In this I conformed to the fashion of the age. I related my past sufferings with a charming fatuity ; I acquainted the reader with a thousand domestic details of the most piquant interest. The description of my mother's bowl filled no less than fourteen chants. I had counted in it the ridges, the holes, the bosses, the bright spots, the splinters, the nails, the stains, the diverse tints, the reflections. I showed the inside, the outside, the edges, the bottom, the sides, the inclined planes. Then passing to the contents, I had studied the blades of grass, the straws, the dry leaves, the bits of wood, the grit, the drops of water, the remains of flies, the feet of broker chafers that occurred there. It was a ravishing description. But don't think I had it printed in an unbroken length. There are impertinent readers who would have skipped it. I skilfully cut it into passages, which I larded into the story so that nothing of it was lost ; and in such a way that, at the most interesting and dramatic moment, there suddenly popped up fifteen pages about the bowl. There you have, I think, one of the great secrets of art, and as I am not avaricious, let any one profit by it who cares.

The whole of Europe was stirred by the appearance of my book. She devoured the intimate revelations that I deigned to communicate. How could it have been otherwise ? Not only did I enumerate all the facts about myself, but I gave the public a complete picture of all the musings that had come into my head since I was two months of age. I had even interposed, in the finest passage, an ode composed in my egg-shell. Of course, I did not neglect to treat by the way the great subject with which so many people are preoccupied; that is to say, the future of humanity. This problem struck me as interesting, and in a moment of leisure I sketched out a solution that generally passed as satisfactory.

Every day I received compliments in verse, letters of felicitation, and nameless declarations of love. As for visits, I rigorously followed the plan I had formed. My door was shut to everybody. I could not, however, refuse to receive two foreigners who announced themselves my relatives. One was a blackbird from Senegal; the other a blackbird from China.

"Ah! sir," they said, almost stifling me in their embrace, "what a great blackbird you are! How well you have depicted, in your immortal poem, the profound sufferings of unrecognized genius! If we had not been already as much misunderstood as possible, we should have become so after reading you. How we sympathize with your griefs, with your sublime scorn of the vulgar herd! We also, sir, understand from our own experience the secret sorrows you have sung. Here are two sonnets we have written, which we beg you to accept."

"Here is also," added the Chinaman, "the melody my wife has composed on some verses of your preface. The intention of the author is wonderfully rendered by the music."

"Gentlemen," I said to them, "so far as I can judge, you seem to me endowed with great hearts and enlightened minds. But pardon me for asking you a question. What is the ground for your melancholy?"

"Look how I am made, sir," answered the native of Senegal. "It is true that my plumage is pleasant to look at, and that I am clothed in the beautiful green colour that is seen shining on drakes. But my beak is too short, and my feet are too long. And look at the tail I have been rigged out in! It is much longer than my body. Isn't that enough to make you sell yourself to the devil?"

"And my misfortune," said the Chinaman, "is still harder to bear. The tail of my companion sweeps the road, but the naughty boys point their fingers at me because I have no tail at all!"

"Gentlemen," I said, "I am sorry for you with all my soul. It is always troublesome to have too much or too little of anything. But permit me to tell you that in the Zoological Gardens there are several persons who resemble you, and yet have bided there a long time comfortably stuffed, in life-like attitudes. Just as it is not sufficient for a woman writer to be a wanton in order to write a fine book, so it is not enough for a blackbird to be discontented in order to be a genius. I am the only one of my species, and I am sorry for it. Perhaps I am mistaken, but it is my privilege. I am white, gentlemen ; become so and then you will know what you can say."

VIII

In spite of the resolution I had taken and the calmness I affected, I was not happy. Glorious as my isolation was, it was none the less painful. I could not think without terror of the necessity in which I was placed of passing my entire life in lonely splendour. The return of springtime, in particular, caused me a mortal uneasiness, and I began to fall again into a deep melancholy, when an unforeseen circumstance changed the course of my existence. It is needless to say that my writings had crossed the Channel, and that the English scrambled after them. The English rush after everything, except that which they understand. One day I received from London a letter from a young blackbird hen.

" I have read your poem," she said to me, " and the admiration I feel has made me resolve to offer you my hand and my person. God has created us for each other ! I am like you—I am a little white blackbird ! "

You will easily guess my surprise and my joy. " A white blackbird hen ! " I said to myself. " Is it possible ? So I am no more alone on this earth ! " I hastened to reply to the unknown beauty, and I did it in a way that showed how much her proposal pleased me. I urged her to come to Paris, or to permit me to fly to her. She replied that she would prefer to come to me, because her parents annoyed her, that she would put her affairs in order, and that I should soon see her. She came, in fact, a few days afterwards. Oh, joy ! she was the prettiest little blackbird in the world, and even whiter than myself.

" Ah ! miss," I cried, " or rather madame, for I regard you henceforward as my legitimate spouse, is it believable that so charming a creature should be found on earth without fame telling me of her existence ! Blessed be my misfortune and the pecks my father gave me, since heaven has reserved for me so unhoped-for a consolation ! Unto this day I thought I was condemned to an eternal solitude, and speaking to you frankly, it was a heavy burden to bear. But I feel, in looking at you, all the qualities of a father of a family. Accept my hand without delay. Let us marry in the English fashion, without ceremony, and set out for a honeymoon in Switzerland."

" I don't look at it in that way," answered the young hen. " I want our wedding to be a magnificent affair, and that all the blackbirds of France of good breeding should solemnly assemble at it. Persons such as we owe something to our own glory, and cannot marry like cats in a gutter. I have brought a supply of bank-notes. Send out your invitations, go and see your tradespeople, and do no tbe stingy about the refreshments."

I blindly obeyed the orders of my bride. Our marriage was an affair of overwhelming luxury. Ten thousand flies were eaten at it, and we received a nuptial benediction from a reverend father Cormorant, who was archbishop *in partibus*. A superb ball brought the day to a close ; nothing was wanting to my happiness.

The more I learnt of the character of my charming wife the more my love for her increased. She united in her little person all the graces of soul and body. She was only a little prudish, but I attributed that to the influence of the English fog in which she had lived, and I did not doubt that the climate of France would soon remove this slight cloud.

One thing that troubled me more seriously was a sort of mystery with which she sometimes surrounded herself in a strange rigour. She locked herself in with her maids, and spent hours, so she pretended, in making her toilet. Husbands do not like this sort of thing. Twenty times have I knocked at my wife's room without her opening the door to me. That cruelly upset me. One day I insisted, in such anger, that she was obliged to give way and let me in, not without bitterly complaining of my importunity. I noticed, in entering, a big bottle full of a kind of paste made of flour and whitening. I asked my wife what she used the mixture for. She said it was a remedy for chilblains, from which she was suffering.

This remedy seemed to me rather suspicious, but how could I mistrust a creature so sweet and so good, who had given herself to me with so much enthusiasm and so perfect a sincerity ? At first I did not know that my beloved was a writer. After some time she admitted she was, and even showed me a novel in which she had imitated both Walter Scott and Scarron. So delightful a surprise gave me much pleasure. I saw that I not only possessed an incomparable beauty, but that the intellect of my wife was worthy of my genius. From that moment we worked together. While I composed my poems, she scribbled away on reams of paper. I recited my verses aloud to her, but that did not prevent her from going on writing at the same time. She produced her novels with almost as much facility as I produced my poems, choosing always the most dramatic subjects—parricides, rapes, murders, and even swindling tricks ; always taking care to attack the Government and to preach the gospel of the emancipation of hen blackbirds. In a word, no effort was painful to her mind, no feat of art to her sense of modesty. She never altered a line or thought out a plan before she started to write. She was the type of the woman of letters.

One day, as she was working with an unusual ardour, I perceived she was perspiring very freely, and I was astonished to see at the same time a large black spot on her back.

" Good heavens ! " I cried.   " What is this ?   Are you unwell ? "
She seemed at first a little frightened, and even dumbfounded, but
her large experience of the world soon enabled her to recover her
admirable self-control.   She said to me that it was a blot of ink
and that she was given to flinging the ink about in her moments of
inspiration.

" Does my wife dye ? " I asked myself.   The thought prevented
me from sleeping.   The bottle of paste came back to my mind.
" Oh, heavens ! " I cried, " what a suspicion.   Can this heavenly
creature be a painted thing, got up to deceive me ?   When I thought
I was pressing to my heart the sister of my soul, the privileged
being created for me alone, was I only marrying flour and
whitening ? "

Pursued by this horrible doubt, I formed a plan to free myself
from it.   I bought a barometer, and eagerly watched for the coming
of a rainy day.   I wanted to take my wife into the country in
doubtful weather, and see what a washing in the rain would do for
her.   But we were in mid-July ; the fine weather continued in a
frightful manner.

The appearance of happiness and the habit of writing had strongly
excited my feelings.   Naïve as I was, it sometimes happened, while
I was working, that my emotion overcame me, and I began to
weep while searching for a rhyme.   My wife loved these rare
occasions.   Every masculine weakness is a delight to feminine
pride.   One night, when I was polishing a correction, after the
precept of Boileau, it happened that my heart opened.

" Oh, you ! " I said to my dear little hen, " you, the only one
and the most beloved !   You, without whom life is a dream !   You
who can change the universe for me with a look, a smile, do you
know how much I adore you ?   A little study and attention will
easily enable me to find words for a commonplace idea already
worn out by other poets.   Where shall I ever find words to express
that which your beauty inspires me with ?   Before you came to
me my isolation was that of an exiled orphan.   To-day it is that
of a king.   In this little feverish brain, in which a useless thought
is fermenting, there can be nothing, my angel, my beautiful one,
that does not belong to you.   Oh, that my genius was a pearl and
you were Cleopatra ! "

In raving thus I wept on my wife and she visibly lost colour.   At
each tear that fell from my eyes a feather appeared, not even black,
but of an old rusty brown tint.   After some minutes of deep
emotion, I found myself face to face with an unwhitened bird,
identically similar to the most ordinary and commonplace of
blackbirds.

What could I do ?   What could I say ?   All reproach was
useless.   I could in truth have considered the case as an annulled

contract and have set aside my marriage. But how could I publish my shame ? Was not my misfortune enough in itself ? Taking my courage in both claws, I resolved to leave the world, to abandon literature and fly to a wilderness, if it were possible, and avoid for ever the face of a living creature.

IX

Thereupon I flew away, always weeping ; and the wind, which is the luck of birds, carried me to the wood of Morfontaine. On this occasion everybody was abed. "What a marriage ! " I said to myself. "What a freak ! It was certainly with a good intention that the poor child whitened herself, but all the same she is none the less a rusty brown, and I am none the less the most miserable creature on earth ! "

The nightingale was still singing. Alone, in the depths of night, he enjoyed with a full heart the gift of God that made him so superior to poets, and gave his thoughts freely to the silence that surrounded him. I could not resist the temptation to go up and speak to him.

"Oh, how happy you are ! " I said to him. "Not only can you sing as much as you like, with everybody listening to you, but you have a wife and children, your nest, your friends, a good pillow of moss, the full moon, and no newspapers. Rubini and Rossini are nothing beside you. I have also sung, sir, and it was pitiable. I ranged my words in order of battle, like Prussian soldiers, and I composed rubbish, while you were singing amid the leaves. Is the source of your inspiration a secret ?

"Not at all," said the nightingale ; "but it is not what you think. My wife bores me, and I do not love her. I am in love with the rose. I sing till I am hoarse all the night for her, but she sleeps on and does not hear me. Her chalice is closed at the present time. She is cradling an old beetle in it ; but to-morrow morning, when I creep back to my bed, worn out with suffering and fatigue, it is then that she will open her petals for a bee that eats her heart out."

CAMILLE

Alfred De Musset

I

The Chevalier des Arcis was a cavalry officer who, having quitted the service in 1760, while still young, retired to a

country house near Mans. Shortly after, he married the
daughter of a retired merchant who lived in the neighbourhood,
and this marriage appeared for a time to be an exceedingly happy
one. Cécile's relatives were worthy folk who, enriched by means of
hard work, were now, in their latter years, enjoying a continual
Sunday. The Chevalier, weary of the artificial manners of Versailles,
entered gladly into their simple pleasures. Cécile had an excellent
uncle, named Giraud, who had been a master-bricklayer, but had
risen by degrees to the position of architect, and now owned
considerable property. The Chevalier's house (which was named
Chardonneux) was much to Giraud's taste, and he was there a
frequent and ever-welcome visitor.

By and by a lovely little girl was born to the Chevalier and
Cécile, and great at first was the jubilation of the parents. But a
painful shock was in store for them. They soon made the terrible
discovery that their little Camille was deaf, and, consequently,
also dumb !

II

The mother's first thought was of cure, but this hope was
reluctantly abandoned ; no cure could be found. At the time of
which we are writing, there existed a pitiless prejudice against those
poor creatures whom we style *deaf mutes*. A few noble spirits, it
is true, had protested against this barbarity. A Spanish monk
of the sixteenth century was the first to devise means of teaching
the dumb to speak without words—a thing until then deemed
impossible. His example had been followed at different times in
Italy, England, and France, by Bonnet, Wallis, Bulwer, and Van
Helmont, and a little good had been done here and there. Still,
however, even at Paris, deaf mutes were generally regarded as beings
set apart, marked with the brand of Divine displeasure. Deprived
of speech, the power of thought was denied them, and they inspired
more horror than pity.

A dark shadow crept over the happiness of Camille's parents. A
sudden, silent estrangement—worse than divorce, crueller than
death—grew up between them. For the mother passionately
loved her afflicted child, while the Chevalier, despite all the efforts
prompted by his kind heart, could not overcome the repugnance
with which her affliction affected him.

The mother spoke to her child by signs, and she alone could
make herself understood. Every other inmate of the house, even
her father, was a stranger to Camille. The mother of Madame
des Arcis—a woman of no tact—never ceased to deplore loudly
the misfortune that had befallen her daughter and son-in-law.
" Better that she had never been born ! " she exclaimed one day.

" What would you have done, then, had *I* been thus ? " asked
Cécile indignantly.

To Uncle Giraud his great-niece's dumbness seemed no such tremendous misfortune. " I have had," said he, " such a talkative wife that I regard everything else as less evil. This little woman will never speak or hear bad words, never aggravate the whole household by humming opera airs, will never quarrel, never awake when her husband coughs, or rise early to look after his workmen. She will see clearly, for the deaf have good eyes. She will be pretty and intelligent, and make no noise. Were I young, I would like to marry her ; being old, I will adopt her as my daughter whenever you are tired of her."

For a moment the sad parents were cheered by Uncle Giraud's bright talk. But the cloud soon redescended upon them.

III

In course of time the little girl grew into a big one. Nature completed successfully, but faithfully, her task. The Chevalier's feelings towards Camille had, unfortunately, undergone no change. Her mother still watched over her tenderly, and never left her, observing anxiously her slightest actions, her every sign of interest in life.

When Camille's young friends were of an age to receive the first instructions of a governess, the poor child began to realise the difference between herself and others. The child of a neighbour had a severe governess. Camille, who was present one day at a spelling-lesson, regarded her little comrade with surprise, following her efforts with her eyes, seeking, as it were, to aid her, and crying when she was scolded. Especially were the music lessons puzzling to Camille.

The evening prayers, which the neighbour used regularly with her children, were another enigma for the girl. She knelt with her friends, and joined her hands without knowing wherefore. The Chevalier considered this a profanation ; not so his wife. As Camille advanced in age, she became possessed of a passion—as it were by a holy instinct—for the churches which she beheld. " When I was a child I saw not God, I saw only the sky," is the saying of a deaf mute. A religious procession, a coarse, gaudily bedizened image of the Virgin, a choir boy in a shabby surplice, whose voice was all unheard by Camille—who knows what simple means will serve to raise the eyes of a child ? And what matters it, so long as the eyes are raised ?

IV

Camille was *petite*, with a white skin, and long black hair, and graceful movements. She was swift to understand her mother's wishes, prompt to obey them. So much grace and beauty, joined to so much misfortune, were most disturbing to the Chevalier.

He would frequently embrace the girl in an excited manner, exclaiming aloud : " I am not yet a wicked man ! "

At the end of the garden there was a wooded walk, to which the Chevalier was in the habit of betaking himself after breakfast. From her chamber window Madame des Arcis often watched him wistfully as he walked to and fro beneath the trees. One morning, with palpitating heart, she ventured to join him. She wished to take Camille to a juvenile ball which was to be held that evening at a neighbouring mansion. She longed to observe the effect which her daughter's beauty would produce upon the outside world and upon her husband. She had passed a sleepless night in devising Camille's toilette, and she cherished the sweetest hopes. " It must be," she told herself, " that he will be proud, and the rest jealous of the poor little one ! She will say nothing, but she will be the most beautiful ! "

The Chevalier welcomed his wife graciously—quite in the manner of Versailles ! Their conversation commenced with the exchange of a few insignificant sentences as they walked side by side. Then a silence fell between them, while Madame des Arcis sought fitting words in which to approach her husband on the subject of Camille, and induce him to break his resolution that the child should never see the world. Meanwhile, the Chevalier was also in cogitation. He was the first to speak. He informed his wife that urgent family affairs called him to Holland, and that he ought to start not later than the following morning.

Madame understood his true motive only too easily. The Chevalier was far from contemplating the desertion of his wife, yet felt an irresistible desire, a compelling need of temporary isolation. In almost all true sorrow, man has this craving for solitude—suffering animals have it also.

His wife raised no objection to his project, but fresh grief wrung her heart. Complaining of weariness, she sank upon a seat. There she remained for a long time, lost in sad reverie. She rose at length, put her arm into that of her husband, and they returned together to the house.

The poor lady spent the afternoon quietly and prayerfully in her own room. In the evening, towards eight o'clock, she rang her bell, and ordered the horse to be put into the carriage. At the same time she sent word to the Chevalier that she intended going to the ball, and hoped that he would accompany her.

An embroidered robe of white muslin, small shoes of white satin, a necklace of American beads, a coronet of violets—such was the simple costume of Camille, who, when her mother had dressed her, jumped for joy. As Madame was embracing her child with the words, " You are beautiful ! you are beautiful ! " the Chevalier joined them. He gave his hand to his wife, and the three went to the ball.

As it was Camille's first appearance in public, she naturally excited a great deal of curiosity. The Chevalier suffered visibly. When his friends praised to him the beauty of his daughter, he felt that they intended to console him, and such consolation was not to his taste. Yet he could not wholly suppress some emotion of pride and joy. His feelings were strangely mixed. After having saluted by gestures almost everybody in the room, Camille was now resting by her mother's side. The general admiration grew more enthusiastic. Nothing, in fact, could have been more lovely than the envelope which held this poor dumb soul. Her figure, her face, her long curling hair, above all, her eyes of incomparable lustre, surprised every one. Her wistful looks and graceful gestures, too, were so pathetic. People crowded around Madame des Arcis, asking a thousand questions about Camille ; to surprise and a slight coldness succeeded sincere kindliness and sympathy. They had never seen such a charming child ; nothing resembled her, for there existed nothing else so charming as she ! Camille was a complete success.

Always outwardly calm, Madame des Arcis tasted to-night the most pure and intense pleasure of her life. A smile that was exchanged between her and her husband was well worth many tears.

Presently, as the Chevalier was still gazing at his daughter, a country-dance began, which Camille watched with an earnest attention that had in it something sad. A boy invited her to join. For answer, she shook her head, causing some of the violets to fall out of her coronet. Her mother picked them up, and soon put to rights the coiffure, which was her own handiwork. Then she looked round for her husband, but he was no longer in the room. She inquired if he had left, and whether he had taken the carriage. She was told that he had gone home on foot.

V

The Chevalier had resolved to leave home without taking leave of his wife. He shrank from all discussion and explanation, and, as he intended to return in a short time, he believed that he should act more wisely in leaving a letter than by making a verbal farewell. There was *some* truth in his statement of that business affair calling him away, although business was not his first consideration. And now one of his friends had written to hasten his departure. Here was a good excuse. On returning alone to his house (by a much shorter route than that taken by the carriage), he announced his intention to the servants, packed in great haste, sent his light luggage on to the town, mounted his horse, and was gone.

Yet a certain misgiving troubled him, for he knew that his Cécile would be pained by his abrupt departure, although he endeavoured to persuade himself that he did this for her sake no less than for his own. However, he continued on his way.

Meanwhile, Madame des Arcis was returning in the carriage, with her daughter asleep upon her knee. She felt hurt at the Chevalier's rudeness in leaving them to return alone. It seemed such a public slight upon his wife and child! Sad forebodings filled the mother's heart as the carriage jolted slowly over the stones of a newly-made road. "God watches over all," she reflected; "over us as over others. But what shall we do? What will become of my poor child?"

At some distance from Chardonneux there was a ford to be crossed. There had been much rain for nearly a month past, causing the river to overflow its banks. The ferryman refused at first to take the carriage into his boat; he would undertake, he said, to convey the passengers and the horse safely across, but not the vehicle. The lady, anxious to rejoin her husband, would not descend. She ordered the coachman to enter the boat; it was only a transit of a few minutes, which she had made a hundred times.

In mid-stream the boat was forced by the current from its straight course. The boatman asked the coachman's aid in keeping it away from the weir. For there was not far off a mill with a weir, where the violence of the water had formed a sort of cascade. It was clear that if the boat drifted to this spot there would be a terrible accident.

The coachman descended from his seat, and worked with a will. But he had only a pole to work with, the night was dark, a fine rain blinded the men, and soon the noise of the weir announced the most imminent danger. Madame des Arcis, who had remained in the carriage, opened the window in alarm. "Are we then lost?" cried she. At that moment the pole broke. The two men fell into the boat exhausted, and with bruised hands.

The ferryman could swim, but not the coachman. There was no time to lose. "Père Georgeot," said Madame to the ferryman, calling him by his name, "can you save my daughter and myself?"

"Certainly!" he replied, as if almost insulted by the question.

"What must we do?" inquired Madame des Arcis.

"Place yourself upon my shoulders," replied the ferryman, "and put your arms about my neck. As for the little one, I will hold her in one hand, and swim with the other, and she shall not get drowned. It is but a short distance from here to the potatoes which grow in yonder field."

"And Jean?" asked Madame, meaning the coachman.

"Jean will be all right, I hope. If he holds on at the weir, I will return for him."

Père Georgeot struck out with his double burden, but he had over-estimated his powers. He was no longer young. The shore was farther off, the current stronger than he had thought. He struggled manfully, but was nearly swept away. Then the trunk of a willow, hidden by the water and the darkness, stopped him suddenly with a violent blow upon the forehead. Blood flowed from the wound and obscured his vision.

"Could you save my child if you had only her to convey?" asked the mother.

"I cannot tell, but I *think* so," said the ferryman.

The mother removed her arms from the man's neck, and let herself slip gently into the water.

When the ferryman had deposited Camille safely on *terra firma*, the coachman, who had been rescued by a peasant, helped him to search for the body of Madame des Arcis. It was found on the following morning, near the bank.

VI

Camille's grief at her mother's loss was terrible to witness. She ran hither and thither, uttering wild, inarticulate cries, tearing her hair, and beating the walls. An unnatural calm succeeded these violent emotions; reason itself seemed well-nigh gone.

It was then that Uncle Giraud came to his niece's rescue. "Poor child!" said he, "she has at present neither father nor mother. With me she has always been a favourite, and I intend now to take charge of her for a time. Change of scene," said Uncle Giraud, "would do her a world of good." With the Chevalier's permission (obtained by letter), he carried off Camille to Paris. The Chevalier returned to Chardonneux, where he lived in deepest retirement, shunning every living being, a prey to grief and keen remorse.

A year passed heavily away. Uncle Giraud had as yet failed utterly to rouse Camille. She steadily refused to be interested in anything. At last, one day he determined to take her, *nolens volens*, to the opera. A new and beautiful dress was purchased for the occasion. When, attired in this, Camille saw herself in the glass, so pleased was she with the pretty picture that, to her good uncle's intense satisfaction, she actually smiled!

VII

Camille soon wearied of the opera. All—actors, musicians, audience—seemed to say to her: "We speak, and you cannot; we hear, laugh, sing, rejoice. You rejoice in nothing, hear nothing.

You are only a statue, the simulacrum of a being, a mere looker-on at life."

When, to exclude the mocking spectacle, she closed her eyes, the scenes of her early life rose before the eyes of her mind. She returned in thought to her country home, saw again her mother's dear face. It was too much! Uncle Giraud observed, with much concern, tears rolling down her cheeks. When he would have inquired the cause of her grief, she made signs that she wished to leave. She rose, and opened the door of the box.

Just at this moment, something attracted her attention. She caught sight of a good-looking, richly-dressed young man, who was tracing letters and figures with a white pencil upon a small slate. He exhibited this slate now and then to his neighbour, a man older than himself, who evidently understood him at once, and promptly replied in the same manner. At the same time the two exchanged signs.

Camille's curiosity and interest were deeply stirred. She had already observed that this young man's lips did not move. She now saw that he spoke a language which was not the language of others, that he had found some means of expressing himself without the aid of speech—that art for her so incomprehensible and impossible. An irresistible longing to see more seized her. She leaned over the edge of the box, and watched the stranger's movements attentively. When he again wrote something upon his slate, and passed it to his companion, she made an involuntary gesture as if to take it. Whereupon the young man, in his turn, looked at Camille. Their eyes met, and said the same thing, " We two are in like case ; we are both dumb."

Uncle Giraud brought his niece's wrap, but she no longer wished to go. She had reseated herself, and was leaning eagerly forward.

The Abbé de l'Epée was then just becoming known. Touched with pity for the deaf and dumb, this good man had invented a language that he deemed superior to that of Leibnitz. He restored deaf mutes to the ranks of their fellows by teaching them to read and write. Alone and unaided he laboured for his afflicted fellow-creatures, prepared to sacrifice to their welfare his life and fortune.

The young man observed by Camille was one of the Abbé's first pupils. He was the son of the Marquis de Maubray.

VIII

It goes without saying that neither Camille nor her uncle knew anything either of the Abbé de l'Epée or of his new method. Camille's mother would assuredly have discovered it, had she lived long enough. But Chardonneux was far from Paris ; the Chevalier did not take *The Gazette*, nor, if he had taken it, would he have read it. Thus a few leagues of distance, a little indolence, or death, may produce the same result.

Upon Camille's return from the opera, she was possessed with but one idea. She made her uncle understand that she wished for writing materials. Although the good man wanted his supper, he ran to his chamber, and returned with a piece of board and a morsel of chalk, relics of his old love for building and carpentry.

Camille placed the board upon her knee, then made signs to her uncle that he should sit by her and write something upon it. Laying his hand gently upon the girl's breast, he wrote, in large letters, her name, *Camille*, after which, well satisfied with the evening's work, he seated himself at the supper-table.

Camille retired as soon as possible to her own room, clasping her board in her arms. Having laid aside some of her finery, and let down her hair, she began to copy with great pains and care the word which her uncle had written. After writing it many times, she succeeded in forming the letters very fairly. What that word represented to her, who shall say?

It was a glorious night of July. Camille had opened her window, and from time to time paused in her self-imposed task to gaze out, although the "view" was but a dreary one. The window overlooked a yard in which coaches were kept. Four or five huge carriages stood side by side beneath a shed. Two or three others stood in the centre of the yard, as if awaiting the horses, which could be heard kicking in the stable. The court was shut in by a closed door and high walls.

Suddenly Camille perceived, beneath the shadow of a heavy diligence, a human form pacing to and fro. A feeling of fear seized her. The man was gazing intently at her window. In a few moments Camille had regained her courage. She took her lamp in her hand, and, leaning from the casement, held it so that its light illuminated the court. The Marquis de Maubray (for it was he), perceiving that he was discovered, sank on his knees and clasped his hands, gazing at Camille meanwhile with an expression of respectful admiration. Then he sprang up, and nimbly clambering over two or three intercepting vehicles, was in a few minutes within Camille's room, where his first act was to make her a profound bow. He longed for some means of speaking to her, and, observing upon the table the board bearing the written word *Camille*, he took the piece of chalk, and proceeded to write beside that name his own —*Pierre*.

"Who are you? and what are you doing here?" thundered a wrathful voice. It was that of Uncle Giraud, who at that moment entered the room, and bestowed upon the intruder a torrent of abuse. The Marquis calmly wrote something upon the board, and handed

it to Uncle Giraud, who read with amazement the following words :
" I love Mademoiselle Camille, and wish to marry her. I am the
Marquis de Maubray ; will you give her to me ? "

The uncle's wrath abated.

" Well ! " remarked he to himself, as he recognised the youth
he had seen at the opera—" for going straight to the point, and
getting through their business quickly, I never saw the like of these
dumb folk ! "

IX

The course of true love, for once, ran smooth. The Chevalier's
consent to this highly desirable match for his daughter was easily
obtained. Much more difficult was it to convince him that it was
possible to teach deaf mutes to read and write. Seeing, however,
is believing. One day, two or three years after the marriage, the
Chevalier received a letter from Camille, which began thus : " Oh,
father ! I can speak, not with my mouth, but with my hand."

She told how she had learned to do this, and to whom she owed
her new-born speech—the good Abbé de l'Epée. She described
to him the beauty of her baby, and affectionately besought him to
pay a visit to his daughter and grandchild.

After receiving this letter, the Chevalier hesitated for a long time.

" Go, by all means," advised Uncle Giraud, when he was consulted.
" Do you not reproach yourself continually for having deserted your
wife at the ball ? Will you also forsake your child, who longs to
see you ? Let us go together. I consider it most ungrateful of
her not to have included me in the invitation."

" He is right," reflected the Chevalier. " I brought cruel and
needless suffering upon the best of women. I left her to die a
frightful death, when I ought to have been her preserver. If this
visit to Camille involves some pain to myself, that is but a merited
chastisement. I will taste this bitter pleasure ; I will go and see
my child."

X

In the pretty boudoir of a house in the Faubourg St. Germain,
Camille's father and uncle found Camille and Pierre. Upon the
table lay books and sketches. The husband was reading, the wife
embroidering, the child playing on the carpet. At sight of the
welcome visitors the Marquis rose, while Camille ran to her father,
who, as he embraced her tenderly, could not restrain his tears.
Then the Chevalier's earnest look was bent upon the child. In
spite of himself, some shadow of the repugnance he had formerly
felt for the infirmity of Camille stirred afresh at sight of this small
being who had doubtless inherited that infirmity.

" Another mute ! " cried he.

Camille raised her son to her arms ; without hearing she had understood. Gently holding out the child towards the Chevalier, she placed her fingers upon the tiny lips, stroking them a little, as if coaxing them to speak. In a few moments he pronounced distinctly the words which his mother had caused him to be taught :

"Good-morning, papa!"

"Now you see clearly," said Uncle Giraud, "that God pardons everything and for ever!"

THÉOPHILE GAUTIER
1811–1872

THE MUMMY'S FOOT

I HAD entered, in an idle mood, the shop of one of those curiosity-vendors, who are called *marchands de bric-à-brac* in that Parisian slang which is so perfectly unintelligible elsewhere in France.

You have doubtless glanced occasionally through the windows of some of these shops, which have become so numerous now that it is fashionable to buy antiquated furniture and that every petty stockbroker thinks he must have his mediæval room.

There is one thing there which clings alike to the shop of the dealer in old iron, the wareroom of the tapestry-maker, the laboratory of the chemist, and the studio of the painter—in all those gloomy dens where a furtive daylight filters in through the window-shutters the most manifestly ancient thing is dust ; —the cobwebs are more authentic than the guimpe laces ; and the old pear-tree furniture on exhibition is actually younger than the mahogany which arrived but yesterday from America.

The warehouse of my bric-à-brac dealer was a veritable Capharnaum ; all ages and all nations seemed to have made their rendezvous there ; an Etruscan lamp of red clay stood upon a Boule cabinet, with ebony panels, brightly striped by lines of inlaid brass ; a duchess of the court of Louis XV. nonchalantly extended her fawn-like feet under a massive table of the time of Louis XIII., with heavy spiral supports of oak, and carven designs of Chimeras and foliage intermingled.

Upon the denticulated shelves of several sideboards glittered immense Japanese dishes with red and blue designs relieved by gilded hatching ; side by side with enamelled works by Bernard Palissy, representing serpents, frogs, and lizards in relief.

From disembowelled cabinets escaped cascades of silver-lustrous Chinese silks and waves of tinsel, which an oblique sunbeam shot through with luminous beads ; while portraits of every era, in frames more or less tarnished, smiled through their yellow varnish.

The striped breastplate of a damascened suit of Milanese armour glittered in one corner ; Loves and Nymphs of porcelain ; Chinese grotesques, vases of *céladon* and crackle-ware ; Saxon and old

Sèvres cups encumbered the shelves and nooks of the apartment.

The dealer followed me closely through the tortuous way contrived between the piles of furniture ; warding off with his hand the hazardous sweep of my coat-skirts ; watching my elbows with the uneasy attention of an antiquarian and a usurer.

It was a singular face, that of the merchant—an immense skull, polished like a knee, and surrounded by a thin aureole of white hair which brought out the clear salmon tint of his complexion all the more strikingly, lent him a false aspect of patriarchal good nature, counteracted, however, by the scintillation of two little yellow eyes which trembled in their orbits like two louis-d'or upon quicksilver. The curve of his nose presented an aquiline silhouette, which suggested the Oriental or Jewish type. His hands—thin, slender, full of nerves which projected like strings upon the fingerboard of a violin, and armed with claws like those on the terminations of bats' wings—shook with senile trembling ; but those convulsively agitated hands became firmer than steel pincers or lobsters' claws when they lifted any precious article—an onyx cup, a Venetian glass, or a dish of Bohemian crystal. This strange old man had an aspect so thoroughly rabbinical and cabalistic that he would have been burnt on the mere testimony of his face three centuries ago.

"Will you not buy something from me to-day, sir ? Here is a Malay kreese with a blade undulating like flame : look at those grooves contrived for the blood to run along, those teeth set backward so as to tear out the entrails in withdrawing the weapon—it is a fine character of ferocious arm, and will look well in your collection : this two-handed sword is very beautiful—it is the work of Josepe de la Hera ; and this *colichemarde*, with its fenestrated guard—what a superb specimen of handicraft ! "

"No ; I have quite enough weapons and instruments of carnage ; I want a small figure, something which will suit me as a paperweight ; for I cannot endure those trumpery bronzes which the stationers sell, and which may be found on everybody's desk."

The old gnome foraged among his ancient wares, and finally arranged before me some antique bronzes—so-called, at least ; fragments of malachite ; little Hindu or Chinese idols—a kind of poussah-toys in jade-stone, representing the incarnations of Brahma or Vishnu, and wonderfully appropriate to the very undivine office of holding papers and letters in place.

I was hesitating between a porcelain dragon, all constellated with warts—its mouth formidable with bristling tusks and ranges of teeth—and an abominable little Mexican fetish, representing the god Vitziliputzili *au naturel* ; when I caught sight of a charming foot, which I at first took for a fragment of some antique Venus.

It had those beautiful ruddy and tawny tints that lend to Florentine bronze that warm, living look so much preferable to the grey-green aspect of common bronzes, which might easily be mistaken for statues in a state of putrefaction : satiny gleams played over its rounded forms, doubtless polished by the amorous kisses of twenty centuries ; for it seemed a Corinthian bronze, a work of the best era of art—perhaps moulded by Lysippus himself.

"That foot will be my choice," I said to the merchant, who regarded me with an ironical and saturnine air, and held out the object desired that I might examine it more fully.

I was surprised at its lightness ; it was not a foot of metal, but in sooth a foot of flesh—an embalmed foot—a mummy's foot : on examining it still more closely the very grain of the skin, and the almost imperceptible lines impressed upon it by the texture of the bandages, became perceptible. The toes were slender and delicate, and terminated by perfectly formed nails, pure and transparent as agates ; the great toe, slightly separated from the rest, afforded a happy contrast, in the antique style, to the position of the other toes, and lent it an aerial lightness—the grace of a bird's foot ; —the sole, scarcely streaked by a few almost imperceptible cross lines, afforded evidence that it had never touched the bare ground, and had only come in contact with the finest matting of Nile rushes, and the softest carpets of panther skin.

"Ha, ha !—you want the foot of the Princess Hermonthis," exclaimed the merchant, with a strange giggle, fixing his owlish eyes upon me—"ha, ha, ha !—for a paper-weight !—an original idea !—artistic idea ! Old Pharaoh would certainly have been surprised had some one told him that the foot of his adored daughter would be used for a paper-weight after he had had a mountain of granite hollowed out as a receptacle for the triple coffin, painted and gilded—covered with hieroglyphics and beautiful paintings of the Judgment of Souls," continued the queer little merchant, half audibly, as though talking to himself !

"How much will you charge me for this mummy fragment ? "

"Ah, the highest price I can get ; for it is a superb piece : if I had the match of it you could not have it for less than five hundred francs ;—the daughter of a Pharaoh ! nothing is more rare."

"Assuredly that is not a common article ; but, still, how much do you want ? In the first place, let me warn you that all my wealth consists of just five louis : I can buy anything that costs five louis, but nothing dearer ;—you might search my vest pockets and most secret drawers without even finding one poor five-franc piece more."

"Five louis for the foot of the Princess Hermonthis ! that is very little, very little indeed ; 'tis an authentic foot," muttered the merchant, shaking his head, and imparting a peculiar rotary motion to his eyes. "Well, take it, and I will give you the bandages into the bargain," he added, wrapping the foot in an ancient damask rag—"very fine ! real damask !—Indian damask which has never been redyed ; it is strong, and yet it is soft," he mumbled, stroking the frayed tissue with his fingers, through the trade-acquired habit which moved him to praise even an object of so little value that he himself deemed it only worth the giving away.

He poured the gold coins into a sort of mediæval alms-purse hanging at his belt, repeating :

" The foot of the Princess Hermonthis, to be used for a paper-weight ! "

Then turning his phosphorescent eyes upon me, he exclaimed in a voice strident as the crying of a cat which has swallowed a fish bone :

" Old Pharaoh will not be well pleased : he loved his daughter— the dear man ! "

" You speak as if you were a contemporary of his : you are old enough, goodness knows ! but you do not date back to the Pyramids of Egypt," I answered laughingly, from the threshold.

I went home, delighted with my acquisition.

With the idea of putting it to a profitable use as soon as possible, I placed the foot of the divine Princess Hermonthis upon a heap of papers scribbled over with verses, in themselves an undecipherable mosaic work of erasures ; articles freshly begun ; letters forgotten, and posted in the table-drawer instead of the letter-box—an error to which absent-minded people are peculiarly liable. The effect was charming, bizarre and romantic.

Well satisfied with this embellishment, I went out with the gravity and pride becoming one who feels that he has the ineffable advantage over all passers-by whom he elbows, of possessing a piece of the Princess Hermonthis, daughter of Pharaoh.

I looked upon all who did not possess, like myself, a paper-weight so authentically Egyptian as very ridiculous people ; and it seemed to me that the proper occupation of every sensible man should consist in the mere fact of having a mummy's foot upon his desk.

Happily I met some friends, whose presence distracted me in my infatuation with this new acquisition : I went to dinner with them ; for I could not very well have dined with myself.

When I came back that evening, with my brain slightly confused by a few glasses of wine, a vague whiff of Oriental perfume delicately titillated my olfactory nerves : the heat of the room had warmed the natron, bitumen and myrrh in which the *paraschistes*, who cut open the bodies of the dead, had bathed the corpse of the princess ;—it was a perfume at once sweet and penetrating—a perfume that four thousand years had not been able to dissipate.

The Dream of Egypt was Eternity ; her odours have the solidity of granite, and endure as long.

I soon drank deeply from the black cup of sleep : for a few hours all remained opaque to me ; Oblivion and Nothingness inundated me with their sombre waves.

Yet light gradually dawned upon the darkness of my mind : dreams commenced to touch me softly in their silent flight.

The eyes of my soul were opened ; and I beheld my chamber as it actually was : I might have believed myself awake, but for a vague consciousness which assured me that I slept, and that something fantastic was about to take place.

The odour of myrrh had augmented in intensity : and I felt a slight headache, which I very naturally attributed to several glasses of champagne that we had drunk to the unknown gods and our future fortunes.

I peered through my room with a feeling of expectation which I saw nothing to justify : every article of furniture was in its proper place ; the lamp, softly shaded by its globe of ground crystal, burned upon its bracket ; the water-colour sketches shone under their Bohemian glass ; the curtains hung down languidly ; everything wore the aspect of tranquil slumber.

After a few moments, however, all this calm interior appeared to become disturbed ; the woodwork cracked stealthily ; the ash-covered log suddenly emitted a jet of blue flame ; and the disks of the pateras seemed like great metallic eyes, watching, like myself, for the things which were about to happen.

My eyes accidentally fell upon the desk where I had placed the foot of the Princess Hermonthis.

Instead of remaining quiet—as behoved a foot which had been embalmed for four thousand years—it commenced to act in a nervous manner ; contracted itself, and leaped over the papers like a startled frog ;—one would have imagined that it had suddenly been brought into contact with a galvanic battery : I could distinctly hear the dry sound made by its little heel, hard as the hoof of a gazelle.

I became rather discontented with my acquisition, inasmuch as I wished my paper-weights to be of a sedentary disposition, and thought it very unnatural that feet should walk about without legs ; and I commenced to experience a feeling closely akin to fear.

Suddenly I saw the folds of my bed-curtain stir ; and heard a bumping sound, like that caused by some person hopping on one foot across the floor. I must confess I became alternately hot and cold ; that I felt a strange wind chill my back ; and that my suddenly-rising hair caused my nightcap to execute a leap of several yards.

The bed-curtains opened, and I beheld the strangest figure imaginable before me.

It was a young girl of a very deep coffee-brown complexion, like the bayadere Amani, and possessing the purest Egyptian type of perfect beauty ; her eyes were almond-shaped and oblique, with eyebrows so black that they seemed blue ; her nose was exquisitely chiselled, almost Greek in its delicacy of outline ; and she might indeed have been taken for a Corinthian statue of bronze, but for the prominence of her cheek-bones and the slightly African fulness of her lips, which compelled one to recognise her as belonging, beyond all doubt, to the hieroglyphic race which dwelt upon the banks of the Nile.

Her arms, slender and spindle-shaped, like those of very young girls, were encircled by a peculiar kind of metal bands, and bracelets of glass beads ; her hair was all twisted into little cords ; and she wore upon her bosom a little idol figure of green paste, bearing a whip with seven lashes, which proved it to be an image of Isis : her brow was adorned with a shining plate of gold ; and a few traces of paint relieved the coppery tint of her cheeks.

As for her costume, it was very odd indeed.

Fancy a *pagne* or skirt all formed of little strips of material bedizened with red and black hieroglyphics, stiffened with bitumen, and apparently belonging to a freshly unbandaged mummy.

In one of those sudden flights of thought so common in dreams I heard the hoarse falsetto of the bric-à-brac dealer, repeating like a monotonous refrain the phrase he had uttered in his shop with so enigmatical an intonation :

" Old Pharaoh will not be well pleased : he loved his daughter, the dear man ! "

One strange circumstance, which was not at all calculated to restore my equanimity, was that the apparition had but one foot ; the other was broken off at the ankle !

She approached the table where the foot was starting and fidgeting about more than ever ; and there supported herself upon the edge of the desk. I saw her eyes fill with pearly-gleaming tears.

Although she had not as yet spoken, I fully comprehended the thoughts which agitated her : she looked at her foot—for it was indeed her own—with an exquisitely graceful expression of coquettish sadness ; but the foot leaped and ran hither and thither, as though impelled on steel springs.

Twice or thrice she extended her hand to seize it, but could not succeed.

Then commenced between the Princess Hermonthis and her foot—which appeared to be endowed with a special life of its own— a very fantastic dialogue in a most ancient Coptic tongue, such as might have been spoken thirty centuries ago in the syrinxes of the land of Ser : luckily I understood Coptic perfectly well that night.

The Princess Hermonthis cried, in a voice sweet and vibrant as the tones of a crystal bell :

" Well, my dear little foot, you always flee from me ; yet I always took good care of you. I bathed you with perfumed water in a bowl of alabaster ; I smoothed your heel with pumice-stone mixed with palm oil ; your nails were cut with golden scissors and polished with a hippopotamus tooth ; I was careful to select *tatbebs* for you, painted and embroidered and turned up at the toes, which were the envy of all the young girls in Egypt : you wore on your great toe rings bearing the device of the sacred Scarabæus ; and you supported one of the lightest bodies that a lazy foot could sustain.

The foot replied in a pouting and chagrined tone :

" You know well that I do not belong to myself any longer. I have been bought and paid for : the old merchant knew what he was about : he bore you a grudge for having refused to espouse him. This is an ill turn which he has done you. The Arab who violated your royal coffin in the subterranean pits of the necropolis of Thebes was sent thither by him : he desired to prevent you from being present at the reunion of the shadowy nations in the cities below. Have you five pieces of gold for my ransom ? "

" Alas, no !—my jewels, my rings, my purses of gold and silver, were all stolen from me," answered the Princess Hermonthis, with a sob.

" Princess," I then exclaimed, " I never retained anybody's foot unjustly ;—even though you have not got the five louis which it cost me, I present it to you gladly : I should feel unutterably wretched to think that I were the cause of so amiable a person as the Princess Hermonthis being lame."

I delivered this discourse in a royally gallant, troubadour tone which must have astonished the beautiful Egyptian girl.

She turned a look of deepest gratitude upon me ; and her eyes shone with bluish gleams of light.

She took her foot—which surrendered itself willingly this time— like a woman about to put on her little shoe ; and adjusted it to her leg with much skill.

This operation over, she took a few steps about the room, as though to assure herself that she was really no longer lame.

" Ah, how pleased my father will be !—he who was so unhappy because of my mutilation ; and who from the moment of my birth set a whole nation at work to hollow me out a tomb so deep that he might preserve me intact until that last day, when souls must be weighed in the balance of Amenthi ! Come with me to my father ; —he will receive you kindly ; for you have given me back my foot."

I thought this proposition natural enough. I arrayed myself in a dressing-gown of large flowered pattern, which lent me a very Pharaonic aspect ; hurriedly put on a pair of Turkish slippers ; and informed the Princess Hermonthis that I was ready to follow her.

Before starting, Hermonthis took from her neck the little idol of green paste, and laid it on the scattered sheets of paper which covered the table.

" It is only fair," she observed, smilingly, " that I should replace your paper-weight."

She gave me her hand, which felt soft and cold, like the skin of a serpent ; and we departed.

We passed for some time with the velocity of an arrow through a fluid and greyish expanse, in which half-formed silhouettes flitted swiftly by us, to right and left.

For an instant we saw only sky and sea.

A few moments later obelisks commenced to tower in the distance : pylons and vast flights of steps guarded by sphinxes became clearly outlined against the horizon.

We had reached our destination.

The princess conducted me to a mountain of rose-coloured granite, in the face of which appeared an opening so narrow and low that it would have been difficult to distinguish it from the fissures in the rock, had not its location been marked by two stelæ wrought with sculptures.

Hermonthis kindled a torch, and led the way before me.

We traversed corridors hewn through the living rock : their walls, covered with hieroglyphics and paintings of allegorical processions, might well have occupied thousands of arms for thousands of years in their formation ;—these corridors, of interminable length, opened into square chambers, in the midst of which pits had been contrived, through which we descended by cramp-irons or spiral stairways ;— these pits again conducted us into other chambers, opening into other corridors, likewise decorated with painted sparrow-hawks, serpents coiled in circles, the symbols of the *tau* and *pedum*—prodigious works of art which no living eye can ever examine—interminable legends of granite which only the dead have time to read through all eternity.

At last we found ourselves in a hall so vast, so enormous, so immeasurable, that the eye could not reach its limits ; files of monstrous columns stretched far out of sight on every side, between which twinkled livid stars of yellowish flame ;—points of light which revealed farther depths incalculable in the darkness beyond.

The Princess Hermonthis still held my hand, and graciously saluted the mummies of her acquaintance.

My eyes became accustomed to the dim twilight ; and objects became discernible.

I beheld the kings of the subterranean races seated upon thrones —grand old men, though dry, withered, wrinkled like parchment, and blackened with naphtha and bitumen—all wearing *pshents* of gold, and breast-plates and gorgets glittering with precious stones ; their eyes immovably fixed like the eyes of sphinxes, and their long beards whitened by the snow of centuries. Behind them stood their peoples, in the stiff and constrained posture enjoined by Egyptian art, all eternally preserving the attitude prescribed by the hieratic code. Behind these nations, the cats, ibixes and crocodiles contemporary with them—rendered monstrous of aspect by their swathing bands—mewed, flapped their wings, or extended their jaws in a saurian giggle.

All the Pharaohs were there—Cheops, Chephrenes, Psammetichus, Sesostris, Amenotaph—all the dark rulers of the pyramids and syrinxes :—on yet higher thrones sat Chronos and Xixouthros—who was contemporary with the deluge ; and Tubal Cain, who reigned before it.

The beard of King Xixouthros had grown seven times around the granite table, upon which he leaned, lost in deep reverie—and buried in dreams.

Farther back, through a dusty cloud, I beheld dimly the seventy-two Pre-adamite Kings, with their seventy-two peoples—for ever passed away.

After permitting me to gaze upon this bewildering spectacle a few moments, the Princess Hermonthis presented me to her father Pharaoh, who favoured me with a most gracious nod.

" I have found my foot again !—I have found my foot ! " cried the princess, clapping her little hands together with every sign of frantic joy : " it was this gentleman who restored it to me."

The races of Kemi, the races of Nahasi—all the black, bronzed, and copper-coloured nations repeated in chorus :

" The Princess Hermonthis has found her foot again ! "

Even Xixouthros himself was visibly affected.

He raised his heavy eyelids, stroked his moustache with his fingers, and turned upon me a glance weighty with centuries.

" By Oms, the dog of Hell, and Tmei, daughter of the Sun and of Truth ! this is a brave and worthy lad ! " exclaimed Pharaoh, pointing to me with his sceptre which was terminated with a lotus-flower.

" What recompense do you desire ? "

Filled with that daring inspired by dreams in which nothing seems impossible, I asked him for the hand of the Princess Hermonthis ; —the hand seemed to me a very proper antithetic recompense for the foot.

Pharoah opened wide his great eyes of glass in astonishment at my witty request.

" What country do you come from ? and what is your age ? "

" I am a Frenchman ; and I am twenty-seven years old, venerable Pharaoh."

" Twenty-seven years old ! and he wishes to espouse the Princess Hermonthis, who is thirty centuries old ! " cried out at once all the Thrones and all the Circles of Nations.

Only Hermonthis herself did not seem to think my request unreasonable.

" If you were even only two thousand years old," replied the ancient King, " I would willingly give you the Princess ; but the disproportion is too great ; and, besides, we must give our daughters husbands who will last well : you do not know how to preserve yourselves any longer ; even those who died only fifteen centuries ago are already no more than a handful of dust ;—behold ! my flesh is solid as basalt ; my bones are bars of steel !

" I will be present on the last day of the world, with the same body and the same features which I had during my lifetime : my daughter Hermonthis will last longer than a statue of bronze.

" Then the last particles of your dust will have been scattered abroad by the winds ; and even Isis herself, who was able to find the atoms of Osiris, would scarce be able to recompose your being.

" See how vigorous I yet remain, and how mighty is my grasp," he added, shaking my hand in the English fashion with a strength that buried my rings in the flesh of my fingers.

He squeezed me so hard that I awoke, and found my friend Alfred shaking me by the arm to make me get up.

" O you everlasting sleeper !—must I have you carried out into the middle of the street, and fireworks exploded in your ears ? It is after noon ; don't you recollect your promise to take me with you to see M. Aguado's Spanish pictures ? "

" God ! I forgot all, all about it," I answered, dressing myself hurriedly ; " we will go there at once ; I have the permit lying there on my desk."

I started to find it ;—but fancy my astonishment when I beheld, instead of the mummy's foot I had purchased the evening before, the little green paste idol left in its place by the Princess Hermonthis.

THE
PAVILION ON THE LAKE

Théophile Gautier

In the province of Canton, some leagues from the town, there lived side by side two rich Chinamen, who had retired from affairs. One was called Tou, and the other Kouan. Tou had occupied a high scientific position. He was a member of the Jasper Chamber. Kouan, in a lower walk of life, had amassed a fortune and won much consideration.

The two Chinamen were distantly related, and had been loving friends. In their younger days they delighted to forgather with some of their old school-fellows; in the autumn evenings they would let their brushes, charged with black ink, fly over the canvas of flowered paper, and celebrate in verse the beauty of the aster flower, while drinking little cups of wine. But their two characters, that first showed scarcely any differences, became, with age, quite opposed to each other. So an almond branch will divide into two stems which, connecting at the bottom, will completely separate at the top, in such a way that, while one sheds its bitter fragrance over the garden, the other will loosen its snow of flowers outside the wall.

From year to year Tou took on seriousness; his stomach swelled out majestically; his chin, with its three folds, shelved out with a solemn air. He wrote nothing except moral couplets suitable for hanging on the posts of pagodas. Kouan, on the contrary, seemed to grow jollier with age. More joyfully than ever, he sang of wine and flowers and swallows. His mind, free from vulgar cares, was keen and alert, like that of a young man; and when the word that he had to enshrine in a verse was given, his hand did not hesitate a single moment.

Little by little the two friends had acquired an animosity against each other. They could no longer speak without scratching each other with sharp words; they were like two hedges of brambles, bristling with thorns. Things came to such a point that they broke off all communication, and each hung on the front of his house a tablet formally forbidding any person of the neighbouring dwelling-place to cross the threshold under any pretext whatever. They would have much liked to be able to take their houses away, and fix them somewhere else. Unhappily, that was not possible. Tou even tried to sell his property, but he could not get a reasonable offer. And besides it would have hurt him to leave the carven wainscotting, the polished tables, the transparent windows, the gilded trellis work, the bamboo seats, the porcelain vases, the cabinets of red and black lacquer, the scrolls of ancient poems, which he had taken so much trouble in arranging. It is always hard to yield to strangers the garden you have planted yourself with willows, peach trees, and plum trees; where you have seen, every springtime, the lovely cherry-blossom open. Each of these objects attaches itself to the heart of a man with a thread finer than silk, but as difficult to break as an iron chain.

At the time when Tou and Kouan were friends, they had each built in their garden a pavilion on the edge of a little lake, common to both estates. It was a pleasure for them to send familiar greetings from the height of the balcony, and to smoke the drop of flaming opium on the mushroom-shaped pipe of porcelain, while exchanging benevolent whiffs. But since their dissensions they had had a wall built that separated the lake into two equal parts. But as the lake was very deep, the wall was supported on piles, forming a kind of low arcade, with arches through which passed a water with long trembling reflections of the opposite pavilion.

These pavilions were in three storeys, with the terraces set back. The roofs, turned up and curved in angles like the toe of a wooden shoe, were covered with round, brilliant tiles, like the scales that cover the stomach of a carp. On each ridge were outlined denticulations in the form of dragons and foliage. Pillars of red varnish, connected by an open-work frieze, like the ivory leaf of a fan, upheld this graceful roofing. Their shafts rested on a little low wall covered with squares of porcelain arranged with delightful symmetry, and edged with a hand-rail of an odd design in such a way as to form an open gallery in front of the body of the building.

This arrangement was repeated on each floor, not without some variations. Here the squares of porcelain were replaced by low reliefs representing scenes of country life ; the network of branches, curiously deformed and making unexpected angles, was used for the balcony ; posts in bright colours served as pedestals for mystical monsters covered with warts and fantastic creatures produced by uniting together every impossibility. The edifice ended in a hollowed-out, gilded cornice, furnished with a balustrade of bamboos with equal knots, adorned at each compartment with a metal bowl. The interior was not less splendid. On the walls the poems of Tou'chi and of Li'tai'pe were written by an agile hand in perpendicular lines of golden characters on a background of lacquer. Sheets of talc let a milky and opalescent light filter through the windows ; and on their ledges, pots of peonies, of orchids, of Chinese cowslips, of erythrina with flowering branches, placed with art, delighted the eyes with their delicate gradations of colour. Squares of silk, magnificently embroidered with foliage, were laid in the corners of each room ; and on the tables, that reflected like looking-glasses, there were always tooth-picks, fans, ebony pipes, porphyry stones, brushes, and all that was needed to write. Artificial rocks, in the chinks of which willows and walnuts plunged their roots, served on the land side as a base for these picturesque constructions ; on the water side, they were carried on posts of indestructible wood.

It was really a charming sight to see the willow fling her filaments of gold and her tassels of silk from the height of these rocks down to the surface of the water, while the brilliant colours of the pavilion glistened in a frame of variegated foliage.

Under the clear water, blue fishes with golden scales gambolled in bands ; flocks of pretty ducks with emerald necks played about in all directions ; and the large leaves of the great water-lily languidly spread out under the diamond-like transparency of this little lake, fed by an underground spring. Except towards the middle, where the bottom was formed of a silver sand of extraordinary fineness, and where the ebullitions of a rising spring prevented any aquatic vegetation from taking root, all the rest of the lake was carpeted with the loveliest green velvet you can imagine, by sheets of perennial cress.

Without the ugly wall raised by the reciprocal inimity of the two neighbours, there would not surely have been in the whole extent of the Celestial Empire, that occupies as you know more than three parts of the world, a more picturesque and more delightful garden.

Each owner would have enlarged his property by the vista of his neighbour's ground, for man here below can only take objects according to their appearance. Such as it was, however, a wise man would not have wished, when ending his life in the contemplation of nature and the amusements of poetry, a more propitious and charming retreat.

Tou and Kouan had by their quarrel obtained only a wall as a perspective, and had deprived each other of the view of the pleasant pavilions, but they consoled themselves with the idea of having injured each other.

This state of things had already obtained for several years. Nettles and weeds invaded the paths that led from one house to the other. Branches of thorny shrubs were interlaced, as though they wished to intercept all communication. It looked as though the plants understood the dissensions that divided the two old friends, and took part in the quarrel, and tried to separate them still more.

During this time the wives of Tou and Kouan had each given birth to a child. Madame Tou was the mother of a charming girl, and Madame Kouan of the prettiest boy in the world. This happy event, which had brought joy to both houses, was ignored by one and the other. For though their estates touched, the two Chinamen lived as remote from each other as though they had been separated by the Yellow River or the Great Wall. Common acquaintances avoided all allusion to the neighbouring house, and the servants, if they chanced to meet, had orders not to speak, under pain of whipping and torture.

The boy was called Tchin-Sing, and the girl, Ju-Kiouan, that is to say, " Pearl " and " Jasper " ; and their perfect beauty justified the choice of these names. As soon as they were able to toddle, the wall that cut the lake in two and unpleasantly stopped the view attracted their attention. They asked their parents what there was behind this barrier so strangely placed in the middle of a sheet of water, and to whom belonged the tall tree whose tops could just be seen. They were told it was the dwelling-place of some odd, crotchety, peevish folk who were very unsociable and that the barrier had been made as a protection against such wicked neighbours.

This explanation was sufficient for the children. They became accustomed to the wall and took no more interest in it. Ju-Kiouan grew in graces and in perfections. She was distinguished in all the works of her sex, and handled the needle with an incomparable skill. The butterflies she embroidered on satin seemed to live and beat their wings. You could have sworn you heard the song of the birds that she fixed on the canvas ; more than one mistaken nose was stuck against her tapestries to smell the fragrance of the flowers she had sewn there. This was not the limit of the talents of Ju-Kiouan. She knew by heart the Book of Odes and the five rules of conduct ; never a lighter hand threw on silk paper clearer and bolder characters. Dragons were not so rapid in their flight as her wrist, when it poured down the black rain of the writing-brush. She knew all the styles of poetry, and composed pieces full of merit on subjects that would naturally strike a young girl—on the return of the swallows, the willows in spring, the asters, and similar subjects. Many a lettered man who thinks himself worthy of bestriding the golden horse could not improvise with so much facility.

Tchin-Sing had profited no less by his studies. His name was found first on the list of examinations. Although he was very young, he was able to put on the black cap ; and already every mother thought that a lad so advanced in the sciences would make an excellent son-in-law, and soon arrive at the highest literary dignities. But Tchin-Sing replied with a merry air to the marriage-brokers that it was too soon, and that he desired to enjoy still longer his liberty. He refused in succession Hon-Giu, Lo-Men-Gli, Oma, Po-Fo, and other young ladies of great distinction. Never, without excepting the handsome Fan-Gan, whose carriage the ladies filled with sweets and oranges when he returned from archery—never was a young man so feasted, watched over, and solicitated ; but his heart seemed insensible to love ; yet not through coldness, for it could be divined by a thousand details that Tchin-Sing had a tender heart, but it seemed as though he remembered some beloved image known in a former life, and that he hoped to find it again in his present existence. It was in vain they boasted to him of eyebrows of willow leaf, of imperceptible feet, of dragon-fly waists belonging to the beauties offered to him in marriage. He listened with a distracted air, as if thinking of something else.

For her part, Ju-Kiouan did not show herself less difficult ; she dismissed all pretenders to her hand. This one saluted without grace, that one was not careful about his clothes ; one had a heavy and commonplace way of writing ; the other did not know the book of verses, or had made a mistake about a rhyme ; in short, they all had some defect. Ju-Kiouan sketched such comical portraits of them that her parents ended by laughing themselves, and, with all politeness, showed to the door the poor aspirant who thought he had already set his foot on the threshold of the eastern pavilion.

In the end, the parents of both children were alarmed at their persistence in rejecting every offer of marriage. Madame Tou and Madame Kouan, occupied no doubt with ideas of marriage, continued in their dreams by night their thoughts of a daytime. One of the dreams which they had impressed them very deeply. Madam Kouan dreamt that she saw on the breast of her son a jasper stone so marvellously polished that it sparkled like a carbuncle. Madame Tou dreamt that her daughter wore on her neck the finest orient pearl, of an inestimable value. What was the meaning of these two dreams ? Did that of Madame Kouan foreshow that Tchin-Sing would win the honours of the Imperial Academy ? Did that of Madame Tou signify that Ju-Kiouan would find some treasure buried in the garden or under a brick of the fireplace ? Such explanations were not unreasonable ; most persons would have been content with them. But these good ladies only saw in their dreams allusions to extremely fine marriages that their children would soon make. Unhappily, Tchin-Sing and Ju-Kiouan persisted more than ever in their resolution, and belied the prophecies.

Although Kouan and Tou had had no dreams, they were astonished at such stubbornness. Marriage was usually a ceremony for which young people did not show so sustained an aversion. They fancied that the resistance was perhaps due to a preconceived inclination ; but Tchin-Sing had not courted any maiden, and no young man walked up and down the trellis work outside Ju-Kiouan's room. Some days of observation sufficed to convince the two families of this. Madame Tou and Madame Kouan believed more than ever in the great destinies foretold in their dreams.

The two women went separately to consult the bonze of the temple of Fo—a fine edifice with carven roofs, round windows, gleaming with gold and varnish, plastered with votive tablets, adorned with masts, from which hung banners of silk embroidered with dragons and monsters, and shadowed by aged trees of enormous thickness. After having burnt gilded papers and perfumes before the idol, the bonze told Madame Tou that the jasper must be joined to the pearl, and informed Madame Kouan that the pearl must be united to the jasper, and that only by this union would all the difficulties be ended. Little satisfied by this ambiguous answer, the two women went home by different paths, without having seen each other in the temple. Their perplexity was much greater than before.

Now it happened that one day Ju-Kiouan was leaning on the balustrade of the pavilion at precisely the hour when Tchin-Sing was doing the same thing behind the wall. The weather was fine—no cloud veiled the sky, there was not enough wind to shake an aspen leaf, and the surface of the pond was more level than a looking-glass. If, in its play, a carp made a leap and traced a circle on the water it soon vanished. The trees by the shore were reflected so exactly that one hesitated between the image and the reality. It looked like a forest planted upside down, and connecting its roots with the roots of a similar mass of trees—a wood that had drowned itself out of unhappy love. The fish seemed to be swimming in the leaves, and the birds to be flying in the water. Ju-Kiouan was amusing herself by studying this marvellous transparency, when, casting her eyes over the part of the lake by the wall, she saw the reflection of the opposite pavilion, which stretched to there, by sliding underneath the arch.

She had never paid attention to this singular play of reflections, and it surprised and interested her. She distinguished the red pillars, the carven frieze, the pots of asters, the gilded vanes, and if the refraction had not reversed them she would have read the sentences written on the tablets. But what astonished her to the highest degree was to see, leaning from the balcony, in a position like her own, a figure that so resembled her own that if it had not come from the other side of the lake she would have taken it for herself. It was the shadow of Tchin-Sing, and if you find it strange that a lad can be taken for a maid, I must explain that Tchin-Sing had taken off his hat, by reason of the heat, and he was extremely young and beardless. His delicate features, his fine colour, and his brilliant eyes easily led to the illusion which, for the rest, did not last long.

Ju-Kiouan, from the movements of her heart, quickly recognised it was not a girl whose image was repeated in the water. Until then she had thought that the earth did not contain a being created for her, and very often she had wished she had at her order one of the horses of Fargana, that cover a thousand leagues a day, to search for a husband in imaginary space. She fancied she was unparalleled in this world, and that she would never know the sweetness of the union of marriage. "Never," she used to say to herself, " shall I consecrate the duck-weed and alasma on the ancestral altar, and I shall enter alone among the mulberry trees and the elms ! "

On seeing the reflection in the water, she understood that her loveliness had a sister, or rather a brother. Far from being angry, she was quite happy. The pride of thinking herself unique quickly gave way to love ; for at this moment the heart of Ju-Kiouan was bound for ever. A single glance, not directly, but a mere reflection, was sufficient for that. And do not accuse her, on this account, of frivolity. It may seem a madness to fall in love with

a young man on seeing his reflection, but except in a long intercourse permitting the study of character, what more do we see
in men ? A purely exterior aspect, like that given by a mirror !
And isn't it proper for young girls to discern the soul of the future
husband by the enamel of his teeth, or the way he cuts his finger-
nails ?

Tchin-Sing had also perceived this marvellous beauty. " Do
I dream wide awake ? " he cried. " This charming figure that
sparkles under the crystal water must have been formed by the
silver rays of the moon, on a night in spring, and the most subtle
fragrance of flowers. Though I have never seen her, I recognise
her : it is she whose image is graven in my heart, the unknown
shape of beauty to whom I address my couplets and quatrains."

Tchin-Sing was still holding forth in a monologue when he heard
his father calling him.

" My son," he said, " it is a very rich and very suitable lady who
is offered to thee by the intervention of my friend, Wing. It is
a girl with imperial blood in her veins, whose beauty is celebrated,
and who possesses all the qualities proper to make a husband happy."

Tchin-Sing, all preoccupied by the adventure of the pavilion,
and burning with love for the image glimpsed in the water, abruptly
refused. His father, wild with anger, threatened most violently.

" Wretched boy ! " cried the old man, " if thou persistest in thy
stubbornnesss, I shall beg the mandarin to have thee sent to that
fortress occupied by the barbarians of Europe, from which a man
can see only mountains capped with clouds, and black water
furrowed by those monstrous inventions of evil spirits that vomit
a smoke and move with wheels. There wilt thou have time to
reflect and amend ! "

These menaces did not greatly frighten Tchin-Sing. He replied
that he would accept the first spouse presented to him, providing
she were not that one.

The next day at the same hour he went to the pavilion, and, as
on the evening before, leant from the balcony. At the end of some
minutes he saw, lengthening out over the water, the reflection of
Ju-Kiouan, like a nosegay of submerged flowers. The young man
put his hand on his heart, and sent kisses from his finger-tips to
the reflection, with a gesture of grace and passion.

A joyful smile opened like a pomegranate bud in the transparence
of the lake and proved to Tchin-Sing that he was not unagreeable to
the unknown beauty. But as a man cannot hold long conversations
with a reflection whose body is unseen, he made a sign that he was
going to write, and withdrew to the interior of the pavilion. After
a little time he came out, holding a square of silvery-tinted paper,
on which he had improvised a declaration of love in verses of seven
syllables. Rolling up his piece of poetry, he enclosed it in the

chalice of a flower, and enveloping it in the large leaf of a water-lily, he placed it all delicately on the waters.

A light breeze, that came very conveniently, pushed his declaration towards one of the arches of the wall, so that Ju-Kiouan had only to stoop in order to gather it. For fear of being surprised, she retired into the innermost chamber, and read with infinite pleasure the expressions of love and the metaphors that Tchin-Sing had used. Besides the joy of knowing she was loved, she experienced the satisfaction of being wooed by a man of merit ; for the beauty of the writing, the choice of words, the exactitude of the rhymes, the brilliance of the images, showed his excellent education. What struck her above all was the name of Tchin-Sing. She had heard her mother speak too often of the dream of the pearl not to be taken with the coincidence. So she did not doubt an instant that Tchin-Sing was the spouse that heaven had destined for her.

The following day, as the wind had changed, Ju-Kiouan sent by the same means, towards the opposite pavilion, an answer in verse, in which, despite the modesty natural to a young girl, it was easy to see that she returned the love of Tchin-Sing. In reading the signature of the letter, the young man could not help an exclamation of surprise : " The Jasper ! Was not this the precious stone that my mother saw in a dream shining on my bosom ? Decidedly, I must present myself at this house, for it is there that the spouse lives, presaged by the nocturnal spirits ! "

As he was about to go out, he remembered the quarrels that divided the two houses, and the prohibitions written on the tablets. Not knowing what to do, he told all the story to Madame Kouan. Ju-Kiouan, for her part, had related everything to Madame Tou. The names of Pearl and Jasper seemed decisive to the two matrons, who returned to the temple to consult the bonze. The priest said that such in effect was the meaning of the dreams, and that the anger of heaven would fall on those who did not conform with it. Touched by the entreaties of the two mothers, and also by the small gifts they made to him, the bonze undertook to deal with Tou and Kouan, and so well did he entangle them that they could not retract when he revealed the true origin of the bride and bridegroom. Meeting again after so long a time, the two old friends could not understand how they had been able to separate on such trivial grounds, and felt how much they lost in being deprived of each other's company. The wedding took place ; and the Pearl and the Jasper could at last talk to one another otherwise than by means of a reflection. Did it make them happier ? That we dare not affirm ; for happiness is only but a shadow in the water.

THE NEST
OF NIGHTINGALES

THÉOPHILE GAUTIER

ROUND the castle there was a beautiful park. In the park were all kinds of birds: nightingales, thrushes, linnets. All the birds of the earth made a meeting-place of the park.

In spring-time you could not hear yourselves speak for the warbling and chirping; every leaf hid a nest, every tree was an orchestra. The little feathered musicians vied with each other in eager rivalry. Some chirped, others cooed; some trilled and executed brilliant shakes, others introduced flourishes, or embellished their songs with rests. Human musicians could not have done as well.

But in the castle were two beautiful cousins who sang better than all the birds in the park. One was named Fleurette, the other Isabeau. Both were beautiful and charming, and on Sundays, dressed in their pretty gowns, had not their white shoulders proved them to be mortals, you would have taken them for angels: only the wings were wanting. When they sang, their uncle, old Sir Maulevrier, often held their hands for fear they should take it into their heads to fly away.

I leave to your imagination the number of lances broken at the tilts and tourneys in Fleurette's and Isabeau's honour. Their reputation for beauty and talent spread over the whole of Europe, and yet they did not become vain. They lived in retirement, seeing no one except the page Valentine, a pretty fair-haired child, and Sir Maulevrier, a white-haired old man, worn and weather-beaten from his sixty years' service in the wars.

They spent their time in feeding the little birds, in saying their prayers, and chiefly in studying the works of the great composers and in practising together some motet, madrigal, villanelle, or other music. There were also the flowers which they watered and tended themselves. Thus they spent their days in sweet and poetical occupations perfectly suited to young girls. They kept themselves retired, and far from the gaze of the world, and yet the world did not let them alone. Neither a nightingale nor a rose can be hidden; they must always be betrayed by their song and their odour. Our two cousins were at once two nightingales and two roses.

Dukes and princes asked them in marriage; the Emperor of Trebizond and the Sultan of Egypt sent ambassadors to Sir Maulevrier with proposals for an alliance. But the two cousins were not weary of a single life, and refused to listen to a word about marriage. Perhaps some secret instinct told them that it was their mission in this world to remain unmarried, and to sing, and that in acting differently they would fail to accomplish it.

They had come to the castle when quite little. The window of their room looked on to the park, and they had been rocked to the tune of the birds' songs. They were scarcely able to stand when their uncle's minstrel, old Blondiau, placed their little hands on the ivory keys of the virginal; that was their baby's rattle. They could sing before they could speak; they sang as others breathed—by nature.

Such an education influenced their characters in a singular fashion. Their melodious childhood differed from the ordinarily turbulent and noisy period of infancy. They had never uttered a shrill cry or a discordant lament: they wept in time, and sobbed in harmony. The musical sense, developed in them at the expense of the others, made them well-nigh insensible to all that was not music. They floated on a sea of melody, and scarcely perceived the actual world except by sounds. They perfectly understood the rustling of the leaves, the murmur of the waters, the striking of the clock, the sighing of the wind in the chimney, the hum of the spinning-wheel, the falling of the raindrop on the vibrating window-pane, all exterior and inferior harmonies. But I must confess a sunset roused no great enthusiasm in them, and they were as little able to appreciate a painting as if their beautiful blue and black eyes had been covered with a thick film. They had the malady of music; they dreamed of it, and could neither eat nor drink: they cared for nothing else in the world. Yes, they cared for two things besides—Valentine and their flowers: Valentine because he resembled the roses, and the roses because they resembled Valentine. But that love was entirely relegated to the second place. It is true Valentine was only thirteen years old. Their greatest delight was to sit at the window of an evening, and sing the music they had composed during the day.

The most celebrated musicians came from far to hear them, and to compete with them. Scarcely had they listened to a few bars than they broke their instruments and tore up their scores, declaring themselves vanquished. It was in fact such wondrous and melodious music that the heavenly angels came to the casement with the other musicians, and learned it by heart to sing to the good God.

One May evening the cousins were singing a motet for two voices; never had so beautiful an air been so splendidly worked out and rendered. A nightingale from the park, snugly perched on a rose-tree, listened to them attentively. When they had finished, he approached the window, and said in his nightingale's language, "I want to enter into a singing competition with you."

The cousins signified their willingness, and that it was for him to begin.

The nightingale commenced. He was a master nightingale. His throat swelled, his wings fluttered, his body trembled. The runs, the intricate passages, the arpeggios, the chromatic scales, seemed never-ending. He ran up and down the scale, he held on the notes, he rounded his cadences with discouraging purity : you would have said that his voice had wings like his body. He stopped, sure of victory.

The two cousins sang in their turn ; they surpassed themselves. By the side of theirs, the nightingale's song seemed but the chirping of a sparrow.

The winged *virtuoso* made a last effort. He sang a romance of love, then executed a brilliant fanfare, ending with a number of shrill and vibrating high notes beyond the range of the human voice.

Undismayed by this master stroke, the two cousins turned the leaves of their music-books, and replied to the nightingale in such a fashion that St. Cecilia, who was listening to them from the distant spheres of heaven, became pale with envy, and let her bass viol fall to the ground.

The nightingale tried to sing again, but the contest had entirely exhausted him : his breath failed him, his feathers were all ruffled ; in spite of himself his eyes closed ; he was dying.

"You sing better than I do," he said to the cousins. "The vanity of wishing to excel you has cost me my life. I ask one boon of you. I have a nest ; in the nest are three little ones ; it is the third wild-rose bush in the broad walk beside the lake. Have them fetched, bring them up, and teach them to sing as you do, for I am about to die."

So saying, the nightingale died. The two cousins wept for him bitterly, for he had sung well. They summoned Valentine, the little fair-haired page, and told him where the nest was. Valentine, who was a clever little fellow, easily found the place ; he put the nest in his doublet, and brought it without accident. Fleurette and Isabeau, leaning against the balcony, impatiently awaited him. Valentine soon arrived, holding the nest in his hands. The three little ones put out their heads, opening their bills wide. The girls pitied the poor orphans, and fed each one in turn. When they were a little older, they began their musical education as they had promised the vanquished nightingale.

It was wonderful to see how tame they were, how well they sung. They flew about the room, perching now on Isabeau's head, now on Fleurette's shoulder. They placed themselves in front of the music-book, and you would have said that they were really able to make out the notes, they looked at the black and white keys with such an air of intelligence. They had learned all Fleurette's and Isabeau's tunes, and began to improvise very pretty ones themselves.

The two cousins lived more and more in solitude, and of an evening sounds of a supernatural melody were heard coming from their rooms. The nightingales, perfectly well educated, took part in the concert, and sang almost as well as their mistresses, who, themselves, had made great progress.

Every day their voices gained extraordinarily in brilliance, and vibrated in a metallic and crystalline fashion above the register of the natural voice. The girls grew visibly thinner; they lost their fine colour, and became pale as agates, and almost as transparent. Sir Maulevrier tried to prevent their singing, but his entreaties were of no avail.

When they had sung a few bars, a little red spot made its appearance on their cheeks, and kept growing bigger and bigger until they had finished. Then the spot disappeared, but a cold perspiration flowed from their skin, and their lips trembled as though they had fever.

However, their singing was more beautiful than ever. It had something that was not of this world; and to hear the sonorous and powerful voices coming from the two frail young girls, it was not difficult to foretell what would happen—the music would destroy the instrument.

They saw this themselves, and began to play on the virginal, an instrument they had neglected for their singing. But one night the window was open, the birds were warbling in the park, the breeze was sighing harmoniously. There was so much music in the air that they could not resist the temptation of singing a duet that they had composed the day before.

It was the song of the swan, a marvellous song steeped in tears, ascending to the most inaccessible heights of the scale, and descending again to the lowest note; a dazzling and marvellous song, a deluge of trills, a burning shower of chromatic passages, musical fireworks, not to be described. But the little red spot grew ever bigger, and almost covered their cheeks. The three nightingales looked at them, and listened with a strange anxiety; their wings fluttered, they flew now here, now there, and could not keep still. At length the girls came to the last bars of the piece, and their voices assumed such a strange sort of sonority that it was easily seen that the singers were no longer living creatures. The nightingales had flown away. The two cousins were dead; with the last note their souls had passed out from them. The nightingales ascended straight to heaven, in order to carry the supreme song to the good God, who kept them in Paradise to perform the music of the two cousins for His delight.

Later, the good God formed out of those three nightingales the souls of Palestrina, Cimarosa, and Gluck.

OCTAVE FEUILLET
1812–1890

CIRCÉ

SCENE—*The Countess's Boudoir.*

THE *Countess.* How do you do, Prince?

Prince. What, not out? Ah, I am fortunate, upon my word!

Countess. But you wrote me that you would come—

Prince. I wrote you that, really? Ah, that's odd. Ah, ah, that is amusing! Madame, your mother is well?

Countess. Very well—a little tired, that's all—she's just going up to her room. But sit down.

Prince (seating himself). Do you know what brings me here?

Countess. What?

Prince. I come to ask your advice. Imagine that I dined at the Embassy. They got talking about little drawing-room comedies, about *proverbes* or parables, about those little things, you know, that they play at private theatricals, and of the difficulty one experiences in finding any that are not too hackneyed, that one has not seen everywhere, and that are agreeable.

Countess. Yes—and then?

Prince. Very well, then. I was in rather a good humour; the spirit was upon me to compose during the week one of those witty trifles. A wager, serious enough, in fact, was connected with it. Briefly, since yesterday I have been thinking, without boring myself about other matters.

Countess. And you have hit upon something?

Prince. I have not yet thought of anything. But it will come. I conceived the idea of talking it over with you. We will do the thing together, if you are quite willing. It is very easy, you will see.

Countess. But I don't know, for my part, that it is so very easy.

Prince. Positively. Nothing more simple. Will you try?

Countess. Mon Dieu, I should like to—but you must hold the pen.

Prince. That's understood.

Countess. There, there's paper and ink—blue ink; is that all right?

Prince. Blue ink will do no harm. (*Places himself at a centre-table.*) There! Sit down in front of me, like a muse, and let us begin without further ceremony, will you?

Countess. Very willingly—but it's rather embarrassing, it seems to me.

Prince. Not at all. It's very easy. Always the same thing: Two people who chat about the rain and about fine weather—more or less wittily, as it happens to come. Well, are you ready?

Countess. Yes, yes—go on.

Prince. First we must write down the persons: "The Count, the Countess——," is it not?

Countess. Yes, of course—but is this to be a *proverbe*?

Prince. Yes, it's a *proverbe*.

Countess. But what *proverbe*? That must be decided first.

Prince. Oh! Mon Dieu, why? It's of no use—it will develop itself in time—it will evolve naturally from the conversation—it will be the finishing touch.

Countess. So be it. Go on.

Prince. "The Count, the Countess. First scene——" Well?

Countess. Hé!

Prince. What is it they say?

Countess. But what is the subject?

Prince. There is no subject! It is a witty trifle, I told you—a nothing—an improvisation without substance—a go-as-you-please conversation. I am not proposing that you should write a play like Molière's *Misanthrope*, remember.

Countess. Yet it is necessary to know what they are to talk about.

Prince. But about nothing—about trifles—you know how those things are!

Countess. But, no, my dear Prince, I know nothing about it—and no more do you, so it would seem.

Prince. Come, dear lady, don't let us quarrel. We said, "The Count and the Countess," is it not so? They are in the country—and the Count is bored, I suppose—

Countess. Yes, that's new enough.

Prince. I do not say that it must be new, but at any rate it is a subject, since you must have one. So then, the Count is bored—and the Countess—the Countess—

Countess. Is bored too, perhaps?

Prince. It's an idea, and with that combination, too, may become original enough. They are both bored— Well, you see, dear madame, we are progressing. Let us pass on to the dialogue— That, that's the easiest— Once in the dialogue it will go by itself— "The Count—" The Count—he enters, doesn't he?

Countess. Quite right.

Prince. And in entering, he says—

Countess. He says?

Prince. What?

Countess. I am asking you.

Prince. Well—he might say, for instance, " Always alone, dear Countess? "

Countess. I see nothing inappropriate in that.

Prince. It's sufficiently the phrase of a bored man—" Always alone, dear Countess? "

Countess. It's a charming phrase— To which the Countess, who is always alone, replies?

Prince. Wait—yes—perhaps—that is to say, no—that will not do.

Countess. Instead of entering the diplomatic service you ought to devote yourself to literature—with your facility.

Prince (rising). It is certain that I am too beastly stupid— dumb as an animal— And then I am thinking of something else— Oh, well, I am going!

Countess. No!

Prince. I assure you that at other times I had a sort of wit— Inquire at the Embassy—they know—But I am altogether changed —Good-night, I am going.

Countess. No!

Prince. I am not going?

Countess. No, I tell you!

Prince. So be it. (*He sits down again.*)

Countess. Let us return. Where were we?— " The Count, the Countess—"

Prince. The truth is, you ought to consider me a regular imbecile.

Countess. Is it the Count says that?

Prince. No, it is I.

Countess. Not at all—I find you only a little odd.

Prince. Odd! You are very kind— But no, really; I beg of you to inquire at the Embassy—they will tell you that I do not lack intelligence, and that at other times I had even a sort of inspiration.

Countess. But, my Prince, I have no need to inquire at the Embassy, I have only to remember. I have known you to be extremely brilliant, several months ago when you were making love to me.

Prince. Brilliant, no; but I was as good as another at any rate.

Countess. Yes, yes, I insist— You were a brilliant young man, sparkling, dreadful!— (*She rubs her hands softly.*)

Prince. You are making fun of me— I was not sparkling, but I had some vivacity—and that was but two years ago! It is true that I had only just arrived at Paris—and that I had not yet passed under the influence of the climate.

Countess. You believe it was the climate—

Prince. What will you have? It must assuredly have been something— It isn't age— I am not thirty years old— At any rate, I think I shall leave Paris, and diplomacy as well— My mother sends for me from Vienna— I received a letter from her this morning— I wanted, also, to show it to you—

(*He fumbles about in his coat pocket and pulls out a letter half-tangled in some black lace.*)

Countess. What lace is that coming out of your pocket?

Prince (*confused*). Lace? Oh! Do you see some lace?

Countess. This— But I say, my Prince, is not this one of my veils, here?

Prince. One of your veils—here?— Are you sure?

Countess. Absolutely!— And I am going to take it back, too, if you will allow me— That's lace of great price, if you have your doubts about it.

Prince. I implore you to believe, indeed, madame, that I did not attach a mercenary value to it. But how do I come to have that veil about me?

Countess. It is very easy to explain. I must have left it at the Embassy on a visit, they charged you to return it to me, and with your usual absent-mindedness, you forgot the commission.

Prince. That's simple. I ask ten thousand pardons. It is perfectly evident! You see I am not myself at all any more. All my faculties—even my memory—are weakening. It is high time I go to recover strength in my native air. You see what my mother tells me?

Countess (*running through the letter*). She has the air of a noble woman, your mother.

Prince. Yes. We two are very fond of each other. She advises me not to have too much success, poor mother! She believes me always irresistible.

Countess. Then you have been so, my Prince?

Prince. Why, yes, a little, up to the day I had the honour of meeting you— Well, what do you advise me?

Countess. To go, since your mother wishes to see you again.

Prince. That's my advice, too, and to tell you the truth, I came this evening specially to bid you good-bye.

Countess. What! to bid me good-bye?— And that *proverbe*? What was the object of that joke?

Prince. That *proverbe*? Come, madame, I want the last impression you receive of me to be pleasant. You will laugh. Here is the history of that *proverbe*. You remember well enough that which passed between us two years ago, after I had vainly offered you my heart and my hand. It so happened that if I wished to continue to regard you as a friend, I must sternly refrain from all allusions to a love definitely repulsed. I gave you my word on the matter, and I expected to have kept it scrupulously.

40*

Countess. That is true.

Prince. Well, then, I made a mistake there. Excuse me, I swear to you that I am going. My discretion and my reserve naturally made you believe that I was cured of my love.

Countess. Naturally.

Prince. Yes. Well, it is a mistake. I love you always. I love you like a fool, like a child, like an angel, like a savage, as you will. Having decided to go away, I wished first to make one supreme effort, a desperate one. The idea of that *proverbe* came to me. Under cover of that *proverbe* I promised myself to set my feelings before you, with so much fire, emotion, eloquence, wit, that you would be infallibly softened, fascinated and overcome. You have seen how successful I was !— Isn't it comic ?— Now, madame, adieu.

Countess. Adieu, Prince.

Prince. One word more. Be gracious enough to tell me why you refused to marry me. My proposal was, in fact, perfectly honest and perfectly worthy of acceptance. Why did you repulse it with so much decision ? Was it from caprice, from antipathy, or did you have some serious reason ?

Countess. I had a serious reason.

Prince. You loved some one ?

Countess. No one.

Prince. Then your heart was free, like your hand. You had not been—you told me so yourself—particularly happy with your husband—although he was charming, from what they say.

Countess. He was charming, altogether charming, sparkling and irresistible—like you—in days gone by.

Prince. In short, you were not happy ; consequently, you had no occasion to torment yourself if you became unfaithful to the memory of the dead. As for me, I had a brilliant name, a fortune, a position. At that time I was not ill and depressed as I am now. I was tolerable in my person.

Countess. Very handsome, indeed.

Prince. I passed for a sufficiently lively talker. I made court to you, if I remember, with—intelligence.

Countess. With much, much wit.

Prince. And you refused me !— Come, now, why ?

Countess. You do not guess ?

Prince. Not at all.

Countess (*she takes his hand and looks him tenderly in the eyes*). It is because I love dumb animals, my friend.

SAVING THE FLAG

OCTAVE FEUILLET

LAST night, after dinner, we scattered in the garden of the château to breathe the cool night air, mingled with the scent of roses and cigars. All the guests chatted in low voices, as though subdued by the beauty of the evening. It was warm and superb. A dazzling moon filled the vast garden with her limpid brightness ; there was a glaze of silver on the water of the lake, in the middle of which two large swans slept motionless in their snowy whiteness. Talking a little about nothing in particular, we came and went, Commandant d'Eblis and I, between the end of the lake and the nearest trees of the avenue that formed, in the midst of all the light, a nave as sombre as a cathedral at midnight. After a silence, I said to Monsieur d'Eblis :

" This sweet and peaceful scene must contrast strangely with your memories of the war, Commandant ! "

" Have you the gift of second sight ? " he said, stopping in his walk.

" I have hardly the gift of first sight," I said laughingly, " for I am short-sighted. But why this question, Monsieur ? "

" Because at this very moment my mind went back to a scene in my military career—an evening just like this, but less beautiful, though quite as peaceful."

" Would you mind telling me ? . . ."

He hesitated, breathed deeply, and then with a slight bow :

" Oh, heavens ! Yes. I was then below Metz. On the evening of which I speak, the 27th of October, I had been charged with carrying some orders, the meaning of which appeared only too clear to me. I had, in particular, to stop in its march one of our regiments, whose number I have forgotten. In fact, I had over- taken it and stopped it. I was going to set off again. I was waiting only till my blown horse had recovered a little. We were then in a plain close to a village called Colombey, I think. The dreadful storms that marked those sinister days had quietened down for a few hours. A tranquil moon was reflected in the pools of water that covered the country. Our imagination brings some strange things together. There is certainly little connection between the smiling scene that surrounds us here and those desolate swamps ;

yet this moonlight on the water just now reminded me of them, . . .
and the lovely swans, sleeping over there made me think of my
escort of dragoons, motionless, like them, in their white cloaks.

"The regiment, while waiting for the new instructions, kept its
formation, rifle in hand. A big bivouac fire had been lighted, and
round it some officers were talking in low voices with mournful
looks. Rumours of surrender had spread through the camps since
the evening before. The colonel, an oldish man, with dark grey
moustache, strode up and down by himself some distance away,
clenching in his hand the order I had brought him. Suddenly he
came up to me and gripped me by the arm.

"'Captain,' he said to me in the tone of a man who is going to
provoke a deadly quarrel with another, 'a word or two with you,
please ! . . . You come from headquarters ; you must know more
than I do. . . . It is the end, isn't it ? '

"'They say so, Colonel, and I believe it.'

"'You believe it ! How can you believe such a thing ? '

"He let go my arm with some violence, walked away, and,
coming back abruptly, looked me in the eyes.

"'Prisoners, then ? '

"'Colonel, I am afraid so.'

"There was another silence ; he stayed some time in front of
me in an attitude of deep thought ; then lifting his head he said
with an extraordinary feeling in his voice :

"'And the flags ? '

"'I don't know, Colonel.'

"'Ah ! You don't know ? '

"Again he left me, and walked by himself for five or six minutes.
Striding then up to his regiment, he said in a tone of command :

"'The flag ! '

"The non-commissioned officer who carried the flag came out
from the ranks. The colonel seized the staff with one hand, and
raising the other to the group of drummers :

"'Open a ban ! ' he said.

"The drums sounded.

"The colonel came up to the fire, carrying the flag on high ; he
dropped the staff on the ground, looked at the circle of officers
and uncovered his head. They all imitated him at once ; the
men, attentive, remained as silent as the dead.

"He then had a moment of hesitation. I saw his lips tremble.
His eyes stared with an expression of anguish at the glorious scrap
of torn silk—sad symbol of the Motherland. At last he came to
a decision : bending the knee, he slowly put the eagle into the fire.
A brighter flame suddenly flared up and lighted more clearly the
pale faces of the officers. Some of them were weeping.

"'Close the ban ! ' said the colonel ; and for the second time there sounded the mournful roll of drumskins soaked by the rain.

"He put on his cap and came towards me.

"'Captain,' he said to me in a hard voice, 'when you go back there—have no scruple—none—tell them what you have seen! Good-bye.'

"'Colonel,' I said to him, 'will you allow me to embrace you?'

"He drew me violently to his breast, and stifling me with his clasp, 'Ah! My poor boy!' he murmured. 'My poor boy!'"

Monsieur d'Eblis turned his head from me when he reached the end of his tale, and I heard a sob. I took his hand.

"Ah," he said, "you understand what a man suffers in a moment like that!"

CONSTANT GUÉROULT
B. 1814

AFTER THE CRIME

It was at the extremity of a village : a window was hurriedly thrown open, and a man appeared at it, his features livid, his eyes haggard, his lips agitated by a convulsive tremor ; his right hand grasped a knife from which blood was dripping, drop by drop. He cast a look into the silent country, then sprang to the ground and set off running away through the fields.

At the end of a quarter of an hour he stopped exhausted, breathless, at the edge of a wood, twenty paces from the highway. He searched for the most closely grown and most impenetrable spot to be found and pressed his way into it, regardless of the thorns that were tearing him ; then he began to dig up the earth with his knife. When he made a hole a foot deep, he placed the weapon in it, and covered it with the soil he had dug out, re-covered it with a grass sod, which he trampled down solidly, after which he sat down upon the wet grass.

He listened, and appeared terrified by the silence which hung upon the country.

It was the hour when the darkness of night is replaced by that grey and uniform tint which is neither day nor night, and through which objects look like phantoms.

It seemed to him that he was alone in this funeral immensity, in the midst of this dumb and dim nature. Suddenly a sound made him start ; it was the axle of a waggon creaking on the road, a league away perhaps ; but in the silence this strange and discordant noise made itself heard with singular distinctness.

Then nature awoke little by little. The lark took flight towards the blue sky, pouring out his notes, at once timid and charming, overflowing with life and happiness ; a winged tribe began to sing and flutter amid the leaves glittering with dew ; on all sides—in the moss on which the golden insect was crawling, to the branch of the highest oak, where the bird voluptuously plumed herself in the ether—arose a morning concert, so harmonious in its confusion, so potent in its delirium, so full of greeting to the first rays coming from the east, that it might well be called a hymn to the sun.

Nature expanded herself, radiant and virginal; all was grace, freshness, sparkle in the forest, where a blue mist still floated; all was calm and hushed in the plain, the great lines of which undulated to infinity, the grey tones of which grew light under the reflection of the blue sky.

The murderer rose; his limbs trembled, and his teeth clattered one against the other.

He cast furtive glances around him, then parted the branches with precaution, stopping, starting, drawing back his head hastily at the least sound; then, at length, he quitted the densely grown thicket in which he had buried his knife.

He pressed forward deeper into the forest, choosing always the most shaded portions and avoiding the open parts and the beaten paths, making frequent stoppages to listen or to examine the ground before him ere he advanced. In this way he walked all day without being conscious of fatigue—so great was the agony which dominated him.

He paused at the entrance to a grove of beeches, whose imposing trunks stood white and smooth, like thousands of columns crowned with foliage. A calm day, a harmonious silence, added to the impression of grandeur and retirement made by this beautiful spot; something animate seemed to throb amid the luminous shade of the motionless boughs, as if a soul were there amid the shadows, murmuring mysterious syllables.

The fugitive felt ill at ease, and, creeping like a reptile, forced his way under a clump of thorn bushes, the density of which completely hid him.

When he was in safety, he first raised his hand to his head and then to his stomach, and muttered, " I am hungry ! "

The sound of his voice made him shudder; it was the first time he had heard it since the murder, and it resounded in his ears like a knell and a menace. For some moments he remained motionless and held his breath, as if in fear of having been heard.

When he had become a little calmer, he felt in his pockets one after the other; they contained a few *sous*.

" That will be enough," he said in a low tone; " in six hours I shall have crossed the frontier; then I can show myself; I can work, and shall be saved."

At the end of an hour he felt the cold begin to stiffen his limbs, for with the coming of night the dew fell, and his only clothes were a linen blouse and trousers of the same material. He rose, and cautiously quitting his thorn bushes, continued his march. He halted at the first signs of dawn. He had reached the limits of the forest, and must now enter upon the open country, must show himself in the full light of day; and, struck with terror by this thought, he dared not advance a step farther.

While he was standing hidden in a thicket the sound of horses' hoofs was heard. He turned pale.

" Gendarmes ! " he gasped, crouching down upon the ground.

It was a farm-labourer going to the fields, with two horses harnessed to a waggon ; he was whistling a country air while re-tying the lash of his whip.

" Jacques ! " a voice cried to him.

The peasant turned round.

" Hallo ! is that you, Françoise ? Where are you going so early ? "

" Oh ! I'm going to wash this bundle of linen at the spring close by."

" I'm going within two steps of it ; put your bundle on one of my beasts."

" Thanks !—that's not to be refused. How's the wife and the little ones—all of them ? "

" I'm the weakest of the family," replied Jacques, laughing loudly ; " all goes well—work, joy, and health."

He tied his lash, and the sharp crack was repeated by echo after echo.

The murderer followed him with his eyes as far as he could see him ; then a deep sigh escaped from his lips, and his gaze turned to the open country spreading before him.

" I must get on," he murmured, " it is twenty-four hours since I——. All is discovered, I am being sought, an hour's delay may ruin me."

He made up his mind resolutely, and quitted the forest.

At the end of ten minutes he came within sight of a church tower. Then he slackened his pace, a prey to a thousand conflicting feelings, drawn towards the village by hunger, restrained by the fear which counselled him to avoid habitations.

However, after a long struggle, during which he had advanced as much as possible under the screen of outhouses and bushes, he was about to enter the village, when he saw something glitter about a hundred paces from him.

It was the brass badge and the pommel of a rural policeman's sabre.

" He may have my description," he murmured with a shudder.

And, shrinking back quickly, he ran to a little wood which extended on his left and hid himself in it, pushing farther and farther into its depths, forgetting his hunger, and thinking only of flying from the village and the rural policeman.

But he speedily reached the end of the wood, which was of very small extent : beyond, the plain began again.

On peering from between the branches he saw a man seated on the grass eating his breakfast. It was Jacques, the farm-labourer.

Nothing could be more pleasant than the corner he had chosen for his breakfast-room. It was a sort of little stony ravine, through which ran two deep wheel-ruts, but carpeted with grass and moss and bordered with creepers, green-leaved, yellow, or purple, according to the caprices of that powerful colourist called Autumn. The wheel-ruts were full of limpid water, at the bottom of which glittered little white stones, smooth and transparent as onyx. Finally, this pretty nest was shaded by a cluster of birch-trees with reddish silvery trunks and foliage light and trembling.

Above this oasis spread ploughed fields on which hung, white and closely woven, the " Virgin-threads," floating and sparkling like an immense silver net.

Jacques' breakfast consisted of a hunch of bread and a piece of cheese, washed down with big draughts of cider claret, which he drank out of a stone pitcher, cooled in the water of the wheel-ruts.

The peasant's strong white teeth buried themselves in the bread with an appetite which might have made a capitalist desire to share his frugal meal which he only interrupted now and then to give a friendly word to his two horses, which, a few paces off, were feeding in brotherly fashion from the same wisp of hay.

" He's happy—he is ! " murmured the murderer. Then, from the depths of his conscience he added : " Yes ! work !—love of family !— peace and happiness are there ! "

He was tempted to accost Jacques and ask him for a piece of bread ; but a glance at his tattered dress forbade him showing himself ; and then it seemed to him that his features bore the stamp of his crime, and must denounce him to whoever looked upon him.

A sound made him turn his head and through the branches he saw an old man covered with rags. He walked bent double, a stick in his hand and a canvas bag slung to his neck by a cord. It was a beggar.

The murderer watched him with envious eyes, and again he murmured :

" What would I not give to be in his place ! He begs, but he is free ; he goes where he pleases in the wide air, in the broad sunlight with a calm heart, with a tranquil conscience, eating without fear and agony the bread given to him in charity ; able to look behind him without seeing a dead body, beside him without dreading to find a gendarme at his elbow, before him without seeing a vision of the scaffold. Yes, he is happy, that old mendicant, and I may well envy him his lot."

Suddenly he turned pale, a nervous trembling agitated all his limbs, and his features were drawn up like those of an epileptic.

" There they are ! " he stammered, his eyes fixed upon a point on the road.

With haggard eye, bewildered, mad with terror, he looked on all sides, seeking to find a place of concealment ; but so strangely was he overcome by fear that his eyes saw nothing, and his mind was incapable of thought.

During this time the gendarmes approached rapidly.

The gallop of the horses and the clanking of arms suddenly brought back to him his presence of mind, and, seeing before him an elm, the foliage of which was dense enough to hide him from sight, he climbed up it with the agility of a squirrel.

He was in safety when the two gendarmes halted on the road a few paces from him.

He listened, motionless, terrified, a prey to emotion so violent that he could hear the beating of the heart within him.

" What if we search this wood ! " said one of the gendarmes.

" It's too small," said the other ; " it's not there that our man would take refuge—rather in a forest."

" Anyhow, it will be prudent to beat it up."

" No," replied his comrade, " it would be time lost, and the assassin has already a ten hours' start of us."

And they went on at a trot.

The murderer breathed again ; he felt a renewed life. But, this agony passed, a suffering, for a moment forgotten, made itself felt anew, and he cried :

" My God, how hungry I am ! "

He had not eaten for forty-eight hours.

His legs gave way under him ; he was seized with giddiness and a humming in the ears. And yet, he no more thought of going to the village for bread. The gendarmes ! the scaffold ! Those two phantoms ceaselessly rose before him, and overmastered even the pangs of famine.

While his restless ears were on the watch for all sounds in the country, the dreary tolling of a bell made him start : it was the bell of the village church sounding the funeral knell. The murderer listened, pale, downcast, suddering at every stroke, as if the clapper of the bell had struck upon his heart. Then big tears fell slowly from his eyes, and streamed down his cheeks unobserved by him, without his making any attempt to stop their flow.

It was because these funeral sounds evoked in his imagination a picture at once terrible and heart-rending. At that same hour the bell of another village church was tolling like this for another death.

" Oh, wretch, wretch that I am ! " sighed the murderer, covering his face with both his hands.

He listened again to the strokes of the church bell, which sounded to him like ths sobs of the poor victim, and he murmured :

" Oh, idleness ! it led me to the tavern—and the tavern, this is what has come of it !—three orphans, a poor wife in the ground, and I !—a monster, hateful to all, hunted like a wild beast, pursued without rest or truce, until the hour when they shall have driven me to the scaffold. Horrible, horrible destiny!—and yet too mild a punishment.

He remained in the tree until night had come. When he saw the stars shine in the sky, when, in the vast solitude around him, he heard nothing but that vague breathing which seems like the respiration of the sleeping earth, then only he ventured to descend to rest himself.

He stretched himself at the foot of the tree, and closed his eyes; but fear which would not quit him, hunger which gnawed at his vitals, kept him constantly awake, and he rose at the first sign of dawn, overwhelmed, bowed down at once by alarm, fatigue, and the fasting of nearly three days.

At the end of a few hours his hunger, sharpened by the exciting air of the wood, ended by overcoming all his terror; and, feeling that his reason was beginning to reel in his brain, he decided to go into the village in search of bread.

He shook off the blades of grass which hung to his clothes, re-tied his neckerchief, passed his fingers through his tangled hair, then resolutely went out into the plain. Five minutes afterwards he entered the village, walking slowly, his head bent down, like a man overcome by fatigue, but casting a furtive and suspicious glance right and left, and ready to take flight at the first appearance of danger.

Not far from the church—that is to say, in the centre of the place —he perceived a tavern, the patriarchal aspect of which seemed to him to be reassuring. After convincing himself that neither cries nor disputes were coming from it—evidence that it was almost empty—he made up his mind to enter.

"What can I give you, my good man?" asked the landlord, a solidly built peasant, with broad shoulders, and a frank and open countenance.

"Bread and wine," replied the murderer, going and seating himself at a table near a window opening on to a garden.

He was speedily served.

"Here you are!" said the landlord, "bread, wine, and cheese."

"I only asked for bread and wine," said the murderer abruptly, hiding his face in his hands.

"Oh! the cheese is of no consequence to me, nor the bread either, for—no offence to you—you don't look too well off, my poor man, and it seems to me that you need to get up your strength; so eat and drink without worrying yourself about the rest."

"Thanks, thanks!"

At that moment the church bells began to ring loudly.

"What is that?" asked the murderer. "Why are the bells ringing in that way?"

"Why! Because the mass is over."

"The mass! What is to-day, then?"

"Sunday. You are not a Christian then? Oh! you'll have companions presently."

The murderer felt himself becoming faint. He was tempted to rush out of the house; but a moment's reflection convinced him that such a course would ensure his certain destruction and that prudence itself called on him to remain where he was.

He had hardly come to this decision when drinkers flocked into the tavern, which presently became full. The murderer began to eat and drink, taking care to keep his face turned towards the window, so as to hide his features as much as possible.

A quarter of an hour passed, an age of torment and anxiety for the fugitive, whom the most insignificant word caused to turn pale and to shudder. At length he was going to rise and leave the tavern, when one of the drinkers cried:

"Hallo! here comes Daddy Faucheux, our brigadier of gendarmerie!"

The murderer started frightfully, and his right hand flew to his head; all his blood had rushed to his heart, and from his heart to his brain, as if he had been stricken with apoplexy.

He came to himself little by little, but without recovering his powers; from the shock he had sustained there remained a weakness and nervous tremor which rendered him wholly incapable of effort.

On seeing the brigadier enter, he leaned his head upon the table, and pretended to fall asleep.

The welcome given to the gendarme attested the esteem in which he was held in the country; every one was eager to offer him a place at his table.

"Thanks, friends," replied Daddy Faucheux, "a glass is not to be refused; but, as to sitting down, and taking it easy with you— the service forbids."

"The service! that's a good one. To-day is Sunday, and thieves require a day of rest as well as other folks."

"Thieves, possibly; but it's different with assassins."

"Assassins! What do you mean by that, Daddy Faucheux?"

"Haven't you heard about the affair at Saint Didier?"

"No; tell us about it."

"The more willingly, because I came in here to give you all a description of the scoundrel we are hunting."

The heart of the murderer throbbed heavily enough to burst his chest.

"He's a stonemason, named Pierre Picard," the brigadier continued.

"And who has he murdered?"

"His wife."

"The beggar! What had she done to him?"

" Cried without complaining when he beat her ; only sometimes she went to the tavern to ask him to give her some money and buy food for her little ones, whom she could not bear to see dying of starvation. That was the whole of her crime, poor creature ! It was for that he killed her on Thursday night last. She was only five-and-twenty. He ought to have kissed the ground she walked on, the wretch ! She spent her life in working and caring for him and the children, and she had never received any other reward save blows and misery."

" The infernal villain ! " cried a young man, striking his fist violently on the table before him ; " I'd think it a pleasure to go and see his head chopped off."

" That's why you all ought to know his description, so as to be able to arrest him if you came upon him ; for we know that he is skulking somewhere hereabouts."

There was a deep silence.

The murderer, he too listened, mastering by a superhuman effort the fever raging in his blood and bewildering his brain.

" This is the description of Pierre Picard," said the brigadier, unfolding a paper : " Middle height, short neck, broad shoulders, high cheek bones, large nose, black eyes, sandy beard, thin lips, a brown mole on the forehead."

Folding up the paper, he added :

" Now you'll be sure to recognise him if you meet him ! "

" With such a description, it would be impossible to mistake him."

" Then, as the song says, ' good-night, my friends ' ; I leave you to go and hunt my game."

The murderer ceased to breathe. While listening to the brigadier's departure, he calculated that a few hours only separated him from the frontier, and already he saw himself in safety.

He was about raising his head, when the heavy boots of the gendarme, taking a new direction, resounded suddenly in his ears.

The gendarme stopped, two paces from the table at which he was seated ; and the murderer *felt* his look turned upon him.

His blood seemed to freeze in his veins. A cold perspiration burst from all his pores, and his heart appeared to him to cease beating.

" By the way," cried the brigadier, " here's a party who is sleeping pretty soundly."

And he struck him on the shoulder.

" Hallo, my friend, hold your head up a little ; I want to see your phiz."

Pierre Picard raised his head sharply ; the expression of his face was frightful. His livid features were horribly contracted, his blood-shot eyes darted flames, and a nervous trembling agitated his thin and close-pressed lips.

" It's he ! " cried ten voices at once.

The brigadier put out his hand to seize him by the collar, but before he could touch him, the murderer struck him two heavy blows with his fist in the eyes and blinded him ; then, springing through the window into the garden, he disappeared.

Recovered from the surprise which had at first paralysed them, twenty young men dashed off in pursuit of him. At a bound he cleared the garden hedge, gained the fields, and in less than ten minutes was half a league away from the village.

After making sure that the unevenness of the ground prevented him from being seen, he paused for a moment to take breath, for he was quite exhausted and would have sunk down senseless if this furious flight had continued twenty seconds longer.

But he had hardly seated himself, before confused cries struck upon his ears. He rose and listened.

It was his pursuers.

What was he to do ? Exhausted, breathless, he could run no farther—and they were there, on his heels. He cast a desperate glance around him. Everywhere he saw the level plain—without a rock, without a hollow, without a clump of trees, in which he could hide himself. Suddenly his eyes fell upon a shining pool of standing water, on the margin of which there was a growth of tall reeds, and he gasped :

" Let's try it."

He dragged himself to the pool, in which he hid himself up to the neck, drawing over his head the reeds and water-plants, then remained as motionless as if he had taken root in the mud.

The water had become still and smooth as a mirror when the twenty peasants arrived at the edge of the pool, preceded by the brigadier, who, thanks, to the care of the landlord of the tavern, had speedily recovered from the stunning effects of the blows he had received.

" Now," cried Daddy Faucheux, from the back of his horse, and examining the country in all directions, " where in the name of wonder can that scoundrel have got to ! "

" It's odd," said a young peasant ; " five minutes ago I saw him plainly—and, now, not a glimpse of him ! and yet the ground's flat and green for three leagues round, without so much as a mole's hole in which he could hide his nose."

" He can't be far off," said the brigadier. " Let us divide and spread over the plain, searching every bit of it, and coming back here last."

Pierre Picard heard the party disperse, uttering threats against him.

Still standing motionless in the pool, he trembled in every limb, and dared not change his position for fear of betraying his presence by agitating the water about him, or by deranging the reeds and water-plants with which he had covered his head.

He passed an hour in this position, studying the sound of the steps crossing each other on the plain, of which his ears, eagerly strained, caught the least perceptible echoes.

At the end of that time the whole of the party were again collected about the pool.

" Thunder and lightning ! " cried the brigadier, furiously ; " the brigand has escaped us, but how the plague could he have done it ? "

" He must be a sorcerer ! " said a peasant.

" Sorcerer or not, I'll not give him up," replied Daddy Faucheux. " I'll just give Sapajou time to swallow a mouthful of water at this pool, and we'll both slip off to the edge of the frontier, towards which the beggar is sure to make his way."

And turning his horse towards the pool, he reined him up just at the spot where the fugitive was hidden amid the tuft of reeds. The animal stretched forward his neck, sniffed the air strongly, then quickly drew back his head and refused to advance. Pierre Picard felt the beast's warm breath upon his cheek.

The brigadier gently flipped Sapajou's ears to force him to enter the pool, but the animal backed a couple of paces, and his master was unable, either by blows or pattings, to induce him to obey.

" Oh ! we are in our tantrums ! " cried the brigadier, furious at a resistance to which he was wholly unused ; " we'll see which of us is going to give in to the other."

And he was preparing to flog poor Sapajou severely, when, as if understanding the impending danger, the animal wheeled suddenly to the left and entered the pool some paces farther off.

" That's all the better for you," said the brigadier. Then, while his horse was drinking, he said to the peasants :

" Now, my good fellows, you can go back to the village ; I and Sapajou will see to the rest."

The peasants moved off, wishing him good luck. Then the horse, having sufficiently satisfied his thirst, left the water and set off across the fields, stimulated by the voice of his master.

The murderer was left alone.

But, though he was benumbed with cold, he allowed more than a quarter of an hour to pass before venturing to quit his retreat. At length he came from the pool, dripping with water, his head and shoulders covered with water-grass and plants which clung to his skin and clothes, his body shivering, his face cadaverous. He cast a long glance over the deserted plain, and tried to speak, but his teeth clattered together so violently that it was some moments before he could articulate a word.

" Saved ! " he gasped at length.

Then he continued, with profound dejection :

" Yes, saved—for the hour ! But the brigadier waits for me on the frontier ; the gendarmerie are warned, the whole population are on foot ; the hunt is going to begin again against the common enemy—against the mad dog. The struggle—for ever the struggle —without cessation, without pity ! All men against me, and God as well ! It is too much—it is beyond my strength ! "

While speaking he mechanically freed himself from the slimy weeds with which he was covered.

He gazed upon the solitude by which he was surrounded, and it appeared to terrify him : he seemed to feel in his heart the same cold, sullen, desolate solitude.

Then he took his head between his hands, and for five minutes remained plunged in his reflections.

" So be it," he said at length, in a resolute tone.

And he set off in the direction of the village from which he had fled.

An hour afterwards he entered the tavern where the brigadier had been so near capturing him.

All the peasants who had pursued him were there.

" The assassin ! " they cried in bewilderment.

" Yes," replied the murderer, calmly, " it is Pierre Picard, the assassin, who has come to give himself up. Go and find the gendarmes."

He seated himself in the middle of the tavern, calm and unmoved.

Two gendarmes speedily arrived. Pierre Picard recognised them as those who, the evening before, had passed close by the elm in which he had taken refuge. He held out his hands to them silently. They placed handcuffs upon his wrists, and led him to a room at the *Mairie*, which was to serve provisionally as his dungeon, before he was transferred to the neighbouring city.

When he found himself alone, shut up securely in this prison, the door of which was guarded by two gendarmes, the murderer sank upon his camp bed, and cried with a sort of fierce enjoyment :

" At last I can rest ! "

THE MIRROR

LETTER I

YOU wish me to write to you, my dear Anaïs—me, a poor blind creature whose hand moves falteringly in the darkness? Are you not afraid of the sadness of my letters, written as they are in gloom? Have you no fear of the sombre thoughts which must beset the blind?

Dear Anaïs, *you* are happy: you can see. To see! Oh, to see! to be able to distinguish the blue sky, the sun, and all the different colours—what a joy! True, I once enjoyed this privilege, but when I was struck with blindness, I was scarcely ten years old. Now I am twenty-five. It is fifteen long years since everything around me became as black as night! In vain, dear friend, do I endeavour to recall the wonders of nature. I have forgotten all her hues. I smell the scent of the roses, I guess its shape by the touch; but its boasted colour, to which all beautiful women are compared, I have forgotten—or, rather, I cannot describe. Sometimes under this thick veil of darkness strange gleams flit. The doctors say that this is the movement of the blood, and that this may give some promise of a cure. Vain delusion! When one has lost for fifteen years the lights which beautify the earth, they are never to be found again except in heaven.

The other day I had a rare sensation. In groping in my room I put my hand upon—oh! you would never guess!—upon a mirror! I sat down in front of it, and arranged my hair like a coquette. Oh! what would I have given to be able to regard myself!—to know if I was nice!—if my skin is as white as it is soft, and if I have pretty eyes under my long lashes!— Ah! they often told us at school that the devil comes in the glasses of little girls who look at themselves too long! All I can say is, if he came in mine he must have been nicely caught—my lord Satan. I couldn't have seen him!

You ask me in your kind letter, which they have just read to me, whether it is true that the failure of a banker has ruined my parents. I have heard nothing about it. No, they are rich. I am supplied with every luxury. Everywhere that my hand rests it touches

silk and velvet, flowers and precious stuffs.   Our table is abundant
and every day my taste is coaxed with dainties.   Therefore, you
see, Anaïs, that my beloved folks are happily well off.

Write to me, my darling, since you are now back from that
aristocratic England, and you have some pity for the poor blind girl.

LETTER II

You have no idea, Anaïs, what I am going to tell you ! Oh ! you
will laugh as if you had gone crazy.   You will believe that with
my sight I must have lost my reason.   I have a lover !

Yes, dear ; I, the girl without eyes, have a wooer as melting and
as importunate as the lover of a duchess.   After this, what is to be
said ?   Love, who is as blind as blind can be, undoubtedly owed me
this as one of his own kind.

How *he* got in amongst us I don't know ;   still less, what he is
going to do here.   All I can tell you is that he sat on my left at
dinner the other day, and that he looked after me with extreme
care and attention.

" This is the first time," I said, " that I have had the honour of
meeting you."

" True," he answered, " but I know your parents."

" You are welcome," I replied, "since you know how to esteem
them—my good angels ! "

" They are not the only people," he continued softly, " for whom
I feel affection."

" Oh," I answered thoughtlessly, " then whom else here do you
like ? "

" You," said he.

" Me ?   What do you mean ? "

" That I love you."

" Me ?   You love *me* ? "

" Truly !   Madly ! "

At these words I blushed, and pulled my scarf over my shoulders.
He sat quite silent.

" You are certainly abrupt in your announcement."

" Oh !   it might be seen in my regards, my gestures, all my
actions."

" That may be, but I am blind.   A blind girl is not wooed as
others are."

" What do I care about the want of sight ? " said he, with a
delightful accent of sincerity ; "what matters it to me if your eyes
are closed to the light ?   Is not your figure charming, your foot
as tiny as a fairy's, your step superb, your tresses long and silky,
your skin of alabaster, your complexion carmine, and your hand
the colour of the lily ? "

He had finished his description before his words ceased sounding in my ears. So then, I had, according to him, a beautiful figure, a fairy foot, a snowy skin, a complexion like a rose, and fair and silky hair. Oh, Anaïs, dear Anaïs, to other girls such a lover, who describes all your perfections, is nothing but a suitor; but to a blind girl he is more than a lover, he is a mirror.

I began again: " Am I really as pretty as all that ? "

" I am still far from the reality."

" And what would you have me do ? "

" I want you to be my wife."

I laughed aloud at this idea.

" Do you mean it ? " I cried. " A marriage between the blind and the seeing, between the day and the night ? Why, I should have to put my orange-blossoms on by groping! No! no! my parents are rich : a single life has no terrors for me ; single I will remain, and take the service of Diana, as they say—and so much the worse for her if she is waited on amiss ! "

He went away without saying a word more. It is all the same : he has taught me that I am nice ! I don't know how it is that I catch myself loving him a little, Mr. Mirror mine !

LETTER III

Oh, dear Anaïs, what news I have to tell you ! What sad and unexpected things befall us in this life ! As I tell you what has happened to me, the tears are falling from my darkened eyes.

Several days after my conversation with the stranger whom I call *my mirror*, I was walking in the garden, leaning on my mother's arm, when she was suddenly and loudly called for. It seemed to me that the maid, in haste to find my mother, betrayed some agitation in her voice.

" What is the matter, mother ? " I asked her, troubled without knowing why.

" Nothing, love ; some visitor, no doubt. In our position we owe something to society."

" In that case," I said, embracing her, " I will not keep you any longer. Go and do the honours of the drawing-room."

She pressed two icy lips upon my forehead. Then I heard her footsteps on the gravel path receding in the distance.

She had hardly left me when I thought I heard the voices of two neighbours—two workmen—who were chatting together, thinking they were alone. You know, Anaïs, when God deprives us of one of our faculties, he seems, in order to console us, to make the others keener ; the blind man has his hearing sharper than his whose gaze can traverse space. I did not lose a word of their remarks, although they spoke in a low tone. And this is what they said :

" Poor things ! how said ! The brokers in again ! "

" And the girl has not the least suspicion. She never guesses that they take advantage of her loss of sight to make her happy."

"What do you mean?"

"There isn't any doubt about it. All that her hand touches is of mahogany or velvet; only the velvet has grown shabby and the mahogany has lost its lustre. At the table she enjoys the most delicious dishes without dreaming, in her innocence, that the domestic misery is kept concealed from her, and that alongside of that very table her father and mother seldom have anything except dry bread."

Oh, Anaïs, you can understand my agony! They have practised on me for my happiness; they have made me live in luxury amidst my darkness—and me alone. Oh! marvellous devotion. All the wealth which a most grateful heart can offer cannot pay this ever-lasting debt.

LETTER IV

I have not told any one that I have guessed this sad yet charming secret. My mother would be overwhelmed to learn that all her trouble to conceal her poverty from me has been useless. I still affect a firm belief in the flourishing condition of our house. But I am determined to save it.

M. de Sauves, as my lover is called, came to see me—and, may Heaven forgive me!—I set myself to play the coquette with him. So I said: "Have you still the same esteem for me?"

"Yes," said he. "I love you because you are beautiful with the noblest beauty, which is pure and modest."

"And my figure?"

"As exquisite and graceful as a vine."

"Ah! and my forehead?"

"Large and smooth as the ivory which it outshines."

"Really?" And I began to laugh.

"What makes you so merry?"

"An idea—that you are my mirror. I see myself reflected in your words."

"Dearest, I would that it might be so always."

"Would you agree, then—?"

"To be your faithful mirror, to reflect your qualities, your virtues. Consent to be my wife. I have some fortune; you shall want for nothing, and I will strive with all my power to make you happy."

At these words I thought of my poor parents, whom my marriage would relieve of an enormous burden.

"If I consent to marry you," I answered, "your self-love, as a man, would suffer. I could not see you."

"Alas!" he cried, "I owe you a confession."

"Go on," I said.

"I am a graceless child of nature. I have neither charm of countenance nor dignity of carriage. To crown my misfortune, a scourge, nowadays made powerless by the art of vaccination, has mercilessly scarred my features. In marrying a blind girl, therefore, I show that I am selfish and without humility."

I held out my hand to him.

"I don't know whether you are too hard on yourself, but I believe you to be good and true. Take me, then, such as I am. Nothing, at any rate, will turn my thoughts from yours. Your love will be an oasis in the desert of my night."

Am I doing right, or wrong? I know not, dear Anaïs, but I am going to my parents' rescue. Perhaps, in my groping, I have found the right way.

LETTER V

I thank you for your kind friendliness, for the compliments and congratulations with which your letter is filled.

Yes, I have been married for two months, and I am the happiest of women. I have nothing to desire ; idolised by my husband and adored by my parents, who have not left me, I do not regret my infirmity, since Edmond sees for both of us.

The day I was married, my mirror—as I call him—reflected complacently my bridal pomp. Thanks to it, I knew that my veil was nicely made, and that my wreath of orange-blossoms was not all on one side. What could a Venetian mirror have done more ?

In the evening we walk out together in the gardens, and he makes me admire the flowers by their perfume, the birds by their song, the fruit by its taste and its soft touch. Sometimes we go to the theatre, and there, too, he reproduces, by his wit, all that my closed eyes cannot see. Oh! what does his ugliness matter to me ? I no longer know what is beautiful, or what is ugly, but I *do* know what is kind and loving.

Farewell, then, dear Anaïs, rejoice in my happiness.

LETTER VI

I am a mother, Anaïs, the mother of a little girl, and I can't see her! They say she looks sweet enough to eat. They make out that she is a living miniature of me, and I can't admire her! Oh, how mighty is a mother's love! I have borne without a murmur not to look upon the blue of heaven, the glamour of the flowers, the features of my husband, of my parents, of those who love me ; but it seems that I cannot bear with resignation not to see my child ! Oh, if the black band which covers my sight would fall for a minute, a second only ; if I could look at her as one looks at the vanishing lightning, I should be happy—I should be proud for the remainder of my life !

Edmond this time cannot be my mirror. It is in vain that he tells me that my cherub has fair curly hair, great wayward eyes, and a vermilion smile. What good is that to me ? I cannot see my little darling when she stretches out her arms to me !

LETTER VII

My husband is an angel. Do you know what he is doing ? He has had me cared for during the past year without my knowing it. He wishes to restore the light to me, and the doctor is—himself !—he who for my sake has adopted a profession from which his sensibility recoils.

"Angel of my life," he said to me yesterday, " do you know what I hope ? "

" Is it possible ? "

" Yes ; those lotions which I made you use under the pretext that they would beautify the skin were really preparations for an operation of a very different importance."

" What operation ? "

" For the cure of cataract."

" Will not your hand tremble ? "

" No ; my hand will be sure, for my heart will be devoted."

" Oh ! " said I, embracing him, " you are not a man you are a ministering angel."

" Ah ! " he said " kiss me once more dearest. Let me enjoy these last few moments of illusion."

" What do you mean, dear ? "

" That soon, with the help of God, you will regain your sight."

" And then—— ? "

" Then you will see me as I am—small, insignificant, and ugly."

At these words it seemed to me as if a flash shot through my darkness : it was my imagination which was kindling like a torch.

" Edmond, dearest," I said, rising, " if you do not trust my love, if you think that, whatever your face may be, I am not your willing slave, leave me in my nothingness, in my eternal night."

He answered nothing, but pressed my hand.

The operation, my mother told me, might be attempted in a month.

I called to mind the details which I had asked about my husband. Mamma had told me that he was marked by small-pox ; papa maintains that his hair is very thin : Nicette, our servant, will have it that he is old.

To be marked by the small-pox is to be the victim of an accident. To be bald is a sign of intellectual power : so said Lavater. But to be old—that is a pity. And then, if, unfortunately, in the course of nature, he were to die before me, I should have less time to love him.

In fact, Anaïs, if you remember the stories in the fairy book which we read together, you with eyes and voice, I in heart and spirit, you will admit that I am rather in the interesting situation of "The Beauty and the Beast" without having the resource of the transformation miracle. Meanwhile pray for me ; for, with God's help, who knows whether I shall not soon be able to read your precious letters !

LAST LETTER

Oh, my friend, don't look at the end of this letter before you have read the beginning. Take your share of my griefs, my vicissitudes, and my joys, by following their natural course.

The operation took place a fortnight ago. A trembling hand was placed upon my eyes. I uttered two piercing cries ; then I seemed to see day, light, colour, sun. Then instantaneously a bandage was replaced upon my burning forehead. I was cured ! only a little patience and a little courage were required. Edmond had restored me to the sweetness of life.

But, must I confess it ? I did a foolish thing. I disobeyed my doctor—he will not know it : besides, there is no danger in my rashness now. They had brought me my little one to kiss. Nicette was holding her in her lap. The child said in her soft voice, "Mamma !" I could resist no longer. I tore off the bandage.

"My child ! oh, how lovely she is !" I cried out. "I see her ! oh, I see her ! "

Nicette quickly put the bandage on again. But I was no longer lonely in the darkness. This cherub face, restored by memory, from that moment lighted up my night.

Yesterday my mother came to dress me. We were long over my toilette. I had on a beautiful silk dress, a lace collar, my hair dressed *à la* Marie Stuart. When my arrangements were complete, my mother said to me :

"Take off the bandage."

I obeyed, and though only a twilight prevailed in the room, I thought that I had never seen anything so beautiful. I pressed to my heart my mother, my father, and my child.

"You have seen," said my father, "everybody but yourself."

"And my husband," I cried out, "where is my husband ? "

"He is hiding," said my mother.

Then I remembered his ugliness, his attire, his thin hair, and his scarred face.

"Poor dear Edmond," I said, "let him come to me. He is more beautiful than Adonis."

"While we are waiting for your lord and master," mamma answered, "admire yourself ; look in the glass. You may admire yourself for a long time without blame, if you are to make up for lost time."

I obeyed ; a little from vanity, a little from curiosity. What if I was ugly ? What if my plainness, like my poverty, had been

LÉO LESPÈS

concealed from me ? They led me to my pier-glass. I uttered a cry of joy. With my slender figure, my complexion like a rose, my eyes a little dazed, and like two shimmering sapphires, I was charming. Nevertheless, I could not look at myself quite at my ease, for the glass was trembling without cessation, and my image reflected on its brilliant surface seemed as if it danced for joy.

I looked behind the glass to see what made it tremble.

A young man came out—a fine young man, with large black eyes and striking figure, whose coat was adorned by the rosette of the Legion of Honour. I blushed to think that I had been so foolish in the presence of a stranger.

" Just look," said my mother to me, without taking any notice of him, " how fair you are ; like a white rose."

" Mamma ! " I cried.

" Only look at these white arms," and she pulled my sleeves above the elbow without the smallest scruple.

" But, mamma," I said, " what are you thinking of, before a stranger ! "

" A stranger ? it is a mirror."

" I don't mean the glass, but this young gentleman who was behind it, like a lover in a comedy."

" Eh ! goose," cried my father, " you need not be so bashful. It is your husband."

" Edmond ! " I cried out, and made a step forward to embrace him.

Then I fell back. He was so beautiful ! I was so happy ! Blind, I had loved in confidence. What made my heart beat now was a new love, swollen by the generosity of this truly noble man, who had ordered every one to say that he was ugly, in order to console me for my blindness.

Edmond fell at my knees. Mamma put me in his arms, as she wiped away her tears.

" How lovely you are," said my husband to me, in an ecstasy.

" Flatterer ! " I answered, looking down at him.

" No, when I alone was your mirror I always told you so—and see ! my colleague, here, whom you have just consulted, is of the same opinion, and declares that I am right ! "

THE GREAT FIND OF
· MONSIEUR BRETONCEL

THE celebrated stockbroker Bretoncel was an amateur of high
curiosities. By that is meant curiosities that are not always
curious but only high in price, so that the people who collect
them think that they are great patrons of art. In their rooms they
heap up enamels, Chinese jades, ancient weapons of war, and
pieces of Venetian crystal until their houses look like curiosity
shops.

In the autumn Monsieur Bretoncel took a month's holiday on a
rich estate by the banks of the Oise, and he did not idle his days
away. There, as in Paris, the mania for curiosities worked in him.
He roamed the country on foot, and objects that he would not
have looked at on a good dealer's recommendation seemed to him
wonderful when he lighted upon them after a day of rummaging.
A hunter who brings nothing back in his game-bag will kill a hedge-
sparrow and have it cooked for breakfast, and find it better than
a woodcock. So it is with collectors of curiosities.

One day the stockbroker had thus tramped about the country
until he was leg weary. It was five o'clock in the evening, and he
was returning sorrowfully to his house with empty hands, when at
the door of a tavern he saw a dresser loaded with common plates
and dishes. He stopped to see if some precious object was not
concealed in the shadow.

"Come in, sir," said the landlady, who, seeing he was tired out,
offered him a chair.

Instead of resting, Monsieur Bretoncel roamed around the room,
casting an anxious look in each smoky corner, and finally stopped
by the mantelpiece, from which hung an old skimmer. He took it
down, turned it over and over, and found there was nothing
interesting about it except that the holes were ingeniously placed
so as to form the name and the date of 1749.

"How much do you want for this skimmer?" he said. The

woman at first was not anxious to sell. The thing came from her grandmother and she did not want to lose it. But as Monsieur Bretoncel so insisted, and offered ten francs, he became the owner of the skimmer, which he studied at his ease sitting by the fireplace and rubbing the copper. Two peasants were also sitting in the tavern before a jug of cider, talking about crops and law-suits.

"What is that man doing?" one of them asked the landlady, who replied that he was a collector of antiquities who had just bought her skimmer for a good sum, that would enable her to get a new one and a pair of hens into the bargain.

"If that is so," said the peasant, raising his voice so as to make himself heard by the fireplace, "I have in my house a famous antiquity!"

Antiquity! The stockbroker at once became interested, and asked the man what he was talking about.

"I don't know what sort of thing you would call it. My children found it in the lumber room, and you may be sure it had been there a long time."

Lumber room! A long time! These were the words that would excite any amateur of curiosities. Monsieur Bretoncel eagerly questioned the peasant.

"All I can tell you, sir, is that it shines. There is a golden angel and some inscription below. It is made of metal."

"Of metal!" cried the stockbroker, opening his eyes wide as though to study this wonderful object of art. "What is the size of it?"

"About as big as the bottom of a saucepan," said the peasant, getting up and slinging over his shoulder his game-bag.

"Are you going already, my dear fellow? Will you take a glass of wine to help you on your way?"

"I have a league to go before I get home, so I will thank you kindly, sir."

The bottle was put on the table.

"You say that there is an angel and some writing?"

"Wait a minute. . . . I remember now, the angel is playing music . . . he is blowing in a trumpet."

"A religious subject," said the stockbroker to himself, "with an explanatory legend. Is it about this size?" he said, taking a saucepan from the fireplace and putting it on the table.

"Just about, sir, except that the upper part is not flat but bulging."

"No doubt hollow underneath?" said the stockbroker.

"My word! You speak like a wizard!"

Monsieur Bretoncel could scarcely conceal his excitement. His breathing was heavy, his heart palpitated, his hands trembled. There was no doubt about it: it was an enamel. The object had been found in a lumber room, where it had been hidden a fine long time, according to the word of the peasant. Thus it was very ancient. It gleamed, it shone. An angel blowing a trumpet was represented, with a golden legend below. The metal was both concave and convex. It was assuredly a marvellous enamel, coming from some old castle or some convent in the neighbourhood. How glorious it would be to recover some admirable masterpiece of Leonard Limousin or Pierre Courtois !

Yet he must not appear excited, lest the countryman should see it. These peasants are so shrewd. He was on the point of making one of the master strokes in the history of collecting ; everything pointed that way.

" Would it be possible to see this en——er-er ? " said the stockbroker, swallowing the last two syllables of the great word.

" Yes, sir. It costs nothing to look at it. You can even give yourself the satisfaction, any day you please, of seeing my kiddies playing at dinner with it."

" The little wretches ! " cried Monsieur Bretoncel. " How can you leave such an object in the hands of mischievous children ? "

" Well, the little ones must amuse themselves."

" But haven't they injured the enam——the thing ! "

" Oh, no ; it is solidly made."

" Are you willing to sell it to me ? " said the stockbroker.

" I am willing, sir. It is the kiddies who hold most by it."

" I have a good mind to go with you."

" I only live a league away," said the peasant.

" Madame," said the stockbroker to the landlady, " let us have three small glasses of your best brandy."

As it was necessary to get on good terms with the peasant, Monsieur Bretoncel drank the brandy, not without a grimace, and touched glasses with the man. Then they set out, but ten steps from the door the peasant went back to see if he had left his pipe behind.

" No harm meant, mother," he said to the landlady, " but how much did the swell give you for the skimmer ? "

" There's the money ! " said the woman, drawing from her pocket the ten-franc piece.

" Good ! " said the peasant, and lighting his pipe he came back with a careless air to his fellow-traveller, puffing out great clouds of smoke.

They spoke about the children. The stockbroker wanted to know how many boys and girls there were, and what their ages were ; and as at the moment they were passing before the general store of the village, Monsieur Bretoncel begged the man to wait, entered the shop, and came out loaded with dolls, funny men, and bags of sweetmeats.

"How you have loaded yourself up, sir!" said the peasant. "Those toys will grow heavier as we walk along."

"Your little girl interests me," replied the stockbroker, "and it will be quite a delight to me to give your children these toys."

"My word, they will think you are Father Christmas! Our kiddies are not used to such gifts."

For half an hour the conversation thus turned on indifferent matters. The stockbroker tried not to speak about the happy chance that, getting him on the track of a marvellous find, led him along the road, weighed down by all sorts of packets. But from time to time he returned to the subject of his search.

"But aren't you afraid to let your children eat out of the copper object?"

"But I tell you, sir, that the hollow part is glazed like the upper part."

"It is certainly an enamel," said the stockbroker to himself.

In the distance the slate roofs of some farm buildings shone between a row of poplars. The heart of the stockbroker expanded. Just a gun-shot's distance, and the marvel would be gleaming beneath his eyes.

"It is not our village," said the peasant. "We have only reached the village we get our provisions from."

Monsieur Bretoncel sighed. The packets of dolls and sweetmeats began to trouble him, and it was necessary to carry them to the little wretches who had perhaps injured a precious work of art. But it was needful to hide his feelings in order to gain the wonderful thing, and the stockbroker repressed the troubles that he felt. The travellers crossed over the village square, where a great wooden stocking stood out from the front of a draper's shop.

"It was here," said the peasant, "that my wife wanted me to buy her a dress. Unhappily there was a bad market to-day and the grains fetched a poor price . . . I shall have to put it off till another time."

The appeal to the generosity of the collector was patent. Still, women are hard in bargaining, and it would be wise to win her favour.

"If your wife would like a dress," said Monsieur Bretoncel, "I shall be delighted to buy her one."

And he entered the big blue stocking shop, and pointed to a roll of dress material.

"Show that enamel," he said.

"Enamel?" repeated the astonished draper.

Dismayed, the stockbroker looked round to see if his companion was listening. But the peasant sat on the doorstep, dreaming of the happy chance that had led him to such a milking cow.

When the material was cut and packed, Monsieur Bretoncel came out with a new packet under his arm.

" Ah, if the fellows of the Stock Exchange saw me in this get-up ! " he said.

The copper skimmer hung from the button of his frock coat. The bags of sweets came half out of his pockets. His two hands gripped the dolls and the funny men ; and under his left arm the stockbroker carried the dress material.

The peasant offered to take half the parcels. But Monsieur Bretoncel, through a superstition common to collectors, would not agree to it. He could make no movement with his arms ; his walk was impeded. But this constraint and worry were not without a charm. The amateur was reminded, at each difficult step, that he was marching to the conquest of a marvel. If his nerves suffered, the enamel gleamed more brightly far ahead.

Monsieur Bretoncel thought of the Duke of Coyon-Latour, whom he had met in the streets of Paris, carrying on his shoulder an enormous bust in marble that he had just acquired. The stockbroker said to himself that he too, while walking in the footsteps of so illustrious a collector, must also share the burden of the passion for curiosities.

" It's a bit of luck my meeting you, sir," said the peasant.

" Have we much farther to go ? "

" Just another half-hour."

" But we have been already two hours on the march."

" Well, sir, I warned you we had a good league to go."

" A good league ! " cried the frightened stockbroker. For if one peasant's league equals two real leagues, how many are there in his " good league " ?

" Patience, sir . . . we shall soon be at Quercy . . . Can't you see the spire ? "

" That spire far away there ? "

" After Quercy, if we make the pace, we can get there in a good quarter of an hour."

At the reference to the good quarter of an hour Monsieur Bretoncel almost fell with all his parcels on the road.

" Happily," said the peasant, " we shall find at the gate of Quercy an inn where they sell a little white wine, dry as gun-flint, that would make a dead man walk."

By a violent effort the stockbroker won to the inn, where he threw on the table dolls, funny men, skimmer, and dress material.

" You are late to-day, Sureau," said the landlady to the peasant. " It will be night before you get home."

" I have been talking with this gentleman," said Sureau.

" Damme ! " said the stockbroker in a burst of anger. " How long will it take us to get to your place ? "

" We should get there in time for supper if we went through Quercy, but I must tell you——"

Sureau scratched his head. " I am obliged to go round by the fields."

" The fields ? "

" No doubt the road is best. But in the middle of the village there is a magistrate's clerk who makes me tremble with anger . . . certainly the road would cut off a good twenty minutes."

" We must follow it," cried the stockbroker, shouldering his parcels. " Let us start."

" But if the magistrate's clerk is before his door I will not answer for myself . . . a misfortune would arise that you would never forget."

" What is the matter ? "

" To tell you the truth, sir, I was behind-hand with a little fine of eighteen francs. Will you believe me that the clerk has already entered me on his book for six francs five sous of extra expense, although I am in the right. A man is a man or he is not . . . if I only saw a picture of the clerk . . . and that's why I always walk another half league every evening to avoid him."

" Another half league ! " said Monsieur Bretoncel. " Go and pay him at once, my good fellow. Here are forty francs ! "

While the peasant was paying the fine, the stockbroker kept saying to himself, " An enamel ! " " An enamel ! " " An enamel ! " Like a drunkard gorging himself with wine from a cask during the absence of the owner, Monsieur Bretoncel pronounced as often as possible the word that should not have come from his mouth till the conclusion of the bargain.

" I have paid them ! " cried the peasant, returning radiant from the house ; " but I gave myself the pleasure of telling the man what I thought of him. There is the receipt in discharge. Ah, law costs, they mount up quicker than a monkey can climb ! "

Though the peasant showed the receipt, he did not show the change from the forty francs. But the stockholder said to himself that he now held in his hand the husband and wife and children, so that there could be no getting out of the sale.

Little by little the night fell. Monsieur Bretoncel dragged his legs along, and for the last time he helped himself with the mirage of the enamel. Finally, worn out with hunger and fatigue, he arrived at the farm.

" Ho ! wife, where are you ? Look at this dress that a gentleman had bought you for a present ! "

The tall thin woman scarcely dared to glance at the material, which seemed to her more brilliant than all the tissues of China.

" What ! You don't open your mouth. . . . Thank the gentleman and give him a seat. . . . He is rather tired."

" It is not worth the trouble. Let us see this——er-er—the object in question."

" Ah ! that's right. . . . Where is it ? . . . the kiddies may have carried the bowl into the orchard. Wife, go and look for the antiquity that the children play with. . . . This gentleman has come from the town to see it. . . ."

The woman remained stuck against the wall.

" I gave it to the pigs," she said.

" An enamel for pigs ! " cried the stockbroker, losing all his self-control.

" As I could not find a pan for the pigs," said the farmer's wife, " I gave them their potatoes in the bowl."

" But they may have destroyed the enamel with their snouts ! " exclaimed Monsieur Bretoncel.

The woman seemed thunderstruck.

" Light the candle, wife, and let us look at the stable," said the peasant.

The door of the stable was opened. The pigs were grunting within. The farmer rained down blows on them to drive them away from their meal.

" Here is the antiquity," he said, after throwing out the bits of potatoes that filled it.

" That ! " cried the stockbroker with a look of stupefaction.

The enamel so much desired was only a fire insurance advertisement. Glazed, gilded, with a golden figure of Fame with her trumpet, lettered below, hollowed out behind and convex in front, it was one of those metal plates that French insurance companies nail on the outside of insured houses. Yet it had all the characters from which Monsieur Bretoncel had inferred that it was an enamel, made by the masters of Limoges.

It is in such circumstances that your amateurs of objects of art return home with their ears down, their eyes sorrowful, ashamed, broken with fatigue, and with no illusion to make them forget the length of the road. And it was thus that Monsieur Bretoncel returned, regretting his gifts and his generosities.

MONSIEUR TRINGLE

CHAMPFLEURY

NEVER was there a happier man than Monsieur Tringle the day he received an invitation to Madame Brou's fancy-dress ball.

M. Tringle lost no time in deciding that he would wear a Mephistopheles costume.

M. Tringle was a bachelor, and desiring to become the possessor of Mlle. Brou, or rather of her dowry, determined to put his fate to the touch on the night of the ball. After dressing at the barber's, who lent the costume on hire, and who greatly admired the fine effect, M. Tringle started in all impatience for the scene of action.

"Your cloak, Monsieur Tringle," cried the barber. "It's cold, I warn you."

But the bachelor was already bounding along the streets, rehearsing as he went a *pas de diable* he had just thought out.

.   .   .   .

He rang the bell.

A slight noise was heard inside, and Mlle. Brou herself opened the door.

"Mademoiselle," said M. Tringle, bending double, so that his tail, starting upwards, was at great pains to be exquisitely polite.

As a rule, Mlle. Brou's face was entirely expressionless, and somewhat resembled a milliner's block looking at the passing of a troop of cavalry from the shop-window. But now she looked immensely astonished.

"Is your mother quite well?" asked M. Tringle, with a further access of affability.

At the same time he entered the hall, and found himself at the dining-room door, where Madame Brou, surrounded by a heap of various stuffs, was sitting at a table lighted by a lamp.

Not without annoyance did M. Tringle say to himself, "I'm too early."

However, he greeted Madame Brou none the less respectfully, and she, glancing aside under her glasses, looked with tightened lips at the extraordinary being who solicited the favour of paying her his compliments.

Mlle. Brou was sitting by her mother, and the two ladies communicated their impressions in dumb show by such looks of astonishment that at first M. Tringle thought some damage must have occurred to his fine devil's costume during his propress along the streets.

An ominous silence followed the awkward arrival, M. Tringle feeling seriously annoyed with himself for coming so early.

"I beg your pardon," said Madame Brou, making visible efforts to enter into conversation.

"Madame——," but in great confusion M. Tringle said no more. Though his eyes were cast down, he felt Madame Brou looking at him from head to foot, from the hoofs to the wig. Uneasy as a soldier before a severe colonel, he asked, "Am I all right?"

Madame Brou, looking at her daughter as if for advice before opening fire, said, "At the first glance I do not recognise you, Monsieur."

This caused M. Tringle to break into uncontrollable fits of laughter.

The effect he desired was obtained !

But the bachelor perceived that Madame Brou did not share his merriment.

The ladies' lips tightened. With a sign of dignity, Madame Brou motioned her daughter to sit up.

They might have been judges about to pronounce sentence.

" What, ladies, don't you recognise me ? " asked M. Tringle, proud of his disguise.

" The ladies are late with their costumes," M. Tringle ventured to say.

But as they did not vouchsafe a reply, the bachelor began to feel annoyed, and to think that for these sorts of entertainments the time ought to be printed on the invitation.

" It's very comfortable here, ladies," he ventured to remark.

Internally the bachelor was hoping to taste some of the refreshments of the evening, for the fatigues of the way had made him exceptionally thirsty.

The ladies did not seem to understand him in the least, and M. Tringle was surprised at the unconcern of the lady of the house, who, at that hour, should surely have been preparing the cakes, lemonade, and punch.

" If only some other mask would arrive ! " said M. Tringle to himself ; " a new costume would take their attention off me."

But the guests did not hurry themselves.

M. Tringle attempted to put some life into the conversation. " Every one is saying, Madame, that your ball will be the most brilliant of the season."

Once again the scissors stopped, and Madame Brou looked at M. Tringle from top to toe.

" Certainly," thought the bachelor, " some unseemly rent must be visible on my person." Aloud, he observed, " The ladies are, doubtless, putting the finishing touches to their dresses." And he expressed his regret that he was not already able to admire the ladies in the full glory of their costumes.

" What's the use of dressing a week before the ball ? " said Mlle. Brou.

" A week before the ball ? " cried M. Tringle. " Ye gods ! "

" We are not invited to the ball to which you are going, Monsieur," said Madame Brou, lighting a candle, and rising to show the unhappy joker that his visit had already been too long.

" The ball's not to-night ? " replied the bachelor in an agitated voice.

" I have the honour to inform you, Monsieur, that we receive on the 18th."

41*

M. Tringle jumped out of his chair.

"The 18th," he cried. "The invitation was dated February 8th. Ah! poor Tringle!"

"What's that?" asked Madame Brou. "You are Monsieur Tringle. What an unfortunate *contretemps!* I was wondering what curious notion could induce a stranger to call on us in that costume."

To dress up like the devil a week before the ball was unheard of. Could he wear so eccentric a disguise twice?

And M. Tringle made countless efforts to hide the tail behind his chair—the tail on whose tricks he had placed all his hopes; but so supple was the spring, that his efforts were not of much avail. At the least movement the ill-behaved little tuft at its end appeared on the arms of the chair, sometimes on one side, sometimes on the other.

M. Brou now returned home, and showed Tringle the door—for ever.

So saying, M. Brou opened the door, and shut it with a bang on terrified M. Tringle.

Philosophers of all nations agree that a misfortune never comes single. What were M. Tringle's feelings when, on attempting to descend the staircase, he found something pulling him back!

His tail was shut in the door!—in the door of a house whence M. Tringle had just been finally dismissed.

At about 2 A.M. he managed to free himself, and on his way home his devil's disguise led him into many extraordinary adventures.

GUSTAVE FLAUBERT
1821–1880

ST. JULIAN
THE HOSPITALLER

I

JULIAN's father and mother lived in a castle girt with woods on the incline of a hill.

The four angular towers had pointed roofs covered with leaden scales, and the base of the walls rested upon shoulders of rock that shelved abruptly to the bottom of the trenches.

The flagstones in the courtyard were stainless as the floor of a church. Long spouts, in the form of dragons with down-stretched necks, sputtered out the rain-water into the cistern ; on the window-sills of every storey, in painted earthen pots, bloomed basil or heliotrope.

A second enclosure, wooden-staked, embraced a fruit orchard, a garden where the flower-beds took the forms of numerals, a vine-arbour with bowers for enjoyment of the air, and a mall which served as a recreation ground for the pages. On the other side stood the kennels, the stables, the bakehouse, the wine-press and the granaries. A pasturage of green turf spread all around, closed in by a stout fence of thorn.

Peace had reigned so long that the portcullis was no more lowered ; the moats were full of water ; swallows made their nests in the loop-holes ; and the archer, who all the day long walked up and down on the curtain-wall, when the sun's rays became too scorching went into the watch-tower and slumbered there like a monk.

Within the castle the iron locks and bolts shone everywhere, tapestries warmed the walls, the cupboards were choked with linen, the cellars were crowded with casks of wine, the oaken money-chests groaned beneath their burden of bags of silver.

In the armoury, between standards and stuffed heads of wild beasts, might be seen a collection of implements of war of all times and all countries, from the slings of the Amalekites and the javelins of the Garamantes, to the short broadswords of the Saracens and the coats of mail of the Normans.

GUSTAVE FLAUBERT

An ox could be roasted entire upon the great spit in the kitchen ; the chapel was as richly adorned as a king's oratory. There was even in a remote part of the building a Roman bath, but from the use of this the lord of the castle abstained, esteeming it a custom of idolaters.

Enveloped always in a cloak made of fox-skins, he would spend his days roaming through his castle, dealing out justice to his vassals, acting as peacemaker in the strife of neighbours. In winter he watched the falling flakes of snow, or had stories read aloud to him. At the first touch of spring he would ride forth on his mule through the narrow by-ways, alongside the fields of sprouting corn, and talk with and counsel the churls. After many amorous adventures, he had taken to wife a damsel of high lineage.

She was very pale and somewhat proud and serious of mien. The horns of her head-dress touched the lintels of the doors ; the train of her robe dragged three paces behind her. Her household was regulated almost like that of a monastery ; every morning she allotted to her servants their several tasks, supervised the making of preserves and ointments ; spun at her distaff, or embroidered altar-cloths. In answer to her prayers God bestowed on her a son.

There were great rejoicings over this, and a banquet was given which lasted three days and four nights ; flowers were strewn upon the floor, harps sounded, there was a continual flare of torches. Rare delicacies were consumed, and fowls as big as sheep ; as a surprise a dwarf was made to step out of a pie ; goblets running short, for the crowd grew continually, they fell to drinking out of horns and helmets.

The young mother took no part in these merry-makings. She kept her bed quietly. One evening, waking up, she saw, in a ray of the moon shining in from the window, what looked like a moving shadow. It was an old man in a russet gown, a rosary at his side, a wallet upon his shoulder, and with all the appearance of a hermit. He drew near to her bed, and said to her without moving his lips apart :

" Rejoice, O mother ! Thy son will be a saint ! "

She was about to utter a cry, but gliding away upon the ray of the moon he rose slowly in the air and vanished. The songs in the banqueting-hall surged up louder than ever. Then she heard the voices of angels, and her head fell back upon the pillow, above which was placed the bone of a martyr in a framework of carbuncles.

On the morrow all the servants, when interrogated, declared that they had seen no hermit. Whether a dream or a reality, it must have been a communication from heaven ; but she was careful to say nothing about it, fearing they would lay it to her vanity.

The guests went off at daybreak, and Julian's father was standing outside the postern-gate, where he had just seen off the last of them, when suddenly a beggar appeared before him in the mist. It was a vagrant with a plaited beard and flashing eyes, wearing silver bangles upon both arms. As though inspired, he gasped out these inconsequent words :

"Ah! Ah! Thy son! . . . Much blood! . . . Much glory! . . . Always happy! The family of an Emperor!"

And stooping to pick up the alms that had been thrown him, he disappeared in the grass and was no more seen.

The good baron glanced to right and left, and shouted at the top of his voice. No answer! The wind whistled and the morning mists began to lift.

He attributed this vision to the weariness of his head from lack of sleep. "If I speak of it, they will laugh at me," he said to himself. Nevertheless the splendours promised to his son dazzled him, vague though the promises had been and doubtful though he remained of having heard them.

Husband and wife guarded their secret. But both of them cherished their son with equal tenderness ; and, venerating him as specially favoured by God, they had for his person an infinite regard. His cradle was stuffed with the finest of down ; a lamp in the form of a dove burned above it perpetually ; three nurses rocked him to sleep ; and tucked up carefully in his swaddling-clothes, with his pink face and blue eyes, his brocaded mantle, and his cap adorned with pearls, he looked like a little infant Jesus. His teeth came without his crying once.

When he was seven years old his mother taught him to sing ; and his father, to make him brave, put him on a big horse. The boy smiled gaily, and it was not long before he had learned everything to do with horsemanship.

A very learned old monk taught him the Holy Scriptures, the Arabic numerals, the Roman characters, and gave him lessons in the art of making small pictures upon vellum. They worked together at the very top of a tower, away from all noise.

The task finished, they went down into the garden, and, walking side by side, studied the flowers.

At times a string of beasts of burden, led by a man on foot in Oriental garb, was to be seen passing along the bottom of the valley. The lord of the castle, recognising a merchant, would despatch a messenger to him. The stranger, thus assured, would turn aside from his route, and, entering the hall, display pieces of silk and velvet, goldsmiths' work, perfumes, and other articles of uses unknown ; it would end by his going off unharmed and loaded with his gains. At other times, a body of pilgrims would knock at the gates. Their soaked garments steamed before the hearth ; and when they had eaten and drunk, they would tell of their adventures :

of their wanderings upon stormy seas, their marches on foot over burning sands, the ferocity of the pagans, the caverns of Syria, of the Crib of Bethlehem, and the Holy Sepulchre. Then they would take shells out of the pockets of their cloaks and give them to the young master.

Often the lord of the castle would entertain his old comrades-in-arms. As they sat and drank together, they would recall the wars in which they had taken part, their assaults on fortresses, their bombardments with catapults, and their prodigious wounds. Julian, listening to them, would cry out excitedly ; and his father would feel assured that the boy would one day be a conqueror. But in the evening, on coming out from the Angelus, when he passed between the rows of the poor kneeling on either side, Julian would put his hand into his purse so simply and with so noble a dignity, that his mother would begin to picture him as a future archbishop.

His place in chapel was beside his parents ; and however long the services might be, he remained kneeling on his prie-dieu, his cap on the ground and his hands joined.

One day, during Mass, happening to raise his eyes, he noticed a white mouse coming out of a hole in the wall. It scampered over the first altar-step, and after two or three quick turns to left and right, fled back again. On the following Sunday he was troubled by the thought that he might see it again. It returned, and every Sunday he found himself on the look-out for it and distracted by it. He became angered against it and resolved to rid himself of it.

Having shut the door, and having strewn crumbs of cake along the altar-steps, he lay in front of the hole, a stick in his hand.

At length a pink nose protruded—then the whole mouse emerged bodily. Julian struck down quickly, then remained stupefied before this little body that no longer moved. A drop of blood stained the floor. He wiped it up quickly with his sleeve, threw the mouse outside, and said nothing about it to anybody.

All sorts of small birds were to be seen pecking the seeds in the garden. It occurred to him one day to put some peas in a reed hollowed out for the purpose. When he heard a twittering in a tree, he drew near it quietly, then raised his tube and blew ; and the little creatures rained down on his shoulders in such numbers that he could not help laughing, mischievously happy.

One morning, when he was returning from the curtain-wall, he saw on the top of the rampart a large pigeon basking in the sun. Julian stood still to look at it ; the wall being broken away at this spot, a bit of stone lay to his hand. He raised his arm and the stone hit the bird, which fell into the moat.

He rushed down, tearing his clothes among the briars, looking for it everywhere as nimbly as a young dog.

The pigeon, its wings broken, hung, palpitating, in the branches of a privet.

The bird's hold upon life irritated the boy. He set about strangling it, and the bird's convulsions made his heart beat, filling it with a savage and tumultuous delight. When at last the victim stiffened in his grasp, a feeling of faintness came over him.

In the evening, during supper, his father declared that a boy of his age should begin to learn the craft of hunting ; and he went in search of an old copy-book which, in the form of questions and answers, contained all the lore of the chase. In this book a master taught his pupil the art of breaking in dogs and training falcons, the setting of snares, and how to distinguish the stag by its scent, the fox by its tracks, the wolf by its scratchings in the earth ; explaining the best way of stalking them all and how to spear them ; telling where their lairs generally might be found, what winds were most propitious for hunting them, enumerating their cries, and giving the rules of the quarry.

As soon as Julian was able to recite all these things by heart, his father started him with a pack of hounds.

First, there were twenty-four Barbary greyhounds, swifter than gazelles, but liable to get out of hand ; then seventeen couples of Breton hounds, red, spotted white, faultless of nose, deep of chest, and great givers of tongue. For boar-hunting, with its risky shifts and doublings, there were forty griffons, as hairy as bears. A number of Tartary mastiffs, standing almost as high as donkeys, flame-coloured, wide-backed, straight-limbed, were destined for the chase of the aurochs. The black coats of the spaniels shone like satin ; the baying of the talbot-hounds rivalled the note of the beagles. In a yard to themselves, growling, rolling their eyes, and dragging at their chains, were eight allain dogs, formidable brutes, that would spring at the stomach of a man on horseback and were not afraid of lions.

They all ate wheaten bread, drank from stone troughs, and had sonorous names.

The falconry was, perhaps, on a yet grander scale than this ; the lord of the castle at a great outlay had procured tiercelets from Caucasus, sakers from Babylonia, gerfalcons from Germany, as well as peregrine falcons, caught upon cliffs overhanging frozen seas in countries far away. They were all kept together in a large thatched shed ; and ranged in order of size upon the perch, with a patch of grass in front of them, on which from time to time they were set to stretch their legs.

Pouches, hooks, traps of all sorts, were made and kept in readiness.

They would often take out ousels, dogs keen and quick at pointing. Then the beaters, advancing step by step, carefully drew an immense net above their motionless bodies. At a word they started barking ; quail flew up and were quickly captured by the hunting party, including the ladies of the neighbourhood invited with their husbands, children, and attendants.

On other occasions there would be a beating of drums to start the hares ; foxes were taken in the moats ; or a trap laid a wolf by the leg.

But Julian regarded these convenient devices with contempt ; he preferred to go out hunting alone, on horseback, with his falcon. He took almost always a great Scythian tarteret, white as snow. Its leather hood was surmounted by a plume, and golden bells trembled upon its blue feet ; it held fast to its master's wrist while his horse went galloping along and the plains unrolled themselves beneath. Julian, unloosing its tether, would let it fly suddenly. Boldly it darted upwards like an arrow ; and two black marks of unequal size could be seen to twist and turn and come together in the azure distance. The falcon would presently return tearing its prey to pieces, and would resume its place upon Julian's gauntlet, its two wings quivering.

Julian took, in this way, heron, kite, crow, and vulture.

He loved, ever and again blowing his horn, to follow the hounds coursing down the hillside, leaping rivulets and heading for the woods ; and when the stag began to groan under their teeth, Julian brought it instantly down, and then gloated over the mastiffs devouring the torn and smoking carcase.

On misty days he would betake him to a marsh after duck, teal, and otter.

Three squires would be in waiting for him from daybreak, at the foot of the steps ; and the old monk, leaning out from his narrow window, beckoned in vain to recall him to his studies. He went out now in all weathers, in the heat of the sun, in rain, even in a storm, quenching his thirst with a hand-scoop of river-water, allaying his hunger with wild apples as he rode, resting under an oak when he was tired ; and he would return home in the middle of the night, blood-stained and covered with mud, thorns sticking in his hair, and the scent of wild beasts clinging to his clothes. He grew like to them. When his mother embraced him he suffered her kisses coldly, seemingly absorbed in profound thought.

He killed bears with the knife, bulls with the axe, and boars with the spear. Once, armed only with a stick, he defended himself against wolves which had been devouring the dead bodies at the foot of a gibbet.

One winter's morning, he set out before daybreak well equipped, a cross-bow on his shoulder, and a quiver full of bolts at his saddle.

His Danish jennet, followed by two basset-hounds, made the earth echo to its even tread. A fierce wind was blowing, and the frost whitened his mantle with pearl-like drops. Presently one side of the horizon was faintly illuminated, and in the pale light of dawn he saw rabbits playing here and there near their burrows. The two hounds made for them, and in another moment had broken the backs of several.

Soon he entered a wood. A heathcock benumbed by the cold was sleeping on the end of a branch, with its head under its wing. Julian, with a backward cut of his sword, slashed off the bird's legs, and without troubling to pick it up continued on his way.

Three hours later, he reached the summit of a mountain so lofty that the sky took a black shadow from it. In front of him sank a rock, shaped like a long wall, overhanging a precipice ; at the end of it two wild goats gazed down into the depths. As he had not his bolts with him (for he had left his horse below), he decided to make his way down to them ; crouching low, bare-footed, he got at last within reach of the nearer of the two and plunged a dagger into its side. The second, terror-stricken, sprang into the void. Julian darted forward to stab it, and his right foot slipping, stumbled over the dead body of its mate, and lay with his arms outstretched, his face downwards over the abyss.

Having descended again into the valley, he followed a line of willows bordering a river. Cranes, flying very low, passed over his head from time to time. Julian brought them down with his whip, missing not one.

By now the air was warmer and the hoar-frost had melted. Clouds of mist floated and the sun came out. He saw a frozen lake gleaming in the distance like a sheet of lead. In the middle of the lake there was a beast that Julian did not know, a black-muzzled beaver. Though it was a long shot, a bolt brought it down, and he was vexed that he could not carry off the skin.

After this he took his way down an avenue of big trees whose topmost branches, meeting, formed a sort of triumphal archway into a forest beyond. A roebuck bounded out of a thicket, a fallow-deer sprang up in a glade, a badger emerged from a hole, a peacock strutting on a grassy patch spread out its tail ; and when he had killed them all, other roebuck, other fallow-deer, other badgers, other peacocks, as well as blackbirds and jays, and polecats, and foxes, and hedgehogs, and lynxes, an infinity of other creatures, made their appearance, their numbers increasing at each step. They circled round him, trembling, their eyes full of gentleness and appeal. But Julian slaughtered them untiringly, alternately fixing his cross-bow, thrusting with his rapier, slashing with his sword, heedless of anything and everything, his mind a blank. He was conscious only of being engaged somewhere in a tremendous hunt, and that this had been so for a period quite indefinite—there he was, and everything seemed to happen with the inexplicable facility

of a dream. An extraordinary spectacle now arrested his attention.
A valley, shaped like a circus, was filled with stags ; and, crowded
close together, they kept each other warm with their breath, which
formed into a cloud above them.

The prospect of carnage upon so great a scale during a space of
minutes almost suffocated him with lust. Then he dismounted,
thrust back his sleeves, and began to shoot.

As the first bolt whistled through the air, all the stags turned
their heads simultaneously. Gaps began to be made in the living
mass, plaintive cries went up, and the whole herd began to move
convulsively.

The rim of the valley was too steep for them to scale. They
bounded hither and thither, trying to escape. Julian continued to
take aim and shoot ; and the bolts rained down like sleet. The
frantic deer reared and pranced and plunged, fighting amongst
themselves, mounting on each other's backs ; and their bodies with
their antlers entangled together made a large mound that fell to
pieces as it moved.

At last they all lay dead upon the sand, foam at their nostrils,
entrails hanging loose, the heaving of their bodies ceasing gradually.
Then all was still.

Night was imminent ; and behind the wood, in the interstices of
the branches, the sky reddened like a clot of blood.

Julian leant against a tree. He gazed with vacant eyes upon
the monstrous massacre, not understanding how he could have
wrought it.

On the far side of the valley, on the edge of the forest, he perceived a stag, a doe and a fawn.

The stag, black and of enormous size, carried sixteen points and
a white beard. The doe, fair with the pallor of dead leaves, browsed
upon the grass, and the spotted fawn sucked at her teats as she
moved about.

The cross-bow whirred again. The fawn fell dead. Then its
mother, gazing heavenwards, gave out a deep-throated, heartbreaking, human cry of anguish. Julian, angered, stretched her on
the earth with an arrow in her chest.

The great stag had seen him and made a bound. Julian let fly at
him his last bolt. It struck him on the forehead and remained
implanted therein.

The great stag seemed not to feel it, and, stepping over the dead
carcases, it advanced continually, and was about to charge him and
tear him open. Julian retreated in indescribable terror. The huge
creature stood still, and with eyes flashing, as solemn as a patriarch
or a law-giver, whilst a bell sounded in the distance, said thrice
over :

" Accursed ! Accursed ! Accursed ! The day will come, ferocious of heart, when thou shalt slay thy father and thy mother ! "

Then the stag's knees gave, its eyelids slowly closed, and it fell dead.

Julian was dumb-struck, then overcome with sudden weariness, and his whole being was pervaded with a sense of unutterable sadness and disgust. He wept for a long time, with his forehead clasped between his hands.

His horse was lost ; his dogs had forsaken him ; the solitude enveloping him seemed to threaten him with vague perils. At last, panic-stricken, he set out across the country-side, chose a path at a venture, and found himself almost immediately at the gate of the castle.

That night he did not sleep. In the flickering light of the hanging lamp he saw always the great black stag. Its prediction obsessed him ; he fought against it. " No, no ! " he cried, " I cannot kill them ! " Then he reflected : " Yet, if I were tempted to . . . ? " . . . and he lay in fear lest the Devil should instil in him the desire.

For three months his mother in anguish prayed at his bedside, and his father walked moaning in the corridors. He summoned the most famous physicians, who prescribed quantities of drugs. Julian's malady, they said, sprang from some evil wind or amorous craving. But the youth, for answer to all questions, shook his head.

His strength came back to him, and he was taken out into the courtyard, his father and the old monk supporting him on either side as he walked.

When he was restored completely to health he had resolved to hunt no more.

His father, thinking to please him, presented him with a great Saracen sword.

It was placed in a panoply, on the top of a pillar. A ladder had to be used to reach it. Julian mounted it. The sword was too heavy for him, escaped from his fingers, and in falling grazed the old lord so closely that it cut his cloak. Julian believed he had killed his father, and fainted.

Thenceforth he stood in fear of arms. The sight of a naked sword made him turn pale. This weakness was a great grief to his family.

At last the old monk commanded him in the name of God, of honour, and of his forebears, to resume his manly sports.

His equerries were in the habit of amusing themselves every day throwing the javelin. Julian joined them in this and soon surpassed them all. He would throw his into the neck of a bottle, or break off the teeth of the weathercocks, or, at a hundred paces, would hit a nail in a door.

One summer's evening, at the hour when the mist makes things indistinct, Julian, being under the trellis in the garden, saw in the distance two white wings fluttering just above the fruit-wall. He made sure it was a stork and threw his javelin.

A piercing scream went forth.

It was his mother. Her hat with its long streamers was pinned to the wall.

Julian fled from the castle and did not return.

II

He joined a body of soldiers who happened to be passing by.

He made acquaintance with hunger and thirst, fevers and vermin. He became inured to the bustle of fighting and the aspect of men stricken to death. The wind tanned his skin. His limbs became toughened by contact with armour ; and as he was of great strength, brave, temperate, and wary, he obtained without difficulty command of a company.

At the outset of a battle he kindled his men with a splendid sweep of his sword. With the help of a knotted rope he climbed up the walls of citadels by night, swung this way and that by the wind, while the sparks of Greek fire fastened on his cuirass, and seething resin and molten lead poured down from the battlements. Time and again his buckler was broken by a stone. Bridges, strained to breaking-point, gave way beneath him. Swinging his mace, he rid himself of fourteen horsemen. He defeated in single combat all those who challenged him. More than twenty times he was thought to be dead.

Thanks to divine favour he escaped always with his life ; for he always protected monks and priests, orphans and widows, and, above all, old men. Whenever he saw an old man walking ahead of him he cried out that he would fain see his face ; it was as though he feared to kill him by mistake.

Fugitive slaves, churls driven to revolt, bastards without means, the daring of all kinds flocked to his banner, and he became the leader of an army.

It grew. He became famous. His support came to be in request.

He went by turn to help the Dauphin and the King of England, the Knights Templars of Jerusalem and the Surena of the Parthians, the Negus of Abyssinia and the Emperor of Calicut. He fought against the Scandinavians in their coats of fish-plate mail, against negroes carrying shields made of rhinoceros hide and mounted upon tawny asses, against Indians with faces the colour of gold who brandished above their diadems deep-bladed sabres that flashed more brightly than mirrors. He vanquished Troglodytes and Cannibals. He traversed regions so hot that in the sun's rays a man's hair took flame of itself, burning like a torch, and others so cold that the arms, coming loose from the body, would fall upon the ground. He visited lands where fogs were so dense that one walked surrounded by phantoms.

Republics had recourse to him in their difficulties. In negotiations with ambassadors he obtained terms favourable beyond all hopes. When some monarch was acting too evilly he would suddenly appear and call him to book. He gave freedom to subjugated races. He delivered queens imprisoned in castles. It was he, and no other, who slew the monstrous serpent of Milan and the dragon of Oberbirbach.

Now, the Emperor of Occitania, having triumphed over the Spanish Mussulmans, had united himself in concubinage with the sister of the Caliph of Cordova ; by her he had a daughter whom he brought up a Christian. But the Caliph, pretending that he wished to become a convert, came on a visit to him accompanied by a numerous suite, massacred his whole garrison, and threw him into a dungeon keep, where he treated him cruelly in the hope of making him yield up his treasures.

Julian hastened to his aid, destroyed the Infidel army, besieged the town, killed the Caliph, cut off his head, and threw it like a ball over the ramparts. Then he took the Emperor from his prison, and set him on his throne again in the presence of his entire Court.

The Emperor, in reward for so great a service, bestowed upon him large quantities of silver in baskets ; Julian would have none of them. Believing he wanted more, the Emperor offered him three-fourths of his riches ; Julian refused again ; the Emperor then asked him to share his kingdom with him ; Julian thanked him ; and the Emperor began to weep with vexation, not knowing how to express his gratitude, until suddenly he struck his forehead and whispered a word in the ear of a courtier ; a tapestry screen was drawn up and a young girl appeared.

Her great dark eyes gleamed gently like two lamps. A bewitching smile parted her lips. The coils of her hair were caught in the jewel-work adorning her partly open robe, and her transparent tunic revealed the youthfulness of her limbs. She was very pretty and plump with a slender waist.

Julian was inebriated with desire, the more so in that he had lived until then with extreme chastity.

So he received the Emperor's daughter in marriage, with a castle which she inherited from her mother ; and, the wedding celebrations over, leave-takings ensued, an infinity of courtesies being exchanged.

It was a palace of white marble, built in the Moorish style on a promontory, in a cluster of orange-trees. Terraces of flowers went down to the shore of a gulf, upon which pink shells cracked beneath the feet. At the back of the castle a forest stretched out in the shape of a fan. The sky was perennially blue, and the trees were stirred in turn by breezes from the sea or by winds from the mountains which closed in the horizon far away.

The dusky rooms borrowed their light from the incrustation of the walls. Lofty columns, slender almost as reeds, supported the vaults of the cupolas, decorated with reliefs in the semblance of stalactites.

There were fountains in the halls, mosaics in the courts, festoons hung from the archways, a thousand delicacies of architecture, and everywhere a silence so profound that you could hear the flutter of a scarf or the echo of a sigh.

Julian waged war no more. He rested, surrounded by a people at peace ; and every day a crowd passed before him, bending their knees and kissing their hands after the manner of Orientals.

Robed in purple, he would stand, leaning forward, in the embrasure of a window remembering his hunts of former days ; and he would long to rush over the desert after gazelles and ostriches, to stalk leopards from hiding-places among the bamboos, to traverse forests full of rhinoceroses, to draw bow at eagles from the highest peaks of the most inaccessible mountains, to join battle with polar bears upon the icebergs of the sea.

Sometimes, in a dream, he pictured himself like our father Adam in Paradise, among all the animals. He had but to lift his arm to kill them. Or, perhaps, he would see them defile before him, two by two, in order of size, from the elephants and the lions down to the ermines and wild ducks, as on the day when they entered into Noah's Ark. From the depths of a cavern he hurled javelins at them with unfailing aim. Then came others. There was no end to them. And he would return to consciousness, rolling his eyes in a frenzy.

Princes whom he counted among his friends invited him to hunt with them. He always refused, hoping by this form of penitence to avert his doom ; for it seemed to him that the fate of his parents was bound up with the slaughtering of animals. But he suffered at never seeing them, and his other yearning began to be intolerable.

His wife, to distract him, sent for jugglers and dancing-girls.

She would accompany him, carried in an open litter, in the country ; at other times, lying on the deck of a sailing-boat, they watched the fish darting this way and that in the pellucid water. Often she would throw flowers at him ; or, crouched at his feet, she played on a three-stringed mandoline. Then placing both her hands together upon his shoulder, she would ask him in a timid voice :

" What is it that troubles you, dear lord ? "

And he would make no answer or would break into sobs. As last, one day, he confessed his terrible thought.

She combated it, reasoning out the matter very wisely : his father and mother were in all likelihood dead ; but if ever he should see them again, by what chance, from what motive, could he perpetrate such an enormity ? His fears were groundless, then, and he should resume the chase.

Julian smiled as he listened to her, but could not decide to yield to his craving.

One evening in August, when they were in their sleeping-room, she had just lain down and he was on his knees in prayer, when he heard the cry of a fox, followed by the sound of light footsteps beneath the window ; and in the darkness he seemed to descry the forms of animals. The temptation was too strong. He took down his quiver.

She seemed surprised.

" I am but obeying you," he said. " I shall be back at dawn."

But she was seized with dread of some disaster.

He reassured her and went out, astonished by her change of mood.

Not long afterwards a page came to her to announce that two unknown visitors, in the absence of the lord, begged to see his lady immediately.

And soon there came into the room an old man and an old woman garbed in cloth, covered with dust, their backs bent, leaning each one on a stick.

They took courage and declared that they came to Julian with news of his parents.

She leaned forward to listen.

But they, gaining confidence at the sight of her, inquired whether Julian still loved his parents, whether he spoke of them sometimes.

" Yes, indeed," she answered.

Then they cried out :

" We are they." And they sank down, being very weary and tired.

The young wife had no means of telling whether her husband was in truth their son.

They gave her proofs, describing particular marks that he had upon his skin.

She jumped up from her bed, called to her page, and food was set before them.

Although they were very hungry they could scarcely eat ; and she, seated apart, noticed how their bony fingers trembled when they raised the goblets.

They asked a thousand questions about Julian. She replied to each, taking care, however, to say nothing of the sinister idea that concerned them.

Seeing no signs of his return, they had left their castle and had been journeying for many years, led by vague traces of him, never losing hope. So much money had gone upon river-tolls and in inns, so much in taxes to princes or in compliance with the demands of robbers, that their purse was empty and they were now begging.

What mattered it now that so soon they were to embrace their son ? They acclaimed his good fortune in having so sweet a wife, and they never tired of gazing on her and of kissing her.

The richness of the apartments set them marvelling ; and the old man, scanning the walls, inquired why they were emblazoned with the arms of the Emperor of Occitania.

She replied :

" He is my father."

At this he began to tremble, recalling the prediction of the vagrant ; and the old woman thought of the words of the hermit. This greatness of her son was doubtless but the dawn of eternal splendours. They both sat open-mouthed beneath the light of the candelabra that illuminated the table.

They must have been very beautiful in their youth. The mother had still her full wealth of hair, and its delicate ringlets, as if modelled in snow, hung down beside her cheeks ; and the father, with his tall figure and flowing beard, looked like a statue in a church.

Julian's wife begged them not to sit up until his return. She put them into her own bed and then closed the window ; they fell asleep. Day was breaking ; outside the windows the little brids were beginning to sing.

Julian had crossed the park ; and he made his way through the forest with vigorous step, enjoying the springy soil and the mild air.

The shadows of the trees stretched out over the heath. Sometimes the moon made white splashes of light in the clearings, and he hesitated to advance thinking he had come upon a pond ; sometimes the surface of still pools was indistinguishable from the colour of the grass. There was everywhere a great silence ; and he could see not one of the animals which, a few minutes earlier, had been wandering round his castle.

The wood thickened, the darkness grew profound. Whiffs of warm air came and went, laden with enervating perfumes. He found his feet sinking into masses of dead leaves, and he leant against an oak to breathe a little.

Suddenly, behind his back, a darker shadow leapt by, a wild boar. Julian had not time to grasp his bow, and grieved over this as a misfortune.

Then, having emerged from the wood, he perceived a wolf making quickly along a hedgerow.

Julian let fly a bolt. The wolf stopped, turned its head round to look at him, and went on its way. It trotted on, keeping always the same distance, stopping now and again, and renewing its flight as soon as Julian had taken aim.

Julian traversed in this way an interminable expanse of ground, then came upon some small sandhills, and finally found himself on a plateau commanding a great space of country. Flat stones lay scattered among ruined vaults. He stumbled over dead men's bones; here and there worm-eaten crosses slanted miserably. But forms seemed to be moving in the indistinct shadows of the tombs; and hyenas issued forth, frightened, panting. Clattering their hoofs on the stones, they came up to him, exposing their gums as they sniffed at him. He drew his sword. They scattered in every direction, and, scampering off on their uneven, headlong way, disappeared far away in a cloud of dust.

An hour later, he encountered in a ravine an angry bull, horns down, scraping the sand with its hoof. Julian struck it under the dewlap with his lance. It broke into pieces as though the animal were made of bronze. He closed his eyes, and waited for his death. When he opened them again, the bull had disappeared.

Then his soul sank with shame. Some stronger power annulled his strength; turning homewards he re-entered the forest.

His path was impeded by climbing plants; he was cutting through them with his sword when a polecat slipped swiftly between his legs, a panther bounded over his shoulder, and a serpent circles up an ash-tree.

From out of the leaves of the ash a hideous jackdaw watched Julian; and here and there among the branches appeared innumerable sparkling lights, as though the firmament had rained down all its stars into the forest.

These were the eyes of animals—wild cats, squirrels, owls, parrots, and apes.

Julian let fly at them with his bolts; the bolts, with their feathers, rested on the leaves like white butterflies.

He threw stones, but the stones hit nothing and fell back upon the ground. He cursed himself, would have liked to strike himself, yelled imprecations, and choked with rage.

And all the animals he had hunted appeared and formed a narrow circle round him. Some of them were standing, others sitting on their haunches. He stood in their midst, frozen with terror, incapable of the slightest movement. At last, by a supreme effort of his will, he took a step forward; those who were perched in the trees opened their wings, those who crowded the earth stirred their limbs; and all went with him.

The hyenas went in front of him, the wolf and the boar behind. The bull, on his right, tossed its head; on his left, the serpent wound its way through the grass; while the panther, arching its back, advanced with long strides and velvet steps. He moved forward as slowly as possible, so as not to anger them; and he saw emerging from the depths of the underwood porcupines, foxes, vipers, jackals, and bears.

Julian began to run ; they ran with him. The serpent hissed ; the animals stank and slobbered. The boar scratched his heels with its tusks ; the wolf the palms of his hands with the bristles of its muzzle. The apes pinched him, making faces at him ; the polecat tumbled about beneath his feet. A bear, with a sweep of its paw, knocked off his hat ; and the panther contemptuously let fall a dart which it had been carrying in its throat.

There was irony in their sinister aspect. And while they watched him out of the corners of their eyes, they seemed to be meditating a plan of vengeance. He, stupefied by the buzz of the insects, battered by the wings of birds, suffocated by the breath of the beasts, moved forward with his arms outstretched and his eyelids closed, like a blind man, without even the strength to cry out for pity !

The crowing of a cock trembled in the air. Others answered ; it was daybreak ; and Julian descried the turrets of his castle above the orange-groves.

Then, at the side of a field, he saw, at a distance of three paces, three red-legged partridges flying about in the stubble. He swung off his cloak and threw it over them like a net.

Lifting it again, he found but one bird beneath it, and it had been long dead and was putrid.

This disappointment exasperated him more than all the others. His craving for carnage taking hold of him anew, and animals failing him, he would fain have slaughtered men.

He went up the three terraces, and broke open the gate with a blow of his fist ; but, at the bottom of the staircase, the memory of his dear wife softened his heart. Doubtless she still slept and he would surprise her.

Having removed his sandals, he gently turned the bolt of the door and entered.

The windows, lined with lead, dimmed the pale light of the dawn. Julian caught his feet in clothes lying on the floor ; a little further, he stumbled against a sideboard, still covered with plates and dishes. " No doubt she has had something to eat," he said, and he advanced towards the bed, that was hidden in the darkness at the other end of the room. When he was beside it, wishing to kiss his wife, he leaned over the pillow upon which the two heads rested side by side. And he felt upon his lips the touch of a beard.

He started back, thinking he had gone mad ; but he drew close to the bed again, and his fingers, groping, came upon tresses of hair that were very long. To convince himself that he had made a mistake, he moved his hand slowly back over the pillow. This time there could be no doubt—it was a beard and a man ! A man in bed with his wife !

Bursting with unbridled rage, he flung himself upon them with his poniard, stamping his feet, foaming at the mouth, uttering cries like a wild beast. Then he stopped. His victims, stabbed to the heart, had not even moved. He listened attentively to their breathing, and as it gradually failed, the sound of another's breathing came to him from afar. Vague at first, this drawn-out, plaintive sound drew nearer and nearer, and, increasing in volume, became painful : and, terrified, he recognised the throating of the great black stag.

And, as he turned, he thought he saw in the framework of the door the phantom of his wife, a light in her hand.

The noise of the murder had brought her to the room. A glance told her all, and fleeing in horror she left the torch fall.

He picked it up.

His father and mother were before him, lying upon their backs, with gaping wounds in their breasts ; and their countenances, filled with a gentle majesty, seemed to be guarding a secret for all time. Spots and splashes of blood bespattered their white skin, the bed-clothes, the ground, the ivory crucifix hanging in the alcove. The window, aglow now through the red dawn, intensified these crimson stains, and flung many others about the room. Julian walked towards the dead bodies, declaring to himself, striving to convince himself that it was not possible, that he was mistaken, that there were sometimes resemblances beyond understanding. At last, bending down to scan the old man's visage, he saw between the eyelids, not yet quite closed, lifeless eyes that burned like fire. Then he went round to the other side of the bed, where lay the second body, the white hair covering part of the face. Julian, placing his hand under the tresses, raised the head ; and he stood looking at it, holding it stiffly at arm's length, while with the other hand he lit up the features with the torch. Drops of blood dripping from the mattress fell one by one upon the floor.

At close of day Julian approached his wife ; and, in a voice unlike his own, he commanded her in the first place to make no answer to him, not to draw near him, not even to look at him ; under pain of damnation she was to carry out all his orders, which were irrevocable.

The funeral obsequies were to be arranged in accordance with instructions which he had left in writing, on a prie-dieu, in the death-chamber. He was leaving her the palace, with his vassals and all his goods, without even retaining the clothes he was wearing, or his sandals, which would be found at the top of the staircase.

She had fulfilled the will of God in bringing about the occasion of his crime ; she must pray for his soul, since henceforth he would cease to be.

The dead were interred with magnificence in the church of a monastery distant three days' journey from the castle. A monk with lowered cowl followed the procession, far from all the others, without any one daring to speak to him.

He remained throughout the Mass prostrated at the entrance to the church, his arms stretched wide, his forehead in the dust.

After the burial, he was seen to take the road which led to the mountains. He looked back several times, and at last disappeared.

III

He went off, begging his way throughout the world.

He held out his hand for alms to riders on the highroads, bent his knee to men gathering in the harvests, or stood motionless before the gates of farmyards; and his face was so sad that no one ever refused him.

In his spirit of humility, he recounted his history; then all fled from him, making the sign of the cross. In villages through which he had passed previously, doors were closed against him as soon as he was recognised, and people threatened him and threw stones at him. The more charitable placed dishes outside their windows, then closed the shutters so as not to see him.

Repulsed by every one, he avoided mankind; he lived on roots plants, odds and ends of fruit, and shellfish picked up along the beaches.

Sometimes, as he passed along the side of a hill, he saw down below a confused mass of roofs, with stone steeples, and towers, and bridges, and dark streets interlacing, whence a continual buzzing mounted to his ears.

The need he felt to mingle in the lives of others caused him to descend into the city. But the brutality of the faces he saw, the din of the crafts, the carelessness of their talk froze his heart. On days of festival, when the bells of the cathedrals set everybody rejoicing from break of day, he would watch the inhabitants issue forth from their houses, and stand looking on at the dances in the market-places and at the fountains of beer at the cross-roads; in the evening, he saw through the ground-floor windows the long family tables at which the grandparents sat, with small children on their knees; sobs choked him, and he went back into the country.

He observed with a rush of affection the colts grazing in the meadows, the birds in their nests, the insects upon the flowers; all, at his approach, ran off, hid themselves in terror, or flew swiftly away.

He sought solitudes. But the wind brought him sounds like those of a death-agony; the falling of drops of dew recalled to him the falling of other drops and heavier. The sun at evening touched the clouds with blood; and every night in his dreams he went through his parricide again.

He made himself a penitential shirt with small iron spikes in it.

He climbed on his knees all hills that had chapels on their summits. But the remorseless memory darkened the splendour of the tabernacles ; no penance could distract him from its tortures.

He did not turn against God, who had destined him to this act, and yet he was in despair at having been capable of committing it.

His own physical being filled him with so much horror that in the hope of ridding himself of it he ventured it in peril. He saved cropples from burning houses, children from the depths of chasms. The abyss gave him back, the flames spared him.

Time brought no relief to his sufferings. They grew unbearable. He resolved to die.

And one day, having come upon a well, and having leant over it to judge the depth of the water, he saw appear before him an emaciated old man, with a white beard, and an aspect so sad that at the sight of him he could not restrain his tears. The old man wept also. Not recognising his own image, Julian recalled vaguely a similar countenance. He uttered a cry : it was his father's. And he put away the thought of killing himself.

In this way, bearing the burden of his memories, he traversed many lands ; and he came at last to a river which was dangerous to cross by reason of its violence and of the great extent of slimy mud upon its banks. For a long time past no one had dared to make the crossing.

An old boat, its stern sunk in the mud, lifted its prow among the reeds. Julian, examining it, found a pair of oars, and the idea came to him that he might devote his life to the service of others.

He began by making a sort of causeway down the bank, enabling people to reach the river ; and he broke his finger-nails in his efforts to shift the huge stones which he carried, holding them against his stomach. Often he lost his footing and slipped into the slime, and narrowly escaped with his life.

Then he repaired the boat with bits of wreckage, and he constructed himself a cabin out of clay and the trunks of trees.

The ferry becoming known, passengers began to appear. From the opposite bank they would hail him by waving flags, and Julian would quickly jump into his boat. It was very heavy ; and it would be weighed down with all kinds of goods and chattels, without counting the beasts of burden, that, restive from fear, encumbered him still more. He asked for no recompense for his labours ; some would give him what was left of the victuals they carried in their wallet, or worn-out garments for which they had no further use. When men of brutal habits broke out in blasphemy, Julian reproved them gently, and they answered him with insults. He contented himself with blessing them.

A small table, a bench, a couch of dead leaves, and three cups made of clay, that was all his furniture. Two holes in the wall served as windows. On one side stretched out barren plains flecked here and there with pools of colourless water; and the great river in front rolled its greenish flood. In the spring the damp earth gave out a putrid odour. Then a violent wind raised whirlwinds of dust. The dust permeated everything; it turned the water he drank into mud, and gritted his gums. A little later there were clouds of mosquitoes, from whose buzzing and stings there was no respite day or night. And then followed terrible frost, which turned things to the hardness of stone and inspired a mad longing to eat meat.

Months passed without Julian's seeing any one. Often he closed his eyes, endeavouring in memory to return to the days of his youth; and the courtyard of the castle came back to him, with the greyhounds upon the steps, attendants in the *salle d'armes*, and, in an arbour of vine-branches, a fair-haired youth seated between an old man covered with furs and a lady wearing a high head-dress; then, in a moment, the two dead bodies were before his eyes. He threw himself face downwards upon his bed, and cried out over and over again, weeping:

"Oh! Poor father! Poor mother! Poor mother!"

And he fell into a troubled sleep in which the dread visions still haunted him.

One night, as he slept, he thought he heard some one calling him. He lent ear, and could distinguish nothing but the roaring of the waters.

But the voice came back:

"Julian!"

It came from the other bank, and this seemed to him extraordinary by reason of the breadth of the river.

A third time it called:

"Julian!"

And this penetrating voice had the tone of a church bell.

Having lit his lantern, he went out of his cabin. A furious gale filled the night. The darkness was profound. Here and there were faint flashes of white waves.

After a minute's hesitation, Julian pushed off. The water became calm immediately, the boat glided across and touched the opposite bank, upon which a man stood waiting.

He was enveloped in ragged garments, his face looked like a death-mask, and his two eyes were redder than live coals. Holding the lantern up to him, Julian perceived that he was covered with a hideous leprosy; nevertheless there was in his bearing something of the majesty of a king.

When he set foot on the boat, it sank deep down beneath his weight, but it righted with a shock and Julian began to row.

At every stroke of the oars the boat rose upon the waves. The water, blacker than ink, swept fiercely past the gunwale, now sinking into gulfs, now rising into mountains ; and the boat leapt over them and sank again into the depths, blown this way and that by the wind.

Julian leant forward, stretched out his arms, and, making sure of his foothold, twisted himself round so as to acquire more power over the boat. The hail stung his hands, the rain poured down his back, the force of the wind made him breathless, and he ceased rowing. Then the boat drifted down-stream. But, feeling that a great matter was at stake, a command which he must not disobey, he seized the oars again ; and their click-clack against the thole-pin cut into the clamouring of the wind.

The little lantern burnt in front of him. Birds flying past obscured it momentarily. But always he saw the eyes of the leper who stood upright at the stern, motionless as a column.

And this lasted a long time, a very long time.

When at last they reached the cabin, Julian closed the door ; he saw the leper sitting on the bench. The shroud-like garments which he wore had fallen to his hips ; and his shoulders, his breast, his meagre arms, were covered with scaly sores. Enormous wrinkles furrowed his brow. Like a skeleton, he had a hole in place of a nose ; and his bluish lips emitted a dense, mist-like, sickening breath.

" I hunger ! " he said.

Julian gave him what he had, an old piece of bacon and some crusts of black bread.

When he had devoured them, the table, the porringer, and the handle of the knife bore the same stains that marked his body.

Then he said, " I thirst ! "

Julian went in search of his jug ; and as he lifted it, there came from it an aroma that distended his heart and his nostrils. It was wine ! What a discovery ! But the leper reached for it and at one draught emptied the jug.

Then he said, " I am cold ! "

Julian, with his candle, lit a bundle of brushwood in the middle of the cabin.

The leper approached it to warm himself ; and, crouching upon his heels, he began to tremble in all his limbs, and to lose strength ; his eyes glowed no longer, his ulcers ran, and, in a voice almost dying, he murmured :

" Thy bed ! "

Julian gently helped him to drag himself to it, and even drew over him his boat cloth as a covering.

The leper groaned. His teeth showed at the corners of his mouth, his breast shook with a thick rattle, and his stomach at every breath he drew became hollow to the spine.

Then he closed his eyes.

" I feel as though I had ice in my veins !   Come near me ! "

And Julian, raising the cloth, lay down upon the dead leaves, close to him, side by side.

The leper turned his head.

" Undress, so that I may have the warmth of thy body ! "

Julian took off his clothes ; then, naked as on the day of his birth, lay down again upon the bed ; and he felt against his thigh the skin of the leper, colder than a snake's and as rough as a file.

He tried to encourage him ; and the leper replied, panting :

" Ah, I am going to die ! . . . Come nearer me, warm me ! Not with thy hands—no, with thy whole body ! "

Julian spread himself all over him mouth against mouth, breast on breast.

Then the leper strained Julian to him and his eyes suddenly took on the radiance of stars ; his hair spread out like rays of sunlight ; the breath from his nostrils had the sweetness of roses ; a cloud of incense rose from the hearth-stone, and the waters sang outside.   And a flood of ecstasies, a joy superhuman, swept through the fainting soul of Julian ; and he whose arms still enfolded him became greater and ever greater, touching with his head and his feet the two walls of the cabin.   The roof flew off, the firmament opened out ; and Julian ascended towards the blue depths beyond, face to face with Our Lord Jesus who carried him to Heaven.

And that, as nearly as may be, is the story of St. Julian the Hospitaller, as it is to be found on a church window in my country.

CHARLES BAUDELAIRE
1821–1867

AN HEROIC DEATH

FANCIULLO was an admirable buffoon, and almost one of the friends of the Prince. But for persons vowed by their positions to the comic side of life, serious things have a fatal attraction ; and though it may appear odd that ideas of liberty and the fatherland should despotically take possession of the brain of an actor, one day Fanciullo joined in a plot formed by several discontented gentlemen.

Everywhere there exists some good man to denounce to the government those individuals of atrabilious humour who wish to depose princes and carry out a change of society without consulting the people. The lords in question were arrested, together with Fanciullo, and condemned to certain death.

I would willingly believe that the Prince was almost sorry to find his favourite comedian among the rebels. The Prince was neither better nor worse than other rulers ; but an excessive delicacy of feeling rendered him in many cases more cruel and more tyrannical than other men in similar positions. A passionate lover of the fine arts, excellent connoisseur besides, he was truly insatiable of pleasure. Fairly indifferent in regard to men and morality, veritable artist himself, he knew no peril except that of boredom. The strange efforts he made to fly or conquer this tyrant of the world would certainly have drawn on him from a severe historian the epitaph of " monster " if it had been permitted in his domains to write anything that did not tend solely to give pleasure or astonishment, which is one of the most delicate forms of pleasure. The great misfortune of the Prince was that he never had a theatre vast enough for his genius. There are young Neros who stifle in too narrow limits and of whose names and good intentions future ages will be ignorant. Unforeseen Providence had given to this man faculties greater than his territories.

Of a sudden the rumour ran that the Prince intended to pardon all the plotters. And the origin of this rumour was the announcement of a grand spectacle, in which Fanciullo would play one of his chief and best parts, with, it was said, the assistance of the condemned gentlemen—an evident sign, added the shallow minds, of the generous intentions of the offended Prince.

On the part of a man so naturally and willingly eccentric, everything was possible—even virtue, even clemency—above all, if he could possibly hope to find in it some unexpected pleasure. But to those who, like myself, had been able to penetrate further into the depths of this sick and curious soul, it was infinitely more probable that the Prince wished to judge the genius for acting in a man condemned to death. He wished to profit by the occasion to make a physiological experiment of capital interest, and verify up to what point the habitual habits of an artist could be changed or modified by the extraordinary situation in which he found himself. Beyond that, did there exist in the soul of the Prince a more or less settled intention to clemency? This is a point that no one has ever been able to clear up.

At last the great day arrived. The little court displayed its full pomp, and it would be hard to conceive, without at least having seen it, all that the privileged class of a little state with restrained resources can show in splendours on an occasion of true solemnity. This was a doubly true solemnity, first from the enchantment of luxury displayed there, and then from the moral and mysterious interest attaching to the affair.

Master Fanciullo excelled especially in dumb rôles, or those lightly charged with words. These parts are often the most important in those pantomime dramas that aim at representing by symbols the mystery of life. He entered the stage lightly and with perfect ease, and this contributed to strengthen in the noble public the idea of gentleness and pardon.

When it is said of a comedian, "There is a good comedian," the saying implies that the man can still be glimpsed beneath the character he plays. That is to say, art, effort, and will power can be guessed at. Now, if an actor succeeded in being, relative to the character he had to express, what the finest statues of antiquity would be—miraculously animated, living, moving, seeing—relative to the general and confused idea of beauty, that would be, without a doubt, a singular and quite unlooked-for event. Fanciullo was that evening a perfect idealisation, which it was impossible not to suppose—living, possible, real. The buffoon came and went, laughed, cried, convulsed himself, with an indestructible halo round his head, a halo invisible to all else but me, in which were mingled in a strange amalgam the beams of art and the glory of martyrdom.

By I know not what special grace, Fanciullo introduced the divine and supernatural into the most extravagant buffooneries. My pen trembles, and tears, born of an emotion always present, rise to my eyes while I seek to describe to you that unforgettable evening. Fanciullo proved to me in a peremptory, irrefutable manner that the intoxication of art is more apt than all other to veil the terrors of the abyss ; that genius can play in comedy at the brink of the grave with a joy that prevents it from seeing the grave, lost, as it is, in a paradise excluding all idea of death and destruction.

All the audience, surfeited and frivolous as it may have been, soon submitted to the almighty power of the artist. No one thought any more of death, of mourning, or of suffering. Each abandoned himself without disquietude to the multiplied delights given by a masterpiece of living art. Explosions of joy and admiration shook again and again the vaults of the building with the energy of continued thunder. The Prince himself, drunk with pleasure, mingled his applause with that of his court. Still, to a clear-seeing eye, his intoxication was not pure of all admixture. Did he feel himself overcome in his power as a despot ; humiliated in his power of terrifying hearts and benumbing minds ; frustrated in his hopes and baffled in his provisions ? Such suppositions, not exactly justified, but not absolutely unjustifiable, crossed my mind, while I contemplated the countenance of the Prince, on which a new pallor was continually added to his habitual pallor, as snow is added to snow. His lips tightened more and more, and his eyes lightened up with an inner fire resembling that of jealousy or spite, even while he was ostensibly applauding the talents of his old friend, the strange jester, who jested so well with death. At a certain moment I saw His Highness lean towards a little page, placed behind him, and speak in his ear. The mischievous face of the pretty child lighted up with a smile, and then he alertly left the royal box as though to carry out some urgent commission.

Several minutes later, the sound of a shrill, prolonged hiss interrupted Fanciullo in one of his best moments, and rent both ears and hearts. And from the place in the hall where this unexpected disapprobation had burst forth, a child ran into a corridor with muffled laughter.

Fanciullo, shaken, roused from his dream, at first shut his eyes, then opened them almost at once, immeasurably enlarged, then opened his mouth in a convulsive breath, staggered a little in front and a little behind, and then fell stone-dead on the planks.

Had the hiss, swift as a sword, really frustrated the headsman ? Had the Prince himself divined all the murderous efficacy of his trick ? It is permitted to doubt it. Did he regret his dear and inimitable Fanciullo ? It is sweet and legitimate to believe it.

The guilty lords had played for the last time in the comic spectacle. On the same night they were effaced from life. Since then, several mimes, justly esteemed in different countries, have come to play before the court, but none of them has been able to remind us of the wonderful talents of Fanciullo, nor rise to the same favour.

THE CORD

Charles Baudelaire

Illusions, said my friend to me, are perhaps as innumerable as the relations of men with men, or of men with things. And when an illusion disappears, that is to say, when we see the man or the thing as it exists outside us, we feel an odd emotion, made up half of regret for the vanished phantom, half of delightful surprise over the novelty of the real fact. For instance, if there exists an evident, commonplace, unchanging phenomenon with a character that it is impossible to deceive oneself about, it is maternal love. It is as difficult to think of a mother without maternal love as of light without heat. Is it not then perfectly legitimate to attribute to maternal affection all the actions and words of a mother in connection with her child? Yet listen to this little story, in which I have been strangely mystified by the most natural of illusions.

My work as a painter leads me to study attentively the faces, the physiognomies, that strike me when I am out walking. You know what delight we get from this faculty which to our eyes makes life more living and more significant than for other men. In the remote part of the town where I live, with large grassy spaces still separating the buildings, I often observed a boy who pleased me from the first by his ardent and mischievous features that distinguished him from all his playfellows. More than once he used to pose for me, and I have transformed him now into a little gipsy, now into an angel, now into mythological Love. I have made him bear the violin of the vagrant, the crown of thorns and nails of the Passion, and the lighted torch of Eros.

At last I took so lively a pleasure in all the drolleries of this urchin that one day I begged his parents—very poor people—to let me look after him. I promised I would feed and clothe him and give him a little money, and not overwork him while cleaning my brushes and running errands for me. The lad, when his face was washed, became charming, and the life he led in my studio seemed to him heavenly in comparison with that which he had known in his dirty hovel of a home. Only I must tell you that this little chap sometimes astonished me by strange moods of precocious melancholy, and that he soon showed an excessive taste for sugar and liqueurs. One day I found that, in spite of my numerous warnings, he had again committed a fresh larceny of this kind, and I threatened to send him back to his parents. Then I went out on some business that took me a pretty long time, and it was late before I got back.

And oh, my horror and astonishment when I entered my house ! The first object that struck my eyes was my little chum, the roguish companion of my life, hanging from the panel of the wardrobe. His feet almost touched the ground ; a chair, that he no doubt had kicked over, was upset by his side. His head leaned convulsively on his shoulder, his swollen face and his eyes, quite wide open with a terrifying fixity, gave me at first an illusion that he was alive. Getting him down was not as easy a task as you would think. He was already very stiff, and I had an explicable repugnance to let him abruptly tumble on the ground. It was necessary to support him with one arm, and cut the cord with the other hand. But when that was done the work was not finished. The little wretch had used a very thin thread that had bitten deeply into his flesh, and it was necessary to search for the cord, with fine scissors, between the two ridges of swollen flesh, in order to free his neck.

I neglected to tell you that I had quickly shouted for help. All my neighbours, however, refused to come to my aid, faithful in that to the habits of civilised man, who will never, I don't know why, have anything to do with a hanging affair. At last the doctor came, and he declared that the child had been dead for some hours. When later we had to undress him for burial, the rigidity of the corpse was such that, despairing of bending the limbs, we had to cut and tear the clothes to get them off.

The police officer to whom, naturally, I had to report the accident, looked at me sideways, and said, " This is very suspicious ! " moved no doubt by an inveterate desire and a habit of mind of making everybody afraid, at all costs, whether innocent or guilty.

There remained a supreme task to accomplish, the mere thought of which gave me terrible pain. It was necessary to inform the parents. My feet refused to take me to them. At last I plucked up courage. But, to my great astonishment, the mother was impassible. Not a tear oozed from the corner of her eye. I attributed this strange thing to the horror she must feel, and I remembered the well-known saying : " The most terrible sorrow is a silent sorrow." As for the father, he contented himself with saying, half brutally, half dreamily, " After all, it is perhaps just as well ; he would always have finished badly ! "

However, the body was stretched on my sofa, and, helped by a serving-maid, I was carrying out the last duties to the dead, when the mother entered my studio. She wished, she said, to see the corpse of her son. I could not in truth prevent her from intoxicating herself with her grief, and refuse her this supreme and sombre consolation. Then she begged me to show her the spot where her little one had hanged himself.

"Oh no, Madame," I answered her, "that would upset you!"

And as my eyes unconsciously turned towards the deadly wardrobe, I perceived, with a mixture of disgust and anger, that the nail remained in the wood, with a long length of cord still trailing from it. I sprang up quickly to get rid of these last traces of the misfortune, and as I was about to fling them away through the open window, the poor woman seized my arm and said in an irresistible voice:

"Oh, sir! Let me have that! I beg you! I implore you, sir!"

It seemed to me that her despair had reached such a point of infatuation that she was now seized with a kind of tenderness for that which had been the instrument of her son's death, and wished to keep it as a dear, horrible relic.

She went away with the nail and the cord; and at last! at last! all was over. I had nothing more to do than to set again to work, harder than usual, to drive away little by little the young corpse that haunted the folds of my brain, and whose phantom, with its large fixed eyes, wore me out. But the next day I received a packet of letters. Some were from the tenants in my house; others from neighbouring houses; one from the first floor; another from the second; another from the third, and so on. Some in a half-joking style, seeking to disguise under an apparent jest the sincerity of the demand; others heavily impudent, and full of bad spelling; but all tending to the same end, that is to say, to obtain from me a piece of the fatal and blessed cord. Among the writers there were, I daresay, more women than men, but they did not all, believe me, belong to the vulgar and lowest class. I have kept those letters.

And then, suddenly, my mind lighted up, and I understood why the mother was so bent on snatching the cord away from me, and by what kind of trade she intended to console herself.

HENRI MÜRGER
1822–1861

FRANCINE'S MUFF

AMONG the true Bohemians of the true Bohemia, I once knew one named Jacques D——; he was a sculptor, and gave promise of showing talent some day. But misery did not give him time to fulfil these promises; he died of exhaustion in the month of March 1844, in the Hospital St. Louis, Ward St. Victoire, bed No. 14.

I knew Jacques in the hospital, where I was myself detained by a prolonged illness. Mademoiselle Francine had been Jacques' sole and only sweetheart; he did not, however, die old, for he was scarcely twenty-three years of age. This love-story was told to me by Jacques himself, when he was No. 14 and I No. 16 of the Ward St. Victoire—an ugly spot in which to die.

Jacques and Francine had met in a house in the Rue de la Tour d'Auvergne, where they had both taken lodgings in the same April quarter. The artist and the young girl were a whole week before they entered into those neighbourly relations into which dwellers on the same floor are almost always forced; yet, without having ever exchanged a word, they already knew one another. Francine knew that her neighbour was a poor devil of an artist, and Jacques had heard that his neighbour was a little dressmaker, who had left her family to escape the unkind treatment of her stepmother. She performed miracles of economy to make both ends meet, as it is called; and as she had never known any pleasures, she did not covet them. This is how it came about that they broke through the restraint of the partition-wall. One evening in the month of April Jacques returned home worn out with fatigue, having fasted since the morning, and intensely sad with that vague sadness which has no exact cause, which comes over us anywhere, at any time—a sort of apoplexy of the heart, to which those unfortunate beings who live alone are particularly subject. Jacques, feeling stifled in his narrow cell, opened the window to breathe a little. The evening was fine, and the setting sun was displaying its melancholy enchantments on the hills of Montmartre. Jacques remained pensively at his casement, listening to the winged choir of springtime harmonies singing in the quiet of eve, and that increased his sadness. Seeing a croaking raven fly before him, he thought of the time when ravens brought bread to Elijah; and he said to himself that ravens are not so charitable now. Then, able to endure this no longer, he closed the window, drew the curtain, and, since he had no money to buy oil for his lamp, he lighted a candle of resin that he had brought back with him from an excursion to the Grande Chartreuse. Growing sadder and sadder, he filled his pipe.

"Fortunately I have still tobacco enough to hide the pistol," he muttered, and began to smoke.

My friend Jacques must have been very sad that evening to think of hiding the pistol. It was his last resource in extreme cases, and it was generally successful. This is how it was done; Jacques smoked tobacco on which he had poured a few drops of laudanum, and he smoked until the cloud of smoke from his pipe had become so thick as to hide from him all the objects in the little room, and especially a pistol that hung on the wall. It needed some ten pipes to do this. When the pistol had become quite invisible, it almost always happened that the smoke and the laudanum combined sent Jacques to sleep; and it happened just as often that his sadness left him on the threshold of his dreams.

But this evening he had used up his tobacco, the pistol was completely hidden, and still Jacques was grievously sad. This evening Mademoiselle Francine, on the contrary, was particularly cheerful on returning home; and there was no cause for her cheerfulness any more than for Jacques' sadness. Hers was the sort of gaiety that drops from heaven, and that God puts into good hearts. Thus Mademoiselle Francine was in a joyous humour, and she sang as she mounted the staircase. But just as she was about to open her door, a gust of wind from the open landing-window suddenly extinguished her light.

"Dear me, how tiresome!" exclaimed the young girl. "Now I shall have to go down and up six flights of stairs again."

Then, perceiving a light beneath Jacques' door, an impulse of laziness, combined with a feeling of curiosity, suggested to her to go and beg a light of the artist. "It is a service that neighbours render one another daily," thought she, "and cannot be misconstrued." She therefore gave two little taps at Jacques' door, which he opened, a little surprised at this late visit. But hardly had she made a step into the room, when the smoke with which it was filled suffocated her; and, without being able to speak a word, she fell fainting into a chair, and let her candle and key fall to the ground. It was midnight, and every one in the house was fast asleep. Jacques did not think it advisable to call for help, for he feared to bring his neighbour into an uncomfortable situation. He therefore merely opened the window to let in a little fresh air; and when he had thrown a few drops of water into the young girl's face, he saw her open her eyes and gradually come to herself.

When, at the end of five minutes, she had entirely recovered consciousness, Francine explained her motive for having come to the artist, and apologised much for what had happened.

"Now I am well again," added she, "I can return to my own room."

And he had already opened the door before she perceived that she had forgotten to light her candle, and had not the key of her room.

"Silly that I am," said she, applying her candle to the resin-taper. "I came in here to fetch a light, and I was going away without it."

But at that very moment the draught in the room, caused by the open door and window, suddenly put out the light, and the two young people were in the dark.

"One might think it was done on purpose," said Francine. "Forgive me, sir, for all the trouble I am giving you; and be so good as to strike a light, so that I may find my key."

"Certainly, mademoiselle," answered Jacques, as he felt about for his matches.

He very soon found them; but a strange idea crossed his mind. He slipped the matches into his pocket, exclaiming:

"Alas, mademoiselle, here is a new difficulty. I have not a single match by me; I used the last when I came in."

"This is an audaciously well-planned artifice," thought he to himself.

"Dear, dear!" exclaimed Francine. "I could easily get back to my room without a light; the room is not so large that I could lose my way in it. But I must have my key. I beg of you, sir, help me to look for it; it must be on the floor."

"Let us look, mademoiselle," said Jacques.

And there were they both in the dark hunting for the object of their search; but, as though they were both guided by the same instinct, it happened that during this search their hands, which were feeling about in the same place, met each other ten times a minute. And as they were both equally clumsy, they did not find the key.

"The moon, which is now hidden by the clouds, shines full on my room," said Jacques. "Let us wait a little; presently it may illuminate our search."

And so, while they awaited the rising of the moon, they began to chat. A chat in the midst of darkness, in a narrow chamber, on a spring night; a chat, which, at first frivolous and insignificant, gradually touches on the chapter of confidences—well, you know to what that leads. Sentences after a while become confused, full of reticence; the voice low; words alternate with sighs; hands meet and complete the thought which mounts from the heart to the lips, and—— Seek the conclusion in your own memory, O young couples! Recall it, young man, recall it, young woman, who walk

42*

to-day hand-in-hand, and who had never seen each other two days ago.

At last the moon unveiled, and its clear light poured into the room. Mademoiselle Francine started from her musings with a little cry.

" What ails you ? " asked Jacques, putting his arm round her waist.

" Nothing," murmured Francine. " I thought I heard some one knock." And, without Jacques observing it, she kicked under a piece of furniture the key she had just perceived.

She did not want to find it.

.   .   .   .   .   .

I have promised you a muff ; and I will give it you presently, as my friend Jacques did to his poor friend Francine, who had become his mistress, as I explained to you in the blank lines above. She was fair, was Francine—fair and lively, which is not usual. She met with Jacques, and she loved him. Their union lasted six months. They had met in the spring ; they parted in the autumn. Francine was consumptive ; she knew it, and her friend knew it too. A fortnight after he became intimate with the young girl he had heard it from one of his friends, who was a doctor. " She will leave you when the leaves are yellow," he had said.

Francine had heard this verdict, and perceived the despair that it caused her friend.

" What matter the yellow leaves ? " she said to him, throwing all her love into a smile. " What matters the autumn ? We are in summer now, and the leaves are green ; let us make use of it, my friend. When you see me ready to leave this life, you will take me in your arms and kiss me, and you will forbid me to go. I am obedient, you know, and I shall stay."

And thus this charming creature encountered during five months the troubles of Bohemian life, with a song and a smile on her lips. As for Jacques, he let himself be blinded. His friend often said to him, " Francine is getting worse ; she needs care." Then Jacques ran about all over Paris trying to obtain the needful means for carrying out the doctor's directions ; but Francine would not have him speak of it, and threw the medicines out of the window. In the night when her cough seized her, she would leave the room and go out on to the landing, so that Jacques might not hear her.

One day, when they had both gone to the country, Jacques perceived a tree whose foliage was turning yellow. He looked sadly at Francine, who walked slowly and somewhat musingly.

Francine saw Jacques turn pale, and she guessed the cause of his pallor.

" Go along with you, you are foolish ! " said she, kissing him. " We are only in July ; there are three months still to October ; and by loving each other night and day, as we do, we shall double the time we have to spend together. And besides, if I should feel worse when the leaves turn yellow, we will go and live together in a pine-wood : there the leaves are always green."

. . . .

In the month of October Francine was obliged to keep her bed. Jacques' friend attended her. The little chamber in which they lodged was situated at the very top of the house and looked out into a yard, whence uprose a tree which daily lost more and more leaves. Jacques had put a curtain before the window to hide this tree from the invalid, but Francine insisted on his drawing back the curtain.

" O my friend," said she to Jacques, " I will give you a hundred times as many kisses as it has leaves." And she would add, " Besides, I am a great deal better. I shall soon go out ; but as it will be cold, and I do not want to have red hands, you shall buy me a muff."

During her whole illness this muff was her only dream.

On All Saints' Eve, seeing Jacques more distressed than usual, she wanted to cheer him ; and to show him that she was better, she got up. The doctor arrived at that moment, and forced her to go back to bed.

" Jacques," he whispered to the artist, " be brave. All is over ; Francine is dying."

Jacques burst into tears.

" You may give her anything she asks for now," added the doctor ; " there is no more hope."

Francine heard with her eyes what the doctor had said to her lover.

" Do not listen to him ! " exclaimed she, stretching out her arms to Jacques ; " do not listen to him, he lies ! We will go out together to-morrow ; it is All Saints' Day. It will be cold ; go and buy me a muff, I beg of you, for I am afraid of getting chilblains this winter."

Jacques was going out with his friend, but Francine detained the doctor.

" Go and get my muff," said she to Jacques ; " get the best, so that it may last a long time." But when she was alone with the doctor, she said, " Oh, sir, I am going to die, and I know it ! But before you go, find me something that will give me strength for one night. I beg of you, make me beautiful for one more night ; and after that let me die, since the Lord does not wish me to live any longer."

As the doctor was consoling her to the best of his power, a north-easterly blast blew into the room, and threw upon the sick-bed a yellow leaf, torn from the tree in the little yard. Francine drew back the curtain, and saw that the tree was now quite bare.

" It is the last," she said, as she placed the leaf under her pillow.

"You will not die till to-morrow," said the doctor; "you have one night more."

"Oh, what happiness!" cried the young girl. "A winter's night! It shall be long."

Jacques came back: he brought a muff.

"It is very pretty," said Francine; "I shall wear it for going out."

Next day, All Saints' Day, while the Angelus bell was ringing, her last agony seized her, and her whole body began to tremble.

"My hands are cold," she murmured; "give me my muff." And she plunged her poor hands into the fur.

"It is over," said the doctor; "go and kiss her."

Jacques pressed his lips on those of his love.

At the last moment they wanted to remove the muff, but she clutched it in her hands.

"No, no," she said; "leave it me; it is winter, and so cold. Ah, my poor Jacques! ah, my poor Jacques! what will become of you? O my God!"

And the next day Jacques was alone.

．　　．　　．　　．　　．　　．　　．　　．　　．

After some silent prayers the procession moved towards the cemetery. When it had come to the appointed grave the Bohemian brotherhood, with bared heads, grouped themselves around it. Jacques stood at the brink; his friend, the doctor, supported his arm. In the midst of his sobs the doctor heard this cry of egotism escape from his lips.

"O my youth! it is you that they bury."

"THE PASSAGE OF THE RED SEA"

HENRI MÜRGER

MARCEL had worked for five or six years upon the famous painting which he said was meant to represent the Passage of the Red Sea; and for five or six years this masterpiece of colour had been obstinately rejected by the jury. Indeed, from its constant journeying back and forth, from the artist's studio to the Salon, and from the Salon to the studio, the painting knew the road so well that you needed only to set it on castors and it would have found its way alone to the Louvre. Marcel, who had repainted the picture ten times, and minutely gone over it from top to bottom, vowed that only a personal hostility on the part of the members of the jury could account for the ostracism which annually turned him away from the Salon, and in his idle moments he had composed, in honour of those watch-dogs of the Academy, a little dictionary of insults, with illustrations of a savage irony. This collection gained celebrity and enjoyed, among the studios and in the École des Beaux-Arts, the same sort of popular success as that achieved by the immortal complaint of Giovanni Bellini, painter by appointment to the Grand Sultan of the Turks ; every dauber in Paris had a copy stored away in his memory.

For a long time Marcel had not allowed himself to be discouraged by the emphatic refusals which greeted him at every exhibition. He was comfortably settled in his opinion that his picture was, in a modest way, the companion piece long awaited by " The Wedding of Cana," that gigantic masterpiece whose dazzling splendour the dust of three centuries has not dimmed. Accordingly, each year, at the time of the Salon, Marcel sent his picture to be examined by the jury. Only, in order to throw the committee off the track and if possible to make them abandon the policy of exclusion which they seemed to have adopted toward " The Passage of the Red Sea," Marcel, without in any way disturbing the general scheme of his picture, modified certain details and changed its title.

For instance, on one occasion it arrived before the jury under the name of " The Passage of the Rubicon " ; but Pharaoh, poorly disguised under Caesar's mantle, was recognised and repulsed with all the honours that were his due.

The following year, Marcel spread over the level plane of his picture a layer of white representing snow, planted a pine-tree in one corner, and clothing an Egyptian as a grenadier of the Imperial Guard, re-christened the painting " The Passage of the Beresina."

The jury, which on that very day had polished its spectacles on the lining of its illustrious coat, was not in any way taken in by this new trick. It recognised perfectly well the persistent painting by, above all, a big brute of a horse of many colours, which was rearing out of one of the waves of the Red Sea. The coat of that horse had served Marcel for all his experiments in colour, and in private conversation he called it his synoptic table of fine tones, because he had reproduced, in their play of light and shade, all possible combinations of colour. But once again, insensible to this detail, the jury seemed scarcely able to find blackballs enough to emphasize their refusal of " The Passage of the Beresina."

" Very well," said Marcel ; " no more than I expected. Next year I shall send it back under the title of ' Passage des Panoramas.' "

" That will be one against them—against them—against them, them, them," sang his friend the musician Schaunard, fitting the words to a new air he had been composing—a terrible air, noisy as a gamut of thunder-claps, and the accompaniment to which was a terror to every piano in the neighbourhood.

"How could they refuse that picture without having every drop of the vermilion in my Red Sea rise up in their faces and cover them with shame?" murmured Marcel, as he gazed at the painting. "When one thinks that it contains a good hundred crowns' worth of paint, and a million of genius, not to speak of all my fair youth, fast growing bald as my hat! But they shall never have the last word; until my dying breath I shall keep on sending them my painting. I want to engrave it upon their memory."

"That is certainly the surest way of ever getting it engraved," said another Bohemian, Gustave Colline, in a plaintive voice, adding to himself, "That was a good one, that was—really a good one; I must get that off the next time I am asked out."

Marcel continued his imprecations, which Schaunard continued to set to music.

"Oh, they won't accept me," said Marcel. "Ah! the government pays them, boards them, gives them the decorations, solely for the purpose of refusing me once a year, on the 1st of March. I see their idea clearly now—I see it perfectly clearly; they are trying to drive me to break my brushes. They hope, perhaps, by refusing my Red Sea, to make me throw myself out of the window in despair. But they know very little of the human heart if they expect to catch me with such a clumsy trick. I shall no longer wait for the time of the annual Salon. Beginning with to-day, my work becomes the canvas of Damocles, eternally suspended over their existence. Henceforward I am going to send it once a week to each one of them, at their homes, in the bosom of their families, in the full heart of their private life. It shall trouble their domestic joy, it shall make them think that their wine is sour, their dinner burned, their wives bad-tempered. They will very soon become insane, and will have to be put in strait-jackets when they go to the Academy, on the days when there are meetings. That idea pleases me."

A few days later, when Marcel had already forgotten his terrible plans for vengeance upon his persecutors, he received a visit from Father Medicis. For that was the name by which the brotherhood called a certain Jew, whose real name was Solomon, and who at that time was well known throughout the Bohemia of art and literature, with which he constantly had dealings. Father Medicis dealt in all sorts of bric-à-brac. He sold complete sets of furniture from twelve francs up to a thousand crowns. He would buy anything, and knew how to sell it again at a profit. His shop, situated in the Place du Carrousel, was a fairy spot where one could find everything that one might wish. All the products of nature, all the creations of art, all that comes forth from the bowels of the earth or from the genius of man, Medicis found it profitable to trade in. His dealings included everything, absolutely everything that exists ; he even put a price upon the Ideal. Medicis would even buy ideas, to use himself or to sell again. Known to all writers and artists, intimate friend of the palette, familiar spirit of the writing-desk, he was the Asmodeus of the arts. He would sell you cigars in exchange for the plot of a sensational novel, slippers for a sonnet, a fresh fish for a paradox ; he would talk at so much an hour with newspaper reporters whose duty was to record society scandals. He would get you a pass to parliament, or invitations to private parties ; he gave lodgings by the night, the week, or the month to homeless artists, who paid him by making copies of old masters in the Louvre. The green-room had no secrets for him ; he could place your plays for you with some manager ; he could obtain for you all sorts of favours. He carried in his head a copy of the almanac of twenty-five thousand addresses, and knew the residence, the name, and the secrets of all the celebrities, even the obscure ones.

Coming among the Bohemians, with that knowing air which distinguished him, the Jew divined that he had arrived at a propitious moment. As a matter of fact, the four friends were at that moment gathered in council, and under the domination of a ferocious appetite were discussing the grave question of bread and meat. It was Sunday, the last day of the month. Fatal day, sinister date !

The entrance of Medicis was accordingly greeted with a joyous chorus, for they knew that the Jew was too sparing of his time to waste it in mere visits of civility ; his presence always announced that he was open to a bargain.

" Good evening, gentlemen," said the Jew ; " how are you ? "

" Colline," said Rodolphe, who was lying in bed, sunk in the delights of maintaining a horizontal line, " practise the duties of hospitality and offer our guest a chair ; a guest is sacred. I salute you, Abraham," added the poet.

Colline drew forward a chair which had about as much elasticity as a mass of bronze and offered it to the Jew. Medicis let himself fall into the chair, and started to complain of its hardness, when he remembered that he himself had once traded it off to Colline in exchange for a profession of faith which he afterwards sold to a deputy. As he sat down the pockets of the Jew gave forth a silvery sound, and this melodious symphony threw the four Bohemians into a pleasant frame of mind.

" Now," said Rodolphe, in a low tone, to Marcel, " let us hear the song. The accompaniment sounds all right."

" Monsieur Marcel," said Medicis, " I have come to make your fortune. That is to say, I have come to offer you a superb opportunity to enter into the world of art. Art, as you very well know, Monsieur Marcel, is an arid wilderness in which glory is the oasis."

" Father Medicis," said Marcel, who was on coals of impatience,

" in the name of fifty per cent, your revered patron saint, be brief."

" Here is the offer," rejoined Medicis. " A wealthy amateur, who is collecting a picture-gallery destined to make the tour of Europe, has commissioned me to procure for him a series of remarkable works. I come to give you a chance to be included in this collection. In one word, I come to purchase your ' Passage of the Red Sea.' "

" Money down ? " asked Marcel.

" Money down," answered the Jew, sounding forth the full orchestra of his pockets.

" Go on, Medicis," said Marcel, showing his painting. " I wish to leave to you the honour of fixing for yourself the price of this work of art, which is priceless."

The Jew laid upon the table fifty crowns in bright new silver.

" Continue," said Marcel ; " that is a good beginning."

" Monsieur Marcel," said Medicis, " you know very well that my first word is always my last word. I shall add nothing more. But think ! fifty crowns ; that makes one hundred and fifty francs ! "

" A paltry sum," answered the artist. " In the robe of my Pharaoh alone is fifty crowns' worth of cobalt. Pay me at least something for my work."

" Hear my last word," replied Medicis. " I will not add a penny more ; but I offer dinner to all your friends, wines included, and after dessert I will pay in gold."

" Do I hear any one object ? " howled Colline, striking three blows of his fist upon the table. " It is a bargain."

" Come on," said Marcel. " I agree."

" I will send for the picture to-morrow," said the Jew. " Come, gentlemen, let us start. Your places are all set."

The four friends descended the stairs, singing the chorus from The Huguenots, " To the table, to the table."

Medicis treated the Bohemians in a fashion altogether splendid. He offered them a lot of things which up to now had remained for them a mystery. Dating from this dinner, lobster ceased to be a myth to Schaunard, and he acquired a passion for that amphibian which was destined to increase to the verge of delirium.

A week after this festivity Marcel learned in what gallery his picture had found a place. Passing through the Faubourg Saint-Honoré, he stopped in the midst of a crowd that was staring at a sign newly-placed above a shop. This sign was none other than Marcel's painting, which had been sold by Medicis to a dealer in provisions. Only " The Passage of the Red Sea " had once again undergone a modification and bore a new title. A steamboat had been added to it, and it was now called " In the Port of Marseilles." A flattering ovation arose among the crowd when they discovered the picture. And Marcel turned away delighted with this triumph, and murmured softly : " The voice of the people is the voice of God ! "

AUGUSTE VITU
1823–1891

THE SECOND VIOLIN

WHILST I was staying at W—— I never missed a single per-
formance at the opera. There was a masterpiece given every night :
*The Freischütz, The Huguenots, Robert le Diable, Don Juan, The
Magic Flute*, etc. All these operas were well put on, great attention
being paid to every detail, so that the whole result was all that
could be desired.

I do not for a moment say that the artists were irreproachable,
and there were certainly not many good soloists in the large orchestra,
but yet they all seemed to understand the thing they were performing,
and to observe most scrupulously the lights and shades as the
composer had meant them, and as, perhaps, only a German or an
Italian orchestra ever does observe them. The baritone, for instance,
did not attempt to drown the tenor, nor the tenor the prima-donna ;
so the general effect was quite satisfactory.

One evening when *The Huguenots* was being given, I set myself
to follow the orchestra in the development of the piece. It is a most
enjoyable occupation to analyse a piece and to study it note by note
when you know the score thoroughly. It always seems to me that
in doing this you obtain the same kind of pleasure as when, after
riding on horseback through a forest, you return to explore it more
thoroughly, and to gather the flowers which you had not noticed the
first time.

My place was in the first row of the orchestra stalls, so that I could
lean on the balustrade which separated me from the musicians, and
when the contra-bass was played I could feel the vibration in my
arms. To my left were the wind instruments, and just in front of
me the second violins. Among the latter I had noticed the very
first night a young man, whose happy-looking face caused me some
surprise.

To my mind there is nothing more unsatisfactory than the part
which the second violin takes. All the lovely melodies belong to the
first violin, and, as though out of compassion, every now and then
the seconds are permitted to attempt a kind of imitation of the air,
then some arpeggios, and the strings are pulled and almost beaten

561

like a drum, whilst the melody itself is taken up by some other instrument. It seems to me, then, that the second violins, condemned thus to do all the filling in, all the servile work as it were, must get morose, taciturn, and spiteful, and I came to the conclusion that this one in the orchestra of the theatre of W—— must be an exception to the rule.

He was young and handsome; he had an oval-shaped face; soft, light curly hair, and such happy-looking blue eyes. He appeared to play with the greatest ease, evidently knowing all by heart, as he only glanced every now and then carelessly at the score. His eyes, and evidently his thoughts too, were elsewhere.

Very soon I thought I had found out, at any rate, where his thoughts were. He was seated to the right of the stage, and, consequently, was exactly opposite the stage-box on the left. He could see everything which went on in this box, and I noticed that he took advantage of his opportunities.

Of course there was a woman in the box, and I observed that she was quite youthful and very beautiful. She was, perhaps, just a trifle over-dressed for one so young. The diamonds in her hair flashed every time she moved, and she appeared to be paying just about as much attention to the stage as the young violinist did to his score. Once I happened to be looking at them when their eyes met, and I saw that her cheeks turned pale just as though all the blood in her veins had suddenly rushed to her heart, while a flush came over the young musician's pale face.

During the interval I overheard several snatches of conversation around me which enlightened me partially. Two young men, who were looking through their glasses into the box on the left of the stage, spoke of this beautiful girl as the Countess Ulrica von Hanzig, and I knew that that family was a branch of the reigning house of W——.

As I said, though, the information only partially enlightened me, for if the beautiful woman with her flashing diamonds were of such high birth, how was it that she could be so interested in a poor violinist? For interested she was, I felt sure from the glance I had seen pass between them.

I immediately began to build up in my own mind a little romance with the Countess Ulrica and the second violin of the orchestra for my heroine and hero. Every time the curtain fell I noticed that my young friend, instead of going out with his fellow-musicians, simply put down his instrument, leaned back in his chair, and gazed up at his idol. This was certainly strange, especially considering that the Countess Ulrica was not alone in her box. There was an elderly man with her, probably either her father or her husband; and he must surely have noticed the admiration expressed on the young violinist's face. It seemed to me once that the elderly man was smiling at him, but afterwards I thought that must surely have been my imagination. Anyhow, the whole affair seemed to me rather mysterious and very interesting to watch.

When the curtain rose, I became so absorbed in the opera that I completely forgot the Countess Ulrica, but, as luck would have it, when I went home that night I was destined to see something else of the little comedy. I was walking leisurely down the wide staircase at the close of the opera, and as I was in no particular hurry, I had stepped aside two or three times to let some of the pushing, scrambling people get out, when I saw in front of me the Countess Ulrica. She was just getting into her carriage as I reached the door, and the elderly man took his seat beside her. The carriage-door was left open, and I noticed that the young Countess kept leaning forward as though looking out for some one.

Presently the violinist I had been watching during the opera appeared on the scene, carrying his instrument in its case under his arm. He stepped into the carriage, sat down opposite the young Countess, took both her hands in his, and then the carriage moved away.

After this, every night I used to watch this trio at the opera, and it seemed to me that the Countess and the violinist were evidently more and more in love with each other every evening, but, of course, I had no means of getting to the bottom of the mystery. One evening I found that my usual place was occupied by a young officer, who appeared to be the centre of attraction to a little group of the most dandified men in W——. The officer was fair, and just the type of a Hanoverian. He looked half German, half English, was very handsome, and had that high and mighty, rather consequential air which women adore, and which exasperates beyond endurance all other men.

I took the nearest seat I could get to my own, and I could not help overhearing the conversation of the little group. It was the usual kind of club talk : horses, women, and society gossip. I could gather from the young officer's questions that he had only arrived that day in W——, after being garrisoned in some other town. Without wishing it in the least, I thus became acquainted with all the gossip going amongst the high life of W——.

Just before the curtain rose, the door of the box on the left of the stage opened and the Countess Ulrica entered with the elderly man, who appeared to follow her about like her shadow. She was more beautiful than ever that night, and I noticed that her appearance caused quite a sensation. I also observed that many people glanced from her to the young violinist, and several ladies put their fans up to hide their smiles. The officer who had taken my place seemed more surprised than any one else. He put his eyeglass on, and then I heard him exclaim :

"By Jove! if there isn't my cousin Ulrica! Let me pass, you fellows: I must go up and speak to her."

The fair-haired warrior went away with a most self-complacent expression on his handsome face, and a minute or two later he appeared in the box in question, evidently to the Countess Ulrica's surprise. He put on a most familiar, almost affectionate, manner, and appeared to be talking to her most confidentially. He had all his trouble for nothing, though, as she kept looking at her violinist. I happened to glance at him too, just as the officer was leaning forward and saying something to the young Countess in the most confidential manner. The violinist's face flushed, and he frowned ominously.

One of my friends who has a great fancy for chemistry said to me one day:

"I do not know anything that has a stronger freezing power than a woman's disdain; in some instances, and under special circumstances, I am sure a woman could ice a bottle of champagne by only looking at it."

That night I had an example of the truth of what my friend asserted, for the refrigerating influence of the Countess Ulrica on the young officer was wonderful. I noticed that he seemed to lose his self-assurance and was reduced to fumbling with his gloves, and when he left the box and came down again to his place he was stroking his moustache nervously.

"Stolberg has had the cold shoulder to-night!" remarked one of the dandies, just before the young officer returned; and the others nodded.

Stolberg, however, not knowing that he had just been the subject of remark, said, as he sat down:

"Why, just think, my cousin Ulrica is married!"

"Ah!" said one of the other young men, half-condescendingly and in a half-jesting tone.

"She gave me the cold shoulder, quite, and I should like to know whether she is angry or whether it was just indifference!"

No one answered, but most of us glanced at the young musician, who was at that moment brandishing his bow over the strings with all the energy of a savage cutting his enemy's throat. There was an awkward pause, and then one of the young officer's friends remarked:

"Then your beautiful cousin was by no means gushing just now, Stolberg?"

"No, indeed, Max, and it is all the more strange that she should behave in that way to *me*, as it is certainly the first time she has treated *me* coldly."

"Since her marriage, you mean?"

"Why, of course, considering that that event has taken place

felt deep gratitude towards him, as, if he had not taken pity on me, I might have had to beg my bread like so many of those of my poor compatriots who escaped the Russian guns had to do.

" Fortunately for me my tastes were simple, and there was nothing repugnant to me in the career which seemed to be my future lot in life. My only ambition was to become some day conductor of the orchestra in the theatre of the Grand Duchy. I was wrapped up in my work and musical studies, and had very little leisure time for thinking of anything else.

" One evening, however, at the opera there was to be a new work given, and the Grand Duke was to be present. All the important families of the Duchy were that evening in their boxes, and I glanced round at the house to see the general effect of the magnificent costumes and the flashing diamonds. I was in reality little interested in all these great people, for I felt myself separated from them by an insurmountable barrier. " You see," he added, smiling bitterly, " the violinist's bow may ennoble the hand of an ordinary citizen provided he be talented, but it only degrades the hand of a fallen count.

" Well, on the evening in question, in a box just opposite to me, a lovely girl was sitting. I was indeed perfectly startled by her beauty, for never in my dreams had I imagined any woman so exquisitely graceful and fascinating. In my delight I know that I smiled, and it seemed to me that she looked down with interest at me. One of my comrades told me that it was the Countess Ulrica von Schaffenbourg, the daughter of one of the Grand Duke's Chamberlains. The thought of my position at once flashed across me, and I felt humiliated to the very dust, and then almost angrily I seized my violin, and during the whole evening I carefully refrained from looking again at that box.

" Ulrica, however, came again several times to the opera, and it always seemed to me that there was the same look of interest on her face whenever our eyes met. I did my utmost not to give way to the kind of magnetism which attracted my eyes to that box, but all in vain. For a whole month things went on like this, and then, as her father had to go abroad on political business, she was placed, in the meantime, at the convent of Meilen.

" I expect you wonder how I found out all these details. And to this day I hardly know myself how I managed to discover everything I wanted to know. One thing is sure, though, that, as far as anything concerning this girl was in question, I should certainly have found a way to baffle the most skilful diplomat in the world.

" Well, I went on thinking about her, dreaming of her, for two long years. I knew nothing of her character, except what I had read in her eyes. I would have given ten years of my life to have heard the sound of her voice. I began to work now in feverish earnest. I had hitherto looked on my violin as the means of earning my daily bread, but now it seemed to me that it must be more to me, and that I must earn distinction through it. I gave myself up entirely to my musical studies, and I got on so well that it seemed as though I had every chance of success.

" The next event in my life was the competition at the Conservatorium, which in Germany is, as you know, of considerable importance. I entered my name, and when the day came there was a large and attentive audience. If I could win distinction that day there was some chance for me. My competitors were heard one after the other, and my name happened to be called last.

" You must forgive me if I sound my own praises, but, inspired as I was by love, I played a theme of Handel's with such feeling that I saw tears in the eyes of some of my judges. My own eyes were moist, too, and I shall never forget the sensation of those few minutes. It was as though all my youth and all my strength were at last having a free course after all the long years that my feelings had been either lying dormant or stifled. I had only the last variation to perform, and my triumph seemed certain. It was a terrible passage, arpeggios, to be played with fearful rapidity from the lowest note to the very highest. It wanted a strong wrist and the lightest fingers. Oh ! the accursed variation ! But still I felt sure of it, and was going to attack it with perfect confidence. I lifted my bow proudly and then, alas ! I suddenly saw Ulrica. The tears were in her eyes, but her face was radiant. All my assurance went, my hand suddenly became feeble, and my fingers uncertain. I hesitated—and that was the end of it, for it was all over with me after that. The concert was over, and there was a murmur of disappointment all through the room, whilst I felt more dead than alive.

" The first prize was, of course, given to another competitor, but out of pity they gave me an accessit. All that did not move me, though ; I had seen Ulrica turn pale with emotion ; I felt, I knew, that she cared for me, and I thought to myself that is surely more than the first prize at the Conservatorium. Directly after, though, a feeling of despair came over me, and I reproached myself bitterly for my weakness. I had proved myself totally unworthy of her, and she was surely worthy of an emperor. And then, too, was it not, after all, a great misfortune, this unhappy love ?—for there was no hope whatever for us. What was to become of me ? Just as I was thinking moodily in this strain the Director of the Conservatorium sent for me.

" ' Albert,' he said, ' you will find a carriage at the door, which is to take you to the Palace of the Grand Duke.'

" My astonishment was extreme, but, notwithstanding, I went down and got into the carriage without staying a minute to reflect.

A major-domo was waiting for me at the door of the palace. He begged me to follow him, and what was my astonishment soon, on finding myself face to face with the Count von Schaffenbourg—Ulrica's father.

" ' Are you Count Albert von Hanzig ? ' he asked, coldly.

" Upon my reply in the affirmative, he continued :—

" ' I sent for you to ask you to give violin lessons to my daughter —the Countess Ulrica von Schaffenbourg.'

" I could not find a single word to say ; I staggered, for I had suddenly turned giddy.

" ' You love her ! ' he said, smiling.

" I did not answer, but I bowed my head, and how it was that I did not there and then lose my senses I have never been able to fathom, for he continued :—

" ' The son of my old friend Louis von Hanzig can marry the daughter of the Count von Schaffenbourg without its being by any means a *mésalliance*.' Those were his very words, and it seems to me that I shall not forget them to my dying day." The young Count stopped for a minute, too deeply moved by these recollections to be able to continue.

" Ulrica became my wife," he said presently, " and all the happiness which true love along can give has been ours. I have been happier than I had thought possible in my very wildest dreams, and yet——" The young Count paused again, and his face clouded over when he continued his story. " Our days were just one long *fête*, and we had so much to say—so much always to tell each other. I told her all about my desolate childhood and then about my work and my struggles, and she told me of all her happy days and of her little schemes and plans in order to bring her father to consent to our union and, what was still more, to get him to send for me and to propose it. Oh ! how gay and happy we were, and how we laughed at each other's stories.

" Our marriage had naturally caused a lot of gossip in W——, but as the Grand Duke himself approved of it, there was nothing further to be said. Gradually people became accustomed to seeing us together in public, and so forgot the romance of it all. *We* had not forgotten, though, and my wife wanted to go again for the first time since our marriage to the opera, where we had first met. We went and we sat in the box on the left of the stage, where you must have seen Ulrica yesterday evening. It was very strange to me at first to find myself up there instead of with my comrades in the orchestra. Ulrica looked down at the music-stand behind which she had always seen me, and I noticed that she seemed very absent-minded and did not pay any attention to the opera. Every time I looked at her, her eyes were fixed on my old place, and yet my successor did not resemble me much."

The Count smiled as he told me all these details, which were evidently quite fresh in his memory.

" My successor," he continued, after a slight pause, " was a little, bald-headed old man, with a very long, red nose, on which rested a pair of enormous gold spectacles. We went constantly to the opera after that evening, and every time my wife was just the same, until at last I begged her to tell me what it was that was troubling her, and why she took no interest in the music.

" ' Albert,' she exclaimed, ' you know I do not care what the world thinks or says. My one wish, my one desire, is to see you there again in your old place and to listen to you, just as I used to, and live over again those days. It would make me so happy. Oh! I wish that by some miracle it could be so ! '

" I did not say anything to my wife, but the next day the little old man with the gold spectacles received his salary to the end of the season, and I, after seeing my wife to her box, left her on some pretence, and then hurried downstairs and took my old place in the orchestra. It was not without a pang that I had decided to do this. I could not help feeling the difference, for I am certain that, no matter in what position in life I had met Ulrica, I should there and then have loved her, and now it seemed to me that if I were to hope to keep her love, I must have recourse to my poor Stradivarius. It was a woman's caprice, her love of the romantic, for now that she was my wife, perfect in every way as she is, I knew that it was from eight o'clock to eleven every night at the opera that I came up to her ideal, and that she loved me with all her soul."

This, then, was what Count von Hanzig had to tell me, and wildly improbable as so much of it sounded, I felt that he was telling me just exactly how matters stood. He was silent again when he had finished his story, and was looking moodily before him. I felt that time was precious, and that I must remind him of the unfortunate business which was now before us.

" And Herr von Stolberg ? " I began.

" Ah ! I had not spoken of him, because he has only crossed my path in life to bring me bad luck. I believe by some family arrangement it had been intended that he should marry Ulrica, and consequently through me, I suppose, he considered his future prospects blighted."

" Do you think that this duel is absolutely obligatory ? "

" What do you think about it as my second ? "

" Well, there was no irreparable insult."

" Ah ! do not let us waste our time discussing useless questions," interrupted the Count impulsively. " You want, of course, to avoid if possible any bloodshed, but in reality you know as well as I do that there is no help for it. The world would never understand any sentimental explanations, and to the world if I, Albert von Hanzig, act as second violin in the orchestra of the opera, why, I am a disgrace to my name and to my rank. Now, if I am either killed by Lieutenant Stolberg in a duel or if I kill him, no one will dare to reproach me with my violin bow when I have shown that I can also wield a sword."

I had felt this myself before the Count had said it, and I knew really that there was no help for it all. We arranged then to take for the other witness a soldier belonging to the Grand Duke's Guards. In the afternoon Herr von Stolberg's seconds came to call on me : the duel was fixed for the following morning, and the weapon chosen was the sword.

I have never yet come across the man who could be present at a duel and keep his *sang-froid*. The two duellists themselves have their honour and their life at stake, and their moral courage, as a rule, keeps them up. The task of the seconds is a most painful one, and nearly always, on meeting the six men concerned in a duel on their way to the place fixed upon, you will find two of them calmer than the others, and, as a rule, those two are prepared to face death.

We had chosen a field where the light and shade were pretty equally distributed, and a ditch marked the limits. Count von Hanzig was calm and serious, but Herr von Stolberg was just as haughty and contemptuous as the other night at the opera. He bowed, however, very politely, and the preliminaries were then arranged. The two adversaries were just about to commence, and there was dead silence, that terrible silence which makes itself felt when one knows that something tragic is about to take place.

Suddenly, at the other end of the field, the branches of the trees were pushed aside and an officer of high rank in the army made his appearance, followed by a detachment of infantry. As he approached we saw that it was an aide-de-camp of the Grand Duke.

" Follow me," he called out, " in the name of His Royal Highness ! "

" Conrad," said Lieutenant Stolberg, turning to one of his seconds, " you'd better call for the fiddlers, the situation is amusing —extremely amusing."

Count von Hanzig did not speak, but his face turned livid with suppressed emotion, and I could see that his hands trembled too.

" I am executing the express order of His Highness, who will not suffer the law as regards duels to be violated in his realm."

" Conrad," said Stolberg again, " the situation is really dramatic : are you not a musician yourself ? "

His friend turned his head away, annoyed at the bad taste displayed by Stolberg, but the latter continued :—

" I pride myself that I am no musician, but it seems to me that a violin duet would be perhaps more easily executed than a sword duet—even if the latter were between men of good blood."

" The Grand Duke has dishonoured me," said Count von Hanzig, bitterly, giving up his sword to the aide-de-camp ; and there was something in the vibration of his voice as he uttered the words that made one feel that the insult was not to be forgotten so easily.

The aide-de-camp took Stolberg's sword too, and then, just as I was going to speak to my new friend and was trying to find something to say which might reconcile him, the officer turned to me and said :—

" The Grand Duke would be glad if you could make it convenient to hasten your departure. He desires me to say that he shall count on your being able to leave within twenty-four hours."

There was no choice left me in the matter. I glanced at Count von Hanzig, and our eyes met in a silent farewell. I then turned and went away, in obedience to the Grand Duke's commands.

A few months ago one of my friends at Constantinople got to know several Hungarian and Polish officers who had served under the command of Georgey, during the struggle taken up by the Magyars against the House of Austria. These refugees used frequently in their long conversations to relate the various romantic or terrible episodes which had come under their notice during that desperate war. One of these stories, which my friend told me after, aroused my attention. It seems that every one had specially noticed in a volunteer corps commanded by Bern two young men, who were both very handsome, and who had displayed marvellous courage and boldness. The taller and older of the two was not only a good soldier but a wonderful musician, and he often charmed the others by playing Polish airs on a violin which he always had with him ; the other one was so fair and delicate-looking that he might have been taken for a woman.

These two friends were both killed by a detachment of the enemy, which had taken them by surprise. When they died, the stronger one had thrown his arms round the other man, as though to protect him. There was a broken violin just near, and a pistol which had recently been fired ; a scrap torn from a letter was there, too, and it had evidently served for loading the pistol. On this scrap of paper the name of Albert von Hanzig could just be read. This indication was, of course, not enough to establish the identity of the young man, and he was buried there where he fell, together with his companion. They both rest there under a grassy mound which is covered every spring with violets and marguerites, and these simple flowers serve as their monument.

THÉODORE DE BANVILLE
1823–1891

TRANSPOSITION

AT the beginning of 1882, Madame Hortense Daffry, already, at the age of twenty, a widow without children or parents, came to live in the Rue de Lille with Madame de Briel, her grandmother. In her company she felt for the last time the true affection and peaceful joys of family life. It was only two years later that the excellent old lady died, mournful and disquietened at leaving her grand-daughter alone and without protection in the world. For, eighty years old, she had seen all those she had loved and known marry and depart, and no one was left to whom she could recommend her darling Hortense.

During the last month of her life, Madame de Briel, feeling her end was near, had put her affairs in perfect order, to avoid all trouble to her grand-daughter. Furthermore, she had carefully sorted out and arranged her papers, burning with her own hands those she did not think worth preserving. During her illness, she kept near to her in the chest of drawers, a lacquer-box, the key of which, threaded with a ribbon, hung from one of the handles of chiselled bronze. Very often Madame de Briel had the box taken out and held it for hours in her hand, as though wishing to come to a decision about it and dispose of its contents. But death at last surprised her before she had done anything with it, and Madame Daffry felt herself troubled and hesitating when the box came into her hands.

It seemed to her that the best thing would be to destroy it piously without seeking to know the secrets it enclosed. But Hortense did not dare to do this, fearing, on the other hand, that she might fail in some duty and escape from some obligation that she ought to undertake. So she opened the box, and found it full of letters, bearing the addresses, not on separate envelopes in modern fashion, but on sheets of letter paper. As she at once saw, the letters were addressed, not to Madame de Briel, but to Madame Eudoxie Tèrrene, the mother of her grandmother. This great-grandmother Hortense had known with her own eyes, for Madame Tèrrene had died only in 1872 at the age of eighty-five.

But, above all, she had often found her again in a family portrait. Baron Gros had made this portrait of the lovely Eudoxie in the days of her triumphant youth.   Now, by the virtue of a strange law whose effects we feel better than we can formulate them, in this image of a great-grandmother, painted fifty-three years before her own birth, Hortense Daffry had recognised her own face, astonishing in its truthfulness and as faithful as a mirror.

For in certain families, at varying intervals, Nature delights in reproducing certain figures, just as a sculptor takes several casts from the same mould, but in these cases, how far does the resemblance go ? Does it tell on the feelings, the thoughts, the most secret fibres of the heart ? This is one of those mysterious problems of modern science that opens to our mind infinite horizons.

Before having read or even looked at the letters written to her great-grandmother, Madame Daffry suddenly saw a medallion which, having slipped down, stood upright against the side of the box, and she took it out.   It was a miniature representing a very young man, in the uniform of an officer of the First Empire, with brown, crisp hair and daring eyes expressing all the ardours of passion and the maddest bravery.   Starting from the top of his forehead and reaching almost to his right eyebrow, a red scar, made by some furious sabre stroke, divided into two parts the large broad forehead of this doer of great deeds.   At her first glance at the portrait, Hortense, attracted, subdued, conquered, felt in her heart a thousand torments and a thousand delights.   She loved.   Whom, however ? A man long since dead, as his dress clearly indicated—a man she would never see on this earth ! But the flame that burns us often makes game of realities and common-sense, and for things to be true it is not at all necessary that they should be possible.

It would not be right to say that Hortense was suddenly struck with love.   She had the sense of an ancient passion, long since known with its joys and its pains, which by an unexplained event had been effaced from her memory, and then suddenly, breaking through a veil, had swept up again into her mind, setting it on fire and lighting it up with the flame.

Then she looked at the letters, all signed with the same name, and read them with feverish eagerness.   It was not difficult to recover the pulsating story from which they were born.   Married quite young to an army contractor, old, selfish, worn out by debauch, Madame Eudoxie Tèrrene was adored by a young lieutenant of Napoleon named Paul Ferrandier.   She was unable to resist the wild passion she had inspired, and the two lovers—handsome, charming, faithful, born for each other—loved like the children they were, and dreamt of eternities of happiness, all the while feeling above their heads the vague beating of the dark wings of Death.

They were soon separated. It was the days of Austerlitz, of Jena, of Eylau, of Friedland, of Wagram. During these glorious years they sometimes met for a few moments; but the rest of the time, between two battles, between two victories, dusty, blood-spattered, broken with fatigue, Ferrandier wrote Eudoxie the rapid, furious, caressing, burning letters that her great-grand-daughter now re-read, her breast heaving and her eyes wet with tears. It was for Eudoxie, as well as for Napoleon, that he fought in battle after battle across Europe, thinking to give his Emperor the last drop of his blood, and win a throne for his beloved.

Contractor Tèrrene died, and mad with hope, Paul Ferrandier thought of returning to his love, when he was killed at Smolensk, struck by a bullet full in the breast. One of his friends, a brother soldier, to whom he had confided the hope of his approaching marriage, wrote to Madame Tèrrene telling her the terrible news; and his letter was placed in the box with those from Paul.

What was veritably strange was that the prayers, the memories, the sobs of grief and the cries of passion contained in the letters seemed to Hortense Daffry to have been addressed to her alone. Her soul, violently liberated from all reality, soared in a dizzying flight, amid the joys of impossibilities. She gave herself, wholly, and with raputre, to Paul Ferrandier, without thinking an instant that he had lived in a vanished era, and that he was dead, more than half a century ago, in the tumult of victory. That she would see him one day, soon perhaps, and shake his hand and hear him speak as he had written, was for her something of which there was no shadow of doubt. She waited for the hour of the meeting with ingenuous confidence.

As in those dreams in which we see the most impossible things happen without being astonished at them, she was exempt from all surprise when, spending an evening with Madame de Simore, she heard the maid announce: " Monsieur Paul Ferrandier."

She saw him enter—the Paul she knew, the Paul she adored—absolutely like his portrait, his dark curly hair, his daring eyes, and the scar down his forehead. The only difference was that he now wore the uniform of a lieutenant of the African Light Cavalry.

No! Madame Daffry was not surprised to see him whom she waited for every minute. But her heart leaped in her white bosom, and she—if there had not been all those men there, all those women in satin and diamonds, a crowd impossible to get through—she would have run to the young man, and fallen in his arms, saying, " Here I am ! "

And Paul Ferrandier, after bowing to Madame de Simore, suddenly saw Hortense. Staggering, distracted, white as a sheet, he dragged himself out of the drawing-room by leaning against the walls, and coming to a boudoir, happily empty, he fell his full length on the carpet in a swoon. Madame de Simore, struck by his strange look, followed behind him, and arrived just in time to see Paul, stretched on the ground, senseless and white as death.

As a cousin of Ferrandier, Madame de Simore could take an interest in him without attracting remarks, and it would have been easy for her to appeal for help to a famous doctor that had come to her party. But with the instinct of a woman, she at once guessed that there was some private trouble that must not be revealed to any one. She knelt down before the young man, moistened his temples and forehead, gave him some strong salts to smell, and, lifting his head in her hands, placed a cushion beneath it.

At last Paul came to, and opened his eyes. Then he took from his breast a portrait ; it was a miniature that he covered with mad kisses and showed to Madame de Simore.

" Ah ! Blanche ! Blanche ! She exists ! " he cried in a frenzy of joy, while his eyes swam with tears.

" Certainly," said Blanche, " Hortense Daffry exists, and she is my closest friend. But I do not understand how you come by her portrait, and why she is dressed like a lady of the First Empire. But you have never seen her ! What is the meaning of the strange attack you have just had ? "

" I have just seen her for the first time," said Ferrandier, " but for years I have loved her with all my soul, with all my strength, with every drop of my blood. It is three years since I first held in my hand this portrait, and it has never left me. In the ambushes, raids, and night-attacks in Africa it has inspired me with courage and scorn of danger and relish for death. For I love her too much to live without her, and, thinking naturally that she was long since old and dead, I never thought it possible to meet her."

" But you have not told me," said Blanche de Simore, " how the portrait came into your hands ? "

" The simplest way in the world," said Paul. " I wanted an old desk in Chinese lacquer that stood in my father's study. He gave it to me at once, and told me that it had been in the family for years. It belonged to one of my great-grand-uncles, named, like myself, Paul Ferrandier. He died at Smolensk, August 17, 1812, lieutenant-colonel in the cuirassiers of the Guards. The keys of the desk were lost ; I had the locks broken open, and in one of the drawers I found this divine portrait, which from the first minute became for ever that of my beloved."

" There is a great deal which is strange about the matter," said Madame de Simore, " but the important thing is that Hortense and you are young, and your own masters, and as free as the air. So there is nothing to prevent you falling in love and finishing your story by a happy marriage."

This prediction was not realised. Hortense and Paul met and

recognised each other, and tasted for a brief while the joys of paradise. But sent to Tonkin with his regiment, Paul Ferrandier died exactly like his great-grand-uncle, struck by a bullet full in the breast.

FIRST LOVE

Théodore de Banville

Madame, said the poet, you ask me at what age love begins. It never begins. For being a lover is the quality of a man, like being a negro, or having a hooked nose. Those who are fated to become lovers have always been so. On this point, as on all others, Shakespeare shows his impeccable genius, by representing Romeo ready to die through the coldness of Rosaline, at the very moment when he is about to meet Juliet. But this needs supporting by a story of our own day. Here it is :

I was educated in the Coriolis boarding-school, in Rue Richer, where a sad and meagre garden, flanked by two flights of steps and planted with rickety trees, was surrounded by the magnificent grounds of some fine mansions that were destroyed when the Rue de Trévise and the Rue Geoffroy-Marie were constructed. It was a school for the children of the rich ; so the life there was extremely fashionable, although they fed us on poor stuff scarcely good enough for men in a convict prison. Among other things, we boys had so much pocket-money that we were able to buy a complete set of stage properties—curtains of red calico, helmets of cardboard covered with gold and silver foil, swords of small size, but made of steel—with which we amused ourselves on Sunday evenings. We played melodramas and tragedies, partly by memory, partly by improvising our parts. The theatre was merely the big class-room, where we pushed the desks together to make an empty space.

Our masters raised no objection ; for on Sunday evenings in winter the boys subscribed to order from Rollet baskets of cakes costing as much as twenty francs. It was, as I have told you, a school where we had the right to dress in the fashion. Boys from families of friends went about together in couples, in the manner of their uncles and fathers, and often took pleasure in wearing the same kind of dress. One of the most charming couples in the school, united by brotherly affection, was that formed by Chéd-'homme and Pessonnaille, both of them sons of wealthy ship-owners of Havre. I can still see them in the playing-ground in green jerseys with small white lines, and in little brown suits in

43

the college classes. My two school-fellows were like myself, about thirteen years old. Chéd'homme had a girl's face, white and clear, with fine fair hair that curled naturally. Pessonnaille had short brushy hair on a little head that was already full of strength and wildness.

One day as we were walking down the long Rue de Provence, Chéd'homme, who sat next to me in class, said with some hesitation that he had a secret to tell me. And speaking in his soft musical voice, he said that he had fallen in love with Rosalie. She was our little linen-maid, thin, dark, with eyes of fire, who mended the sheets and serviettes. Chéd'homme had gone into the linen-room to get a new tie, and dropping a pin, he had knelt down to pick it up. Then Rosalie had put her two hands over his eyes and kissed his hair. They had sworn to love each other for ever, and were arranging a meeting-place when Aunt Bégat, the withered housekeeper of the school, entered and interrupted the love affair.

He told me all this in broken words, in the delightful fever of adolescence. It was early in April; the air was full of the warm exhalations of spring; puffs of fragrance came to us from the neighbouring gardens, and on the theatre posters we read the title of romantic tragedies. I eagerly drank in the words of Chéd'homme. They fell on my heart like fire on a trail of gunpowder; for I was in love also, but with Chloe, with Pyrrha, with Phyllis—with all the women of the odes of Horace.

The drama developed with surprising rapidity. I was separated for some days from Chéd'homme; my play-time was spent in writing pensums that I had earned by an ode of three syllables found in my desk; and we were not placed together when we went out. I found myself at last by his side, ten days after our first talk. He was pale, upset, and so angry that he could scarcely speak to me.

" He has betrayed me," he said. " Pessonnaile ! My friend, my brother ! He has done it ! "

Vainly I tried to interrupt him.

" I will kill him," he said.

Then he told me all. A duel had been arranged between him and Pessonnaille for the next day. During the lesson from twelve to one, they would both go out and fight in the garden, having for witnesses the fifty boys of the class, who, through the curtainless windows, could easily see them. As for Duriez, the master of the class, they counted on his invincible imbecility, and they were certain that he only would not see anything.

As you can imagine, I used every possible argument to make him give up his plans.

" And my honour ! " he cried, like the juvenile lead on the stage, shaking his pretty curls. " But it isn't that," he added, bursting into tears ; " but since Rosalie has deceived me, I must die. You see, I love her ! " And again he wept abundantly.

I never had for a moment the idea of denouncing my chum. For I used to think then—as I do still—that the end never justifies the means.

But what is very strange is that the scheme of these poor children was carried out, point by point, without any difficulty. The next day, during the lesson, both of them found a pretext to leave the room. We soon saw them in the garden, in shirt and trousers, mounted on one of the gymnastic apparatus, and holding in their hands their naked swords—the little swords taken from our stage properties. They arranged to fight at this height, so that they should be clearly seen by all of us. Our fifty chests panted. Duriez could not understand the general inattention to the lesson ; but thanks to his supernatural stupidity, he did not perceive the ardent looks that, one after the other, we cast by stealth towards the garden.

Brave, furious, bathed in sunlight, our two friends were as pretty as angels. The duel opened, violent and atrocious, for they knew nothing, or next to nothing, of the art of fencing ; and in their anger they did not notice the cuts they received, and the blood that stained their shirts. Finally, by a horrible stroke, Chéd'homme, struck on the forehead by Pessonnaille's sword that made a large hole and broke in the wound, fell backward from the top of the wooden horse. Pessonnaille sprang down to him, weeping and staunching the flow of blood. An immense cry rose from all our throats. We jumped over the tables and flung ourselves in a crowd into the garden, and there at the same time arrived Monsieur and Madame Coriolis, the Demoiselles Coriolis, the professors, Aunt Bégat, the servants, everybody in the place.

You can guess the terror and the fright of this drama. For when Chéd'homme was put in bed, not in the infirmary, but in a bedroom given up by one of the Coriolis girls, he fell into a profound swoon, and the doctors could not say that he would live. Two months passed, during which the whole school lived as in a dream, full of anguish and agitation, before he was sufficiently well to be sent away to his parents. As for Pessonnaille, the very day of the fight, he was put in a coach, with a professor entrusted with taking him to Havre and giving him up to his family, to punish or not as they pleased.

Well, Madame, thirty-eight years passed after these events of our childhood before I met Chéd'homme. He had become the celebrated traveller whose achievements are not unknown to you. He had struggled, fought, worked, suffered, won fame, and undergone amazing disasters. Roasted on a spit pretty well by the natives of Africa, baked with the sun, struck down with hunger and fever

in the great desert, he had escaped from a thousand deaths. His
charming lovely wife had perished in a shipwreck, and his son
had been slaughtered in our last war. Yet, as soon as he saw me
at Nice on the English promenade, he ran up to me and seized my
hand with an air of infantile joy.

"You remember," he said to me, "the tress of Rosalie's hair?
She did not give it to Pessonnaille. He stole it from a drawer.
I met him last year at Rio, and he admitted it all to me."

Looking at Chéd'homme I saw his old neck, where the wrinkles
formed a pattern like watered silk, jerk with joy, and his skull,
smooth and bare, brown as a death's head carved in boxwood,
lightened up.

THE CAB

THÉODORE DE BANVILLE

WHO doesn't know the composer Janoty? Although he is as poor
as Job, and his operas have as yet only been heard at a very
minor theatre, this man with his colourless hair and complexion,
afflicted with one of those faces that Heine called "superfluous,"
was a month ago loved for himself, and was the happy owner of
that rarer thing than rhymes to *triumph*—a faithful wife. Now
all is changed, and you shall learn how he came by his tragic fate.

Colette was an adorable little woman, forcing herself to believe
in her husband's genius, keeping the house clean and nice without
the aid of a servant, economising on nothing at all, fabricating
delicious dishes out of chimerical ingredients, always amiable, good
tempered, and cheerful, playing Janoty's compositions on the piano
as often as he liked, even a hundred times following. To make the
boiled beef palatable, she provided sauces fit for an archbishop, of
ideal and divine flavour, drawn solely from her own imagination.
She would walk in the hot sun to the Batignolles market, where
lobsters are sometimes to be bought for a halfpenny. Janoty was
perfectly happy, beloved, cherished, caressed, and fed as well as
a rich abbot. How did it happen then that in less than five
minutes all this was changed? That is just what I'm going to tell you.

Tata, the *prima donna* of the minor theatre where Janoty's compositions were performed, had an immense success with the song,
"My brother pumps, pumps, pumps," and she came to ask Janoty
to write an air for her in the new piece which should be, and yet
should not be, "My brother pumps, pumps, pumps." Our *maestro*
had just the very talent that those sorts of compositions require.

Colette opened the door to her; she was washing vegetables, and held a dishcloth in her hand.

"Announce me," said Tata, spreading out her train, and Colette, who never gave herself airs, announced her. While Tata was putting forth all her arts to dazzle Janoty, down came one of those showers which, during the past month, have spoiled so many hats and brought into bloom so many roses.

"Good gracious! how it's coming down," said Tata. "May I trouble you to let your maid fetch me a cab?"

There was a fine opportunity for Janoty to prove himself a courageous, or merely an honest man, and to say, "I haven't a maid, it's my wife." He was a coward, and replied, "Certainly." Then, twirling his thumbs, he went into the dining-room, which did duty for a hall, where Colette was washing her vegetables more industriously than ever, rubbing and scraping away like the worthy housewife she was. "Mademoiselle Tata," he muttered, "is wearing a satin gown and satin shoes. It is pouring cats and dogs; it would be very kind of you to go——"

"And fetch a cab?" asked Colette, giving her husband a flaming glance that ought to have made him sink into the earth. "Fetch a cab! Well, I never! Directly!"

She went, getting her only pair of boots quite wet, and even taking the coppers that Tata slipped into her hand for her trouble. And from that moment Janoty, without leaving the house, could witness every day a pantomime in five hundred tableaux, with most extraordinary transformation scenes. He made the acquaintance of iced soup and warmed-up wine, of the lamp exchanged for a guttering candle, and as he was sitting down to dinner the meal would be replaced by a piece of sausage wrapped in paper. Colette, who used to rise with the lark, could now be awakened with difficulty at eleven o'clock, and would then murmur, "Surely it's not daylight yet." The house, formerly so spotless that you would have sought a grain of dust in vain, resembled an Italian city in the hands of the Goths. There were cobwebs in the plates, and saucepans on the clock. Coats and shirts were buttonless, and stockings full of holes. And instead of performing her husband's compositions, she played nothing but Wagner.

Her irritating hands evoked the stormiest sounds; the piano was full of Tannhausers, Walkyries, Rheingolds and Götterdammerungs, and when Janoty in despair held his head and cried, "That music gives me a fearful headache," Colette sweetly replied, "I fetched the cab." And those words formed the refrain of all their conversations. "Colette, the soup is cold." "I fetched the cab." "There are no buttons on my shirt." "I fetched the cab." "You don't love me any more; you never kiss me." "No, my dear, but I fetched the cab!"

ALEXANDRE DUMAS THE YOUNGER
1824–1895

THE
HANGING AT LA PIROCHE

Do you know La Piroche?

No? Neither do I. So I shall not abuse my privilege as an author by giving you a description; especially since, between you and me, they are very tiresome, those descriptions. Unless it be a question of the virgin forests of America, as in Cooper, or of the Mississippi, as in Chateaubriand, that is to say, countries that are not close at hand, and in regard to which the imagination must be assisted by those poetical voyagers who have visited them, in general descriptions are not of much consequence except to be skipped by the reader. Literature has this advantage over painting, sculpture, and music; the threefold advantage of being able to paint by itself a picture in a single word, to carve a statue in one phrase, to mould a melody on one page; it must not abuse itself of that privilege, and one should leave to the special arts a little of their own prerogative.

I own, then, for my part, and for lack of better advice, that when I find that I have to describe a country which does not differ from our own, I prefer to leave to my reader the pleasure of recalling it if he has seen it, or of imagining it if he does not yet know it. The reader likes well enough to be left to do his share of the work he is reading. It flatters him and makes him believe that he is capable of doing the rest. And it is an excellent thing to flatter your reader. Moreover, the whole world in reality knows what the sea is like—a plain, a forest, a blue sky, an effect of sun, an effect of the moon, or an effect of storm. Of what use to dwell upon it? It would be far better to trace a landscape in one stroke of the brush like Rubens or Delacroix; this should be said without comparison and keep the whole value of your palette for the figures you wish to reanimate.

When you blacken with descriptions page after page of paper, you don't give the reader an impression equal to that experienced by the most artless bourgeois who walks through the Bois de Vincennes on a soft April day, or by an unlettered girl who strolls in June, on the arm of her fiancé, at eleven o'clock at night, through the shady vistas of the woods of Romainville or the park of Enghien. We all have in our minds and hearts a gallery of landscapes made from memory, and which serves as background for all the stories of the world. There is but one word to use—day or night, winter or spring, calm or storm, wood or plain—to evoke at once a most finished landscape.

So I have only to tell you this : that at the moment when the story I am about to tell you begins it is noon, that it is May, that the highway we are going to enter is bordered on the right with furze bushes, on the left by the sea ; you know at once all that I have not told you, that is to say, that the bushes are green, that the sea is murmuring, that the sky is blue, that the sun is warm, and that there is dust on the road.

I have only to add that this highway that winds along the coast of Brittany runs from La Poterie to La Piroche ; that Piroche is a village about which I know nothing, but which must be more or less like all villages, that we are in the beginning of the fifteenth century, in 1418, and that two men, one older than the other, one the father of the other, both peasants, are following the highway mounted on two nags trotting along comfortably enough under the weight of two peasants.

" Shall we get there in time ? " said the son.

" Yes, it is not to take place until two o'clock," replied the father, " and the sun marks but a quarter after noon."

" Oh, but I am curious to see that ! "

" I can well believe it."

" So he will be hanged in the armour that he stole ? "

" Yes."

" How the devil did he get the idea of stealing armour ? "

" It's not the idea that is hard to get——"

" It's the armour," interrupted the boy, who wanted his share in making a part of that joke.

" And that, too, he didn't get."

" Was it fine armour ? "

" Splendid, they say, all shining with gold."

" And did they catch him as he was carrying it away ? "

" Yes, you know as well as I do that armour like that never goes astray without raising a great outcry ; it can't escape its proper owner all by itself."

" So, then, it was of iron ? "

" They woke up in the château at the noise they heard."

" And did they arrest the man ? "

" Not at once ; they began by being afraid."

" Of course, it's always that way that people who have been robbed begin when they are in the presence of thieves ; otherwise there would be no object in being a thief."

" No, nor any pleasant excitement in being robbed ! But those
brave folks had no idea that it was an affair of robbery."

" Of what, then ? "

" Of a ghost. That wretched, most vigorous fellow was carrying
the armour in front of him, holding his head at the height of the loins
of the armour so effectively that he acquired gigantic proportions in
the corridor where he passed. Add to this a clattering noise which
the rascal made behind him, and you will appreciate the fright of the
valets. But, unfortunately for him, he woke up the Seigneur of La
Piroche, he who has fear of neither the dead nor the living, who easily,
and all by himself, arrested the thief and handed him over, bound,
to his well-deserved justice."

" And his well-deserved justice ? "

" The condemned man is to be hanged clothed in the armour."

" Why that clause in the sentence ? "

" Because the Seigneur of La Piroche is not only a brave captain,
but a man of common sense and of spirit, who wished to draw from
this just condemnation an example for others and an advantage for
himself. Why, don't you know that whatever touches a hanged man
becomes a talisman for him who possesses it ? So the Seigneur of
La Piroche has ordered that the thief should be hanged dressed in his
armour, so as to reclaim it when the man is dead and have a talisman
to wear during our next wars."

" That is very ingenious."

" I should think so."

" Let's make haste, for I am so anxious to see the poor man
hanged."

" We have plenty of time ! We must not wear our beasts out. We
are not going to stop at La Piroche ; we will have to go on a league
farther, and then return to La Poterie."

" Yes, but our beasts will rest for five or six hours, for we do not
return until evening."

The father and son continued on their way, talking, and half an
hour later they reached La Piroche.

As the father had said, they arrived in time. Have fathers always
the privilege of being right ?

There was an immense concourse of people on the great square in
front of the château, for it was there that the scaffold had been
erected, a splendid gallows, in faith, of sound oak, not very high, it is
true, since it was intended for a wretched, obscure criminal, but high
enough, nevertheless, for death to do its work between earth and
the end of the rope which was swinging in the fresh sea breeze like
an eel hanging by its tail.

The condemned man was certain of having a beautiful view at the
moment of death, for he was to die with his face turned toward the
ocean. If this view could be any consolation to him, so much the

better, but, for my part, I doubt it.

And all the while the sea was blue, and from time to time between the azure of the sky and that of the sea floated a white cloud, like an angel on its way to heaven, but whose long robes still trailed upon the earth it was quitting.

The two companions approached as near as possible to the scaffold, so as to miss nothing that was going on, and, like all the rest, they waited, having this advantage over the others, that they were mounted on two nags and could see better with less fatigue.

They had not long to wait.

At a quarter of two the gates of the château opened, and the condemned man appeared, preceded by the guards of the Seigneur of La Piroche and followed by the executioner.

The thief was dressed in the stolen armour and was mounted reversed on the bare back of a jackass. He rode with vizor down and head lowered. They had tied his hands behind him, and if they wish for our opinion in the matter we have no hesitation in saying that, judging by his position, in default of his face, which could not be seen, he ought to have been very ill at ease, and indulging at that moment in very sad reflections.

They conducted him to the side of the scaffold, and a moving picture hardly pleasant for him began to silhouette itself against the blue sky. The hangman set his ladder against the scaffold, and the chaplain of the Seigneur of La Piroche, mounted on a prepared platform, delivered the sentence of justice.

The condemned man did not move. One might have said that he had given the spectators the slip by dying before he was hanged.

They called to him to descend from his ass and deliver himself to the hangman.

He did not move. We understand his hesitation.

Then the hangman took him by the elbows, lifted him off the ass, and set him upright on the ground.

Fine fellow, that hangman !

When we say that he set him upright, we do not lie. But we would lie in saying that he remained as they placed him. He had in two minutes jumped two-thirds of the alphabet ; that is to say, in vulgar parlance, that instead of standing straight like an I, he became zigzag like a Z.

During this time the chaplain finished reading the sentence.

" Have you any request to make ? " he asked of the culprit.

" Yes," replied the unfortunate, in a voice sad and low.

" What do you ask ? "

" I ask for pardon."

I do not know if the word " joker " was invented in those days, but then or never was the time to invent it and to speak it.

The Seigneur of La Piroche shrugged his shoulders and ordered the executioner to do his duty.

The latter made ready to mount the ladder leaning against the gibbet, which, impassive, was about to draw with extended arm the soul out of a body, and he attempted to make the condemned mount in front of him, but it was not an easy thing to do. One does not know, in general, what obstacles those condemned to death will put in the way of their dying.

The hangman and the man there had the air of passing civilities one to another. It was a question of who should go first.

The hangman, to make him mount on his ladder, returned to the method he employed in making him descend from his ass. He seized him around the middle of his body, balanced him on the third rung of the ladder, and began to push him up from beneath.

" Bravo ! " cried the crowd.

He ought to have mounted well.

Then the executioner adroitly slipped the running noose, which adorned the end of the rope, around the neck of the culprit, and, giving the latter a vigorous kick in the back, he flung him out into space, which strongly resembled Eternity.

An immense clamour greeted this looked-for dénouement, and a shudder passed through the crowd. Whatever may be the crime he had committed, the man who dies is always at the moment greater than those who watch him die.

The hanged man swung for three or four minutes at the end of his rope, as he had a right to do, danced, wriggled, then hung motionless and rigid.

The Z had become an I again.

They gazed a while longer on the culprit, whose gilded armour glistened in the sun, then the spectators divided themselves, little by little, into groups, and went their way home, chatting about the event.

" Pooh ! a horrid thing is death ! " said the son of the peasant, as he continued his journey with his father.

" In good faith, to hang one for not having succeeded in stealing a piece of armour, that's expensive. What do you think ? "

" I wonder, I do, what they would have done to him if he had really stolen the armour ? "

" They would not have done anything to him, for if he had really stolen the armour he would have been able to escape from the château. Then, possibly, he would not have returned to be arrested."

" Yet he is punished more for a crime that he has not committed than he would have been if he had committed the crime ! "

" But he had the intention of committing it."

" And the intention was accounted as a fact——"

"That is perfectly just."

"But it isn't pretty to look at."

And since they found themselves on rising ground, the two companions turned to contemplate for the last time the silhouette of the unfortunate.

Twenty minutes later they entered the little town where they were to receive certain moneys, and which they were to leave that evening in order to accomplish the return home that same night.

On the morrow, at break of day, the guards sallied out from the château of La Piroche for the purpose of taking down the corpse of the hanging man, from which they intended to recover the armour of the Seigneur, but they discovered something which they had been far from anticipating, that is to say, the gibbet was there, as always, but the hanged man was not there.

The two guards rubbed their eyes, believing themselves to be dreaming, but the thing was very real. No more hanged man, and naturally no more armour.

And what was extraordinary, the rope was neither broken nor cut but just in the condition it was before receiving the condemned.

The two guards ran to announce this news to the Seigneur of La Piroche. He was not willing to believe it, and proceeded to assure himself of the truth of the facts. So puissant a lord was he that he was convinced the hanged man would reappear for him there ; but he saw what all the rest had seen.

What had become of the dead ? For the condemned had certainly died the day before, before the eyes of the whole village.

Had another thief profited by the night to get possession of the armour that covered the corpse ?

Possibly—but in taking the armour he would naturally leave the corpse, for which he had no use.

Had the friends or relations of the culprit wished to give him Christian burial ?

Nothing impossible in that if it were not for the fact that the culprit had neither friends nor relations, and that people who had had religious sentiments like that would have taken the culprit and left the armour. That, then, was no longer to be thought of. What should one believe, then ?

The Seigneur of La Piroche was in despair. He was all for his armour. He made promise of a reward of ten gold crowns to any one who should deliver to him the thief, dressed as he was in dying.

They ransacked the houses ; they found nothing.

No one presented himself.

They caused a wise man of the town of Rennes to be sent for, and they propounded this question to him :

"In what way does a dead man who has been hanged manage to

free himself from the rope that holds him in the air by the neck ? "

The wise man demanded eight days to ponder over the question, at the termination of which he replied :

" He cannot do it."

Then they propounded this second question :

" A thief, unsuccessful in stealing while alive, and having been condemned to death for stealing, can he steal after his death ? "

The wise man replied :

" Yes."

He was asked how it could be done. He replied that he knew nothing about it.

He was the greatest sage of his time.

They sent him home and contented themselves with believing, for those were the days of witchcraft, that the thief was a wizard.

Then they said masses to exorcise that evil spirit, which was without doubt taking his revenge upon the Seigneur who had ordered his death and upon those who had come to see him die.

A month passed in fruitless search.

The gibbet still stood there as always, humiliated, gloomy, and discredited. Never had a gibbet committed such a breach of confidence.

The Seigneur of La Piroche continued to clamour for his armour from man, God, and the devil.

Nothing.

At last he was beginning, without a doubt, to make the best of this strange event, and of the loss which had been the result, when one morning, as he was waking, he heard a great commotion on the square where the execution had taken place. He was making ready to inform himself of what was passing when his chaplain entered the room.

" Monseigneur," said he, " do you know what has happened ? "

" No, but I am going to ask."

" I can tell you, I can."

" What is it, then ? "

" A miracle from heaven ! "

" Really ! "

" The hanged man—— "

" Well ? "

" He is there ! "

" Where ? "

" On the scaffold."

" Hanging ? "

" Yes, Monseigneur."

" In his armour ? "

" In your armour."

" True, for it *is* mine. And is he dead ? "

" Absolutely dead—only—— "

" Only what ? "

" Did he have spurs on when they hanged him ? "

" No."

" Well, Monseigneur, he has them, and in place of having the casque on his head, he has placed it with great care at the foot of the gibbet, and left his head hanging uncovered."

" Let us see, Mr. Chaplain, let us see, straight off ! "

The Seigneur of La Piroche ran to the square crowded with the curious.   The neck of the hanged man had passed again into the running noose, the corpse was there at the end of the rope, and the armour was there on the corpse.

It was astounding.   So they proclaimed it a miracle.

" He has repented," said one, " and has come to hang himself over again."

" He has been there all the time," said another ; " only we did not see him."

" But why has he got spurs ? " asked a third.

" No doubt, because he has come from afar and wished to return in a hurry."

" I know well, for my part, that far or near, I would not have needed to put on spurs, for I would not have come back."

And they laughed, and they stared at the ugly face the dead man made.

As for the Seigneur of La Piroche, he thought of nothing but of making sure that the thief was quite dead, and of securing his armour.

They cut down the corpse and stripped it ; then, once despoiled, they hung it up again, and the ravens investigated so thoroughly that at the end of two days it was all jagged, at the end of eight days it had only the appearance of a rag, and at the end of fifteen days it had no longer the appearance of anything at all ; or, if it did resemble anything it was only those impossible hanged men we used to make pictures of on the first page of our text-book, and below which we would write :

> Behold Pierrot suspendered,
> Who has not his Latin rendered.
> But 'twas otherwisely fated :
> Pierrot was the one translated.

But what had the hanged man been doing during his month of absence ? How did it happen that he escaped, and, having escaped, that he hanged himself again ?

We will give below the three versions which have been presented to us.

A magician, a pupil of Merlin, declared that if at the moment of dying the culprit has had the will to disappear and the ability to absorb his body into his will, the will being an immaterial thing, invisible, and impalpable, the body, which finds itself absorbed by it, and consequently hidden in it, becomes by that means also impalpable, immaterial, and invisible, and that if the body of a thief has reappeared at the end of a month, and at the end of a rope, it is because at that supreme moment his will, troubled by his conscience, has not had sufficient force for eternal absorption.

This may not be a good version, but it is one.

The theologians affirm that the culprit did succeed in vanishing, but that, pursued by remorse and being in haste to reconcile himself with God, he could not endure the life longer than one month, and, full of repentance, came to execute upon himself that justice which he had escaped the first time.

That, perhaps, is not the true version, but it is always Christian logic, and as a Christian we will not dismiss it altogether.

Finally, they declared that our two peasants in returning home that evening, and passing close to the gibbet heard lamentations, a rattling, and something like a prayer ; that they piously crossed themselves and demanded what was the matter ; that they received no reply ; but the lamentations continued, and it seemed to them that they came from the corpse that was above their heads. Then they took the ladder that the hangman had left at the foot of the scaffold, rested it against the arm of the gibbet, and the son, having mounted to the level of the condemned, said to him :

" Is it you who are making these complaints, poor man ? "

The condemned gathered all his strength together and said :
" Yes."

" Then you are still alive ? "

" Yes."

" You repent of your crime ? "

" Yes."

" Then I will loosen you, and since the Evangelist commands us to give succour to those who suffer, and that you suffer, I am going to succour you and bring you to life in order to bring you to good. God prefers a soul that repents to a corpse that expiates."

Then the father and the son cut down the dying man, and saw how it was that he still lived. The rope, instead of tightening about the neck of the thief, had tightened at the base of the casque so effectually that the culprit was suspended but not strangled, and, occupying with his head a kind of vantage-point in the interior of the casque, he was able to breathe and to keep alive up to the time our two companions passed by.

The latter took him down and carried him home with them, where they gave him into the care of the mother and the young daughter.

But he who has stolen will steal.

There were but two things to steal at the peasant's, for the money he had brought back with him was not in his house. These two things were his horse and his daughter, a fair-haired girl of sixteen.

The ex-hanged decided to steal both the one and the other, for he was covetous of the horse and had fallen in love with the daughter.

So one night he saddled the horse, buckled on the spurs to make him ride faster, and went to take the young girl while she was asleep, and lift her up on to the crupper.

But the girl awoke and cried out.

The father and the son came running up. The thief tried to escape, but he was too late. The young girl told about the attempt of the hanged man ; and the father and the son, seeing well that no repentance was to be expected from such a man, resolved to execute justice upon him, but more effectually than the Seigneur of La Piroche had allowed himself to do it. They bound the thief to the horse which he had saddled himself, led him to the square of La Piroche, and strung him up there where he had been hanged, but placed his casque on the ground to make sure that he should not vanish again ; then they returned home quietly.

There is the third version. I do not know why I believe it to be the most probable, and that you would do well, like me, to give it preference over the other two.

As for the Seigneur of La Piroche, as soon as he had secured a real talisman, he went happily off to the wars, where he was the first to be killed.

ERCKMANN-CHATRIAN
1822–1899

MY INHERITANCE

AT the death of my worthy uncle, Christian Haas, mayor of
Lauterbach, I was already music conductor to the Grand
Duke Yeri Peter, and I had fifteen hundred florins as salary.
That did not prevent me from being in very low water. Uncle
Christian, well aware of my position, never sent me a penny, so I
cannot help shedding a few tears in learning his posthumous
generosity. I inherited from him, alas ! . . . two hundred and fifty
acres of good plough-land, vineyards, orchards, a bit of forest, and
his fine mansion of Lauterbach.

"Dear uncle," I said to myself with much feeling, "now I see
the extent of your wisdom, and glorify you for keeping your purse-
strings tied up. If you had sent me any money, where would it
be now ? In the hands of the Philistines ! Little Kate Fresserine
alone could have given any news about it. But now, by your
caution, you have saved the situation. All honour to you, dear
Uncle Christian ! . . . All honour to you ! "

And having said all this and much more, not less touching or
less sincere, I set off on horseback for Lauterbach. It was very odd !
The demon of avarice, with whom I never had any dealings, almost
made himself master of my soul.

"Kasper," he whispered in my ear, "now you're a rich man. Up
to the present you have only pursued vain phantoms. Love and
pleasure and the arts are only smoke. A man must be mad to
think anything of glory. There is no solidity about anything
except lands, houses, and money out on first mortgages. Give
up your illusions ! Push forward your fences, widen your fields, heap
up your money, and you will be honoured and respected. You will
become mayor like your uncle, and the people, when you approach,
will take off their hats a mile away, saying, "Here comes Herr Kasper
Haas . . . the rich man . . . the warmest gentleman in the country ! "

These ideas came and went in my head like figures from a magic
lantern, and I found they had a reasonable, serious look, and I was
much taken with them.

It was in mid-July. In the heaven the lark poured out his

unending music; the crops undulated in the plain; the warm
puffs of light wind carried to me the love-cries of the quail and the
partridge in the corn; the foliage twinkled in the sunlight; the
Lauter murmured in the shadow of the large old willows. But
I saw or heard nothing of all that. I wished to be the mayor;
I stuck out my abdomen; I puffed out my cheeks, and I repeated
to myself, " Here comes Herr Kasper Haas . . . the rich man . . .
the warmest gentleman in the country! Ho! Ho! Ho!"

And my little mare galloped on. I was anxious to try on the
three-cornered hat and the great red waistcoat of my Uncle
Christian, for I thought that if they suited me it would save me
buying others. About four in the afternoon the little village of
Lauterbach appeared, nestling in the valley; and it was with some
emotion that I looked at the large fine mansion which was to be
my residence, the centre of my estate and my power. I admired
its picturesque situation on the dusty highway, the immense roof
of grey tile, the sheds with their vast wings brooding over carts and
wagons and crops, with a farmyard behind, then the kitchen
garden, the orchard, the vineyards on the hill slope, the meadows
in the distance. I thrilled with pleasure at the spectacle.

And as I went down the main road of the village, old women,
with nose and chin meeting like nut-crackers, bare-headed, rumpled
children, men in big otter-skin hats, a pipe with a silver chain in
their mouths—all these good folks looked at me and greeted me:

" Good day, Herr Kasper! Good day, Herr Haas!"

And all the little windows fill with astonished faces. I already
feel at home. It seems to me I have always been a great landowner of Lauterbach. My life as a musical conductor is no more
than a dream—my enthusiasm for music a folly of youth. How
money does alter a man's way of looking at things!

However, I stopped before the house of Notary Becker. He has
the deeds of my property, and must give them to me. Tying my
horse to the ring by the door, I jumped on the step, and the old
lawyer, his bald head uncovered, his thin spine clad in a long green
dressing-gown with a flower pattern, came out to welcome me.

" Herr Kasper Haas! I have much honour in greeting you!"

" Your servant, Master Becker!"

" Will you deign to enter, Herr Haas?"

" After you, Master Becker, after you."

We crossed the hall, and I saw at the end a little bright airy room,
a well-set out table, and, near the table, a pretty girl, graceful and
sweet, her cheeks touched with a modest blush.

" Herr Kasper Haas!" said the venerable notary.

I bowed.

" My daughter Lothe!" added the worthy man.

While I was feeling my old artistic inclinations revive within me, and admiring the little nose, the scarlet lips, and large blue eyes of Fräulein Lothe, her slender waist, and her little dimpled plump hands, Master Becker invited me to take my place at the table, saying that, as he knew I was about to arrive, he had had a little meal prepared for me.

So we sat down and talked about the beauties of nature. I thought of the old father, and began to calculate what a notary would earn in Lauterbach.

"Fräulein, may I have the pleasure of helping you to the wing of a chicken?"

"Sir, you are very good. With pleasure."

Lothe lowered her eyes. I filled her glass, and she moistened her red lips with the wine. Father was joyful, and talked about hunting and fishing.

"You will no doubt take up the pleasures of a country life. Our rabbit warrens are splendid, and the streams are full of trout. There is some fine hunting in the forest, and in the evening there is good company at the tavern. The inspector of woods and waters is a charming young man, and the magistrate is an excellent hand at whist."

I listened, and thought this calm and peaceful sort of life was delicious. Fräulein Lothe seemed to me charming. She talked little, but her smile was so sweet and frank that she must be very loving, I fancied.

At last the coffee and the liqueur arrived. The young lady retired, and the old lawyer got on to serious business affairs. He spoke to me of my uncle's estate, and I listened very attentively. No will, no legacies, and no mortgage! Everything clear, straightforward, regular! "Happy Kasper!" I said to myself. "Happy Kasper."

Then we entered the study to deal with the title-deeds. The closeness of the air, the piles of documents, the rows of law books, quickly chased away the day-dreams of my amorous fantasies. I sat down in a big arm-chair, and Master Becker thoughtfully fixed his horn spectacles on his long curved nose.

"Here are the title-deeds to your Eichmatt meadowlands, a hundred acres of the best soil in the parish, and splendidly watered. Three crops of hay in a year. It will bring you in four thousand francs. Here are the deeds for your Grünerwald farms, and those for your Lauterbach mansion. It is by far the largest in the village, dating from the sixteenth century."

"The devil! Master Becker, that is nothing in its favour."

"On the contrary. It is in a perfect state of repair. It was built by Hans Burckart, the Count of Barth, as his hunting-house. It is true, a good many generations have passed since then, but the upkeep and repair have never been neglected."

With more explanations, Master Becker handed me the title-deeds of my other properties ; and having put the parchments in a bag lent to me by the worthy man, I took leave of him, more convinced than ever of my new importance. Arriving at my mansion, I inserted the key in the lock, and kicking the step, I cried, " This is mine ! " I entered the hall, " This is mine ! " I opened the wardrobes, and seeing the linen piled to the top, " This is mine ! " I mounted to the first floor, repeating always like a madman, " This is mine ! This is mine ! Yes, I am the owner ! "

All my cares for the future, all my fears for the morrow are dissipated. I figure in the world, no longer by the feeble merit men allow me, by the caprice of the fashion of the day, but by the possession of things that everybody covets. Oh, poets ! . . . Oh, artists ! . . . what are you beside this stout owner of land, who nourishes you by the crumbs from his table ? You are only the ornament of his banquet . . . the distraction of his moods of boredom . . . the songbird on his hedgerow . . . the statue decorating his garden. . . . You exist only by him and through him. . . . Why should you envy him the fumes of pride and vanity . . . he who owns the only realities in this world !

If in this moment the poor Musical Conductor Haas had appeared before me, I should have looked at him over the shoulder, and asked myself, " Who is this fool ? What has he in common with me ? "

I opened the window. Night was falling. The setting sun gilded my orchards, my vineyards that lost themselves in the distance. On the summit of the hill a few white stones indicated the cemetery. I turned round. A vast Gothic hall, the ceiling adorned with heavy mouldings, took my eye. I was in the hunting-lodge of Hans Burckart, the Count of Barth. An antique spinet was placed between two of the windows. I passed my fingers over the keys absent-mindedly. The slack wires knocked together with the strange, twangling, ironic voice of teethless old women humming over the melodies of their youth.

At the end of the hall was the half-vaulted alcove, with great red curtains and a four-poster bed. The sight reminded me that I had been six hours in the saddle. And, undressing with a smile of unspeakable satisfaction, " This is the first time," I said, " I have slept in my own bed." And lying down, my eyes bent on the immense plain, already bathed in shadows, I felt my eyelids grow heavy in pleasant fashion. Not a leaf murmured ; the noises of the village died one by one away . . . the sun had sunk . . . some golden gleams marked his trail in infinite space. . . . I soon fell asleep.

It was night, and the moon shone in all her glory when I awoke with no apparent cause. The vague fragrances of summer came through the window to me. The air was filled with the sweet scent of the new hay. I stared around in surprise, for when I tried to get up to close the window, by some inconceivable thing, my body slept on, heavy as lead, while my head was perfectly free. With all my efforts to rise, not a muscle responded. I felt my arms by my side completely inert . . . my legs were stretched out, motionless ; my head moved in vain. The deep, cadenced breathing of my body frightened me . . . my head fell back on the pillow, exhausted by its efforts. " Am I paralysed in my limbs ? " I asked myself. ' Kasper Haas, the master of so many vineyards and fat pasturages, cannot even move this clod of clay that he really owns ? O God ! . . . What does it mean ? "

And as I was thinking in this melancholy way, a slight sound attracted my attention. The door of my alcove opened ; a man dressed in some stiff stuff like felt, as the monks of Saint Gualber in Mayence are . . . a large grey felt hat with a hawk's plume in it . . . his hands buried to the elbow in hide gloves . . . entered the hall. His bell-shaped boots came above his knees ; a heavy gold chain, charged with decorations, hung from his neck. His tanned bony face, with hollow eyes, wore a look of keen sadness, and there were horrible greenish tints on it.

He walked the hall with hard, firm step, like the tick-tack of a clock ; and with his hand on the guard of an immense sword, striking the floor with his heel, he cried, " This is mine ! . . . Mine . . . Hans Burckart. . . . Count of Barth ! "

It was like an old rusty machine grinding out necromantic words. It made my flesh creep. But at the same time the door at the other end opened, and the Count of Barth disappeared through it. I heard his automatic step descend a stair that never seemed to come to an end. The sound of his footfall on each step grew fainter and fainter, as though he were descending to the fiery depths of the earth.

As I still listened, hearing nothing, lo ! suddenly the great hall was filled with many people. The spinet sounded . . . they danced . . . they sang . . . made love and drank good wine. I saw against the blue background of the moon, young ladies loll round the spinet ; their cavaliers, clad in fabulous lace, and numberless knick-knacks, sat with crossed legs on gold-fringed stools, leaning forward, tossing their heads, waddling about, making themselves pleasant. The little withered fingers of an old lady, with a nose like a parrot's beak, clicked on the keys of the spinet ; bursts of thin laughter rocketed left and right, ending in a mad rattle that made the hairs stand up in my neck.

All this society of folly and grace and fine manners exhaled a smell of rose water and mignonette soured by old age. I made again some superhuman efforts to get rid of this nightmare

Impossible! But at the same moment one of the young ladies said:

"Gentlemen, make yourselves at home.... This domain—"

She did not have the time to finish. A silence of death followed her words. I looked around. The phantasmagoria had disappeared.

Then the sound of a horn struck my ears. Outside, horses were prancing, dogs barking, and the moon, calm, contemplative, shone into my alcove. The door opened, as by a wind, and fifty hunters, followed by young ladies, two hundred years old, with long trailing gowns, filed majestically from one hall to the other. Four serfs also passed, bearing on their stout shoulders a stretcher of oak branches, on which rested—bleeding, frothy at the mouth, with glazed eyes—an enormous wild boar. I heard the sound of the horn still louder outside. Then it died away in the woodlands like the sleepy cry of a bird ... and then ... nothing!

As I was thinking of this strange vision, I looked by chance in the silent shadows, and was astonished to see the hall occupied by one of those old Protestant families of bygone days, calm, dignified, and solemn in their manners. There was the white-haired father, reading a big Bible; the old mother, tall and pale, spinning the household linen, straight as a spindle, with a collar up to her ears, her waist bound by fillets of black ratteen; then the chubby children with dreaming eyes leaning on the table in deep silence; the old sheep dog, listening to his master; the old clock in its walnut case, counting the seconds; and farther away, in the shadow, the faces of girls and the features of lads in drugget jackets and felt hats, discussing the story of Jacob and Rachel by way of declaring their love.

And this worthy family seemed to be convinced of the holy truths; the old father, with his cracked voice, continued the edifying story with deep emotion:

"This is your promised land ... the land of Abraham and Isaac and Jacob ... which I have designed for you from the beginning of the world ... so that you shall grow and multiply there like the stars of the sky. And none shall take it from you ... for you are my beloved people, in whom I have put my trust."

The moon, clouded for a few moments, grew clear again, and hearing nothing more I turned my head. The calm cold rays lighted up the empty hall; not a figure, not a shadow.... The light streamed on the floor, and, in the distance, some trees lifted their foliage, sharp and clear, against the luminous hillside.

But suddenly the high walls were hidden in books. The old spinet gave way to the desk of a learned man, whose big wig showed to me above an arm-chair of red leather. I heard the goose-quill scratching the paper. The writer, lost in thought, did not stir. The silence overwhelmed me. But great was my surprise when the man turned in his chair, and I recognised in him the original of the portrait of the Jurist Gregorius that is No. 253 in the Hesse-Darmstadt Picture Gallery. Heavens! how did this great person descend from his frame? That is what I was asking myself when in a hollow voice he cried, "Ownership, in civil law, is the right to use and abuse so far as the law of nature allows." As this formula came from his lips, his figure grew dimmer and dimmer. At the last word he could not be seen.

What more shall I tell you, my dear friends? During the following hours I saw twenty other generations succeed each other in the ancient castle of Hans Burckart. . . . Christians and Jews, lords and commoners, ignorant people and learned, artists and philistines, and all of them claimed the place as their legitimate property. All thought themselves the sovereign masters of the property. Alas! the wind of death blew them out of the door. I ended by becoming accustomed to this strange procession. Each time one of these worthy persons cried, "This is mine!" I laughed and murmured, "Wait, my friend, wait, you will vanish like the rest."

I was weary when, far away, very far away, a cock crowed, and with his piercing voice awoke the sleeping world. The leaves shook in the morning wind, and a shudder ran through my body. I felt my limbs were at last free, and rising on my elbow I gazed with rapture over the silent countryside. . . . But what I saw was scarcely calculated to make me rejoice. All along the little hill-path that led to the graveyard climbed the procession of phantoms that had visited me in the night. Step by step they advanced to the lichen gate, and in their silent march, under the vague grey shadowy tints of the rising dawn, there was something terrible. As I looked, more dead than alive, my mouth gaping, my forehead bathed in a cold sweat, the leaders of the procession seemed to melt into the old weeping willows. There remained only a little number of spectres. And I was beginning to recover my breath, when my uncle Christian, the last figure in the procession, turned round under the old gate, and motioned to me to come with him. A voice, far away . . . ironical, cried:

"Kasper. . . . Kasper. . . . Come. . . . This land is ours!"

Then everything disappeared, and a purple line, stretching across the horizon, announced the dawn. I need not tell you that I did not accept the invitation of Master Christian Haas. It will be necessary for some one more powerful than he to force me to take that road. But I must admit that my night in the castle of Burckart has singularly altered the good opinion I had conceived of my own importance. For the strange vision seemed to me to signify that if the land, the orchards, the meadows do not pass away, the owners vanish very quickly. It makes the hair rise on your head when you think on it seriously.

So, far from letting myself slumber in the delight of an idle country life, I took up music again, and I hope next year to have an opera produced in Berlin. The fact is that glory, which common-sense people regard as moonshine, is still the most solid of all forms of ownership. It does not end with life. On the contrary, death confirms it, and gives it a new lustre. Suppose, for example, that Homer returned to this world. No one would think of denying him the merit of having written the *Iliad*, and each of us would hasten to render to this great man the honours due to him. But if by chance the richest landowner of his age returned to claim the fields, the forests, the pasturages, which were the pride of his life, it is ten to one he would be treated as a thief, and perish miserably under the blows of the Turks.

UNCLE BERNARD'S SHELL

ERCKMANN-CHATRIAN

UNCLE BERNARD had a large shell on his chest of drawers. A shell with rosy edges is not common in the forest of Hundsruck, at a hundred and fifty leagues from the sea; Daniel Richter, an old soldier of the Empire, had brought this from the ocean as an eternal memorial of his voyages.

You can imagine with what admiration we village children contemplated this wonderful object. Each time that Uncle went out on his round of visits, we entered the library—cotton caps on the back of our heads, hands in the slits of our blue blouses, noses against the slab of marble, we stared at the "American snail," as it was called by the old servant Gredel.

Ludwig said it must have lived in the hedges; Kasper held it swam in the rivers; but none of us knew really what the facts of the case were. Now, one day Uncle Bernard, finding us disputing as usual, began to smile. He put his three-cornered hat on the table, took the shell between his hands, and sitting in an arm-chair, said:

"Listen to what is going on inside there!"

Each of us applied his ear to the shell, and we heard a great noise, a complaint, a murmur, like a gust of wind far away in the depths of the wood. And all of us stared at each other wonder-struck.

"What do you think of that?" said Uncle; but none of us knew what to reply.

Then he said to us in a grave voice :

" Children, this big voice that murmurs there is the noise of your blood flowing in your head, in your arms, in your heart, in all your limbs. Here it runs like a little fountain, there like a torrent, there like brooks and great streams. It bathes all your body inside, so that everything there can live and prosper and grow larger, from the tip of your hairs to the sole of your feet. You know the echo of the Hollow Rock that sends you back your shout when you cry, your song when you sing, and the sound of your horn when you lead your goats from the Altenberg at evening ? Well, this shell is an echo similar to that of the Hollow Rock. Only, when you bring it close to your ear, it is the noise of what is passing within you that it gives back, and this noise resembles all the voices of the sky and the earth ; for each of us is a little world. If a man could see a hundredth part of the marvels that take place in his head in a single second, to make him live and think, and of which he only hears the murmur in the depth of the shell, he would fall on his knees and weep a long time, thanking God for His infinite goodness.

" Later, when you are men, you will understand my words better, and recognise that I am right. In the meantime, my dear friends, watch over your souls, keep them without stain, for it is by the soul that you live. The Lord has put it in your little world to light it up, as He has put the sun in the sky to illumine and warm the universe. Avoid idleness, gluttony, disobedience and lies. All these ugly things are like clouds that rise from below and end by darkening the light that the Lord has given you. If you keep your soul above these clouds, it will shine always like a clear sun and you will be happy ! "

Thus spoke Uncle Bernard, and each of us listened and resolved to follow his good advice, and not allow the vapours from below to overcloud his soul.

How often since have I not leant my ear to the humming of the marvellous shell ! Every evening, in the fine autumn weather, in returning from the pastures, I took it on my knees, and with my cheek against its rosy enamel I listened in deep thought. I pictured to myself the wonders that Uncle Bernard had told us, thinking, " If we could see those things through a little hole, it would be splendid ! "

But what astonished me more than all the rest was that, through continually listening, I seemed to be able to distinguish, amid the humming of the shell, the echo of all my thoughts. Some sweet and tender, others joyful ; they sang like tits and blackcaps at the return of springtime, and that delighted me. I would have remained there for hours, my mouth half open, my eyes staring, scarcely breathing in order to hear better, if our old Gredel had not shouted to me, " Fritzel, what are you thinking about ? Take that shell away from your ear for a little while, and put on the table-cloth. For here is the doctor coming back!"

Then I placed the shell on the drawers with a sigh, and laid the cloth for myself and my uncle at the end of the table, and, taking the large decanter, fetched some water from the well.

One day, however, the shell of Uncle Bernard gave me back less agreeable sounds; its music became severe, and put me in the greatest fright. It was because I had no reason to be satisfied with myself; dark clouds covered my soul; I had done wrong, very great wrong. But I must tell you that from the beginning. This is how it all happened. Ludwig and I, in the afternoon, were looking after our goats on the plateau of the Altenberg. We platted the cord of our whips, we whistled and thought of nothing. The goats climbed to the top of the rock, their necks outstretched, their beards standing out against the blue sky. Our old dog, Bockel, quite toothless, slumbered, with his long wolfish head between his paws. We were lying in the shadow of a clump of small firs, when suddenly Ludwig stretched his whip towards the ravine, and said to me, "Look down there, at the edge of the big rock, on the old beech tree; there is a nest of blackbirds."

Then I saw the old blackbird darting from branch to branch, because he knew we were looking at him. A thousand times Uncle Bernard had forbidden me to rob birds' nests; and, moreover, the nest was above the precipice, in the fork of a big mouldering branch. For a long time I looked at it all, musing. Ludwig said to me, "There are young ones. While I was gathering blackberries in the brambles this morning, I heard them chirping for food. To-morrow they will fly away, for they must be feathered."

I still said nothing, but the devil pushed me on. I rose up and went to the tree, in the midst of the heather, and tried to clasp it round. It was too big. Unhappily, close by grew a smaller tree all green. I climbed on it, and, making it bend over, I reached the first branch of the big beech. I mounted up. The two blackbirds circled about the foliage with plaintive cries. I paid no attention to them, and got astride the mouldering bough leading to the nest, which I could see very well. In it were three nestlings and an egg, and that made me feel plucky. The little ones stretched out their necks, and opened their large yellow beaks to the bottom of their throats, and I was sure of getting them. But, as I went forward, my legs hanging down and my hands clutching in front, suddenly the bough broke clean off and I had only the time to cry, "Oh, my God!"

I made two turns through the air, and fell on a big bough below, to which I clung with all my strength. The tree trembled to the roots, and the upper branch went down, dragging the rocks with it with a noise that made the hairs of my head stand on end. In spite of myself I looked at it descending the ravine. It splashed into the torrent, and went spinning away in the foam towards the big whirlpool, where it disappeared. Then I carefully climbed up the trunk, my knees well pressed together, and I let myself slide, trembling and sick, into the heather. The two old blackbirds still hovered above me with mournful cries. Ludwig had run away; but as he was going down the path from the Altenberg, he chanced to turn his head, and seeing me safe and sound came back, shouting breathlessly, "There you are! You didn't fall from the rocks?"

"Yes," I answered, almost unable to move my tongue. "Here I am. . . . The good Lord has saved me. . . . But let us go away. . . . Go away. . . . I am afraid!"

It was about seven in the evening, the red sun was setting between the pines. I had enough that day of looking after goats. The dog drove along our flock that took the dusty path down to Hirschland. Neither Ludwig nor I blew joyfully in our horn, as on other evenings, to get an answer from the echo of Hollow Rock. Fear was upon us, and my legs were still trembling. Reaching the village, where the goats went to left and right bleating at all the doors of the stables, I said to Ludwig:

"You will not say anything?"

"No. Be easy about it."

And I went home to Uncle Bernard. He had gone on the mountains to see an old, sick wood-man. Gredel prepared the table. When Uncle did not return by eight o'clock, we supped alone. We did this as usual. Then Gredel took the plates away and washed up in the kitchen, and I entered the library, and took up the shell, not without anxiety. God in heaven, how it murmured! I heard the torrents and the rivers roaring, and in the midst of it all the sorrowful cries of the old blackbirds, the noise of the falling branch dragging down the rocks, and the shivering of the old rocking beech tree. And as I pictured to myself the poor little nestlings crushed on a stone! . . . it was terrible . . . terrible! I ran into my little bedroom above the barn and got into bed. But I could not sleep. Fear was still upon me.

About ten o'clock I heard Uncle trot up in the silence of the night. He stopped at our door, led his horse to the stable, and then entered. I heard him open the kitchen cupboard and take a snack, as was his custom when he came back late.

"If he knew what I had done!" I said to myself. At last he went to bed. In vain I turned from one side to the other. I was too agitated to sleep. It seemed to me that my soul was as black as ink, and I wanted to cry. At midnight my despair became so great that I preferred to confess everything. Rising up, I went down in my shirt to Uncle's bedroom, who was sleeping with a night-light on the table. I knelt down by his bed. He woke up with a start, and raising himself on his elbow looked at me in astonishment.

"Fritzel!" he said. "What is the matter, my child?"

"Uncle Bernard," I sobbed, "pardon me, I have committed a great sin."

"What have you done?" he said tenderly.

"I climbed on a beech on the Altenberg to rob a blackbird's nest, and the bough broke."

"Broke? Oh, my God!"

"Yes, but the Lord saved me by allowing me to get caught on a lower branch. Now the old blackbirds keep asking me for their little ones. They fly around me, and will not let me sleep."

My Uncle remained silent for some time. I wept passionately.

"Uncle," I said again, "this evening I listened in the shell. Everything is broken, everything is upset. It can never be put right."

Then he took me in his arms, and said in a grave voice:

"I pardon you, my boy! Now be calm. But let it serve as a lesson to you. Think how sad I should have been if you had been brought back dead! Well, the poor father and the poor mother of the little blackbirds are as sad as I should have been myself. You did not think of that. And now that you are sorry, we must all pardon you."

Rising up, he gave me a glass of sugared water, saying, "Now go and sleep. The poor blackbirds will not trouble you any more, and God has pardoned you because you are sorry. So now you can sleep quietly. But from to-morrow you will not tend the goats. A boy of your age ought to go to school."

I went back to my room more at ease, and slept quite happily. The next morning Uncle Bernard took me to our old schoolmaster, Tobie Veyrius. Speaking truly, it seemed hard to me at the beginning to remain shut up in a room from morn to eve, without daring to stir. Yes, it struck me as very hard. I longed to get back to the open air; but on this earth you arrive at nothing without giving yourself considerable trouble, and then the work ended by becoming a pleasant habit. It is even, all things considered, the purest and most solid of our pleasures.

Now Uncle Bernard is very old. He spends his time sitting in a big arm-chair behind the stove in winter, and in summer on the stone bench before the house, in the shadow of the vine that covers the front. And I am a doctor. I take his place. At dawn in the morning I get on horseback, and I do not come back till the evening, worn out with fatigue. It is a hard life, especially in the season of the deep snowstorms. And yet that does not prevent me from being happy.

The shell is always in its place. Sometimes, after my rides in the mountains, I take it up, as in the golden days of my childhood, and listen to the murmuring echo of my thoughts. They are not always joyful. At times they are very sad, when one of my poor patients is in peril of death, and I can do nothing to help. But never are they so threatening as on the evening of the adventure with the blackbird's nest. He alone is happy, my dear friends, who can listen without fear to the voice of his conscience. Rich or poor, he experiences the most complete felicity it is given man to know in this world.

THE INVENTOR

Erckmann-Chatrian

On the twenty-ninth day of July 1835, Kasper Boeck, a shepherd of the village of Hirchwiller, his large felt hat hanging upon his shoulders, his canvas wallet hanging by his side, and followed by his great yellow-pawed dog, presented himself about nine o'clock in the evening at the house of Burgomaster Petrousse, who had just finished supper, and was helping himself to a glass of kirschenwasser to aid his digestion.

The Burgomaster was a tall thin man, and wore on his lip a large grizzly moustache. He had, in former days, served in the army of the Archduke Charles; and, while possessed of a good-natured disposition, he ruled the village of Hirchwiller with a wag of his finger and a nod of his head.

"Burgomaster!" cried the shepherd in a state of excitement; but Petrousse, without waiting to hear him further, frowned and said:

"Kasper Boeck, begin by taking off your hat; send out your dog, and then speak plainly without spluttering, in order that I may understand you."

Whereupon the Burgomaster, standing near the table, quietly emptied his glass, and sucked the fringe of his great moustache with an air of indifference.

Kasper sent out his dog and returned, cap in hand.

"Now," said Petrousse, seeing the shepherd somewhat composed, "tell me what has happened."

"The ghost has appeared again in the ruins of Geirstein!"

"Ah! I doubt that very much. Have you seen it, Kasper?"

"That I have, Burgomaster, very plainly."

"What was it like?"

" It looked like a little man."

" Good."

Then the old soldier, unhooking his gun from above the door, slung it over his shoulder and addressed the shepherd :

" Go and tell the constable to meet me directly in the little lane of the hollies," said he. " Your ghost is likely to prove some vagabond rascal ; but if it should turn out to be only a fox, I'll make its skin into a cap with long ears for you."

So saying the Burgomaster strode out, followed humbly by Kasper Boeck.

The weather was charming. Whilst the shepherd hastened to knock at the door of the constable, Petrousse ensconced himself in a grove of elders which skirted the back of the old village church. Two minutes later Kasper and Hans Goerner, his short sword dangling by his side, joined the Burgomaster at a sharp trot. The three advanced towards the ruins of Geirstein.

These ruins, situated at about twenty minutes' walk from the village, appeared insignificant enough, consisting of several fragments of a broken-down wall, some four or six feet in height, which made themselves barely visible amidst the brushwood. Archæologists called them the aqueducts of Seranus, the Roman camp of Holder-loch, or the vestiges of Theodoric, according to their fancy. The only remarkable feature about these ruins was the flight of stairs of a cavern cut in the rock. Contrary to most winding stairs, instead of the concentric circles contracting at every downward sweep, the spiral of this hollow increased in width in such a manner that the bottom of the hollow became three times as large as the outlet.

Could this be a caprice of architecture ? or what other strange cause determined so odd a structure ? It is a matter which need concern us little ; sufficient for the present is the fact, that in the cavern might be heard that vague murmur which any one may hear by applying the hollow of a shell to his ear : you could hear also the step of the wayfarer upon the gravel, the sighing of the breeze, the rustling of the leaves, and even the conversation of the passers-by.

The three travellers ascended the little footpath which lay between the vines and the cabbage-gardens of Hirchwiller.

" I can see nothing," broke forth the Burgomaster turning up his nose mockingly.

" Nor I either," Hans chimed in, imitating the tone of his superior.

" Oh, it is in the hole," murmured the shepherd.

" We shall see, we shall see," the Burgomaster replied confidently. And after this fashion in about a quarter of an hour they reached the mouth of the cavern.

I have said that the night was clear, bright, and perfectly calm. The moon, as far as the eye could reach, lit with bluish tints one of those nocturnal landscapes clothed with silvery trees, the shadows of which upon the ground seem traced in the firm dark lines of a pencil. The heath and the broom in blossom perfumed the breeze with an odour sharpened by the night air ; and the frogs of a neighbouring marsh croaking their hoarse strains broke from time to time the silence of the night.

But all these appearances escaped the attention of our worthy rustics ; they thought only of laying hands upon the ghost.

Arriving at the cavern mouth the three halted and listened. Then they looked into the darkness : nothing could be seen, nothing stirred.

"Confound it," exclaimed the Burgomaster, " we have forgotten to bring a bit of candle with us. Get down the stair, Kasper, you know the way better than I do ; I will follow you."

At this proposal the shepherd recoiled hastily. If he had followed his own inclination the poor fellow would have taken to his heels : his piteous looks caused the Burgomaster to fall into fits of laughter.

"Very well then, Hans, since Kasper is afraid to descend, you must lead the way."

"But—but, good Burgomaster," expostulated the constable, " you know there are some of the steps awanting. We run the risk of breaking our necks."

"Then send on your dog, Kasper," continued the Burgomaster.

The shepherd called his dog : he showed him the stairs, he urged him forward, but the dog no more than the men inclined to make the venture.

At this moment a brilliant idea occurred to Hans.

"Ha ! Mister Petrousse," he exclaimed, " suppose you fire a shot into the cave ? "

"By my faith," cried the Burgomaster, " you are right. We shall see clearly at any rate."

And without hesitating the bold man approached the staircase holding his gun. But by reason of the acoustic effects which have been already pointed out, the ghost, the vagabond, or whatever it was occupied the cavern, heard all that had passed. The idea of receiving the report of a gun did not seem to suit his tastes, for in a small shrill voice he cried :

"Hold ! do not fire ! I ascend to you ! "

Then the three besiegers regarded each other, subduing their laughter, and the Burgomaster again bending over the hollow shouted in rude tone :

"Make haste, rascal, or I fire ! "

He shouldered his gun. The click of the lock seemed to hasten the ascent of the mysterious individual, and several stones, detached in his haste, were heard to roll to the bottom. Nevertheless, more than a minute elapsed before any one appeared, the cavern being at least sixty feet in depth.

What could engage that man in the midst of such darkness? Surely he must be some great criminal! Thus thought at least the Burgomaster and his attendants.

At length a vague form emerged from the shade. Then slowly, step by step, a little lean red-haired man, four and a half feet in height, his complexion sallow, his eyes sparkling like a magpie's, his hair in disorder, and his clothes in tatters, issued from the cavern crying:

" By what right, wretches, do you come to disturb my studies? "

This authoritative speech was not at all in keeping with the dress and figure of the little fellow, so the Burgomaster replied indignantly:

" Make haste to prove yourself an honest man, you wretched imp, or I shall begin by giving you a thrashing."

" A thrashing! " cried the manikin, dancing with rage and drawing himself up under the nose of the Burgomaster.

" Yes, a thrashing," replied Petrousse, who, nevertheless, could not help admiring the courage of the dwarf, " if you do not reply in a satisfactory manner to the questions I am about to put to you. I am the Burgomaster of Hirchwiller; here is the constable, the shepherd and his dog; we are stronger than you, observe; be wise, therefore, and tell me peaceably what you are, what you do here, and why you do not appear in the light of day. After that we shall see what is to be done with you."

" All that does not concern you," replied the little man in his harsh voice; " I will not answer you."

" In that case then, forward march! " the Burgomaster responded, seizing him by the neck, " you shall take up your quarters in prison."

The little fellow struggled and twisted like a weasel: he even attempted to bite, and the dog was already manifesting designs upon his calves, when, thoroughly exhausted, he said, not without a certain dignity:

" Release me, sir, I yield to force; I shall follow you."

The Burgomaster, not wanting in courtesy, became more calm in turn.

" You promise me that," said he.

" I promise you."

" That is well: walk then in front of us."

And this is how, on the night of the twenty-ninth of July 1835, the Burgomaster of Hirchwiller effected the capture of a little red-haired man, issuing from the ruins of Geirstein.

On reaching the village the constable ran to seek the key of the prison, and the captive was shut in under double lock.

The next day, towards nine o'clock, Hans Goerner, having

received orders to lead the prisoner to the court-house in order to submit him to a new interrogation, betook himself with four stout fellows to the cell. They opened the door, full of curiosity to see the ghost, but what was their surprise to see him hanging by his cravat to the railing of the skylight window. Without delay they set off to the house of the Burgomaster, to apprise him of the event.

The justice of peace and the doctor of Hirchwiller drew up in legal form a deposition of the witnesses of the catastrophe; then they buried the unknown one in a neighbouring clover-field, and so the matter ended.

But about three weeks after these events I went to see my cousin Petrousse, of whom I happened to be the nearest relative and heir, circumstances which maintained between us an attachment of the closest kind. We were dining together and talking of various subjects, in the course of which he related to me the preceding history, just as I have reported it.

"It is strange, cousin," said I to him, "very strange! and you have no other trace of that mysterious being?"

"None."

"You have learned nothing which can give you a hint of his intentions?"

"Absolutely nothing, Christian."

"But what could he be doing in the cave? what could be the object of his life?"

The Burgomaster shrugged his shoulders, refilled our glasses, and replied:

"Your health, cousin."

"And yours."

We remained silent for some minutes. It was impossible for me to be satisfied with the sudden termination of this adventure, and in spite of myself I fell into a dreamy melancholy, thinking of the sad fate of certain men who appear and disappear in the world like the flowers of the field, without leaving behind them the least remembrance or the least regret.

"Cousin," I at length inquired, "how far may it be from here to the ruins of Geirstein?"

"Twenty minutes' walk at farthest. Why do you ask?"

"Just that I wish to see them."

"You know that to-day we have a meeting of the council, and that I cannot accompany you."

"Oh!" I replied, "I shall easily find them myself."

"That is unnecessary," he said, "Hans will show you the way; he has nothing better to do." And my cousin, having tapped upon his glass, called his servant and said:

"Katel, go seek Hans Goerner; let him make haste; it is now two o'clock and I must be going."

The domestic departed, and Hans arrived without delay. He received instructions to conduct me to the ruins, and, whilst the Burgomaster proceeded leisurely to the council chamber, we mounted the brow of the hill. Hans Goerner pointed out to me with his hand the remains of the aqueduct. At this moment the rocky edge of the plateau, the blue mountains of Hundsrück, the sadly dilapidated walls covered with sombre ivy, the clang of the village bell calling the worthies of Hirchwiller to council, the panting constable clinging to the brushwood, all produced within me a sad and sombre impression I could hardly account for, unless it might be the history of the poor suicide casting a shadow on the horizon.

The staircase of the cavern appeared to me extremely curious, its spiral form elegant. The rough shrubs springing from the fissures at almost every step, and the desolate aspect of the place, accorded with my sadness.

We descended, and soon the luminous point of the opening above, which appeared to become more and more narrow, taking the form of a star with diverging rays, alone lent us its pale light.

On reaching the bottom of the cave it was a wondrous sight which the whole flight of steps presented, lighted from above and casting their shadows with a marvellous regularity. I now heard the resonance Petrousse had spoken of to me; the immense granite shell had as many echoes as stones.

"Has any one descended here since the little man was discovered?" I inquired of Hans Goerner.

"No, sir, the peasants are afraid; they imagine that the ghost has gone back again. No one ventures into the Screech-owl's Ear."

"Do they call this the Screech-owl's Ear?"

"Yes."

"It resembles that closely," said I, lifting my eyes. "This vault reversed forms the concha or outer part, underneath the stairs we have the tympanic cavity, and the windings of the staircase represent the cochlea, the labyrinth, and the vestibule of the ear. Here, then, is the cause of the murmur which is heard: we are at the base of a colossal ear."

"It is very likely," replied Hans, who seemed to understand nothing of my observations.

We prepared to ascend, and I had already mounted a few steps when I felt something crumble under my foot. Bending down to see what it might be, I perceived at the same time a white object before me, which proved to be a tattered sheet of paper. As for the hard substance which had been broken, I recognised in it a kind of glazed brown stone jug.

"Oh, ho!" I cried, "this may throw some light upon the Burgomaster's story," and I rejoined Hans Goerner, who already awaited me at the mouth of the cavern.

" Now, sir," he said to me, " where do you wish to go ? "

" In the first place," said I, " let us rest a little : we shall consider presently.

I sat down upon a stone, while Hans cast his falcon eye round about the village in search of plunderers in the gardens, if any such could be discovered.

I examined carefully the stone vase, of which only a fragment remained. That fragment presented the form of the mouth of a trumpet lined with down. Its use I could not make out. I then read the fragment of the letter, which was written in a steady flowing hand. I have transcribed it word for word. It seems to form a continuation of another portion of the sheet, which I have since sought for unsuccessfully in and about the ruins.

" My micracoustic cornet has therefore the double advantage of multiplying infinitely the intensity of sounds, and of introducing into the ear nothing which will in the least annoy the observer. You could hardly credit, my dear master, the delight which one experiences in distinguishing the thousand imperceptible noises which, in the beautiful summer days, combine to form one immense hum. The bee has his song, like the nightingale ; the wasp is the linnet of the mosses ; the grasshopper the twittering swallow of the tall grass ; the gnat resembles the wren in the same degree ; its voice is only a sigh, but that sigh is melodious.

" This discovery, from a philosophic point of view, which makes us share in the life universal, surpasses in importance all that I am able to say of it.

" After so much suffering, privation, and weariness, how glorious it is to gather in at last the reward of our labours. With what thankfulness the soul lifts itself towards the divine Author of these microscopic worlds, the magnificence of which has been revealed to us ! What are now the long hours of anguish, of hunger, of scorn, which formerly overwhelmed us ? Nothing, my dear master, nothing ! Tears of gratitude moisten our eyes. We are proud of having bought by suffering new joys for humanity and of having contributed to its elevation. But however vast, however admirable may be these first results of my micracoustic cornet, its advantages do not stop there. There are others more positive, more material, so to speak, and which are demonstrable by figures.

" Just as the telescope enables us to discover myriads of worlds accomplishing their harmonious revolutions in space, so does my micracoustic cornet carry the sense of hearing beyond the bounds of the possible. Thus, sir, I do not stop at the circulation of the blood and the humours of the living body. You may hear them rush along with the impetuosity of cataracts, you may perceive them with a distinctness that would astonish you. The least irregularity in the pulse, the slightest obstacle in its course, strikes you, and produces the effect of a rock against which are dashed the waters of a torrent!

"This is unquestionably an immense gain in the development of our physiological and pathological knowledge, but it is not on this point I insist.

"On applying your ear, sir, to the ground, you can hear the hot mineral waters springing up at immense depths; you can estimate their volume, their currents, their obstacles. Do you desire to go further? Descend into a subterranean vault so constructed as to collect a considerable quantity of appreciable sound; then at night, when all sleep, and nothing disturbs the interior sounds of our globe, listen!

"My dear master, all that I can say at this moment—for in the midst of my deep misery, of my privations, and often indeed of my despair, there is left for me only a few lucid moments in which I can pursue my geological observations—all it is possible for me to tell you is, that the bubbling of flaming lava and the uproar of elements in ebullition is something awful and sublime, and which can only be compared to the feelings of the astronomer sounding with his glass the depths of space and infinitude. Nevertheless I must confess to you, that these experiences have need of being further studied and classified in methodic manner, in order to draw from them reliable conclusions. Also, as soon as you have deigned, my dear and worthy master, to forward to me at Newstadt the small sum I have asked of you to meet my pressing wants, we shall come to an understanding, with the view of establishing three subterranean observatories—one in the valley of Catane, the other in Iceland, and the third in one of the valleys of Capac-Uren, of Songay, or of Cayembe-Uren, the deepest in the Cordilleras, and consequently . . ."

Here the letter ended! My hands fell by my sides, I was stupified. Had I been reading the ravings of a madman or the realised inspirations of a genius? What could one say? What could one think? This miserable man living at the bottom of a pit, dying with hunger, had been perhaps one of those chosen ones whom the Supreme Being sends upon the earth to enlighten future generations. This man had hung himself in disgust. His prayer had not been responded to, although he asked only a morsel of bread in exchange for his discovery. It was a horrible thought. Long I remained there, lost in reverie and thanking Heaven for not having willed to make of me a leading man in the community of martyrs. At length

Hans Goerner, seeing me with eyes fixed and mouth agape, ventured to touch me on the shoulder.

" Sir," said he, " it grows late ; the Burgomaster by this time will have returned from the council."

" Ah ! you are right," I exclaimed, crumpling the paper in my hand ; " let us go."

We descended the bank. My cousin met us on the threshold, a smile upon his face.

" Well, friend Christian ! you have found nothing of the simpleton who hung himself ? "

" No."

" I thought as much," continued the Burgomaster. " He was doubtless some lunatic escaped from Stefansfeld or other madhouse. By my faith, he did well to hang himself. When one is good for nothing, that is the wisest thing he can do."

THE PAPERS
OF MME JEANNETTE

Erckmann-Chatrian

EVERY day after school I used to go and see Jean Pierre Coustel, the turner, at work at the end of the village. He was an old man, half bald, his feet in big torn shoes, and a rat-tail wig frisking about his back. He loved to talk about his campaigns along the Rhine and the Loire and in Vendée. Then he would look at you and laugh softly. His little wife, Madame Jeannette, spun behind him in the shadow. She had large black eyes and hair as white as flax. She would stop spinning and listen every time Jean Pierre spoke of Nantes. They were married there in 1793.

I can see it all as if it were yesterday ; the two little windows surrounded with ivy ; the three hives on a plank above the old, worm-eaten door ; the bees fluttering in a sunbeam on the thatched roof ; Jean Pierre, his back curved, turning chair-legs or bobbins ; the shavings curling up like corkscrews. . . . It is all before me !

And I can see at evening, Jacques Chatillon, the timber merchant, with his big red whiskers, coming in the evening, his measure under his arm ; the gamekeeper Benassis, his bag on his hip and his little cap over his ear ; Monsieur Nadasi, the sheriff's officer, walking with his nose in the air, spectacled, his hands in his tail pockets, as though he was proclaiming to the world, " I am Nadasi who carries summonses to men who will not pay their debts " ; then my uncle Eustache, and many others, without speaking of the wife of the little tailor Rigodin, who came to fetch her husband at nine o'clock, in order to be treated to a drink. For in addition to being a turner, Coustel kept a wine-shop, and a fir-branch hung from his little house. In the winter, when it was raining or the snow was banked up to the windows, it was pleasant to sit in the old hovel, and listen to the fire humming to the spinning-wheel of Jeannette, whole gusts of wind outside swept through the village.

I, quite a child, never stirred from my corner until Uncle Eustache, knocking the ashes out of his pipe, said to me, " Come, Francis, let us be off ! Good-night to you all." How all these far-off things come back to me, fresh and vivid, when I think of them. But what I remember above all is the story of the marshes of old Jeannette —the lands she possessed along the sea-shore in Vendée, which might have made the Coustels rich if they had claimed their property sooner.

It appears that in 1793 a good many people were drowned at Nantes, and principally the old nobility. They were bound together, and thrown in a boat, and taken out to the Loire, and there the boats were sunk. It was in the days of the Terror, and the peasants of Vendée also shot all the Republican troops they could get. Both parties were bent on exterminating the other ; there was no pity for any one. But each time a Republican trooper offered to marry some noble girl who was going to be drowned, and the unhappy creature agreed to take him as her husband, she was at once released. And that was how Madame Jeannette became the wife of Coustel. She was on one of the boats at the age of sixteen—an age when it is terrible to die ! White with fear, she looked around to see if there was any one to take pity on her. Jean Pierre Coustel, who was passing, his gun on his shoulder at the moment when the boat was leaving, saw the young girl and cried :

" Stop a moment ! . . . Citizeness, will you take me ? I will save your life ! "

And Jeannette, almost dead with fright, fell in his arms, and he took her away and they were married at the town hall.

Old Jeannette never talked about her former life. She had been very happy in her girlhood. She had had a maid and servants, horses and carriages, and then she had become the wife of a poor devil of a Republican trooper. She had cooked his food and mended his ragged clothes ; her old ideas of castles and manor-houses and curtseying peasant women in Vendée faded from her mind . . . So things go in this world ! And sometimes Nadasi would mock the poor old woman.

" Your ladyship, half a pint ! . . . Your ladyship, a glass of wine ! " He would ask her what was the latest news from her estates. She would look at him with tightening lips; her pale cheeks would flush, and it would seem as if she were going to make some reply; but in the end she would lower her head, and go on spinning in silence.

If Nadasi had not spent a fair amount of money in the wine-shop, Coustel would have thrust him out of the door. But when you are poor, there are many things you must put up with, and the cads know it. They never insult any one like my uncle Eustache, who would pull their ears for them; they are too cunning for that. But we all know this sort of creature, and I will go on with my story.

One evening we were sitting in the wine-shop towards the end of the autumn of 1830; it rained in floods, and at eight o'clock the gamekeeper Benassis entered, saying, "What weather! If this continues the three ponds will overflow."

He shook his cap and drew his blouse over his shoulders to dry it behind the stove. Then he sat down at the end of the bench, telling Nadasi to move further up.

In spite of the rain the gamekeeper was in a good humour. He said a flock of wild geese had settled on the ponds, and that the shooting over the marshes would soon being. Uncle Eustache said he would willingly join the shooting party in a boat, but that wading through the mud, with the risk of dropping head over heels into it, was not the kind of sport that amused him. Everybody was having his say on the matter, and old Jeannette, sunk in thought, began to murmur:

"I also had marshes . . . ponds!"

"Ho!" cried Nadasi with a jeering air, "listen to this! Dame Jeannette had marshes of her own!"

"Undoubtedly I had," she said.

"Where, most noble lady?"

"In Vendée, by the sea-shore."

And as Nadasi shrugged his shoulders, as though saying, "The old woman is mad!" Jeannette went up the little wooden ladder at the back of the hovel, and then came down with a basket full of odds and ends—cotton, needles, spools, and yellow parchments.

"Here are our papers," she said. "The marshes, the ponds, and manor-house are mentioned with the other things. We tried to claim them under Louis the Eighteenth, but my relatives would not give them back to us, because I had dishonoured the family by my marriage. It would have been necessary to bring a lawsuit, and we hadn't the money. Isn't that true, Coustel?"

"Yes," said the turner quietly.

Among all those present nobody thought anything of these things, any more than of the bundles of paper money of the time of the First Republic that are found in many old chests. The old paper money is valueless, so the old deeds. . . .

Nadasi, still with a grin on his face, opened one of the parchments, and, lifting his nose, started to read it with the idea of getting more fun out of Jeannette. But his look suddenly became serious ; he wiped his spectacles, and turned towards the poor old woman who had resumed her spinning.

" Do you mind my taking this away and studying it, Madame Jeannette ? " he said.

" My God ! do what you like with it," she replied. " We have no further use for it, and besides, Coustel and myself, we cannot read."

Nadasi, with a grave air, folded the parchment up, and put it in his pocket with several others, saying :

" I will look into it. It is just striking nine. Good-night."

He went out, and the others soon followed him. But eight days afterwards Nadasi set out for Vendée. He had got Coustel and Jeannette to sign the power of attorney, with which he could recover, alienate, and sell all their property on their behalf. The rumour spread through the village that Madame Jeannette was of noble birth, that she had a castle in Vendée, and that the Coustels would receive an immense fortune. But Nadasi wrote that he had come six weeks too late, and that the brother of Madame Jeannette had shown him some documents proving that he had held the marshes for more than thirty years, and that when any property had been occupied without protest for more than thirty years, the absent owner lost all right to it. So that the Coustels, having let their noble relative keep possession of the estate, had surrendered all claim to it.

The poor couple, who had thought they were rich and who had been complimented and flattered by all the villagers, felt their poverty far more keenly than they had done before. It was not long before they died, one after the other.

Nadasi never came back to the village. No doubt he found something that paid him better than trotting about with summonses.

A good many years passed by. Louis Philippe went away ; the Second Republic rose and fell, and the Third Napoleon reigned over France. The bones of the Coustels had moulded into dust in their grave on the hill. I occupied my grandfather's position at the post office, and Uncle Eustache, as he used to say himself, had taken his passport. It was then, one morning during the watering season at Baden, that something astonishing happened that still gives me food for reflection. Several postchaises had passed down the street, and about eleven o'clock a courier came to tell me that the Baron de Roselière, his master, was approaching.

I was breakfasting, but I at once rose to see to the relay. When the horses were being harnessed, a head looked out from the carriage —an old head, deeply wrinkled, with hollow cheeks, and golden spectacles on the nose. It was the face of Nadasi, but aged, worn out, and tired. Behind him was the head of a young girl. I was bewildered.

" What is the name of this village ? " he said, yawning behind his hand.

" Laneuville, my lord."

He did not recognise me and sat down. Then I saw an old lady in the depths of the carriage. The horses were harnessed, and they went away.

God pardon me if I am wrong, but I still think that Nadasi sold the documents of poor Jeannette and then got a new skin for himself, like many other swindlers, by taking a noble name to cover his tracks ! Who could have stopped him ? Didn't he have all the titles, all the parchments, and the general power of attorney ? Poor old Jeannette ! . . . What miseries we meet in life ! . . . And to think that God lets it all go on !

EDMOND ABOUT
1828–1885

WHICH
WAS THE MADMAN?

I

I AM sure that you have passed Doctor Auvray's house twenty times without supposing that miracles are performed there. It is a modest-looking house, without any display or any sign : it does not even bear on its door the unattractive inscription—*Maison de santé*. It is situated near the end of the Avenue Montaigne, between Prince Soltikoff's Gothic palace and the great Triat's gymnasium where they regenerate mankind on the trapeze. A gate, painted in imitation of bronze, opens upon a little garden of lilacs and roses. The porter's lodge is at the right ; the building at the left contains the doctor's rooms, and those of his wife and daughter. The principal building is at the remote end : it turns its back upon the avenue, and opens all its windows to the south-east on a little park, well planted with chestnuts and lindens.

There the doctor treats, and often cures, people who have lost their minds. I would not take you into his establishment if you ran any risk of meeting all kinds of insanity ; but do not be afraid ; you will not have the distressing spectacle of imbecility, paralytic insanity, or even utter loss of intelligence. M. Auvray has created for himself what is called a specialty : he treats monomania. He is an excellent man, full of intelligence and learning : a real philosopher and pupil of Esquirol and Laromiguière. If you were ever to meet him, with his bald head, well-shaven chin, black vestments, and placid face, you would not know whether he were a doctor, professor, or priest. When he opens his heavy eyes, you expect him to say, " My child ! " His eyes are not ugly, considering how they protrude, and they throw around him glances comprehensive, limpid, and serene, beneath which you see a world of kindly thoughts. Those large eyes are the open doors of a beautiful soul.

M. Auvray's vocation was decided when he was at the medical school. He gave himself up passionately to the study of monomania —that curious disturbance of the faculties which is seldom due to a physical cause, which does not answer to any perceptible lesion in the nervous system, and which is cured by moral treatment. He was seconded in his observations by a young female superintendent of one of the wards, who was quite pretty and very well educated. He fell in love with her, and as soon as he got his degree married her. It was a modest entrance upon life. Nevertheless, he had a little property which he devoted to founding the establishment you know. With a touch of charlatanism, he could have made a fortune ; he was satisfied to make his expenses. He avoided notoriety, and whenever he attained a marvellous cure he did not proclaim it from the house-tops. His reputation made itself, and almost in spite of him. His treatise on *Monomanie raisonnante*, which he published through Baillière in 1842, is in its sixth edition without the author having sent a single copy to the papers. Modesty is certainly good in itself, but it ought not to be carried to an extreme. Mlle Auvray has not more than twenty thousand francs dowry, and she will be twenty-two years old in April.

About a fortnight ago (it was, I think, on Wednesday, December 13th) a cab stopped before M. Auvray's gate. The driver rang, and the gate was opened. The carriage went on to the doctor's house, and two men briskly entered his office. The servant begged them to sit down and wait till the doctor had finished his rounds. It was ten o'clock in the morning.

One of the strangers was a man of fifty, large, brown, full-blooded, of high colour, passably ugly, and specially ill-made ; his ears were pierced, his hands large, and his thumbs enormous. Fancy a workman dressed in his employer's clothes : such is M. Morlot.

His nephew, François Thomas, is a young man of twenty-three, hard to describe, because he is just like everybody else. He is neither large nor small, handsome nor ugly, developed like a Hercules nor spindled like a dandy, but, maintaining the happy medium throughout, unobtrusive from head to foot, hair of no particular colour, and mind and clothes of the same. When he entered M. Auvray's house he seemed very much agitated ; he walked up and down apparently in a rage, would not keep still anywhere, looked at twenty things at once, and would have handled them all if his hands had not been tied.

"Calm yourself," said his uncle ; "what I'm doing is for your good. You'll be happy here, and the doctor will cure you."

"I'm not sick. Why have you tied me ? "

"Because you would have thrown me out of the carriage. You're not in your right mind, my poor François ; M. Auvray will restore you."

"I reason as clearly as you do, uncle, and I don't know what you're talking about. My mind is clear, my judgment sound, and my memory excellent. Would you like me to repeat some verses ?

Shall I translate some Latin ? Here's a Tacitus in this bookcase. . .
If you would prefer a different experiment, I can solve a problem in
Arithmetic or Geometry. . . . You don't care to have me ? Very well !
Listen to what we have done this morning :

" You came in at eight o'clock, not to wake me, for I was not
asleep, but to get me out of bed. I dressed myself, without
Germain's help ; you asked me to go with you to Dr. Auvray's ;
I refused ; you insisted ; I got angry ; Germain helped you to tie
my hands ; I'll discharge him to-night. I owe him thirteen day's
wages : that is thirteen francs, as I engaged him at thirty francs a
month. You owe him damages : you are the cause of his losing
his Christmas gift. Is this reasoning ? And do you still think you
can make me out crazy ? Ah ! my dear uncle, take a better view
of things ! Remember that my mother was your sister ! What
would she say—my poor mother !—if she were to see me here ? I
bear you no ill-will, and everything can be arranged pleasantly.
You have a daughter, Mlle Claire Morlot. . . ."

" Ah ! there I have you ! You see clearly enough that you are
out of your head. I have a daughter ? I ? But I'm a bachelor.
A confirmed bachelor ! "

" You have a daughter," replied François mechanically.

" My poor nephew ! Let us see. Listen to me carefully. Have
you a cousin ? "

" A cousin ? No. I have no cousin. Oh ! you won't find me
out of my reckoning ; I have no cousins of either sex."

" I am your uncle ; isn't that so ? "

" Yes, you are my uncle, although you forgot it this morning."

" If I had a daughter she would be your cousin ; now you have
no cousin, therefore I have no daughter."

" You're right. I had the happiness of seeing her this summer
at Ems Springs, with her mother. I love her ; I have reason to
think that I am not indifferent to her, and I have the honour to ask
you for her hand."

" Whose hand ? "

" Mademoiselle's hand—your daughter's."

" Well, so be it," thought M. Morlot ; " M. Auvray will be very
skilful if he cures him. I will pay six thousand francs board from
my nephew's income. Six from thirty leaves twenty-four. I shall
be rich. Poor François ! "

He seated himself and casually opened a book. " Sit down there,"
he said to the young man ; " I'll read you something. Try to
listen : it will calm you down." He read :

" Monomania is the persistence of one idea, the exclusive domination of a single passion. Its seat is in the heart ; there it must
be sought and there it must be cured. Its cause is love, fear, vanity,
ambition, remorse. It displays itself by the same symptoms as

passion generally; sometimes by joy, gaiety, daring, and noise; sometimes by timidity, sadness, and silence."

During the reading, François seemed to grow quiet and drop asleep. "Bravo!" thought M. Morlot. "Here's a miracle performed by medicine already: it puts a man to sleep who has been neither hungry nor drowsy." François was not asleep, but he played possum to perfection. He nodded at proper intervals, and regulated the heavy monotone of his breathing with mathematical accuracy. Uncle Morlot was taken in: he continued reading in a subdued voice, then yawned, then stopped reading, then let his book slip down, then shut his eyes, and then went sound asleep, much to the satisfaction of his nephew, who watched him maliciously out of the corner of his eye.

François began by moving his chair: M. Morlot budged no more than a tree. François walked about the room, making his shoes creak on the inlaid floor: M. Morlot began snoring. Then the crazy man went to the writing-table, found an eraser, pushed it into a corner, fixed it firmly by the handle, and cut the cord which bound his arms. He freed himself, recovered the use of his hands, repressed a cry of joy, and stealthily approached his uncle. In two minutes M. Morlot was firmly bound, but with so much delicacy that his sleep was not even troubled.

François admired his work, and picked up the book which had slipped to the floor. It was the last edition of the *Monomanie raisonnante*. He took it into a corner, and set to reading like a bookworm, while he awaited the doctor's arrival.

II

It now becomes necessary for me to recount the antecedents of François and his uncle. François was the son of a late toy dealer in the Passage du Saumon named M. Thomas. Toy selling is a good business; a hundred per cent is cleared on almost every article. Since his father's death, François had enjoyed a competence of the degree called "honourable," undoubtedly because it obviates the necessity of doing dishonourable things; perhaps, too, because it makes practicable the doing of the honours to one's friends: he had thirty thousand francs income.

His tastes were extremely simple, as I think I have told you. He had an innate preference for things which are not glaring, and naturally selected his gloves, vests, and coats from the series of modest colours lying between black and brown. He did not remember having dreamed of plumes, even in his tenderest childhood, and the ribbons most desired had never troubled his sleep. He never carried an opera-glass, because, he said, his eyes were good: nor wore a scarf-pin, because his scarf would keep in place without a pin; but the real reason was that he was afraid of attracting attention. The very polish of his boots dazzled him. He would have been doomed to wretchedness if the accident of birth had afflicted him with a noticeable name. If, for the sake of giving him one, his sponsors had called him Americ or Fernand, he would never have signed it in his life. Happily, his names were as unobtrusive as if he had chosen them himself.

His timidity prevented him from entering upon any career. After crossing the threshold of his baccalaureate, he stopped in that great door which opens upon everything, and stood rapt in contemplation before the seven or eight roads which were lying before him. The bar seemed to him too boisterous, medicine too devoid of rest, a tutorship too arrogant, commerce too complicated, the civil service too constraining.

As to the army, it was useless to think of that : not that he was afraid to fight, but he trembled at the idea of wearing a uniform. He remained, then, in his original way of life, not because it was the easiest, but because it was the most obscure : he lived on his income.

As he had not earned his money himself, he lent it freely. In return for so rare a virtue, Heaven gave him plenty of friends. He loved them all sincerely, and acceded to their wishes with very good grace. When he met one of them on the Boulevard, he was always the one to be taken by the arm, turned about, and taken where his friend desired. Don't think that he was either foolish, shallow, or ignorant. He knew three or four modern languages, Latin, Greek, and everything else usually learned at college ; he had some ideas of commerce, manufactures, agriculture, and literature, and he estimated a new book well, if there was nobody near to listen to his opinion.

But it was among women that his weakness showed itself in its full strength. It was a necessity of his nature always to be in love with somebody, and if in rubbing his eyes in the morning he saw no gleam of love on the horizon, he got up out of sorts and infallibly put his stockings on wrong side out. Whenever he was at a concert or a play, he began by searching among the audience for some face that pleased him, and was in love with it the whole evening. If he found one to suit him, the play was fine, the concert delicious ; otherwise, everybody played badly or sang false. His heart so abhorred a vacuum, that in presence of a mediocre beauty it spurred him to believe her perfect. You will realise without my help that this universal susceptibility was by no means licentiousness, but innocence. He loved all women without telling them so, for he had never dared to speak to one. He was the most candid and inoffensive of roués ; Don Juan, if you please, but before Doña Julia.

When he was in love, he rehearsed to himself courageous declarations, which regularly died upon his lips. He paid his court ; laid open the very bottom of his soul ; held long conversations and charming dialogues, in which he made both the questions and replies.

He made appeals energetic enough to soften rocks, and warm enough to melt ice ; but no woman was drawn towards him by his mute aspirations : one must *want*, to be loved. There is a great difference between desiring and wanting ; desiring floats easily upon the clouds : wanting runs on foot among the flints. One watches for every chance, the other demands nothing but its own existence ; wanting marches straight to its point over hedges and ditches, ravines and mountains ; desiring remains seated at home and cries for the moon in its sweetest voice.

Nevertheless, in the August of this very year, four months before pinioning his uncle's arms, François had dared to love face to face. At the Ems Springs he had met a young girl almost as shy as himself, whose shuddering timidity had given him courage. She was a Parisienne, frail and delicate as fruit grown on the shady side of a wall : transparent as those lovely children whose blue blood can be seen distinctly under their skin. She accompained her mother, whom an inveterate disorder (a chronic trouble of the throat, if I am not mistaken) obliged to take the waters. Mother and daughter must have lived apart from the world, for they regarded the boisterous crowd of bathers with long looks of astonishment. François was casually presented to them by one of his friends, who had become cured and was going to Italy through Germany. He attended them assiduously for a month, and was virtually their only companion. For sensitive souls, the crowd is a vast solitude ; the more noise the world makes around them, the more do they shrink into their corner to whisper into each other's ears.

The young Parisienne and her mother went straight into François' heart as naturally as from one room to the next, and found it pleasant there. Every day they discovered new treasures, like the navigators who first set foot in America : they wandered with ever fresh delights over this mysterious and virgin land. They never asked themselves if he were rich or poor ; they were satisfied to know that he was good ; and nothing they might find could be more precious to them than that heart of gold. On his side, François was inspired with his metamorphosis.

Has any one ever told you how spring breaks upon the gardens in Russia ? Yesterday the snow covered everything : to-day comes a ray of sunshine which puts winter to flight. At noon the trees burst their buds : by night they are covered with leaves : to-morrow they almost bear fruit. So did François's love bloom and bear its freight of promise. His coldness and constraint were carried away like icicles in a thaw ; the shamefaced and pusillanimous boy in a few weeks became a man. I do not know who first uttered the word *marriage*, but what difference does it make ? The word is always understood when two true hearts speak of love.

François was of age and his own master, but his beloved depended upon a father whose consent it was necessary to obtain. There the unfortunate youth's timidity mastered him again. It was well enough for Claire to say to him, " Write unhesitatingly ; my father is already notified : you will receive his consent by return mail." He wrote and re-wrote this letter over a hundred times, without being able to make up his mind to send it. Nevertheless, it was an easy task, and the most ordinary intelligence would have performed it with credit. François knew the name, position, fortune, and even the temperament of his future father-in-law. They had let him into all the domestic secrets ; he was almost one of the family. What was left for him to do ? To state, in a few words, what he was and what he had ; the reply was not doubtful.

He hesitated so long, that at the end of a month Claire and her mother were forced to entertain misgivings regarding him. I think they would have still been patient for a fortnight longer, but the paternal wisdom did not permit it. If Claire was in love, if her lover had not decided to make a formal declaration of his intention, the thing to do was, without losing any time, to get the girl in a safe place in Paris. Possibly then M. François Thomas would make up his mind to ask her in marriage : he knew where to find her.

One day when François went to take the ladies out walking, the hotel-keeper told him that they had left for Paris. Their rooms were already occupied by an English family. Such a rude blow, falling suddenly upon such a delicate head, destroyed his reason. He went out like an idiot, and began looking for Claire in all the places where he had been used to taking her. He went to his lodgings with a violent pain in his head, which he treated, God only knows how. He had himself bled, took boiling hot baths, applied ferocious sinapisms, and, in short, revenged on his body the tortures of his soul. When he considered himself cured, he started for France, resolved to apply for Claire's hand before changing his coat. He hurried to Paris, sprang from the car, forgot his baggage, jumped into a cab, and cried to the driver :

" To *her* ! Gallop ! "

" Where to, boss ? "

" To Monsieur ——, Rue ——, I don't know any more." He had forgotten the name and address of the woman he loved. " Go ahead to my house ; I'll find it again." He gave the coachman his card and was taken home.

His concierge was a childless old man named Emmanuel. On meeting him, François bowed low and said :

" Monsieur, you have a daughter, Mlle. Claire Emmanuel. I wanted to write you to ask for her hand ; but I thought it would be better to make the request in person."

They realised that he was crazy, and ran to the Faubourg St. Antoine to find his Uncle Morlot.

Uncle Morlot was the most honest man in the Rue de Charonne, which is one of the longest streets in Paris. He made antique furniture with ordinary skill and extraordinary conscientiousness. It was not his way to represent stained pear-wood as ebony, or a cabinet of his own make as a mediaeval piece ! Nevertheless, he knew as well as anybody the art of cracking new wood and making it appear full of worm-holes of which worms were entirely innocent. But it was his principle and his law to wrong nobody. With a moderation almost absurd in the manufacture of articles of luxury, he limited his profits to five per cent. over and above the general expenses of his establishment ; consequently he had gained more respect than money. When he made out a bill, he went over the addition three times, so fearful was he of misleading somebody to his own advantage.

After thirty years of this business, he was just about as rich as when he left his apprenticeship. He had made his living like the humblest of his employees, and he asked himself, with a touch of jealousy, how M. Thomas had managed to lay up money. His brother-in-law looked down on him a little, with the vanity natural to parvenus, but he looked down upon his brother-in-law more effectually, with the pride of a man who never cared to become a parvenu. He made a parade of his mediocrity, and said with plebeian self-conceit, " At least I'm sure that I've nothing that belongs to anybody else."

Man is a strange animal : I am not the first who has said so. This excellent M. Morlot, whose super-scrupulous honesty amused the whole faubourg, felt an agreeable tickling at the bottom of his heart when they came to tell him of his nephew's disorder. He heard an insinuating little voice saying to him, very low, " If François is insane, you'll be his guardian." Probity hastened to reply, " We won't be any richer."—" How ? " answered the voice. " Certainly an insane man's board never costs thirty thousand francs a year. Moreover, we shall have all the trouble ; we'll have to neglect our business ; we deserve more compensation ; we won't wrong anybody."—" But," replied Disinterestedness, " one ought to help his relations without charging them for it."—" Certainly," murmured the voice.—" Then why didn't our family ever do anything for us ? "—" Bah ! " responded the goodness of his heart. " This won't amount to anything, anyway ; it's only a false alarm. François will be well in a couple of days."—" Possibly, however," continued the obstinate voice, " the malady will kill the patient, and we'll inherit without wronging anybody. We've worked thirty years for the sovereign who reigns at Potsdam ; who knows but what a blow on a cracked head may make our fortune ? "

The good man stopped his ears ; but his ears were so large, so ample, so nobly expanded, like a conch-shell, that the subtle and persevering little voice always slipped into them in spite of him. The factory in the Rue de Charonne was left to the care of the foreman, and the uncle established his winter quarters in his nephew's pretty rooms. He slept in a good bed, and liked it. He sat at an excellent table, and the cramps in the stomach which he had complained of for many years were cured by magic. He was waited upon, dressed, and shaved by Germain, and he got used to it. Little by little he consoled himself for seeing his nephew sick. He fell into the habit of thinking that perhaps François never would get well ; nevertheless, he repeated to himself now and then, to keep his conscience easy, " I'm not injuring anybody."

At the end of three months, he grew tired of having a crazy man in the house, for he began to feel as if he were at home there himself. François's perpetual drivelling, and his mania for asking Claire in marriage, came to be an intolerable burden to the old man ; he resolved to clear the house and shut the sick man up at M. Auvray's. " After all," he said to himself, " my nephew will get better care there, and I shall be more at ease. Science has recognised that it is well to give the insane change of scene to divert them : I'm doing my duty."

With such thoughts as these he went to sleep, when François took it into his head to tie his hands ; what an awakening !

III

The doctor came in with apoligies for keeping them waiting. François got up, put his hat on the table, and explained matters with great volubility, while striding up and down the room.

"Monsieur," said he, " this is my maternal uncle, whom I am about to confide to your care. You see in him a man of from forty-five to fifty, hardened to manual labour and the privations of a life of hard work ; as to the rest, born of healthy parents, in a family where no case of mental aberration has ever been known. You will not, then, have to contend against an hereditary disorder. His trouble is one of the most curious monomanias which you ever had occasion to examine. He passes with inconceivable rapidity from extreme gaiety to extreme depression ; it is a singular compound of monomania proper and melancholy."

" He has not entirely lost his reason ? "

" No, monsieur, he's not absolutely demented ; he's unsound on but one point, so he comes entirely within your specialty.

" What's the characteristic of his malady ? "

" Alas, monsieur, the characteristic of our times—cupidity. The poor fellow is certainly the man of the period. After working from childhood, he finds himself poor. My father, starting where he did, left me considerable property. My uncle began by being jealous ; then realising that he was my only relative, and would be my heir in case of death, or my guardian in case of insanity, as a weak mind easily believes what it desires, the unhappy man persuaded himself that I had lost my reason. He has told everybody so : will say the same to you. In the carriage, although his own hands were bound, he thought that it was he who was bringing me to you."

" When was the first attack ? "

" About three months ago. He went down and said to my concierge, with a frightened air, ' Monsieur Emmanuel, you have a daughter ; leave her in your lodge, and come and help me bind my nephew.' "

" Does he realise his condition ? Does he know that he is not himself ? "

" No, monsieur, and I think that's a good sign. I'll tell you, moreover, that he has some remarkable derangements of the vital functions, and especially of nutrition. He has entirely lost appetite, and is subject to long periods of sleeplessness."

" So much the better. A deranged person who sleeps and eats regularly is almost incurable. Let me wake him up."

M. Auvray gently shook the shoulder of the sleeper, who sprang to his feet. His first movement was to rub his eyes. When he found his hands bound, he realised what had happened while he slept, and burst out laughing.

" That's a good joke ! " he said.

François drew the doctor aside.

" You see. Well, in five minutes he will be raving."

" Leave him to me. I know how to take them." He approached his patient smiling as one does upon a child whom he wishes to amuse. " My friend," he said, " you woke up at the right time. Did you have pleasant dreams ? "

" I ? I've not been dreaming. I laughed at seeing myself tied up like a bundle of sticks. People would take me for the crazy one."

" There ! " said François.

" Have the kindness to let me loose, doctor. I can explain matters better when I'm free."

" My child, I'm going to untie you ; but you must promise to be very good."

" Why, monsieur, do you really take me for a madman ? "

" No, my friend, but you're not well. We'll take care of you and cure you. Hold still. Now your hands are free. Don't abuse it."

" Why, what the devil do you suppose I'll do ? I've brought you my nephew——"

" Very well," said M. Auvray, " we'll talk about that in good time. I found you asleep ; do you often sleep in the daytime ? "

" Never ! This stupid book——"

" Oh ! oh ! " said the author, " the case is serious. And so you think your nephew is mad ? "

" Mad enough to be tied up, monsieur ; and the proof is, that I had fastened his hands together with this rope."

" But you're the one whose hands were tied. Don't you remember that I set you free ? "

" It was I ? It was he ! But let me explain the whole affair."

" Tut, my friend, you're getting excited : you're very red in the face. I don't want you to tire yourself. Just be content to answer my questions. You say that your nephew is ill ? "

" Crazy, crazy, crazy ! "

" And you are satisfied to see him crazy ? "

" I ? "

" Answer me frankly. You're not anxious for him to get well : isn't that so ? "

" Why ? "

" So that his fortune can remain in your hands. You want to be rich. You don't like having worked so long without making a fortune. You think it's your turn now ? "

M. Morlot did not answer. He kept his eyes fixed on the floor. He asked himself if he were not having a bad dream, and tried to make out what was real in this experience of pinioned hands, cross-examinations, and questions from a stranger who read his conscience like an open book.

" Does he hear voices ? " asked M. Auvray.

The poor uncle felt his hair stand on end. He remembered that persistent little voice which kept whispering in his ear, and he answered mechanically, " Sometimes."

" Ah ! he has hallucinations ? "

" No, no ! I'm not ill ; let me go. I'll lose my senses here. Ask all my friends ; they'll tell you that I'm in full possession of my faculties. Feel my pulse ; you'll see that I've no fever."

" Poor uncle ! " said François. " He doesn't know that insanity is madness without fever."

" Monsieur," added the doctor, " if we could only give our patients fever, we'd cure them all."

M. Morlot threw himself on the sofa ; his nephew continued to pace the doctor's study.

" Monsieur," said François, " I am deeply afflicted by my uncle's misfortune, but it is a great consolation to be able to entrust him to such a man as yourself. I have read your admirable book on *La Monomanie raisonnante* ; it is the most remarkable book that has been written on the subject since the *Traité des Maladies mentales*, by the great Esquirol. I know, moreover, that you are a father to your patients, so I will not insult you by recommending M. Morlot to special care. As to the expense of his treatment, I leave that entirely to you." He took a thousand-franc note from his pocketbook, and quietly laid it on the mantel. " I shall have the honour to present myself here in the course of next week. At what hour is access to the patients allowed ? "

" From noon till two o'clock. As for me, I'm always at home. Good-day, monsieur."

" Stop him ! " cried the poor uncle. " Don't let him go ! He's the crazy one ; I'll explain his madness ! "

" Pray calm yourself, my dear uncle," said François, going out ; " I leave you in M. Auvray's hands ; he'll take good care of you."

M. Morlot tried to follow his nephew. The doctor held him back.

" What awful luck ! " cried the poor uncle. " He won't say a single crazy thing ! If he would only lose his bearings a little, you'd see well enough that it's not I who am crazy."

François already had hold of the door-knob. He turned on his heel as if he had forgotten something : marched straight up to the doctor, and said to him :

" Monsieur, my uncle's illness is not the only motive which brought me here."

" Ah ! ah ! " murmured M. Morlot, who thought he saw a ray of hope.

The young man continued :

" You have a daughter."

" At last ! " cried the poor uncle. " You'll bear witness that he said, ' You have a daughter ! ' "

The doctor replied to François, " Yes, Monsieur. Explain—"

" You have a daughter, Mlle Claire Auvray."

" There it is ! There it is ! I told you that very thing ! "

" Yes, monsieur," said the doctor.

" Three months since she was at the Ems Springs with her mother."

" Bravo ! bravo ! " yelled M. Morlot.

" Yes, monsieur," responded the doctor.

M. Morlot ran up to the doctor and said, " You're not the doctor ! You're one of the patients ! "

" My friend," replied the doctor, " if you don't behave yourself, we'll have to give you a shower-bath."

M. Morlot recoiled, frightened. His nephew continued :

" Monsieur, I love Mademoiselle—your daughter. I have some hope that I'm loved in return, and if her sentiments have not changed since September, I have the honour to ask you for her hand."

The doctor answered, " This is Monsieur François Thomas, then, with whom I've the honour of speaking ? "

" The same, monsieur, and I ought to have begun by telling you my name."

" Monsieur, permit me to tell you that you've decidedly taken your own time."

At this moment, the doctor's attention was drawn to M. Morlot, who was rubbing his hands with a sort of passion.

"What's the matter with you, my friend ? " he inquired in his sweet and paternal voice.

"Nothing ! Nothing ! I'm only rubbing my hands."

"But why ? "

"There's something there that bothers me."

"Show it to me ; I don't see anything."

"You don't see it ? There, there, between the fingers. I see it plainly, I do ! "

"What do you see ? "

"My nephew's money. Take it away, doctor ! I'm an honest man ; I don't want anybody's property."

While the doctor was listening attentively to these first aberrations of M. Morlot a strange revolution took place in the appearance of François. He grew pale and cold, his teeth chattered violently. M. Auvray turned towards him to ask what had happened.

"Nothing," he replied. "She's coming. I hear her. This is joy . . . but it overcomes me. Happiness falls upon me like snow. The winter will be hard for lovers. Doctor, see what's going on in my head."

M. Morlot ran to him, saying :

"Enough ! Don't be crazy any more ! I no longer want you to be an idiot. People will say that I stole your wits. I'm honest, doctor ; look at my hands ; search my pockets ; send to my house, Rue de Charonne, in the Faubourg St. Antoine ; open all the drawers ; you'll see that I've nothing that belongs to anybody else."

The doctor stood much perplexed between his two patients, when a door opened, and Claire came in to tell her father that breakfast was waiting.

François jumped up as if propelled by a spring, but only his wishes reached Mlle Auvray. His body fell heavily on the sofa. He could scarcely murmur a few words.

"Claire ! It is I. I love you. Will you ? . . ."

He passed his hand over his brow. His pale face flushed violently. The temples throbbed fiercely, and he felt a heavy oppression over his eyelids. Claire, as near dead as alive, caught up his two hands. His skin was dry, and his pulse so hard that the poor girl was terrified. It was not thus that she had hoped to see him again. In a few minutes a yellowish tinge spread about his nostrils ; then came nausea, and M. Auvray recognised all the symptoms of a billious fever. "What a misfortune," he said, " that this fever didn't come to his uncle ; it would have cured him ! "

He pulled the bell. The maid-servant ran in, and then Mme Auvray, whom François scarcely recognised, so much was he overcome. The sick man had to be put to bed, and that without delay. Claire offered her chamber and her bed. It was a pretty little couch with white curtains ; a tiny chamber and chastely attractive, upholstered in pink percale, and blooming with great bunches of heather, in azure vases. On the mantel appeared a large onyx cup. This was the only present which Claire had received from her lover ! If you are taken with fever, dear reader, I wish you such a sick-room.

While they were giving the first cares to François, his uncle, beside himself, flurried around the chamber, getting into the doctor's way, embracing the patient, seizing Mme Auvray's hand, and crying in ear-splitting tones, " Cure him quick, quick ! I don't want him to die ; I won't permit his death ; I've a right to oppose it ; I'm his uncle and his guardian ! If you don't cure him, they'll say I killed him. I want you all to bear witness that I don't claim to be his heir. I'll give all the property to the poor. A glass of water, please, to wash my hands with.

They had to take him into the sick-wards of the establishment. There he raved so that they had to put him in a strong canvas waistcoat laced up behind, with the sleeves sewed together at the ends : that is what they call a strait-jacket. The nurses took care of him.

Mme Auvray and her daughter took devoted care of François, although the details of the treatment were not always the most agreeable ; but the more delicate sex takes naturally to heroism. You may say that the two ladies saw in their patient a son-in-law and a husband. But I think that if he had been a stranger, he would have scarcely lost anything. St. Vincent de Paul invented only a uniform, for in every woman, of any rank, or any age, exists the essential material of a sister of charity.

Seated night and day in this chamber, filled with fever, mother and daughter employed their moments of repose in telling over their souvenirs and their hopes. They could not explain François's long silence, his sudden return, or the circumstances that had led him to the Avenue Montaigne. If he loved Claire, why had he forced himself to wait three months ? Did he need his uncle's illness to bring him to M. Auvray's ? If his love had worn out, why did he not take his uncle to some other doctor ? There are enough of them in Paris. Possibly he had thought his passion cured until Claire's presence had undeceived him ! But no, for before seeing her he had asked her in marriage.

All these questions were answered by François in his delirium. Claire, hanging on his lips, eagerly took in his lightest words ; she talked them over with her mother and the doctor, who was not long in getting at the truth. To a man accustomed to disentangle the most confused ideas, and to read the minds of the insane like a partly obliterated page, the wanderings of fever are an intelligible language, and the most confused delirium is not without its lights. They soon knew that he had lost his reason, and under what circumstances, and they even made out how he had been the innocent cause of his uncle's malady.

Then began a new series of misgivings for Mlle Auvray. François had been insane. Would the terrible crisis which she had unwittingly brought on cure him ? The doctor assured her that fever had the privilege of indicating the exact nature of mental disturbance, that is to say, of curing it. Nevertheless, there is no rule without exceptions, especially in medicine. Suppose he were to get well, would there be no fear of relapses ? Would M. Auvray give his daughter to one of his patients ?

"As for me," said Claire, sadly smiling, " I'm not afraid of anything : I would risk it. I'm the cause of his sufferings ; ought not I to console him ? After all, his insanity is restricted to asking for my hand : he'll have no more occasion to ask it when I'm his wife ; then we'll not have anything to fear. The poor child is sick only from excess of love ; cure it, dear father, but not too thoroughly. I want him always to be mad enough to love me as I love him."

"We'll see," responded M. Auvray. "Wait till the fever is past. If he's ashamed of having been ill, if I find him sad or melancholy when he gets well, I can't answer for anything. If, on the other hand, he looks back upon his disorder without shame or regret, if he speaks of it resignedly, if he meets the people who have been taking care of him without repugnance, I can laugh at the idea of relapses."

"Ah, father, why should he be ashamed of having loved to excess ? It is a noble and generous madness which never enters petty souls. And how can he feel repugnance on meeting those who have nursed him ? For they are we ! "

After six days of delirium, an abundant perspiration carried off the fever, and the patient began to convalesce. When he found himself in a strange room, between Mme and Mlle Auvray, his first idea was that he was still at the hotel of the Quatre Saisons in the principal street of Ems. His feebleness, his emaciation, and the presence of the doctor, led him to other thoughts ; he had his memory, but vaguely. The doctor came to his aid. He opened the truth to him cautiously, as they measure out food for a body enfeebled by fasting. François commenced by listening to his own story as to a romance in which he had not played any part ; he was another man, an entirely new man, and he came out of the fever as out of a tomb. Little by little the gaps in his memory closed up. His brain seemed full of empty places, which filled up one by one without any sudden jars. Very soon he was quite master of himself, and fully conscious of the past. The cure was a work of science, but, above all, of patience.

It is in such particulars that the paternal treatment of M. Auvray is so much admired. That excellent man had a genius for gentleness. On the 25th of December, François, seated on the side of his bed, and ballasted with some chicken soup and half the yolk of an egg, told, without any interruption, trouble, or wandering, without any feeling of shame or regret, and without any other emotion than a tranquil joy, the occurrences of the three months which had just passed. Claire and Mme Auvray wept while they listened. The doctor acted as if he were taking notes or writing from dictation, but something else than ink fell upon the paper. When the tale was told the convalescent added, by way of conclusion :

"To-day, the 25th of December, at three o'clock in the afternoon, I say to my excellent doctor, to my beloved father, M. Auvray, whose street and number I shall never forget again, ' Monsieur, you have a daughter, Mlle Claire Auvray ; I saw her last summer at the Ems Springs with her mother ; I love her ; she has given me abundant proof that she loves me, and if you are not afraid that I will get sick again, I have the honour to ask you for her hand.' "

The doctor only made a little motion of the head, but Claire passed her arm around the convalescent's neck, and kissed him on the forehead. I care for no other reply when I make a similar demand.

The same day, M. Morlot, calmer and freed from the strait-jacket, got up at eight in the morning. On getting out of bed, he took his slippers, turned them over and over, shook them carefully, and passed them to the nurse, begging him to see if they did not contain thirty thousand francs income. Not till then would he consent to put them on. He combed himself for a good quarter of an hour, repeating, "I don't want anybody to say that my nephew's fortune has got into my head." He shook each of his garments out of the window, after examining it down to its smallest wrinkle. As soon as he was dressed, he asked for a pencil, and wrote on the wall of his chamber :

"COVET NOT THAT WHICH IS ANOTHER'S."

Then he commenced to rub his hands with incredible energy to satisfy himself that François's fortune was not sticking to them. He scraped his fingers with his pencil, counting them from one up to ten, for fear that he should forget one. He thought he was in a police court, and earnestly demanded to be searched. The doctor got him to recognise him, and told him that François was cured. The poor man asked if the money had been found. "As my nephew is going to leave here," he said, "he'll need his money ; where is it ? I haven't got it, unless it's in my bed." And before any one had time to prevent him, he pulled his bed topsy-turvy. The doctor went out after pressing his hand. He rubbed this hand with scrupulous care. They brought him his breakfast ; he commenced by examining his napkin, his glass, his knife, his plate, repeating that he did not want to eat up his nephew's fortune. The repast over, he washed his hands in enormous quantities of water. "The fork is silver," said he ; "perhaps there's some silver sticking to my hands ! "

M. Auvray does not despair of saving him, but it will take time. Summer and autumn are the seasons in which doctors are most successful with insanity.

GUSTAVE DROZ
1832-1895

THE SEMPSTRESS'S STORY

" YES, Ma'm'selle Adèle," said the sempstress, " the real happiness of this world is not so unequally distributed after all." Louise, as she said this, took from the reserve in the bosom of her dress a lot of pins, and applied them deftly to the trimming of a skirt which I was holding for her.

" A sufficiently comfortable doctrine," I answered, " but it does seem to me as if some people were born to live and to die unhappy."

" It is only folks who never find anybody to love enough ; and I think it's nobody's fault but their own."

" But, my good Louise, wouldn't you have suffered much less last year, when you came so near losing your boy, if you hadn't cared so much for him ? "

I was only drawing her on, you see : Louise's chat was the greatest resource to me at that time.

" Why, Ma'm'selle Adèle, you are surely joking. You'd as well tell me to cut off my feet to save my shoes. You'll know one of these days—and not so far off neither, maybe—how mighty easy and sensible it would be not to love your children. They *are* a worry, too ; but oh, the delight of 'em ! I'd like to have had anybody tell me not to love my darling because it might grieve me, when he lay there in his mother's lap, with blue lips, gasping for his breath, and well-nigh dead ; his face blackish, and his hands like this piece of wax. You could see that everything was going against him ; and with his great big eyes he was staring in my face, until I felt as if the child was tugging at my very heart-strings.

" I kept smiling at him, though, through the tears that blinded me, hard as I tried to hide them. Oh ! such tears are bitter salt indeed, ma'm'selle ! And there was my poor husband on his knees, making paper figures to amuse him, and singing a funny song he used to laugh at. Now and then the corners of his mouth would pucker, and his cheeks would wrinkle a little bit under the eyes. You could tell he was still amused, but in such a dreamy way. Oh ! our child seemed no longer with us, but behind a veil, like. Wait a minute. You must excuse me, for I can't help crying when I think of it."

And the poor creature drew out her handkerchief and fairly sobbed aloud. In the midst of it, however, she smiled and said, "Well, that's over now ; 'twas nothing, and I'm too silly. And, ma'm'selle, here I've gone and cried upon your mother's dress, and that's a pretty business."

I took her hand in mine and pressed it.

"Aren't you afraid you'll stick yourself, ma'm'selle ? I've got my needle in that hand," she said playfully. "But you did not mean what you said just now, did you ? "

"What did I say ? "

"That it would be better not to love your children with all your heart, on account of the great anxiety. Don't you know such thoughts are wicked ? When they come into your head your mind wants purifying. But I'm sure I beg your pardon for saying so."

"You are entirely right, Louise," I returned.

"Ah ! so I thought. And now, let me see. Let's fix this ruche ; pull it to the left a little, please."

"But about the sick boy. Tell me about his recovery."

"That was a miracle—I ought to say two miracles. It was a miracle that God restored him to us, and a miracle to find anybody with so much knowledge and feeling—such talent. Such a tender heart, and so much, so much—I'm speaking of the doctor. A famous one he was, too, you must know ; for it was no less than Doctor Faron. Heaven knows how he is run after ; and how rich and celebrated he is ! Aren't you surprised to hear that it was he who attended our little boy ? Indeed, the wonders begin with that. You may imagine my husband was at his wits' end when he saw how it was with the child ; and all of a sudden I saw him jump up, get out his best coat and hat, and put them on.

" ' Where are you going ? ' I asked.

" ' To bring Doctor Faron.'

"Why, if he had said, ' To bring the Prime Minister,' it would have seemed as likely.

" ' Don't you believe Doctor Faron is going to trouble himself about the likes of us. They will turn you out of doors.'

"But 'twas no use talking, my dear. He was already on the stairs, and I heard him running away as if the house was on fire. Fire, indeed ; worse, far worse than any fire !

"And there I was, left alone with the child upon my knees. He wouldn't stay in bed ; and was quieter so, wrapped up in his little blanket. Here will he die, I thought. Soon will his eyes close, and then it will be all over ; and I held my own breath to listen to his feeble and oppressed pantings.

"About an hour had passed, when I heard a rapid step on the stairs—(we are poor, and live in the attic). The door opened, and my husband came in, wet with perspiration and out of breath. If I live a century I'll not forget his look when he said :

"'Well?'

"I answered, 'No worse. But the doctor?'

"'He's coming.'

"Oh! those blessed words! It actually seemed as if my child were saved already. If you but knew how folks love their little ones. I kissed the darling, I kissed his father, I laughed, I cried, and I no longer felt the faintest doubt. It is by God's mercy that such gleams of hope are sent to strengthen us in our trials. It was very foolish, too ; for something might easily have prevented the doctor's coming, after all.

"'You found him at home, then?' I inquired of my husband.

"Then he told me, in an undertone, what he had done, stopping every now and then to wipe his face and gather breath :

"'I ran to the Children's Hospital, which he manages, hoping to find him there. The porter showed me a low door at the end of the courtyard. I knocked and was let into a room full of young fellows, all smoking, talking and laughing away at a great rate.'

"Ah! the wretches! and with dying folks all round 'em."

"Don't say that until you know all. 'What do you want here, friend?' says a tall one in a white apron and black sleeves, and who, seeing my troubled looks, took me on one side. 'What's the matter?'

"'I'm sorry to trouble you, sir,' I began.

"'No ceremony, man. Speak out.'

"'I'm looking for Doctor Faron, to come and save my child, sir. He's dying with croup. I'm not rich, but all I can raise I will give.'

"'Oh! that's all right,' says he. 'How old's the child.'

"'Four years old, sir.'

"'Who's been attending it?'

"'A doctor who gives him little white pills in a heap of water, sir.'

"'Ah! hah!' says he, smiling ; 'well, don't be downhearted,' and with that he threw off his apron and black sleeves, and wrote something on a bit of paper.

"'Take this to Doctor Faron. That's his address. Where do you live? I'll come when I get my coat on.'

"'Oh! how kind, sir!'

"I could have hugged him. But he said, 'Come, no nonsense, friend. Away with you!' So I hurried off to Doctor Faron's house with the note ; but he was dining out.

"'Where?' I asked, as the servant held the door ajar.

"'Don't know,' says he, very short ; and shut the door in my face.

" At that I got angry, and it seemed to me the child came before my eyes. I pushed open the door, and in I went.

" ' That won't do,' I said. ' One of the hospital doctors sent me here, and I *must* know where to find your master, and quick, too.'

" Seeing that I wouldn't stand trifling, he gave me the direction, and growled, ' now clear out, and shut that door.'

" So I rushed away to the Rue de Lille. The courtyard was full of carriages, and the windows all in a blaze of light ; but in I went, for all that.

" ' My boy will die !—my boy will die ! ' I kept repeating, as I elbowed through the people. An old servant stopped me in the ante-chamber. ' Where now ? ' says he.

" ' I want to speak to Doctor Faron,' says I ; ' I *must* speak to him. Get him to come out here, won't you, please ? '

" The old fellow looked at me hard, and then said very kindly, ' Sit down there an instant, and I'll try.'

" What possessed me to sit there and cry, with all those servants hurrying about with plates and dishes, I can't tell ; but I couldn't help it.

" In a minute or so, here comes a large gentleman with a white cravat on. ' Where's the man that wants me ? ' he asks in a gruff voice. Then seeing me there in the corner in such a state, with a searching look at me, he took the note, read it, and said quietly, ' Ah ! the noble boy.' Then, turning to me, ' Go home, my man ; I'll be there directly. Cheer up ; I'll lose no time.' "

" My husband had scarcely uttered these words," continued Louise, " when I heard a step on the stairs. It was he ! it was that blessed angel of a doctor come to help us in our sore distress.

" And what do you think he said in his deep voice when he got into the room ?

" ' God bless you, my friends, but I nearly broke my neck on those stairs. Where's that child ? '

" ' Here he is, my dear, darling doctor.' I knew no better way to speak to him, with his dress-cravat showing over his great-coat, and his decorations dangling like a little bunch of keys at his button-hole.

" He took off his wrappings, stooped over the child, turned him over, more gently even than his mother could have done, and laid his own head first against his back, then against his breast. How I tried to read his eyes ! but they know how to hide their thoughts.

" ' We must perform an operation here,' says he ; ' and it is high time.'

" Just at this moment the hospital doctor came in, and whispered to him, ' I am afraid you didn't want to be disturbed, sir.'

" ' Oh, never mind. I am sorry it wasn't sooner, though. Get everything ready now.'

" But, Ma'm'selle Adèle, why should I tell you all this? I'd better mind my work."

" Oh! go on, Louise, go on!"

" Well, then, ma'm'selle, if you believe me, those two doctors—neither of e'm kin, or even friends till then—went to work and made all the preparations, while my husband went off to borrow lights. The biggest one tied a mattress on the table, and the assistant spread out the bright little knives.

" You, who have not been through it all, ma'm'selle, can't know what it is to have your own little one in your lap, to know that those things are to be used upon him, to pierce his tender flesh, and, if the hand that guides them be not sure, that they may kill him.

" When all was ready, Doctor Faron took off his cravat, then lifted my child from my arms and laid him on the mattress, in the midst of the lamps, and said to my poor man:

" 'You will hold his head, and your wife his feet. Joseph will pass me the instruments. You've brought a breathing tube with you, my son?'

" 'Yes, sir.'

" My husband was as white as a sheet by this; and when I saw him about to take his place with his hands shaking so much, it scared me, so I said:

" 'Doctor, please let me hold his head!'

" 'But, my poor woman, if you should tremble?'

" 'Please let me do it, doctor!'

" 'Be it so then,' and then added, with a bright look at me, and a cheering smile, ' We shall save him for you, my dear; you are a brave little woman, and you deserve it.'

" Yes, and save him, did he! God bless him! saved him as truly as if he had snatched him from the depths of the river."

" And you didn't tremble, Louise?"

" You may depend on that. If I had, it would have been the last of my child."

" How in the world did you keep yourself steady?"

" The Lord knows; but I was like a rock. When you must, you must, I suppose."

" And you had to behold every detail of that operation?"

" Yes, indeed; and often have I dreamed it over since. His poor little neck laid open, and the veins, which the doctor pushed aside with his fingers and the little silver tube which he inserted, and all that; and then the face of the child, changing as the air passed into his lungs. You've seen a lamp almost out, when you pour in oil? It was like that. They had laid him there but half alive, with his eyes all but set; and they gave him back to me, pale and with bloodless lips, it is true, but with life in his looks, and breathing—breathing the free, fresh air.

"'Kiss him, mother,' says the doctor, 'and put him to bed. Cover the place with some light thing or other, and Joseph must stay with you to-night; won't you, Joseph? Ah, well, that's all arranged.'

"He put on his things and wrapped himself up to go. He was shaking hands with my husband, when I seized one hand, and kissed it—like a fool, as I was—but I didn't stop to think. He laughed heartily, and said to my husband, 'Are you not jealous, friend? Your wife is making great advances to me. But I must be off now. Good-night, good people.'

"And from that night he always talks so friendly to us, not a bit contemptuously either, but as if he liked us, and was glad to be of service to us.

"The next morning, at half-past five, there he was, as fresh as a rose, and larger, as it seemed to me, than before. And no wonder, neither, for don't you think he had brought four bottles of old Bordeaux! two in his pockets and two under his arms.

"'The little fellow must take this,' says he. 'Everything gone on well in the night, eh?'

"'Admirably well, sir,' answered Mr. Joseph. I call him Mr. Joseph, but I have since found out that he was a rising physician, nephew to the old doctor, and 'way above the common run. But he always spoke to the other like a soldier to his general.

"Well, that's not all the doctor did; for during the entire week after he came every day, and when I would hear his carriage rumbling over our poor little street, I would say, 'Heaven knows what we shall ever do to pay him.' For we well knew that Doctor Faron attended dukes and noblemen, and charged them by the thousand.

"We had some hundred francs in the Savings, to be sure, but I was thinking what we should do if he charged two or three times as much. You can understand how very awkward it would have been. It fairly made me sick.

"At last, one morning when my husband was at home, I mustered up all my courage and began:

"'Doctor Faron, you have been so good, too good to us. You have saved our boy's life.'

"'You may prate over that just as much as you please, my dear; but recollect it is my trade to cut up such little chaps.'

"'But not those who live on the fifth floor in the Rue Serpente, sir.'

"You see, ma'm'selle, how I was leading up to the question?

"'How's that? how's that? Why, what are you talking about? Those before anybody else, to be sure. Are they not most in need?'

"'I know you have the best heart in the world, doctor; but that's not what I mean. Now, that the child is well, we want to— we are not rich—but still——'

" By this time I was as red as a cock's comb, and the more I tried to express myself the worse it got.

" ' You want to pay me. I see, I see,' said he suddenly. ' Well, you owe me precisely nothing, if you don't think that too much.'

" ' Oh ! doctor ! we couldn't—we must—— '

" ' Let us pay according to our means, doctor,' says my husband.

" ' Well, then, I don't want to wound you, my friends. If you prefer to pay something, my charge is just fifty francs. And now don't bother me any more about it. (He pretended to be angry, and it was so droll). Don't bother me, I say, you lunatics. Fifty francs, I tell you, and not a copper less ; in specie, too ; no paper money for me. Next Sunday dress the little man, and have him ready ; for I wish him to take a turn in the Bois de Boulogne.'

" ' Ah ! there's no end to your kindness, doctor.'

" ' Don't interrupt me, I say. After his drive, bring him to see me ; and let him fetch the money himself. Do you hear ? '

" Well, ma'm'selle," added Louise, " that very evening here comes a basket of wine, although we hadn't finished the other. What a man ! you may well say. And I declare to you, if he had wanted my right arm, I should have said, ' Cut if off, sir.'

" Fifty francs, indeed ! It wasn't the twentieth of what we owed him ; and he only took that to save our feelings. And seeing this, I was still more anxious to please him ; so I bought some linen, the finest I could get, and didn't I make him an elegant set of shirts ! "

" Why, how did you get his measure ? "

" Ah ! that *was* hard ; but when I make up my mind nothing stops me. I went to his valet—who knew me, because he had brought the wine—and I told him the doctor wanted me to look over his linen in the wash. So I got to the laundress, and I made her think he had ordered some shirts like those she had in hand, and so I got the pattern.

" I was full of work at that time, but I made all those shirts at night ; and it gave me such satisfaction to think, " Ah ! you won't let us pay you—you obstinate man—but you can't prevent my sitting up and working for you the livelong night ; and the way I worked ! you should have seen me at it !

" You may depend on it there was plenty of hem-stitching on those shirts, and you know when I try I *can* hem-stitch.

" But I am trifling away my time, and this dress will never be done."

ANDRÉ THEURIET
1833–1907

A SENTIMENTAL JOURNEY

WHEN the train left the station of Sisteron, the artist, Esprit Capdenave, saw that all the travellers in his second-class compartment had got out, with the exception of a girl who occupied the corner opposite to his. Capdenave had got in at Pertuis at dawn, and, at once snuggled down in his corner, had continued the sleep interrupted by his sudden early departure. Now he rubbed his eyes, shook himself, and, cheered by a ray of sunlight, resumed possession of his faculties of observation. Like himself, the girl opposite had just opened her sleepy eyes. She freed herself from a shawl of thick black lace, tidied her fair scattered hair, and with the help of a pocket-mirror did her best to smarten herself up.

She seemed to be about twenty-four ; fresh, healthy, plump, she had fine flower-blue eyes and a little beauty-spot of a mole on her upper lip. The artist remarked with pleasure her slim waist, her enticing rounded bosom, and her finely-moulded hands in cotton gloves. While he slyly examined her, he saw her search in her travelling-bag and take out a roll. She hoped no doubt to find something more appetising than dry bread ; for, after upsetting the contents of the bag, she gave a little disillusioned pout.

Seeing this, Esprit, obeying an impulse of compassion, opened his own bag, displayed a tablet of chocolate still wrapped in silver paper, and gallantly presented it to the young lady, saying, " Madame . . . or Mademoiselle . . . "

" Mademoiselle," she replied, a little astonished. A smile of good nature played over the lips of the artist, and was lost in his short curly beard.

" Very well, Mademoiselle," he continued, " permit me to offer you a little chocolate to replace that which you have forgotten."

The girl, after a moment's hesitation, accepted it with thanks, and proposed to give in exchange half her roll. They both began to eat with a good appetite, while the train steamed along the Buech Valley. While crunching, they looked out of the window at the mountains fading, one over the other, in the distance ; the terraced orchards, all snowy with flowering plum and cherry trees ; and, here and there on slopes watered by gleaming brooks, the young grass of the meadows starred with white narcissi.

The frugal repast in common broke the ice. They became more communicative. Esprit Capdenave, with a view to gaining the confidence of his fellow-traveller, told her his age, his profession, and his business. He came from Saint Raphael and was going to Grenoble, where he had a commission for some portraits—the whole of a family of glove-makers, ugly as sin, but possessing money and paying well. With exuberant gestures, the blarney of the Southerner, and a droll gift of pantomime, he gave a jesting description of his future models. The girl laughed heartily, and became more and more friendly.

" So you paint portraits ? " she asked.

" At your service, Mademoiselle. What is your Christian name ? "

" Louise."

" Well, Mademoiselle Louise, if you will only stop two days at Grenoble, I will paint your portrait with the greatest pleasure. My word ! That would be an agreeable relief from my family of glove-makers ! "

" Thank you," she said with a blush, " but I am not going so far. I am getting out at Monestier de Clermont."

Then she told him the story of her life. She was a governess at Aix, in a magistrate's family. Orphan, she had no other relations than an aunt and uncle living at Monestier, who had arranged a marriage between her and a well-to-do trader of the town, a widower without children, who was called Léchaudel. She was profiting by her Easter holidays to visit her relations, and meet at their house this Monsieur Léchaudel, of whom she had only seen a photograph.

" He is rather old for me," she added frankly, " and he seems to have a very ordinary appearance. But I am tired of being under others. It is so sad to live alone, without the slightest sign of affection. Provided that this gentleman is not very displeasing, I think I shall accept him."

While making this confidence, she sighed, and her red soft lips half opened, discovering the whiteness of her teeth. At the same time, Esprit observed in the blue pupils of the girl that humid, brilliant languor particular to the eyes of women tormented by the need for love. This humid gleam of her glance, this red mouth of hers, unconsciously asking for kisses, her frank confessions of her weary solitude, awoke in him the desire to flirt with her, and made him suddenly wishful to supplant this unknown pretender, to whom the governess was preparing with resignation to yield her alluring youth.

" What ! " he cried, " you will not condemn yourself to marry an old ugly shop-keeper, and wall yourself up in a hole of a village ! It is not possible ! A pretty girl has not the right to sacrifice herself

45

in this way with a light heart. Do not commit this madness, I pray you ! "

To strengthen his pleading, he took the hands of the governess, who at first laughed, and let him go on, then little by little, frightened by his prolonged clasp, tried in vain to free her fingers. During this time the train ran over a high tableland, full of floating mist, then came out in full sunlight among the meadow-lands, full of music of cowbells. A brisk air blew into the carriage some of the white falling petals of the cherry trees, and this snow of petals carried with it the exciting exhalations of spring-time. Suddenly the train burried itself in the sonorous darkness of a tunnel, and the painter profited by it to use more tender caresses. The girl, in its obscurity, found herself still more agitated, and scarcely defended herself. Esprit was sitting beside her, his arm around her waist, when suddenly they came out into full sunlight.

" Oh ! If we should be seen ! "

" By whom . . . the birds of the air ? Don't trouble about them, and let me love you ! "

Again the train entered a tunnel. Louise, scared, felt the invisible lips of her audacious companion placed on her eyes, on her mouth. An anxious and yet sweet emotion came over her. Her head turned, and she resisted more weakly. Happily for her, the glittering daylight reappeared, the train stopped before a little station to the cry of " Clelles ! Clelles ! "

" My God ! " she sighed, recoiling, ashamed, and trembling. " We will soon be to Monestier ! Leave me alone, I beg you ! "

Still trembling she rose to her feet, took her hat, and hastily did her hair up.

" What matters Monestier ! " said Capdenave with passion, taking her again in his arms. " I love you. I cannot leave you, and I must take you with me ! "

" You are mad ! " she stammered. " Keep quiet."

The train steamed along a wooded slope. Louise half freed herself and leaned from the window. She could already see the sunlit village in the middle of fields and pine woods, with its single long, steep street. Then she could discern the station, isolated in the country, and on the platform three silhouettes, growing more and more distinct, grouped in an attitude of expectation.

" I recognize my aunt and uncle," said the governess. " The gentleman who accompanies them must be Monsieur Léchaudel."

" It is ugly enough for him ! " replied Esprit, cunningly getting between the girl and the door.

With an abrupt action he shut the window, and planted himself resolutely before the door, that he hid with his big shoulders.

" No," he affirmed, " I will not let you immolate yourself to such a villain. I love you and I will keep you."

After slowly slackening down, the train stopped dead, and the voice of the guard ran along the carriages : " Monestier de Clermont ! " The governess, thinking it was all a joke, took up her bag and umbrella.

" Come, sir, do be serious ! Open the door for me."

" Never, on my life ! " swore the painter, drawing her to him, and stifling her protestations with kisses.

Outside there could be heard the uncle and aunt, anxiously looking in the carriages and calling, " Louise ! Louise ! " But they called in vain, and the large back of Capdenave prevented them from seeing their niece.

" They are looking for me ! They are calling me ! " murmured Louise in tears. " This is unworthy of you ! Open the door, sir, I beg you ! "

A whistle ; the train went on, and the station of Monestier soon disappeared like a dream. Enervated and tired by the useless struggle the governess fell back on the seat. Esprit tried again to encircle her with his arms, but she rejected him in anger, and threw herself at the other end of the carriage. Hiding her face in her hands, she sobbed, suffocating :

" No ! it is too much ! Go away ! I detest you ! "

He sat down opposite to her, and sought to console her by tender words. She kept in an attitude of dislike, savagely silent, and thus they reached the station of Vizille. The door opened, and the compartment was filled with travellers who were going to spend the Sunday at Grenoble. This was like a shower-bath on the effervescent Capdenave, and compelled him to keep silent. The governess in her corner half turned her back on him, and looked at the door sullenly. Esprit, condemned to remain mute, began to reflect more cooly on the consequences of his escapade, and the responsibility he had assumed. They did not exchange another word, and on reaching Grenoble he silently aided the girl to get down, and took charge of her bag.

Confused, Louise looked at what he did in a sort of stupor, and followed him with the docility of a frightened animal. Outside the station the artist took her arm, and led her to a hotel just opposite. When the waiter took them to a room, and they were alone, Louise sank down on a chair, and was taken with a sudden fit of crying. She wrung her hands desperately, and her breast was shaken with deep sobs.

It was the turn of Esprit to become frightened. He had not expected this explosion of profound grief. Kneeling down by the governess, he tried to quieten her with caresses, but it was labour in vain. The sobs of Louise redoubled, and she rejected him with horror.

" Go away ! " she moaned. " If you have any feeling at all, do not do anything more. Ah! God! God! What a misfortune! My relatives will write to Aix, and the people there will have a fine opinion of me. I shall be shamefully dismissed and be without a situation. All that through your fault. Because you have treated me as if I were a bad woman, and now I am lost! lost! . . ."

Her tears flowed again. Esprit, upset with himself, thought, "Yet she is right, and I have acted like a blackguard!" He was not a bad fellow, and though he was not remarkable for the austerity of his manners, he was no wise inclined to compromise a woman against her will. It hurt him to think he had done any wrong to this pretty weeping creature. He saw she was absolutely sincere, and this sincerity awoke in him the beginnings of remorse. He suddenly seized the hands of the governess.

"Forgive me," he said humbly, "and do not upset yourself so, Mademoiselle Louise. I will lead you back to the station. You can take the first train starting for Monestier; and you can make things all right by telling your people that you fell asleep and did not wake up till you got to Grenoble. Dry your eyes. I am a terrible fool, but I am also a decent man."

Thereupon he led her back to the station. A train was just about to start in the direction of Monestier. Capdenave got a ticket, and put the governess in a carriage, with some sweets and fruit and cakes. Now that she felt that she was saved, Louise was quite recovered. Her flower-blue eyes shone with a humid brilliance, and her soft red lips formed a malicious smile to thank the artist when he shut the door of the carriage.

Capdenave looked at the train, rolling away with its long plume of steam.

"What a pity!" he sighed, sorrowful; "she will marry Monsieur Léchaudel. . . . What a pity!"

LA BRETONNE

André Theuriet

One November evening, the eve of Saint Catherine's Day, the gate of the Auberive prison turned upon its hinges to allow to pass out a woman of some thirty years, clad in a faded woollen gown and coiffed in a linen cap that framed in a singular fashion a face pale and puffed by that sickly-hued fat which develops on prison regimen. She was a prisoner whom they had just liberated, and whom her companions of detention called La Bretonne.

Condemned for infanticide, it was exactly, day for day, six years ago that the prison van had brought her to the Centrale. Now, in her former garb, and with her small stock of money received from the clerk in her pocket, she found herself free and with her road-pass stamped for Langres.

The courier for Langres, however, had long since gone. Cowed and awkward, she took her way stumblingly toward the chief inn of the borough, and with trembling voice asked shelter for the night. But the inn was crowded, and the landlady, who did not care to harbour " one of those birds from over yonder," counselled her to push on to the tavern at the far end of the village.

La Bretonne passed on, and, more trembling and awkward than ever, knocked at the door of that tavern, which, properly speaking, was but a dram-shop for labourers. The proprietor also eyed her askance, scenting doubtless a " discharged " from the Centrale, and finally refused her on the plea that there was no bed to give her.

La Bretonne dared not insist, but with bowed head pursued her way, while at the bottom of her soul rose and grew a dull hatred for that world which thus repulsed her.

She had no other resource than to gain Langres afoot.

Towards the end of November, night comes quickly. Soon she found herself enveloped in darkness, on a greyish road that ran between two divisions of the forest, and where the north wind whistled fiercely, choked her with dust, and pelted her with dead leaves.

After six years of sedentary and recluse life her legs were stiff, the muscles knotted, and her feet, accustomed to sabots, pinched and bruised by her new slippers. At the end of a league she felt them blistered and herself exhausted. She dropped upon a pile of stones by the wayside, shivering and asking herself if she was going to be forced to perish of cold and hunger in this black night, under this icy breeze, which froze her to the marrow.

All at once, in the solitude of the road, she seemed to hear the droning notes of a voice singing. She listened and distinguished the air of one of those caressing and monotonous chants with which one soothes young children.

She was not alone, then !

She struggled to her feet and in the direction from which the voice came, and there, at the turn of a cross-road, perceived a reddish light streaming through the branches. Five minutes later she was before a mud-walled hovel, whose roof, covered by squares of sod, leaned against the rock, and whose window had allowed to pass that beckoning ray.

With anxious heart she decided to knock.

The chant ceased instantly and a woman opened the door, a peasant woman, no older than La Bretonne herself, but faded and aged by work. Her bodice, torn in places, displayed the skin tanned and dirty ; her red hair escaped dishevelled from under a soiled stuff cap, and her grey eyes regarded with amazement the stranger whose face had in it something of touching loneliness.

" Good evening ! " said she, lifting yet higher the sputtering lamp in her hand ; " what do you desire ? "

" I am unable to go on," murmured La Bretonne, in a voice broken by a sob ; " the city is far, and if you will lodge me for the night, you will do me a service. . . . I have money ; I will pay you for the trouble."

" Enter," replied the other, after a moment's hesitancy ; " but why," continued she, in a tone more curious than suspicious, " did you not sleep at Auberive ? "

" They would not give me a lodging," lowering her blue eyes and taken with a sudden scruple, " be—because, see you, I come from the Maison Centrale."

" So ! the Maison Centrale ! but no matter—enter—I fear nothing, having known only misery. Moreover, I've a conscience against turning a Christian from the door on a night like this. I'll give you a bed and a slice of cheese."

And she pulled from the eaves some bundles of dried heather and spread them as a pallet in the corner by the fire.

" Do you live here alone ? " demanded La Bretonne timidly.

" Yes, with my kiddie, going on seven years now. I earn our living by working in the wood."

" Your man, then, is dead ? "

" Yes," said the other brusquely, " the kiddie has no father. Briefly, to each his sorrow ! But come, behold your straw, and two or three potatoes left from supper. It is all I can offer you—— "

She was called by a childish voice coming from a dark nook, separated from the room by a board partition.

" Good-night ! " she repeated, " the little one cries ; I must go, but sleep you well ! "

And taking up the lamp she passed into the closet, leaving La Bretonne crouched alone in the darkness.

Stretched upon her heather, after she had eaten her supper, she strove to close her eyes, but sleep would not come to her. Through the thin partition she heard the mother still softly talking to the child, whom the arrival of a stranger had wakened, and who did not wish to go to sleep again.

The mother soothed and fondled the child with words of endearment that somehow strangely disturbed La Bretonne. That outburst of simple tenderness seemed to waken a confused maternal instinct in the soul of that girl condemned in the past for having stifled her new-born.

" If things had not gone so badly with me," thought La Bretonne sorrowfully, " *it* would have been the same age as this little one here."

At that thought and at the sound of that childish voice a sickening shudder seemed to shake her very vitals ; something soft and tender to spring up in that soured heart, and an increasing need for the relief of tears.

" But come, come, my little one," the mother cried, " to sleep you must go ! And if you are good and do as I say, to-morrow I'll take you to the Saint Catherine's Fair ! "

" The feast-day of little children, mamma ; the feast-day of little children, you mean ? "

" Yes, my angel, of little children."

" And the day when the good Saint Catherine brings playthings to the babies, mamma ? "

" Sometimes—yes."

" Then why doesn't she bring playthings to our house, mamma ? "

" We live too far away, perhaps ; and then—we are too poor."

" She brings them only to rich babies, then, mamma ? But why, mamma, why, I say ? I should love to see playthings ! "

" Very well ! some day you may, if you are very good—to-night, perhaps, if you are good and go to sleep soon."

" I will, then, mamma, I will go to sleep now, so she can bring them to-morrow."

The little voice ceased ; there was a long silence ; then a long breath, even and light !

The child slept at last—the mother also.

La Bretonne, only, did not sleep ! An emotion, at once poignant and tender, tore at her heart, and she thought more than ever of that other little one, whom they said she had killed. . . . This lasted till dawn.

Mother and child slept still, but La Bretonne was up and out, gliding hurriedly and furtively in the direction of Auberive and slackening her pace only when the first houses of the village came in sight.

Soon she had reached and was traversing its only street, walking slowly now and scanning with all her eyes the signs of the shops. One at last seemed to fix her attention. She knocked at the shutter and presently it opened. A mercer's shop, apparently, but also with some toys and playthings in the window—poor, pitiful trifles, a pasteboard doll, a Noah's ark, a woolly, stiff-legged little sheep !

To the astonishment of the merchant, La Bretonne purchased them all, paid, and went out. She had resumed the road to the hovel in the wood, when suddenly a hand fell heavily upon her shoulder, and she was face to face with a brigadier of police.

The unhappy one had forgotten that it was forbidden to liberated prisoners to loiter near the Maison Centrale.

"Instead of vagabondising here, you should already be at Langres," said the brigadier gruffly. "Come, march, be off with you! To the road, to the road, I say!"

She sought to explain. Pains lost. At once a passing cart was pressed into service, La Bretonne bundled into it, and in charge of a policeman once more en route for Langres.

The cart jolted lumberingly over the frozen ruts. The poor La Bretonne clutched with a heart-broken air her bundle of playthings in her freezing fingers.

All at once, at a turn of the road, she recognised the cross-path that led through the wood. Her heart leaped and she besought the policeman to stop only one moment. She had a commission for La Fleuriotte, the woman that lived there!

She supplicated with so much fervour that the man, a good fellow at heart, allowed himself to be persuaded. They stopped, tied the horse to a tree, and ascended the pathway.

Before the door La Fleuriotte hewed the gathered wood into the required fagots. On seeing her visitor return, accompanied by a policeman, she stood open-mouthed and with arms hanging.

"Hush!" said La Bretonne, "hush! the little one—does it sleep still?"

"Yes—but——"

"Then, here, these playthings, lay them on the bed and tell her Saint Catherine brought them. I returned to Auberive for them; but it seems I had no right to do it, and they are taking me now to Langres."

"Holy Mother of God!" cried the amazed La Fleuriotte.

"Hush! be still, I say!"

And drawing near the bed herself, followed always by her escort, La Bretonne scattered upon the coverlet the doll, the Noah's ark, and the stiff-legged, woolly, and somewhat grimy little lamb, bent the bare arm of the child till it clasped the latter, then turned with a smile.

"Now," said she, addressing the policeman, vigorously rubbing his eyes with the cuff of his jacket—the frost, it seemed, had gotten into them—"I am ready: we can go!"

LUDOVIC HALEVY
1834–1908

THE GRAND MARRIAGE

Nov. 25th, 1893.   *4 o'clock.*

THIS morning at ten o'clock I was just settling down to attack Beethoven's Twenty-fifth Symphony, when the door opened, and who should walk in but mamma. Mamma awake and stirring at ten o'clock ! And not only awake and stirring, but dressed and ready to go out—mantled and bonneted.

I could not remember ever to have seen her stirring so early before. She never manages to get to church on Sunday before the middle of the one o'clock mass. The other evening she said, laughingly, to Abbé Pontal :

"Monsieur l'Abbé, our dear religion would be absolutely perfect if you substituted a mass at two for that at one. Then the concerts at the Conservatoire could be put an hour later, and Sunday in winter would be all that could be desired."

At mamma's entrance I was stupefied, and exclaimed, " You are going out, mamma ? "

" No, I've just come in."

" You've just come in ? "

" Yes, I had something to do this morning—to choose some stuffs for the hangings—that blue, you know, which is so difficult to find."

" Have you found it ? "

" No—no. But they say they can get it for me—and I hope that—— They are going to send it by the day after to-morrow at the latest."

Mamma got quite confused in her explanation. She finally announced that we were going to an evening party at the Mercereys'. There was to be a little music. She had known of it for several days, but had forgotten to mention it to me before. I didn't show the slightest sign of surprise, but while listening to mamma, I studied her carefully, and thought to myself, " What's the meaning of all this ? Mamma rambling about at this unearthly hour, matching blues ! A *soirée musicale* at the Mercereys' ! Mamma evidently confused, too ! There's something hidden."

45*

So I let her flounder and never uttered a sound. When she had finished she took a few steps toward the door, just as actors do in a theatre when they pretend they are going out, then she turned back and tried to say with an air of indifference, as if the thought had only just occurred to her, " Which gown do you think of putting on to-night ? "

" To-night, mamma ? Really, I don't know. I might put the grey on—or the blue—or the rose."

" No, no ; not the rose. Put the blue on. You looked quite nice in it the day before yesterday at Aunt Clarice's. Besides, your papa doesn't like the rose, and as he is going with us to the Mercereys'——"

" Papa going to the Mercereys' ! "

" Yes, certainly."

" Does he know there's to be some music ? "

" Yes."

" He knows—and yet he is going ? "

" Yes. What is there surprising in that ? "

" Oh, nothing, mamma ; nothing at all."

Whereupon she really left the room, and I was quite alone. Then, without a moment's hesitation, I said to myself, " A marriage is in the air. They're going to show me off to some one. *That's* why papa is obliged to go."

Fancy papa letting himself be dragged by mamma to a *soirée musicale* ! The whole world will seem topsy-turvy. There are only three places which he finds tolerable in the evening—the club, the opera during the ballet, and the little theatres where people go to laugh and amuse themselves generally—the theatres where young girls are not allowed to go, but where I intend to go when I am married.

Yes, I'm sure there's an interview in the wind. It must be something of great importance, for mamma has been in a state of the highest excitement ever since this morning. She ate no breakfast, and didn't manage to conceal her unrest at all. Not only has she inspected my blue dress carefully, but she has also examined me with equal thoroughness. She fell into a fit of veritable despair on verifying the fact that there was a slight flaw on my features.

" What's that ? " she cried.

" Where ? What ? mamma ! "

" On the tip of your nose."

" Have I anything on the tip of my nose ? "

" Yes, a horrid gash."

" Oh, good gracious ! A gash ? "

Quite horrified, I rushed to the mirror. Then I breathed freely again. It was the merest trifle—where the kitten had given me a pat with its paw. Nothing worth mentioning—a little reddish mark that was hardly visible to the naked eye, and which could easily be got rid of before evening.

But in mamma's solicitous eyes the little mark assumed the proportions of a disfiguring wound. The tip of my nose has never received so much touching attention before. Mamma made me sit still in an arm-chair during half of the day, with cold-water cloths fixed like a pair of goggles on the tip of the afore-mentioned nose.

Poor mamma! She's so anxious to see me married. It's quite natural, after all. She looks very well herself yet in the evening, and it is awkward to have to drag a big marriageable daughter around her heels.

I don't like it, either, for that matter. I know that I make her look older, and, therefore, as soon as we enter a room in the evening I slip away from her, and try to see as little as possible of her afterward until the carriage is announced. So each goes her own way, and interferes as little as possible with the other.

She's a dear, good old soul. There are mothers who simply bully their daughters, and worry them into marrying at five minutes' notice. Quite a leap in the dark. Mamma isn't one of them.

Besides, she knows I have made up my mind not to be hurried— and not to decide carelessly. Marriage is not a trifling thing. If a mistake is made it is for life; so it's well to know what one is doing when one takes the plunge. When I get married it will be in all seriousness. I don't intend to tumble head over ears in love with the first newcomer, fair or dark, who says to his mother, " I've found the girl of my choice. I love her, and her alone. I'll have her or nobody."

Oh, no! I'm not going into that stupidity. I intend to keep my eyes open, and my wits about me.

Last spring I declined five very likely wooers simply because none of them offered all the advantages of birth, fortune, and position which I consider I am justified in demanding.

I shall follow the same course of action during the winter campaign—the same calm prudence. I am not yet twenty, so I can afford to wait.

Since this morning I have felt highly satisfied with myself—*very* highly satisfied. I have not been in the least affected by mother's open agitation. To-day, as usual, I have glanced through my notes.

On my eighteenth birthday I find I wrote the following simple words on the first page of my notebook, which I still keep carefully under lock and key:

MY MARRIAGE.

" And so five have bitten the dust already." I'm sure there'll be a sixth combatant in the lists to-night. Is he the one who will finally become my very humble and very obedient servant and lord?

In any case, he had better get ready to undergo the most rigorous and searching examination.

I'm not like mamma. I don't lose *my* head.

Nov. 26*th. Four o'clock.*

I wasn't mistaken. It *was* the sixth.

But let me be orderly, and write the events, both small and great, in their due sequence.

After dinner mamma and I went upstairs to dress. I took a long time over it, and was very careful too. I may as well tell the truth. I worked at my toilet. It took me an hour and a half to dress to my own complete satisfaction. On coming downstairs I found all the doors open, and as I noiselessly approached the drawing-room I heard papa and mamma talking. Papa said :

" You think it *absolutely* necessary, then ? "

" *Absolutely* necessary. Just think of it. Your presence is indispensable."

The temptation was too great. I stopped to listen. Was it not right, or at least justifiable curiosity on my part ?

" Why indispensable ? " replied papa. " I know the young fellow. I've often met him at the club. I've even played whist with him. He doesn't play badly, either. He saw Irene on horseback, and thought she was superb. That settles the whole affair as far as I am concerned. What business is it of mine ? It's only your affair— yours and Irene's.

" My dear, I assure you that propriety demands——"

" Well, well ; I'll go, I'll go."

Then silence fell. Not another word was spoken. I waited to hear the man's name, but it didn't come. My heart beat a little quicker as I stood there in expectancy—in fact, I distinctly heard its tick-tack. I stood two or three minutes, but as they did not think fit to resume the conversation, I entered, and had to pretend to know nothing.

But I did know something, and that something was of importance, too. He is a member of the Jockey Club. To me that means every-thing. If I attach too much importance to it, it is papa's fault, for he thinks that any one who is not a member of the Jockey Club is simply nobody. The world, as far as papa is concerned, begins with the Jockey Club, and ends at those who are not of the charmed circle. I have been brought up with those ideas. My husband must be a member of the Jockey Club.

Well, the three of us set off in the landau—papa gloomy, depressed, silent ; mamma in the same state of eager excitement ; I outwardly cool and indifferent, but thinking hard all the same.

What could be the meaning of so much mystery ? This gentleman has seen me on horseback, and had thought I was bewitching, which was very sweet of him. Was it he who had asked to see me in a brilliantly-lighted room—*décolletée*?

That, it seemed to me, was scarcely the correct thing. He ought to have been shown to *me* before I was so liberally shown to him on horseback and on foot. But, after all, it didn't matter much.

We got to the Mercereys' at half-past ten. I was very sorry for papa, for it really was a *soirée musicale*, and there was a quartette, too, which is about the most trying thing in the world for one who does not care for music, and has not been broken in into bearing it. In addition, the music was highly and wearily classical.

There were not many people present—only about a score. The company was very mixed, and it was evident that the affair had been arranged in a hurry, for the people seemed to have been picked up haphazard, with no thought for their peculiarities and idiosyncrasies —nobody knew anybody, and there was an evident lack of sympathy.

We entered just when the andante movement of a sonata was in full swing, and we went on tiptoe to seats. I settled myself snugly in a quiet corner and cast a rapid, furtive glance round the battlefield. At first I only saw a few old men—bored-looking persons—evidently not for me.

Then, in the opposite corner, I noticed a little knot of four young men. There could be no doubt that there was the enemy.

Yes, but which of the four? In my simplicity I thought, " It must be he who is looking at me most devotedly and attentively." I modestly lowered my eyes, and assumed the attitude of a saint listening with inward rapture to the austere strains of a Haydn sonata.

Then suddenly I raised my eyes and let them fall full upon the group of young men. But I had to drop them more quickly than I had raised them, for all the four young men were studying me with an equal amount of curiosity and evident approbation. I let the sonata go a little longer, and again renewed the experiment—with the same result. The four pairs of eyes were fixed unflinchingly upon me.

I don't think I was much put out by so much attention. In fact, I wasn't at all put out. It was pleasant, very pleasant ; and I rather liked it than otherwise.

The country did wonders for me last summer. I have grown a little—ever so little—fatter. Virginie, my maid, said to me the other evening while dressing me :

" Ah ! Mademoiselle, you don't know how the summer has improved you." In which Virginie was very much mistaken. Mademoiselle *did* know it very well. One always notices such things first one's self.

The quartette at last came to an end, and the usual confusion of tongues followed. I took mamma aside and said :

" Mamma, do point him out."

" Why, you little minx, have you guessed ? "

" Yes, I've guessed. Show me him—quick—the music's going to start again."

" That's he—the tall dark man, on the left there—the man standing under the Meissonnier. Don't look just now. He's looking at you."

" He's not the only one. They're all doing that."

" He's not looking now, though. There he is. He's going to papa. He's talking to him."

" He's not bad looking."

" I should rather think he isn't ! "

" But his mouth's too large."

" I don't think so."

" Oh, yes it is. But that's a trifle. On the whole, he'll do."

" Oh, if you only knew all—birth, fortune everything you could wish for. It was such an extraordinary accident, too—quite romantic."

" What's his name ? "

" Comte de Martelle-Simieuse. Don't look at him ; he's beginning to look at you again. As I was saying, he is a Martelle-Simieuse, and the Martelle-Simieuses are cousins of the Landry-Simieuses, and of the Martelle-Jonzacs. You know the Martelle-Simieuses ? "

At this point one of the musicians tapped on his desk, and mamma's flow of genealogical eloquence was stopped. We resumed our seats, and the music began. Mozart this time. I sank back into my corner and settled down to my reflections. It was evident to me that he must be a splendid catch, for mamma was so excited.

Comtesse de Martelle-Simieuse. Two names. Just what I had dreamt of and longed for. Of course, I should have preferred to be a duchess ; but then there are so few real dukes left—only twenty-two, I believe—so that is practically out of the question. But a countess is passable.

Comtesse de Martelle-Simieuse. The name would sound well, I thought, and I repeated it several times to convince myself. I paid no attention whatever to Mozart. At first I scarcely realised that the musicians were playing Mozart—it might have been Wagner. All that I knew was that the musicians were playing a melody which seemed to fit in with the words, " Madame la Comtesse de Martelle-Simieuse."

After all a name *is* a matter of great importance, and particularly a name which goes well with a title. He is titled as well as a member of the Jockey Club. *He* must be titled. I wouldn't become plain " Madame "—no, not for a fabulous fortune. Comtesse de Martelle-Simieuse. Yes, certainly, that sounded very well.

When the quartette was over the conversation was renewed. Papa turned toward mamma, so did I. As soon as I reached her, she said, excitedly, " The affair is going splendidly. He has asked to be introduced to you, and papa noticed that his voice trembled—didn't it ? "

" Yes," replied papa, " his voice trembled."

" Your papa is going to bring him up to introduce him. If you are not satisfied with him, don't stay at my side. If you are satisfied, stay."

" Of course I shall stay, mamma ; but it must be understood that I shall have due time for reflection afterward. You have promised not to hurry me."

" You will be quite free. But don't forget that it is a chance in a hundred thousand. If you only knew his relatives, and how well they are married. His mother was a Précigny-Laroche. Think of that ! A P——"

" Yes, yes. I see."

" There is no better blood than that of the Précigny-Laroches."

" Keep calm, mamma. Don't get so excited. People are looking at you." Then papa fetched him, and we had a nice chat in the interval. It was evident that he was affected. He had had courage to stare at me from a distance, but close at hand he daren't look at me. I had to lead the conversation, and I managed in ten minutes, while chatting apparently about the most trivial topics, to learn all that was absolutely necessary that I should know before letting things go farther.

He loves Paris—so do I. He detests the country—so do I. He thinks Trouville is very amusing—so do I. He doesn't like shooting —nor do I. On the other hand, he is passionately fond of horses and hunting—just as I am. It is well that we agree on that point. How many times have I said to myself, " My husband will have a hunting-seat." He has one. He rents a forest which is only ten leagues from Paris. You leave Paris at half-past eight in the morning from the Gare du Nord—the most convenient of stations—and at half-past ten you are on horseback. And unless the hunt is a very long one, you are back in Paris in the evening for the theatre or a ball.

Then again, his time, his fortune, as well as he himself, are entirely at his own disposal. He has neither father nor mother. He has only a younger brother, who is at present serving in an artillery regiment, and a very rich and very old aunt, who has no children. So he is the head of the family. Martelle-Simieuse belongs to him. It is an estate somewhere out in Vendée. Of course, I have not the remotest idea of going and burying myself out in Vendée for half of the year ; but it's quite necessary to have a country-seat, and Vendée is just as good as anywhere else.

All which information I picked up in the short space of ten minutes or a quarter of an hour at the outside. Madame Mercerey, seeing that we were engaged in a serious conversation, lengthened the interval

for the benefit of us four—I might say of us three, for papa never
uttered a word—might even say of us two, for mamma didn't say
much either.

All the information I obtained by skilfully turning the conversation in the most natural manner, and without asking a single
question.

This morning mamma told me that she was absolutely shocked
at my calmness and precision last night. Yes, I have a practical side
to my nature. I am anxious to place my life in certain unassailable
conditions of independence and security, without which there could
be neither happiness nor love, nor anything else worth having.

For instance, I'm determined not to have a mother-in-law.
I don't know what I wouldn't give *not* to have a mother-in-law.
I don't intend to have to quarrel with one. At home a wife should
be at home, and only have her husband to deal with.

It was on account of that decision that I rejected the little Marquis
de Marillac last year. He was one of the five. I could have loved
him ; really, I had already begun to. Then I saw his mother.
I stopped.

She was a terrible creature—strict, lugubrious, and ferociously
pious. She expected her daughter-in-law to go and bury herself in
the depths of Britanny for eight months out of the twelve. Certainly
it would have been a saving—but at what a cost ! What slavery !
Besides, what would be the good of getting married, if, the day after
leaving girlhood, the wife had to become a child and go back into
leading-strings again the next day ?

Now let me see. Where was I ? I've really quite forgotten.
Oh, I remember. The music began again, as I said. It was the last
piece. We four sat down in a row in the following order : I, mamma,
papa, and he. It was scarcely an hour before that I had first set eyes
on him, and we were already quite a little family party, we four,
sitting stupidly and stiffly in a straight line on our chairs.

Some short waltzes of Beethoven were played, with intervals of
one minute between. During the first interval mother said to me :

" Well, what do you think of him, now that you have seen him ? "

" The same as before, mamma."

" Is he all right ? "

" He'll do."

" Then your father may venture to ask him to dinner ? "

" Wouldn't that be hurrying matters rather too much ? "

" We must hurry matters."

" Why, mamma ? "

" 'Sh ! They're going to begin again."

I was somewhat put out. What was the reason for such unseemly haste ? I was quite shocked by it. It seemed really as if
I were being thrown at the gentleman's head. I was in a hurry to

know the why and the wherefore. I thought the concert would never end.

After ages of waiting the second interval came, and I began again :

" Mamma, tell me why."

" I can't tell you anything just now. It would take too long. I'll tell you all presently, when we get home. But if he's invited it must be to-night ; and there's not a minute to lose—yes or no ? "

" Mamma, you're hurrying me."

" No, I'm not hurrying you. You are at liberty to decline."

" Very well, then—yes."

" Dinner on Thursday ? "

" Thursday will do very well."

Between the third and fourth waltzes, mamma said hurriedly to papa :

" Invite him to dinner."

" What day ? "

" Thursday."

" All right."

Papa has behaved with admirable docility and resignation. I never saw him in such a serious *rôle* before. It is true that the music seemed to bewilder him so that he scarcely knew what he was doing. I felt restless, and thought, " There, now, he'll go and invite the wrong one." Nothing of the sort. He gave the invitation quite correctly, and it was accepted with enthusiasm.

We left at midnight, and before we had fairly got away from the Mercerey's I said to mamma :

" I see clearly that you are as anxious as possible that I should accept this man."

" Certainly."

" Then tell me——"

" Just let me get my breath first. I am quite exhausted. I'll tell you everything when we get home."

An hour later I knew all. It was the most extraordinary thing in the world. Yesterday morning at eight o'clock a maid awoke mamma, and gave her a note marked " Important." It was from Madame de Mercerey, and was as follows :

" I have a headache and cannot leave my room. Come—come at once to see me. A splendid stroke of luck for Irene."

Mamma at once got up and went to Madame Mercerey.

But I must leave the rest till to-morrow. We dine at eight o'clock.

November 27th.

Well, mamma went off post-haste, and this is what she heard from Madame Mercerey : " The two Martelle-Simieuses, the elder,

insurrection, but he soon found out whom he had to deal with. Monsieur Coates was very much pleased with me.

"This morning," said he, "you ride superbly—like an angel"—which was also the opinion of my second, self-appointed groom, who kept saying to himself :

"How well she rides ! How well she rides ! "

That was the idea which filled his head during the ride, and he compared me with Catherine de Puymarin.

The ride finished, I went and found Miss Morton, got into the dog-cart, and set off for the Rue de Varennes. Young Martelle-Simieuse trotted behind and acted as my escort home.

He waited until the door was opened and we had entered, then he satisfied himself that I lived in a good house, in a good street, and that from all appearances I was no adventuress.

What he then wanted was the name of the intrepid Amazon. A very simple idea occurred to him. What does the name matter for the moment ? He returned home, got the directory—Rue de Varennes, 49 *bis*, Baron and Baronne de Léoty. That is how he discovered the name of her who will perhaps become the faithful partner of his joys and sorrows. Baron de Léoty. He knew papa from the club. But had papa a daughter ? The mystery had to be solved.

It was very soon solved, for that evening Adrien dined at the Mercereys', and during a lull in the conversation he said carelessly to Madame Mercerey, "Do you happen to know a Monsieur de Léoty ? "

"Quite well."

"Has he a daughter ? "

"Yes."

"How old is she ? "

"About twenty."

"Very pretty, isn't she ? "

At which, it appears, there was a general and enthusiastic outburst in my honour. He was the only one present who didn't know me, poor fellow. Madame de Mercerey wanted to know the reason for all his inquiries. So he recounted the story of the morning's ride, my horse's obstinacy, my firmness, my hair flying in the wind—in fact, it was quite a lyrical description, which caused general stupefaction, for he had never been heard to sing in that strain before.

Whereupon Madame de Mercerey showed presence of mind which was as rare as it was admirable. *En passant* it must be observed that she loves mamma and hates the Puymarins heartily, although, until about six weeks ago, they were the best of friends. She really has good cause to be offended with them, though.

The Puymarins have given three *soirées* this year—the Orleans princes were at one, and the Grand Duke Vladimir at another, while the third was made up of nobodies. Well, the Duchess invited the Mercereys with the nobodies. Now, considering their birth and fortune, they might reasonably have expected more consideration than that. For that reason they are very angry—and justifiably so.

Now comes Madame de Mercerey's stroke of genius. Taking the ball, as it were, on the rise, without a moment's hesitation, she said, in the presence of her husband, who was stupefied at the assertion, that on the following evening they were going to have a few friends, among whom Madame and Mademoiselle Léoty were invited, and that Monsieur de Martelle-Simieuse would be welcome if he cared to come. There would be some music, and he would have an opportunity of seeing his fair heroine of the Bois. Monsieur de Mercerey was thunderstruck.

" Aren't you mistaken in the date, my dear ? " he said. " We were surely going to the Gymnase to-morrow night to see the new piece of Octave Feuillet."

" No, my dear ; that is for the day after to-morrow."

" I thought that—I ordered the box myself."

" It is for the day after to-morrow, I tell you."

Upon which Monsieur subsided and got no further explanation of the riddle until dinner was over. Madame de Mercerey's exertions did not stop at that. She took possession of Monsieur de Martelle-Simieuse, and treated him to a eulogy of me.

" Irene de Léoty is just the girl to suit you—just the wife you want. The meeting this morning was clearly the work of Providence."

He repeated as refrain :

" How well she rides ! "

Yesterday, after having seen mamma, Madame de Mercerey, in spite of her headache, courageously set to work and took the field to get people together—engaged musicians and got programmes printed. What admirable activity !

On what insignificant trifles our destiny hangs. If Virginie had fastened my hair up properly, if Triboulet had been quiet, if the Puymarins had not put the Mercereys among the nobodies—Monsieur de Martelle-Simieuse would not have been invited to dine at our house to-morrow, and I should not be asking myself the question :

" Shall I or shall I not be Comtesse de Martelle-Simieuse ? "

Poor Puymarins ! They have come to Paris for the sole purpose of exhibiting their phenomenon. Poor Catherine de Puymarin ! Shall I let her keep her count, or shall I take him myself ?

I don't yet know. But I do know that the sixth has not made a bad start, and if I *had* to bet on the result, I would not give odds.

November 29th.   Ten o'clock in the morning.

What deliberations there were about the dinner. Should it be a big affair or a small one ? Where should *he* be placed ? Opposite me or at my side ? Mamma at first held out for opposite. She maintained that I produce a much better effect full face than in profile, especially when I am *décolletée*, and of course I *was décolletée*. I stuck out for being at his side. I didn't feel at all nervous at the idea of having him near me. It was necessary to make him talk, so as to be able to take his measure. I still held to my resolution of not getting married without knowing what I was doing. So, of course, he was put at my side—on my right. So as not to be too hungry, and to have plenty of time for cross-questioning, I had a pretty substantial lunch at five o'clock. That left me free to turn the conversation as I wished—which I did.

We were at table over an hour and a half, and at the end of that time I was convinced that we were made for each other. We first talked about carriages and hunting. It was a splendid start. I discovered immediately that his ideal of a horse is just the same as mine—not too thin, and not too high—light certainly, but not too slim ; elegant, but well formed. I think he was somewhat surprised to find that I was *au fait* in such matters. About carriages and gear our ideas are exactly the same.

He was both surprised and charmed. When dinner began he was evidently excited and ill at ease, but as we chatted, and I put him at his ease, the conversation began to go swimmingly. We spoke the same language. We were made to understand each other.

He hunts boars with a pack of eighty hounds—magnificent animals of the best breed. He described his hunting suit minutely—coat *à la française*, colour of dead leaves, facings and pockets of blue velvet. It would be charming to have a costume to harmonise with the dead leaves. I have already an idea for a little hat—a dainty little thing.

One reason which induces me to favour him is that, as a rule, we have to choose our husbands from among men who have nothing to do, and who live lives of the most appalling idleness. That is the reason why boredom and fatigue ruins so many happy households.

His time is, however, quite occupied. He hasn't a single minute of free time which he can really call his own. His energy and intellect are employed in pursuits which are at the same time useful and elegant. He is one of the leaders of a very smart coterie, which has just been organised ; member of the committee of a pigeon-shooting society, and of a skaters' league ; he is interested in a society for steeple-chasing, and is part owner of a stud of race-horses. With so many irons in the fire it is evident that he is fully occupied.

All which I had learned in half an hour. Then I passed on to politics, and catechised him thereon. This is a very, very important question, and I have fully made up my mind to have no misunderstandings on that head. Poor mamma has suffered cruelly, and I am resolved not to expose myself to like annoyances.

Mamma has been very happy with papa—except from a political standpoint. She was very young when she was married. Her family was an ancient one, and of strict monarchical principles. So was papa. So far, so good. But toward the end of 1865 papa went over to the Empire. It was not because his opinions had changed—he took the step out of goodness of heart. Poor papa is *so* good—too good in fact. His change in politics was due to his devotion to my uncle Armand, his brother, who is now general of division. He was only a captain then, and had had no promotion for ages. He was not in favour because papa refused to set foot in the Tuileries, in spite of the many advances made to him. So at last papa, who adored Uncle Armand, accepted an invitation and promised to present mamma. That was a veritable triumph for the Empire, for there is no bluer blood in France than that of mamma's family.

Mamma passed the day of the presentation in tears. She was, however, forced to obey, but on the way there was a frightful scene in the landau. Mamma became obstinate, and declared that she would not be presented. She wanted to get out of the carriage into the street, although she was wearing white satin shoes and a crown of roses, and it was snowing heavily at the time. At length she became quieter, and resigned herself to her fate.

A fortnight afterward Uncle Armand received a decoration, and at the end of six months was chief of a squadron. But the affair caused many doors to be shut against papa and mamma. That caused him no trouble—not a bit ; in fact, he was rather pleased than otherwise. He detests society, and always has his club. But society is mamma's life-breath, and she is not a member of the Jockey Club, so she suffered cruelly.

Nearly all the doors which were shut have since been opened—that is to say, since the establishment of the Republic, because since then many things have been forgotten. The remainder would be thrown open to me were I once Comtesse de Martelle-Simieuse. I should be received everywhere with open arms. Since the beginning of the century the political attitude of the Martelle-Simieuses has been irreproachable. It did not even trip during the Empire.

The Martelle-Simieuses can trace their pedigree, fairly and without any trickery, back to the fourteenth century. Adrien's mother—there, I am already calling him Adrien—Adrien's mother was a Précigny-Laroche, and as for his father—Adrien has published a little book about his genealogy. Only a hundred copies were printed and distributed among his friends. Madame de Mercerey has a copy of it, which she lent to mamma. I have read it, and re-read it, until I know it by heart. It proves incontestably that Adrien is the third in rank among the counts of France—not fourth, but third.

Of course, one must naturally consider nobility of heart and elevation of character in the first place, but one must not forget to attach their real importance to these other things. They are of enormous interest in life, and especially at this particular moment, in the midst of this flood of self-styled nobility, in the presence of Spanish dukes and Italian princes, who are easily able, if we cannot prove that we are really of noble family, to steal a march on us, and usurp our position in society. I couldn't bear the thought of being put at a table at dinner with money-makers and literary persons.

Another point demands attention, for nothing is too trifling to notice when it is a question of making certain definite arrangements for the comfort and pleasure of after-life. One ought firmly to secure what one wants. Mamma has a box at the opera every Monday. It has been understood, for some time past, that when I marry I am to go halves on that box. Mamma will have it one Monday, and I the next. That's a very good arrangement, and I am quite satisfied with it.

Now, if I marry Adrien, I shall have a box in the first row, in front, at the Théâtre Français, every Tuesday from December to June. This is how it will be arranged. He has an aunt, a dear old aunt, very rich, without children (so he is her heir), very old, asthmatic, and she has the said box at the Théâtre Français. She is quite willing to hand it over to him, for she never uses it. She has not been in the theatre for over three years. What a dear old aunt she is !

All that information I got out of him between the soup and the cheese. So, when, after dinner, mamma rushed to me and said, " Well ? " I replied :

" I don't think I could find a better."

" Then it's settled ? "

" Two are necessary for a marriage."

" Oh, you may set your mind at rest on that score. You are two. I have been watching you the whole time during dinner. His head is quite turned."

That was my opinion, too. When mamma rushed to me, he rushed off to Madame Mercerey, who, of course, was of the party. He loved me to distraction ; adored me, would marry only me—me and nobody else. And he besought Madame Mercerey to go and demand me from mamma at once.

She had to try to pacify him, and to show him that one must not act too rashly. Mamma, for her part, would have been quite contented to settle the affair at once. She had a dread of the machinations of the Puymarin clique.

I didn't share her fear in the least. I recognised clearly what an effect I had produced, and I felt that I was mistress of the situation. So I reminded mamma of her promises, and of my resolution only to come to a decision when I had carefully weighed the pros and cons, and said that I had only seen him twice—each time in evening dress.

I was determined to see him twice in the daytime, and in frock coat. I knew how Cousin Mathilde had managed. She saw her husband twice in the daytime—once in the Louvre and once at the Hippodrome. As there was no Hippodrome where I could see Adrien, I would substitute the museum at Cluny. I was determined, however, to have my two interviews in broad daylight.

So Madame Mercerey arranged an accidental meeting at the Louvre for to-day at three o'clock punctually, in front of Murillo's " Virgin."

The same day. Five o'clock.

We have just returned from an hour's stroll in the galleries, where we did not pay much attention to the pictures. I imagine that he is surprisingly ignorant of pictures. But then I have no thought of marrying an art critic. He has such a fine figure, and dresses so well. He speaks very little, is very reserved, but very correct ; and above all, never makes stupid remarks. Taking him altogether, I am quite contented.

As soon as we were alone in the carriage in the Rue Rivoli, I had to repulse another attack from mamma :

" He's simply charming. I should think that you would never insist on Cluny now."

" No. I waive that. Never mind Cluny."

" That's right. Then you've decided ? "

" Not yet, mamma ; not yet. One oughtn't to rush madly into marriage after having got a little information about a man's fortune and situation."

" But what more do you want ? "

" To see him on horseback. He's seen me riding, but I haven't seen him."

In short, Madame de Mercerey, whose devotion is indefatigable, is going to advise him to-night to go and ride about at the entrance of the Avenue des Acacias about ten o'clock to-morrow morning. As inducement she will hint delicately that he may possibly meet papa and me. For papa—I must say that papa astonishes me—he is acting the *rôle* of a father who has a marriageable daughter to perfection. He hasn't mounted a horse for four years, but to-morrow he is going to risk a broken neck.

November 30th.

We had a ride round the Bois—all three of us—papa, he, and I. *He* looks very well on horseback. He rode a splendid bay mare. I will take her for myself, and will pass Triboulet on to him, for I know Triboulet too well, and am tired of him.

On my return I flung my arms round mamma's neck.

" Yes, a thousand times," I said.

And with tears in my eyes, I thanked her for having been so indulgent, so good, so patient.

December 4th.

To-day at three o'clock the old aunt who has the box at the theatre on Tuesdays is to come to demand my hand officially, and so before the 10th of January (that will be absolutely necessary because of the grandmother's will) I shall be Comtesse de Martelle-Simieuse. Adrien will get the one and a half millions and me into the bargain, as extra consolation prize. I think it will be money easily gained. I don't think that he is much to be pitied.

December 11th.

The wedding is fixed for January 6th. It is absurd to get married at such a time, but it couldn't be arranged otherwise. The will ! The will ! Besides, after all, the date doesn't displease me so very much. We shall have a short—a *very* short—honeymoon—a few days at Nice—ten days at the outside.

After that Paris in full swing, with all the theatres open. The unfortunate Louise de Montbrian got married last spring—at the end of May, and returned to Paris after a six-weeks' honeymoon only to find the city torrid and sinister.

We shall be supremely happy—of that I haven't the slightest doubt. He adores me. And I ! Do I love him ? Well, I must be candid with myself, and it would not be true if I declared, in the phrases so common in English novels, that I love him madly ; that I only really live when he is present ; that I tremble at the sound of his footsteps, and start when I hear his voice.

Oh, no ! I am not so easily moved. My heart can't be expected to go at that rate. But I already like him very much. Love will come in time, I have no doubt.

Love is such an economiser in a household. I bring a million, and we can reckon on an income of about 230,000 francs. That may at first sight seem a very large income, but it isn't really so. First of all we must deduct about 80,000 francs for the keeping up of Simieuse, our château in Vendée, and for hunting. That will leave only 150,000 francs for living expenses, which amount will be sufficient if we love each other and pull together like good chums.

But if, on the contrary, we begin after a short time—and this is the history of many households—to pull in opposite directions, we shall only have 75,000 francs each, and that will mean pinching—supposing that theatres—leaving the opera and the Théâtre Français out of the reckoning—cost 2000 or 3000 francs a year if we go together, it would at once be double that sum if we went separately. And so with everything else—the expenditure doubled.

Take, for instance, Caroline and her husband. They have only 100,000 francs per annum, but they live well, and without economising. Why ? Because they love each other. They have quite a small house, and naturally don't require a host of servants. They receive little, and rarely go out. The more they are with each other, the more they see of each other, the more they are satisfied. Caroline is quite content, too, with 12,000 francs for her toilet.

Take Adèle as an example of the contrary. Poor girl, she married very much against her own will and judgment. Her mother was dazzled by the title. Certainly a title is something—in fact, it is a great deal—but it is not exactly everything. Well, her marriage with Gontran turned out badly. Things went wrong from the first week. Consequently they find themselves pinched in spite of their great income of 250,000 francs. She spends a fortune on clothes, on stupid whims. It costs her much more to satisfy the whole world than it would to please one individual. The Duke, in consequence, has taken to play, and has already squandered half of his fortune.

Caroline said to me recently :

" As soon as you are married try to love your husband. In our set that means a saving of at least 100,000 per annum, and even if people can't love each other for love's sake, they ought to for convenience."

" Oh, yes ! I'll love him. I'll love him. Besides, it's only the 11th of December. Between now and the 6th of January I have still twenty-six days before me."

THE DREAM

Ludovic Halévy

THE day before yesterday my friend Raoul was married at Sainte Clotilde's. On arriving at the church I found a great crowd and the ceremony already in progress. The priest finished his address thus : " Be then united on earth until you are definitely united in heaven."

I could scarcely restrain an exclamation. Raoul was not marrying a spinster, but the pretty little Countess Jeanne de Charmelieu, the widow of my friend Gaston de Charmelieu. That charming woman was destined to make my friends happy. Raoul after Gaston. On earth, nothing could be simpler. Gaston having withdrawn, Raoul remained ; but for the definite union above, in heaven, there will be two, Gaston and Raoul, the first and second husband.

I left the church, paid two or three calls, returned home, dined at the club, went to the opera, and was everywhere pursued by the ridiculous idea, " How will Raoul and Gaston arrange things in the other world ? "

I went to bed and slept. Then the dream began.

I was in Paradise, at the railway station. A great bustle of trains. The carriages left empty, and returned more or less full. St. Thomas was the station-master. I had a chat with him, and he very kindly explained the organisation. He went on talking, but I ceased to listen, for at the door of a saloon carriage I saw the pretty head of my widow of Sainte Clotilde's, Gaston's wife, Raoul's wife. And she rushed about, crying out, " Paradise, where is Paradise ? Here's my ticket."

And St. Peter came to her and said, " Your ticket, madame ; kindly show me your ticket."

" Here it is, Monsieur."

" Quite correct, you may pass. Here is the entrance to Paradise." I was seized with an immense desire to follow her.

Who knows ? Perhaps Raoul was dead, and my widow would find herself between her two husbands.

I asked St. Thomas if he could allow me to enter.

" Easily," he replied.

" Yes, but at most for an hour. I don't want to be compelled to stay. I shall be able to leave. Because, don't you know, however pleasant Paradise may be, if I'm still good for a few years on earth, I don't want to lose them. Life only comes once, and Paradise is for ever."

" Be assured, you will be able to come out again." And he took me to St. Peter : " You will know this gentleman again," he said ; " he wants to have a look round, and come out again."

" Pray go in, Monsieur ; I shall know you again."

There I was in Paradise. Just in the nick of time. Raoul and Gaston, who had been eagerly scanning the new arrivals, had already rushed up to *their wife.*

Gaston had seized her right hand and was drawing her to one side, saying, " Jeanne, my dearest Jeanne."

Raoul had seized her left hand, and was pulling her towards the other side, saying, " Marthe, my dearest Marthe."

She had two Christian names, and she had thought it better for her second husband to use the one that had not served for the first. She was a charming creature, with exquisite delicacy of feeling.

Neither Raoul nor Gaston, however, appeared disposed to give way.

" Jeanne ! "

" Marthe ! "

" I am your first husband."

" I am your second husband."

" My right is indisputable."

" Monsieur, leave this lady alone."

" I am not speaking to you, Monsieur, I do not know you ! "

I do not know you! Now on earth, when they were alive, they were intimate and inseparable friends. Raoul, the second husband, was always to be found at Gaston's, and ill-natured gossips said— but as if one can believe everything ill-natured gossips say!

However, the dispute between Raoul and Gaston waxed hotter. Their voices became louder. Life in heaven is pleasant, but just a little monotonous ; and the least event has something of the effect of a carriage accident in a small provincial town. The elect ran up from all sides. Some took the part of the first husband, others that of the second. Jeanne did not move ; she had freed her hands, and did not speak either to Raoul or to Gaston.

St. Thomas had accompanied me into Paradise.

" You must often have similar cases," I said. " Women with two husbands are not uncommon on earth."

" True ! But what is unusual, absolutely unusual, is that the two husbands should fight over the wife. Ordinarily, in such circumstances, the husbands don't want the wife again."

" And when the situation is reversed ? when there are two wives for one husband ? "

" Oh ! that's quite a different thing. It's the women who are anxious to catch the husband. Women are mad about marriage even in Paradise."

At that moment St. Thomas was interrupted by a loud shout from the crowd of the elect. " The holy father ! the holy father ! " He chanced to be passing that way, and hearing the noise, came up.

A dream, this is merely a dream that I cannot get out of my mind.

He stopped and asked what was going on. The affair was shortly told him.

" Well," said the holy father, " what could be simpler ? The lady is here as a reward for her piety and Christian sentiments. She has every right to absolute and long-lasting happiness. Let her make her choice between the two gentlemen."

" But," remarked Gaston, " what of the one who comes in a bad second ? "

You observe how Gaston, who, when alive, had kept a racing stud, preserved, even after his death, deplorable habits of speech.

" Well," replied the holy father, " I'll give him one of the unclaimed women who crowd Paradise. Come, madame, do not waste any time ; make your choice."

Silent, motionless, Jeanne stood between her two husbands, and then Gaston and Raoul in turn, like an ancient Greek play, sought words which might most surely move their wife's heart.

.   .   .   .

" Really, Monsieur," interrupted Raoul, " such recollections are out of place——"

"Possibly, Monsieur, but I am permitted to recall—to speak of my love, and also of my trust. My confidence was to be admired! How many persons came to me and said perfidiously, 'Give heed to Raoul. Observe him carefully. He is of course very fond of you; but there's one person he likes better, and that is your wife.' I paid no attention to such idle tales."

"I also proved valiant in the matter of confidence. Later, Monsieur, when, after you, I was in my turn the husband, gossip still went its way. People spoke to me of Monsieur de Séricourt, of Séricourt, my best friend; what an absurdity!"

I noticed that at the name of Séricourt Jeanne could not repress a slight start. But I was the only one who observed it; Raoul remarked nothing, and continued:

"And when Séricourt was killed in Mexico, when the unexpected news caused you most natural and legitimate grief, I received an abominable anonymous letter, stating that my wife wept for the friend more than she would weep for the husband. I never mentioned the letter to you. To suspect you! To suspect Séricourt!"

"Who may Séricourt be?" cried the holy father. "Is he a third husband? I'm fairly puzzled by all this."

"One word in conclusion, holy father, just one word more. On my wedding-day an excellent priest assured me at Sainte Clotilde's that our provisory union on earth would be followed by a definite union in heaven."

"And me, holy father," replied Gaston, "on my wedding-day, at the Madeleine, a bishop, do you mark—not a priest, a bishop—made me the same promise in exactly the same terms."

"Dear me, this becomes very embarrassing, very embarrassing," said the holy father. "My representatives on earth sometimes act very thoughtlessly. But, madame, it is for you to decide."

And then the little widow, blushing, and with much emotion, said, "If you are of infinite goodness, Lord, you will allow me to go to M. de Séricourt, who is in that little cloud to my left; he has been making signs to me for the last quarter of an hour."

I turned my head and saw Séricourt performing a gallant and expressive pantomime in his little cloud.

Another friend, Séricourt! I repeat that this charming woman was destined to make all my friends happy, even to eternity, both in this world and the next.

"Why didn't you say so at once?" replied the holy father. "That settles everything. Make yourself happy with M. de Séricourt. Since you were a good Christian, my only desire is that you should have a good time in Paradise."

And thereupon I awoke with a start.

ÉMILE GABORIAU
1835–1873

THE ACCURSED HOUSE

THE Vicomte de B——, an amiable and charming young man, was peacefully enjoying an income of 30,000 livres yearly, when, unfortunately for him, his uncle, a miser of the worst species, died, leaving him all his wealth, amounting to nearly two millions.

In running through the documents of succession, the Vicomte de B—— learned that he was the proprietor of a house in the Rue de la Victoire. He learned, also, that the unfurnished building, bought in 1849 for 300,000 francs, now brought in, clear of taxes, rentals amounting to 82,000 francs a year.

" Too much, too much, entirely," thought the generous vicomte, " my uncle was too hard ; to rent at this price is usury, one cannot deny it. When one bears a great name like mine, one should not lend himself to such plundering. I will begin to-morrow to lower my rents, and my tenants will bless me."

With this excellent purpose in view, the vicomte sent immediately for the *concierge* of the building, who presented himself as promptly, with back bent like a bow.

" Bernard, my friend," said the vicomte, " go at once from me and notify all your tenants that I lower their rents by one-third."

That unheard-of word " lower " fell like a brick on Bernard's head. But he quickly recovered himself ; he had heard badly ; he had not understood.

" Low—er the rents ! " stammered he. " Monsieur le Vicomte deigns to jest. Lower ! Monsieur, of course, means to raise the rents."

" I was never more serious in my life, my friend," the vicomte returned ; " I said, and I repeat it, lower the rents."

This time the *concierge* was surprised to the point of bewilderment—so thrown off his balance that he forgot himself and lost all restraint.

" Monsieur has not reflected," persisted he. " Monsieur will regret this evening. Lower the tenants' rents ! Never was such a thing known, monsieur ! If the lodgers should learn of it, what would they think of monsieur ? What would people say in the neighbourhood ? Truly——"

"Monsieur Bernard, my friend," dryly interrupted the vicomte, "I prefer, when I give an order, to be obeyed without reply. You hear me—go!"

Staggering like a drunken man, Monsieur Bernard went out from the house of his proprietor.

All his ideas were upset, overthrown, confounded. Was he, or was he not, the plaything of a dream, a ridiculous nightmare? Was he himself Pierre Bernard, or Bernard somebody else?

"Lower his rents! lower his rents!" repeated he. "It is not to be believed! If indeed the lodgers had complained! But they have not complained; on the contrary, all are good payers. Ah! if his uncle could only know this, he would rise from the tomb! His nephew has gone mad, 'tis certain! Lower the rents! They should have up this young man before a family council; he will finish badly! Who knows—after this—what he will do next? He lunched too well, perhaps, this morning."

And the worthy Bernard was so pale with emotion when he re-entered his lodge, so pale and spent, that on seeing him enter, his wife and daughter Amanda exclaimed as with one voice:

"Goodness! what is it? What has happened to you now?"

"Nothing," responded he, with altered voice, "absolutely nothing."

"You are deceiving me," insisted Madame Bernard, "you are concealing something from me; do not spare me; speak, I am strong—what did the new proprietor tell you? Does he think of turning us off?"

"If it were only that! But just think, he told me with his own lips, he told me to—ah! you will never believe me——"

"Oh, yes; only do go on."

"You will have it then!— Well, then, he told me, he ordered me to notify all the tenants that—*he lowered their rents one-third!* Did you hear what I said?—*lowered* the rents of the tenants——"

But neither Madame nor Mademoiselle Bernard heard him out—they were twisting and doubling with convulsive laughter.

"Lower!" repeated they; "ah! what a good joke, what a droll man! Lower the tenants' rents."

But Bernard, losing his temper and insisting that he must be taken seriously in his own lodge, his wife lost her temper too, and a quarrel followed! Madame Bernard declaring that Monsieur Bernard had, beyond a doubt taken his fantastic order from the bottom of a litre of wine in the restaurant at the corner.

But for Mademoiselle Amanda the couple would undoubtedly have come to blows, and finally Madame Bernard, who did not wish to be thought demented, threw a shawl over her head and ran to the proprietor's house. Bernard had spoken truly; with her own two ears, ornamented with big, gilded hoops, she heard the incredible

word. Only, as she was a wise and prudent woman, she demanded
" a bit of writing " to put, as she said, " her responsibility under
cover."

She, too, returned thunderstruck, and all the evening in the lodge,
father, mother, and daughter deliberated.

Should they obey ? or should they warn some relative of this mad
young man, whose common sense would oppose itself to such
insanity ?

They decided to obey.

Next morning, Bernard, buttoning himself into his best frock
coat, made the rounds of the three-and-twenty lodges to announce
his great news.

Ten minutes afterward the house in the Rue de la Victoire was in
a state of commotion impossible to describe. People who for forty
years had lived on the same floor, and never honoured each other with
so much as a tip of the hat, now clustered together and chatted
eagerly.

" Do you know, monsieur ? "

" It is very extraordinary."

" Simply unheard of ! "

" The proprietor's lowered my rent ! "

" One-third, is it not ? Mine also."

" Astounding ! It *must* be a mistake ! "

And despite the affirmations of the Bernard family, despite even
the " bit of writing " " under cover," there were found among the
tenants doubting Thomases, who doubted still in the face of everything.

Three of them actually wrote to the proprietor to tell him what
had passed, and to charitably warn him that his *concierge* had wholly
lost his mind. The proprietor responded to these sceptics, confirming
what Bernard had said. Doubt, thereafter, was out of the question.

Then began reflections and commentaries.

" *Why* had the proprietor lowered his rents ? "

" Yes, *why ?* "

" What motives," said they all, " actuate this strange man ? For
certainly he must have grave reasons for a step like this ! An
intelligent man, a man of good sense, would never deprive himself of
good fat revenues, well secured, for the simple pleasure of depriving
himself. One would not conduct himself thus without being forced,
constrained by powerful or terrible circumstances."

And each said to himself :

" *There is something under all this !* "

" But what ? "

And from the first floor to the sixth they sought and conjectured
and delved in their brains. Every lodger had the preoccupied air of
a man that strives with all his wits to solve an impossible cipher, and

everywhere there began to be a vague disquiet, as it happens when one finds himself in the presence of a sinister mystery.

Some one went so far as to hazard :

" This man must have committed a great and still hidden crime ; remorse pushes him to philanthropy."

" It was not a pleasant idea, either, the thought of living thus side by side with a rascal ; no, by no means ; he might be repentant, and all that, but suppose he yielded to temptation once more ! "

" The house, perhaps, was badly built ? " questioned another, anxiously.

" Hum-m, so-so ! no one could tell ; but all knew one thing—it was very, very old ! "

" True ! and it had been necessary to prop it when they dug the drain last year in the month of March."

" Maybe it was the roof, then, and the house is top-heavy ? " suggested a tenant on the fifth floor.

" Or perhaps," said a lodger in the garret, " there is a press for coining counterfeit money in the cellar ; I have often heard at night a sound like the dull, muffled thud of a coin-stamper."

The opinion of another was that Russian, maybe Prussian, spies had gained a lodgment in the house, while the gentleman of the first storey was inclined to believe that the proprietor purposed to set fire to his house and furniture with the sole object of drawing great sums from the insurance companies.

Then began to happen, as they all declared, extraordinary and even frightful things. On the sixth and attic floors it appeared that strange and absolutely inexplicable noises were heard. Then the nurse of the old lady on the fourth storey, going one night to steal wine from the cellar, encountered the ghost of the defunct proprietor —he even held in his hand a receipt for rent—by which she knew him !

And the refrain from loft to cellar was :

" There *is* something under all this ! "

From disquietude it had come to fright ; from fright it quickly passed to terror. So that the gentleman of the first floor, who had valuables in his rooms, made up his mind to go, and sent in notice by his clerk.

Bernard went to inform the proprietor, who responded :

" All right, let the fool go ! "

But next day the chiropodist of the second floor, though he had naught to fear for his valuables, imitated the gentleman beneath him. Then the bachelors and the little households of the fifth storey quickly followed his example.

From that moment it was a general rout. By the end of the week, everybody had given notice. Every one awaited some frightful catastrophe. They slept no more. They organised patrols. The terrified domestics swore that they too would quit the accursed house and remained temporarily only on tripled wages.

Bernard was no more than the ghost of himself ; the fever of fear had worn him to a shadow.

" No," repeated his wife mournfully at each fresh notification, " no, it is *not* natural."

Meanwhile three-and-twenty " For Rent " placards swung against the façade of the house, drawing an occasional applicant for lodgings.

Bernard—never grumbling now—climbed the staircase and ushered the visitor from apartment to apartment.

" You can have your choice," said he to the people that presented themselves, " the house is entirely vacant ; all the tenants have given notice as one man. They do not know why, exactly, but things have happened, oh ! yes, *things !* a mystery such as was never before known—*the proprietor has lowered his rents ! "*

And the would-be lodgers fled away affrighted.

The term ended, three-and-twenty vans carried away the furniture of the three-and-twenty tenants. Everybody left. From top to bottom, from foundations to garret, the house lay empty of lodgers.

The rats themselves, finding nothing to live on, abandoned it also.

Only the *concierge* remained, grey-green with fear, in his lodge. Frightful visions haunted his sleep. He seemed to hear lugubrious howlings and sinister murmurs at night that made his teeth chatter with terror and his hair erect itself under his cotton nightcap. Madame Bernard no more closed an eye than he. And Amanda in her frenzy renounced all thought of the operatic stage and married— for nothing in the world but to quit the paternal lodge—a young barber and hairdresser whom she had never before been able to abide.

At last, one morning, after a more frightful nightmare than usual, Bernard, too, took a great resolution. He went to the proprietor, gave up his keys, and scampered away.

. . . .

And now on the Rue de la Victoire stands the abandoned house, " The Accursed House," whose history I have told you. Dust thickens upon the closed slats, grass grows in the court. No tenant ever presents himself now ; and in the quarter, where stands this Accursed House, so funereal is its reputation that even the neighbouring houses on either side of it have also depreciated in value.

Lower one's rents ! ! Who would think of such a thing ! ! !

COUNT VILLIERS DE L'ISLE-ADAM
1835-1889

A TORTURE BY HOPE

BELOW the vaults of the *Oficial* of Saragossa one nightfall long ago, the venerable Pedro Arbuez d'Espila, sixth Prior of the Dominicans of Segovia, third Grand Inquisitor of Spain—followed by a *fra redemptor* (master-torturer), and preceded by two familiars of the Holy Office holding lanterns—descended towards a secret dungeon. The lock of a massive door creaked ; they entered a stifling *in pace*, where the little light that came from above revealed an instrument of torture blackened with blood, a chafing-dish, and a pitcher. Fastened to the wall by heavy iron rings, on a mass of filthy straw, secured by fetters, an iron circlet about his neck, sat a man in rags : it was impossible to guess at his age.

This prisoner was no other than Rabbi Aser Abarbanel, a Jew of Aragon, who, on an accusation of usury and pitiless contempt of the poor, had for more than a year undergone daily torture. In spite of all, " his blind obstinacy being as tough as his skin," he had refused to abjure.

Proud of his descent and his ancestors—for all Jews worthy of the name are jealous of their race—he was descended, according to the Talmud, from Othoniel, and consequently from Ipsiboe, wife of this last Judge of Israel, a circumstance which had sustained his courage under the severest of the incessant tortures.

It was, then, with tears in his eyes at the thought that so steadfast a soul was excluded from salvation, that the venerable Pedro Arbuez d'Espila, approaching the quivering Rabbi, pronounced the following words :

" My son, be of good cheer ; your trials here below are about to cease. If, in presence of such obstinacy, I have had to permit, though with sighs, the employment of severe measures, my task of paternal correction has its limits. You are the barren fig-tree, that, found so oft without fruit, incurs the danger of being dried up by the roots . . . but it is for God alone to decree concerning your soul. Perhaps the Infinite Mercy will shine upon you at the last moment ! Let us hope so. There *are* instances. May it be so ! Sleep, then, this evening in peace. To-morrow you will take part in the *auto da fé*, that is to say, you will be exposed to the *quemadero*, the brazier premonitory of the eternal flame. It burns, you are aware, at a certain distance, my son ; and death takes, in coming, two hours at least, often three, thanks to the moistened and frozen clothes with which we take care to preserve the forehead and the heart of the holocausts. You will be only forty-three. Consider, then, that, placed in the last rank, you will have the time needful to invoke God, to offer unto Him that baptism of fire which is of the Holy Spirit. Hope, then, in the Light, and sleep."

As he ended this discourse, Dom Arbuez—who had motioned the wretched man's fetters to be removed—embraced him tenderly. Then came the turn of the *fra redemptor*, who, in a low voice, prayed the Jew to pardon what he had made him endure in the effort to redeem him ; then the two familiars clasped him in their arms : their kiss, through their cowls, was unheard. The ceremony at an end, the captive was left alone in the darkness.

Rabbi Aser Abarbanel, his lips parched, his face stupefied by suffering, stared, without any particular attention, at the closed door. Closed ? The word, half unknown to himself, awoke a strange delusion in his confused thoughts. He fancied he had seen, for one second, the light of the lanterns through the fissure between the sides of this door. A morbid idea of hope, due to the enfeeblement of his brain, took hold on him. He dragged himself towards this strange thing he had seen ; and, slowly inserting a finger, with infinite precautions, into the crack, he pulled the door towards him. Wonder of wonders ! By some extraordinary chance the familiar who had closed it had turned the great key a little before it had closed upon its jambs of stone. So, the rusty bolt not have entered its socket, the door rolled back into the cell.

The Rabbi ventured to look out.

By means of a sort of livid obscurity he distinguished, first of all, a half-circle of earthy walls, pierced by spiral stairways, and, opposite to him, five or six stone steps, dominated by a sort of black porch, giving access to a vast corridor, of which he could only see, from below, the nearest arches.

Stretching himself along, he crawled to the level of this threshold. Yes, it was indeed a corridor, but of boundless length. A faint light —a sort of dream-light—was cast over it ; lamps suspended to the arched roof, turned, by intervals, the wan air blue ; the far distance was lost in shadow. Not a door visible along all this length ! On one side only, to the left, small holes, covered with a network of bars, let a feeble twilight through the depths of the wall—the light of sunset apparently, for red gleams fell at long intervals on the flag-stones. And how fearful a silence ! . . . Yet there—there in the depths of the dim distance—the way might lead to liberty ! The wavering hope of the Jew was dogged, for it was the last.

Without hesitation he ventured forth, keeping close to the side
of the light-holes, hoping to render himself indistinguishable from
the darksome colour of the long walls. He advanced slowly, dragging himself along the ground, forcing himself not to cry out when
one of his wounds, recently opened, sent a sharp pang through him.

All of a sudden the beat of a sandal, coming in his direction,
echoed along the stone passage. A trembling fit seized him, he
choked with anguish, his sight grew dim. So this, no doubt, was
to be the end! He squeezed himself, doubled up on his hands and
knees, into a recess, and, half dead with terror, waited.

It was a familiar hurrying along. He passed rapidly, carrying
an instrument for tearing out the muscles, his cowl lowered; he
disappeared. The violent shock which the Rabbi had received had
half suspended the functions of life; he remained for nearly an
hour unable to make a single movement. In the fear of an increase
of torments if he were caught, the idea came to him of returning
to his cell. But the old hope chirped in his soul—the divine
" Perhaps," the comforter in the worst of distresses. A miracle
had taken place! There was no more room for doubt. He began
again to crawl towards the possible escape. Worn out with suffering
and with hunger, trembling with anguish, he advanced. The
sepulchral corridor seemed to lengthen out mysteriously. And he,
never ceasing his slow advance, gazed forward through the darkness, on, on, where there *must* be an outlet that should save him.

But, oh! steps sounding again; steps, this time, slower, more
sombre. The forms of two Inquisitors, robed in black and white,
and wearing their large hats with rounded brims, emerged into the
faint light. They talked in low voices, and seemed to be in con-
troversy on some important point, for their hands gesticulated.

At this sight Rabbi Aser Abarbanel closed his eyes, his heart beat
as if it would kill him, his rags were drenched with the cold sweat
of agony; motionless, gasping, he lay stretched along the wall,
under the light of one of the lamps—motionless, imploring the God
of David.

As they came opposite to him the two Inquisitors stopped under
the light of the lamp, through a mere chance, no doubt, in their
discussion. One of them, listening to his interlocutor, looked straight
at the Rabbi. Under this gaze—of which he did not at first notice
the vacant expression—the wretched man seemed to feel the hot
pincers biting into his poor flesh; so he was again to become a living
wound, a living woe! Fainting, scarce able to breathe, his eyelids
quivering, he shuddered as the robe grazed him. But—strange at
once and natural—the eyes of the Inquisitor were evidently the
eyes of a man profoundly preoccupied with what he was going to
say in reply, absorbed by what he was listening to; they were
fixed, and seemed to look at the Jew *without seeing him.*

And indeed, in a few minutes, the two sinister talkers went on their way, slowly, still speaking in low voices, in the direction from which the prisoner had come. They had not seen him ! And it was so, that, in the horrible disarray of his sensations, his brain was traversed by this thought : " Am I already dead, so that no one sees me ? " A hideous impression drew him from his lethargy. On gazing at the wall, exactly opposite to his face, he fancied he saw, over against his, two ferocious eyes observing him ! He flung back his head in a blind and sudden terror ; the hair started upright upon his head. But no, no. He put out his hand, and felt among the stones. What he saw was the *reflection* of the eyes of the Inquisitor still left upon his pupils, and which he had refracted upon two spots of the wall.

Forward ! He must hasten towards that end that he imagined (fondly, no doubt) to mean deliverance ; towards those shadows from which he was no more than thirty paces, or so, distant. He started once more—crawling on hands and knees and stomach—upon his dolorous way, and he was soon within the dark part of the fearful corridor.

All at once the wretched man felt the sensation of cold *upon* his hands that he placed on the flag-stones ; it was a strong current which came from under a little door at the end of the passage. O God, if this door opened on the outer world ! The whole being of the poor prisoner was overcome by a sort of vertigo of hope. He examined the door from top to bottom without being able to distinguish it completely on account of the dimness around him. He felt over it. No lock, not a bolt ! A latch ! He rose to his feet ; the latch yielded beneath his finger ; the silent door opened before him.

" Hallelujah ! " murmured the Rabbi, in an immense sigh, as he gazed at what stood revealed to him from the threshold.

The door opened upon gardens, under a night of stars—upon spring, liberty, life ! The gardens gave access to the neighbouring country that stretched away to the sierras, whose sinuous white lines stood out in profile on the horizon. There lay liberty ! Oh, to fly ! He would run all night under those woods of citrons, whose perfume intoxicated him. Once among the mountains, he would be saved. He breathed the dear, holy air ; the wind reanimated him, his lungs found free play. He heard, in his expanding heart, the " Lazarus, come forth ! " And to give thanks to God who had granted him this mercy, he stretched forth his arms before him, lifting his eyes to the firmament in an ecstasy.

And then he seemed to see the shadow of his arms returning upon himself ; he seemed to feel those shadow-arms surround, enlace him, and himself pressed tenderly against some breast. A tall figure, indeed, was opposite to him. Confidently he lowered his

eyes upon this figure, and remained gasping, stupefied, with staring
eyes and mouth drivelling with fright.

Horror! He was in the arms of the Grand Inquisitor himself,
the venerable Pedro Arbuez d'Espila, who gazed at him with eyes
full of tears, like a good shepherd who has found the lost sheep.

The sombre priest clasped the wretched Jew against his heart
with so fervent a transport of charity that the points of the monacal
hair-cloth rasped against the chest of the Dominican. And, while
the Rabbi Aser Abarbanel, his eyes convulsed beneath his eyelids,
choked with anguish between the arms of the ascetic Dom Arbuez,
realising confusedly *that all the phases of the fatal evening had been
only a calculated torture, that of Hope!* the Grand Inquisitor, with
a look of distress, an accent of poignant reproach, murmured in his
ear, with the burning breath of much fasting: " What! my child!
on the eve, perhaps, of salvation . . . you would then leave us ? "

ERNEST DAUDET
B. 1837

THE VENGEANCE OF
THE ADMIRAL

LIKE a citadel, the manor-house was planted on the crest of a bare rock that dominated the shore. On one side it overlooked the open sea, with a sky-line closed by the red band of the sunset. On the other side was the roadside of Brest ; and at the end of the roadside the port, above which rose chimneys and the masts of the ships, gleaming in the last flicker of the dying light.

Its narrow windows, with pointed arches, framed bits of the sea, like pieces of greenish silk, along which passed grey sails bellying out in the cool evening wind. Its heavy embattled towers, with their regular indentations, stood out against the stormy sky. The rare shrubs, growing around the walls, had their branches spun out by strong western winds, like the wild sinister tresses of the spectre of a woman fleeing in the night. As twilight deepened, the sky grew heavy with storm-clouds. The gale that shrieked over the sea drove against the rock high white waves that rose and fell with a sound of thunder.

In his study on the first floor, Admiral the Marquis de Bec'Hellouin was sitting alone before a table ; over it was scattered some open letters, many of them yellow with age, and among the letters were some withered flowers, a knot of blue ribbon, and a locket. By the side, half open and empty, was a box of carven ivory, from which the Admiral had taken these relics of love. There was a deep sadness in his face, and, at times, a quick sudden flash of anger lightened in his eyes.

A grand old man, the Admiral. A lean bony face, dull eyes, skinny limbs, all the body exhausted by the malady that was killing him. The famous sailor had even lost the imperious, thundering voice that once sounded over the noises of the storm. Of his strength that was the admiration of the men of the fleet, of his old daring and courage displayed in both battle and tempest—of these nothing remained. Stricken by the deadly disease he was no more than a shadow. And now that death already had him by the throat, he

46*   681

seemed to have left only just enough energy to examine the evidence of the crime he had just discovered, and to dream of avenging himself.

\Early that morning he had received an anonymous letter from Nice, where for six weeks the Marquise de Bec'Hellouin had settled for the winter, as she did every year. The letter ran : " It is now fourteen years that your wife has been unfaithful to you. You are the only person who does not know that all this time she has been carrying on with Captain Faucheron, your former aide-de-camp. If wou wish to know the truth of the matter, go into the bedroom of the Marquise. At the head of the bed, under the hangings, there is a little box in the wall. Force the lock and read what you find, and you will know the truth."

On receiving this blackguardly letter, the work of some dismissed servant, the Admiral at first rubbed it feverishly between his hands, driving away the suspicions it provoked. But, beset by these suspicions that tortured his heart, he had read it again, doubting for the first time the fidelity of his wife. Then, under the empire of this terrible doubt, he had staggered from his bed, and dragged himself into the empty bedroom, and there, in the spot indicated, he had found the overwhelming proof of his misfortune.

Now he was groaning over the clear evidence of the dishonour that had fallen on his house. He built up, year by year, the story of shame, and went back to the beginning of the long series of outrages of his honour. Then, driven to the edge of the grave by the blow that had just struck him, he asked himself what vengeance he could take on the guilty couple before he died.

Oh, the wretches ! How they had betrayed his trust and repaid, one, his love, the other, his kindness and help ! This Faucheron, always treated like his son, who owed everything in his brilliant career to him ! And his wife ! the miserable woman ! She was twenty when he married her, and he was, it is true, fifty. But to the poor, lovely orphan he had brought a glorious name and much wealth ; he had assured her his protection while he lived, and an independent life in the future when he was gone. And she had married him freely of her own choice. Since, adored, spoilt, tended, she had had all she could wish for. Her desires became orders, and her caprices were realised as soon as they were expressed. In summer, on the country estate, in winter in the splendid mansion at Paris or the graceful villa at Nice—everywhere, she was a queen of society ; everywhere, the fame and name of her husband gave her the highest rank. And while, always trustful and always loving, far away or near, he brooded over her with profound tenderness, rejoiced in her successes, and took pride in her beauty, she was betraying him. For forty years he had served his country, fought in Africa, in the Crimea, in Mexico, winning promotion at the sword's point, and amassing glory for his son—and now, suddenly, at the very end of so full a life, he was covered with dishonour by the fault of this creature.

And she condemned him to a still more horrible torture, to a doubt that filled all his heart and brain, and darkened the world to him. His Patrick, the pride and the joy of his life ! Was he his son ? Was he the son of Faucheron ? Patrick had grown up in freedom in the old manor-house, where his mother, every winter, left him in the care of the priest, and where his father came, between two cruises, to embrace him. He was as strong and as upright as a tree. Under his tanned skin, with his deep eyes glowing with pride in his awakening strength, with his brown hair thick on his forehead, his fine figure and lissom limbs, he had the beauty of a young god. He passionately admired the old man whose name he bore ; he loved him still more passionately. Between them there was always an exchange of intimate confidences, in which the heart of the father melted in the caresses of the boy. This paternal happiness, these memories of the deepest of joys, which were the best part of the Admiral's life, had now been overthrown by the crime of the wife.

The unhappy man pressed his trembling hands against his head, that felt as if it would burst. The fever burned in his blood and a shudder ran through his flesh ; and thus he sat, stunned, strengthless, beaten, stammering, " I will avenge myself ! "

But how ? Kill them who had dishonoured his name ? They were far away. Recall them ? But before they arrived, he would be dead. He sought for some means of vengeance. Night came, but he had not found what he wanted. He dragged himself to his bed a broken man.

At dawn the next morning, the medical man of the cruiser *Inflexible*, that had long borne the flag of the Admiral, came to Brest to see his chief, as he did every day. He was terrified on observing what progress had been made in a single day by the disease he was trying to overcome. His face betrayed his terror.

" It is all over, doctor, isn't it ? " said the Admiral.

" Oh ! I have not lost all hope, sir. You are in a bad way, but——"

" No lies. I have faced death before now, and I will not let him take me by surprise at last. The truth ! I order you ! "

The doctor remained silent for two minutes ; then seriously, he said :

" Unless a miracle happens, Admiral, this evening you will stand before your Maker."

The Admiral received the blow calmly.

" Very well," he said. " You will come back, won't you ? "

" I will come back, my Admiral. Would you not like to warn Madame la Marquise ? "

" It is useless. Besides, she is at Nice. I wanted to spare her the sight of my agony. She thinks me unwell, and will always learn soon enough that she is a widow. She will be told when I am dead."

The doctor withdrew.

" How is my father ? " said Patrick, on meeting him outside the door.

The surgeon-major did not answer. But his deep sigh told the boy what was the matter, and the little lad ran towards his father, wild with grief.

" Come to me, my son," said the Admiral. Half rising, his elbow on the pillow, his hand supporting his terribly pale face, he spoke to the boy :

" You are twelve years old, Patrick—only a child. But I am obliged to treat you like a man. I have something to tell you."

It did not take long. When he had finished a sombre fire shone in the eyes of the child. He was so thoughtful and cold and serious that it looked as though the death which was stealing on his father was ageing him and ripening his intelligence, and that in a few minutes he had passed from childhood to manhood, carried along by grief and trouble.

. . . .

The following year, at the end of autumn, less than ten months after the death of the Admiral, people began to speak in society about the marriage of his widow with the handsome Faucheron. They spoke about the matter with a smile, as an event long expected. It was in fact so. After a long separation, necessitated by social custom, the lovers were about to unite for life in proper form. One morning Captain Faucheron arrived at the manor-house, where the Marquise, since the death of her husband, lived in retirement, devoting herself entirely to her son, while waiting for the return of the man she loved. During the day Patrick came to her, carrying himself with a seriousness beyond his age.

" Is it true," he asked, " that you are now about to marry Captain Faucheron, mother ? "

" Who told you ? " she said, in a troubled voice.

The child was silent. She continued :

" A son should not question his mother."

" I do not intend," said Patrick resolutely, " that Captain Faucheron shall take the place of my father."

" You do not intend ! . . . What is the meaning of this action ? " and pointing to the door with an angry gesture, she added, " Leave the room at once, sir ! "

He went out. In a few minutes, after going to his own room, he abruptly entered, without knocking, the Captain's room, one hand in his trousers pocket.

Faucheron was shaving himself before the looking-glass. He turned round, saw Patrick, and said :

" You should have knocked before you came in."

" This is my house, and I want to speak to you."

" You want to speak to me ? . . . Speak ! "

" I know why you are here. What you want to do cannot be done. You will leave this night, and you will never return. I forbid you to marry my mother."

" But the child is mad ! "

" Will you obey me ? "

" Obey you ! " exclaimed Faucheron stupefied, his face pale and his eyes angry. " Be off, you silly little wretch ; I will box your ears ! "

He strode with raised hand towards Patrick. The boy stepped back, drawing from his pocket the thing he had hidden there. It was a revolver. He lifted his arm, sighted, and fired. The Captain swung round and fell sprawling, a bullet-hole in his forehead. A shriek was heard. The Marquise, entering, had seen everything.

" What have you done ! Unhappy boy ! " she shrieked, throwing herself on her son to disarm him.

Patrick let her take his weapon ; then, as she flung herself with passionate frenzy on the corpse, he said savagely :

" Before my father died, he revealed to me that this man was your enemy and mine. He ordered me to watch over you, to protect you, and if need be to free you. I have obeyed."

It is thought by most people that Captain Faucheron committed suicide.

ARMAND SILVESTRE
1839–1891

THE STORM

I

It was at the little hamlet of Pilhoël, one of the wildest on the coast of Britanny, savage in its environment of blue rocks, the rugged crests of which were reddened by the setting sun, with the sea, rampant like a chained lion, or furious and hurling its sonorous waves to the very thresholds of the houses above ; while, inland, the country was sheltered and smiling with flowers in all seasons, as in a green-house—a sunny zone, where camellias blossomed in the open air.

At that time Pilhoël was a corner unknown to tourists, and a few painters who went there to sketch took care not to lead thither the importunate crowd of fashionable people. Fifty houses at most, all inhabited by fishermen, stood under the shadow of the ruined church, the cracked bell of which frightened even the sea-gulls on the shore. During the working days of the week none but women with children hanging to their skirts were to be seen moving about between the dwelling-places. All the men were away fishing.

On Sundays their long nets were spread along the weather-stained white of the house-walls, holding in their meshes silver spangles which glittered in the light ; and there was a world of poor people, all resigned, pious, and knowing nothing of the unwholesome dreamings of city dwellers, but full of faith and courage.

There is in France—at least on the borders of the sea—no village, however humble, which has not its pearl of beauty. It was no untruth so to call Jeanne, the prettiest girl in Pilhoël. The humblest garments—for she was one of the poorest girls in the hamlet—could not disguise her inherent grace and beauty. Her superbly-designed bare feet, her little hands, which hard toil had often wounded, were signs unconquerable of natural aristocracy. Good and modest above all the girls about her, she had, none the less, a love-secret in her heart.

She was sixteen, and he whom she loved was four years older ; a handsome youth who, equally with herself, felt the flow of noble blood in his veins. Something of instinctive worth was betrayed in his least gestures, and a proud melancholy was strongly expressed in his face. He was skilful in his calling, and bravest of the brave ; with all that, a dreamer, taking little part in the Sunday sports on the square in front of the church, but oftener, at the hour when Jeanne was listening to the vespers and singing the verses, re-entering the holy building, and at the foot of a pillar contemplating her in the shadow scarcely penetrated by the yellow rays of the altar candles ; or wandering away to the deserted sea-shore to think of her, the music of the waves seeming to bear away to far-off horizons the frail bark of his unspoken hopes.

What was it separated these two human beings, so completely made to unite their laborious and resigned existence ? Their common poverty. Both were orphans. Loëhic had earned his scanty living in service on the boats, and only at last had been able to buy one for himself, and such a boat !—the oldest and most sea-battered of the little fleet.

As to Jeanne, she had been reared by her old Aunt Mathurine, who had brought her up with infinite tenderness, but at the same time promising herself not to allow her niece to marry any but a man who would be in a position to assure her (Mathurine) a comfortable provision for her old age. For there is always a basis of selfishness in our devotion.

This man she had chosen without saying anything about it : it was Mathias, the pilot, who was looked up to by the whole fishing community of the little hamlet. A rough man, with his weather-beaten face and hands of bronze, yet hale and hearty in spite of his fifty years ; who had often faced Death, from whom he had snatched his intended victims ; and who had made enough fortune to insure his ease and allow him to retire from his perilous calling. He had known Jeanne in her infancy, had danced her on his knees, and had seen her grow with increasing and affectionate interest. And Mathurine, who had the natural sharpness of all peasants, had guessed that the old pilot was in love with this flower of grace, slowly expaning under his eyes.

But Mathias was no fool, and when he thought of his age he laughed at himself, and again became paternal with the young girl, who, innocent creature, had never even suspected the combat that was being waged in the old sailor's heart. With him she was always the same—simple, frank, and sometimes cruelly charming ; admiring him, but in the way in which patriarchs are venerated.

All her tenderness was reserved for Loëhic, and, knowing that her aunt was opposed to her marriage with him, she had resolved to remain unwed rather than become the wife of any other man. She had sworn it to him one evening when they had met upon the shore in the soft moonlight, broken by the sea into a rain of gold ; at one of those mysterious hours, sweet to lovers, when their hearts seem to open widest to solemn confidences, when their souls bathe deliciously in the same concert of abandonment and sincerity ; she had even placed upon his finger a ring in remembrance of her promise—a poor brass ring, but one which Monseigneur the bishop had blessed at the last confirmation.

" Before God I am your betrothed," she had said to him, all her soul vibrating in her voice, " and death alone can part my thoughts from yours ! "

And both had melted into tears, the bitter drops of which ran down to their lips, mingling with the salt vapours rising from the waves and the tossing seaweeds of the shore. And from the shelter of a block of granite in the moorland he had plucked a wild flower and given it to her, and she had placed it between two leaves of her poor " Book of Hours," the face towards a picture of the Virgin bearing this epigraph : " Ave maris stella." And she turned her eyes towards a star, on the golden eyelashes of which a tear of pity seemed to tremble.

Both had moved away, overcome by this idyll, but confident in each other, expecting nothing of men, but everything from some marvellous and heavenly intervention, which would not permit the future viewed by them with a like tenderness to be for ever destroyed, or that such a dream as theirs should be the eternal despair of their lives.

After that supreme interview, existence had, so to speak, returned to them. Loëhic every day, without rest or truce, risked his life in his miserable boat for trifling gains ; and Jeanne repaired the nets of old or unmarried fisherman for a small piece of money, which Aunt Mathurine dropped into the throat of a nearly empty purse.

II

There was a festival that day at Pilhoël. The pilot, Mathias, had solemnly retired. He had said farewell to the fleet he had commanded, and his old companions, to do him honour, and in gratitude for the services he had rendered them, had organised a series of rejoicings.

As soon as it was daylight they went to his cottage to play the drum and fire guns and pistols under his windows. Then the maidens brought him a large bouquet, which was presented by Jeanne ; which made the old sailor's tanned face blush as red as a peony with pleasure. Then full cups of the best cider—which had been bottled months before in anticipation of the event—were drained, and the glory of the old pilot commemorated in song.

Loëhic had not been the least active in all these proceedings ; for he felt towards Mathias a childlike admiration mixed with a confiding sympathy. Many times he had been on the point of confessing to him his tenderness for Jeanne and asking his advice— for how could he for a moment imagine that venerable Mathias had ever regarded her with other than fatherly feelings ? At twenty, people think those who are fifty years of age veritable Methuselahs.

As was proper, this touching ceremony was not left without its comic side. This was secured to it by Aunt Mathurine, by the offering of a pair of slippers embroidered by herself—a garden in tapestry, with roses resembling cabbages and birds that might readily be mistaken for gnats : for Mathurine had in her youth been in service in one of the large towns, and had acquired genteel accomplishments. The old sailor, who had never in his life worn anything but sabots, felt an enormous temptation to burst into a roar of laughter.

" If it makes no difference to you, Mathurine," he said, " I'll wear 'em on my hands in winter-time, to play the dandy in at the High Mass."

And, by way of thanks, he clapped on the old girl's two cheeks a pair of such hearty kisses as, for a moment, made her teeth rattle in her head like castanets.

Everybody had that morning made holiday for this rejoicing, which was followed by a copious repast, and ended with a rigadoon, accompanied by Mathurine on the guitar—a superannuated instrument which had been given to her by one of her old employers, and which distilled under her meagre fingers some vinegary notes, falling drop by drop, as it were, into the tormented ear. But they had no refined notions as to music at Pilhoël, and so this performance of Aunt Mathurine, embroidered by the gruntings of a bagpipe, played by a lad whose execution had come to him naturally and wholly without study seemed to all who heard it as charming as any music could be.

All this revelling had filled the morning down to one o'clock, and the time was then come for putting off to sea, to make up for the early lost hours of the day.

It was in the month of September, and the forenoon had been particularly bright. The sun had risen over the ocean in mist, which had speedily been consumed by its rays and had melted, like the last cloud of smoke at a conflagration, into the rosy light. The intense azure of the zenith paled down to the horizon, where the blue of the sea blended with that of the sky in a long kiss—the insensible line between reality and dream, between the region of stars and the region of tempests.

The mild air—too warm, perhaps, for the season—was scarcely tinctured with salt, but laden with the life-giving perfumes, the nourishing breath of the immense living thing which breathes along the land and warms it with the beatings of its heart. On seeing the few tiny copper clouds which the dawn had rapidly driven before it, some of the weather-prophets had said that the day would not pass without a storm.

But this threat seemed to have withdrawn behind the glittering curtains of the firmament, and in the gaieties of Mathias's *fête* had passed from the minds of all. Joyously, therefore, the sails had been unbound from the masts, dressed with flags for the occasion, when, suddenly and unexpectedly, they were caught by a rude puff of wind and filled even before they were completely spread, while a violet-hued vapour rose above the horizon, presently shaping itself into a long, slate-coloured blade, widening itself obliquely, and cutting the azure sky as with a shadowy knife.

" There'll be a tempest presently ! " said Mathias. " Take care of yourselves, boys ! "

" Ah ! you have done well to quit the business, my good Mathias ! " Aunt Mathurine murmured softly in his ear.

Jeanne looked sadly on while Loëhic adjusted, as well as he could the rough and torn sail which, like a wounded wing, was to bear him out to sea. His soul was heavily oppressed by melancholy. When he had wished to dance with Jeanne, old Mathurine had made at him through her diabolical spectacles such a pair of eyes that he had not dared to invite the young girl. At table, before that, they had been placed as far as possible apart from each other ; so that what had been a pleasure to everybody else, had been for him nothing but a punishment.

Never had he felt so completely downcast. So, when passing near him, while her aunt was offering a pinch of snuff to Mathias, Jeanne had said to him :

" Don't go out to sea, my Loëhic, I beg of you ! "

The only reply he had been able to make to her was :

" Oh, let me go !—I wish to die."

III

A heavy gloom poisoned the departure after the gaiety of the morning, and many a furtive tear mingled with the farewells along the range of boats into which the men were climbing, to go in quest of the daily bread for which they daily prayed.

The prediction of Mathias had troubled the minds of the most courageous ; the old pilot knew so well the ocean and its treasons ! But all had solid boats, and well fitted to withstand the onslaughts of the waves. Then, they were not going far out, but meant to content themselves with fishing within sight of the coast, ready for a prompt return, in case the winds and waves should prove too hostile. Loëhic alone, in his shattered boat, would run any real danger.

" Take my better boat, lad," said Mathias, with rough tenderness.

But, for the first time, the poor young fellow had noticed the old man's assiduities to Jeanne, and with what fond eyes he had gazed upon her, and he answered, shortly :

" No, thank you ; I don't want it."

And with a last look, charged with agony, cast upon his loved one, he threw himself into his leaky boat, and his tattered sail, filling with the rest, bore him away. The wind grew every moment stronger, and one by one the boats disappeared into the violet mist, their grey sails looking to the end like the wings of frightened gulls.

Mathias and Mathurine had retired into the cottage of the latter, who had prevailed on him to partake of a last pitcher of cider ; for she could think of no better artifice for drawing to her house the only nephew she could hope to secure in this country, so far removed from the shores of Pactolus. Moreover, the moment appeared to her an excellent one for making a first trial. The old sailor had given up the sea ; it was the very time for him to take to himself a wife. Jeanne was the prettiest girl in Pilhoël ; Mathias was the richest fisherman there.

These two aristocracies were made for one another evidently. The match-maker, therefore, set about diplomatising, commencing the campaign by a significant enumeration of her niece's virtues ; she augured well from the enthusiasm with which Mathias declared that she had still fallen short of the truth.

During this conversation, in which she was so much concerned, Jeanne had remained on the sea-shore, anxiously, and with moistened eyes, peering into the horizon overspread by a dark curtain which had at length veiled the whole sky. Suddenly this veil was torn by a flash of lightning, skimming the dense green surface of the sea afar off ; followed by a scarcely perceptible rumble, after a long interval. The storm was yet distant.

But she already felt its commotions, and a chill fell on her heart. The light had faded out of the sky. Heavy drops of rain fell upon the sands, tinting them grey. A fresh zig-zag of fire rent the air, reflecting itself on the face of the deep water, and the voice of the thunder immediately followed.

Jeanne uttered a cry of agony.

"We had better go and see what it was, perhaps," said Mathias, emptying a last glass of cider to the health of Jeanne.

"Nonsense—stay where you are," said Mathurine, restraining him.

Like a flight of pigeons regaining the dovecots, pressing closely one against the other, white, and rapidly increasing in size, the sails of the fishermen appeared, all low upon the water, all flying before and under the stress of the tempest. A third burst of thunder had brought all the women and children in terror to the beach.

In spite of Mathurine, Mathias had hurried down to the shore, his rough face expressing a strange anxiety. This one and that one uttered cries of relief and joy on receiving those belonging to them. The wind came in aid of the courage of the sailors ; a powerful gust threw the whole fleet on to the shore in safety.

On all sides kisses, embracings, sobs of joy, hand-graspings of friends lost and restored.   One sail alone was behind—a rag of canvas on a raft, for the gunwale of the boat had all been torn away by the waves ; and against it the figure of a young man struggling to keep it standing against the fury of the wind.   Jeanne recognised in him Loëhic, and, with blanched features and clenched hands, felt as if Death had laid his hands upon her.

" He is lost ! " was the cry of all.

" There is only one man who can save him ! " cried a fisherman.

" Mathias, alone, could make head against such a sea ! " cried another.

Mathias had already stripped off his waistcoat and thrown it on the ground.   He was going to launch his own boat.

" Unhappy man—I forbid you ! " screamed Mathurine, clinging to the pilot's shirt-sleeve.

Mathias looked at Jeanne.

There are moments, solemn, mysterious, when language becomes useless, when souls understand each other in silence, when hearts open themselves, dumb, but readable as widespread books.   The young girl went to the pilot and said to him, in a voice so low that none but he could hear her :

" Save him, and I will be your wife."

For that look—that one look—had, in an instant, revealed to her the pilot's passion.

With a vigorous movement, Mathias threw off Mathurine—so vigorous, indeed, that her clutch carried away with it a shred of the shirt-sleeve on which it had been fastened—and sprang into his boat, already moving out through the surf.   A turn of the helm—a white furrow in the sea—then a cry of agony and admiration !

The storm raged more furiously than ever.   The old pilot's boat had reached Loëhic's shattered vessel in the midst of a cloud of spray, which at moments hid both from view.   The mingled forms of two men stood out against the grey tumultuous background—Mathias holding Loëhic, insensible, in his stalwart arms.   The double shadow stoops—the shadow of a single man rises : Mathias has laid in the bottom of his own boat the body of the man he has saved.   Another turn of the helm, and in a few seconds the rescuer lands the still insensible form of Loëhic on the beach.

A ringing outburst of hurrahs !—the horny hand of the old pilot passed from lip to lip ; his name murmured by all mouths in bene-diction.   The women on their knees put up thanks to the Virgin also.

Jeanne, pale, motionless as death ; Mathias turns upon her a look appealing for thanks.   A pained smile passes to the young girl's lips, and Mathurine makes everybody laugh by breathlessly bringing to the pilot a glass of hot sugared wine, which, in spite of all the old girl's protestations, he insists on forcing between the lips of Loëhic, who has not yet returned to consciousness.

IV

At the end of six weeks, Loëhic, saved and sheltered by Mathias, has slowly recovered the reason of which for awhile he had been bereft by excess of emotion. After many days of delirium, during which his life had been in suspense, consciousness had returned to his mind, but on his heart had fallen the shadow of an incurable sadness.

Mathurine had only permitted Jeanne to come and see him once ; and Mathias—strange as it seemed—had not sought to break through that cruel decree, but appeared to be completely in agreement on the subject. The reason was that in his sick dreams poor Loëhic had so often repeated the name of Jeanne, and with such despairing tenderness in the tones of his voice, that the old pilot feared he had discovered that love existed between them. Jeanne, whom he saw every day at her aunt's, appeared, however, firmly resolved to keep her promise. She had allowed her hand to be officially asked of Mathurine, and, without making the least objection, proceeded with the preparation of her trousseau.

The young girl listened to the pilot's projects of happiness without responding, but with a vague smile upon her lips which he might take for contentment.

One day she was kneeling in prayer as he entered, and in rising let a faded flower fall from the " Book of Hours." Mathias stooped for the purpose of picking it up and returning it to her ; but before he could reach it she had snatched it up and jealously hidden it in her bosom.

The eagerness of her action attracted the old sailor's attention.

" Who gave you that flower ? " he asked, uneasily, without knowing why.

" Loëhic gave it to me."

And, as a look of anguish passed into the pilot's eyes, she added : " God does not forbid remembrance."

Mathias did not insist, but a terrible doubt had entered his heart. An hour later, on taking his place by the bed of Loëhic, now convalescent, he said to the young man :

" How would you answer me, Loëhic, if I, who have saved your life, were to ask something of you in return ? "

" I should answer you : ' Mathias, my life is yours ; dispose of it as you please.' "

After an interval of painful silence, and with a faltering voice, the pilot continued :

" It is not much I have to ask of you, lad ; give me only the worthless brass ring you always wear on your finger."

Loëhic started in his bed and became very pale.

" That ? Never ! " he cried, an angry light flashing from his eyes.

" It was Jeanne, then, who gave it to you ? " replied Mathias, his voice choking with pain.

" *Why* do you ask me, since you know ? " rejoined Loëhic, closing his eyes and overcome by this sudden trial of emotion.

The pilot rose, his eyes full of tears. He kissed the forehead of the young man, who had fallen suddenly into a kind of sleep. He listened, and assured himself that he was really sleeping.

" Forgive me ! " he murmured.

Then, in a corner of the room, before a crucifix, he knelt and besought God to give him courage. Calmed, a look of admirable resignation on his brow, he put on his heavy woollen cap and returned to the house of Mathurine, whom he found working with feverish ardour at the white bridal dress.

" Well—will the trousseau be ready soon ? " he cried, in a voice which he rendered almost rough from trying too much to make it gay.

" You have become very pressing all of a sudden, Master Mathias," replied Aunt Mathurine. " For when do you want it ? "

Very simply, this time, in the admirable tone of sacrifice, the pilot answered, looking at Jeanne :

" For when Loëhic is well again."

ALPHONSE DAUDET
1840–1897

THE POPE'S MULE

OF all the clever sayings, proverbs, or saws with which our Provence peasants embellish their discourse, I know of none more picturesque or more peculiar than this. Within a radius of fifteen leagues of my mill, when anybody mentions a spiteful, vindictive man, he will say : " Look out for that man ! he is like the Pope's mule, that keeps her kick for seven years."

I tried for a long time to find out the source of that proverb, what that Papal mule might be, and that kick kept for seven years. No one here was able to give me any information on that subject, not even Francet Mamaï, my fife-player, who, however, has the whole legendary history of Provence at his finger-ends. Francet agrees with me that there is probably some old tradition of Provence behind it ; but he has never heard it mentioned except in the proverb.

"You won't find that anywhere except in the Grasshoppers' Library," said the old fifer, with a laugh.

I thought the suggestion a good one, and as the Grasshoppers' Library is right at my door, I shut myself up there for a week.

It is a wonderful library, splendidly stocked, open to poets day and night, the attendants being little librarians with cymbals, who play for you all the time. I passed some delightful days there, and after a week of investigation—on my back—I ended by discovering what I wanted to know, that is to say, the story of my mule and of that famous kick stored up for seven years. The tale is a pretty one, although slightly ingenuous, and I am going to try to tell it to you as I read it yesterday morning in a manuscript of the colour of the weather, which had a pleasant smell of dry lavender, with long gossamer-threads for book-marks.

He who never saw Avignon in the time of the Popes has seen nothing. Never was there such a city of gaiety, life, animation, and a succession of *fêtes*. There were, from morning till night, processions, pilgrimages, streets strewn with flowers and carpeted with magnificent tapestries, cardinals arriving by the Rhône, with banners flying ;

gaily bedecked galleys, the soldiers of the Pope singing in Latin on
the squares, and the bowls of mendicant friars ; and then, from roof
to cellar of the houses that crowded humming about the great Papal
palace, like bees about their hive, there was the tick-tack of the
lace-makers' looms, the rapid movement of the shuttles weaving
gold thread for the vestments, the little hammers of the carvers of
burettes, the keyboards being tuned at the lute-makers', the songs
of the sempstresses ; and, overhead, the clang of the bells, and always
a tambourine or two jingling down by the bridge. For with us, when
the common people are pleased, they must dance and dance ; and as
the streets in the city in those days were too narrow for the farandole,
the fifes and the tambourines stationed themselves on Avignon
Bridge, in the cool breezes from the Rhône ; and there the people
danced and danced, day and night. Ah ! the happy days ! the
happy city ! Halberds that did not wound, state prisons where they
put wine to cool. No famine ; no wars. That is how the Popes of
the Comtat governed the people ; that is why the people regretted
them so bitterly.

There was one especially, a good old fellow, whom they called
Boniface. Ah ! how many tears were shed in Avignon when he died !
He was such a good-natured affable prince ! He laughed so heartily
from the back of his mule ! And when you passed him—though you
were simply a poor little digger of madder, or the provost of the
city—he would give you his blessing so courteously ! He was a
genuine Pope of Yvetot, but of a Provençal Yvetot, with a something
shrewd in his laughter, a sprig of marjoram in his biretta, and never
a sign of a Jeanneton. The only Jeanneton that the old man had
ever been known to have was his vineyard, a tiny vineyard which he
had planted himself, three leagues from Avignon, among the myrtles
of Château Neuf.

Every Sunday, after vespers, the excellent man went to pay court
to it ; and when he was there, seated in the warm sun, with his mule
by his side and his cardinals lying at the foot of the stumps all about,
then he would order a bottle of native wine opened—that fine ruby-
coloured wine which was called afterwards the Château Neuf of the
Popes—and he would drink it in little sips, looking at his vineyard
with a tender expression. Then, when the bottle was empty and the
day drew to a close, he would return merrily to the city, followed by
all his chapter ; and when he rode over Avignon Bridge, through the
drums and farandoles, his mule, stirred by the music, would fall into
a little skipping amble, while he himself marked the time of the
dance with his cap, which scandalised his cardinals terribly, but
caused the people to say : " Ah ! the kind prince ! Ah ! the dear
old Pope ! "

Next to his vineyard at Château Neuf, the thing that the Pope loved best on earth was his mule. The good man fairly doted on the beast. Every night before going to bed he would go to see if his stable was securely fastened, if anything was lacking in the crib ; and he never rose from the table until a huge bowl of wine *à la Française*, with plenty of sugar and spices, had been prepared under his own eye, which he carried to the mule himself, despite the comments of his cardinals. It should be said, too, that the beast was worth the trouble. It was a fine black mule, dappled with red, sure-footed, with a glossy coat, a broad, full rump ; and she carried proudly her slender little head, all bedecked with plumes, and ribbons, and silver bells and streamers ; and as gentle as an angel withal, with a mild eye and two long ears always in motion, which gave her a most amiable aspect. All Avignon respected her, and when she passed through the streets there was no attention which the people did not pay her ; for they all knew that that was the best way to be in favour at court, and that, with her innocent look, the Pope's mule had led more than one to wealth ; witness Tistet Védène and his wonderful adventures.

This Tistet Védène was in truth an impudent rascal, whom his father, Guy Védène, the gold-carver, had been obliged to turn out of his house, because he refused to do any work and led the apprentices astray. For six months he was seen dragging his jacket through all the gutters of Avignon, but principally in the neighbourhood of the Papal palace; for the rogue had had for a long while a scheme of his own about the Pope's mule, and you will see what a mischievous scheme it was.

One day, when his Holiness all alone was riding by the ramparts on his steed, behold my Tistet approaches him, and says, clasping his hands with an air of admiration :

" Ah ! *mon Dieu !* what a fine mule you have, Holy Father ! Just let me look at her. Ah ! what a lovely mule, my Pope ! the Emperor of Germany has not her like."

And he patted her and spoke softly to her, as to a maiden :

" Come, my jewel, my treasure, my pearl."

And the excellent Pope, deeply moved, said to himself :

" What a nice little fellow ! How nice he is with my mule ! "

And what do you suppose happened the next day ? Tistet Védène exchanged his old yellow jacket for a fine lace alb, a violet silk hood, and shoes with buckles ; and he entered the household of the Pope, to which only sons of nobles and nephews of cardinals had ever been admitted. That is what intrigue leads to ! But Tistet Védène did not stop there. Once in the Pope's service, the rascal continued the game that had succeeded so well. Insolent with everybody else, he reserved his attention and care for the mule alone ; and he was always to be seen in the courtyard of the palace, with a handful of oats or a bunch of clover, whose purple clusters he shook as he glanced at the Holy Father's balcony, as if he would say : "Look! for whom is this?" The result was that the excellent Pope finally, feeling that he was growing old, left it to him to look after the stable and to carry the mule her bowl of wine *à la Française* ; which did not make the cardinals laugh.

Nor the mule either—it did not make her laugh. Now, when the time for her wine arrived, she always saw five or six little clerks of the household enter her stable and hastily bury themselves in the straw with their hoods and their lace ; then, after a moment, a delicious odour of caramel and spices filled the stable, and Tistet Védène appeared, carefully carrying the bowl of wine *à la Française*. Then the poor beast's martyrdom began.

That perfumed wine which she loved so dearly, which kept her warm, which gave her wings, they had the fiendish cruelty to bring to her manger, to let her inhale it, and then, when her nostrils were full of it, off it went ! the beautiful rose-coloured liquor disappeared down the throats of those young rogues. And if they had only contented themselves with stealing her wine ! but all those little clerks were like devils when they had been drinking. One pulled her ears, another her tail ; Quiquet mounted her back, Béluguet tried his cap on her head, and not one of the scamps reflected that with a sudden kick the excellent beast could have sent them all into the polar star, or even farther. But no ! not for nothing is one the Pope's mule, the mule of benedictions and in-dulgences. Let the boys do what they would, she did not lose her temper, and she bore a grudge to Tistet Védène alone. But he—when she felt him behind her, her hoofs fairly itched, and in good sooth there was reason for it. That ne'er-do-well of a Tistet played her such cruel tricks ! He conceived such fiendish ideas after drinking !

Would you believe that one day he took it into his head to make her go up with him into the belfry, away up to the highest point of the palace ! and this that I am telling you is not a fable—two hundred thousand Provençals saw it. Just imagine the terror of that wretched beast, when, after twisting blindly about for an hour on a winding staircase, and climbing I know not how many stairs, she suddenly found herself on a platform dazzling with light ; and a thousand feet below her, a whole fantastic Avignon, the stalls in the market no larger than walnuts, the Pope's soldiers in front of their barracks like red ants, and yonder, over a silver thread, a little microscopic bridge where the people danced and danced. Ah ! the poor creature ! what a panic ! All the windows in the palace shook with the bray that she uttered.

"What's the matter? What are they doing to her?" cried the good Pope, rushing out upon the balcony.

" Ah ! Holy Father, this is what's the matter ! Your mule—
mon Dieu ! what will become of us !—your mule has gone up into
the belfry."

" All alone ? "

"Yes, Holy Father, all alone. See ! look up there. Don't you
see the ends of her ears hanging over, like two swallows ! "

" Merciful Heaven ! " exclaimed the poor Pope, raising his eyes.
" Why, she must have gone mad ! Why, she will kill herself ! Will
you come down here, you wretched creature ? "

Pécaïre ! She would have asked nothing better than to have
come down ; but how ? As to the staircase, that was not to be
thought of ; it is possible to go up such things ; but in going down
there is a chance to break one's legs a hundred times. And the
poor mule was in despair ; as she wandered about the platform
with her great eyes filled with vertigo, she thought of Tistet Védène.

" Ah ! You villian, if I escape, what a kick to-morrow morning ! "

That idea of a kick restored a little of her courage ; save for that,
she could not have held out. At last they succeeded in taking her
down ; but it was a difficult task. They had to lower her in a litter,
with ropes and a jack-screw. And you can imagine what a humiliation it was for the Pope's mule to be suspended at that height,
swinging about with her hoofs in the air, like a butterfly at the end
of a string. And all Avignon looking at her !

The wretched beast did not sleep that night. It seemed to her
all the time that she was walking about on that infernal platform,
with the city laughing below her ; then she thought of that infamous Tistet Védène, and of the dainty kick that she proposed to
give him in the morning. Ah ! my friends, what a kick ! they would
see the smoke at Pampérigouste.

Now, while this pleasant reception was in store for him at the
stable, what do you suppose Tistet Védène was doing ? He was
going down the Rhône, singing, on one of the Pope's galleys, on
his way to the Court of Naples, with a party of young nobles whom
the city sent every year to Queen Joanna, for training in diplomacy
and in refined manners. Tistet was not of noble birth ; but the
Pope desired to reward him for the care he had bestowed upon his
mule, and above all for the activity he had displayed during the
day of rescue.

Imagine the mule's disappointment the next morning !

" Ah ! the villain ! he suspected something ! " she thought, as
she shook her bells savagely ; " but never mind, you scoundrel !
you shall have it when you come back, that kick of yours ; I will
keep it for you ! "

And she did keep it for him.

After Tistet's departure, the mule resumed her quiet mode of
life and her former habits. No more Quiquet or Béluguet in her

stable. The blissful days of wine *à la Française* had returned, and
with them good-humour, the long siestas, and the little dancing
step when she crossed Avignon Bridge. Since her misfortune, however, she was always treated rather coldly in the city. People
whispered together as she passed ; the old folks shook their heads,
and the children laughed as they pointed to the belfry. Even the
worthy Pope himself had not his former confidence in his friend,
and when he allowed himself to take a little nap on her back, on
Sundays, when he returned from his vineyard, he always had this
thought : " Suppose I should wake up on the platform up there ! "

The mule saw that and she was unhappy over it, although she
said nothing ; but when the name of Tistet Védène was mentioned
in her presence, her long ears quivered, and with a short laugh she
would sharpen the iron of her little shoes on the pavement.

Seven years passed thus ; and then, at the end of those seven
years, Tistet Védène returned from the Court of Naples. His time
there was not at an end ; but he had learned that the Pope's chief
mustard-bearer had died suddenly at Avignon, and as the office
seemed to him a good one, he returned in great haste to apply for it.

When that schemer of a Védène entered the great hall of the
palace, the Holy Father had difficulty in recognising him, he had
grown so tall and so stout. It should be said also that the Pope
had grown old too, and that he could not see well without spectacles.

Tistet was not frightened.

" What ? don't you recognise me, Holy Father ? It is Tistet
Védène."

" Védène ? "

" Why yes, you know, the one who used to carry French wine
to your mule."

" Oh, yes ! I remember. A good little fellow, that Tistet Védène !
And what does he want of us now ? "

" Oh ! a mere nothing, Holy Father. I came to ask you—by
the way—have you still your mule ? And is she well ? Good !—
I came to ask you for the place of the chief mustard-bearer, who
has just died."

" You, chief mustard-bearer ! why, you are too young. How
old are you ? "

" Twenty years and two months, illustrious pontiff ; just five
years older than your mule. Ah ! blessed palm of God ! the excellent beast ! If you only knew how I loved that mule ! how I
sighed for her in Italy !—Won't you let me see her ? "

" Yes, my child, you shall see her," said the kind-hearted Pope,
deeply touched. " And as you are so fond of the excellent beast,
I propose that you shall live near her. From this day I attach you
to my person as chief mustard-bearer. My cardinals will make an
outcry, but so much the worse ! I am used to it. Come to us to-

morrow, when vespers is done, and we will deliver the symbols of your office, in the presence of our chapter, and then—I will take you to see the mule, and you shall come to the vineyard with us both. Ha! ha!—Now go!"

If Tistet Védène was pleased when he left the great hall, I need not tell you how impatiently he awaited the ceremony of the morrow. Meanwhile, there was some one in the palace still happier than he and even more impatient; that was the mule. From the hour of Védène's return until vespers of the following day, the bloodthirsty creature did not cease stuffing herself with oats, and kicking at the wall with her hind feet. She, too, was preparing for the ceremony.

On the morrow, then, when vespers was at an end, Tistet Védène entered the courtyard of the Papal palace. All the high clergy were there, the cardinals in their red robes, the advocate of the devil in black velvet, the convent abbés with their little mitres, the church-wardens of the Saint-Agrico, the violet hoods of the household, the lower clergy too, the Pope's soldiers in full uniform, the three brotherhoods of penitents, the hermits from Mount Ventoux with their fierce eyes, and the little clerk who walks behind them carrying the bell, the Flagellants naked to the waist, the red-faced sacristans in gowns like judges—all, yes, all, even to those who hand the holy-water, and he who lights and he who extinguishes the candles; not one was missing. Ah! it was a grand installation! Bells, fireworks, sunlight, music, and, as always, those mad tambourine-players leading the dance yonder on Avignon Bridge.

When Védène appeared in the midst of the assemblage, his presence and his handsome face aroused a murmur of admiration. He was a magnificent Provençal, of the blond type, with long hair curled at the ends and a small, unruly beard which resembled the shavings of fine metal from the graving-tool of his father the gold-smith. The report was current that the fingers of Queen Joanna had sometimes toyed with that light beard; and Sire de Védène had in truth the vain-glorious air and the distraught expression of men whom queens have loved. That day, to do honour to his nation, he had replaced his Neapolitan clothes by a jacket with a pink border à la Provençale, and in his hood floated a long plume of the Camargue ibis.

Immediately upon his entrance, the chief mustard-bearer bowed with a noble air, and walked toward the high daïs, where the Pope awaited him, to deliver the symbols of his office: the spoon of yellow wood and the saffron-coloured coat. The mule was at the foot of the staircase, all saddled and ready to start for the vine-yard. When he passed her, Tistet Védène smiled affably and stopped to pat her two or three times in a friendly way on the back looking out of the corner of his eye to see if the Pope noticed him.

"Perhaps you are tied too short; do you want me to lengthen the rope?"

"It isn't worth while, Monsieur Seguin."

"What is it that you want, then?"

"I want to go to the mountain, Monsieur Seguin."

"Why, you wretched creature, don't you know that there is a wolf in the mountain? What will you do when he comes?"

"I will butt him with my horns, Monsieur Seguin."

"The wolf doesn't care for your horns. He has eaten goats with horns much longer than yours. Don't you remember poor Renaude who was here last year? A fine goat, as strong and ill-tempered as any he-goat. She fought with the wolf all night, and then in the morning the wolf ate her.

"*Pécaïre!* poor Renaude! but that doesn't make any difference to me, Monsieur Seguin; let me go to the mountain."

"Divine mercy!" exclaimed Monsieur Seguin; "what on earth does somebody do to my goats? Still another one that the wolf will end by eating! But no! I will save you in spite of yourself, you hussy! and as I am afraid that you will break your rope, I am going to shut you up in the stable, and you shall always stay there."

Thereupon Monsieur Seguin carried the kid to a dark stable, the door of which he locked securely. Unluckily he forgot the window and he no sooner had his back turned than the little creature took her leave.

Do you laugh, Gringoire? Parbleu! of course you do; you are of the faction of the goats, against poor Monsieur Seguin. We will see if you laugh in a moment.

When the white kid arrived in the mountain there was general rejoicing. Never had any of the old fir-trees seen anything so pretty. They welcomed her like a little queen. The chestnuts bent to the ground to caress her with their branches. The golden heather opened for her to pass, and gave forth the sweetest perfume that it could. The whole mountain celebrated her arrival.

You can imagine, Gringoire, whether our kid was happy! No more ropes, no more stakes, nothing to prevent her from gambolling and grazing at her pleasure. That was the place where the grass grew! above the tips of her horns, my dear fellow! And such grass! fine and sweet, made up of a thousand different plants. It was a very different thing from the grass in the enclosure. And the flowers— great blue bell-flowers, purple foxgloves with long stamens, a whole forest of wild flowers, overflowing with intoxicating juices.

The white kid, half tipsy, played about there with her legs in the air, and rolled down the slopes, with the falling leaves and the chestnuts; then, of a sudden, she sprang to her feet with one leap. Away she went, with her head thrust forward, through the under-brush and the thickets, sometimes on a peak, sometimes in the bottom of a ravine, up and down and everywhere. You would have said that there were ten of Monsieur Seguin's kids in the mountain.

The fact is that Blanquette was afraid of nothing. She crossed with one bound broad torrents which spattered her, as she passed, with misty spray and foam. Then, dripping wet, she stretched herself out on a flat rock and allowed the sun to dry her. Once, as she crept to the edge of a plateau with some clover in her teeth, she spied below her, in the plain, Monsieur Seguin's house with the enclosure behind it. That made her laugh until she cried.

"How tiny it is!" she said; "how was I ever able to live there?"

Poor dear! finding herself perched up there so high, she believed herself to be at least as large as the world.

In fact that was a great day for Monsieur Seguin's kid. About mid-day, as she ran to right and left, she happened upon a band of chamois which were busily engaged in eating wild grapes. Our little white-robed vagrant created a sensation. They gave her the best place at the vine, and those gentlemen were all very gallant. Indeed it seems—this between ourselves, Gringoire—that a young chamois with a black coat had the good fortune to please Blanquette. The two lovers lost themselves in the woods for an hour or two, and if you would know what they said to each other, go ask the chattering streams that flow invisibly under the moss.

Suddenly the wind freshened. The mountain turned purple; it was evening.

"Already!" said the little kid; and she stopped, much surprised.

The fields below were drowned in mist. Monsieur Seguin's enclosure disappeared in the haze, and of the cottage she could see only the roof, with a thread of smoke. She listened to the bells of a flock being driven home, and her heart was heavy. A falcon, flying homeward, brushed her with his wings as he passed. She started. Then there arose a howl in the mountain:

"Hou! hou!"

She thought of the wolf; during the day the wild creature had not given him a thought. At the same moment a horn blew in the valley. It was good Monsieur Seguin making a last effort.

"Hou! hou!" howled the wolf.

"Come back! come back!" cried the horn.

Blanquette longed to go back; but when she remembered the stake, the rope, and the hedge about the enclosure, she thought that she could never again become accustomed to that life, and that it was better to stay where she was.

The horn ceased to blow.

The kid heard a rustling of leaves behind her. She turned and saw in the darkness two short, straight ears, and two gleaming eyes. It was the wolf.

He sat there on his haunches, enormous, motionless, gazing at the little white kid and licking his chops in anticipation. As he felt sure that he should eat her, the wolf was in no hurry ; but when she turned, he began to laugh wickedly.

" Ha ! ha ! Monsieur Seguin's little kid ! " and he passed his great red tongue over his lean chops.

Blanquette felt that she was lost. For a moment, as she remembered the story of old Renaude, who had fought all night only to be eaten in the morning, she thought that it would be better to be eaten then ; then, thinking better of it, she stood on guard, her head down and her horns forward, like the brave Seguin goat that she was. Not that she had any hope of killing the wolf—kids do not kill wolves—but simply to see if she could hold out as long as Renaude.

Thereupon the monster came forward and the little horns began to play.

Ah ! the dear little kid, how courageously she went at it ! More than ten times—I am not lying, Gringoire—she compelled the wolf to retreat in order to take breath. During these momentary respites, the little glutton hastily plucked another blade of her dear grass ; then she returned to the battle with her mouth full. This lasted all night. From time to time Monsieur Seguin's kid glanced at the stars dancing in the clear sky and said to herself :

" Oh ! if only I can hold out until dawn ! "

One after another the stars went out. Blanquette fought with redoubled fury with her horns, the wolf with his teeth. A pale gleam appeared on the horizon. The hoarse crowing of a cock came up from a farm.

" At last ! " said the poor creature, who was only awaiting the dawn to die ; and she lay down in her lovely white coat all spotted with blood.

Thereupon the wolf threw himself upon the little kid and ate her.

Adieu, Gringoire !

The story you have heard is not a fable of my invention. If ever you come to Provence our farmers will often speak to you of " the goat of Monsieur Seguin, that fought the wolf all night, and then, in the morning, the wolf ate her up."

You understand, Gringoire :

" And then, in the morning, the wolf ate her up."

OLD FOLKS

ALPHONSE DAUDET

" A LETTER, Father Azan ? "

" Yes, monsieur, it comes from Paris."

He was as proud as a peacock that it came from Paris, was excellent Father Azan. But not I. Something told me that that Parisian epistle from Rue Jean-Jacques, falling upon my table unexpectedly and so early in the morning, would make me lose my whole day. I was not mistaken ; see for yourself :

" You must do me a favour, my friend. You must close your mill for one day and go at once to Eyguières—Eyguières is a large village three or four leagues from you, just a pleasant walk. On arriving there, you will ask for the orphan convent. The next house to the convent is a low house with grey shutters, and a small garden behind. You will go in without knocking—the door is always open—and as you enter, you will say in a very loud voice : ' Good day, my good people ! I am Maurice's friend ! ' Then you will see two old folks— oh ! very old, immeasurably old—who will hold out their arms to you from the depths of their great easy-chairs, and you will embrace them for me, with all your heart, as if they were your own people. Then you will talk ; they will talk about me ; nothing but me ; they will tell you a thousand foolish things, which you will listen to without laughing.—You won't laugh, will you ?—They are my grandparents, two people whose whole life I am, and who have not seen me for ten years. Ten years is a long while ! but what can you expect ? Paris holds me tight, and their great age holds them. They are so old, that if they should come to see me they would fall to pieces on the way. Luckily, you are in the neighbourhood, my dear miller, and, while embracing you, the poor people will think that they are embracing me to some extent. I have so often written to them of you and of the warm friendship——"

The devil take our friendship ! It happened to be magnificent weather that morning, but not at all appropriate for walking on the road ; too much mistral and too little sunshine—a genuine Provençal day. When that infernal letter arrived, I had already chosen my *cagnard* (place of shelter) between two rocks, and I was dreaming of staying there all day, like a lizard, drinking light, and listening to the song of the pines. However, what was I to do ? I closed the mill, grumbling, and put the key under the door. My stick and my pipe, and I was off.

I reached Eyguières about two o'clock. The village was deserted ; every soul was in the fields. Under the elms of the farmyards, white with dust, the grasshoppers were singing as in the heart of Crau. There was an ass taking the air on the square, in front of the mayor's office, and a flock of pigeons on the church fountain ; but no one to point out to me the way to the orphanage. Luckily an old fairy appeared of a sudden, sitting in her doorway and spinning. I told her what I was looking for ; and as that fairy was very powerful, she had only to raise her distaff : instantly the orphan convent rose before me as if by magic. It was a high, gloomy, dark building, proud to be able to show, above its ogive doorway, an old cross of red sandstone with some Latin word around it. Beside it, I saw another smaller house. Grey shutters and a garden behind. I recognised it instantly, and I entered without knocking.

As long as I live I shall never forget that long, quiet, cool corridor, with its pink walls, the little garden quivering at the rear through a curtain of light colour, and over all the panels faded flowers and lyres. It seemed to me as if I were entering the house of some old bailiff of the days of Sedaine. Through a half-opened door at the end of the corridor, on the left, I could hear the ticking of a big clock, and the voice of a child, but of a child of school age, reading and pausing after each word : " Then—St.—I-re-næ-us—cried—I—am—the—grain—of—the—Lord.—I—must—be—ground—by—the—teeth—of—these—an-i-mals."

I approached the door softly and looked in.

In the peaceful half-light of a small bedroom, a good old man with red cheeks, wrinkled to the ends of his fingers, was sleeping in an easy-chair, with his mouth open and his hands on his knees. At his feet a little girl dressed in blue—big cape and little cap, the costume of the convent—was reading the life of St. Irenæus from a book larger than herself. That miraculous reading had produced its effect upon the whole household. The old man was sleeping in his chair, the flies on the ceiling, the canaries in their cage at the window. The great clock snored, tick-tack, tick-tack. There was nothing awake in the whole chamber save a broad band of light which entered, straight and white, through the closed shutters, full of living sparks and microscopic waltzes. Amid the general drowsiness, the child gravely continued her reading : " In-stant-ly—two—li-ons—rushed up—on—him—and—ate—him—up." It was at that moment that I entered. The lions of St. Irenæus rushing into the room would not have produced greater stupefaction than I did. A genuine stage effect ! The little girl shrieked, the great book fell, the flies and canaries woke, the clock struck, the old man sat up with a start, greatly alarmed, and I myself, slightly disturbed, halted in the doorway and shouted very loud :

" Good day, good people ! I am Maurice's friend."

Oh, if you had seen the poor old man then ; if you had seen him come towards me with outstretched arms, embrace me, shake my hands, and run wildly about the room, exclaiming :

" *Mon Dieu ! mon Dieu !* "

Every wrinkle in his face laughed. His cheeks flushed, and he stammered :

" Ah ! monsieur ; ah ! monsieur."

Then he hurried towards the end of the room, calling :

" Mamette ! Mamette ! "

A door opened, there was a mouselike tread in the hall ; it was Mamette. Nothing could be prettier than that little old woman, with her shell-shaped bonnet, her nun's gown, and the embroidered handkerchief which she held in her hand, to do me honour, after the ancient fashion. It was a most touching thing—they actually resembled each other. With a tower of hair and yellow shells, he too might have been named Mamette. But the real Mamette must have wept bitterly during her life, and she was even more wrinkled than the other. Like the other, too, she had with her a child from the orphanage, a little nurse in a blue cape, who never left her ; and to see those two people cared for by those two orphans was the most touching picture that one could imagine.

When she came in, Mamette began by making me a low reverence, but the old man cut it in two by a word :

" This is Maurice's friend."

Instantly she began to tremble and weep, she lost her handkerchief, turned red, red as a peony, even redder than he. Those old people had but a single drop of blood in their veins, and at the slightest emotion it rushed to their faces.

" Quick, quick, a chair ! " said the old woman to her little one.

" Open the shutters," cried the old man to his.

And, each taking me by a hand, they trotted to the window, which was thrown wide open that they might the better see me. The easy chairs were brought, and I stationed myself between them on a folding-chair, the little blue girls behind us, and the questioning began.

" How is he ? What is he doing ? Why doesn't he come to see us ? Is he happy ? " and *patati !* and *patata !* that sort of thing for hours.

For my part I answered all their questions to the best of my ability, giving such details concerning my friend as I knew, and unblushingly inventing those that I did not know ; above all, being careful not to confess that I had never noticed whether his window closed tightly, or what colour the paper was on the walls of his bedroom.

"The paper of his bedroom! it is blue, madame, a light blue, with flowers."

"Really?" said the poor old woman, deeply moved; and she added, turning towards her husband: "He is such a good boy!"

"Oh, yes; he is a good boy!" said the other, enthusiastically.

And all the time I was talking, they exchanged little nods of the head, little sly laughs, and winks, and significant glances; or else the old man would stoop over and say to me:

"Speak louder. She's a little hard of hearing."

And she, on her side:

"A little louder, please! he doesn't hear very well."

Thereupon I would raise my voice; and both would thank me with a smile; and in those faded smiles, leaning towards me, seeking in the depths of my eyes the image of their Maurice, I, for my part, was deeply moved to find that image in theirs—vague, veiled, almost intangible, as if I saw my friend smiling at me a long way off, in a mist.

Suddenly the old man sat erect in his chair.

"Why it just occurs to me, Mamette—perhaps he has not breakfasted!"

And Mamette, in dismay, tossed her arms into the air:

"Not breakfasted! Great Heaven!"

I thought that they were still talking about Maurice, and I was about to reply that that excellent youth never waited later than noon for his breakfast. But no, they were talking about me; and you should have seen the commotion when I confessed that I was still fasting.

"Lay the table quick, my little blues; the table in the middle of the room, and the Sunday cloth, the flowered plates. And let's not laugh so much, if you please; and make haste."

I should say that they did make haste. They had hardly had time to break three plates when the breakfast was ready.

"A nice little breakfast," said Mamette, as she led me to the table, "but you will be all alone. We have already eaten this morning."

Poor old people! at no matter what time you take them, they have always eaten that morning.

Mamette's nice little breakfast consisted of two fingers of milk, some dates, and a *barquette*, something like a shortcake; enough to support her and her canaries for at least a week. And to think that I alone consumed all those provisions; What indignation about the little table! How the little blues whispered as they nudged each other; and yonder in their cage, how the canaries seemed to say to each other: "Oh! see that gentleman eating the whole *barquette*!"

I did eat it all, in truth, and almost without noticing it, occupied as I was in looking about that light, peaceful room, where the air was filled with an odour as of ancient things. Above all, there were two little beds from which I could not remove my eyes. Those beds, almost cradles, I imagined as they looked in the morning at day-break, when they were still hidden behind their great French curtains. The clock strikes three. That is the hour when all old people wake.

"Are you asleep, Mamette ? "

"No, my dear."

"Isn't Maurice a nice boy ? "

"Oh ! he is a nice boy, indeed."

And I imagined a long conversation like that, simply from having seen those two little beds standing side by side.

Meanwhile, there was a terrible drama taking place at the other end of the room, before the cupboard. It was a matter of reaching on the top shelf a certain jar of branded cherries, which had been awaiting Maurice ten years, and which they desired to open in my honour.

Despite the entreaties of Mamette, the old man had insisted upon going to get the cherries himself ; and, having mounted a chair, to his wife's great alarm, he was trying to reach them. You can imagine the picture—the old man trembling and standing on tiptoe, the little blues clinging to his chair, Mamette behind him, gasping, with out-stretched arms, and over all a faint perfume of bergamot, which exhaled from the open cupboard and from the great piles of unbleached linen. It was delightful.

At last, after many efforts, they succeeded in taking the famous jar from the cupboard, and with it an old silver cup, all marred and dented, Maurice's cup when he was small. They filled it for me with cherries to the brim ; Maurice was so fond of cherries ! and while serving me the old man whispered in my ear with the air of an epicurean :

"You are very lucky, you are, to have a chance to eat them. My wife made them herself. You are going to taste something good."

Alas ! his wife had made them, but she had forgotten to sweeten them. What can you expect ? People become absent-minded as they grow old. Your cherries were atrocious, my poor Mamette. But that did not prevent me from eating them to the last one, without a wink.

The repast at an end, I rose to take leave of my hosts. They would have been glad to keep me a little longer, to talk about the good boy ; but the day was drawing to a close, the mill was far away, and I must go.

The old man rose as I did.

"My coat, Mamette. I am going with him to the square."

Surely Mamette believed in her heart that it was already a little cool for him to escort me to the square, but she made no sign. However, while she was helping him to put his arms into the sleeves of his coat, a fine coat of the colour of Spanish snuff, I heard the dear creature whisper to him :

" You won't stay out too late, will you ? "

And he, with a little sly look :

" Ha ! ha ! I don't know—perhaps."

At that they looked at each other with a laugh, and the little blues laughed to see them laugh, and the canaries in their corner laughed also in their way. Between ourselves, I believe that the odour of the cherries had intoxicated them all a little.

The night was falling when the grandfather and I went out. The little blue followed us at a distance, to take him home ; but he did not see her, and he was as proud as possible to walk on my arm, like a man. Mamette, with radiant face, saw that from her doorstep, and as she watched us, she nodded her head prettily, as if to say :

" Never mind, he can still walk, my poor old man ! "

THE TWO INNS

Alphonse Daudet

I was returning from Nîmes one July afternoon. The heat was overwhelming. The scorching white road stretched out as far as the eye could see, a dusty line, between gardens of olive-trees and of scrub-oaks, beneath a huge sun of dull silver, which filled the whole sky. Not a sign of shade, not a breath of wind. Nothing save the vibration of the hot air, and the shrill cry of the grass-hoppers, a mad, deafening music, at a hurried tempo, which seemed the very resonance of that boundless, luminous vibration. I had been walking through this desert for two hours, when suddenly a group of white houses detached itself from the dust of the road before me. It was what is called the relay of St. Vincent : five or six farmhouses, long, red-roofed barns, a watering-trough without water, in a clump of meagre fig-trees, and, on the outskirts of the hamlet, two large inns looking at each other from opposite sides of the street.

There was something striking in the proximity of those two inns. On one side, a large new building, full of life and animation, all the doors thrown open, the diligence stopping in front, the steaming horses being unharnessed, the passengers drinking hastily on the road, in the short shadow of the walls ; the courtyard crowded with mules and vehicles ; carters lying under the sheds, awaiting the cool of the evening. Within outcries, oaths, blows of fists on the tables, the clinking of glasses, the clicking of billiard-balls, the popping of corks, and above all that uproar, a jovial, ringing voice, singing so loud that the windows shook :

> " Pretty little Margoton,
> As soon as dawn was waking,
> Took her silver pitcher,
> And went off to the well."

The inn opposite, on the contrary, was silent and seemed deserted. Grass under the gateway, shutters broken, over the door a rusty twig of holly hanging like an old plume, the door-step strewn with stones from the road. It was all so poverty-stricken, so pitiful, that it seemed an act of charity to stop there and drink a glass.

On entering, I found a long room, deserted and dismal, which the dazzling light, entering through three curtainless windows, rendered even more dismal and deserted. A few rickety tables, on which stood broken glasses dull with dust, a dilapidated billiard-table, holding out its four pockets as if asking alms, a yellow couch, an old desk, slumbered there in an oppressive and unhealthy heat. And the flies ! flies everywhere ! I had never seen so many : on the ceiling, clinging to the windows, in the glasses, in swarms. When I opened the door, there was a buzzing, a humming of wings as if I were entering a hive.

At the end of the room, in a window-recess, there was a woman standing close to the window, busily occupied in looking out. I called her twice :

" Ho there ! hostess ! "

She turned slowly, and showed me the face of a poverty-stricken peasant woman, wrinkled and furrowed, earth-coloured, framed by long lappets of rusty lace, such as the old women in our neighbourhood wear. She was not an old woman, though ; but much weeping had faded her completely.

" What do you want ? " she asked, wiping her eyes.

" To sit down a moment and drink something."

She gazed at me in amazement, without moving from her place, as if she did not understand me.

" Isn't this an inn ? "

The woman sighed.

" Yes, it is an inn, if you choose. But why don't you go opposite, like all the rest ? It is much more lively."

" It is too lively for me. I prefer to stay here with you."

And without waiting for her reply, I seated myself at the table.

When she was quite sure that I was speaking seriously, the hostess began to go and come with a very busy air, opening doors, moving bottles, wiping glasses, and disturbing the flies. It was clear that a guest to wait upon was an important event. At times the unhappy creature would stop and take her head in her hands, as if she despaired of ever accomplishing anything.

Then she went into the rear room ; I heard her shaking great keys, fumbling with locks, looking into the bread-box, blowing, dusting washing plates. From time to time a deep sigh, a sob ill stifled.

After a quarter of an hour of this business, I had before me a plate of raisins, an old loaf of Beaucaire bread, as hard as sandstone, and a bottle of sour new wine.

" You are served," said the strange creature ; and she turned back at once to her place at the window.

As I drank, I tried to make her talk.

" You don't often have people here, do you, my poor woman ? "

" Oh, no ! never any one, monsieur. When we were alone here, it was different ; we had the relay, we provided hunt-dinners during the ducking-season, and carriages all the year round. But since our neighbours set up in business we have lost everything. People prefer to go opposite. They consider it too dull here. It's a fact that the house isn't very pleasant. I am not good-looking, I have fever and ague, and my two little girls are dead. Over yonder, on the contrary, they are laughing all the time. It is a woman from Arles who keeps the inn, a handsome woman with laces, and three bands of gold beads round her neck. The driver of the diligence, who is her lover, takes it to her place. And then she has a lot of hussies for chambermaids, so that she gets lots of custom ! She has all the young men from Bezouces, Redessan, and Jonquières. The carters go out of their way to pass her house. And I stay here all day without a soul, eating my heart out."

She said this in a distraught, indifferent tone, with her forehead still resting against the glass. There was evidently something which interested her at the inn opposite.

Suddenly, on the other side of the road, there was a great commotion. The diligence moved off through the dust. I heard the cracking of the whip, the postillion's bugle, and the girls who had run to the door calling out :

" *Adiousias ! adiousias !* " And over it all the stentorian voice that I had heard before, beginning again, louder than ever :

> " She took her silver pitcher,
> And went off to the well ;
> From there she could not see
> Three soldiers drawing near."

At that voice the hostess trembled in every limb, and, turning to me, she said in an undertone :

" Do you hear ? That's my husband. Doesn't he sing well ? "

I gazed at her in stupefaction.

"What? Your husband? Do you mean to say that he goes there too?"

Thereupon, with a heart-broken air, but with the utmost gentleness, she replied:

"What can you expect, monsieur? Men are made that way; they don't like to see people cry; and I cry all the time since my little girls died. And then this great barrack, where nobody ever comes is so melancholy. And so, when he is bored too much, my poor José goes across the road to drink, and as he has a fine voice, the woman from Arles makes him sing. Hush! there he goes again."

And she stood there, as if in a trance, trembling, with her hands outstretched, and tears rolling down her cheeks, which made her look uglier than ever, to hear her José singing for the woman from Arles:

> "The first one said to her:
> ' Good day, my pretty dear!'"

THE ELIXIR
OF FATHER GAUCHER

Alphonse Daudet

"Drink this, neighbour, and tell me what you think of it."

And drop by drop, with the painstaking care of a lapidary counting pearls, the curé of Graveson poured out for me two fingers of a golden-green, warm, sparkling, exquisite liqueur. My stomach was as if bathed in sunlight.

"This is Father Gaucher's elixir, the joy and health of our Provence," said the worthy man, with a triumphant air; "it is made at the convent of Prémontrés, two leagues from your mill. Isn't it better than all the chartreuses on earth? And if you knew how interesting the story of this elixir is! Listen."

Thereupon, as artlessly as possible, without the slightest tinge of irony, in that parsonage dining-room, so placid and calm, with its *Road to the Cross* in tiny pictures, and its pretty light curtains ironed like surplices, the abbé began a somewhat sceptical and irreverent anecdote, after the fashion of a tale of Erasmus or d'Assoucy.

"Twenty years ago, the Prémontrés, or the White Fathers, as we Provençals call them, had fallen into utter destitution. If you had seen their convent in those days it would have made your heart ache.

"The high wall, the Pacôme Tower, were falling in pieces. All around the grass-grown cloisters the pillars were cracked, the stone saints crumbling in their recesses. Not a stained-glass window whole, not a door that would close. In the courtyards, in the chapels, the wind from the Rhône blew as it blows in Camargue, extinguishing the candles, breaking the leaden sashes of the windows, spilling the water from the holy-water vessels. But the saddest of all was the convent belfry, silent as an empty dove-cote ; and the fathers, in default of money to buy a bell, were obliged to ring for matins with clappers of almond-wood !

"Poor White Fathers ! I can see them now, in the procession on Corpus Christi, pacing sadly along in their patched hoods, pale and thin, fed on pumpkins and water-melons ; and behind them monseigneur the abbé, marching with downcast head, ashamed to exhibit in the sunlight his tarnished crook and his worm-eaten mitre of white wool. The ladies of the fraternity wept with compassion in the ranks, and the stout banner-bearers whispered sneeringly to one another as they pointed to the poor monks :

"'The starlings grow thin when they fly in flocks.'

"The fact is, the unfortunate White Fathers had reached the point where they asked themselves if they would not do better to fly out into the world and to seek pasturage each for himself.

"Now, one day when this grave question was being discussed in the chapter, the prior was informed that Brother Gaucher desired to be heard in the council. I must say for your information that this Brother Gaucher was the drover of the convent ; that is to say, he passed his days waddling from arch to arch through the cloister, driving before him two consumptive cows, which tried to find grass between the cracks of the flagstones. Supported until he was twelve years old by an old madwoman of the Baux country, called Aunt Bégon, then taken in by the monks, the wretched drover had never been able to learn anything except to drive his beasts and to repeat his paternoster ; and even that he said in Provençal, for his brain was thick and his mind as dull as a leaden dagger. A fervent Christian, however, although somewhat visionary, comfortable in his haircloth shirt, and inflicting discipline upon himself, with sturdy conviction, and such arms !

"When they saw him come into the chapter-hall, simple and stupid of aspect, saluting the assemblage with a leg thrown back, prior, canons, steward, and everybody began to laugh. That was always the effect produced by that good-natured face with its grizzly, goatlike beard and its slightly erratic eyes, whenever it appeared anywhere ; so that Brother Gaucher was not disturbed thereby.

"'Reverend fathers,' he said in a wheedling voice, playing with his chaplet of olive-stones, 'it is quite true that empty casks make the best music. Just imagine that, by dint of cudgelling my poor brain, which was already so hollow, I believe that I have thought out a way to help us out of our poverty.

"'This is how. You know Aunt Bégon, that worthy woman who took care of me when I was small—God rest her soul, the old hag! she used to sing some very vile songs after drinking.—I must tell you then, reverend fathers, that Aunt Bégon in her lifetime knew as much about the mountain herbs as an old Corsican blackbird, and more. In fact, towards the end of her life, she compounded an incomparable elixir by mixing five or six kinds of simples that we picked together in the mountains. That was a good many years ago ; but I believe that, with the aid of St. Augustine and the permission of our worshipful abbé, I might, by careful search, discover the composition of that mysterious elixir. Then we should only have to bottle it and sell it at a rather high price, to enable the community to get rich as nicely as you please, like our brothers of La Trappe and La Grande——'

"He was not allowed to finish. The prior sprang to his feet and fell upon his neck. The canons seized his hands. The steward, even more deeply moved than all the rest, kissed respectfully the ragged edge of his cowl. Then they all returned to their chairs to deliberate ; and the chapter decided on the spot that the cows should be entrusted to Brother Thrasybule, so that Brother Gaucher might devote himself exclusively to the compounding of his elixir.

"How did the excellent monk succeed in discovering Aunt Bégon's recipe ! At the price of what efforts, of what vigils ? History does not say. But this much is sure, that after six months the elixir of the White Fathers was very popular. Throughout the Comtat, in all the Arles country, there was not a farmhouse, not a granary, which had not in the depths of its buttery, amid the bottles of mulled wine and the jars of olives à la picholine, a little jug of brown earthenware, sealed with the arms of Provence, and with a monk in a trance on a silver label. Thanks to the popularity of its elixir, the convent of the Prémontrés grew rich very rapidly. The Pacôme Tower was rebuilt. The prior had a new mitre, the church some pretty stained windows ; and in the fine open-work of the belfry a whole legion of bells, large and small, burst forth one fine Easter morning, jingling and chiming with all their might.

"As for Brother Gaucher, that unfortunate lay brother, whose rustic manners amused the chapter so much, was never spoken of in the convent. Henceforth they only knew the Reverend Father Gaucher, a man of brains and of great learning, who lived completely apart from the trivial and multifarious occupations of the cloister, and was shut up all day in his distillery, while thirty monks hunted the mountain for him, seeking fragrant herbs. That distillery, which no one, not even the prior, had the right to enter, was an old abandoned chapel, at the end of the canons' garden. The simplicity of the worthy fathers had transformed it into something mysterious and redoubtable ; and if by chance some audacious and inquisitive young monk happened to get as far as the rosework of the doorway, he retreated very quickly, terrified by the aspect of Father Gaucher, with his sorcerer's beard, leaning over his furnaces, scales in hand ; and all about him retorts of red sandstone, huge alembics, serpentine glasses, a whole strange outfit, flaming as if bewitched, in the red gleam of the stained glass.

" At nightfall, when the last Angelus rang, the door of that abode of mystery would open softly, and the father would betake himself to the church for the evening service. You should have seen the welcome that he received when he passed through the monastery ! The brethren drew up in two lines for him to pass. They said to one another :

" ' Hush ! he knows the secret ! '

" The steward followed him and spoke to him with downcast eyes. Amid all this adulation, the father walked along, mopping his forehead, his broad-brimmed, three-cornered hat placed on the back of his head like a halo, glancing with an air of condescension at the great courtyards full of orange-trees, the blue roofs surmounted by new weathervanes ; and, in the cloister, glaringly white between the gracefully carved pillars, the monks, newly dressed, marching two by two with placid faces.

" ' They owe all this to me ! ' the father would say to himself ; and every time that thought caused his bosom to swell with pride.

" The poor man was well punished for it, as you will see.

" Imagine that one evening, during the service, he arrived in the church in a state of extraordinary excitement : red-faced, breathless, his hood awry, and so perturbed that when he took his holy water he wet his sleeves to the elbow. They thought at first that his excitement was due to being late ; but when they saw him make profound reverences to the organ and the galleries instead of saluting the main altar, when they saw him rush through the church like a gust of wind, wander about the choir for five minutes looking for his stall, and, when once seated, bow to the right and left with a beatific smile, a murmur of amazement ran through the three naves. From breviary to breviary the monks whispered :

" ' What can be the matter with our Father Gaucher ? What can be the matter with our Father Gaucher ? '

" Twice the prior, in his annoyance, struck his crook on the flagstones to enjoin silence. In the choir the psalms continued ; but the responses lacked vigour.

" Suddenly, in the very middle of the *Ave verum*, lo and behold Father Gaucher fell backward in his stall and chanted in a voice of thunder :

> " ' In Paris there is a White Father—
> Patatin, patatan, tarabin, taraban.'

" General consternation. Everybody rose.

" ' Carry him away ! he is possessed ! ' they cried.

" The canons crossed themselves. Monseigneur's crook waved frantically. But Father Gaucher neither saw nor heard anything ; and two sturdy monks were obliged to drag him away through the small door of the choir, struggling like one bewitched and continuing his *patatans* and his *tarabans* louder than ever.

" The next morning, at daybreak, the poor wretch was on his knees in the prior's oratory, confessing his sin with a flood of tears.

" ' It was the elixir, monseigneur, it was the elixir that took me by surprise,' he said, beating his breast. And seeing him so heart-broken, so penitent, the good prior was deeply moved himself.

" ' Come, come, Father Gaucher, calm yourself ; all this will dry up like the dew in the sunshine. After all, the scandal was not so great as you think. To be sure, there was a song which was a little—however, we must hope that the novices did not hear it. Now, tell me just how the thing happened to you. It was while you were trying the elixir, was it not ? Your hand was a little too heavy. Yes, yes, I understand. It was like Brother Schwartz, the inventor of powder ; you were the victim of your invention. And tell me, my dear friend, is it really necessary that you should try this terrible elixir upon yourself ? '

" ' Unluckily, yes, monseigneur. The test-tube, to be sure, gives me the strength and degree of heat of the alcohol ; but for the finishing touch, the velvety smoothness, I can trust nothing but my tongue.'

" ' Ah ! very good. But listen to what I ask. When you taste the elixir thus as a duty, does it taste good to you ? Do you enjoy it ? '

" ' Alas ! yes, monseigneur,' said the unhappy father, turning as red as a beet ; ' for two evenings now I have found such a bouquet, such an aroma in it ! It is certainly the devil who has played me this vile trick. So I have determined only to use the test-tube henceforth. If the liqueur is not as fine, if it is not as smooth as before, so much the worse ! '

" ' Do nothing of the sort,' interrupted the prior earnestly. ' We must not take the risk of displeasing our customers. All that you have to do now that you are warned is to be on your guard. Tell me, how much do you need to drink, for your test ? Fifteen or twenty drops, is it not ? Let us say twenty drops. The devil will be very smart if he can catch you with twenty drops. Moreover, to avert all chance of accident, I excuse you from coming to church henceforth. You will repeat the evening service in the distillery. And now, go in peace, my father, and above all things count your drops carefully.'

"Alas! the poor father counted his drops to no purpose; the demon had him in his clutch, and he did not let him go.

"The distillery heard some strange services!

"In the daytime everything went well. The father was tranquil enough; he prepared his retorts, his alembics, carefully assorted his herbs—all Provençal herbs, fine and grey, and burned with perfume and sunlight. But at night, when the simples were steeped and the elixir was cooling in great basins of red copper, the poor man's martyrdom began.

"'Seventeen, eighteen, nineteen, twenty.'

"The drops fell from the tube into the silver goblet. Those twenty the father swallowed at one draught, almost without enjoyment. It was only the twenty-first that aroused his longing. Oh! that twenty-first drop! To avoid temptation, he would go and kneel at the end of the laboratory and bury himself in his paternosters. But from the still warm liqueur there ascended a wreath of smoke heavily laden with aromatic odours, which came prowling about him, and drew him back towards the basins, whether he would or no. The liqueur was a beautiful golden green. Leaning over it, with distended nostrils, the father stirred it gently with his tube, and it seemed to him that he saw, in the sparkling little spangles on the surface of the emerald lake, Aunt Bégon's eyes laughing and snapping as they looked at him.

"'Nonsense! just one more drop!'

"And from drop to drop the poor wretch ended by filling his goblet to the brim. Then, at the end of his strength, he would sink down in an easy-chair; and his body relaxed, his eyes half closed, he would enjoy his sin by little sips, murmuring to himself with ecstatic remorse:

"'Ah! I am damning myself! I am damning myself!'

"The most terrible part of it was, that in the depths of that diabolical elixir he remembered, by some witchery or other, all Aunt Bégon's naughty songs: 'There was three little gossips, who talked of giving a feast'; or, 'Master André's shepherdess goes to the woods alone'; and always the famous one of the White Fathers: 'Patatin, patatan!'

"Imagine his confusion the next day when his old neighbours said to him with a sly expression:

"'Ha! ha! Father Gaucher, you had grasshoppers in your head when you went to bed last night.'

"Then there were tears, despair, fasting, haircloth, and penance.

But nothing could prevail against the demon of the elixir ; and every evening at the same hour the possession began anew.

"Meanwhile, orders rained upon the abbey like a blessing from Heaven. They came from Nîmes, from Aix, from Avignon, from Marseilles. From day to day the convent assumed the aspect of a factory. There were packing brothers, labelling brothers, brothers to attend to the correspondence, drayman brothers ; the service of God lost a few strokes of the bell now and then, to be sure, but the poor people of the neighbourhood lost nothing, I assure you.

"But one fine Sunday morning, while the steward was reading to the chapter his annual inventory, and the good canons were listening with sparkling eyes and smiling lips, behold Father Gaucher rushed into the midst of the conference, exclaiming :

"'It is all over ! I can't stand it any longer ! give me back my cows.'

"'What is the matter, pray, Father Gaucher ?' asked the prior who had a shrewd idea what the matter might be.

"'The matter, monseigneur ? The matter is that I am laying up for myself an eternity of hell-fire and blows with the pitchfork. The matter is that I am drinking, drinking like a miserable wretch.'

"'But I told you to count your drops.'

"'Count my drops ! Oh, yes ! I should have to count them by goblets now. Yes, my fathers, I have reached that point. Three flasks an evening. You must see that that cannot last. So let whomsoever you choose make the elixir. May God's fire consume me if I touch it again !'

"The chapter laughed no longer.

"'But you are ruining us, unhappy man !' cried the steward, waving his ledger.

"'Do you prefer that I should damn myself for ever ?'

"Thereupon the prior rose.

"'My fathers,' he said, putting forth his beautiful white hand, upon which the pastoral ring glistened, 'there is a way to arrange everything. It is at night, is it not, my dear son, that the demon tempts you ?'

"'Yes, monsieur prior, regularly every evening. So now, when night comes, a cold sweat takes me, saving your presence, like Capitou's donkey when he saw the saddle coming.'

"''Tis well ! be comforted. Henceforth every evening, at the service, we will repeat in your favour the prayer of St. Augustine, to which plenary indulgence is attached. With that, whatever happens, you are safe. It affords absolution during sin.'

"'Oh, well ! in that case, thanks, monsieur prior !'

"And, without asking anything more, Father Gaucher returned to his laboratory, as light-hearted as a lark.

"And in truth, from that day forward, every evening at the end of the complines, the officiating father never failed to say :

"' Let us pray for our poor Father Gaucher, who is sacrificing his soul in the interest of the community. *Oremus, Domine*——'

"And while the prayer ran quivering over those white hoods, prostrate in the shadow of the nave, as a light breeze rushes over the snow, yonder at the other end of the convent, behind the flaming stained glass of the distillery, Father Gaucher could be heard singing at the top of his lungs :

> "' In Paris there is a White Father,
> Patatin, patatan, tarabin, taraban ;
> In Paris there is a White Father
> Who dances with the nuns,
> Trin, trin, trin, in a garden,
> Who dances with the——' "

Here the good curé stopped, in dismay.

"Merciful Heaven ! " he exclaimed, "suppose my parishioners should hear me ! "

THE POPE IS DEAD

Alphonse Daudet

I passed my childhood in a large provincial town cut in two by a much-travelled, very restless river, where I early acquired a taste for wandering and a passion for life on the water. There was especially a corner of a certain wharf near a foot-bridge called St. Vincent, of which I never think, even to-day, without emotion. I see again the sign nailed to the end of a yard : *Cornet, boats to let ;* the little ladder going down into the water, slippery and blackened with moisture ; the fleet of little boats, freshly painted in bright colours, lying in a line at the foot of the ladder, swaying softly from side to side, as if made buoyant by the pretty names painted in white letters on their sterns : *The Humming-bird, The Swallow,* and so forth.

And then, among the long oars gleaming with white lead, which were drying against the bank, Father Cornet walking about with his pail of paint, his long brushes, his tanned, furrowed, wrinkled face, with a thousand little dimples, like the river on an evening when the wind is fresh ! Oh ! that Father Cornet ! He was the Satan of my existence, my sorrowful passion, my sin, and my re-morse. What crimes he has caused me to commit, with his boats ! I stayed away from school, I sold my books. What would I not have sold for an afternoon of boating !

With all my books in the bottom of the boat, my jacket off, my hat thrown back, and the pleasant, fanlike breeze from the river in my hair, I clung tightly to my oars, drawing my eyebrows together to give myself the aspect of an old sea-wolf. As long as I was in the town, I kept to the middle of the river, at an equal distance from both banks, where the old sea-wolf might have been recognised. What a triumph to mingle with that great procession of boats, of rafts, of logs, of steamboats which glided by, skillully avoiding one another, separated only by a narrow streak of foam ! There were heavy boats, which turned in order to make the most of the current, and thereby displaced a multitude of others.

Suddenly the wheels of a steamer would beat the water near me ; or else a heavy shadow would fall upon me : the foresail of an apple-boat.

" Out of the way, you little brat ! " a hoarse voice would shout ; and I would struggle and sweat, entangled in the ceaseless going and coming of that life of the stream, which the life of the streets constantly crossed, on those bridges and foot-bridges which cast reflections of omnibuses over the strokes of the oars. And the current that was so strong under the arches ; and the eddies, the famous hole of La Mort-qui-trompe ! I tell you that it was no small matter to guide one's self through that, with arms of twelve years and no one to hold the tiller.

Sometimes I had the luck to meet the *chain* there. I would quickly hook on at the end of those long lines of boats which it was towing, and with my oars idle, reaching out like soaring wings, I would let myself go with that silent swiftness which cut the river in long ribbons of foam, and made the trees on both banks and the houses on the quay hurry by. Before me, far, very far away, I could hear the monotonous beating of the screw, a dog barking on one of the tow-boats, where a thin thread of smoke rose from a low funnel ; and all that gave me the illusion of a long voyage, of real life on board ship.

Unluckily, these meeting with the *chain* were rare. Generally I had to row, and row in the hours when the sun was hottest. Oh, that noonday sun falling perpendicularly upon the river ! It seems to me that it burns me now. Everything glared and glistened. Through that blinding and sonorous atmosphere, which hovers over the waves and vibrates with their every movement, the short strokes of my oars, the tow-lines rising from the water all dripping, would cause vivid flashes of polished silver to pass. And I would row with my eyes closed. At times on account of the vigour of my efforts and the rush of the water under my boat, I imagined that I was going very fast ; but on raising my head, I always saw the same tree, the same wall opposite me on the bank.

At last, by tiring myself out, I would succeed in leaving the city all dripping and flushed with heat. The uproar of the cold baths, of the laundresses' boats, of the landing-floats, diminished. The bridges stretched across the broadening river here and there. Suburban gardens, a factory chimney, were reflected in the water at intervals. Green islands trembled on the horizon. Then, unable to row any more, I would draw up against the bank, amid the reeds all buzzing with life ; and there, overcome by the sun, fatigue, and the heavy heat that rose from the water studded with great yellow flowers, the old sea-wolf would bleed at the nose for hours at a time. My voyages never had any other end. But what would you have ? I called that delightful.

But the terrible part was the return to the town and home. In vain would I row back with all my strength ; I always arrived too late, long after the school was dismissed. The impression of the falling night, the first jets of gas in the fog, all augmented my fear and my remorse. The people who passed, returning tranquilly to their homes, aroused my envy ; and I would run along, with an aching head, full of sunshine and water, with roaring of shells in my ears, and on my face the blush for the lie that I was going to tell.

For I had to tell one every time, to meet that terrible " Where have you been ? " which awaited me at the door. It was that question on my arrival that frightened me most. I had to reply on the spot, on my feet ; always to have a story ready, something to say, and something so surprising, so impressive, that the surprise cut short all the questioning. That gave me time to go in and to take breath ; and to attain that end, nothing cost too much. I invented terrible tales : revolutions, a whole quarter of the town on fire, the railway bridge fallen into the river. But the worst thing that I invented was this :

That evening I arrived home very late. My mother, who had been expecting me for an hour, was standing at the top of the stairs watching for me.

" Where have you been ? " she cried.

Tell me what deviltry a child's head may not hold. I had thought of nothing, prepared nothing. I had come too fast. Suddenly a wild idea passed through my head. I knew that the dear woman was very pious, as fervent a Catholic as a Roman, and I answered in all the breathlessness of intense emotion :

" O mamma ! If you knew ! "

" What ? What is it now ? "

" The Pope is dead."

" The Pope is dead ! " exclaimed my poor mother, and she leaned against the wall, as pale as death. I hurried into my room, a little frightened by my success and the enormity of the lie. But I had the courage to maintain it to the end. I remember a dismal but pleasant evening ; my father very serious, my mother crushed. They talked in undertones at the table. I lowered my eyes, but my escapade was so entirely buried in the general desolation that no one thought about it.

They vied with one another in citing some instance of the virtue of poor Pius IX. ; then, little by little, the conversation strayed back through the history of the popes. Aunt Rose spoke of Pius VII., whom she remembered very well to have seen in the south, in a post-chaise, between gendarmes. Somebody recalled the famous scene with the Emperor : *Comediante ! tragediante !* It was fully the hundredth time that I had heard that terrible scene described, always with the same intonations, the same gestures, and the stereotyped formula of family traditions which one generation bequeaths to another, and which never change, as childish and as purely local as convent stories.

However, it had never seemed so interesting to me.

I listened with hypocritical sighs, frequent questions, an assumed air of interest, and all the time I was saying to myself :

" To-morrow morning, when they learn that the Pope is not dead, they will be so glad that no one will have the courage to scold me."

Thinking thus, my eyes closed in spite of myself, and I had visions of little boats painted blue, with little corners of the Saone made drowsy by the heat, and long claws of water-spiders darting in every direction and cutting the glassy river like diamond-points.

THE LITTLE PIES

ALPHONSE DAUDET

I

THAT morning, which was a Sunday, Sureau, the pastry-cook on Rue Turenne, called his apprentice and said to him :

" Here are Monsieur Bonnicar's little pies ; go and take them to him and come back at once. It seems that the Versaillais have entered Paris."

The little fellow, who understood nothing about politics, put the smoking hot pies in the dish, the dish in a white napkin, and balancing the whole upon his cap, started off on a run for Île St. Louis, where M. Bonnicar lived. It was a magnificent morning, one of those bright, sunny May mornings which fill the fruit-shops with clusters of cherries and bunches of lilac. Despite the distant cannonading and the bugle-calls at the corners of the streets, that whole ancient quarter of the Marais retained its peaceful aspect.

There was Sunday in the air ; bands of children in the yards, tall girls playing battledore in front of the door, and that little white silhouette, trotting along in the middle of the deserted roadway, amid a pleasant odour of hot pies, put the finishing touch of artlessness and Sunday merriment to that morning of battle. All the life of the quarter seemed to have betaken itself to Rue de Rivoli. Cannon were being drawn thither and barricades thrown up ; groups of people at every step, National Guardsmen full of business. But the little pastry-cook did not lose his head. Those children are so accustomed to walking in the midst of crowds and the uproar of the street ! On saints' days and holidays, when the streets are so crowded, early in the year, and on Sundays, they have the most running to do ; so that revolutions hardly surprise them.

It was really pleasant to see the little white cap dodge about amid the helmets and bayonets, avoiding collisions, maintaining its equilibrium, sometimes very rapidly, sometimes with a compulsory slowness in which one was conscious still of a longing to run. What difference did the battle make to him ? The important thing was to arrive at Bonnicar's on the stroke of noon, and to run away at once with the little fee which awaited him on the small table in the reception-room.

Suddenly there was a terrible pressure in the crowd, and wards of the Republic passed at the double-quick, singing. They were lads of twelve to fifteen years, arrayed in helmets, red belts, and high boots ; as proud of being disguised as soldiers as when they run about on Mardi gras with paper caps and a strip of a fancy pink umbrella, in the mud of the boulevards. This time, in the midst of the crowd, the little pastry-cook had much difficulty in keeping his balance ; but his dish and he had slipped so many times upon the ice, had played so many games of hop-scotch on the sidewalk, that the little pies escaped with a fright. Unluckily that excitement, those songs, those red belts, combined with admiration and curiosity, aroused in the apprentice the desire to march a little way in such goodly company ; and passing the Hôtel de Ville and the bridges leading to Île St. Louis without noticing them, he found himself carried I know not whither, in the dust and the wind of that wild march.

II

For at least twenty-five years, it had been the custom of the Bonnicars to eat little pies on Sunday. At precisely twelve o'clock, when the whole family, great and small, was assembled in the salon, a sharp and merry ring at the bell would cause them all to say :

" Ah ! there's the pastry-cook."

Thereupon, with a great moving of chairs, the rustle of Sunday clothes, the expansive joy of laughing children about the well-laden table, all those happy bougeois would take their places around the little pies, symmetrically heaped upon the silver chafing-dish.

That day the bell remained dumb. Monsieur Bonnicar, scandalised, looked at his clock, an old clock surmounted by a stuffed heron, which had never in its life gained or lost. The children yawned at the windows, watching the corner of the street where the apprentice usually appeared. Conversation languished, and hunger, which noon with its twelve strokes digs in the stomach, made the dining-room look very large and very dismal, despite the antique silver plate glistening on the damask cloth ; and the napkins all about, folded in the shape of little stiff white horns.

Several times already the old cook had come to whisper in her master's ear : the joint burned, the peas cooked too much. But Monsieur Bonnicar was obstinately determined not to take his place at the table without the little pies ; and furiously angry with Sureau, he resolved to go himself to see what such an unheard-of delay could mean. As he went out, brandishing his cane, hot with indignation, some neighbours warned him :

" Take care, Monsieur Bonnicar ; they say that the Versaillais have entered Paris."

He refused to listen to anything, even to the cannonading which came from Neuilly, even to the alarm guns from the Hôtel de Ville, which shook all the windows in the quarter.

" Oh ! that Sureau ! that Sureau ! "

And in his excitement he talked to himself, fancied himself already in the middle of the shop striking the floor with his cane, making the mirrors in the show-window and the plates of sweetmeats tremble. The barricade on Pont Louis Philippe cut his wrath in two. There were some confederates there, of ferocious mien, strutting about in the sun on the unpaved ground.

" Where are you going, citizen ? "

The citizen explained, but the story of the little pies seemed suspicious, especially as Monsieur Bonnicar had on his fine Sunday coat, his gold spectacles, and wore every appearance of an old reactionary.

" He's a spy," said the confederates ; " we must send him to Rigault."

Whereupon four enthusiasts, who were not sorry to leave the barricade, pushed the unfortunate, exasperated man before them with the butts of their guns.

I know not how they accomplished it, but half an hour later they were all captured by troops of the line, and were sent off to join a long column of prisoners about to start for Versailles. Monsieur Bonnicar protested more and more loudly, brandished his cane, told his story for the hundredth time. Unfortunately the fable about the little pies seemed so absurd, so incredible in the midst of that intense excitement, that the officers simply laughed.

728   ALPHONSE DAUDET

"That's all right, that's all right, old fellow. You can explain at Versailles."

And through the Champs-Élysées, still white with the smoke of the firing, the column moved off between two rows of chasseurs.

III

The prisoners marched five by five, in close, compact ranks. To prevent the escort from being separated, they were obliged to walk arm in arm; and the long human flock, tramping along through the dust of the road, made a noise like a heavy shower.

The unfortunate Bonnicar thought that he was dreaming. Perspiring, puffing, beside himself with alarm and fatigue, he trailed along at the end of the column, between two old hags who smelt of petroleum and brandy; and from the words, "Pastry-cook, little pies," which constantly occurred in his imprecations, everybody about him thought that he had gone mad. In truth, the poor man's head was in a whirl. When they went up or down hill, and the ranks of the escort separated a little, he actually imagined that he saw, in the dust which filled the gaps, the white jacket and cap of the little apprentice at Sureau's! And that happened ten times on the road. That little white flash passed before his eyes as if to mock at him; then disappeared amid the swell of uniforms, blouses, and rags.

At last, at nightfall, they arrived at Versailles; and when the crowd saw that old fellow with spectacles, dilapidated, dust-covered, and haggard, everybody agreed that he had the face of a villain. They said:

"It's Felix Pyat—no, it is Delescleuze."

The chasseurs of the escort had much difficulty in landing him safe and sound in the court of the Orangery. Not until then could the poor flock scatter, stretch itself out on the ground, and draw breath. There were some who slept, others who swore, others who coughed, others who wept; but Bonnicar neither slept nor wept. Seated on a step, with his head in his hands, three-fourths dead with hunger, shame, and fatigue, he reviewed in his mind that unlucky day, his departure from his house, his anxious guests, that meal delayed until evening and still awaiting him; and the humiliation, the insults, and the blows with the butts of muskets, all because of an unpunctual pastry-cook.

"Monsieur Bonnicar, here's your little pies!" suddenly said a voice close beside him; and the good man, raising his head, was greatly surprised to see the little apprentice from Sureau's, who had been arrested with the wards of the Republic, remove his cap, and hand him the dish which was concealed under his white apron. Thus it was that, despite the riot and his imprisonment, Monsieur Bonnicar had his little pies on that Sunday as on others.

THE SIEGE OF BERLIN

ALPHONSE DAUDET

WE were going up the Champs Élysées with Doctor V——, gathering from the walls pierced by shell, the pavement ploughed by grape-shot, the history of the besieged Paris, when just before reaching the Place de l'Étoile the doctor stopped and pointed out to me one of those large corner houses so pompously grouped around the Arc de Triomphe.

" Do you see," said he, " those four closed windows on the balcony up there ? In the beginning of August, that terrible month of August of '70, so laden with storm and disaster, I was summoned there to attend a case of apoplexy. The sufferer was Colonel Jouve, an old Cuirassier of the First Empire, full of enthusiasm for glory and patriotism, who, at the commencement of the war, had taken an apartment with a balcony in the Champs Élysées—for what do you think ? To assist at the triumphal entry of our troops ! Poor old man ! The news of Wissembourg arrived as he was rising from table. On reading the name of Napoleon at the foot of that bulletin of defeat he fell senseless.

" I found the old Cuirassier stretched upon the floor, his face bleeding and inert as from the blow of a club. Standing, he would have been very tall ; lying, he looked immense ; with fine features, beautiful teeth, and white curling hair, carrying his eighty years as though they had been sixty. Beside him knelt his grand-daughter in tears. She resembled him. Seeing them side by side, they reminded me of two Greek medallions stamped with the same im-press, only the one was antique, earth-stained, its outlines somewhat worn ; the other beautiful and clear, in all the lustre of freshness.

" The child's sorrow touched me. Daughter and grand-daughter of soldiers—for her father was on MacMahon's staff—the sight of this old man stretched before her evoked in her mind another vision no less terrible. I did my best to reassure her, though in reality I had but little hope. We had to contend with hæmoptysis, from which at eighty there is small chance of recovery.

" For three days the patient remained in the same condition of immobility and stupor. Meanwhile came the news of Reichshofen—you remember how strangely ? Till the evening we all believed in a great victory—20,000 Prussians killed, the Crown Prince prisoner.

" I cannot tell by what miracle, by what magnetic current, an echo of this national joy can have reached our poor invalid, hitherto deaf to all around him ; but that evening on approaching the bed I found a new man. His eye was almost clear, his speech less difficult, and he had the strength to smile and to stammer :

" ' Victory, victory.'

" ' Yes, Colonel, a great victory.' And as I gave the details of MacMahon's splendid success I saw his features relax and his countenance brighten.

" When I went out his grand-daughter was waiting for me, pale and sobbing.

" ' But he is saved,' said I, taking her hands.

" The poor child had hardly courage to answer me. The true Reichshofen had just been announced, MacMahon a fugitive, the whole army crushed. We looked at each other in consternation, she anxious at the thought of her father, I trembling for the grandfather. Certainly he would not bear this new shock. And yet what could we do ? Let him enjoy the illusion which had revived him ? But then we should have to deceive him.

" ' Well, then, I will deceive him,' said the brave girl, and hastily wiping away her tears she re-entered her grandfather's room with a beaming face.

" It was a hard task she had set herself. For the first few days it was comparatively easy, as the old man's head was weak, and he was as credulous as a child. But with returning health came clearer ideas. It was necessary to keep him *au courant* with the movements of the army and to invent military bulletins. It was pitiful to see that beautiful girl bending night and day over her map of Germany, marking it with little flags, forcing herself to combine the whole of a glorious campaign—Bazaine on the road to Berlin, Frossard in Bavaria, MacMahon on the Baltic. In all this she asked my counsel, and I helped her as far as I could, but it was the grandfather who did the most for us in this imaginary invasion. He had conquered Germany so often during the First Empire. He knew all the moves beforehand. ' Now they should go there. This is what they will do,' and his anticipations were always realised, not a little to his pride. Unfortunately, we might take towns and gain battles, but we never went fast enough for the Colonel. He was insatiable. Every day I was greeted with a fresh feat of arms.

" ' Doctor, we have taken Mayence,' said the young girl, coming to meet me with a heartrending smile, and through the door I heard a joyous voice crying :

" ' We are getting on, we are getting on. In a week we shall enter Berlin.'

" At that moment the Prussians were but a week from Paris. At first we thought it might be better to move to the provinces, but once out of doors, the state of the country would have told him all, and I thought him still too weak, too enervated, to know the truth. It was therefore decided that they should stay where they were.

"On the first day of the investment I went to see my patient— much agitated, I remember, and with that pang in my heart which we all felt at knowing that the gates of Paris were shut, that the war was under our walls, that our suburbs had become our frontiers.

"I found the old man jubilant and proud.

"'Well,' said he, 'the siege has begun.'

"I looked at him stupefied.

"'How, Colonel, do you know?'

"His grand-daughter turned to me, 'Oh, yes, Doctor, it is great news. The siege of Berlin has commenced.'

"She said this composedly, while drawing out her needle. How could he suspect anything? He could not hear the cannon nor see that unhappy Paris, so sullen and disorderly. All that he saw from his bed was calculated to keep up his delusion. Outside was the Arc de Triomphe, and in the room quite a collection of souvenirs of the First Empire. Portraits of marshals, engravings of battles, the King of Rome in his baby-robes; the stiff consoles, ornamented with trophies in brass, were covered with Imperial relics, medals, bronzes; a stone from St. Helena under a glass shade; miniatures all representing the same becurled lady, in ball-dress, in a yellow gown with leg-of-mutton sleeves and light eyes; and all—the consoles, the King of Rome, the medals, the yellow ladies with short waists and sashes under their arms—in that style of awkward stiffness which was the grace of 1806.—Good Colonel! it was this atmosphere of victory and conquest, rather than all we could say, which made him believe so naïvely in the siege of Berlin.

"From that day our military operations became much simpler. Taking Berlin was merely a matter of patience. Every now and then, when the old man was tired of waiting, a letter from his son was read to him—an imaginary letter of course, as nothing could enter Paris, and as, since Sedan, MacMahon's aide-de-camp had been sent to a German fortress. Can you not imagine the despair of the poor girl, without tidings of her father, knowing him to be a prisoner, deprived of all comforts, perhaps ill, and yet obliged to make him speak in cheerful letters, somewhat short, as from a soldier in the field, always advancing in a conquered country. Sometimes, when the invalid was weaker than usual, weeks passed without fresh news. But was he anxious and unable to sleep, suddenly a letter arrived from Germany which she read gaily at his bedside, struggling hard with her tears. The Colonel listened, religiously, smiling with an air of superiority, approving, criticising, explaining; but it was in the answers to his son that he was at his best. 'Never forget that you are a Frenchman,' he wrote; 'be generous to those poor people. Do not make the invasion too hard for them.' His advice was never-ending ; edifying sermons about respect of property, the politeness due to ladies—in short, quite a code of military honour for the use of conquerors. With all this he put in some general reflections on politics and the conditions of the peace to be imposed on the vanquished. With regard to the latter, I must say he was not exacting :

" ' The war indemnity and nothing else. It is no good to take provinces. Can one turn Germany into France ? '

" He dictated this with so firm a voice, and one felt so much sincerity in his words, so much patriotic faith, that it was impossible to listen to him unmoved.

" Meanwhile the siege went on—not the siege of Berlin, alas ! We were at the worst period of cold, of bombardment, of epidemic, of famine. But, thanks to our care, and the indefatigable tenderness which surrounded him, the old man's serenity was never for a moment disturbed. Up to the end I was able to procure white bread and fresh meat for him, but for him only. You could not imagine anything more touching than those breakfasts of the grandfather, so innocently egotistic, sitting up in bed, fresh and smiling, the napkin tied under his chin, at his side his grand-daughter, pale from her privations, guiding his hands, making him drink, helping him to eat all these good, forbidden things. Then, revived by the repast, in the comfort of his warm room, with the wintry wind shut out and the snow eddying about the window, the old Cuirassier would recall his Northern campaigns and would relate to us that disastrous retreat in Russia where there was nothing to eat but frozen biscuit and horse-flesh.

" ' Can you understand that, little one ? We ate horseflesh.'

" I should think she did understand it. For two months she had tasted nothing else. As convalescence approached our task increased daily in difficulty. The numbness of the Colonel's senses, as well as of his limbs, which had hitherto helped us so much, was beginning to pass away. Once or twice already, those terrible volleys at the Porte Maillot had made him start and prick up his ears like a war-horse ; we were obliged to invent a recent victory of Bazaine's before Berlin and salvoes fired from the Invalides in honour of it. Another day (the Thursday of Buzenval I think it was) his bed had been pushed to the window, whence he saw some of the National Guard massed upon the Avenue de la Grande Armée.

" ' What soldiers are those ? ' he asked, and we heard him grumbling beneath his teeth :

" ' Badly drilled, badly drilled.'

" Nothing came of this, but we understood that henceforth greater precautions were necessary. Unfortunately, we were not careful enough.

" One evening I was met by the child in much trouble.

" ' It is to-morrow they make their entry,' she said.

" Could the grandfather's door have been open ? In thinking of it since, I remember that all that evening his face wore an extraordinary expression. Probably he had overheard us ; only we spoke of the Prussians and he thought of the French, of the triumphal entry he had so long expected, MacMahon descending the Avenue amidst flowers and flourish of trumpets, his own son riding beside the marshal, and he himself on his balcony, in full uniform as at Lützen, saluting the ragged colours and the eagles blackened by powder.

" Poor Colonel Jouve ! He no doubt imagined that we wished to prevent his assisting at the defile of our troops, lest the emotion should prove too much for him, and therefore took care to say nothing to us ; but the next day, just at the time the Prussian battalions cautiously entered the long road leading from the Porte Maillot to the Tuileries, the window up there was softly opened and the Colonel appeared on the balcony with his helmet, his sword, all his long unused but glorious apparel of Milhaud's Cuirassiers.

" I often ask myself what supreme effort of will, what sudden impulse of fading vitality, had placed him thus erect in harness.

" All we know is that he was there, standing at the railing, wondering to find the wide avenue so silent, the shutters all closed, Paris like a great lazaret, flags everywhere, but such strange ones, white with red crosses, and no one to meet our soldiers.

" For a moment he may have thought himself mistaken.

" But no ! there, behind the Arc de Triomphe, there was a confused sound, a black line advancing in the growing daylight—then, little by little, the spikes of the helmets glisten, the little drums of Jena begin to beat, and under the Arc de l'Étoile, accompanied by the heavy tramp of the troops, by the clatter of sabres, bursts forth Schubert's Triumphal March.

" In the dead silence of the streets was heard a cry, a terrible cry :

" ' To arms !—to arms !—the Prussians.' And the four Uhlans of the advance guard might have seen up there on the balcony a tall old man stagger, wave his arms, and fall. This time Colonel Jouve was dead."

THE BOY SPY

Alphonse Daudet

His name was Stenne : they called him Little Stenne.

He was a thorough child of Paris ; delicate-looking, pale, about ten years old—perhaps fifteen—one never can tell the ages of these

scaramouches. His mother was dead ; his father, an old marine,
used to guard a square in the Temple quarter. Babies, nursemaids,
the old women with folding-chairs, poor mothers—all the leisurely-
moving world of Paris which puts itself out of the way of carriages
in those gardens—knew Father Stenne, and worshipped him.
People knew that under that bristling moustache, the terror of
dogs and tramps, there lurked a tender, pleasant, almost a maternal
smile ; and that to see it one had only to say to the good man :
      " How is your little boy ? "
      Father Stenne was very fond of his son. He was never so happy
as in the evening after school when the little fellow came to fetch
him, and when they went together round the walks, halting at every
bench to speak to the regular loungers, and to reply to their civil
greetings.
      With the siege all this unfortunately changed. The square was
closed ; petroleum had been stored in it, and poor Stenne, obliged
to keep watch incessantly, passed his life amid the deserted, and
partly destroyed, clumps of trees without being able to smoke, and
without the company of his son until he returned home late in the
evening. You should have seen his moustache when he spoke of
the Prussians !
      Little Stenne, however, did not complain very much of this
new life. A siege is such fun for the street boys ! No more school ;
no lessons ; holidays all the time, and the streets just like a fair !
The lad stayed out all day till quite evening, running about. He
would accompany the battalions of the quarter on their turn
of duty to the ramparts, choosing those especially which had good
bands ; and on this question little Stenne was quite critical. He
would have told you plainly that the band of the Ninety-sixth was
not good for much ; but that the Fifty-fifth had an excellent one.
At other times he watched the mobiles drilling, and then there
were the *queues* to occupy him.
      With his basket on his arm he would take his place in the long
lines which, in the half-light of the winter mornings—those gasless
mornings—were formed outside the gates of the butchers and bakers.
There the people, waiting for rations, their feet in the puddles, talked
politics and made acquaintances ; and, as the son of M. Stenne, every
one asked the lad his opinion. But the greatest fun of all was the
cork-throwing parties—the famous game of *galoche*—which the
Breton mobiles had introduced during the siege. When little Stenne
was not on the ramparts, or at the distribution of rations, you would
surely find him in the Place Château d'Eau. He did not play *galoche*
himself, you must understand : too much money was needed for that.
He contented himself by watching the players " with all his eyes."
      One lad—a big fellow in a blue jacket—who never ventured aught
but five-franc pieces, especially excited the admiration of little

Stenne. When this fellow moved about you could hear the coins jingling in his pocket.

One day, when picking up a piece that had rolled to the feet of our hero, the big boy said to him :

" Ah ! that makes your mouth water, eh ? Well, if you wish, I will tell you where to find some like this."

When the game was finished he led Stenne to a corner of the Place, and proposed that he should go with him and sell newspapers to the Germans—at thirty francs the trip ! At first Stenne indignantly refused, and he did not go again to watch the game for three whole days—three terrible days. He no longer ate nor slept. At night he had visions of heaps of *galoches* at the foot of his bed, and five-franc pieces rolling and shining brightly. The temptation was too strong. On the fourth day he returned to the Château d'Eau, saw the big boy again, and permitted himself to be led astray !

One snowy morning they set out carrying a linen bag, and with a number of newspapers stuffed under their blouses. When they reached the Flanders Gate it was scarcely daylight. The big boy took Stenne by the hand, and approaching the sentry—a brave " stay-at-home," who had a red nose, and a good-natured expression —said to him, in a whining tone :

" Let us pass, good sir ; our mother is ill, papa is dead. We are going—my little brother and I—to pick up some potatoes in the fields."

He began to cry. Stenne, shame-faced, hung down his head. The sentry looked at the lads for a moment, and then glanced down the white, deserted road.

" Get on with you, quick ! " he said, turning away ; and then they were in the Aubervilliers road. The big boy laughed heartily !

Confusedly, as in a dream, little Stenne saw the factories, now converted into barracks ; abandoned barricades decked out with wet rags, and high chimneys, now smokeless, standing up, half in ruins, against the misty sky. At certain distances were sentries ; officers, cloaked and hooded, sweeping the horizon with their field-glasses ; and small tents saturated by the melting snow beside the expiring watch-fires. The big boy knew the paths, and took his way across the fields so as to avoid the outposts.

Presently, however, they came upon a strong guard of Franc-tireurs, and were unable to pass by unnoticed. The men were in a number of small huts concealed in a ditch full of water all along the line of the Soissons railway. Here it was no avail for the big boy to tell his story ; the Franc-tireurs would not let him pass. But while he was lamenting, an old sergeant, with white hair and wrinkled face, came out from the guard-house ; he was something like Father Stenne.

" Come, come, you brats, don't cry any more ! " he said. " You may go and fetch your potatoes ; but first come in and warm yourselves a little. The youngster there looks nearly frozen ! "

Alas ! little Stenne was not trembling from cold, but for fear, for very shame !

In the guardhouse were some soldiers huddled round a very poor fire—a true " widow's fire," at which they were toasting biscuits on the points of their bayonets. The men sat up close to make room for the boys, and gave them a drop of coffee. While they were drinking it an officer came to the door and summoned the sergeant of the guard. He spoke to him very rapidly in a low tone and went off in a hurry.

" My lads," said the sergeant, as he turned round with a beaming countenance, " *There will be tobacco* to-night ! The watchword of the Prussians has been discovered, and this time we shall take that cursed Bourget from them ! "

There was an explosion of " bravos " and laughter. The men danced, sang, and clashed their sword-bayonets, while the lads, taking advantage of the tumult, wended on their way.

The trench crossed, the plain lay extended in front of them ; beyond it was a long white wall, loopholed for musketry. Towards this wall they made their way, halting at every step, pretending to pick up potatoes.

" Let us go back ; do not go there," little Stenne kept saying. But the other only shrugged his shoulders, and continued to advance.

Suddenly they heard the click of a fire-lock.

" Lie down," cried the big boy, throwing himself flat on the ground as he spoke.

As soon as he was down he whistled. Another whistle came across the snow in reply. The boys crawled on. In front of the wall, on the level of the plain, appeared a pair of yellow moustaches under a dirty forage-cap. The big boy leaped into the trench beside the Prussian.

" This is my brother," he said, indicating his companion.

He was so small, this little Stenne, that the Prussian laughed when he looked at him, and he was obliged to lift him up to the embrasure.

On the farther side of the wall were great mounds of earth, felled trees, dark holes in the snow, and in every hole was a dirty cap and a yellow moustache, whose wearer grinned as the lads passed.

In one corner stood a gardener's cottage, casemated with trunks of trees. The lower storey was filled with soldiers playing cards, or busy making soup over a clear fire. How good the cabbage and bacon smelt ! What a difference from the bivouac of the Franc-tireurs ! Upstairs the officers were quartered. Some one was playing a piano, while from time to time the popping of champagne corks was also audible.

When the Parisians entered a cheer of welcome assailed them. They distributed their newspapers, had something to drink, and the officers " drew them out." These officers wore a haughty and disdainful air, but the big boy amused them with his street slang and vulgar smartness. Little Stenne would rather have spoken, to have proved that he was not a fool, but something restrained him. Opposite to him was seated a Prussian older and more serious than the rest, who was reading, or rather pretending to read, for his gaze was fixed on little Stenne. In his steadfast look were tenderness and reproach, as if he had at home a child of the same age as Stenne— as if he was saying to himself :

" I would rather die than see my own son engaged in such a business ! "

From that moment Stenne felt as if a heavy hand had been laid upon his heart, and that its beatings were checked—stifled.

To escape from this terrible feeling he began to drink. Soon the room and its occupants were turning round him. In a vague way he heard his companion, amidst loud laughter, making game of the National Guard—of their style of drill ; imitating a rush to arms ; a night alarm on the ramparts. Subsequently the " big fellow " lowered his tone, the officers drew nearer, their faces became more grave. The wretch was about to tell them of the intended attack of the Franc-tireurs.

Then little Stenne stood up in a rage, as his senses returned to him ; he cried out, " None of that, big one, none of that ! " but the other only laughed and continued. Ere he had finished, all the officers were on their feet. One of them opened the door.

" Get out," he said to the boys. " Be off ! "

Then they began to converse among themselves in German. The big boy walked out as proud as the Doge, clinking his money in his pocket. Stenne followed him with drooping head, and as he passed the elderly Prussian, whose glance had so discomposed him, he heard him say in a sad tone in broken French, " This is bad ! Very bad ! "

Tears came into Stenne's eyes. Once in the plain again, the lads set out running, and returned quickly. The bag was full of potatoes which the Prussians had given them, and with it they passed the Franc-tireurs unmolested. The troops were preparing for the attack that night ; bodies of men were coming up silently and massing themselves behind the walls. The old sergeant was present, engaged in posting his men, and seemed quite happy. As the lads passed he nodded at them, and smiled kindly in recognition.

Ah ! how bad Stenne felt when he saw that smile : he felt inclined to cry out :

" Don't advance yonder ; we have betrayed you ! "

But the " big one " had told him that if he said anything they would both be shot ; and fear restrained him.

At La Courneuve the pair went into an empty house to divide the money. Truth compels me to state that the division was honourably made, and little Stenne did not feel his crime weigh so heavily on his mind when he heard the coins jingling in his pocket, and thought of the prospective games of *galoche*!

But—unhappy child!—when he was left alone! When, after they had passed the gate, and his companion had left him—oh, then his pocket weighed heavily, and the hand which pressed upon his heart was hard indeed! Paris was no longer the same. The people passing looked at him severely, as if they were aware of his mission. The word *spy* seemed to ring in his ears, and he heard it above the din of carriages, and in the rolling of the drums along the canal.

At length he reached home, and was very glad to find that his father had not yet come in. He hurried upstairs to his room to hide the crowns which had become so burdensome to him.

Never had Father Stenne been in such spirits, never in such good humour, as on that evening when he returned home. News had come in from the provinces: things were going better. As he ate his supper the old soldier gazed at his musket which was hanging on the wall, and exclaimed: "Hey, my lad, how you would go at the Prussians if you were big enough!"

About eight o'clock the sound of cannon was heard.

"That's Aubervilliers; they are fighting at Bourget," said the good old man, who knew all the forts. Little Stenne turned pale, and feigning fatigue went to bed, but not to sleep. The thunder of the cannon continued. He pictured to himself the Franc-tireurs marching in the darkness to surprise the Prussians, and falling into an ambuscade themselves. He recalled the sergeant who had smiled, and pictured him, with many others, extended lifeless on the snow. The price of all this blood was then under his pillow, and he—he, the son of M. Stenne, a soldier—what had he done? Tears choked him. He could hear his father walking about in the next room; he heard him open the window. In the Place below the *rappel* was being beaten; a battalion of mobiles was mustering. Yes, it was a real battle—no mistake about it! The unhappy lad could not repress his sobs.

"Why, what's the matter?" cried Father Stenne, coming into the bedroom.

The lad could bear it no longer; he jumped out of bed, and was about to throw himself at his father's feet when the silver coins rolled out upon the floor.

"What's this? Have you robbed any one?" asked the old soldier in a tremulous voice.

Then, all in a breath, little Stenne told him how he had gone to the Prussian lines and what he had done. As he continued to speak the weight on his heart grew less—it was a relief to accuse himself.

Father Stenne listened ; his face was terrible to see. When the lad had finished his narrative the old man buried his face in his hands and wept aloud.

" Oh, father ! father !——"

The boy would have spoken, but the old man pushed him aside and picked up the money without a word.

" Is this all ? " he asked.

Little Stenne made a sign in the affirmative. The old soldier took down his musket and cartouche-box, and putting the silver money in his pocket, said calmly :

" Very well ; I am going to pay it back to them ! "

Then, without another word, without even turning his head, he descended the stairs, and joined the mobiles who were marching out into the darkness.

No one ever saw him again !

BELISAIRE'S PRUSSIAN

Alphonse Daudet

Here is a story which I heard this very week in a drinking-shop at Montmartre. To do the tale justice I ought to possess the faubourg accents of Master Belisaire, and his great carpenter's apron ; and to drink two or three cups of that splendid white wine of Montmartre, which is capable of imparting a Parisian accent to even a native of Marseilles. Then I might be able to make your flesh creep, and your blood run cold, as Belisaire did when he related this lugubrious and veracious story to his boon companions.

" It was the day after the ' amnesty ' (Belisaire meant armistice). My wife wished me to take our child across to Villeneuve-la-Garenne to look after a little cottage we had there, and of which we had heard and seen nothing since the siege had commenced. I felt nervous about taking the little chap with me, for I knew that we should fall in with the Prussians ; and as I had not yet encountered them, I was afraid that something unpleasant would happen. But his mother was determined. ' Get out ! ' she cried. ' Let the lad have a breath of fresh air ! '

" And the fact is he wanted it badly, poor little chap, after five months of the siege operations and privations.

" So we started off together across the fields. I suppose he was happy, poor mite, in seeing the trees and the birds again, and in dabbling himself with mud in the ploughed land ; but I was not so

comfortable myself; there were too many spiked helmets about for
me. All the way from the canal to the island we met them every
moment; and how insolent they were! It was as much as I could
do to restrain myself from knocking some of them down. But I did
feel my temper getting the better of me as we reached Villeneuve,
and saw our poor gardens all in disorder, plants rooted up, the houses
open and pillaged, and those bandits established in them! They
were shouting to each other from the windows, and drying their
clothes on our trellises. Fortunately the lad was trotting along close
beside me, and I thought when I looked at him, if my hands itched
more than usual, ' Keep cool, Belisaire; take care that no harm
befall the brat!'

" Nothing but this feeling prevented me from committing some
foolish act. Then I understood why his mother had been so determined about my bringing the boy out.

" The hut is at the end of the open space, the last on the right hand
on the quay. I found it empty from top to bottom, like all the others.
Not an article of furniture, not a pane of glass, was left in it! There
was nothing except some bundles of straw and the last leg of the big
arm-chair, which was smouldering in the chimney. These signs
were Prussian all over; but I could see nothing of the Germans.

" Nevertheless it seemed to me that somebody was stirring in the
basement. I had a bench down there at which I used to amuse
myself on Sundays. So I told the child to wait for me, and went
down.

" No sooner had I opened the door than a great hulking soldier
of William's army rose growling from the shavings and came at me
his eyes staring from his head, swearing strange oaths which I did
not understand. I could perceive that the brute meant mischief, for
at the first word that I attempted to speak he began to draw his
sword.

" My blood boiled in a second. All the bile which had been
aroused during the previous hour or so rushed to my face. I seized
the bench-iron and struck him with it. You know, my lads, whether
my fist is usually a light one, but it seemed to me that that day I had
a thunderbolt at the end of my arm. At the first blow the Prussian
measured his length upon the floor. I thought he was only stunned.
Ah! well, yes! But all I had to do was to clear out, to get myself
out of the pickle.

" It seemed queer to me, who had never killed anything—not even
a lark—in my life, to see the great body lying there. My faith! but
he was a fine fair-haired fellow, with a curly beard like deal shavings.
My legs trembled as I looked—and now the brat upstairs was
beginning to feel lonely, and to yell out, ' Papa, papa!' at the top
of his voice.

" There were some Prussians passing along the road. I could see

their sabres and their long legs through the casement of the underground room. Suddenly the idea struck me—' If they enter the
child is lost.' That was enough. I trembled no longer. In a second
I dragged the corpse under the bench, covered it with planks and
shavings, and hurried up the stairs to join the child.

" ' Here I am ! ' I said.

" ' What is the matter, papa ?   How pale you are ! '

" ' Come, let us go on ! '

" I declare to you that the ' Cossacks ' might hustle me, or regard
me with suspicion, but I would not take any notice of them. It
seemed that some one was running after me, and crying out behind
us all the time. Once when a horseman came galloping up, I thought
I would have fallen down in a faint ! However, after I had passed
the bridges I began to pull myself together. Saint Denis was full of
people. There was no risk of our being fished out of the crowd.
Then I only thought of our little cottage. The Prussians would
surely burn it when they found their comrade, to say nothing of
the risk of Jaquot, my neighbour, the water-bailiff, who, being the
only Frenchman left in the hamlet, would be held responsible for the
dead soldier ! Truly it was scarcely plucky to save myself in such
a way !

" I felt that I must arrange for the concealment of the body some-
how ! The nearer we came to Paris the closer I cherished this idea.
I could not leave that Prussian in my basement. So at the ramparts
I hesitated no longer.

" ' You go on,' I said to the brat, ' I have another place to visit
in Saint Denis.'

" I embraced him, and turned back. My heart was beating rather
fast, but all the same I felt easier in my mind, not having the child
with me then.

" When I again reached Villeneuve, night was approaching.
I kept my eyes open, you may depend, and advanced foot by foot.
The place seemed quiet enough, however. I could discern the hut
still standing yonder in the mist. There was a long black line, or
row, upon the quay. This ' palisade ' was composed of Prussians
calling the roll. A splendid opportunity to find the house deserted.
As I made my way along I noticed Father Jaquot engaged in drying
his nets. Decidedly nothing was known yet. I entered my house,
I went down into the basement and felt about among the shavings.
The Prussian was there ! There were also a couple of rats already
busy at work at his helmet, and, for a moment, I had a horrible
fright, when I felt his chin-strap move ! Was he reviving ?   No ;
his head was heavy and cold.

" I crouched in a corner and waited. I had the idea to throw the
body into the Seine when the others were all asleep.

" I do not know whether it was the proximity of the dead,

but I was uncommonly sorry when the Prussians sounded the
'retreat.'

"For some five minutes I heard the clanking of sabres, the
tapping at doors; and then the soldiers entered the courtyard
and began to shout:

"'Hofmann! Hofmann!'

"Poor Hofmann remained quiet under his shavings; but 'twas
I who was on the alert. Every instant I expected to see the guard
enter. I had picked up the dead man's sabre, and there I was
ready, but saying to myself, 'If you get out of this scrape, my boy,
you will owe a splendid wax taper to Saint John the Baptist of
Belleville!'

"However, after they had called several times my tenants
decided to return. I could hear their heavy boots upon the staircase, and in a few moments the whole house was snoring like a
country clock. This was all I had been waiting for. I looked out.

"The place was deserted; all the houses were in darkness.
Good for me! I re-descended quickly, drew my Hofmann from
beneath the bench, stood him upright, raised him on my back,
like a burden, or a bale. But wasn't he heavy, the brigand! What
with his weight, my terror, and the want of food, I was afraid
that I should not have strength to reach my destination. Then
no sooner had I reached the centre of the quay than I heard some
one walking behind me. I turned round. There was no one!
The moon was rising. I said to myself, 'I must look out; the
sentries will fire!'

"To add to my trouble the Seine was low. If I had cast the
corpse on the bank it would have remained there as in a cistern.
I went on; no water! I could not go out any farther: my breath
came thick and short. I panted. At length when I thought I had
gone far enough, I threw down my load. There he goes into the
mud! I pushed and pushed! *Hue!* There!

"Fortunately a puff of wind came up from the east, the river
rose a little, and I felt the 'Maccabee' leave his moorings gently.
Pleasant journey to him! I took a draught of water, and quickly
mounted the bank.

"As I passed the bridge at Villeneuve the people were gazing at
something black in the water. At the distance it had the appearance of a wherry. It was my Prussian, who was coming down on
the current, in the middle of the stream!'"

MOTHERS

Alphonse Daudet

THAT morning I had gone to Mount Valérien to see our friend
B——, the painter, a lieutenant in the battalion of the Seine.
The excellent fellow happened to be on guard at the time. He
could not leave his post. So we had to remain there, pacing back
and forth like sailors on watch, in front of the postern of the fort,
talking of Paris, of the war, and of our absent dear ones. Suddenly
my lieutenant, who, beneath his soldier's tunic, had always remained the enthusiastic art student of the old days, interrupted me,
struck an attitude, and seizing my arm, said to me in an undertone :
" Oh ! what a fine Daumier ! "
And while the corner of his little grey eye suddenly lighted up
like the eye of a hunting-dog, he pointed to two venerable silhouettes which had just made their appearance on the plateau
of Mount Valérien.

A magnificent Daumier, in very truth. The man, in a long,
chestnut-coloured coat, with a collar of greenish velvet that seemed
to be made of old wood-moss ; short and thin, with a red face,
low forehead, round eyes, and a nose like an owl's beak. A
wrinkled bird's face, solemn and stupid. To complete the picture,
a bag of flowered carpet, from which protruded the neck of a bottle,
and under the other arm a box of preserves, the everlasting tin
box which no Parisian will ever be able to look upon again without
thinking of the five months of siege. Of the woman we saw at
first only an enormous cab-like hat, and an old shawl wrapped tightly
about her from neck to heels, as if sharply to outline her poverty ;
then, from time to time, between the faded ruffles of the hood,
the sharp end of a nose peered out and a few poor, grizzled locks.

On reaching the plateau the man stopped to take breath and
to wipe his forehead. It was not very hot up there in the late
November fog, however ; but they had come so fast.

The woman did not stop. Walking straight to the postern, she
gazed at us a moment hesitatingly, as if she wished to speak to
us ; but, held in awe doubtless by the officer's straps, she preferred
to apply to the sentinel, and I heard her timidly asking permission
to see her son, a Parisian infantryman of the 6th Regiment of the
Third.

" Stay here," said the sentry, " and I will send for him."

Overjoyed, she ran to her husband with a sigh of relief, and they sat down together on the edge of a slope.

They waited for a long while. Mount Valérien is so large, such a labyrinth of courtyards, of glacis, of bastions, of barracks and casemates ! It is a hard task to find a soldier of the 6th in that entangled city, suspended between heaven and earth, and hovering in a spiral column amid the clouds, like the island of Laputa—to say nothing of the fact that at that hour the fort was full of drums and trumpets, and soldiers running, and canteens jingling. The guard was being changed, the tasks allotted, and rations distributed ; a spy covered with blood, driven in by sharp-shooters with the butts of their guns ; peasants from Nanterre coming to complain to the general ; an orderly arriving at a gallop, the man worn out, the horse steaming ; and litters returning from the outposts, with the wounded swaying from side to side on the mule's backs and groaning softly like sick lambs ; sailors hauling a new gun to the sound of fifes and cries of " Heave ho ! " the flock of sheep belonging to the fort driven in by a shepherd in red trousers, with a switch in his hand and his helmet slung over his shoulder ; all these going and coming, passing one another in the courtyards, disappearing under the postern, as through the low doorway of an Eastern caravansary.

" If only they don't forget my boy ! " said the poor mother's eyes meanwhile ; and every five minutes she rose, walked softly towards the gate, cast a furtive glance into the outer courtyard, peering out from behind the wall ; but she dared not ask any more questions for fear of making her child ridiculous. The man, who was even more timid than she, did not move from his corner, and each time that she returned to her seat with a heavy heart and a discouraged look, we could see that he scolded her for her impatience, and that he gave her abundant explanations about the needs of the service, with the gestures of a fool trying to play the pundit.

I have always been much interested in these silent scenes of private life. which one divines rather than sees, these pantomimes of the street which elbow you when you walk abroad, and reveal a whole existence with a gesture ; but what captivated me especially in this episode was the ingenuousness and awkwardness of the characters, and I was genuinely moved in following through their pantomime, as clear and expressive as the soul of two of Seraphin's actors, all the changes of an interesting family drama.

I imagined the mother saying to herself one fine morning :

" I'm tired of this General Trochu, with his orders. It's three months since I've seen my boy. I propose to go and embrace him."

The father, timid and awkward in the affairs of life, alarmed at the thought of the steps he would have to take to procure a permit, tried at first to argue with her :

" Why, you mustn't think of such a thing, my dear! That Mount Valérien is as far away as the devil. How will you ever manage to get there, without a carriage ? Besides, it's a citadel! Women can't go in ! "

" I will go in," said the mother ; and as she does whatever she wishes, the man started off ; he went to the *secteur*, to the mayor's office, to staff headquarters, to the commissary, perspiring with fear, freezing, running into everything, mistaking the door, waiting two hours in line at a department which proved to be the wrong one. At last, at night, he returned with a permit from the governor in his pocket. The next day they rose early in the cold, by lamplight. The father broke the crust to warm himself, but the mother was not hungry. She preferred to breakfast yonder with her son. And to treat the poor soldier a little, they hurriedly piled in the basket the ban and arrière-ban of the siege provisions—chocolate, preserves, sealed wine, everything, even to the box, a box that cost eight francs, which they had treasured carefully for days of great want. And then they started. As they reached the ramparts, the gates were just opened. They had to show the permit. Then it was the mother who was frightened. But no, it seems that it was all right.

" Let them pass ! " said the adjutant on duty.

Not until then did she breathe freely.

" That officer was very polite."

And away she trotted, as active as a partridge, in hot haste. The man could hardly keep up with her.

" How fast you go, my dear ! "

But she did not listen. Up yonder, in the vapour of the horizon, Mount Valérien beckoned to her :

" Come quick, he is here."

And now that they had arrived, there was a new period of agony. Suppose they did not find him ! Suppose he did not come !

Suddenly I saw her start, touch the old man's arm and spring to her feet. At a distance, under the arched postern, she had recognised his step.

It was he ! When he appeared, the front of the fort was all lighted up by him. A tall, fine-looking fellow, on my word ! Erect, with his knapsack on his back and his musket over his shoulder. He approached them, his face wreathed in smiles, and said in a manly, joyous voice :

" Good day, mother."

And instantly knapsack, coat, helmet, everything disappeared in the great cab-like hat. Then the father had his turn, but that was not long. The hat wanted everything for itself ; it was insatiable.

48*

"How are you? Are you warmly clothed? How are you off for linen?"

And I could feel, beneath the ruffles of the hood, the long, loving glance with which she enveloped him from head to foot, amid a rain of kisses, of tears, and of little laughs : the arrears of three months of motherly affection paid all at once. The father, too, was deeply moved, but he was determined not to show it. He realised that we were looking at him, and he winked in our direction, as if to say to us :

"Excuse her, she's a woman."

Excuse her !

A bugle-blast suddenly blew cold upon that exuberant joy.

"There goes the recall," said the boy. "I must go."

"What ! aren't you going to breakfast with us?"

"Why, no ! I can't. I am on duty for twenty-four hours, at the top of the fort."

"Oh !" exclaimed the poor woman ; and she could say no more.

They stood for a moment looking at one another, all three, with an air of consternation. Then the father spoke.

"At least take the box," he said in a heartrending voice, with an expression of martyred gluttony, at once touching and comical. But lo, in the confusion and excitement of the parting, they could not find the cursed box ; and it was pitiful to see those feverish, trembling hands seeking and groping ; to hear those voices, broken with tears, ask : "The box? Where is the box?" with no shame at intruding that little housekeeping detail upon their great grief. When the box was found, there was a last long embrace and the son ran back into the fort.

Remember that they had come a long distance for that breakfast, that they had made a great occasion of it, that the mother had not slept the night before ; and tell me if you can imagine anything more heartrending than that abortive expedition, that corner of paradise barely glimpsed and suddenly closed so brutally.

They waited some time, without moving, on the same spot, with their eyes still fixed upon that postern through which their boy had disappeared. At last the man shook himself, turned half about, coughed two or three times with a very brave air, and said aloud and very jauntily, his voice steadied at last :

"Come, mother, let's be off !"

Thereupon he made us a low bow and took his wife's arm. I followed them with my eyes to the bend in the road. The father acted like a madman. He brandished the basket with desperate gestures. The mother seemed calmer. She walked besides him with her head hanging, her arms close to her sides. But at times I fancied that I could see her shawl quiver convulsively on her narrow shoulders.

THE LAST LESSON

Alphonse Daudet

I started for school very late that morning and was in great dread of a scolding, especially because M. Hamel had said that he would question us on participles, and I did not know the first word about them. For a moment I thought of running away and spending the day out of doors. It was so warm, so bright! The birds were chirping at the edge of the woods; and in the open field back of the saw-mill the Prussian soldiers were drilling. It was all much more tempting than the rule for participles, but I had the strength to resist, and hurried off to school.

When I passed the town-hall there was a crowd in front of the bulletin-board. For the last two years all our bad news had come from there—the lost battles, the draft, the orders of the commanding officer—and I thought to myself, without stopping:

" What can be the matter now ? "

Then, as I hurried by as fast as I could go, the blacksmith, Wachter, who was there, with his apprentice, reading the bulletin, called after me:

" Don't go so fast, lad ; you'll get to your school in plenty of time ! "

I thought he was making fun of me, and reached M. Hamel's little garden all out of breath.

Usually, when school began, there was a great bustle, which could be heard out in the street, the opening and closing of desks, lessons repeated in unison, very loud, with our hands over our ears to understand better, and the teacher's great ruler rapping on the table. But now it was all so still! I had counted on the commotion to get to my desk without being seen ; but, of course, that day everything had to be as quiet as Sunday morning. Through the window I saw my schoolmates, already in their places, and M. Hamel walking up and down with his terrible iron ruler under his arm. I had to open the door and go in before everybody. You can imagine how I blushed and how frightened I was.

But nothing happened. M. Hamel saw me and said very kindly:

" Go to your place quickly, little Franz. We were beginning without you."

I jumped over the bench and sat down at my desk. Not till then,

when I had got a little over my fright, did I see that our teacher
had on his beautiful green coat, his frilled shirt, and the little black
silk cap, all embroidered, that he never wore except on inspection
and prize days. Besides, the whole school seemed so strange and
solemn. But the thing that surprised me most was to see, on the
back fences that were always empty, the village people sitting
quietly like ourselves ; old Hauser, with his three-cornered hat,
the former mayor, the former postmaster, and several others besides.
Everybody looked sad ; and Hauser had brought an old primer,
thumbed at the edges, and he held it open on his knees with his
great spectacles lying across the pages.

While I was wondering about it all, M. Hamel mounted his
chair, and, in the same grave and gentle tone which he had used
to me, he said :

" My children, this is the last lesson I shall give you. The order
has come from Berlin to teach only German in the schools of
Alsace and Lorraine. The new master comes to-morrow. This
is your last French lesson. I want you to be very attentive."

What a thunder-clap these words were to me !

Oh, the wretches ; *that* was what they had put up at the town-
hall !

My last French lesson ! Why I hardly knew how to write ! I
should never learn any more ! I must stop there, then ! Oh, how
sorry I was for not learning my lessons, for robbing bird's eggs, or
going sliding on the Soar ! My books, that had seemed such a
nuisance a while ago, so heavy to carry, my grammar, and my
history of the saints, were old friends now that I couldn't give up.
And M. Hamel, too ; the idea that he was going away, that I should
never see him again, made me forget all about his ruler and how
cranky he was.

Poor man ! It was in honour of this last lesson that he had put
on his fine Sunday clothes, and now I understood why the old
men of the village were sitting there in the back of the room. It
was because they were sorry, too, that they had not gone to school
more. It was their way of thanking our master for his forty years
of faithful service and of showing their respect for the country that
was theirs no more.

While I was thinking of all this, I heard my named called. It
was my turn to recite. What would I not have given to be able to
say that dreadful rule for the participle all through, very loud and
clear, and without one mistake ? But I got mixed up on the first
words and stood there, holding on to my desk, my heart beating,
and not daring to look up. I heard M. Hamel say to me :

" I won't scold you, little Franz ; you must feel bad enough.
See how it is ! Every day we have said to ourselves : ' Bah ! I've
plenty of time. I'll learn it to-morrow.' And now you see what

we've come to ! Ah, that's the great trouble with Alsace ; she puts off learning till to-morrow. Now those fellows out there will have the right to say to you : ' How is it ; you pretend to be Frenchmen, and yet you can neither speak nor write your own language ? ' But you are not the worst, poor little Franz. We've all a great deal to reproach ourselves with.

"Your parents were not anxious enough to have you learn. They preferred to put you to work on a farm or at the mills, so as to have a little more money. And I ? I've been to blame also. Have I not often sent you to water my flowers instead of learning your lessons ? And when I wanted to go fishing, did I not just give you a holiday ? "

Then, from one thing to another, M. Hamel went on to talk of the French language, saying that it was the most beautiful language in the world—the clearest, the most logical ; that we must guard it among us and never forget it, because when a people are enslaved, as long as they hold fast to their language it is as if they had the key to their prison. Then he opened a grammar and read us our lesson. I was amazed to see how well I understood it. All he said seemed so easy, *so* easy ! I think, too, that I had never listened so carefully, and that he had never explained everything with so much patience. It seemed almost as if the poor man wanted to give us all he knew before going away, and to put it all into our heads at one stroke.

After the grammar, we had a lesson in writing. That day M. Hamel had new copies for us, written in a beautiful round hand : *France, Alsace, France, Alsace.* They looked like little flags everywhere in the schoolroom, hung from the rod at the top of our desks. You ought to have seen how every one set to work, and how quiet it was ! The only sound was the scratching of the pens over the paper. Once some chafers flew in ; but nobody paid any attention to them, not even the littlest ones, who worked straight on tracing their fish-hooks, as if that was French, too. On the roof the pigeons cooed very low, and I thought to myself :

"Will they make them sing in German, even the pigeons ? "

Whenever I looked up from my writing I saw M. Hamel sitting motionless in his chair and gazing first at one thing, then at another, as if he wanted to fix in his mind just how everything looked in that little schoolroom. Fancy ! For forty years he had been there in the same place, with his garden outside the window and his class in front of him, just like that. Only the desks and benches had been worn smooth ; the walnut-trees in the garden were taller, and the hop-vine that he had planted himself twined about the windows to the roof. How it must have broken his heart to leave it all, poor man ; to hear his sister moving about in the room above, packing their trunks ! For they must leave the country next day.

But he had the courage to hear every lesson to the very last.

After the writing, we had a lesson in history, and then the babies chanted their *ba, be, bi, bo, bu*. Down there at the back of the room old Hauser had put on his spectacles and, holding his primer in both hands, spelled the letters with them. You could see that he, too, was trying ; his voice trembled with emotion, and it was so funny to hear him that we all wanted to laugh and cry. Ah, how well I remember it, that last lesson !

All at once the church-clock struck twelve. Then the Angelus. At the same moment the trumpets of the Prussians, returning from drill, sounded under our windows. M. Hamel stood up, very pale, in his chair. I never saw him look so tall.

" My friends," said he, " I—I—" But something choked him. He could not go on.

Then he turned to the blackboard, took a piece of chalk, and, bearing on with all his might, he wrote as large as he could :

" *Vive La France !* "

Then he stopped and leaned his head against the wall, and, without a word, he made a gesture to us with his hand :

" School is over—you may go."

THE
DEATH OF THE DAUPHIN

Alphonse Daudet

The little Dauphin is ill. The little Dauphin is going to die. In all the churches of the kingdom the Holy Sacrament remains exposed night and day, and tall candles burn for the recovery of the royal child. The streets of the old capital are sad and silent ; no bells sound ; carriages move slowly. At the approaches to the the palace, the curious townspeople see, through the ironwork gates, the beadles with gilded paunches talking in the courtyard with an important air.

All the castle is in a flutter of anxiety. Chamberlains and major-domos mount and descend the marble stairs at a run. The galleries are full of pages and courtiers in silken garments, who go from one group to the other, seeking news in whispers. On the large staircase, weeping maids-of-honour make deep curtseys, wiping their eyes with pretty embroidered handkerchiefs.

In the Orangery there is a numerous assembly of long-robed doctors. They can be seen through the window-panes, agitating their wide black sleeves, and learnedly inclining their clapper wigs. The governor and the squire of the little Dauphin walk up and down before the door, awaiting the decisions of the Faculty. Scullions pass by them without saluting. The squire is swearing like a pagan ; the governor recites some verses of Horace. Meanwhile, down there by the side of the stables, a long plaintive neigh is heard. It is the chestnut of the little Dauphin, that the g ooms have forgotten, and that sadly complains before his empty manger.

And the King ! Where is His Majesty the King ? The King has shut himself up alone in a room at the end of the castle. Royal persons do not like to be seen weeping ! But as for the Queen, that is another thing. Sitting by the pillow of the little Dauphin, her lovely face streaming with tears, she sobs aloud before every-body, as a tradesman's wife would do.

In his cot of lace the little Dauphin, whiter than the cushions on which he is stretched, rests with closed eyes. It is thought he is sleeping ; but no! The little Dauphin is not asleep. . . . He turns towards his mother, and seeing her tears, he says to her, " Madame the Queen, why do you weep ? Do you really think, like all the others, that I am going to die ? " The Queen tries to answer ; sobs prevent her from speaking.

" Do not cry, Madame the Queen ! You forget that I am the Dauphin, and that Dauphins cannot die in this way." The Queen sobs still more, and the little Dauphin begins to be frightened. " Stop ! " he says, " I do not want Death to come and take me, and I know quite well how I can hinder him from coming here. Order at once forty of our strongest halberdiers to mount guard round our bed ! Let a hundred big cannon and their gunners, with lighted matches, stand night and day under our windows ! And woe to Death if he dares to draw near us ! "

To humour the royal child the Queen gives the order. At once there is heard the big cannon rolling in the courtyard ; and forty tall halberdiers, halberds in hand, enter and range themselves round the room. They are all veterans, with grey moustaches. The little Dauphin claps his hands when he sees them. He recognises one of them, and calls to him : " Lorrain ! Lorrain ! " The soldier makes a step towards the bed. " I like you very much, my old Lorrain. Let me see your great sword. If Death wishes to take me, you will kill him, won't you ? " Lorrain answers, " Yes, sir. . . ." And two big tears run down his tanned cheeks.

At this moment a priest approaches the little Dauphin, and speaks to him for a long time in a low voice, showing him a crucifix. The little Dauphin listens with an air of great astonishment ; then all of a sudden interrupting him : " I understand quite well what you say to me, but, after all, could not my little friend Beppo die in my place, if we gave him a great deal of money ? " The priest continues to speak to him in a low voice, and the astonishment of the little Dauphin increases.

When the priest has finished, the little Dauphin says with a big sigh, " All that you tell me is very sad, sir. But one thing consoles me—that is, above there, in the paradise of stars, I shall still be the Dauphin. . . . I know that God is my cousin, and will not fail to treat me according to my rank." Then he adds, turning towards his mother, " Let them bring me my finest clothes, my doublet of white ermine, and my pumps of velvet. I wish to dress up for the angels, and enter Paradise in a becoming manner ! "

For the third time the priest leans towards the little Dauphin, and speaks to him for a long time in a low voice. . . . In the middle of his discourse the royal child angrily interrupts him : " But then," he cries, " being the Dauphin is nothing at all ! " And without wishing to hear any more, the little Dauphin turns his face to the wall, and he weeps bitterly.

THE
MAGISTRATE IN THE FIELDS

ALPHONSE DAUDET

HIS Worship the Magistrate is on circuit. Coachman in front, lackey behind, the Government barouche carries him majestically to the district meeting of Combe-aux-Fées. For this memorable affair His Worship the Magistrate has put on his fine embroidered coat, his top hat, his tight breeches with silver bands, and his gala sword with a pearl handle. On his knees rests a large portofolio of goffered shagreen, at which he looks sadly.

His Worship the Magistrate looks sadly at his portfolio of goffered shagreen. He thinks of the famous speech which he is about to declaim before the inhabitants of Combe-aux-Fées. . . . " Gentlemen under my jurisdiction . . ." But in vain he twists the blonde silk of his whiskers, and repeats twenty times in sequence. . . . " Gentlemen under my jurisdiction . . ." The rest of the speech will not come.

The rest of the speech will not come. It is so hot in this barouche. As far as eye can see, the road to Combe-aux-Fées shines, dry and dusty, under the southern sun. The air is on fire, and on the elms by the roadside, all covered with white dust, thousands of cicadas answer each other from tree to tree. All of a sudden His Worship the Magistrate gives a start. Below there, at the foot of a hill, he perceives a copse of green oak trees that seems to signal to him.

The copse of green oak trees seems to signal to him : " Do come here, Your Worship the Magistrate, to compose your speech ! You will be much better inspired under my trees. . . ." His Worship the Magistrate yields to the seduction. He leaps down from his barouche, and tells his men to wait for him, while he composes his speech beneath the oak trees.

Beneath the oak trees there are violets and sweet grasses and murmuring springs, and birds are singing in the branches. When they see His Worship the Magistrate with his handsome breeches, and his portfolio of goffered shagreen, the birds are afraid and stop singing. The springs do not dare to make any noise, and the violets hide themselves in the grass. . . . All this little world has never seen a Magistrate before, and they all ask in a low voice, " Who is this fine lord who walks about in silver breeches ? "

In a low voice, under the green leaves, they ask themselves, " Who is this fine lord in silver breeches ? . . ." Meanwhile, His Worship the Magistrate, delighted with the silence and the coolness of the trees, lifts up the skirts of his coat, puts his top hat on the grass, and sits down on the moss at the foot of a young oak. Then he opens on his knees his great portfolio of goffered shagreen, and draws from it a large sheet of Government paper. " It is an artist ! " says the finch. " No," says the bullfinch, " it is not an artist, since he wears silver breeches ; it is rather a prince."

" It is rather a prince," says the bullfinch. " Neither an artist nor a prince," interrupts an old nightingale, who once sang for a whole season in the gardens of some Government offices. . . . " I know what it is ; it is a Magistrate ! " And all the little wood goes whispering, " It is a Magistrate ! It is a Magistrate ! " " How bald he is ! " says the crested lark. The violet asks, " Is it a wicked being ? "

" Is it a wicked being ? " ask the violets. The old nightingale replies, " Not at all ! " And on this assurance, the birds begin again to sing, the springs to flow, the violets to scent the air, as if the gentleman was not there. . . . Impassible in the midst of all this pretty uproar, His Worship the Magistrate invokes in his heart the muse of agricultural associations, and, with pencil raised, begins to declaim in his most ceremonious tones, " Gentlemen under my jurisdiction . . ."

" Gentlemen under my jurisdiction," says the Magistrate in his most ceremonious tones. . . . A burst of laughter interrupts him ; he turns round and sees nothing but a big woodpecker, who looks at him with a smile, perched on his top hat. The Magistrate shrugs his shoulders, and tries to continue his speech ; but the woodpecker again interrupts him, and cries from the distance, " What is the good of it ! " " How ! What is the good of it ? " says the Magistrate, becoming quite red in the face. And, driving away with a gesture this impudent bird, he continues, " Gentlemen under my jurisdiction . . ."

" Gentlemen under my jurisdiction," the Magistrate says once more. But look ! the little violets are rising towards him on the end of their stalks, and saying to him very softly, " Your Worship the Magistrate ! Can you smell how beautiful we are ? " And the springs under the moss make a divine music for him ; and in the branches above his head a flock of finches come and sing to him their prettiest airs, and all the little wood conspires to prevent him from composing his speech.

All the little wood conspires to prevent him from composing his speech. His Worship the Magistrate, drunk with perfumes, intoxicated with music, vainly tries to resist the new charm that steals over him. He leans on the grass, unbuttons his fine coat, and stammers still two or three times : " Gentlemen under my jurisdiction . . . Gentlemen under my juri— . . . Gentlemen und— . . ." Then he sends everybody under his jurisdiction to the devil, and the muse of agricultural associations has nothing left to do but to veil her face.

Veil thy face, O muse of the agricultural associations ! When, at the end of an hour, the coachman and lackey, anxious about their master, come into the little wood, they see a spectacle that makes them recoil with horror. His Worship the Magistrate is lying on his stomach in the grass, as barely clad as a gipsy. He has taken off his coat, and, while chewing violets, he is composing verses.

AT THE PALAIS DE JUSTICE

Alphonse Daudet

I know not if it be from lack of habit, but I can never enter the Palais de Justice without an uneasiness, an inexplicable heart pang. That grating, those great courts, that stone staircase so vast that every one mounts it in isolation, enveloped in his individual torment. The antiquity of the structures, the melancholy clock, the height of the windows, and also the mist of the quay, that moisture that clings to walls that skirt the water, all give you a foretaste of the neighbouring prison. In the halls the impression is the same, or more vivid still, because of the peculiar company which peoples them, because of those long black robes which make the solemn gestures, because of those who accuse, and the unintelligible records, the eternal records spread out everywhere on the tables, carried under the arms in enormous bundles, overflowing.

There are great green doors, noiseless and mysterious, from whence escape—when they are ajar—gusts of voices severe or weeping, and visions of school benches, platforms black with caps, and great crucifixes leaning forward. Muskets ring out on the flags. Sinister rumblings of carriages pass shaking the arches. All these noises blended together are like a respiration, the panting breath of a factory, the apparatus of justice at work. And hearing this terrible law machine at labour, one desires to shrink within himself, to dwindle for fear of being caught, even by a hair, in this formidable. gearing which one knows to be so complicated, tenacious, destructive.

I was thinking of this the other morning, in going to see an examining magistrate before whom I had, in behalf of a poor devil, to recommend a stay of proceedings. The hall of witnesses, where I was waiting, was full of people, sheriff's officers, clerks engrossing behind a glass partition, witnesses whispering to each other in advance of their depositions, women of the people, impressive and garrulous, who were telling the officers their entire lives in order to arrive at the affair that had brought them there. Near me an open door lit the sombre lobby of the examining magistrate, a lobby which leads everywhere, even to the scaffold, and from which the prisoners issue as accused. Some of these unfortunates, brought there under a strong escort by way of the staircase of la Conciergerie, lay about on the benches awaiting their turn to be interrogated, and it is in this ante-chamber of the convict prison that I overheard a lovers' dialogue, an idyl of the faubourg, as impassioned as Theocritus' poem, but more heartbreaking—Yes, in the midst of this shadow, where so many criminals have left something of their shuddering, of their hopes, and of their rages, I saw two beings love, and smile ; and however lowly was this love, however faded was this smile, the old lobby must have been as astonished by it as would a miry and black street of Paris, if penetrated by the cooing of a turtle-dove.

In a listless attitude, almost unconscious, a young girl was seated at the end of a bench, quiet as a working woman who waits the price of her day's labour. She wore the calico bonnet and the sad costume of Saint Lazare with an air of repose and of well-being, as though the prison régime were the best thing she had found in all her life. The guard, who sat beside her, seemed to find her much to his taste, and they laughed together softly. At the other end of the lobby, wholly in the shadow, was seated, handcuffs on wrists, the lover of this girl. She had not seen him at first ; but as soon as her eyes became accustomed to the darkness, she perceived him and trembled : " Why, that's Pignou—Hé ! Pignou ! "

The guard silenced her. Prisoners are expressly forbidden to talk to each other.

" Oh ! I beg of you, only one word ! " she said, leaning far forward toward the remotest part of the lobby.

But the soldier remained inflexible. " No—no—it can't be done—only if you have some message to give him, tell it to me, I will repeat it to him.

Then a dialogue was entered into between this girl and her Pignou, with the guard as interpreter.

Much moved, without heeding those about her, she began :

" Tell him I have never loved any one but him ; that I will never love another in all my life."

The guard made a number of steps in the lobby, and redoubling his gravity as though to take from the proceeding all that was too kindly, he repeated : " She says she has never loved but you, and that she'll never love another."

I heard a grumbling, a confused stammering which must have been the response of Pignou, then the guard went back with measured step toward the bench.

" What did he say ? " demanded the child all anxious, and as though waiting were too long : " Well, tell me what he said now ! "

" He said he was very miserable ! "

Then, carried away by her emotion and the custom of the noisy and communicative streets, she cried out loud :

" Don't be weary, my friend—the good days will come again ! "

And in this voice, still young, there was something piteous, almost maternal. Plainly this was the woman of the people with her courage under affliction and her dog-like devotion.

From the depths of the lobby a voice replied, the voice of Pignou, wine-soaked, torn, burned with alcohol :

" Go on ! the good days—I'll have them at the end of my five years ! "

He knew his case well, that one !

The guards cried : " Hush !—Keep quiet ! " But too late.

. . . .

A door had opened, and the examining magistrate himself appeared on the sill.

Skull-cap of velvet, grizzled whiskers, mouth thin and evil, the eye scrutinising, distrustful, but not profound, it was just the type of an examining magistrate, one of those men who thinks he has a criminal before him always, like those doctors of the insane who see maniacs everywhere. That one in particular had a certain way of looking at you, so annoying, and so insulting, that you felt guilty without having done anything. With one glance of the eye he terrified all the lobby: " What does all this noise mean ? Try to do your duty a little better," he said, addressing the guards. Then he closed his door with a sharp click.

. . . .

The municipal guard taken to task, red, mortified, looked around a moment for some one upon whom to lay the blame. But the little girl said nothing more, Pignou sat quiet on his bench. All at once he perceived me, and as I was at the door of the hall, almost in the lobby, he took me by the arm and jerked me around brutally.

" What are you doing there, you ? "

THE BENEFICENT GOD OF CHEMILLÉ

ALPHONSE DAUDET

THE priest of Chemillé had to carry the Holy Sacrament to a sick man.

It was very sad that any one should die on such a lovely summer's day, and just at noon too, when everything was life and light.

It was also very sad that the poor priest should be obliged to start directly after dinner, at the very time he was in the habit, breviary in hand, of taking a bit of a nap under the shade of his arbour, in the fresh air and repose of a pretty garden full of ripe peaches and hollyhocks.

" For Thy sake, O Lord ! " thought the holy man, with a sigh ; and, mounted on a grey ass, with the holy crucifix in front of him across the saddle, he followed the narrow pathway made half-way up the hillside between red rock, covered with flowering mosses, and the stony slope and tall brushwood stretching down to the plain.

The ass, likewise, the poor ass sighed, " For Thy sake, O Lord ! " after his fashion, lifting up now one ear, now the other, to keep off the flies that were tormenting him.

How wicked and worrying those noontide flies are ! and added to that there was the hill to go up and the priest of Chemillé to carry— no light weight, especially after a meal.

Occasionally peasants passed by, and the priest returned their greeting on the part of the holy cross without exactly knowing what he was doing, for his head began to be heavy with sleep.

Past Villandry, where the rock becomes higher and the steep path narrower, the priest of Chemillé was rudely awakened from his slumbers by the " Hoi ! hoi ! " of a waggoner coming towards him. The cart was heavily laden with hay, and leaned to the side at every turn of the wheel.

It was a critical moment. Even by crouching as close as possible to the rock, there was not room for two abreast in the path. Go down again to the high road ? The priest could not do it. He had taken this short cut for the sake of speed, knowing his sick man to be at the last extremity. He tried to explain this to the waggoner, but the rustic refused to listen.

" I'm sorry, sir," he said, without removing his pipe from his mouth, " but it's too hot for me to return to Azay by the side-path. But for you, jogging along quietly on your ass, it's all right."

" But, wretched man, don't you see what I've got here, the holy crucifix, the Beneficent God of Chemillé, you bad Christian you, that I'm taking to a dying man."

" I belong to Villandry," retorted the waggoner, " and have nothing to do with the God of Chemillé. Hoi ! hoi ! " and the heathen whipped up his horse at the risk of sending the ass and all upon it rolling down to the foot of the hill.

Our priest was not exactly patient. " Ah ! that's it, is it ? Very well, wait a moment," and dismounting, he carefully placed the holy crucifix on a bed of wild thyme.

Then the holy man fell on his knees, and offered up this short prayer : " Beneficent God of Chemillé, thou seest what has happened, and how I am forced to bring this recreant to his senses. And I can do it without assistance from any one, for I have strong fists and right on my side. Stay quietly there, look on at the fight, and be neither for nor against. I shall soon settle his business."

The prayer ended, he got up, and began turning up his sleeves. Then above his hands, his beautiful priestly hands, soft and smooth with many benedictions, there appeared two baker's wrists firm and strong as knots of ash.

Crash ! crash ! At the first blow the waggoner's pipe was broken between his teeth, at the second he found himself lying at the bottom of the ditch, humiliated, bruised, motionless.

Then the priest dragged the waggon back, and very carefully placed it along the slope with the horse's head in the shade of a mulberry-tree. He proceeded at a brisk trot to his sick man, whom he found sitting up under his chintz bed-curtains, recovered from his fever as if by a miracle, and in the act of uncorking an old bottle of sparkling Vouvray in order to celebrate his return to life. I leave you to guess whether our priest assisted in the operation.

From that time the Beneficent God of Chemillé has been very popular in Touraine, and it is he that the good people of that place invoke in all their quarrels, saying : " O Beneficent God of Chemillé, be neither for nor against ! "

He is the true God of Battles, who favours nobody and lets each triumph according to his strength and right. So, when the day dawns—you know, my friends, what I mean—we must not address our prayers to the sanguinary friend of Augusta and Wilhelm who is to be won over by Te Deums and masses set to music. No ! we must not pray to the Lord God of Sabaoth, but to the Beneficent

God of Chemillé. And this is what we shall say to him :

PRAYER

" Beneficent God of Chemillé, the French are praying to thee. Thou knowest what those people over there have done to us. Now the day of vengeance has come. To take it we need no help from any one, having, this time, good guns, buttons on all our gaiters, and right on our side. Remain then at thy ease and watch our battles and be neither for nor against us. The business of those beggars will soon be settled. So be it ! "

ÉMILE ZOLA
1840–1902

THE SHOULDERS OF THE MARQUISE

I

THE Marquise is sleeping in her big bed, beneath large curtains of yellow satin. At noon, at the clear chime of the clock, she decides to open her eyes. The chamber is warm. The carpets, hangings, doors and windows make it a soft, delightful nest, where the cold does not enter. Perfumes and warm airs float about. Here eternal springtime prevails.

As soon as she is well awake, the Marquise seems to be seized by a sudden anxiety. Throwing back the counterpane, she rings for Julie.

" Did Madame ring ? "

" Say, is it thawing ? "

Oh, the good Marquise ! With what a troubled voice she asks this question ! Her first thought is for this terrible frost, this keen north wind that she does not feel herself, but which must blow so cruelly into the hovels of the poor. And she asks if the heavens have been pitiful, if she can warm herself without remorse, without thinking of all those who are shivering outside.

" Has it thawed, Julie ? "

Her maid brings her her morning dressing-gown, which has been warmed before the big fire.

" Oh, no, Madame ! It is not thawing. On the contrary, it is freezing harder. A man has just been found frozen to death on an omnibus."

The Marquise is possessed by a childish joy : she claps her hands.

" Ah ! so much the better. I shall be able to skate this afternoon," she says.

II

Julie draws the curtain softly, so that no sudden brightness should hurt the tender eyes of the delicious Marquise. The bluish reflection of the snow fills the room with a blithe radiance. The sky is grey, but such a pretty tint of grey that it reminds the Marquise of the gown of pearl-grey silk she wore last night at the Ministerial ball. This gown was trimmed with white lace, similar to the network of snow she sees on the edge of the roofs, against the paleness of the sky.

Last night she was charming with her new diamonds. She went to bed at five o'clock : so her head is still somewhat heavy. However, she has sat down before a mirror, and Julie has lifted up the blonde waves of her hair. The dressing-gown slips : her shoulders remain bare down to the middle of her back. Quite a generation has grown old enjoying the spectacle of the shoulders of the Marquise. Since, thanks to a strong Government, ladies with a joyous nature can uncover their necks and dance at the Tuileries, she has carried her shoulders through the rout of the official drawing-rooms with an assiduity that has made her the living sign-board of the charms of the Second Empire. It has been necessary for her to follow the fashion and cut down her gowns, now as far as the small of her back, now as far as the points of her bosom ; so that the dear woman has, dimple by dimple, unveiled all the treasures of her bust. The shoulders of the Marquise, largely displayed, are the blazon of the reign of the Third Napoleon.

III

It is useless to describe the shoulders of the Marquise. They are as popular as the Pont Neuf. For eighteen years they have been part of the public spectacles. You need only to perceive the slightest tip of them, in a drawing-room, at the theatre or elsewhere, to exclaim : " Look ! the Marquise ! I recognise the dark mole on her left shoulder ! " Moreover, they are very lovely shoulders, white, plump, enticing. The glances of a Government have passed over them, giving them more fineness, like those paving-stones that the feet of the crowd polish in the course of time. If I were the husband or the lover, I would prefer to go and kiss the crystal door-handle of a Minister's study, worn by the hands of solicitors of favour, rather than touch with my lips these shoulders over which has passed the warm breath of all the gallantry of Paris. When you think of the thousand desires that have trembled above them, you ask yourself of what clay must nature have moulded them that they are not as corroded and crumbled as those nudities of statues, exposed to the open air of gardens, and with all their contours eaten away by the winds.

The Marquise has put her modesty elsewhere, and made her shoulders an institution. And how she has fought for the Government of her choice ! Always in the breach, everywhere at once, at the Tuileries, with the Ministers, in the embassies, among the simple millionaires, rallying the hesitators with smiles, supporting the throne with her alabaster breast, displaying in days of peril the little hidden delicious corners, more persuasive than the arguments of orators, more decisive than the swords of soldiers, and threatening, in order to win a vote, to cut down her under-linen until the wildest members of the Opposition admit they have been convinced! Always the shoulders of the Marquise have remained whole and victorious. They have borne up a world, without a single wrinkle appearing on their marble whiteness.

IV

This afternoon, on coming from the hands of Julie, the Marquise clad in a delicious Polish costume, has gone skating. She skates, adorably. At the Bois it was cold enough to freeze a wolf. The north wind stung the lips and noses of the ladies, just as if sharp sand were being blown in their faces. The Marquise laughed : it amused her to feel cold. Now and then she went to warm her feet at the braziers, lighted on the edge of the little lake. Then she returned in the icy air, spinning away like a swallow that skims the ground.

Ah, what an enjoyable afternoon! And how lucky it is that the thaw has not yet set in ! The Marquise will be able to skate all the week.

In coming home the Marquise saw in a by-way of the Champs Élysées a poor woman, shivering at the foot of a tree, half dead with cold.

" The unhappy creature ! " she murmured, in a sorry voice.

And as the carriage was going too quick, the Marquise, not being able to find her purse, threw her bouquet to the beggar-woman, a bouquet of white lilac well worth a hundred francs.

THE PARADISE OF CATS

ÉMILE ZOLA

An aunt has left me an Angora cat that is really the stupidest beast I know. This is what my cat told me, one winter evening, before the fire :

I

I was then two years old, and I was the plumpest and most simple cat ever seen. At this tender age I showed all the presumption of an animal that scorns the sweetnesses of home life. And yet what gratitude I owed to Providence for having placed me with your aunt ! The worthy woman adored me. I had, in the depths of a cupboard, a veritable bedroom—feather cushion and a triple coverlet ! The food was equal to the room. Never bread, never soup, nothing but meat, good red meat.

And well ! in the midst of all this luxury, I had only one desire, one dream—to slip through the open window and run away on the roofs. Caressing was without pleasure to me, the softness of my bed nauseated me, and my fatness sickened me. I was bored all day long through being happy. I must tell you that, in stretching out my neck, I had seen from the window the opposite roof. Four cats that day were fighting there, their fur bristling, their tails up, rolling on the blue slates in the broad sunlight, swearing with joy. Never had I contemplated a sight so extraordinary. Henceforward my beliefs were fixed. True happiness was upon that roof, behind the window they shut so carefully. I remembered as proof of this that they just as carefully shut the cupboards in which meat was hidden.

I drew up a plan of flight. There must be in life something else than red meat. There was the unknown, the ideal. One day they forgot to shut the kitchen window. I jumped on a little roof just below it.

II

How fine the roofs were ! Large gutters edged them, giving forth delicious smells. I followed joyfully these gutters, where my paws sunk in a fine mud that had an inexpressible sweetness and warmth. It seemed to me I was walking on velvet. And the sun gave a good heat, a heat that melted my fat.

I shall not conceal from you that I trembled in all my limbs. There was terror in my joy. I especially recollect a frightful feeling that almost made me tumble on the pavement. Three cats, who rolled from the top of a house, came up to me caterwauling hideously. And as I almost fainted with fear, they treated me as an utter fool, and said they had only mewed in fun. I began to mew with them. It was charming. The jolly fellows had not my stupid fat. They jeered at me when I slid like a ball on the plates of zinc, warmed by the strong sun. An old tom-cat of the merry band became very friendly with me. He offered to complete my education, and I accepted his good offices with gratitude.

Ah, how far off was the cosiness of your aunt ! I drank from the gutters, and never had sugared milk seemed so sweet ! Everything appeared to me good and fine. A she-cat passed, a ravishing she-cat, and the sight of her filled me with an unknown emotion. Only in dreams alone, up to then, had I seen these exquisite creatures, with spines of adorable suppleness. We rushed to greet the newcomer, my three companions and myself. I raced ahead of the others, and was about to pay my compliments to the delightful beauty, when one of my comrades bit me in the neck. I gave a cry of pain.

"Bah !" said the old tom-cat to me, dragging me off. "We shall see plenty of others ! "

III

After a ramble of an hour I had a ferocious appetite.

"What is there to eat on the housetops ? " I asked my friend.

"What you find," he replied sagely.

This answer troubled me, for though I searched well I found nothing. At last I saw a young working-woman in a garret, preparing her lunch. On the table below the window was a fine cutlet of an appetising redness. "Here is your affair!" I said to myself in all simplicity. And I leaped on the table and seized the cutlet. But the woman, having seen me, struck me on the spine a terrible blow with a broom. I dropped the meat and fled, giving a terrified oath.

"Why do you go outside your own village?" said the tom-cat. "Meat that is placed on a table is meant to be desired afar. You must search in the gutters."

Never could I understand that meat in kitchens did not belong to cats. My stomach began to worry me seriously. The tom-cat completely made me despair by saying that we should have to wait till night. Then we should go down to the streets and ransack the rubbish heaps. Wait till the night! He said that tranquilly, like a hardened philosopher. I—I felt ready to faint at the mere thought of this prolonged fast.

IV

Night slowly came, a night of drizzle that chilled me. Then the rain soon fell, sharp, penetrating, whipped by sudden gusts of wind. We descended by the skylight of a staircase. How ugly the street seemed to me! There was no more of the warm sunlight, the large sun, the roofs white with radiance, where you could bask so delightfully. My paws slid over the greasy pavement. I recollected with bitterness my triple coverlet and my feather cushion.

Scarcely had we reached the street than my friend the big tom-cat began to tremble. He hunched himself up, small, very small, and shot stealthily along the houses, telling me to follow him quickly. As soon as he found a coach door, he hastily hid there, with a purr of satisfaction. I asked him what was the reason for our flight.

"Did you see that man with a basket and a hooked stick?" he said.

"Yes."

"Well! if he had seen us he would have knocked us on the head, and eaten us roasted!"

"Eaten us roasted!" I cried. "Then the street does not belong to us? We do not eat, and yet we are eaten!"

V

However, people had emptied their rubbish before their doors. I ransacked the heaps with despair. I found two or three small, meatless bones that had been dragged through the cinders. It was then I understood how succulent are fresh liver and lights! My friend the tom-cat scratched over the rubbish like a craftsman. He kept me on the run till the morning, visiting each pavement, and never hurrying. For nearly ten hours I was in the rain ; I shivered all over. Accursed streets, accursed freedom ! Oh, how I longed for my prison !

At dawn, the tom-cat, seeing I staggered :

" You have had enough ? " he asked, with a strange look.

" Yes," I replied.

" Would you like to go home ? "

" Certainly. But how can I find the house ? "

" Come with me. Seeing a fat cat like you coming out this morning. I felt sure you were not made for the harsh joys of liberty. I know your lodging. I will take you to the door."

He said it quite simply, the worthy fellow. When we arrived :

" Good-bye ! " he said, without the least show of emotion.

" No ! " I cried. " We cannot leave like this. You must come with me. We will share the same bed and the same meat. My mistress is a good woman . . ."

He did not let me finish.

" Be quiet ! " he said sharply. " You are a fool. I should die amid your feather cushions. Your way of life is good enough for mongrel cats. Free cats would never buy your bed and meat at the price of a prison. Good-bye ! "

And he scrambled back on the roofs. I saw his great, lean silhouette shivering with pleasure in the light of the rising sun. When I entered, your aunt took the whip and gave me a beating that I received with deep joy. I relished the pleasure of being warm and beaten. While she struck me, I thought of the delights of the meat she would presently give me.

You see, concluded my cat, stretching himself out before the flames, true happiness, paradise, my dear master, is to be shut up and beaten in a room where meat is.

I speak for the cats.

THE LEGEND OF LITTLE BLUE RIDING-HOOD

Émile Zola

I

SHE was born, the lovely girl with red hair, one December morning, as the snow fell slow and virginal. There were certain signs in the

air that announced the mission of love she had come to fulfil: the
sun shone rosy upon the white snow, and over the roof there floated
the scent of lilac and the song of bird, as in springtime. She came
into the world in the depths of a hovel, no doubt by humility, in
order to show that she wished only for the riches of the heart.
She had no family; so she could love the whole of mankind, having
arms supple enough to embrace the world. As soon as she had
reached the age of love, she left the shadow, where she had been
meditating, and began to walk the roads, seeking for starved hearts
that she satisfied with her glances.

She was a tall, strong girl with black eyes and red mouth. Her
flesh was of a dead pallor, covered with a light down tnat made her
skin a white velvet. When she walked, her body undulated in a
tender rhythm. Besides, on leaving the straw in which she was
born, she understood that it comported with her mission to clothe
herself in silk and lace. Here she was inspired by her white teeth
and her rose-coloured cheeks; she knew how to find necklaces of
pearl, white as her teeth, and petticoats of satin as rosy as her
cheeks. When she was fully adorned, it was good to meet her on a
path on a clear morning of May. Her heart and her lips were open
to all comers. When she found a beggar on the edge of a ditch
she questioned him with a smile: if he complained of burnings
and fevers at the heart, she gave him alms at once from her mouth,
and the misery of the beggar was assuaged.

All the poor of the parish knew her. They crowded to her door,
awaiting the distribution. She came down morning and evening,
dividing her treasures of love, serving to each his part. She was as
good and as sweet as white bread, and the beggars called her Little
Blue Riding-Hood of Love.

II

Now it happened that a terrible plague desolated the country.
All the young men were struck down by it, and the greater number
were dying. The symptoms of the malady were terrifying. The
heart ceased to beat, the head grew empty, the dying man became
stupefied. Young fellows, resembling ridiculous dancing puppets,
walked about sneering, buying hearts at the fairs, as children buy
sticks of barley-sugar. When the plague attacked good honest
lads, the disease was manifested in a black melancholy, a mortal
despair. Artists wept, powerless, before their works; lovers went
and threw themselves in rivers.

You can imagine that the beautiful child knew how to play her
part in this sombre event. She established ambulances, she tended
the sick night and day, using her lips to close their wounds, and
thanking heaven for the great task that had been given her. She
was a Providence for the young unfortunates. She saved a great
number of them. Those whose hearts she could not cure were those

who no longer had any heart. Her treatment was simple : she gave the sick men her helpful hand and her warm breath. Never did she ask a recompense. She ruined herself cheerfully, giving alms without a thought. So the misers of the time shook their heads when they saw the young spendthrift disperse in this way the great fortune of her graces. They said to one another :

" She will die on the straw. She gives her heart's blood away without ever weighing the drops."

III

Indeed, one day as she searched her heart, she found it empty. She had a shudder of terror ; there scarcely remained to her a few grains of love. And the plague was still raging.

The girl revolted, thinking no longer of the immense fortune she had dissipated, feeling the need of poignant charity that made her poverty harder to bear. It was so sweet, in warm sunny weather, to go in quest of beggars ; so sweet to love and be loved ! And now, she was obliged to dwell in the shadow, waiting in her turn for alms that perhaps would never come. For a moment she entertained the wise resolution to guard preciously the little that still remained to her, and spend it with great care. But she grew so cold in her lonely retreat that she ended by coming out and searching for the sunshine of spring.

On her way, at the first boundary stone, she met a young man whose heart was evidently dying of inanition. At this sight her ardent charity awoke. She could not belie her mission. And radiant with goodness, and rising higher in her abnegation, she put all the rest of her heart on her lips, and bending down sweetly, she kissed the young man saying, " There is my last gift. Give me back all you can spare me."

The young man returned her all he could. That evening she sent a letter to her circle of poor, telling them that she was obliged to suspend her alms. There was left to the dear girl just enough to live on in honest ease, with the last hungry creature she had succoured.

This legend of the Little Blue Riding Hood of love has no moral.

ACKNOWLEDGMENTS

To the WALTER SCOTT PUBLISHING CO., LTD., London
and Felling-on-Tyne,
> For the translations of " The Nest of Nightingales "
> by Théophile Gautier, "Monsieur Tringle" by
> Champfleury, " The Cab " by Théodore de Banville,
> " The Dream " by Ludovic Halévy, and " The
> Beneficent God of Chemillé " by Alphonse Daudet,
> here reprinted by arrangement from *The Humour
> of France* by Elizabeth Lee.

To Messrs. GEORGE NEWNES, LTD., London,
> Under arrangement with whom the translations of
> " After the Crime " by Guéroult, " The Mirror " by
> Léspès, " A Torture by Hope " by Villiers de l'Isle-
> Adam, " The Storm " by Armand Silvestre, " The
> Boy Spy " and " Belisaire's Prussian " by Alphonse
> Daudet are here reprinted from the *Strand Magazine*.

To Messrs. G. P. PUTNAM'S SONS, London and New York,
> For permission to use the following translations by
> George Burnham Ives of stories by Alphonse Daudet
> from their series of *Little French Masterpieces* :—
> " The Pope's Mule," " Old Folks," " Mothers,"
> " The Little Pies," " The Goat of Monsieur
> Seguin," " The Pope is Dead," " The Two Inns,"
> and " The Elixir of Father Gaucher."

To Messrs. CHATTO & WINDUS, London,
> For their courtesy in permitting the use of
> " Francine's Muff " by Henri Mürger, from *Half-
> Hours with Foreign Novelists* by Alice and Helen
> Zimmern.

To Messrs. T. C. & E. C. JACK, London and Edinburgh,
> For permission to reprint Mr. Frederic Whyte's
> translation of Flaubert's " St. Julian the Hospitaller "
> from their series of *The World's Story-Tellers*.

*Made and printed in Great Britain by Hazell, Watson & Viney, Ltd.,
London and Aylesbury*